THE HUNT

THE HUNT

Cover Design: Selkkie Designs www.selkkiedesigns.com
Map Design: Rob Seib www.mindfruit.games
Editing: Yoanna Stefanova | Enchanted Ink Publishing
Book Design and Typesetting: Enchanted Ink Publishing
www.enchantedinkpublishing.com

The text type was set in Garamond Premier Pro

ISBN: 978-1-0693441-1-3 (E-book)
ISBN: 978-1-0693441-0-6 (Paperback)

First Edition 2025

Thank you for your support of the author's rights.

WWW.NAOMITIESSENAUTHOR.COM

To all the queens fearful of wearing their crowns:
You can bear its weight. You are strong enough.

To all the kings with flowers in their veins:
Strength takes many forms. Let yours bloom countless gardens.

CONTENT WARNING

The Hunt contains instances of explicit language, violence, gore, death, and sexual content, which might be considered disturbing to some readers. If these are sensitive topics for you, please only read if you are safe to do so.

They come out at night,
They'll give you a fright,
If you choose to swim in the dark.
So swim if you dare,
But you better take care,
For you shall become their mark.
With cold dead hands they'll grab you,
Your fears of death will come true,
You can't scream, cry, or hide.
They'll pull you down,
Until you drown,
Your corpse shall be their bride.
So do not swim in the dark.

THE BARRENS' LULLABY

Ocean Kingdom

Garden

Cave

Palace

Training Grounds

Coral Fields

To Leth

The Barrens

Evanora & Grayson's Beach

Howler's Hill

Tully

Fenharrow

Floria Sea

Hannigan's Cove

to Evanora's Home

Maude

Fariid

Asylum

Black Sands Beach

Balafor Ocean

N

W   E

S

The Barrens

THE HUNT

NAOMI TIESSEN

CHAPTER ONE

GRAYSON

I WAS DYING AGAIN.

My ma's cold fingers pressed against my throat, holding me beneath the Balafor Ocean's hammering fists. Icy rain pelted my face whenever I broke the surface for a second to catch my stolen breath. The water numbed my senses, but my wrists—bleeding from the trail of her knife—felt like they were on fire. Crimson danced with the chilling black of night, mixing with the waves that threatened to carry me away.

I wanted to cry out, to scream at her to stop, stop, *stop*. But every time I opened my mouth, seawater flooded in, heavy with salt and decay. I fought to reach the surface, but everything was distorted in the water, upside down, a riddle. Was I getting closer to breaking the water's edge or tumbling toward the unending ocean floor? Was I dizzy from disorientation or blood loss?

Please, I thought, fighting to find my ma in the dark. *Please stop!*

And then I heard them.

At first, it was faint—a low, thrumming whisper that tore through the waters, rippling along my skin. Fear squeezed at my heart as the voices darted around the inky black, searching, *hunting*. It clicked and sighed, haunting and hungry as it drew closer, eager to find me, its prize. Ma's grip tightened, and I sank lower.

Please stop!

There was silence, and then a deep, guttural moan reverberated in my ears, echoing in the night.

The sound pressed against my thrashing body, threading itself along every fiber of my being until it was just me, the feral water, and the darkness within it.

They had found me.

The shadows in the water shifted, coming alive, claws and fangs surging toward me with a thousand wailing voices.

Please!

Terror clung to me as the darkness reached out. Closer, closer, its long, icy fingers brushing against mine, a shadow of death etched into my skin. It caressed my bleeding arm, almost tenderly, before it sank its claws into me, vicious and predatory. It wanted my death.

Stop!

I shot up in bed, gasping for air. My blurred gaze swept over my surroundings as I grasped for something real: A desk smothered in papers. A shelf cluttered with dusty books and jars stuffed with herbs. Warrick's bed, untouched and dusty, opposite mine. A wheezing sigh escaped through my clenched teeth. I was in my room, and judging by the gloom pouring through the cracked window above my desk, dawn had not yet even thought about breaking.

It was all a dream, a half-forgotten memory—one that I had not dared to think of for a while. It was already fading into the crevices of my mind, but the fear remained, clinging to me like a second skin. Sweat plastered my messy brown curls to my forehead, and my nightshirt stuck to my damp skin. Shuddering, I climbed out of bed. Mornings in Tully were stubbornly chilly, and the coolness of the floorboards shot a shiver up my spine, coating my arms in goose bumps as I carefully peeled off my pajamas. We were nearly in April, the promise of warmer weather and longer days beyond the frost-nipped grass and bitter wind.

But the thought of spring sent another shiver through me, one that had nothing to do with the cold.

Pinching my lips together, I pushed the intrusive thoughts away, focusing on my feet as I willed them to move. Pa's snoring fluttered through the timber walls of our home, and I crept quietly, hopping into dusty black pants and buttoning up my long-sleeve cotton shirt. At least *one* of us was having a decent sleep.

As I fastened my suspenders over my shoulders, I glanced back to the window. My shift at the Tully docks wasn't for another two hours, but there was no sense in being idle, waiting for daylight to catch up to my unusually early start. Giving Pa's room a wide berth, I tiptoed through the hallway, tucking myself into the kitchen at the front of the house. The fire in the cast-iron stove had withered to spiteful embers, leaving the room damp and dim. Dried Arctic thyme, witch hazel, and spearmint hung in clumps from hooks on the low ceiling, and the crumb-covered countertops were littered with dirty dishes. As I grabbed my bag from the round table in the center of the room, my stomach grumbled. It wasn't much of a breakfast—it didn't even look edible—but I took the bruised apple from the counter and the suspiciously hard bread beside it.

Breakfast of champions, I thought wryly as I placed the food into the bag and made my way to the mudroom. Slipping into my thick flannel jacket and lacing up my scuffed black boots, I couldn't help but think that if Ma were home, I'd be having a completely different breakfast. Pancakes maybe, with whipped cream smiles and blueberry eyes. Not an expiring apple and bread hard enough to chip teeth. Once upon a time, my ma, Persephone, would've wanted to celebrate this day, even if I didn't.

After tucking a log into the simmering stove to make it feel better about itself, I forced myself outside, letting the frigid morning engulf me. I sucked in a breath, then watched as it escaped in a little cloud. The ground crunched under my feet, and the birch trees surrounding my moss-eaten home were dusted with a light frost, their weathered branches stiff with cold.

I hurried to the barn beside the house. Calling it a barn was generous; the cracked wooden walls and slanted roof made it more of a shed. I couldn't even tell what color Warrick had painted it anymore.

I pushed the creaking door to the side and was instantly greeted with a wave of musty heat and a cacophony of noise. I wasn't the only one awake. And hungry.

The chickens flapped away, but the goats immediately began to sniff out the edges of my jacket. I paid them no mind as I high-stepped over upturned buckets and wads of hay to the last stall of the barn.

"Good morning, Penny," I said, leaning over her stall gate with my arms folded over the top.

The Clydesdale graced me with a scowl from over her large gray shoulder before returning to look at the wall.

I sucked on my teeth, keeping my eyes on her as I pushed a nosy goat away with my leg. "No love for me today?"

Penny huffed, her long white tail swishing and snapping. I leaned back to avoid getting whipped.

"Oh, come on." I laughed. "Are you really going to give me the silent treatment?"

Stomping her shaggy hoof, Penny threw me another sour look, as if to say, *Are you really going to keep me in here with all these other animals?*

With impeccable timing, a goat thumped its horned head against the backs of my legs, nearly causing my knees to buckle. I straightened, frowning at the bleating animal. "Wait your turn, Simon." I turned back to Penny. "If you aren't going to say hello, I'll be forced to eat my breakfast alone." I pulled the apple from my bag. Penny's ears perked up, but that was her only movement. I turned it over in my hands tentatively, and when Penny still refused to come my way, I took a bite. Overly sweetened juice squirted into my mouth. I gagged at the squishy texture but forced out a strained, "Mmm."

Thankfully, I didn't have to take a second bite; Penny slowly turned and lumbered toward me.

"There's my girl," I murmured, holding out the apple for her to take.

Penny wasn't nearly as picky as I was when it came to apples and gladly accepted the gift. I scratched at her white-speckled neck as she ate, juice clinging to her whiskers. My eyes trailed down her legs, where an angry lesion rested just behind her elbow. I sighed, my hand stilling. "Not getting any better, is it?" A hint of annoyance bristled in my veins at the sight of the oozing sore.

Penny, now finished with the apple, began sniffing for more treats. I snorted as her wet whiskers tickled my ear. "Sorry, girl. That's all I've got." I leaned away from the stall. "I'll make you a salve for that sore tonight."

After filling Penny's grain bucket and shuffling out feed for the rest of the begging animals, I left the barn and made my way through the woods that circled behind our house. There was no path, but I didn't need one. I stepped over moss-drenched rocks and skipped over exposed roots, pausing periodically to inspect the plant life that cluttered around my feet. I hobbled over the footbridge made of wooden planks woven together with birch branches. The stream beneath gurgled and bubbled as it spilled over algae-covered stones, too busy to notice me.

A gentle breeze pushed through the trees looming above, the shy wisteria buds dancing in dewdrops. Pushing aside some bishop's-weed, I plucked a sprig of angelica root, twirling the green stem between my fingers, the white sprouts flailing delicately. Carefully packing the herb into my bag, I pressed on. The witch hazel I had back at the house would help Penny's persistent girth gall, but angelica root might work better. I had to get on top of the lesion before it got any worse. Annoyance bloomed again. *If Pa stopped treating her like a cart pony.*

Smells of flowers and new life changed into brine and dead seaweed. The trees began to thin before petering out entirely, giving way to a small patch of earth, wide where the tree line ended and narrowing to a needle point as it stretched out toward the horizon and surrounding ocean. The lush moss and grass were replaced with piles of volcanic rock and dirt before ending abruptly, revealing long black basalt columns that plummeted down, down, down, straight into the water below.

As I walked gingerly to the edge of the island, I heard a mournful wail trickling along the tail of the breeze. The wind swirled around me, and the faint cry shifted in pitch, transitioning from eerily high notes to low, solemn ones. I sat down, kicking my feet over the cliff's ledge. Howler's Hill was one of my favorite places on all of Lethe. Birds had drilled holes into the basalt columns long ago in hopes of nesting, and the wind would echo through the rock channels, making haunting melodies. But I liked their morbid songs. They reminded me of Ma.

Pulling the bread from my bag, I gnawed on the crust as I fished for my pencil and journal. I hunched forward and sketched the angelica root I had found, then jotted down the plant's medicinal properties that I could remember off the top of my head: respiratory ailments, infections, digestion. Bread hanging from my mouth, I paused, tapping the tip of my pencil along the paper. There were more. I'd have to go to the library and finish the list there.

I sat up straight, stretching my back with a groan. Giving up on the bread—the thing was *never* going to soften up enough to be edible—I traced the horizon with my gaze. The sky slowly brightened in hues of pink and orange. I could hear the gentle *shhh-shhh* of the waves below. Holding my breath, I leaned forward, peering down. Dark gray waves pelted the shoreline before retreating and stretching out. Hunks of ice cluttered the shore, reminders of the particularly brutal winter we were trying to leave behind. The ice reached out, a hardened ring that trapped the island in a limbo, the inky-blue water locked underneath. My eyes drifted along the ring, tendrils of unease flickering in my veins.

It was going to melt soon.

Remnants of my dream scuttled along the threads of my subconscious, feeding the lingering fear like a pestering ache. I shoved them aside, rubbing my wrists as I spotted the thick band of dark water that coiled around the island like an ugly scar. The place where the ice stopped.

The Barrens.

The stretch of dark water that circled all of Lethe. Blacker than ink, an endless void in the ocean. It reached for the horizon, sinking its shadowy fingers into the flanks of the waves. There were fairy tales about that dark scar, lullabies sang to children about the monsters lurking there and what they would do to you if you swam at night.

The Hunt, on the other hand, wasn't some fairy tale. It wasn't some verse in an age-old lullaby or a myth whispered in the halls of the Rose Hill Asylum. It was real, and it was celebrated.

The wind whistled around me, and the cliffs screamed in response. I shuddered, burying my face into the collar of my jacket. My ears had gone numb the second I stepped out of the house, and my nose felt like it was well on its way to sprouting icicles.

And in the broken quiet of the dawn, the fragmented peace I had carefully collected, I finally allowed the thought I had been refusing to acknowledge all morning snake its way through my mind, sharp and barbed with hate.

It was my birthday.

B Y THE TIME I MADE MY WAY OUT OF THE WOODS AND HURRIED along the winding dirt road that led to Tully, I'd managed to settle my nerves and go back to pretending that I was not officially eighteen.

It was just another day at the Tully docks. I would keep my head down, mend the nets, try to stay out of Mr. Brightly's way, and go home. And that would be that.

Tully had the biggest fishery on Lethe. Seated on the west side of the island, the range of fish we received was startling. Bluefin tuna, herring, even the occasional swordfish—Tully always pulled in heavier nets than our competing fishery in Fariid. I always figured it was due to the ferry polluting the Floria Sea. Mr. Brightly told me I was simple for thinking like that and to consider reading a book on currents and migration, which was ironic; I doubted that man was even literate.

Tully also saw a lot more mermaids than anywhere else. Some saw it as a bad omen. Many saw it as a blessing. And when the Hunt arrived, most would be bringing their boats to Tully shores.

The mist clinging to the water's surface was starting to lift as I stepped onto the boardwalk. For the most bountiful fishery on Lethe, you wouldn't know it by looking at our docks. The ramshackle lodge that served as both Mr. Brightly's office and storage for rowboats and nets leaned heavily to one side, looming over the wooden piers. It was going to tumble into the ocean one day. The roof had missing shingles, and the shed attached to its side sank further into the water every year. Graham Brightly, ever frugal, was never one to spend money on useless things like comfort—even when the chimney collapsed, brick by brick.

Stuffing my hands into my pockets, I strode down the stairs, stomping the numbness out of my feet. Jasper Warren looked up from his spot on the docks, offering me a lopsided smile. "Morning," he drawled, dragging out the word so it was four syllables instead of two.

Jasper was leaning heavily on a broom. I glanced down at the wooden planks, where a puddle of fish heads, blood, and guts were strewn at his feet. I stifled a gag, my stomach immediately churning. "What's all this?" I asked, busying myself with the net hanging over one of the dock pillars so I didn't have to keep staring at the gore.

Jasper blew out a breath, sending his frizzy ginger hair in all directions. "A prank gone wrong." He began sweeping the chum into a neat circle. "As it turns out," he grunted, leaning down and scooping a handful of fish heads into the steel bucket next to him, "Sebastian isn't a fan of finding blood and guts in his shoes."

The net nearly slipped from my hands. "Sebastian? As in Mr. Brightly's *nephew*?"

Jasper shrugged. "It was all in fun."

"Jasper," I said with a grimace, slowly sinking into my chair, "that's *gross*."

"Yeah, well, apparently, Sebastian thought so too." He limped over to the edge of the dock, where a glob of entrails tried to escape through the cracks. He swept it back into formation with the rest of the chum. "Mr. Brightly made me clean out the shoes, then forced me to pour the entire bucket out here *just* so I could clean it back up. To *teach me a lesson* or something," he said, mimicking Mr. Brightly's gruff baritone voice. He gave me a pained look. "The shoes were made of *velvet*, Grayson. Velvet!" Jasper made a disgusted noise and resumed sweeping.

I watched in silence, biting back a smile. "You really ought to be nicer to Sebastian."

Jasper snorted, straightening. "To *that* prissy mainlander? No way."

"He didn't ask to be here."

"Well," Jasper grumbled, sweeping with renewed vigor, "he knows where the ferry terminal is." As he spoke, the broom slipped from his slimy grip, connecting with the steel bucket and sending its innards scattering all over the pier.

The laughter that had been hanging on to the tip of my tongue sputtered out, and I slapped a hand over my mouth, trying to silence it. Jasper paused from gawking at the mess to throw a dirty look my way, but as he opened his mouth to spew something colorful and clever, another voice rang out like cannon fire. "Mr. Warren! Ya better be cleanin' up that chum like I asked and not playin' around with it in hopes of gettin' outta work!"

I swore I could feel the dock boards vibrate as Mr. Brightly spoke. I looked up to see the rotund man standing on the cobblestone street sidling the boardwalk. He had his hands on his plump hips, his umber skin an unusual shade of purple to match his poorly restrained anger. The mustard-yellow sailor's tuque on his head was slightly askew, hanging low over his thick eyebrows. His clenched jaw twitched from underneath his scraggly black beard, the vein in his wide neck bulging.

Jasper gripped the broom and nodded fervently. "Absolutely, Mr. Brightly!" He quickly got to work on sweeping up the freshly spilled entrails, hobbling to snag the fish heads out of reach. "No playing around here, sir!"

Mr. Brightly's good eye darted between me and Jasper, his other permanently squinted shut. I averted my gaze, giving the net in my hands all my attention. Out of the corner of my eye, I saw Mr. Brightly cross his arms and shake his head.

"Boys pretendin' to be men," he muttered. "If I sense any more horseplay outta ya, ya best believe you'll find yer payroll lackin', Mr. Warren."

Jasper picked up his pace, nearly sending the bucket skittering once more. "Yes, sir, Mr. Brightly!"

The dock manager stood at the edge of the street for a handful of minutes just to show he meant business. I tended to my net. Jasper swept with conviction. When he finally stomped away, Jasper made sure to sweep vigorously for another minute before leaning against the broom, gingerly folding his bad leg over the other. I watched him rub his thigh. It had become a habit; I didn't even think Jasper realized he rubbed the place where the bone had once broken through the skin.

I swallowed, gesturing to the broom. "Want some help?"

Jasper looked at his hand on his leg and quickly pulled it back like he had touched something hot. "Help cleaning up *my* mess? No way!" He began sweeping again, albeit a little slower. "Can't have your precious net-mending hands get a splinter or something," he added with a wink.

A rush of warmth coated my cheeks, and I ducked my head, scoffing. Using a hook, I plucked at the fraying knots lying in a heap on my lap. Jasper liked to remind me that I was one of the better net menders in Tully. I was quick with my hands, strategic with my bell and ribbon placements, and a quick learner when it came to different types of knots. Pa had taught me a lot when I was young, but it was Warrick who had gotten me a job with him at the docks. I was good, but Warrick was better. Mr. Brightly used to enjoy reminding me of that whenever he got the chance, hoping it would stir my motivation to work harder.

When Warrick died, so did Mr. Brightly's snarky remarks. I knew he was thinking them though; whenever he saw me struggling to pick apart a particularly cruel knot or loosen the drawstring around a purse-knit net, his eyes said everything his twisted mouth didn't.

Jasper gasped, halting the broom mid-sweep. "I almost forgot!" He stared at me, his hazelnut eyes wide and eager. "Happy birthday, champ!"

I groaned, prying at a knot with weak enthusiasm. "Don't remind me."

Jasper grinned, wrinkling his freckle-spattered nose mischievously. Clearing his throat, Jasper fluttered a hand to his chest and began to sing. Loudly. "*Happy birthday to you! Happy birthday to—*"

I shot my head up, putting a finger to my lips. "Not so loud!" I pleaded as fishermen and dockworkers began looking over from the nearby piers.

"Oh, come on!" Jasper laughed. "You can't pretend that it's not your birthday. And not just any birthday." He inhaled deeply, standing tall. "*The* birthday!" Jasper reached forward, slapping a hand onto my shoulder. "You're finally eighteen! And you know what that means!"

"I'm old enough to drink?" I mumbled, not quite meeting his gaze.

Jasper snorted, smacking my shoulder again. "No, stupid. You can finally join the Hunt!"

My stomach dropped at the mention of it. I shifted uncomfortably in my seat, looking anywhere but at his eager expression. "I just . . ." I sighed, inwardly begging my heart to stop drumming against my rib cage. I tried again. "The entire island doesn't need to know it's my birthday."

Jasper gave me a pointed look. "People are going to find out, Grays. They're going to see your name on the betting board." He widened his eyes. "You *are* signing up for this year's Hunt, right?"

I swallowed hard, trying to ignore the tightness in my chest. "Of course."

Jasper relaxed with a sigh of relief. He ran his hand through his hair, causing the wiry strands to stick up. "Thank goodness! I mean, we never actually *talked* about it or anything. I just thought, you know." He shrugged. "It was sort of a given for you. What with Warrick and all."

I gripped the net tightly. "We don't know if a mermaid killed him."

Jasper scoffed, but his smile became fixed. "Grayson, come *on*. Of *course* it was a mermaid. He went out in the dead of night and was never seen again. What else could it be?"

He was saying things I knew I was expected to understand, to believe. But he was also wrong.

"What about the Barrens?" I asked tentatively. "What about the . . . thing that lives in there?"

Jasper made an annoyed sound, staring up at the cloudy sky. "Grayson," he groaned. "That's just a fairy tale—something our great-great-grandparents made up to scare us."

"Is it?"

A snort. "Yes, obviously."

"People have *seen* it though." I pointed to the ocean. "At night, people have seen it."

"Yeah, the crackpots down in Maude." Jasper scrunched up his face, looking like he wanted to apologize. He chose not to. Biting his lip, Jasper stared down at the fish remains still coating the dock. "The big bad *whatever* in the Barrens isn't real. Mermaids are, and they are *not* innocent creatures. Don't defend them."

Despite the morning chill, beads of sweat began to line the nape of my neck. "I'm not."

Jasper held my gaze for a long second before offering a real smile. "Just think," he breathed, "*finally* being able to join the Hunt. No more sitting on the sidelines for us chumps!" He strode forward, clamping a hand on my shoulder. "Imagine the festivals, the challenges! All the pretty girls in their pretty dresses just waiting to be wooed during Hunting Month until the big finale."

Girls. It was always about girls with Jasper. Girls and glory.

"And come May 1"—Jasper leaned into his hand, his face inches from mine—"we claim our birthright of this island." His fingers turned into claws as he grinned. "I can already feel the blood of those sorry, stupid mermaids on my hands. I'm going to kill so many! I'll get the victor pot for sure!"

I frowned at the net in my hands, fingering one of the brass bells tied into a weakening knot. I wanted to throw up. "Right."

The sound of hurried footsteps pounding down the boardwalk met my ears. Eager to exit the conversation with Jasper, I stood up, the net dropping to my feet. I peered into the mist through narrowed eyes, latching on to Mr. Brightly as he lumbered our way.

Jasper began sweeping the wooden planks aggressively.

Mr. Brightly rushed down the boardwalk, huffing as he held his tuque in place with one hand, the other gripping his drooping trousers. When he reached our pier, he shuffled to a stop and bent over, hands on his knees. Amidst his deep gasps for breath, his beady black eye landed on the chum still strewn on the dock, then fixed on Jasper in a scorching glare.

I cleared my throat. "News, Mr. Brightly?"

Jasper, not faltering from his sweeping, cast me a thankful smile.

Mr. Brightly let out a heavy breath. "Aye, news indeed." He pointed a finger over his shoulder. "Somethin' got caught in our cargo net near Bristlin' Bay." His eye gleamed with sick delight. "Somethin' big."

Jasper gasped, dropping the broom. "Something big?"

Mr. Brightly grinned. "Aye, somethin' big." He nodded to me and Jasper. "Now get a move on. We need all hands for this."

Jasper hobbled hurriedly to Mr. Brightly's side, throwing on his navy-blue plaid jacket as he fought to catch up. "Do you think it's a mermaid?" he asked in a hushed voice.

Mr. Brightly nodded gruffly. "If we're lucky." He rubbed his callused hands together. "And I feel lucky today!"

I couldn't move. I felt as though I had been pinned to the dock. I watched as other fishermen and dockworkers began to stumble down the boardwalk, whispering excitedly as they wrestled with their gloves and armed themselves with spears.

"Grayson?" Jasper and Mr. Brightly had stopped at the end of the pier, staring back at me. Jasper was still fighting to get his arms into the jacket. "Aren't you coming?"

I looked down at my clasped hands. "What are you going to do with it? If . . . it's a mermaid?" I asked, unsure if I truly wanted to know the answer.

Mr. Brightly choked out a dubious laugh. "What do ya think we're gonna do with a mermaid, Mr. Shaw?"

I shrugged stiffly. "It's illegal to catch a mermaid outside of the Hunt." I nodded in the direction of Bristling Bay. "Shouldn't you just . . . let it go?"

Jasper visibly wilted next to Mr. Brightly, looking embarrassed for my sake. Mr. Brightly stared hard at me, any form of mirth gone from his face. "Let it go, ya say?" He scratched his chin. "Sounds like a waste of money to me."

"I just thought—"

Mr. Brightly waved a hand, silencing me as he turned away. "Come if ya like, Mr. Shaw. Or don't. Regardless, you've lost yer pay for the day." He pushed Jasper forward, causing him to stumble. "Let's go, Jasper," he grunted, marching away.

Jasper offered me one last pained look before floundering after the dock manager. The embarrassment he had felt earlier finally settled on me, and my cheeks and ears burned from it. I watched helplessly as the docks emptied out until I was the only one there. Nothing but me and the waves against the seawall. I made my feet step over the net and trudge back to the boardwalk. But that was all I could force them to do. They would not follow the others, not willingly walk in the direction of bloodshed and torture.

With a heavy sigh, I turned away from the docks, away from Bristling Bay, and aimed myself for town.

CHAPTER TWO

EVANORA

THE WATERS WERE QUIET.

Too quiet.

I poked my head out from the dull green strands of seaweed where I had been hiding, flicking my gaze left and right. I held my breath and paused. My parents' garden lay before me, the circle of seagrass and surrounding anemones swaying with the undercurrent. The only movement was a school of fish lazily zigzagging through the space. It was empty. I was alone.

I darted forward, my tail propelling me to the sacred space with ease. The fish scattered as I swept through them. There was no time for apologies, unfortunately. Aiming for the boulders that bordered the garden, I dove behind the largest one, curling my long tail against my chest. My iridescent fluke quivered with anticipation, sending up clouds of sand with its flowing fins. I wrapped my arms around the folds of my tail, trying to smooth out the scales that had grown stiff, and willed myself not to panic.

And then I waited.

I squeezed my eyes shut, fearful that even my shallow, uneven breaths would give me away. I pressed myself against the boulder, trying to become smaller, invisible.

It wasn't enough.

After a beat of tense silence, I felt it: a long, thin arm suctioning itself to my naked collarbone. The tip snaked up my neck, grazing my jawline, then my cheek.

My violet eyes snapped open as I sucked in a breath.

And promptly let it out in a spew of bubbles, an annoyed growl on my tongue.

I raised a thin white eyebrow at the pale octopus attached to me. "Found me, have you?" I sighed, prying the creature off my neck and cradling it in my hand. "I fear you're much better at this game than I am."

The small beast stared at me with its ancient eyes, its siphon undulating gently as it wrapped its sleek arms around my fingers. I stroked its smooth head, watching the ripples of color that danced across its skin.

"Now, if I could change color like you, maybe I'd be harder to find. Though"—I extended my tail and eyed its length—"being my size hardly helps. Your small stature makes it nearly impossible to track you down."

The octopus unsuctioned itself from me and unfurled its many arms, hovering just above my hand as it stretched itself taut. I laughed, resting my head against the boulder. "My mistake. How large and grand you are!"

The creature lingered above my hand for a moment more before fluttering its limbs, sailing away from me in long, graceful strides. It shifted colors as it swam, a swift ensemble of yellows, blues, and reds. "Show-off," I teased.

I sat there, my back against the boulder, staring into the space where the octopus had once been. The game was over, but I was in no mood to return home. Silence drifted around me, the soothing *whoosh* of the undercurrent singing its familiar lullaby. I closed my eyes, embracing the serenity I always felt upon entering my parents' garden. My fluke twitched sharply. *My garden*, I corrected myself sternly.

The ice overhead groaned, and I opened one eye reluctantly. The surface above me was shifting, splitting. My stomach clenched as a large crack splintered through the ice, sending a ripple across its brittle center. The anemones reached toward the light. Even the seaweed seemed to stretch taller, yearning for the warmth of the surface.

Despite the beauty around me, dread spooled in my veins. Every day, the sun gained strength, and the ice—the barrier separating us from the surface—weakened. Soon it would cleave itself in two, shatter into a million pieces, turn to dust and diamond shards, and we would be exposed.

Exposed to them. Humans.

Spring was here, which meant—

Another sound snagged my attention—not the creaking of ice or the swell of the undercurrent. I paused, listening.

A low, moaning whisper, drifting along the ebb and flow of the water.

It twisted through the reeds, danced along the sand, rippled through the schools of fish. It was steady, a humming of words sewn together with no need for pause, for breath. It was ongoing, and unending. It wasn't meant to be understood, but simply *heard*. I bit my lip, forcing myself to look at the source of the noise.

There, past the garden, through the seaweed, and around the lanterns marking the edge of our land. At the ocean's floor, where it fell into a jagged cliff. The darkest dark. Where no light could reach and no one dared enter.

The Barrens.

The whispering shuddered through me, tugging at my heart and teasing the blood in my veins. I could feel it searching my soul, pulling at the threads of fear that always bristled at the very mention of the Barrens. I stared into the darkness, and it stared right back.

The whispers grew louder and more insistent as they hungered for my attention. I knew I should look away, turn my back on the Barrens, to not show the entity lurking within my fear. But they continued to sing to me, and I listened.

"Evanora." A voice reverberated within my mind, startling in its sudden intrusion.

The void of black hissed, the sound like a toxin in my bloodstream. The multitude of voices riddled in death and decay swept for me, desperate to make my fear fester into a full-blown panic.

"Evanora," the voice tried again. *"Where are you?"*

I pushed myself back against the rock, breathing hard. The jolting movement caused my hair to float into my face. I pushed it away hurriedly, trying to collect myself and stifle the nausea clinging to my throat.

Jorah. How long had I been away from the pod? Certainly not long enough for my advisor to worry about me. Granted, that frail old fish worried about everything. I swallowed hard, rubbing at the fins on my forearms; they had grown rigid in my alarm.

"I'm here," I replied inwardly, letting out a shaky breath.

"And . . . where is here?" my advisor asked, and I swore I could hear his impatience in the telepathic words.

I rolled my eyes. My fins were smooth once more, and my heart had returned to a steadier beat. *"I'm on my way."*

There was a pause. Then, firmly: *"Hurry."*

I pushed myself off the boulder and tore through the water. It wasn't long before the garden was far behind me and the glittering city loomed before me. I undulated my tail confidently, twisting through the seaweed forest, following the old lava-rock path that weaved along the ocean floor.

Jorah was swimming in slow careful circles around the statue of my parents that sat at the base of the palace steps. He was hunched forward in thought, rubbing gingerly at his elbow as he swam. His long blue tail dragged along the smooth lava rock, the tips of his paling fluke drooping from fatigue. He straightened when he spotted me, his steel-gray eyes twinkling with relief. "Your—Evanora," he said clumsily, placing a hand on his chest and dipping his head.

I eyed the old mermaid for a long second before clucking my tongue in annoyance and mirroring him. Only when I had mine against my scaled chest did Jorah slide his hand downward, swooping it gracefully to his side, palm up.

A greeting for royalty. I hated it.

Jorah knew how much I didn't like it. I suspected that was why he did it every chance he got.

"What is it, Jorah?" I asked, smiling politely at pod members as they swam by. "Why have you called for me?"

"Where were you?" he asked, ignoring my question.

I groaned, swimming away. "Just . . . out."

Jorah pushed himself forward, maintaining my pace. "Out?"

"Is that not a good-enough answer?"

Jorah pressed his lips together, his brow furrowing. "For any common mermaid, yes. For the last royal member of our pod? Absolutely not."

I rolled my eyes, somersaulting playfully until I was swimming in circles around my advisor. "Come now, Jorah. Where's your sense of adventure?"

"It left"—he narrowly avoided the flick of my fluke by his face—"when I realized that a *merling* had been left in my care instead of a queen."

I stuttered to a stop. Jorah kept swimming. I scrunched up my face and raced forward to catch up. "Well, you're no fun."

Jorah offered me a weary smile. "I'm your advisor, Evanora. I'm not allowed to be *fun*." As he spoke, Jorah's hand drifted to his elbow.

I watched out of the corner of my eye as he rubbed at the cracked scales, marred with oozing boils and blisters. My heart pinched tightly in my chest.

"Don't look at me like that," Jorah said within my mind.

I turned my attention forward, fighting against the shudder that ached to crawl up my dorsal fin. Sometimes I hated that Jorah was a mind bender. Why couldn't he be a water wielder, or even a siren? It would be a lot easier to keep secrets from him.

"Like what?" I asked innocently.

Jorah reached forward, gripping my arm and pulling me to a halt. "Like I'm a wounded animal," he said aloud.

I tried not to look at his rotting elbow. "Won't you let me heal you?" I asked lightly, trying to keep the edge of begging out of my words. "You are always telling me to practice my Gift."

Jorah looked at me for a moment, a hint of sadness folding itself into the creases next to his eyes. "Your Gift is needed elsewhere today." He tugged on my arm, pulling me forward. "Come. Your pod needs you."

My advisor led me through our city's alleys, between crumbling white cylindrical homes, around decaying coral. He took me to a house in the back of the tiered structure the homes were built upon, cascading down until the last row touched the city square. The domed homes, covered in a gentle blue bioluminescent glow, often reminded me of teeth with their towering trunks, rounded tops, and flat bases.

Strategic, my appah, Rainos, had once told me.

Cluttered, I had replied.

Many of the homes were now abandoned. Whether from death or crumbling structures, it all meant the same thing: The pod was struggling. Mermaids had clustered together, cramming into the few homes still standing, those closest to the square and still holding firm against the water. Safety in numbers.

"Evanora," Jorah murmured, pulling me from my thoughts of rot and decay. "We are here."

I blinked, remembering myself, and looked down at the mermaid curled up on a bed of seaweed.

She was huddled tightly into a ball, guarding her abdomen, her face contorted into a grimace. Her fluke shifted from side to side with unease, rubbing itself raw against the rocks circling her. The mermaid's mate sat next to her, his tail folded up neatly underneath him as he rubbed her arm. His tightly drawn face was next to her pointed ear, and he was speaking to her in a hushed tone. He pulled her straggly black hair off her forehead, placing a delicate kiss on her temple.

A knot twisted in my gut, but I forced a smile as I sank to the ocean floor next to the mermaids. I carefully unfurled my hands from the fists I had unknowingly clenched them into and pressed my palms together. Dipping my head low, I uttered softly, "My path has led me to you."

The female only groaned in response, but her mate met my eyes with his worried ones. He slowly straightened to return my greeting. "May our ances-

tors' light guide you home," he answered, clasping his hands together. "She is
not well, Your Majesty," he said quietly, his shoulders drooping.

I nodded, a swell of pain blooming within me. "What is her name?" I
asked gently.

"Safra, Your Majesty," the mermaid said. "I am Braemos."

I offered an encouraging smile. "Safra," I said as I leaned forward, trying
to meet the mermaid's pained gaze, "may I see what troubles you?"

Safra winced, her chapped lips wobbling as she slowly withdrew her
arms from her stomach. I had to swallow down the sudden presence of bile
in my mouth. The purple scales that were meant to glide from her tail and up
her hips and abdomen were shredded off, replaced by bleeding pustules and
spiteful blisters ready to burst. I stared, careful to keep my face pleasant. All
I really wanted to do was look away, *swim* away. The smell that wafted to my
nose was nearly as bad.

"When did you last bathe in sunlight?" I asked.

Behind me, Jorah clucked his tongue.

Braemos grimaced. "Before the ice was created last year, when the nights
were short and the waters warm."

I blinked, surprised. "Summer? You haven't been to the surface since
summer?" No wonder Safra was in such a state; she hadn't seen the sun in
months.

Safra moaned again, her entire body twitching.

Jorah cleared his throat. "Stay on track, Your Majesty," he uttered around
a strained smile.

"Well?" Braemos asked hesitantly. "Can you heal her?" He looked at the
angry wound on Safra's stomach, then back at me. "You can, can't you?"

Swallowing hard, I nodded again. "Yes," I whispered, hoping I sounded
more confident than I felt.

My fingers itched. I didn't want to touch the rotten flesh. I wanted to
be back in the garden, playing with the octopus, pretending I wasn't the last
surviving healer in my pod.

Willing my hands to stop shaking, I hovered them over Safra's stomach,
offering the mermaid one last smile. "I need you to stay very still, Safra."

Safra whimpered but nodded. Braemos took her hands, and he, too,
went very still.

I took a deep breath and closed my eyes. Within seconds, I could feel the
gentle hum of my magic stir within me. My fins fluttered with it, my long hair
dancing in the current my Gift was creating. The magic trailed through my
veins, singing in my blood, traveling through my nervous system before pool-

ing into my fingertips. I cracked my eyes open. Light began to shine from my outstretched hands, glistening onto Safra's stomach as my magic melted into her skin. Safra's sores shifted before my eyes, her broken skin stitching itself back together. Safra grunted but remained still like I had asked.

It's working, I breathed inwardly, relieved. *Thank the ancestors.*

And then . . . nothing.

My magic sputtered out, the light flickering from my fingers as the humming within me dimmed.

I could feel Jorah's gaze on me. I bit my lip, my eyes narrowed in concentration as I stared at the wound. *Poseidon drown me!* I wiggled my fingers. *Please work.*

The light at my fingertips sparked back to life, and the humming in my heart resumed. I exhaled sharply, quickly returning my attention to Safra.

Within minutes, her wounds had closed over. Tiny red marks dotted where the blisters and pustules had once been, her skin tender and swollen from my magic. Safra closed her eyes, her face no longer pinched. Her breathing became less shallow, less erratic. She leaned back, resting her head against Braemos's tail. "Thank you," she sighed deeply. "I had forgotten what this felt like. To be"—she waved a hand weakly in the water—"pain-free."

I placed my hands against my tail. Now they most definitely *were* shaking. "Your scales will eventually grow back," I reassured her. "I'll have Mavi create a salve that you can place on your stomach to reduce the redness and swelling." I leaned forward, squeezing her arm warmly. "I'll bring it before nightfall."

As Safra slipped into sleep, I bid Braemos farewell. Jorah and I swam back toward the city square, and I made sure that a safe distance was between us and the pair before I spoke. "I've dulled her pain, but only temporarily." I glanced down at my hands, still trembling at my sides. "It won't last very long. If she remains in the dark, if she refuses to seek the sun . . ." I gazed at the breaking ice overhead, sighing. "It'll only get worse. I fear Dark Madness is just around the corner for her."

Jorah stiffened at my side, his fins growing rigid on his arms. Still, despite the tales of fear his body was telling, he smiled at me, placing an arm on my shoulder. "It's enough for now." He gave me an affectionate squeeze. "Your Majesty."

I scoffed, swatting his arm away. "And that's enough of that, thank you."

Jorah chuckled, swimming ahead. I trailed behind, feeling my soul lighten, rising precariously from the base of my stomach where it had plummeted the second I had seen Safra's wounds. But when Jorah spoke again, down it went with a heavy crash. "Are we going to talk about that flicker?"

My smile slipped right off. "We are not."

"You cannot show weakness like that, Evanora. Your pod looks to you for strength. You are their queen! They expect you to—"

"Act like it," I interjected with a sigh. "I know."

Jorah softened. "It is a large responsibility," he admitted quietly, sounding more like the mermaid who had helped raise me and less like the crotchety advisor he had become in recent years. "While each of your pod members has but one Gift, you are the only one who has been blessed by the ancestors with two."

I never understood why the royal members of our pod received two magical elements. It seemed like a cruel joke that I was given the Gifts of light bringer and healer when I could hardly do either. "Yes," I purred sarcastically. "Positively blessed."

Jorah winced, his wrinkled face puckering. "If you just took my advice for once and stopped acting like you still had spots, you'd learn to harness your Gifts. You'd learn to love leading."

I bit my lip, giving him a pointed look. "If I had more control," I ventured carefully, "I might learn to love it sooner."

Jorah's hand fluttered to his elbow as he clucked his tongue. "You'll receive more control when you are ready. Right now, you are far from ready." His words were as prickly as an urchin. "I am here to help you. To guide you until you are fit to rule on your own."

I almost laughed. *To suffocate me, you mean.*

Jorah's head whipped in my direction, a flash of anger in his ancient eyes. "To *guide* you," he corrected sternly. "Not suffocate you. There is a difference."

A rush of heat coated my pale cheeks, but I held his stare. "Is there?" I asked out loud. *"Stay out of my head,"* I demanded inwardly.

Jorah blinked at me, realizing his breach in my privacy. He pinched his thin lips together, his pale blue forearm fins flaring in the undercurrent. "I'm only trying—"

"Evanora!" a voice rang out, pulling me out of a conversation with Jorah that would have surely killed me and my immortal soul.

I turned away to see Mavi racing toward us, breathless and wearing a massive grin. I smirked, shedding my ill mood like dead scales. "Well, hello there!"

Mavi clasped my hands in hers, her honey-brown skin a stark contrast to my nearly transparent ivory. "I have the *best* news!"

Jorah's frown grew impossibly deeper. He cleared his throat expectantly.

Mavi looked over my shoulder at him before ducking her head, causing her curly brown hair to bob with her. Letting go of me, Mavi quickly placed a hand on her chest before swinging it clumsily to her side. "Your Majesty," she hummed, batting her eyelashes at me.

I bit back a snort. "My Mavi," I replied, tugging her in for a quick hug. I swore I could feel Jorah glaring daggers at the back of my head.

Pulling away with a laugh, Mavi spared a glance at Jorah. "I must steal the royalty for a second." She took my hand, lightly tugging me away. "Urgent news to discuss and all that."

My advisor opened his mouth to protest. I held up a finger. "Only for a second!" I repeated before letting my dear friend tow me away.

When Jorah was out of view, I allowed the giggles I had been holding at bay loose. "What is all this about?" I asked between breaths. "What is your news?"

Without letting go of my hand, Mavi turned to face me, swimming backward. "Oh," she said, making a face, "no news. I thought you simply needed to escape that old blowfish."

My mouth dropped open. "Mavi!" I scolded. "You can't call my advisor such names!" Still, another spurt of laughter erupted from me. "Honestly," I said, wiping at my eyes, "what has you so excited?" When Mavi said nothing, I folded my arms against my chest, feigning annoyance. "If you don't tell me right this instant, I promise I'll be very cross with you."

Mavi pursed her plump lips together, pouting. The facade was quick to break, however, as her infectious grin made another appearance. She swam up to me, her hands clasped against her chest. "It's the ice."

I cocked my head to the side. "The ice?" I asked hesitantly.

Mavi's golden eyes shone with contagious joy. "The ice," she breathed. "It's finally broken by the shoreline." Her grin grew. "Which means . . ." She raised her eyebrows as her sentence petered out.

But she didn't need to finish her sentence. My heart jumped in my chest.

It was time to seek the sun.

CHAPTER THREE

GRAYSON

T HE BELL ABOVE THE BUTCHER SHOP DOOR SIGNALED MY arrival enthusiastically. The air was thick with the pungent scent of blood. I cringed, instinctively covering my nose. It seemed like cruel punishment for Pa to work in a butchery, considering my aversion to blood and gore.

There was a sleepy chirp, and a light pressure intertwined itself between my legs. I looked down to see a tailless black-and-white cat weaving around me, letting out a purr that was much larger than its small body. I chuckled, crouching to pet its torn ears. "Hello, Phineas."

We weren't really sure where the cat had come from, only that one day he wasn't at the butcher shop, and the next, he was. When Pa found him tucked away in the back room, licking up a pool of drying blood on the ground, the poor thing was in rough shape; both ears were tattered beyond repair, he was dangerously thin, and his tail looked like it had been made into a stump unnaturally. There was blood all over him, but it was difficult to detect whether it was from a fight he had lost or from the slab of beef hanging over his head.

Pa had been seconds away from shooing the cat out the door, but I had cried about the injustice of it all. Warrick had come to my aid and, despite his allergies, had charmed Pa enough to agree to keep him around for mousing—though it quickly became apparent that the cat wasn't all that good at it. Pa kept him around all the same. Sometimes I caught him feeding Phineas meat scraps.

Phineas becoming a member of the Shaw family was one of my fondest memories. It was before everything went to shit.

There was the sound of heavy footsteps as Rowan Shaw appeared from the back room, a smile on his face as he wiped at his bloody hands with a bloody rag. When his heavy brown eyes landed on me—his son and not a waiting customer—the smile promptly vanished. "You're off early," he noted gruffly, slapping the damp rag over his broad shoulder and crossing his tattooed arms against his chest.

Heat immediately sputtered to my cheeks. Avoiding eye contact, I turned my attention back to Phineas. "Mr. Brightly let me go home early. Maybe it was his version of a birthday present."

Pa let out a sardonic laugh. "Graham Brightly handing out birthday presents? What a wild concept." He paused. "With pay?"

I winced, my gaze darting to my pa's. "Not exactly."

His face turned to stone. "So, you were dismissed, is what you're telling me."

I didn't know my cheeks could get any warmer. But as I stared at Pa and felt his disappointment waft off him in waves, I realized they could. Pa growled darkly, taking the towel from his shoulder and wringing it in his callused hands before slapping it onto the counter with a *crack*. I tried not to flinch. "Every penny counts, Grayson. You know that."

Phineas, done with my attentiveness, returned to his perch at the butchery's large window facing Tully's main street. I stood, my heart pounding. "I know."

Pa rubbed at his creased forehead, his fingers getting tangled in the coils of brown curls that had fallen out of the high knot his hair was pulled into. "I just don't understand how you can be so careless. How many times do I have to tell you that—"

"Money is tight," I finished for him, staring at my feet.

Pa nodded, wiping his hands on the stained apron around his waist. "*Especially* in the offseason. With the ferry being closed for winter and without the onslaught of tourism from the mainland . . . How are the two of us going to make ends meet if you keep finding ways to leave the docks?"

I kicked a lone dust bunny. "It's not like I had a choice," I mumbled.

To say that I instantly regretted uttering such words would be a vicious understatement.

Pa tilted his head, his hardened stare piercing straight through me. "Does your leaving have anything to do with mermaids?" he asked quietly.

When I didn't reply, Pa groaned, letting his neck go slack so that he was staring at the low-hanging ceiling. "For Pete's sake, Grayson."

"I know," I blurted, stepping forward. "I know, and I'm sorry." I spread my hands on the cool countertop. "It's just that . . . It's just that they might've caught one over at Bristling Bay. I didn't know what to do. Everyone was so excited about it, but I couldn't go. Even if I wanted to, I couldn't make my feet move, Pa! I just—"

"Panicked." My pa sighed, dropping his chin and looking at me with disappointment. "Like you always do."

I swallowed, biting at the insides of my cheeks. "I'm sorry," I said again.

But the words didn't mean anything to him. A heavy silence settled between us, thick with words left unsaid and feelings ignored. Phineas's steady purr rattled from the windowsill. I picked at the lint on my sleeve, feeling unmoored. "Pa, I—"

"Go on home." He sighed again, heading for the back room. "You're no use to me here."

My heart was pounding so hard that I could feel it in my wrists. The room was quiet, and despite Pa being only one room over, I felt more alone than I had all day.

THE WEATHER WAS BEGINNING TO TURN. THE ONCE-CLEAR SKIES were now marbled with clouds in every shade of blue. Foul forecasts were part of Lethe's charm—its weather was as temperamental as a turning tide. I shoved my hands into my pockets and walked down the cracked sidewalk.

Stores flanked me as I walked, offering coffee and treats and gifts from the mainland. Carts wheeled by me on the flagstone road, horses working hard to pull mounds of dirt, bricks, and hay bales. The occasional car puttered by, spewing clouds of exhaust. They were growing more popular on our archaic island, but their heavy mechanical smells still made my nose burn.

I paused, noting a *BUSINESS IS CLOSING* sign posted outside one of Tully's fabric shops. A chill prickled my skin. That was the second store to close this year. I swallowed hard and kept walking. It wasn't just Pa and me scraping by. I doubted Mr. Grieves, one of Lethe's wealthiest men and owner of several struggling businesses, would let the butcher shop close. The butchery was a staple; apparently, fancy fabric wasn't.

A hand pressed against my shoulder, startling me.

Holly Warren quickly jumped back. "I'm sorry!" she squeaked.

I blinked down at her. Holly's thick ginger hair had been collected into two long braids that sat over her shoulders. Her fingers darted back and forth between fidgeting with her hair and the knot of the gray wool shawl draped over her tiny frame. Her large hazelnut eyes stared up at me, her thin lips looking like they were torn between pulling up into a smile or wobbling with the frazzled nerves she was radiating like a furnace.

"Hi there, Holly," I said, forcing a smile.

Holly grinned then, her freckled face lighting up. She nodded at the store I had stopped in front of. "Doing some window-shopping?"

I looked to the store she was pointing at. I hadn't even realized that I had stopped moving again. My heart sank as I took in the dimly lit store full of porcelain figurines and mannequins covered in silk, all imported from the mainland.

It had been Ma's favorite store once. When I was younger, we would go there every Sunday after church service. Warrick and Pa would immediately head home, blasphemously bashing Pastor Kline's message, but I always made sure to leave with Ma, even if their ranting made for great entertainment.

Ma would drift between the rows of clothing, her fingers grazing the lace edges of dresses far beyond our means. "I'm touching part of the mainland," she'd say with a smile. I didn't quite understand her words; whenever I touched the cloth with my grubby little hands, all I felt was scratchy fabric that smelled of heavy perfume.

Whenever we left the shop to trudge back to our shabby cottage atop the hill, Ma's smile would fade. I'd watch her shoulders slump and feel an ache settle into my chest, as though I'd failed her somehow. By the time I was old enough to work at the docks, I'd resolved to bring that smile back. I saved every penny Mr. Brightly paid me, hoarding my earnings until I could afford something—anything—from that import store.

It wasn't fancy, just a simple silver bracelet etched with the constellation Orion's Belt. I liked it best because the star pattern matched the freckles dotting my left cheek. Dangling from it was a single octopus charm on a silver loop.

I never got a chance to give it to her. By the time I could afford the bracelet, Ma had been sent to Maude. Eight years later, it still sat in a box, waiting for her wrist.

"Grayson?" Holly's voice broke through my thoughts.

I gave my head a quick shake, chuckling as heat warmed my ears. "I'm sorry," I said. "I just don't know where my head is at today."

Holly twirled a braid around her finger, her deep green gingham dress twisting as she swayed from side to side. "You're a goof, Grayson Shaw."

I scratched the back of my neck, hoping to rub the blush off. "You are correct, Holly Warren."

Holly's cheeks reddened at the sound of her name on my lips. She suddenly straightened. "Oh!" she cried. "I almost forgot." Holly pulled her other arm out from behind her back, producing a black leather-bound journal. She bit her lip, grinning up at me, bouncing lightly in place. "Happiest of birthdays."

I looked at the journal, a frown on my lips.

Holly's bouncing faltered. "You don't like it?"

"No!" I insisted, choking on a stunned laugh. "No, I love it." I took the journal, twisting it back and forth to admire the black leather. "It's just a surprise, that's all." I ran a finger along the spine. "Not even your brother thought to get me a gift."

Holly's smile returned. "Open it!"

Raising an eyebrow, I slowly cracked the journal open. Tucked against the cover was a crumpled-up daisy. It hadn't been pressed correctly, so several of the vibrant white petals were torn and crooked.

"Daisies are my *favorite*," Holly said as I looked at the wilted flower.

I closed the journal, hugging it to my chest. "What a thoughtful gift, Holly. Thank you."

Holly's response was a squeal so loud that I nearly dropped the journal. "The festival!" she breathed, glancing my way. "How exciting!"

She pointed to the poster plastered onto the brick siding of Mott's Pharmacy. Speckled colors resembling crude fireworks took up most of the advertisement. In big cursive lettering, it boasted music, treats, and liquor from Lyre Brewery. *Start Hunting Month off right with the First Festival—April 1*, the bottom caption read.

Holly clasped her hands together dreamily. "I just adore the First Festival." Her large eyes flicked to mine hesitantly. "Don't you?"

Nope. I had stopped liking it when Warrick died. It wasn't long after his passing that I'd stopped going altogether. I smiled. "Will you be going?"

Holly immediately drooped, bowing her head until it rested against the windowpane. "No," she huffed, straightening just so she could stomp her feet. "I have to stay home to watch the twins."

I tucked the journal underneath my arm and planted my hands into my jacket pockets as a rush of wind swept by us. "There's no age restriction to the festival."

Holly scoffed, trying in vain to corral her hair back into place. "Mom thinks the fireworks would startle them too much." She sighed, rolling her eyes. "And since it's Jasper's first Hunt, he obviously gets to go. So, that just leaves me." She pointed at herself, disgust written along her dainty face. "The less important, least favorite child."

I knew she was joking. Still, I couldn't stifle the threat of nausea that cinched my throat. "I know the feeling." A fat raindrop pelted the top of my head. I looked up at the ripe clouds. "I should go. Don't want the rain ruining this journal before I get a chance to use it."

Holly nodded, though the disappointment flickering in her eyes was palpable. She leaned forward, squeezing my arm. "Happy birthday again, Grayson!"

We parted ways, and I hurried down the street, dodging the puddles pooling in the flagstones. As Main Street gave way to the dirt path leading up the hill to our home, I stole a glance at the docks.

Even from a distance, I could hear the fishermen shouting, see them bustling on the boardwalk. Whatever Mr. Brightly had caught must've been worth the overtime he was paying.

I closed my eyes, turning away.

Despite it being my birthday, I was beginning to wonder if there was truly anything happy about it.

CHAPTER FOUR

EVANORA

N o."

"Jorah," I growled, flopping into the throne of curved glass that sat in the middle of the room. "Have you heard *anything* I've said?"

"Yes," Jorah replied, clasping his hands behind his back as he swam in front of the coral dais where I was perched. "You said the ice is melting. You said that we must seek the sun before more mermaids succumb to fin rot and bloat like Safra. What you *didn't* say"—Jorah stopped in front of me—"is that it is far too dangerous to bathe in sunlight. Any sane mermaid would realize that the risks are far too great."

I held back another growl. "We *need* to bathe in sunlight. It is essential for our health."

"No," Jorah bit out. "*You* are essential for our health. With your Gift as healer, we no longer need the sun."

I laughed coldly. "Try telling that to Safra!" I pointed at his arm. "Try telling that to yourself." I shook my head. "Jorah, I may be a healer, but I can only do so much. You've witnessed that my magic has limitations." I leaned back into the throne. "The sun can do so much more for us than my half-hearted Gift. We've been without it for far too long." I didn't need to go on further, not when the reason behind our lack of visits to the surface was swimming right in front of me, rubbing at his inflamed elbow.

"But at the risk of your own pod getting caught while sunbathing?" Jorah resumed his pacing. "No. Absolutely not. Out of the question."

I took a breath, then let it out slowly. "Fine," I said, my fingers splayed against the shell armrests. "Then we must expand our borders."

Jorah laughed incredulously. "Absolutely *not*!" he said again.

I pushed myself off the throne, swimming until I was in front of him. "If you refuse to let us seek the sun, then at least you can let us forage in locations we haven't picked clean. We need more food, more medicinal plants to make salves, more—"

"I will not allow you to send some poor soul on a fool's errand!"

"Then *I'll* go!" I growled with exasperation.

Jorah laughed again. "Neptune spear me. Evanora—"

"I would be quick," I promised. "I would be careful. Just a scouting mission to start. I wouldn't get caught!"

Jorah tried to swim around me, but I wouldn't let him.

"You are needed here." He pointed a gnarled finger to the front of the throne room, past the marble pillars bordering the palace's entrance, past the chipped steps leading down to the city square, to the glowing kingdom beyond. "*They* need you here." His gaze lingered on the unlit lanterns that lined the lava-rock streets before fanning out, bordering the city in a large strategic loop.

I didn't need to be a mind bender to know what he was thinking. I bristled, my fins flaring. "I would be back before nightfall," I defended, the confidence in my words dwindling.

Jorah narrowed his deep gray eyes at me. "Can you truly guarantee that, Your Majesty?" When I said nothing, he sighed, running a hand through his thinning hair. "Do I need to remind you of what lives in the Barrens?"

I couldn't stop the shudder that ran up my dorsal fin. Darkness. Death. Soul-feasters and fear-eaters. "No."

"And do I need to tell you what happens at nighttime?"

"It doesn't matter," I snapped, shaking my head. "I would be back—"

"And if you aren't?" Jorah cut in, his voice as sharp as the edge of a broken shell. He clasped his hands behind his back and began circling me, slow and deliberate. "The Cursed Beings won't wait for you." He gestured toward the entrance. "The moment the sun sets, the evil lurking in the Barrens will stir. They'll kill every creature unlucky enough to cross their path, revel in the carnage, and still crave more."

He came closer, gripping my arms just shy of where my fins bristled, their tips razor-sharp. "You are our pod's last light bringer," he said, his voice low and unyielding. "You alone can protect us from the night, from the creatures that thrive in its depths. Lighting those lanterns is not a choice—it's your duty, your responsibility. If something happens to you out there, we'll all pay the price."

His hands dropped to his sides, his posture softening, though his tone did not. "As your advisor, I cannot allow it. I forbid you from leaving."

I swallowed hard, my throat tight. The mention of the Cursed Beings—those deathless predators that prowled the Barrens—sent a shiver through me. They were a constant reminder of our fragile existence, trapped between their territory and the human island that wished us extinct.

"I am your queen," I said, though my voice wavered like a brittle reef in a storm. "You cannot forbid me. You—" I forced a shaky laugh. "You cannot control me!"

Jorah turned away, swimming to one of the dining tables nestled in the far side of the room. He leaned against the stone slab heavily. "Cursed Beings aside, the dangers have amplified with the upcoming Hunting Month." His gaze trickled to the vaulted ceiling, where the fading light poured through the skylight above the throne. "If the ice had melted earlier, then maybe I would allow these childish notions."

I surged forward, the water rippling with my ferocity. "The Hunt is exactly why we *need* to act now. You saw Safra today. You saw her wounds." I grabbed the limp bag next to Jorah's hand and held it in front of his face. The gentle *clink* of jars flowed through the water between us. The last batch of salves Mavi had made, and it was dangerously light. "Our resources have grown heavily depleted over the winter. If feeding on sunlight is no longer an option, we need more plants if we wish to survive the Hunt with limited casualties."

"The pod doesn't need plants and sunshine. They need their leader." He leaned away from the bag to give me a pained look. "Their *healer*."

"The sunlight helps. The plants help!" I insisted, rattling the bag again.

"But you can help more." Jorah's fingers began to trace along the red patch of skin at his elbow. "You need to stop focusing on ways to skirt around your responsibilities and lean into your calling as the ruler of this pod. Forget about Mavi's ridiculous salves and potions and being the reckless hero. Become the stronger healer your city deserves."

His words sliced into me, cleaving through my heart and sending the shredded pieces into my stomach. I pressed a hand against my chest, where it suddenly felt barren and hollow. *"I'm trying,"* I said inwardly, sending my thoughts Jorah's way. *"Don't you see that? I'm trying."*

Jorah watched me carefully. His shoulders sagged, and he groaned, rubbing a hand over his tightly pinched face. "If you are so desperate that you won't see reason, then I suppose I could allow you to send Illeron and his squadron of warriors tomorrow morning. He is more than capable of scouting."

I bit out a laugh. "That uptight sea urchin? No thank you."

Jorah shrugged. "That is my only compromise. It is just too dangerous, Evanora." He looked up at the throne. "If you refuse to let your best warrior go, then *no one* will go."

I clenched my fists at my sides, squeezing the bag tightly. "Oh," I seethed, my voice shaking, "you insufferable fish!"

Jorah flinched at my words but said nothing. He only cocked his head to the side and stared at me with the same tired look I was quickly beginning to loathe.

I turned with a choked growl, taking the bag with its few precious salves and storming out of the throne room.

The water was growing cool with the approaching dusk. It wouldn't be long before the fall of night. I still had to light all the lanterns bordering our city, take one of Mavi's salves to Braemos and Safra, and send my prayers to the ancestors.

And yet, I found myself swimming listlessly, in no particular direction, replaying Jorah's words in my head.

It is just too dangerous.

I gritted my teeth. Mavi was waiting in the square for good news I didn't have. I turned in the opposite direction, my tail moving with reluctant flicks.

You are needed here.

I knew that. But if I didn't act, there would soon be no one left to need me.

Passing beneath a crumbling archway, I scowled at its disrepair. The shadows deepened as I swam into an alley littered with shards of sea glass from broken roofs. The sun's reach faltered, and the temperature dipped. Goose bumps rippled across my skin, and I quickened my pace.

Our city hadn't always been this way—decrepit, lifeless.

Once, it was the gem of the Balafor, a shimmering beacon in the depths. Smooth white towers with sea-glass roofs stretched toward the surface, their light rivaling the stars above. Lava-rock paths weaved through lush seaweed forests, leading to an onyx fountain that pulsed like the city's very heart.

Our kingdom was once beautiful, strong, *mighty*.

But that was a long time ago. Back when my parents were alive and ruling, when there was peace between us and the humans.

When the Initial War hadn't happened yet and the Hunt didn't exist.

Every year, the humans yearned for our blood and rejoiced in our pain. Every year, our pod suffered, our great numbers declining at an alarming rate.

And this year, I was alone.

I no longer had someone to hide behind, someone to fight in the battle I was too young and too ill-prepared for.

I hated humans with every scale on my body, and I would not, *could not*, sit by and watch my pod die in the shadows.

But it wasn't going to be enough. The hatred, the loathing, wasn't going to stop the fin rot from blooming, or the hunger from eating away at bloated bellies, or the Dark Madness from settling into vulnerable minds.

I needed to do more.

I forbid you from leaving.

I paused, shifting to look at the palace at the crest of our city. My lower lip began to wobble, the sting of salty tears mingling with my pale white eyelashes. A sob stuck in my throat, I sank onto a broken crate, letting my frustration get the better of me.

"Why are you sad, Your Majesty?"

I rubbed my cheeks and turned swiftly to see who had snuck up on me.

Solandis hovered near the archway, her hands fidgeting nervously at her hip fins. Her large green eyes were wide as they hesitantly flitted from me to the brokenness that surrounded us.

I blinked away the last of my tears and forced a smile. "It's this blasted salt water. It always makes my eyes prickle." I sucked in a breath, my shoulders heaving as I reined in my emotions. "What are you doing here, Solandis? You know it is unsafe to play near the abandoned houses."

Solandis tucked a long strand of black hair behind her pointed ear. "I saw you swimming this way. I followed you."

"Whatever for?"

Solandis shrugged, her spotted green tail swishing up dust and debris. "You seemed troubled."

Without question. I nodded. "Well, I'm fine." I plastered on a bright smile. "Don't I appear fine?"

Solandis scrunched up her face, seeing the cracks that spread across my facade. "I'm told that lying is frowned upon."

Unable to help it, I let out a spurt of laughter. I wasn't supposed to have favorites amongst the merlings, but Solandis had carved a special place in my heart. "Perceptive little one, aren't you?" I sighed, motioning her forward. "You're right," I admitted when Solandis got close, her wide eyes fixed on mine. "I am a little blue in the gills. But do you know what would make me feel better?" I wrapped an arm around her small frame and squeezed her lightly. "A song."

Solandis frowned. "A song?"

"A song," I repeated. "Come now, let me see how your Gift is faring."

Solandis bit her lip, her eyebrows knitting together worriedly. "Surely there's another more talented siren you'd rather listen to?"

I shook my head vigorously. "No. I want to hear you." I offered a small smile, dipping my face low to meet her evading gaze. "Please?"

Solandis swallowed hard. "I'm not very good."

"That's not what Andoras tells me."

Solandis jolted, whirling around to face me at the mention of the water-wielding merling. "Really?"

I nodded. "He's saying you're the best siren out of all the merlings."

Solandis pressed a fist to her lips and tried to hide her grin; it was like the sun withholding its rays. "All right," she said, turning away from me. "But only for a second or two."

Solandis squeezed her eyes shut, opened her mouth, closed it, and then opened it again. Her throat began to glow as the first few notes drifted off her tongue, a mournful little squeak that sent the waters around us shuddering with her awakening magic.

"*Ancestors guide our pod to thee . . .*"

She tried again, her voice carrying more force as the song pulsated from her small frame, encompassing us in a ripple of bubbles.

"*To the light we may be free . . .*"

As the music came more freely, her neck and mouth began to shine, a beacon in the shadows of the alley. The undercurrent pulsated, churning with the force of Solandis's words.

"*May our journey be clean of strife . . .*"

The song wrapped around us, warm and encompassing, pulling me into memories of long ago. My ammah's voice echoed in my mind, singing the same lullaby as she held me close on stormy days, on the eve of the Hunt, and on nights when the lanterns didn't work.

"With our ancestors we claim eternal life."

I had become so wrapped up in the memories of me curling against Ammah's tail as she sang those very same words that I hadn't realized Solandis had stopped. The bubbles were already dissipating, the wall of music crumbling. I grasped the memory of my ammah as long as I could until it, too, disappeared with the undercurrent.

Solandis's hands were clutched together, her breath coming out in sharp bursts. "I can only do the first verse," she admitted quietly, sneaking a peek at me. "Oh. You're crying again."

My hands fluttered to my face. "Happy tears, I promise." I reached forward and squeezed Solandis's tightly bound hands. "It was lovely. No siren could have sung it better."

Solandis's fins relaxed from their taut state. "I wanted to be brave for you."

A wobbly smile graced my lips. "You were the bravest. Thank you."

Solandis's shoulders bowed slightly. "It's hard being brave sometimes."

"Yes, it is," I agreed.

Solandis's mouth quirked to the side. "I think it's a little easier when the mermaid you want to be brave for deserves it."

I froze, the sting of Jorah's words entering my mind.

Become the stronger healer your city deserves.

Becoming the healer my city deserved meant I had to be brave too.

My home. My pod. My crumbling kingdom.

I could be brave. I would not fail them.

I rose from my seat. "Forgive me, Solandis, but I must go." I leaned down, smiling as I cupped her delicate cheek. "You've given me the courage to do something I wasn't sure I could do."

Solandis's eyebrows rose in confusion, but she nodded.

Sucking in a breath, I retrieved the bag and hurled myself out of the shadows.

Straight for the island.

IT WAS NEARLY SUNSET BY THE TIME THE GLOWING LIGHTS OF THE island loomed before me. I remained confident; I could find an area ripe with plants and return to the city in time to light the lanterns. But I couldn't waste time. In the ever-darkening waters, my nerves were wild, sending my iridescent glow radiating off me in waves. I was an easy target for both humans and the hungry creatures within the Barrens.

I could hear their ominous whispers as I raced away from our kingdom's borders, their haunting lullaby calling out to me. When night approached, they'd grow louder, more insistent in their cacophonic chaos.

I had never seen a Cursed Being before, had only heard them calling from the dark. I didn't wish for that to change.

It wouldn't change. Not today. I had time.

Fins twitching in anticipation, I scoured the sun-soaked waters, trying to spot anything that would prove useful to the pod. My ears pricked, trying to listen for the scuttle of crabs, the whisper of plants in the waves. I was met with silence and disappointment.

I tilted my head, gazing at the surface. Maybe if I was higher up . . .

Retrieving my bravery, I pushed upward, stopping just before I touched the edge of the water. Glancing around, I took a deep breath, squeezed my eyes shut, and forced myself out of the wave's caress. A chilled spring breeze whispered over the top of my head and tips of my shoulders. The water was warmer, and my scales seemed to sigh with relief after being in the frigid depths for so long. I had nearly forgotten what warmth felt like.

I was closer to the island than I had realized. Pushing aside a drifting chunk of ice, I peered at the shoreline.

My gaze settled on something steaming and crackling, flickering dully with bursts of orange and red. A fire. It was nestled over to the side of the beach, where the coarse sand curved to meet a wall of rock that dipped into the ocean, forming large crevices and caves that got swallowed by the tide. The fire was dying, and I didn't see anyone tending to it.

The beach was empty.

Then I saw it—a soft glow near the water's edge where land kissed ocean. Prayer reeds. Their faint hum reached my ears even from the water. Rare and prized amongst mermaids, the reeds only grew in shallow waters, making them both precious and dangerous to collect.

And they were bursting with healing properties.

Hurried footsteps shattered the quiet. I dipped beneath the waves, the fins along my forearms flaring taut and sharp, ready to defend. The sound was muffled by sand but unmistakably close.

A shadow burst into view, pacing the waterline and yelping at the waves as they pummeled the beach. I relaxed, my fins slackening. It was an animal with shaggy black fur and a large pink tongue. The beast trotted and jumped, biting at the evading water and sniffing at the wet trail it left behind on the sand. I observed from below the surface, biting back a smile.

Then there was another sound. A voice.

My fins flared again as a man strode down the wooden stairs carved into the hillside at the edge of the beach. He whistled, calling to the beast as he patted his thighs. The animal ignored him, bolting past the steps to chase the waves farther down the shore. It glanced back at him, its tongue lolling in a playful grin.

The man gazed longingly at the fizzling fire, then back to his escaping companion. But he began to jog after the beast, calling out for it as he ambled into the shadows, out of sight.

Too dangerous. This was too *dangerous*.

I had done my job. I had scouted a location outside our borders and found victory. The uptight Illeron and his warriors could come back another time to grab the prayer reeds.

I bit my lip, staring longingly at the glowing plants, their luminescent colors drifting in the waves.

Or I could just grab them now.

Heart pounding up my throat, I scanned the beach once more to make sure the coast was still clear. I couldn't hear the barking of the animal or the heavy footsteps of the man. This was it. This was my chance.

Adrenaline bursting through me, I darted toward the prayer reeds, zigzagging through the seagrass, narrowly avoiding clusters of coral. In a matter of seconds, I was upon the plants, their faint glow kissing my skin, their humming fluttering to my ears. I reached forward, my fingers brushing against the smooth leaves.

And then I stopped.

Looked up.

The man was standing over me, silhouetted by the sunset. He was a tower, an impenetrable force as he stared down at me.

No. Not at me. At the prayer reeds.

The man crouched low, inspecting them. He cocked his head to the side, and I sucked in a breath as his hands dipped into the water, reaching for the plants. His large fingers brushed against the same leaves I had been going for, and the plants hummed louder at his touch. I swore I could feel his fingers drag against mine, and I bit back a hiss, fighting against the desire to rip my hand away. I remained still, even though everything inside me screamed at me to move, to fight, to flee.

At last, the man straightened, turning his hand to inspect the gleaming residue on his fingers. His beast barked in the distance, and he glanced toward the sound, hesitating before retreating down the beach.

Only when his shadow faded into the dusk did I dare to move.

My heart pounded against my ribs as I yanked handfuls of prayer reeds and stuffed them into my bag. The plants' hum seemed to echo my panic. When the bag was full, I pushed off the sandy floor and darted toward the depths, kicking up a spray of water and sand.

I was too loud, but I didn't care. I needed to escape, to put this nightmare behind me. My light flared in waves, illuminating my path through the darkening waters.

The sun slipped over the horizon. Night had officially fallen.

And the whispers began.

My light began to shift and crackle around me, coating me in an icy glow as I swam faster, faster, *faster.* The whispers grew louder. Was I going in the direction of home, or deeper into the darkness, toward the Barrens? I arched, turning sideways, trying a different direction. My electrifying light was nearly blinding. The Cursed Beings' voices ate at my mind, stealing my focus. I couldn't concentrate. Fear gripped at me as I twisted again, trying to find my bearings.

There was a mournful wail, sharp and piercing as it rippled the waters right beside me. The sound was close.

Too close.

The Cursed Beings had found me. They were *hunting* me.

I somersaulted, bending my body as I propelled myself in the opposite direction. Everything around me became blurred and distorted. *Get away from the sound!*

Suddenly, the beach came back into view in streaming colors of white sand, burnt fires, and colossal rock walls.

I was going too fast. If I didn't stop, I would crash onto the sand. Gritting my teeth, I swung my tail out, tangling in the water's current. The fins on my hips and forearms shook as the water pummeled into them.

There was a warbled *snap* as something solid coiled itself around my tail and wrapped around my body. It was thick and cold and reeked of humans.

And then I was no longer swimming. In fact, I had come to a painful dead halt.

Gasping, I grabbed at the strong rope cords that snaked across me, trying to pry them away, pull them apart, *something.* The braided strands only cinched tighter, ignoring my protests to escape. Barbed wires bit into my skin the harder I fought, and my tail quickly began to ache from being unnaturally folded around me. My bag was pinned against my side, digging into my ribs and squishing the valuable plants within. I whimpered, pressing my fingernails into the rope. This wasn't happening. This *couldn't* be happening!

As the sand around me settled, my light slowly began to dim, and my breathing turned shallow, the reality of my situation sank into my bones, cold and uninvited.

I was in a net. I was trapped. I could not get out.

CHAPTER FIVE

GRAYSON

CERTAIN SOUNDS BROUGHT ME COMFORT.

The whisper of waves crashing outside my bedroom window.

The soft whickering of Penny when she wanted more food.

The scraping of a pestle against plants in the mortar.

I found music in these sounds, melodies in what others might consider noise. They calmed me, grounded me.

Concentrating, I sank deeper into my chair. Clumps of witch hazel and angelica root lay scattered across the wooden surface of my desk. My journal, propped against the window ledge, displayed a recipe for a new salve I was trying to make. Squinting at the hurriedly scribbled words, I grabbed a handful of pink echinacea petals and dropped them into the mortar.

A bead of sweat slid down my cheek, and I paused to swipe it away. My fingers ached from gripping the pestle, but the plants refused to break down. Grinding harder, I ignored the dull throb in my knuckles.

My pa's footsteps outside my bedroom door—*that* was a sound I never enjoyed.

I heard the protesting creaks of my door being opened, followed by the sudden appearance of Pa's shadow on my wall. My back tightened in response, but I continued to focus on the plants.

Pa's shadow shifted as he slowly walked into the room, coming to stand just behind me. "You're up late," he said, placing his iron-reeking hands on the back of my chair and leaning forward, inspecting my desk and the chaos strewn upon it.

I picked up a chunk of witch hazel, dropping it into the mortar. Why were my fingers trembling? I gripped the pestle harder, grinding the plants into a pulp. I savored the sound of stone scraping stone for a second longer before answering. "I need to set this before the plants dry out, otherwise the salve is useless." I tossed a careful stare over my shoulder. "Penny's girth gall isn't getting any better, so I figured I could make her something to ease the pain."

Pa furrowed his brow, ignoring my pointed look. "She's a tough old bird. She'll be okay."

I broke apart some angelica root, mixing it in. "Not if you keep working her the way you do."

Pa pulled away from my chair, chuckling dryly as he circled around. "Always looking out for others, aren't you? Even on your birthday."

I tried not to cringe. It was well into the evening—in a few more hours, my birthday would be over, and I could pretend the day had never even happened.

I jumped as my pa dropped something hard and heavy onto my desk. He was kind enough not to hit the mortar, but the plants covering the wooden top weren't so lucky, and quickly deflated underneath the object's weight.

My heart stuttered to a stop as I flicked my gaze to the thing invading my desk and squishing my precious plants.

A hunting knife.

A *large* and *angry*-looking hunting knife.

Pa stepped back, folding his arms against his chest as he grimaced at me. I think it was meant to be a smile. "Happy birthday, son," he said.

I stared at the knife, dumbfounded. The blade glinted in the light of the flickering candle perched on my desk. The handle, smooth and white, looked like it had been carved from bone, and the flecks of glitter had me instantly thinking of mermaid scales. My stomach flipped; I didn't want to know where—or what—the bone had come from.

"Well, go on, then," Pa urged, gesturing eagerly to the knife. "Pick it up! See how it feels."

My hands were coated with sweat as I tentatively reached for the handle, holding it at arm's length between my thumb and index finger.

Pa clucked his tongue, shaking his head. "No, not like that. Like this." He leaned forward, clasping his hand around mine, adjusting my grip so that the handle was wholly pressed against my palm, my fingers encircling the cool bone. "Come on," he said, pinching my fingers in his grasp. "It won't bite you."

Oh, I very much doubt that, I thought.

His hand lingered a moment before he stepped back, nodding in approval. "A knife fit for a hunter," he said, his eyes alight with pride. "What do you think?"

A shiver ran through me. The knife's weight dragged at my arm, the bone handle cold and alien in my grasp. "It's . . . large."

Pa nodded, his mustache twitching with what might have been a grin. "And the weight?"

I wanted nothing more than to put it down, shove it as far from me as I could. "It's a little heavy," I admitted, my arm quivering under the strain.

When Pa's smile faltered, his eyes dimming, I quickly added, "I'll get used to it, I'm sure. With training."

Pa's face relaxed. "Oh, without a doubt. Soon you'll be wielding that knife like the best of them." He clapped a hand onto my shoulder, his satisfaction unmistakable. "My boy, finally joining me in the Hunt. I thought this day would never come."

A sigh slipped through my teeth. Setting down the knife, I picked up the pestle and mortar and began grinding at the pulp.

Pa's grip on my shoulder grew tighter, though I didn't think he realized he had done it. "Aren't you happy with your gift?"

I quickened my pace with the pestle, sparing Pa a brief glance before returning my attention back to the recipe. "No, I am. Really. It's just—"

"The plants. I know." Pa removed his hand from my clammy shoulder and walked over to Warrick's bed. He sat down heavily, the wooden frame groaning from his weight. Running a hand through his hair, he laughed quietly, the sound lacking mirth. "Warrick would have appreciated it." He sighed. "I don't know what I was thinking, giving you such a thing."

A pang of agony blistered underneath my skin. I bent forward, focusing on the mixture of plants in the mortar. "Well, I'm not Warrick, am I?"

I wanted to say more. That he was wrong—that Warrick would have hated the hunting knife even more than I did. That Warrick would have refused to acknowledge the Hunt, let alone take part in it. But I bit my tongue, swallowing the venom before it could spill out.

Pa sucked in a breath, dropping his head. "No," he muttered. "No, I guess you're not."

Silence permeated the air. I closed my eyes for a heartbeat, listening for the waves, for the *squish* and *squelch* of pulverizing plants, trying to find the comfort that had evaded me the second my pa entered the room.

With his head still down, Pa spoke again. "Warrick . . . The mermaids murdered him, Grayson. It didn't matter that he was young, or that he was innocent, or that he carried a heart that loved everything about the world." He lifted his head, piercing me with a hardened stare. "They murdered your brother because they are vicious, *heartless* creatures. They murdered him because they *could*."

My hands stilled. Wrong again.

Pa stood from the bed. "They hunted us, so now we hunt *them*." He clenched his fists, his knuckles cracking. "We are repaying the pain they've caused us. All the lives they've taken, the innocent bloodshed—we are simply returning it. *That* is what the Hunt is all about." He cleared his throat and the emotions lodged in it. "We are doing it for Warrick. Don't you think he deserves that much?"

When I didn't say anything, Pa sighed, rubbing at his misty eyes. "I was wrong about all of this." He stalked toward me, reaching for the hunting knife. "You're not ready for this. You're not ready for the Hunt."

Something sprang loose inside me. Impulsively, I slapped a hand on top of Pa's before he could take the blade away. "No! I am!" I pleaded. "I swear I am!"

What was I doing? What was I saying? My pa was right—no part of me was ready for this, or even *wanted* this.

Pa pressed his lips together, his brow drooping low over his eyes as he evaluated me carefully.

I tightened my grip on Pa's callused and scarred hand. "Please. I want to do this. I want to help."

Good God, what was happening?

Pa cocked his head to the side. "You're saying you want to enter the Hunt?"

I don't. "I do," I pushed. "For Warrick. You're right—he deserves that much."

Pa remained still for a moment before huffing, pulling out of my grasp, and heading for the door. "After the Symbolic Sign-In, there will be no turning back. You won't be able to change your mind."

"I won't," I said, my voice firmer than I felt. "I want to join."

He lingered in the doorway, one hand on the knob, his sharp eyes still watching me. "Be ready."

When the door closed, my breath escaped in a shaky rush. My shoulders sagged, and I buried my face in my hands before running them through my curls. My gaze drifted to the drying plants, then to the knife. A weight settled in my chest as I slumped forward, pressing my forehead against the desk.

Me, entering the Hunt. What an astronomically bad idea. Even the waves couldn't comfort me. *What have I done?*

CHAPTER SIX

EVANORA

"DON'T PANIC," I BREATHED. "DON'T PANIC, DON'T PANIC, don't panic."

You're panicking, my heart muttered within its bony cage.

I let out an aggravated growl, thudding my head against the back of the net.

How long had I been trapped? The sky was beginning to stir from its starry slumber, and the tide was retreating, inching back into the ocean. Time was slipping away.

My hands, blistered and raw, trembled as I stared at the ropes. This net wasn't ordinary—it was crafted specifically for mermaids. Unique to Lethe, its barbed wires reinforced the fibers, making it nearly impossible to tear apart. Not even my teeth and razor fins could break through. But that didn't stop me from trying.

The bells tied into the knots jingled with my every movement, their eerie chime like a mocking lullaby. Designed to lure us out of hiding, the bells now seemed to mock my struggles.

I clenched my hands into fists, ignoring the biting pain. I *had* to keep trying. Smothering my pride, I called out to Jorah in my mind, hoping he was close enough to hear my message.

"Stuck. Net. Daylight. Help."

I held my breath, waiting.

Even the silence had begun to taunt me; I was too far away. Jorah could not hear me.

Which meant I was as good as dead.

I shook my head in sharp, quick movements. No, I couldn't think like that. There was still time. I could still get out of this.

I pressed my palms against the ropes and closed my eyes. My magic flared within me, surging into the net in a burst of crackling white light. It immediately sputtered out, fizzling to nothing more but a limp flame. I sighed, slouching back. My Gift was spent; I couldn't rely on it to get me out or to heal the rope burns on my body.

What if someone finds you? my heart whispered, sending a bolt of icy fear down my back. *What if the owner of this net comes to check it?*

I pushed the damning thoughts aside. The algae and seaweed tangled in the thick cords told me that this net wasn't tended to frequently. It might've even been abandoned. I was much more likely to die of starvation than at the hands of a human.

That was, of course, unless someone came down to the beach for a morning stroll and spotted me.

I hissed, pushing against the barbed rope. In response, the ropes cinched tighter around me—another charming quality the nets possessed. The more I pushed, the tighter it got. I immediately relaxed my taut arms, steadying my breath as I closed my eyes.

What would happen to the pod if I didn't return? Jorah would take charge, but the old fish was only a shadow of his former self. The sores on his elbow worried me. Fin rot, the result of neglecting sunbathing, was the first sign that Dark Madness was closing in. It wouldn't be long before he succumbed entirely, slipping into the darkness eager to claim him.

How much longer before he started having delusions? How much longer before he looked at me—his queen, his *friend*—and didn't recognize me?

And even if Jorah were capable of tending to the pod without me, there was no one left to keep the Cursed Beings at bay. I bit my lip. How had they fared without me last night? If by some miracle I was able to escape, would I return home to find blood sifting through the water and the lifeless bodies of my pod floating like debris, all the light and life drained from them?

A sharp breath escaped me as my eyes snapped open. *No. Stop.* I couldn't afford to think like that. I *had* to get out.

I pressed my shredded hands against the ropes again, willing my magic to awaken. A faint spark flickered to my fingers, only to fizzle out. My grip on the net loosened as despair settled in. My Gift, like my hope, was fading.

Above me, the sky brightened, soft pinks and oranges chasing away the dark blues and grays of night. Tears pricked my eyes, unwelcome and uninvited. I blinked them back, frustration bubbling in my chest.

It was hard not to feel sorry for myself, trapped in a net of my own making. If only I'd listened to Jorah. If only I'd learned more from my parents before they died. Maybe things would have been different.

But they weren't. I was in a prison of rope, and the sun was rising, and my pod was left defenseless in my absence. And it was all my fault.

As the first rays of light pierced the horizon, and the tide continued to pull away from the beach, exposing the tip of my head to the cool spring air, I allowed myself to panic.

CHAPTER SEVEN

GRAYSON

APRIL 1 – MORNING

I WAS FAIRLY CONFIDENT THAT I HADN'T SLEPT EVEN A SINGLE minute last night.

The conversation with Pa replayed in my head on a torturous loop. No matter how many times I picked it apart, I still didn't understand why I'd agreed to join the Hunt. What was I thinking? I wanted nothing to do with it. Pa had even given me the chance to back out.

Part of me wondered if his seemingly gracious gesture was actually a trap, one laced with guilt. With all that had occurred in our family, our relationship was rocky at the best of times, and I didn't want to do anything to make it worse. Not participating in the Hunt felt like a surefire way to teeter our relationship into earthquake territory.

I blinked, staring hard at the bookshelf in front of me. My stomach churned sourly at the sight. Books of all shapes and sizes swarmed before my eyes. Tips on winning the Hunt and scoring high on the betting board. The Initial War that had ruined our fragile peace with the mermaids. The best way to harvest mermaid organs. On and on the grotesque titles went. I had never even been in this section of the library before, and for good reason.

"Excuse me, sir, but I believe the botany section is three aisles over," a voice whispered in my direction.

Holly was peeking out from the end of the bookshelf I was glued in front of.

I laughed awkwardly, scratching the back of my head. "I thought I'd try something new. You know"—I grabbed a hefty book from the shelf and waved it at her—"do some light reading."

Holly clasped her hands behind her back and strode toward me, her brown cognac boots shuffling along the worn carpet. She peered at the book I was holding, biting back a giggle. "You look like a fish out of water."

I sighed, plunking the book back onto the shelf. "Is it that obvious?"

Holly's mouth twisted to the side, and after a moment of thoughtful silence, she plucked out a smaller, less intimidating book two shelves over. "Here," she said, handing it to me. "This one suits you better, I think."

I scanned the cover. "*The Art of Combat*," I read aloud. "*A beginner's guide to wielding a weapon.*" I whistled, looking over the top of the book to meet Holly's watchful stare. "Will this help me become a hunter?" I asked, half joking.

Holly grimaced. "At the very least, it'll help you not cut yourself." Her eyes trailed down to my leg. "Especially with a blade that size. Jasper will be jealous."

For a blissful moment, I had forgotten about the hunting knife strapped to my hip and thigh. The weight of it was suddenly unbearable.

"And we all know what happens when you see blood, don't we, buttercup?" a voice called out from behind the bookshelf.

Holly and I turned to see Jasper saunter into the aisle, a cocky grin plastered across his face. Leaning against the shelf, he mimicked a fainting swoon. "You turn into a regular damsel in distress!"

I rolled my eyes, turning my attention back to the book. "That's a little excessive."

"Not in the slightest." Jasper pushed off the shelf, smirking. "Even Holly doesn't faint like you do." His gaze landed on the knife, and his grin faltered, his jaw going comedically slack.

Holly tsked. "Jasper speechless. There's a first."

Jasper gave his head a quick shake, hitting me with a bewildered look before limping forward. "Look at the size of that thing!" he crowed. "You'll take your own eye out for sure!"

Mrs. Humphries looked up from her perch behind the front desk. The cranky librarian's beady eyes pinned each of us with heat, though she had to lean around a mountain of books to do it.

Holly ducked her head, her fair cheeks quick to flush. "Jasper! Inside voice!"

Jasper paid Holly no mind, pushing around her to get to me. "Let's have a look, then," he gushed, his fingers tugging on the clasp.

I pulled away, clamping a hand over Jasper's. "Jasper, no."

"Oh, come on!" Jasper whined. "You can't keep all the fun to yourself. I just want to look."

Holly tugged at the brooch pinned at her neck, glancing hurriedly toward Mrs. Humphries, who was now standing with her hands planted on the desk.

"*Jasper!*" she hissed.

"Just a peek!" Jasper urged, prying my fingers away and trying at the clasp with a surge of enthusiasm.

The clasp popped out of place, and Jasper hooted victoriously. Images of bleeding fingers swam in my mind, and I jerked my hands away as Jasper pulled the knife out of its sheath. He whistled through his teeth, lifting the blade to his eyes. "This is *nice*," he breathed.

"Thank you," I said, my voice strained. "Now give it back."

Jasper jabbed at the air a couple times, swinging the blade back and forth before pausing to inspect it again. "Heavy too!" He swung it again, narrowly missing the bookshelf. "Must've cost a pretty penny."

If I didn't hate birthdays and the Hunt before, I certainly loathed them now. "It's not a *toy*, Jasper," I seethed, leaning away as he struck the air between Holly and me.

Mrs. Humphries was stomping our way. Dropping my book, I reached for the knife, thought the better of it, and aimed for Jasper's wrist. "All right. Time to give it back."

Jasper flinched away, dragging me with him. "But I'm not done with it!"

I spared a fleeting glance at Holly, who looked about as petrified as I felt. "I am. *We* are."

Jasper tried to wrench himself free from my clammy grasp, sending us both into the shelf. Several books burst from the rows, flopping to the ground and sending up clouds of dust.

"Boys!" Mrs. Humphries barked from her looming position beside Holly. "That is quite enough!"

I straightened quickly, my back going rigid beneath my sweat-soaked shirt. I bumped into Jasper, causing him to drop the knife. The blade sank into the carpet between his feet. Jasper's eyes dropped to the discarded knife, then to me, and together, we slowly turned to face the librarian.

Mrs. Humphries planted her hands on her thick hips. "Unsheathed weapons are strictly prohibited in the library!" She scowled, glaring at us through her horn-rimmed glasses. "Put that thing away before someone gets hurt!"

Jasper lunged for the knife, but I got there first. My fingers gripped the hilt, and I gave it a yank. It didn't budge. A helpless laugh escaped me as I wrapped both hands around the hilt and tried again. With a loud *riiiiip*, the blade finally came free—along with a chunk of jade-green carpet.

I stared in horror as the shredded piece of flooring slid off the blade and flopped onto my boot. *Mortifying. This is mortifying.* I glanced down at the fresh hole in the library floor, wishing it would widen enough to swallow me whole.

Mrs. Humphries gawked at the wad of carpet next to my boot. "The . . . The floor!" She took a stumbling step forward, her hands outstretched to the hole. "The *carpet*!"

Jasper made a hearty *ah!* sound and lurched down, picking up the chunk and handing it to Mrs. Humphries. "There you go!" he chirped, smiling sweetly and looking proud of himself.

Mrs. Humphries cradled the carpet with shaking fingers. She stared at it for so long that her glasses slipped off her hooked nose and clattered to the floor, next to the hole. When she looked back up at us, she was baring her yellowing teeth. "You should be *ashamed* of yourselves!"

I cringed against the words, and Jasper's smile flattened out. Holly fussed with her burnt-orange skirts and avoided my pleading gaze. Her lips were pinched to keep from wobbling.

"Roughhousing and damaging village property!" Mrs. Humphries went on, crumbling the carpet in her balled-up fist. "Why they let *boys* participate in the Hunt stands for beyond reason."

Jasper, dear oblivious Jasper, frowned. "But we're not boys—"

I elbowed him sharply, and the rest of his sentence ended in a cough. "We're so sorry, ma'am," I said earnestly.

I elbowed Jasper again, and he repeated the words with a lot less enthusiasm.

Mrs. Humphries was in the process of turning into a tomato. Her skin was taking on a shiny red tinge that matched her ill-fitting dress. The dark mole between her eyebrows had a pulse of its own. "Both of you, out. Now." She pointed a finger at the door. "Before I report you to Mr. Grieves."

Jasper opened his mouth to speak, but I yanked on his arm, tugging him toward the exit. "Sorry again!" I called over my shoulder, picking up my pace before the librarian exploded.

Holly didn't meet my eyes once.

Jasper and I walked in silence. I was trying not to be mad, but it was really, really hard.

Jasper was the first one to speak. "Well, that escalated quickly!" he said, kicking at a stone on the sidewalk.

I stuffed my hands into my pockets and tilted my head to the side, offering Jasper a shriveling stare. "It didn't have to escalate at *all.*"

"Oh, it was just a little fun."

"Holly didn't seem to think so."

Jasper winced. "Yeah . . . I guess I'll be getting the silent treatment for a while."

I thought back to the shame she had worn like a second skin, the hate in her eyes as she played with the fabric of her skirt. A pang of guilt fluttered through my chest. "I hope she isn't in too much trouble."

Jasper threw his head back to guffaw at the sky. "I wouldn't worry too hard about her. She's a good girl. They need her there too, what with so many people leaving for the mainland."

My frown deepened, unease unfurling within my gut like a poisonous vine. "The cost of the damage to the floor might come out of her own pocket, you know."

"Oh, please." Jasper rolled his eyes. "Mr. Moneybags Grieves hasn't borrowed a book from the library in *years*. I doubt he knows the place still exists."

She couldn't even look at me. Another fear sprang to mind. "You don't think she'll give me the silent treatment too, do you?"

A sardonic chuckle escaped Jasper's lips. "You? No. She could never be mad at you."

"But—"

Jasper grunted, throwing an arm around my shoulders and pulling me close. "Listen," he said, interrupting my anxiety, "if I were you, I'd focus less on my sister, and more on tonight." He sighed dreamily, resting his head against my shoulder. "The First Festival—the beginning of the best time of our lives! I've been waiting for this moment for *years*." His head rolled to the side, a huge grin plastered onto his face. "Our first Hunt is *finally* here."

"Yay," I responded with absolutely no enthusiasm.

Jasper, oblivious to my rapidly souring mood, nodded jubilantly. "We are doing such a good deed for our island. The more hunters, the more mermaids dead. And the more mermaids dead, the better the tourist season. We can finally give back to society, do our part in fighting for our right to survive." He glanced at me dolefully, batting his light eyelashes. "You're still coming tonight, right? I'll let you be my wingman!"

I forced a weak smile, jostling him off my shoulder. "If only to help you get laid."

Jasper straightened, beaming at me. "Attaboy!"

We went our separate ways—but not before Jasper made me swear up and down that I was *actually* going to help him find a girl with desperately low standards—and with a wavering breath, I stepped off the sidewalk and weaved through the carts bustling by. I crossed the road that caressed the hill my house sat upon and kept walking.

I could hear the water long before I could see it, and my nerves immediately began to bristle to attention. As the flagstone road eventually crumbled away to a simple dirt path nearly overrun with dead grass, and the din of Main Street was eaten away by the roar of the waves and whisper of the wind, I could feel the familiar pull on my heart as my feet carried me to the ocean.

After Warrick died, after Ma, I had become deathly afraid of water. And yet, I was drawn to it. Like a masochistic moth to a flame, I allowed the waves to sing me their lullaby, soothing my soul and the worries burdening it. *Come closer, closer, closer*, the ocean seemed to say to me. And I would listen. But rarely had I fully succumbed to its call. I couldn't. It was a rare occurrence to go any deeper than my knees.

I was drawn to the water, but I also wasn't stupid enough to trust its siren call.

I wandered down the embankment, the dirt path gradually giving way to uneven stairs. Soon, even the stairs disappeared, replaced by coarse sand choked with tufts of wildflowers and weeds. Hannigan's Cove wasn't special—not like the black sands and turquoise waves of Fariid's beaches, or the white sands of Fenharrow Bay that turned crimson when wet. Aside from the basalt columns eroded into caves and craters, it was unremarkable. The brittle sand rubbed your feet raw, the westward wind cut against your face, and the ever-present stench of fish from the Tully docks clung to the air.

Still, it was home.

I closed my eyes and drew in a deep breath of salt-laden air. The wind nipped at my nose and tore at my clothes, but I welcomed it. Pulling off my boots and peeling away my threadbare socks, I rolled up my trousers and let my toes sink into the biting sand. Its coolness sent a shiver up my spine, but it felt grounding, calming.

The waves danced along the shore, a swirling mix of grays and deep blues that swelled and crested before crashing into the earth. Slowly, the tension of the library faded, my shoulders loosening with each brush of wind, each breath of the Balafor Ocean.

Feeling more like myself, I began to hunt for plants to inspect. I crouched, plucking a deep purple one and holding it close to my face. The petals splayed outward, revealing the flower's vibrant orange insides. *A violet, perhaps?* I chewed on my lower lip, my brow furrowing. *A bog iris?* I brought the flower to my nose, hoping to catch a scent before the wind stole it away.

There was a heavy splash, shattering through the rhythmic thrum of the waves.

I froze. The sound was close. Too close.

I wasn't alone.

CHAPTER EIGHT

GRAYSON

APRIL 1 – MORNING

I SHOT TO MY FEET, MY HEART IN MY THROAT AS I SCANNED the water. The wind gusted around me, causing the sand to spin at my feet. I paid the icy breeze no mind as my eyes trailed along the water, searching for the source of the noise. Rocks jutted from the churning surface, clumps of seaweed drifted through the foam, a chorus of seagulls chimed overhead as they searched for their next meal.

Then I saw her.

A mermaid, tangled in a net.

A gasp tore from my throat. The flower slipped from my grasp, landing forgotten at my feet.

A mermaid. A real mermaid. Here, in front of me.

The tide had gone out, exposing the mermaid in her roped prison from the waist up.

She had gone deathly still, her vibrant violet eyes fixed on me, unblinking. I was frozen in place, stuck in her silent stare. I could feel my legs quake as tremors laced through my joints, feeding the chill that crawled up my spine. My mind was swimming with scattered thoughts, each fragmented end chasing the next, everywhere at once, going nowhere.

We stared at each other for an infinity. Neither one of us moved. Neither one of us breathed.

Then the mermaid thrashed her tied-up tail, a quiet hiss seeping from her snarling lips.

I began to run.

Spinning on my toes, I raced up the hill, leaving my boots and socks, the flower, and the mermaid behind. *Move.* I gritted my teeth, pushing myself faster. *Move!*

I was halfway up the sandy embankment when a mournful shriek pierced the air, riding on the back of the wind. My pace faltered. She howled again, a high-pitched keening sound that was a mixture of a woman wailing and wind chimes caught in a storm. I slowed to a stop. Against the warnings wreaking havoc in my mind, I turned.

Even from the embankment, I could see that the mermaid was tired. She was panting from exertion, the shimmering scales on her arms and face dry and cracking from being out of the water. How long had she been stuck there? I glanced up the embankment as she screamed again. How long before people came to investigate the unearthly noise? How long before she was found, dragged to shore, and killed?

Sucking in a breath, I was moving again.

Not up the embankment, but down it.

Toward the mermaid.

I ran as fast as my feet could carry me, stumbling as I fought against the sand's sinking pull. *Stupid*, I thought, ripping off my jacket and throwing it onto the ground. *This is so, so stupid!*

The mermaid screeched, recoiling as I reached out. The net cinched tighter with her struggles, forcing her shoulders inward and her head down. Her tail flailed in the shallow water, splashing against my thighs.

"Be still!" I barked, gripping the slick ropes.

My words only spurred her on, her thrashing frantic and wild. The net groaned under the strain, its barbed edges nearly slicing my fingers.

The ropes were old, the braids fraying. If I could loosen the strands enough, I might be able to create a gap for her to escape. But how?

Then I felt it—the knife at my hip.

With one hand clamped around the net, I reached down and unclasped the knife strapped to my leg. At the sight of the blade, the mermaid screamed. Shrill and long and without end. She writhed heavily against the roped cage, showering us both in waves of water and sand. I grunted, looping my arm into one of the net's holes. *Stupid. This is stupid!* The mermaid was a wild, unpredictable beast. One wrong move and she'd tear my arm off. Or worse— she'd cinch the net so tight that I ended up getting pinned there with her.

"Please stop!" I pleaded, adjusting the blade in my hand and aiming for the net. "I'm trying to help you!"

The mermaid stilled, but only for a heartbeat. Thankfully, it was long enough for me to wedge the knife into the reinforced braids. Gritting my teeth, I twisted the blade. The fibers groaned in protest before snapping apart, one by one. Tossing the knife behind me, I dug my shaking fingers into the small gap I'd created and pulled with everything I had.

A guttural moan escaped her—the sound raw and feral, clawing its way into my ears. My stomach turned, but I didn't stop.

The ropes began to fray and tear, loosening under the strain. Rising clumsily, I planted my foot on the exposed net and yanked upward, forcing the hole wider. Little by little, it stretched, wobbling open like a crooked smile. When the net finally sagged, the mermaid sucked in a shuddering breath, her chest heaving with relief.

But she made no move for the opening. I panted, holding the net's hole as high as my cramping arms would allow.

"Can you get out?" I asked tentatively.

The mermaid looked up at me. She bared her teeth, her porcelain body vibrating. She remained tucked into the farthest corner of the net, her long white tail curled awkwardly around her.

There was nothing. No movement, no words, nothing but sounds of heavy breathing and the water colliding with the shore.

Then, without warning, she lunged.

The mermaid tore through the opening with a deep growl, her claws raking against the ropes as she dragged herself free. Her tail thrashed wildly, sending sprays of sand into the air. I stumbled back with a startled cry, the adrenaline that had propelled me moments before now draining away, leaving me hollow. My knees buckled, and I collapsed into the wet sand.

She didn't stop.

I scrambled backward, my hands and feet slipping in the damp grit. My eyes locked on hers, wide and unblinking.

Her body rippled with inhuman strength, her movements smooth and deliberate despite her exhaustion. Her face, framed by long tangled white hair clinging to her sharp cheekbones, twisted into a mask of rage.

The mermaid froze, her chest rising and falling in ragged bursts. Her piercing gaze pinned me in place. Then she turned her head and let out a mournful wail. It sliced through the wind, raw and unrelenting.

Her tail.

The net had collapsed when I dropped it, ensnaring the fluke. She twisted and dragged herself along the sand, but the wad of ropes trailed after her. Straining, she reached back with her webbed hands, her body twisting at an awkward angle. But she couldn't reach—not without making herself vulnerable. Her dorsal fin trembled, and a choked sound—half sob, half growl—escaped her lips. She sank to her forearms, defeated.

I held my breath, watching as the mermaid bowed her head, the gills on her neck working furiously. She was so close to getting free, too close to give up now. Steeling my unraveled nerves a final time, I crawled until I was within reach of the net. Keeping my eyes on the mermaid, I hooked my hands into the rope's ripped opening once more and lifted it. My fingers grazed the mermaid's tail, slipping along the cool, silky scales. They shimmered under my touch.

The mermaid hissed, whipping around and striking me. The movement was lightning fast. I had no time to react. The fin on her forearm had been soft and fragile only moments earlier. Now it was rigid and razor-like as it sliced along my arm.

I yelped and let go of the net, dragging myself back and clutching my arm against my chest. Thankfully, the hole remained open long enough for the mermaid to pull her tail out; I didn't know if I had the strength to try again.

Now free, the mermaid flopped her tail, lifting it up into the air and slapping it hard against the sand, almost like she was stretching. She cocked her head to the side and inspected me with a calculating gaze. I cowered back, a whimper oozing past my tightly clenched lips. But I couldn't look away. I couldn't blink.

The mermaid's lips curled into a snarl. Her tail smacked the ground again, sending vibrations that scuttled up my arms.

And then she was gone.

As a large wave crashed into the sand, the mermaid twisted around and dove into it, following the rush of water as it hurried away from the shore.

I panted against the ground, my heart a foul beast in my chest. It was going to stop working, I just knew it. I sputtered out a breath, a mixture of a groan and gasp intermingling with it. As I forced myself to sit up, I searched the cascading waves for her. Was she going to come back? Realize that it was a mistake keeping me alive and return to slit my throat? When I was only met with the lulling waves and the whispers of the wind, I heaved a long sigh and flopped back onto the sand, staring up at the sky. Clouds drifted lazily along their vibrant blue background, ignoring the state I was in.

I raised my arm and eyed up the large slice in my shirt. Quaking, I traced my fingers along my skin, expecting to be met with the warmth of blood and shredded flesh.

My arm was cold, wet, and intact.

"Oh," I wheezed, dropping my hand back onto my chest, "thank God."

I had to move. If anyone came down and saw me next to the wrecked net, they would immediately be suspicious. But I was absolutely drained, nothing left in my system save for frazzled nerves and overflowing relief that I had survived such a vicious encounter.

I was also fairly confident that I had pissed myself.

Under my other hand, I could feel the cold bone hilt of my discarded hunting knife. I plucked it up, examining the large blade with a new outlook. Perhaps it had its uses after all.

I grunted, sitting back up. My body ached in protest, but I ignored its chirps and whines for rest and staggered to my feet. As I brushed the sand from my pants, hair, and face, I glanced at the net. Something was still tangled in it. I waded back into the water, plunging my fingers into the mass of rope until I snagged the soft fabric. Pulling it out, I watched as it twisted slowly in my hands.

A bag.

Hesitantly, I opened the top, peering inside.

It held a couple jars with green mush trapped inside and a handful of freshly plucked plants. I frowned. I'd seen them around the island. They grew in the shallow waters, and while I enjoyed the soft glow their leaves emitted, I had always assumed they were poisonous. I closed the bag, gazing out to the ocean once more, feeling the familiar thread of longing pull at my heartstrings as the water sang to me.

So, I wondered, *what did she want with them?*

CHAPTER NINE

EVANORA

APRIL 1 – MORNING

I RACED HOME AS FAST AS MY TAIL WOULD PROPEL ME, BUT IT never felt fast enough. No matter how much distance I put between myself and the beach, I could still feel the ropes biting into my skin, still smell the metallic sting of barbed wire embedded in my flesh. I had escaped, but in my mind, I was still trapped—still tangled in that net, stranded in a prison built just for me.

Not escaped, per se, I reminded myself. *Rescued. By a boy.*

My veins flared with hate at the thought. The fact that I couldn't free myself was embarrassing enough. But saved by a human? Absolutely deplorable.

And, *gods*, the bag. In my hurry to leave, I had left it behind. I stifled a growl. Mavi's remaining jars of salves, the freshly procured prayer reeds I had risked everything to grab . . .

I had been reckless, a fool, and now I had nothing to show for it.

The kingdom was barren when I arrived. The sun shimmered through the water, reaching for the lava-rock streets, tumbling across the marble pillars lining the entrance to the palace. But it was quiet. Not a soul lingered within the glowing streets, the cramped homes, or the forests of seaweed surrounding the city. There was no one training in the weaponry in the south and no one hunting in the coral to the west.

My home was abandoned.

I circled the statue in the city square, hands running through my hair. I denied myself the panic that begged to swell in my throat and forced my heart to resume its painfully steady rhythm. The pod was safe—that much was certain. There would've been blood in the water if death and destruction had entered the kingdom. I bit my lip, my eyes frantically searching the empty space. *But . . . where are they?*

I straightened, twisting to look at the obscured path beyond the crumbling homes. *The cave.* I breathed a sigh of relief, the muscles in my neck loosening. *Of course!*

I swam as hard as I could, pushing through the long reeds of seaweed that stretched along the northeastern part of the kingdom. Schools of fish scattered out of my way, and a pair of porpoises looked particularly perturbed at my hurry. I pushed on, picking up my speed when the cave came into view. *Please be in there!*

Without hesitation, I aimed for the section of rock that was cluttered in sweeping vines and wild water flowers. My tail whipped behind me, strong and sure. They were going to be in the cave system my parents had created to ensure our safety in times of emergency. I couldn't bear to think anything different.

Holding my breath, I squeezed my eyes shut and collided with the curtain of plants.

The pod was tucked into the folds of the cave, cowering against the shadows and pressed into the dark tunnels that stretched away from the main chamber. They collectively shrieked when I burst through the entrance, curling into one another, trying to become smaller, invisible.

There was silence save for my heavy gasping. And then—

"Evanora!" Mavi cried, pulling herself out of the throng of mermaids and racing toward me, arms outstretched, her eyes coated with unshed tears.

Relief flooded me as Mavi wrapped her shaking arms around my waist and squeezed hard. "I'm here," I gulped, pressing my face into her tightly coiled hair. "I'm back!"

The pod, realizing it was me and not a predator—or something worse—instantly relaxed. Small cries of joy echoed in the cave as they crowded closer, drawn to the faint light my nervous glow cast. How long had they been here, hiding in the dark? How long had they been afraid to leave the safety of the chamber?

Mavi released me, her hands roving over my face, my neck, my arms, her endless honey-gold eyes filled with worry as they assessed every cut, every burn, every tear.

I chuckled, gripping her hands in mine. "It's all right, Mavi. I'm still in one piece."

Mavi's shoulders shook as she crumpled forward. "I thought you were dead." She glanced over her shoulder at the mermaids surrounding us. "We all did."

I let out a shuddering breath, the memory of the net still fresh on my skin. "I almost was," I admitted.

Mavi sniffled, blinking through another onslaught of tears. "What happened?"

Casting a hurried look through the crowd, I dipped my head, my voice dropping with the movement. "I went to forage, and—"

"Of all the *selfish* things!" Jorah's growl cut through my hushed words.

My advisor pushed through the crowd of mermaids, wedging himself between me and Mavi. The snarl on his face was scathing, and I fought to not shrink back. Still, my fins wilted, giving my true feelings away.

"How could you be so reckless?" Jorah snapped. "After I specifically forbade you from going!"

My scales bristled at his tone. I crossed my arms over my chest. "I was doing it for the pod."

Jorah looked so tired, worn thin, whittling away to nothing. "On the first day of Hunting Month, no less." He pointed a shaking finger at me. "You knew how dangerous it could be, and you went anyway. Foolish girl!"

I raised my arms, gesturing to the mass of mermaids circling us. "Jorah, the Hunt is the entire reason *why* I went. We need to forage, more than ever. To ensure that we are safe and protected when the time of the Hunt arrives!" I swallowed. "I even found some prayer reeds."

Jorah tilted his head to the side, his eyes dragging along my naked arms. "And? Where are these prized *lifesaving* plants? The ones you felt the irresponsible need to get, putting your entire pod in danger?"

I bit my lip, rubbing the soft fins at my forearms. "I might've forgotten them."

Mavi stiffened. "My bag?" she squeaked.

I couldn't look at her as I shook my head, ashamed.

Jorah gave a barking laugh that carried very little warmth. He spun in a sharp circle, touching his elbow. "Oh, that is *rich*."

I flinched at the words but didn't offer a defense. He was right, after all. I would hold off on telling him about the net and the boy. That would just make everything worse, add fuel to his hurricane temper. Instead, I reached forward, taking his arm.

"Jorah," I said, "there is no reason to continue with this scolding." I placed a hand over my heart. "I have learned my lesson, and you did a wonderful job taking my place as leader."

Jorah narrowed his eyes at me. "Flattery will not aid you right now, Your Majesty."

I shook my head, softening my mouth into a smile. "My words are genuine. The pod is safe because of you." I looked around, my glow bouncing off the low ceiling, illuminating the crowd. "With your guidance, everyone was able to make it into the cave."

Jorah bristled in my grasp. "No." He sighed. "Not everyone."

A bolt of alarm speared through my bloodstream. I let go of him, turning to look at the mass of mermaids. Her name was on my tongue as my eyes scanned the crowd, drifting into the tunnels, along the walls. Everyone looked back at me expectantly, and when I finally found Solandis peeking out from underneath a rocky overhang, her large green eyes red from crying, her lips swollen from biting back whimpers, I allowed myself to loose the breath I had been holding.

I searched again, trying to find the missing piece, the hole in my memory. And then I realized it. The answer was obvious.

Safra and Braemos.

I shifted sharply to Jorah. "What happened?"

Jorah had gone back to rubbing at the oozing sores that seemed to be crawling over his fins and up his arms. "There was no time," he breathed. "They were too weak. Without your light in the lanterns, the darkness closed in too quickly." He shook his head, his shoulders sagging. "I couldn't stop it. I tried, but . . . without the lanterns, the Cursed Beings . . ." He began to shake. "They swept in, and—"

I rushed out of the cave, Jorah's cries of protest following me through the entrance as I raced back to the city. A deep rage bloomed within me, festering in my gut and burning in my veins as I tore through my home, diving through the alleys, ducking under caving archways, until I made it to the back row of houses. To the place I had visited what felt like lifetimes ago.

There, lying in the same bed of seaweed they had been in when I had come to act as a healer, were Safra and Braemos.

They were tangled together, their arms jutting out at awkward angles, bones poking from scaled skin. Their tails were torn, fins shredded. Blood still seeped from their mouths, their noses, from their eyes, wide and unseeing. Braemos was clutching Safra, his hand pressed against her waist, where her flesh—still pink and swollen from when I had healed her—was ripped away, exposing bloated intestines, a crab feasting on her stomach lining, and a sea of blood from a heart no longer beating.

Dead. They were dead because of me.

CHAPTER TEN

GRAYSON

APRIL 1 – EVENING

I T WAS WELL PAST NIGHTFALL, AND I WANTED NOTHING MORE than to crawl into bed and fall into a sleep that would make the dead jealous. But it was April 1, and I knew that I wouldn't be sleeping for a while.

I sighed, stretching out my shoulders. The events of the day had left me feeling stupidly sore. After my run-in with the mermaid, I'd left Hannigan's Cove a frazzled mess, only to return to retrieve the ruined net. I didn't want someone stumbling upon it and seeing the huge hole I had put in it. But now that it was in the loft of the barn, I wasn't sure what to do. Keeping it was not an option. Completely destroying it just seemed wrong. Repairing it and returning it to the beach *also* seemed wrong, but also like the lesser of two evils. Damn me and my good heart.

I twisted my back, earning several cricks and crunches along my spine. The old rotary phone on our kitchen counter had yet to ring, and I was getting tired of standing and staring at it. Jasper had promised to call before swinging by to grab me. I knew he was pretending to be nice, but really, all he was doing was making sure I couldn't back out of going to the festival.

I narrowed my eyes at the phone, willing it to ring. The festival was in Fariid. Walking there would take over an hour. That was if it was daylight and the weather was cooperating. The time was cut in half if you owned a vehicle—a luxury Pa and I didn't have. I looked down at my clothes. The dark brown trousers could hide the mud and dirt I'd accumulate with walking, but the off-white long-sleeve cotton shirt wouldn't. I fidgeted with the buttons of my navy-blue vest and glared at the phone again.

The ancient machine chirped in its receiver, startling me and the silence I had been tucked into. I ripped the phone off the hook hurriedly. "Hello?"

"Can you take a call from the Warren residence?" the operator asked in a voice thick with smoke.

I clutched the phone to my ear. "Yes!"

The operator sighed tiredly. "One moment please."

Silence. And then: "Grayson!" a scratchy voice called out from the other end.

I closed my eyes and exhaled slowly, stifling my impatience. "Jasper, where *are* you?"

Jasper groaned on the other end, fading in and out with the bad connection. "It's not my fault! It's crazy over here, Grays. The twins knocked milk onto my dress jacket, and Holly is going on strike about having to stay home to babysit, and now Ma and Pa are talking about canceling the night altogether!" He took a deep breath. "It's general anarchy over here. I'm sorry, Grayson, but you'd have better luck going with your pa in the butcher cart."

I pinched the bridge of my nose, leaning against the wall with a huff. "Pa's already in Fariid with Penny. He's been there all day, setting up the booth to sell jerky and candied meats."

I heard Jasper curse on the other end—rebellious, but low enough so his parents didn't hear. "Then I think you'll have to walk."

"I don't know, Jasper. Maybe I'll—"

"Don't even *think* about not going!" Jasper hollered. "You promised you'd go!"

"And *you* promised to pick me up. It's a stalemate."

There was some shuffling on the other phone, followed by some raised voices. "I gotta go, Grays, see if I can talk some sense into my parents or something. If, by some miracle, I make it to the festival and you aren't there, I won't let you hear the end of it, I swear!"

The phone went dead, a solemn dial tone ringing in my ears. I gritted my teeth and placed the phone back on the wall.

Walking. Great.

T HE AIR WAS BRISK AS I MADE MY WAY DOWN THE HILL. THE FES-
tival would be in full swing by the time I got to Fariid. I tucked my chin
into the collar of my coat, quickening my pace. I could've been back home,
playing with my plants, going to bed at a decent hour. Instead, I was walking
to a party I didn't even want to go to. *In the cold.* I tripped over a hidden
rock, then another. *And in the dark.*

I was nearing Tully's village borders when there was the noise of wheels
crunching along the road and the huffing and whickering of a horse. I stepped
to the side and looked up as a simple carriage hobbled by. I nodded at the
driver, who was cloaked in the darkness of the night. But instead of pulling
by me, the driver mustered up a "Whoa!" and yanked on the reins, easing the
horse to a halt. The driver set the reins down and leaned over, peering at me.
"Young Shaw, is that you?"

I squinted up at the driver. The voice was familiar. The same one
I had heard rasping behind a splintered pulpit every Sunday. "Pastor
Kline?" I tried.

Pastor Kline guffawed and slapped his knee. "So, it is you!" he croaked.
"What is a smart lad like you doing out on a cold dark night like this?"

I gestured down the road with a nod of my head. "Just trying to make my
way into Fariid."

He tipped his large-brimmed felt hat back, rubbing his wrinkled forehead. "Fariid? At this hour? And on foot?" His frown deepened. "You
wouldn't be wandering off to the festival, would you?"

I shrugged, putting my hands into my pockets. They were already getting
cold. "I guess it's a little ambitious of me."

Pastor Kline chuckled merrily and scooted down the bench. "Well, it just
so happens that I'm also heading there!" He grabbed the reins and grinned
widely at me, his yellowing teeth looking like they'd never experienced a
toothbrush before.

When I said nothing, Pastor Kline patted the space next to him on the
bench. "Hop on up, young sir!"

Pa thought Pastor Kline was a crackpot and a drunk. Both might have
been true. Pastor Kline always gave me the creeps, with his wiry gray hair
that burst out from underneath his hat like bean sprouts, his pale blue eyes
and tiny pupils, and his overly large smile that looked like he could eat a child
in a single bite.

I smiled politely. "I should be fine on foot, thanks." Even as I said the
words, I eyed the wagon, desperately wanting to climb onto it.

"Oh, ta!" Pastor Kline tutted, smacking the bench a little harder. "The festival will be over by the time you get there."

I opened my mouth to reply, but the pastor shook his head.

"Now, I won't take no for an answer. I can't, in good conscience, leave you to fend for yourself in the dead of night, especially with all the reports of missing people fluttering around as of late."

I blinked. Crackpot or not, a free ride was a free ride.

With a grunt, I pulled myself into the front of the wagon. Pastor Kline patted my shoulder encouragingly before snapping the reins, sending us jolting down the road. I tried to ignore the smell of alcohol that rolled off the pastor with every bump and jostle of the wagon.

"What's this about missing people?"

Pastor Kline tilted his head, looking at me from underneath the brim of his hat. "You haven't heard?"

I shook my head, my hand shooting out to grip the edge of the bench as the wagon thudded into a large hole. "Do you mean people disappearing to the mainland?"

"Oh, heavens no!" Pastor Kline adjusted the stiff white collar clinging to his neck. "It's tragic, really. Truly heartbreaking." He reached underneath his black cloak, pulling something from his pocket. "Here," he said, handing me a folded-up piece of paper. "This is the most recent poor soul who's gone missing." He clucked his tongue, shaking his head. "So young too."

I unfolded the paper, gazing at the bright young face grinning up at me. "Harland Finch?" I frowned. "Who was he?"

"*Is*," Pastor Kline corrected sternly. "Good God, boy." His eyes briefly searched the skies as if waiting for a sudden strike of lightning. After a couple seconds full of silence and no blasphemous smiting, he continued. "Harland Finch has only been missing for a couple days. That is hardly enough time to declare him deceased. He is a boy from Fariid. Went to school one day and failed to return home." He sighed sadly. "The boy is deaf as an adder but as sweet as they come. Just look at that smile!"

I handed the paper back. "What do you think happened to him?"

Pastor Kline patted his sweaty cheeks with the back of his gloved hand. "Everyone assumes it's the mermaids behind the dirty deed, what with the Hunt just around the corner." With a grunt, Pastor Kline stuffed the paper back into his pocket, and when he removed his hand, he was holding a flask. Avoiding my wide-eyed stare, he unscrewed the cap and took a vigorous swig. "The Hunt," he coughed out, wiping his mouth. "Ghastly business, that thing."

I picked at the dried skin on my lower lip, refraining from touching the place on my arm where the mermaid had struck. "I didn't realize you had ill feelings toward the event."

Pastor Kline took another sip from the flask before burying it back into his pocket. He eyed me carefully as he took up the reins again. "It's a necessary evil. A cleansing, you know. A tradition passed down by our ancestors, and we honor them by carrying it forward. A future without mermaids—that's what they wanted. And that's what we strive for."

The hope of not being different, of not being alone, died on my tongue, and I snapped my mouth shut.

Pastor Kline shook the reins, urging the horse over the large cobblestone bridge that connected one side of the island with the other. Between the mountains looming around us, I could just make out the lights of Fariid. I scooted up on the bench, clutching my hands to my chest and leaning forward to get a better view.

Pastor Kline chuckled at my interest. "Have you been to Fariid, young Grayson?"

I peeled my eyes away from the glowing distance. "When I was younger. It's been a couple years."

"Tully can't really compete with Fariid, can it?"

I rubbed the frown off my face, feigning an itchy nose. "Tully is fine."

Pastor Kline sniffed, like he took offense to my tone despite living in Tully himself, not to mention leading the only church we had. "How is Persephone?" he asked, changing the subject. The smile on his face was sympathetic, if a little nosy. "I haven't been able to pay any visits to the asylum lately. Is she well?" His bushy eyebrows pulled together, peeking out from underneath the hat. "Truly, I'm terribly sorry for what has happened to your poor family."

I could feel my hackles rise with the goose bumps on my arms. "It was a long time ago."

"But I'm sure it still weighs heavily on your mind," Pastor Kline pried.

I didn't reply, partially because I didn't know what to say and largely because whatever did come to mind wasn't very nice.

The horse wheezed, the mountains sidled beside us quietly, and thankfully, the lights grew closer. After a long chunk of awkward silence, hints of music began to drift in the air. I closed my eyes, breathing in the scents of sweet pastries, chocolate scones, and roasting meats. I hated the Hunt, but God, I had forgotten how sinfully delicious the First Festival was.

The wagon jolted to a halt. "We are here, young sir!" Pastor Kline announced.

I opened my eyes, blinking against the swaying lights circling Fariid's city square. They looked like fireflies strung over the vendors, crisscrossing throughout the opening before all meeting in the middle, resting on top of the fountain in the center. It was like a circus canopy of twinkling lights. Bonfires were scattered around the square, surrounded by bodies swaying to the music playing on the wooden stage at the front. The festival was well underway, and the large space was packed full of dancing people, booming laughter, and the crows of vendors seeking coins for their goods.

As I hopped off the wagon, Pastor Kline reached over and tapped my shoulder. "Just a minute, Mr. Shaw."

I watched as he slipped his hand into his pocket once more. For a second, I was worried he was going to offer me his flask. But then, to both my embarrassment and relief, he opened his palm. Four coins tumbled out. My mouth dropped open as I stared at the money.

"Thank you for the fine company," Pastor Kline said. "Now be a good boy and buy yourself something tasty!"

I knew I shouldn't accept. But a waft of sweet tarts assaulted my senses, and I closed my hand around the coins. "Thank you, Pastor Kline."

The pastor winked. "Just don't go spending it on alcohol. Deadly stuff, that nectar."

My lips pinched to the side, biting back a smile as I nodded. With a jerk of the reins, Pastor Kline was leading his wagon away, leaving me alone in the square.

I quickly put the money to use, buying a large blackberry pastry with icing that dripped all over my fingers the second I grabbed it. I took a bite, savoring the burst of sweet jam filling and the fluffy golden pastry that melted in my mouth. I groaned with pleasure. If I could live off sweets, I would die young but very, very happy.

Someone bumped into my shoulder, and I stumbled forward. Mr. Brightly, holding a large pewter mug of beer, scowled down at me through his one good eye. I swallowed the bite of pastry I had been working on. "Evening, Mr. Brightly."

Mr. Brightly frowned at me, his big beard glistening with beer foam. "Yer the last Shaw boy I'd expect to see here."

That makes two of us. I looked around, taking in the ambiance of the square. "It is unfortunate that Warrick never got a chance to participate in the Hunt. He would have loved it."

A full-blown lie, but Mr. Brightly didn't need to know that.

Mr. Brightly made a weird snorting sound, but the way he aggressively nodded his head made me think that he was agreeing with me. "So, *you'll* be joinin' the Hunt, then, is what yer tellin' me?"

"For Warrick, yes."

Mr. Brightly whistled. "Well then," he said, adjusting the tuque on his head, "that's a decent surprise."

When I nodded, Mr. Brightly let out a sharp laugh. "I didn't think ya had it in ya."

I mustered a smile. "Neither did I."

This caused Mr. Brightly to laugh again. For being a crotchety old man, he certainly was in good spirits. Likely because of the beer in his hand.

"I'm sorry for leaving work early the other day," I said, careful to make it sound like it had nothing to do with Mr. Brightly's stingy behavior and piss-poor attitude. "What did you end up catching in Bristling Bay?"

Mr. Brightly shrugged, causing the beer to slosh over the lip of the mug. "Just a whale. The thing was already dead. Useless to us." He sighed loudly. "All bloated and the like. Looked like somethin' had tried to make a meal outta it too."

A streak of ice crawled up my spine. Whales were the largest animal roaming our portion of the ocean. *What could make a meal out of one?*

Mr. Brightly was already beginning to lose interest in our conversation. I followed his gaze to where he was having a staring contest with a girl with long hair, large breasts, and an even larger smile. Heat fluttered to my cheeks, and I cleared my throat. "Have a wonderful evening, Mr. Brightly."

He didn't notice as I slipped away, deeper into the crowd. I licked the icing from my fingers, swaying past a couple dancing, their laughter blending with the music. Pa's booth was off to the side. He was leaning over the counter, holding out a meat skewer to a man while pounding his fist on the wooden top, laughing at something the man had said. I ducked my head, veering away. I didn't want him to see that I had left the hunting knife at home.

A sharp voice pierced the air, commanding and shrill. "If I have to repeat myself to you rambunctious lot one more time, no one's getting a treat after the play!"

I looked up from my pastry to see Mrs. Sybil Morris just ahead of me, herding a group of children in handmade costumes toward the stage. Her crown of graying hair was perched high on her head, each curl and braid held fast with pins. The jewels around her neck and fingers glittered in the festival lights.

I raised my clean hand and waved. "Mrs. Morris!"

My old schoolteacher paused from her herding to look up, and her green eyes sparkled when she saw me. "Grayson Shaw! What a surprise."

I smiled, scooting closer. "So I keep hearing."

Mrs. Morris brushed a stray lock of hair out of her eyes, looking me up and down. "You barely reached my hip the last time I saw you." She ruffled my hair with a grin. "You've certainly seen a growth spurt or two."

I nodded. "Still helping out with the festival play?"

"One of my many duties." She sighed, wiping her hands on her beige apron. "But enough about me—I'm old and boring. What great and terrible things have you been up to, Mr. Shaw?"

I filled Mrs. Morris in on the *great and terrible* things. The list wasn't very long. Mrs. Morris's eyes glazed over when I mentioned my job at the docks, and she wasn't surprised—or impressed—to hear that I was still friends with Jasper. She cooed appreciatively when I brought up how I still read and practiced my cursive despite having been out of the classroom for a handful of years. But she positively lit up when I told her of my interest in plant life and the healing qualities they possessed.

"Oh!" Mrs. Morris exclaimed, clapping her hands together. "That's wonderful news! We could use more ethnobotanists around here."

I wanted to smile at her praise, but felt a frown forming instead. "It's a hobby. Just small things, like salves for rope burns and oils for sores."

Mrs. Morris placed her hands on her hips. "Now, Mr. Shaw. I won't have you condemning your gift just because it's a hobby. Great things can come out of hobbies." She peered at me, her eyes shining. "Do you wish to spend your life at the docks, wasting away until you are nothing but arthritic hands and a bad back, because it's what you think you should be doing? Or do you want to do something more with your life?" With a good-natured smile, she tapped me lightly on the chest, just above my heart. "What do *you* want to do?"

Before I could answer, a hand clapped sharply against my shoulder.

"Cripes, the play!" Jasper gasped, looking around Mrs. Morris at the children. "Remember the play, Grayson?"

Mrs. Morris stiffened at Jasper's intrusion. "Hello, Mr. Warren."

"Hiya," Jasper said, paying our old teacher no mind. He grinned at me, slapping my shoulder again. "Remember when we were that young, running around in our little sailor costumes, forgetting our lines and nearly puking onstage?"

"If I remember correctly, *you* were the one vomiting everywhere," I said, removing his heavy hand. "Not to mention, you *still* act young enough to be in that play."

Jasper rolled his eyes. He had a very obvious stain on his bright blue dress jacket and a smudge that suggested that he had tried—and failed—to get it off. "I'll bet it hasn't changed a bit since when we were in it."

A child began to scream as another one, clad in a mermaid costume, pulled on her hair. Mrs. Morris sighed, turning away from us. "I best get back before there's a mutiny." She glanced over her shoulder to flash me one last smile. "Always a pleasure, Mr. Shaw!"

Jasper jutted out his lower lip, pouting as Mrs. Morris strode back to the children and ripped the mermaid off the sailor. "How come she didn't say goodbye to me?"

"Probably because your presence isn't always a pleasure?"

Jasper gasped, whirling to face me. "I'm a regular delight, I'll have you know!"

I laughed, leaning away. "Of course you are. Nice to see you made it. Is your whole family here, then?"

Jasper nodded, and as if on cue, I spotted Holly lurking near one of the fires, staring at me. Her fingers were fiddling with her long braids, her face unreadable as she watched me from the distance. I wondered if she was still mad at me.

The crowd erupted into cheers, and the music came to an abrupt halt. I tore my gaze away from Holly's entrancing eyes. The mayor of Lethe was hobbling up the stage steps, struggling to lift the hem of his long black cloak to avoid tripping. He looked like a delicate maiden as he clutched the fabric to his chest. The stage's garland of ferns and twigs, decorated with large flowers and fake gems meant to represent mermaid scales, caught on the cloak, its gnarled fingers twisting into the fabric. Despite only having five steps to climb, the mayor stopped on each one, as if to steady himself.

Once he reached the top, Mayor McCoy dropped the cloak, adjusted the leafy wreath perched atop his balding head, and strode to the podium, smiling and waving to the crowd. He was a frail twig of a man, barely visible behind the wooden podium. His oversized cloak nearly swallowed him whole. He waved his hands in the air, laughing merrily as the crowd's cheers subsided into quiet murmurs.

"Welcome, people of Lethe," he called out jovially, "to this year's First Festival!"

The crowd boomed again, and I flinched against the sudden crack of noise. Jasper crowed beside me, jumping and pumping a fist into the air. He had to keep a hand on my arm to keep himself balanced.

Mayor McCoy waited for the mass to settle once more. "What a sight to see! What a turnout! Thank you all for coming to such a joyous occasion."

My heart pressed against my rib cage. Joyous? There was nothing joyous about the Hunt. The pastry suddenly felt like a rock in my hand, and my hunger for it dwindled.

"I hope your enthusiasm can carry us through the month of April," the mayor continued, "until it is time for us to retrieve our spears, pull our boats into the treacherous waters, and claim our birthright!"

The crowd went wild. At first, I thought it was from Mayor McCoy's idea of a stirring speech. But then I saw a man strut toward the stage, climb up the stairs with ease, and sway his way to where the mayor was perched.

Mr. Silas Grieves smiled smoothly as he shook Mayor McCoy's hand, then turned and dazzled the crowd with the same smug look. The wealthiest man on all of Lethe had enough swagger and charm to sink an entire fleet of ships.

"Thank you for such a powerful speech, Mayor McCoy!" Mr. Grieves crooned, squeezing the mayor's shoulder before stepping in front of the podium. "Truer words couldn't have been spoken."

"Oh, you're too kind!" Mayor McCoy stuttered as he stepped away from his perch. "But . . . But I wasn't quite done—"

"Brothers and sisters of Lethe," Mr. Grieves announced from the podium, ignoring the squeaking mayor, "the time has come."

The mass of people went deathly silent, hanging on to Mr. Grieves's ominous words. I was afraid to breathe. There was something about Mr. Grieves that seemed . . . dark, dangerous. The man felt as ominous as the Barrens. When I looked at Mr. Grieves, my heart screamed at me to run, run, run.

Mr. Grieves leaned against the podium, the gold embroidery on his dark gray suit dancing in the bonfire light. He stared each and every one of us down. "The time has come to make our stand once more. A year has passed, and we have waited." He pounded a fist against the podium, causing several members of the crowd to jump. "But no more!"

There was a rush of murmurs amongst the people, the nodding of heads. Pinpricks of unease bit at my skin.

"It is time we remind those disgusting creatures that we are the better species, the stronger species, the *right* species. No longer will we hide in our homes, fearful to venture into the water. No longer will dust linger on our spears. This April, this Hunting Month, we shall prepare. We'll sharpen our minds, strengthen our bodies, and come May 1, we will drag our boats into the ocean, and we will show those mermaids what happens when they wrong us."

The crowd hummed their agreement. Jasper nodded his head viciously. I swallowed bile.

Mr. Grieves sighed, bowing his head. "I'm tired of losing poor, innocent souls to those thieving beasts." He wiped his tearless eyes with a golden handkerchief, shaking his head sorrowfully as he tucked it back into his breast pocket. "Many of which were too young, too full of life. The list of bloodshed is endless and full of agony." He paused, pressing a fist to his mouth and releasing a shuddering breath around it. "Please, I'm asking you—no, *begging* you—to join me on April 5 at the Symbolic Sign-In. Let us all come together to take an oath, as brothers and sisters, to make those mermaids wish they had never drawn our blood." He raised a shaking fist into the air. "Fight with me!"

The crowd roared, and the sound was deafening.

Mr. Grieves closed his eyes, letting out a low breath. And when his eyes snapped open, they were feral with hunger.

But his smile—his cool, calculating, cutthroat smile—was far worse.

Pastor Kline stumbled up the stage's stairs next. He managed to slur through half of his painfully long prayer before a blast of fireworks cut him off. They exploded in the air, showering us in pinks, purples, blues, and greens.

The music resumed, and the festival was back in full swing.

Jasper smoothed out his shirt's ruffles. "Well, I know there's some girl out there just *dying* to dance with me." He sucked on his teeth as he eyed the moving bodies and shimmy of skirts. "Now all I need to do is find her."

Jasper, smelling of desperation and expired milk, limped away with a wave of his hand.

"Good luck!" I called out, frozen to my spot near the stage.

Alone and feeling a lot less confident for it, I rotated in a small circle, unsure of where to go. My hands were sticky and coated in bits of icing and pastry. My eyes fell to the fountain, and as I contemplated risking the embarrassment and washing my hands in the water, I felt a gentle tap on my shoulder.

Holly's hands were playing with the daisies braided into her hair as she swished in place, her pale pink dress lazily following her movements.

"Holly," I said, "hello!"

Holly frowned at me. "You have jelly on your cheek."

I blinked. "What?"

Holly bit back a smirk, her eyes dancing in the festival lights. "Jelly," she repeated, pointing to her face, "on your cheek."

"Oh, jeez." I cringed, scrubbing at my face with my clean hand. How long had it been there? And why hadn't Jasper warned me?

Holly sighed, rolling her eyes. "It's not coming off. Here." Without waiting for my reply, Holly licked her thumb, then pressed it into my left cheek. "It's been there for a while. I could see it from across the square."

I squeezed my eyes shut, blush creeping up my neck. "Well, that's embarrassing."

I could feel Holly's fingernail scratch against my cheek, rubbing my skin raw. "There!" she said, pulling away to admire her handiwork. "Fixed."

I mumbled my thanks, having a hard time meeting her searching gaze. My cheek pulsed from the pressure of her touch. "Are you still upset about the library?" I asked quietly.

Holly scrunched her face. "What?"

The music swelled, and I leaned closer to her ear. "I'm sorry about what happened at the library," I said, fighting to be heard above the band. "Are you upset with me?"

When I leaned back, I noticed Holly had gone stiff, waves of heat radiating from her. She quickly shook her head, her fingers fluttering to the curls framing her face. "No!" she squeaked. Then, with a small nod, she added, "I mean, yes, I am. Terribly so, actually." She raised an eyebrow at me, a coy smile tugging at her lips. "But I'd consider it water under the bridge if you danced with me."

For some strange reason, the second those words left Holly's lips, I suddenly found myself thinking about the mermaid I had saved earlier.

Her plump lips, peeled back in a hiss.

The wild fear in her violet eyes.

The feel of her smooth scales underneath my fingers.

How—impossibly, stupidly, desperately—I wanted to see her again.

And what a thought that was, to come face-to-face with death and still long to catch a glimpse of it again.

My hand drifted to my arm, and I rubbed at the sensitive skin coated with goose bumps.

Say yes, my mind begged. *Just say yes and forget about that mermaid.*

"I'm sorry," I found myself saying, offering an apologetic smile. "I'm really not much of a dancer."

Holly's face crumpled, the entire sun that seemed to shine within her snuffing out.

I took a step forward, and she stumbled back. "Holly," I started, "please, don't—"

Holly spun around so quickly that her braids slapped me in the face, sending a flurry of flowers scattering through the air. Without another word, she vanished into the crowd, retreating from the hurt I had caused her. I watched her go, torn between chasing after her or leaving her be. I wasn't good at reading people or knowing what to say, but even the village idiot could tell that what I had just done was a colossal mistake.

A sudden *crash* splintered through the music, followed by a howling wail. I whirled around to see one of Mrs. Morris's students, clad in a mermaid costume, at the bottom of the stage's steps in a crumpled heap. The fabric of the tail had gotten caught in the garland, and the child was in the unfortunate state of nearly being upside down, her little legs flailing against the steps as she fought to get free.

My mind instantly filled with images of the captured mermaid again. *No time for that right now.*

Springing to action, I dropped the pastry and raced to the child, sitting her upright and freeing her tail. "Are you all right?" I asked hurriedly. "Are you hurt?"

"The ... The ... The costume!" the child cried out between sobs. "It's ... It's *ruined*!"

I clucked my tongue, wiping the sweaty hair off her forehead, narrowly avoiding the plastic gemstones glued to her skin. "There, there," I soothed, racing to find any words of comfort. "The tear is hardly noticeable."

"Nooooo," she cried, rubbing her glittery sleeve across her nose. "It's not that."

I sat up, my face pinched together in confusion. The girl sniffled, straightening her legs so I could look at her stomach.

At the deep shade of crimson bleeding through the fabric, pooling on the ground beneath us.

At the blood smothering my hands.

"Oh, God." I sucked in a breath, turning my head.

"Heavens!" Mrs. Morris tutted, rushing around the stage and sinking to the ground next to us. Her beige apron immediately began wicking up the flood of red. "What on God's good earth happened here?"

"I'm sorry, Mrs. Morris," the girl whimpered. "The tail got caught, and I . . . I . . . I fell!"

Mrs. Morris scoffed, rubbing a hand over her face. "I knew those garlands would be a nuisance. Susie, love, stop your crying. It's nothing a little water can't fix. Grayson, relax; it's only paint."

I swallowed around the lump in my throat, not trusting myself to look at my old teacher. "You're sure?"

Mrs. Morris chuckled dryly. "I made the costumes, didn't I? Yes, I'm sure. Paint in a bag for theatrical purposes." With a grunt, she picked Susie up, nestling the child against her chest. "Thank you for helping, Mr. Shaw, but I can take it from here." She smiled thinly at me, glancing down at my dirty hands. "I do hope to see you at the Symbolic Sign-In."

As Mrs. Morris trotted away with Susie, calling out for a wet cloth, all I could do was stare numbly at my soaked hands, at the red stones underneath my feet. I couldn't breathe.

Jasper was wrong. The play had changed a lot since the last time we were in it.

CHAPTER ELEVEN

EVANORA

APRIL 2 – MORNING

"YOU DIDN'T HAVE TO COME WITH ME."

The warrior, Illeron, only grunted.

I cast a scathing glare in his direction. "I don't need a protector. I can protect myself."

Illeron, the powerful strokes of his silver-and-crimson tail not faltering, slowly tilted his face to look at me. "Clearly."

I scoffed, rolling my eyes at him. "I can!"

Illeron broke our stare, a tight grin cracking through his frown. "If thinking of me as your protector damages your pride, perhaps think of me more as a merling sitter?"

A dark growl erupted through my bared teeth. I couldn't believe I had once been friends with this clown fish. It was a long time ago, before I was ruler, and before he got all brooding and handsome. "*Ugh*," I groaned, "this is torture."

Illeron shifted, the armor on his shoulders gleaming. He adjusted the leather strap on his chest holding the metal in place. "I wouldn't disagree, Your Majesty."

I shot him another seething look and quickened my pace. The faster we swam, the faster we got to the prayer reeds, and the faster we could get home, where I could pretend that being chaperoned by my kingdom's greatest warrior hadn't happened. In truth, I would have preferred to go alone to get the reeds, but I knew I was already pushing my luck by forcing Jorah to let me go. I had offered to let Mavi tag along, but both Jorah and I knew that Mavi was all things sweet and innocent and pure and likely useless with a weapon.

Jorah had chosen Illeron to be my guide. He wanted me to be safe, but the old fish also wanted to teach me a lesson.

Wordlessly, Illeron and I skirted around a wall of sea rock, ducking under the natural tunnel it had eroded into. We were nearly there, having left at first light in hopes of finding the reeds before humans found us instead. I had wanted to leave yesterday, but by the time we had buried Braemos and Safra, the sun was already in its descent, and it would've been too risky.

I shuddered, remembering how Jorah and I had carefully wrapped their lifeless bodies in a blanket of seaweed and flowers, how their blood leaked through the cracks, how Safra's hand tumbled out of the blanket, like she was trying one last time to escape. How I had cast a prayer into the waters, wishing that even in death, the couple chose light.

I hated that prayer. How could we choose light when we were cursed to live in darkness? Mermaids were meant to be immortal, yet death clung to us, hunted us, yearned for us. Death by humans. Death by Cursed Beings. There was no light. Not anymore.

"Evanora," Illeron growled.

I snapped myself back into focus. "What is it?"

Illeron cocked his head to me, his mouth pinched into a thin line. "Please get out of your thoughts."

A rush of warmth spattered against my pale cheeks. "I forgot you can . . ."

"Yes," the warrior bit out. "So, please do us both a favor and think of something more cheerful, maybe?"

I sniffed, pointing my gaze forward. I attempted to think of nothing at all for a small period of time, just to let Illeron know what not being a mind bender felt like, but temptation ate away at my willpower. "Have you ever seen them?"

"Seen who?" Illeron asked, careful to keep his face blank, which was infuriating.

"The Cursed Beings." I waved my hand dismissively. "You know, for being able to read minds, you are terrible at following conversation, both spoken and not."

Illeron said nothing, but his grip on his spear tightened. He was silent for several heavy seconds before responding. "When I was a merling, a small group of us swam to the edge of the Barrens. We wanted to see what the elders were so frightened of." His mouth twitched, pulling at his pointed jaw. "It was so dark at the cliff, we couldn't see anything. But we could hear them." A shiver ran through him, and he shook his head. "It was unlike anything I've ever heard. A low hum, like a multitude of voices whispering. It was constant, a wave of hunger. I didn't understand it, not fully, but I could feel what it wanted. What it desired."

"Death," I offered quietly. "It desires death."

"Yes." Illeron rubbed his face, softening his sharp features. "But not just our death. Death to everything, to everyone. Even death to itself, I think, to the curse." He shrugged. "I decided then that I didn't truly care to meet with one after that." Illeron's ruby-red eyes darted to mine reluctantly. "I think . . ." He paused, letting out a breath that seemed to carry a terrible weight. "I think it knows what we desire too."

My blood ran cold. "The Cursed Beings?"

Illeron nodded. "When you failed to return from your adventures—I had begun to round up the pod and send them to the cave. On the cusp of day meeting night, when I was doing a final perimeter check, I heard them. I was so caught up in the chaos, I hadn't realized that I had completely swum out of borders." His jaw clenched. "It wasn't like before, when the merlings and I tested our grit; we went to the Barrens during the day. I think, even then, we knew better than to tempt fate. But at night . . ." He drew in a sharp breath. "Their incoherent whispers and wails . . . I don't know . . . They made *sense*, Evanora. I could *hear* them speaking. Speaking to me."

I swallowed hard, fighting the tendrils of fear pushing at my scales. "What were they saying?"

Illeron's gaze hardened, his eyes cutting through me like steel. "They told me things about myself that I had never told another soul. My secrets, my desires, my worst fears." He shrugged, the movement stiff. "It was like they had pulled my heart out of my chest and presented it back to me, taunting me with it. I could tell that they wanted me to enter the Barrens, to discover what else they knew about me, what they could do to make my dreams a reality, but I . . . I hurried away before they could say anything else."

I shifted closer to Illeron. "And?"

"And what?"

"What are your biggest fears?"

The warrior frowned at me. "Having to put up with you for the rest of my miserable life, Your Majesty."

I gave Illeron a withering glare. "Thank you for the reminder of how painful it is to have me as your ruler."

Illeron flashed a sarcastic smile, placing a hand to his chest. "My pleasure."

I flicked my fluke, whipping Illeron's shoulder. The warrior shifted, his smile turning, just for a moment, into something genuine. I could tell he was thankful for the conversation shift, even if he didn't say it. Illeron barrel-rolled, swimming on his back, spinning his spear expertly over the arm braces cinched just below his forearm fins. "What did your parents teach you about them?"

"Not much," I admitted. "They had suspicions that the Cursed Beings hunted by scent, hearing, and touch. But what does that mean? Are they blind?" I bit my lip, shuddering. "Do they even have eyes?"

"No one who has seen one has lived to tell us," Illeron said, sighing.

I nodded. "Exactly. And we know that they come out at night, so what do they do during the day? Are they just . . . waiting? For the cover of darkness?"

Illeron shifted closer to me, avoiding a bundle of coral. His crimson fins brushed against mine. "After all this time, we are still in the dark."

"Clever."

"I try."

I rolled my eyes. "And obviously, there is the tale of the curse itself. Ammah and Appah drilled it into me like a religion." I fluttered a hand to my chest. "Instead of a bedtime story, I was told of the tragic tale of the boy and his mermaid."

Illeron sighed heavily. "I'll bet your completely justifiable tears of boredom slipped right off your silky seaweed bed."

I paused for a beat before flashing Illeron a sharp smile. Clearing my throat, I spoke, loud and robust. *"When two young souls, their love entwined . . ."*

I waited, looking at Illeron expectantly. When the warrior returned my stare with a blank one of his own, I groaned, throwing my head back. "Come on, Illeron. Your turn."

"I respectfully decline."

I raised my eyebrows, then fed him the next line. *"Set out to sea on night divine. One mermaid, the other human—race knowing no bounds; their love reached craters of the earth unfound."*

Illeron frowned at me. "With the utmost respect, Your Majesty, you are acting like a merling."

I flipped onto my back, my tail undulating lazily behind me. I reached up, stretching for the surface with my fingertips. *"But the love was betrayed—no one knows by who. Blood was met with blood, a love torn in two."*

"Is this how every excursion is going to be with you?"

I grinned and replied with, "*Their blood fed the darkness, full of bitterness and hate. It sank into the Barrens, giving way to a hunger that nothing could satiate.*"

A muscle tightened in Illeron's jaw. "I'll take that as a resounding *yes.*"

"*And from their deaths, new life arose, an evil lurking deep. The Cursed Beings now rule the night . . .*" I drifted into poignant silence, glancing mournfully at the warrior. When he didn't rise to the challenge, I puckered my lips into a pout.

Illeron clucked his tongue disapprovingly. "*Their presence will make you weep,*" he finished begrudgingly.

I giggled, flipping back over. "See? That wasn't so difficult!"

"Oh, Neptune spear me." The warrior gave me a thin smile. "Our definitions of *difficult* are very different."

The ground began to slant upward. I hardened my features, nodding to Illeron. "We're close."

The sky was beginning to turn from a dusty gray to a blushing pink. It would be daylight soon; we had to move quickly.

We paused at a place where the island jutted outward into the water, creating a barricade of rocks that ate into the ocean's waves. I peeked above the surface, my eyes darting along the beach. I couldn't see anyone, but that hardly offered comfort. I hadn't seen the man with his beast—or the net—until it was nearly too late.

I took a breath, my gills flaring, and ducked underneath the waves. Illeron stared at me, his face tight, his red eyes gleaming with concern. "Well?" he whispered.

I shook my head. "No signs of life." I gathered my hair, twisting it into one giant lock over my shoulder. *"Wait here and be on the lookout. I won't be long."*

Illeron immediately shook his head, his lips curling back to show his pointed canines. "No," he ground out. "Absolutely not."

"You sound like Jorah," I snapped before mentally reeling back, composing myself. I closed my eyes for a pounding heartbeat, inhaling deeply. "I'll be fine," I said quietly. "I don't need you to hold my hand for everything." Illeron opened his mouth, but I placed a hand on his raised spear, lowering it. "I'll be *fine,* Illeron."

The warrior jutted out his chin, a tremor lacing through it. After a long pause, he relaxed. "You are done when I say you are done. Come back as soon as I call for you."

I nodded sharply, but as I turned away, Illeron reached out, gripping my arm and pulling me back. "As soon as I call you, Evanora," he warned again, searching my eyes with a ferocity that made my heart squeeze.

Swallowing, I nodded with a little less enthusiasm. I glanced down at his long fingers wrapped around my wrist. "I can't exactly go *anywhere* with you holding me hostage, can I?"

With a grunt, Illeron released me, and I took pleasure in seeing the gentle blush that coated his shimmering cheeks. Illeron tucked himself next to the rocky ledge, holding the spear tightly, his eyes wary as they scoured the waters.

I shook my arms, ridding them of the nerves that tingled along my fins. My heart was a steady drum, ricocheting off my rib cage, singing to my blood. "Enjoy the sun. Relax," I said, knowing it was physically impossible for the warrior to do either of those things. I steeled myself one last time, then surged forward, racing deftly along the sand.

I focused on the remaining prayer reeds, yanking out as many as I could carry. The plants hummed against my chest, their soft glow beginning to fade in the growing morning light. I worked quickly until the patch was cleared, relief flooding my veins with every reed I gathered. This would be enough for several batches of salves. *Finally*, I sighed inwardly, *I'm doing something right—something good.*

As I turned to Illeron, showing him my full arms and my cheeky grin, I saw it.

The bag, sitting on the shore. It was perched upright, like it was politely waiting for me. It sat at the edge of the waves, the water lapping at the faded brown fabric.

I bit my lip, considering. Grabbing it would make the return journey home a lot easier, but it meant I had to go above the surface, which was growing increasingly risky with the rising sun. I eyed the rays of light dancing off the waves above me.

"Don't even think about it," Illeron's voice snarled in my mind.

I turned to look at him, frowning. "Stay out of my head."

Illeron swept forward. "Evanora," he warned, "don't."

"I'm just going to *look*," I replied quickly.

Before Illeron could scold me again, I tilted my head back and breached the surface.

The beach was quiet, the town still asleep. The sun was a glorious crown on my head, and I had to fight the urge to close my eyes and bask in its warmth. With one last glance around, I swam closer. I dropped the prayer reeds onto the sand and hauled myself forward, inching closer to the abandoned bag. I grabbed it quickly, panting as I pulled it onto my waist and hugged it tightly, sending a silent thank-you to the gods that it was safe.

The jars were still in there, as well as the reeds I had picked. Now dry, the plants were shriveled, dead and dark and absolutely useless to me. Not allowing myself to mourn their waste, I pulled them out and made room for the new ones. Once they were all tucked inside, I flopped the flap back into place and buttoned it closed. As I did, one of the pockets lining the outside of the bag fumbled open, revealing a single purple flower.

I frowned at the pocket. I didn't remember popping something in there. I didn't exactly have time. With shaking fingers, I hesitantly plucked the vibrantly colored flower out and brought it up to my face, squinting at it.

It looked like the one the boy had been analyzing that morning, before I had distracted him. I froze, my blood shifting to ice. Had that boy saved my bag? Had he put the flower in it? For me?

I shook my head, a choked laugh escaping my constricted throat. What a ridiculous thought.

I twirled the flower between my fingers, watching the petals dance and sway, the flash of orange at its center. Land flowers were so dainty and fragile, unlike the ones that grew near my home, which were thick petaled and slimy and not nearly as vibrant. A thought drifted through my mind, and I lifted the flower to my nose. Closing my eyes, I inhaled deeply.

The smell was like pure sunshine.

I hummed with delight, savoring the smell like it was a delicacy.

When I opened my eyes, I found myself staring at him.

The boy.

The boy with soft hurricane eyes and gentle hands. The boy who had saved me.

He was standing a short distance in front of me.

And he was holding a net in his hands.

CHAPTER TWELVE

GRAYSON

APRIL 2 – MORNING

WE LOCKED EYES WITH EACH OTHER FOR A FROZEN second.

I couldn't breathe, couldn't think, couldn't speak. All I could do was look into those deep, endless violet eyes. The ones I had dreamt of the second my head hit my pillow last night.

I stepped forward, tentative, and the moment shattered.

The mermaid hissed, abruptly dropping the flower, grabbing her bag, and tearing back into the water.

"No, please wait! Please!" Throwing the net to the ground, I tumbled to the water's edge. "I didn't mean to scare you!"

But she was already beneath the waves by the time my boots hit the wet sand. I stopped just short of entering the ocean, fear sparking as the water lapped against me, trying to pull me in. Stuck on solid ground, I watched helplessly as she became a streak of white, disappearing into the foam. When she veered around the rocky cove, my shoulders sagged under the weight of my disappointment. I sighed, dipping my head. "Well, that went horribly."

I glanced at the net I had carelessly discarded on the embankment. I'd managed to drag myself out of bed to repair it enough to resemble the old abandoned pile of ropes it had once been. I had left the house before dawn, not expecting to encounter anyone, let alone a mermaid, at Hannigan's Cove.

I bit my lip, a tremor running down my fingertips. I couldn't deny that seeing her again thrilled me, but I wasn't sure the feeling was mutual.

I hadn't gotten a good look at her when she had been trapped in the net, but now, seeing her on the beach—her glistening face upturned to the sun, a soft smile on her lips as she inhaled the scent of the flower I had picked for her, her long ivory hair cascading over her slender shoulders, shimmering scales adorning her hips . . .

It felt like my body was on fire, a match struck a thousand times and yet still burning.

The mermaid was breathtaking beyond any rational reason.

H OWLER'S HILL WAS ESPECIALLY LOUD TODAY.
Penny was back at the tree line, sniffing at roots and picking at the good clumps of grass. I liked taking her with me from time to time; I could trust her not to be stupid enough to inspect the heights. I sat at the edge of the cliff, my feet hanging over the rocky ledge, kicking listlessly. A gentle pressure had been building up in my chest since the second I sat down; the ocean pulled at my heart, whispering at me to come closer. My eyes scoured the water, stretching along the base of the island to the border of the Barrens, looking for the pale mermaid, for any sign that she was out there and that this morning hadn't been some fever dream I had desperately made up in my head. All I could see was the violent churning of white-capped waves.

There was a heavy thud as my pa settled at my side, carefully lowering his legs over the edge. He leaned back on his hands, his red plaid shirt rolled up at the sleeves, his tan vest unbuttoned. He eyed the infinite horizon. "Some party last night," he said in greeting.

"How did the booth fare?" I asked, not taking my gaze off the water.

Pa chuckled, tilting his head back to look at the darkening sky. "Just fine." His eyes were as sly as the grin on his face when he looked over at me. "I couldn't help but notice that you turned down that Warren girl." When I didn't say anything, he continued. "Looked like you broke her heart clean in two."

I closed my eyes, shrinking in my seat. "Pa," I groaned, "please don't."

"It was just a dance she wanted. Would it have really killed you?"

It's a lot more than a dance she wants. I swallowed, turning my face into the wind, trying to drown out the sound of my pa's teasing words.

"Well," Pa tried again, "what did you think about the rest of the festival? What of Mr. Grieves's speech?"

"Invigorating."

"About as stimulating as Pastor Kline's prayer," Pa added.

I was hoping Pa would take my silence as a hint and leave me alone. I had no idea what he was doing at Howler's Hill; he never visited me when I was out here. All he did was grumble and complain about having my head either floating in the clouds or stuck in a botany book, never facing forward, paying attention. Maybe he needed Penny for something. I was just about to point out her whereabouts when he spoke again.

"Did you know that this is where I proposed to your ma?"

His voice had changed. It was hardly noticeable; I could just make out the soft edges of his words, where razor sharpness usually lay.

I instantly perked up, angling my body to face him. Pa *never* talked about Ma unless it was to scold me for wanting to see her, or to curse her for simply existing.

Pa chewed on his lip thoughtfully. "The early years of my life were some of the best ones because of her." He smirked, the corners of his eyes crinkling at buried memories. "We never had much, but it was more than enough for the two of us."

A million questions pounced onto my tongue. I had to be careful—one wrong move, one poorly worded question, and the conversation would be over before it even started. I wrung my hands together, the dry skin pinching and pulling. "Wasn't Ma from a wealthier family?"

Pa nodded, loosing a heavy breath. "She lost it all when she ran away with me." He threw me a wry glance. "She was engaged to a mainlander when we met."

I choked on a sudden burst of laughter. "No way."

"I'm not joking," he urged, chuckling quietly. "She was practicing her walk down the aisle when I bumped into her. I was working as the butcher shop's delivery boy at the time, and was carrying about three crates full of filleted fish down Main Street. I didn't see her around the crates, and . . ." Pa cringed, gesturing in a sweeping motion down his body. "I absolutely smothered her in fish."

My mouth dropped open. "You didn't!"

"It was disgusting," Pa agreed. His mirth slowly dwindled into a sad smile. "But it was also love at first sight, if you can believe that."

I could. The love Pa had for my ma was the stuff of fairy tales. It was a wildfire love, always burning and smoldering and heating up the rooms they were in. But even wildfires were eventually snuffed out.

My pa looked out into the ocean. "When your ma told her parents about me, well . . ." He snorted bashfully. "They were less than impressed. Trading in her wealthy fiancé for a delivery boy?" He waved a hand dismissively. "It was unheard of. She lost everything. Her dowry, her inheritance, her passport to travel to the mainland." He shook his head. "But it didn't matter. None of that did."

"So, what happened?" I asked hesitantly.

Pa shrugged. "We bought the shabby little shack that sat alone on a hill, slowly made it into a home. It took her some time getting used to the countryside; she didn't know how to cook, or clean, or how to manage livestock. But she wasn't afraid to get her hands dirty. She wasn't afraid to try." His expression darkened, and for a moment, pain flashed across his face.

The wind tangled with the silence between us. Pa didn't need to finish the story—I knew how it ended. When Warrick died, it felt like Ma died with him. She became a shell, a recluse. She stopped eating, stopped sleeping, stopped pretending everything was fine. Living with her was like living with a ghost, watching her drift through our home with a dead look in her eyes. Always searching for something and never finding it.

Eventually, it drove her mad. She embraced that madness. When she finally cracked, she nearly dragged me into the hell she'd made for herself. If Pa hadn't found us on the beach when he did, I would've been dead. And so would she.

I looked down at my wrists, carefully tucked beneath my sleeves. "I miss her," I admitted quietly.

Pa glanced at me sharply, his brow wrinkled with tension. After a moment, he softened, his gaze turning back to the ocean. "So do I."

I slowly turned to him, offering a small smile. "We could go see her, you know."

Pa, who had been buttoning his vest back up, went painfully still. "Please, God, tell me I didn't just hear you say that."

The smile dripped off my face, but I tried again. "You said yourself that you miss her."

"Of *course* I miss her. She was my wife."

I brought my knees up, hugging them against my chest. "Just because she's stuck in Maude doesn't mean she isn't still a part of this family."

Pa pinched the bridge of his nose, squeezing his eyes shut. "She chose to not be in this family the second she pulled you into the ocean." He crumpled forward, holding his head in his hands as he rested his elbows against his thighs. His shoulders heaved as he said, "After everything she did to us? To you? You *still* want to see her?"

Instinctively, I grazed the warped flesh at my wrists. The twisted scars snaked across the entire width of both my arms, thick white lines holding the memory of the knife that had once been there. I forced out a choked laugh to combat the swelling of my throat. "You talk about her as though she's dead."

"Because she is dead!" Pa shouted, standing abruptly, towering over me. "The woman I married is gone. The woman I loved, the one who gave me Warrick and you, is gone. That woman in the asylum," he panted, his voice rough, "is not my wife. She's a monster." The wind tore through his hair, scattering strands across his face. "I don't want you seeing her. Not now, not ever. Do you hear me?" He drew in a sharp breath, shaking his head. "She's brought nothing but pain and heartache to this family. We're at rock bottom because of her. Our name is ruined because of her." He stared at me, his eyes hard. "And you're broken because of her."

I shrank back, surprised by the sudden threat of tears lurking on my bottom eyelashes. I willed them to stay put. To cry now would only prove his point, and I'd be damned if I gave him the satisfaction. Pa, my only family left, the one who thought I was *broken*, turned away from me.

"You need to stop being so soft," he grumbled, stomping for the tree line and grabbing at Penny's reins. "You're a hunter now, and you need to toughen up like one. Stop living in this fantasy world, believing that Persephone will get better and come home. She won't. She doesn't want to."

CHAPTER THIRTEEN

EVANORA

APRIL 2 – AFTERNOON

THE REEDS HUMMED IN MY HANDS, THEIR SOFT GLOW painting my fingers, mixing with my own light.

The throne room was silent save for the quiet song of the prayer reeds. I hovered near one of the long tables, plucking each colorful leaf off the plants. Mavi sat beside me, stuffing them into jars. Illeron lingered by the palace entrance, looking utterly bored.

The sun's rays filtered around the entrance's white pillars, rippling along the marble floor. My fingers had started getting sticky hours ago. Now I was convinced that the goo from the prayer reeds would simply remain stained onto my skin forever. But I didn't mind. My heart buzzed contentedly with each jar I filled, every leaf I plucked off, every time the reeds hummed.

The pale octopus scuttled across the tabletop, eyeing up the jars with its giant eyes. It wrapped a long, thin limb around one and flung it upward, sending it floating across my face. I calmly retrieved the escaping jar and placed it back onto the table without missing a beat. The octopus shifted colors rapidly, as if to say, *Well, you're no fun!* and went for another one.

Mavi shooed the octopus away when it went for the jar in her hands. "What's *he* doing here?" she asked quietly.

I knew she wasn't referring to the octopus. I rolled my eyes, grabbing another bundle of prayer reeds.

"Her punishment was increased after that little stunt today. She is clearly not capable of making sound decisions." Jorah's voice filled the throne room, the disappointment echoing into the domed ceiling as he swam in from the back halls. "It was bad enough that I let you twist my tail into going back for the reeds." Jorah sighed, rubbing his temples. "A vulnerable moment on my part. It won't happen again."

I concentrated on the leaves. "I was grabbing my bag."

"And you were spotted by a human!" Jorah bit back, his hand swooping away from his face to point at me. "I don't think you understand the weight of that problem, Your Majesty."

My heart thudded at the memory of seeing the boy again. "I think he was harmless."

"He was holding a net," Illeron chimed in from his place by the entrance.

I glared at the warrior, my fingers stilling against the reeds. "He was just a *boy*."

A boy who had carefully laid my bag onto the sand in case I came back to grab it. A boy who had placed a purple flower in the side pocket for me to enjoy. I mourned the loss of that flower. It wouldn't have survived in the harsh depths of the ocean, but I would have cherished it until it died.

I looked at the prayer reeds, their splashes of pinks and greens coating my fingers. It wasn't just that I believed the boy was harmless. No. I had felt something—something strange, something I couldn't quite put my finger on. It had been there the first day I had met him, though I'd been too shaken up about the net to really think about it. But that morning, when I saw him standing there, staring at me with those painfully blue eyes and that hesitant smile, I knew I wasn't wrong.

The boy wasn't just harmless. There was more to it than that. There was something there, hidden in the tendrils of fear and uncertainty—a thread that twisted from my heart and stretched to his. A connection, a voice telling my quivering soul that this boy was important, that he *would* be important. I just had to figure out *how*.

"Those *boys* become the very beasts who kill us," Jorah pushed, forcing me out of my thoughts.

"Or," Illeron added from his post, "have you forgotten what happened to your parents?"

I slammed my hands onto the table and whirled to face the warrior. A hiss slipped off my tongue as my magic crackled over my rigid fins. "You have no right to bring up my parents so casually. Watch yourself, warrior."

Illeron's mouth twitched into a thin line, and his steely gaze returned to the throne's yawning entry.

The room grew quiet. No one but Jorah met my searching gaze. "Yes," I said, my voice cold, "Appah was murdered by humans during last year's Hunt. But Ammah . . ." My heart tightened. "We don't truly know what happened to her."

Silence hung in the air. I turned slowly, struggling to keep my composure. By the time I faced Jorah again, my fins had wilted. "I know you all think I'm unfit to lead," I said, my voice wavering with poorly concealed fury. "That I'm reckless, immature, and not worthy of my title. Me grabbing my bag shouldn't be a surprise to any of you."

"No," Illeron agreed stiffly, "we aren't surprised. We are, however, disappointed."

I spun to face him, my face giving away the anger I was desperately trying to contain. "Will you be silent for *one* moment so the rest of us can talk?"

Illeron clucked his tongue but did as I demanded.

Jorah's brow creased. "Illeron lacks sensitivity. It's just that . . ." He winced, poking at his rotting elbow. "You are so very young, and leading an entire pod is a monumental task that one shouldn't take lightly." He offered a half-hearted laugh. "You won't even wear your ammah's crown."

I pulled away from the hand he had stretched toward me, bumping into the table and sending the jars wobbling. The octopus took off in a cloud of ink. I stared at Jorah, my chest heaving. It was always the same conversation, the same fight. We both knew it by heart. "I don't wear it because I don't deserve it."

"The pod will take you more seriously if you wear it," Jorah pressed. "*I* will take you more seriously."

"And it's not like Nereida is coming back to claim it," Illeron muttered.

I shook my head. "You don't know that."

"It's been eight years. Yes, I do," Illeron said.

"I'm not ready to bear its weight," I countered.

"Evanora," Mavi whispered, "it's just a crown."

"One that has been collecting barnacles on your bedside table," Illeron added.

"It's *yours* now." Mavi was already drifting to the hallway behind the dais. "I can retrieve it for you!"

"I'm not ready!" I snapped, my Gift fluttering out of my scales in a lightning-sharp crack.

Illeron let out a groan. "Poseidon drown me—don't be so dramatic."

I laughed, sharp and biting. "I'm being dramatic? You all believe that a piece of jewelry is suddenly going to change me into this amazing leader. I am *not* Nereida! I am *not* Rainos! I am Evanora. And I am trying my best." My bottom lip began to wobble. "Why is my best not good enough?" I finished, the words becoming soft and warbled around the edges.

Jorah opened his mouth as Mavi swam forward. Even Illeron looked particularly apologetic.

I needed to be alone. Before Jorah could say another damning thing, or Mavi could lock me into a smothering hug, or Illeron could soften from his rock-hard state, I surged out of the palace.

I blinked through my tears as I twisted along the path, aiming for my parents' garden. My thoughts were a special breed of hatefulness, spreading through my body like a virus, clawing through my scales, through my blood, through my tangled nerves. I hated everyone at that moment. I hated Jorah, my pod, that innocent boy on the beach, and myself.

The garden was quiet when I slipped into the center of the rock circle, my tail brushing against the fine white sand that coated the floor. The coral was bright in the day's last light, shimmering like jewels in the water. A bundle of seahorses whistled by, swinging in the soft undercurrent. I nestled onto the ground, curling my tail around myself. As I listened to the stillness, I let my tears fall, and I allowed myself to admit that Jorah was right.

I blinked up at the surface above, my fingers dipping into the sand in slow, fluid circles. I wasn't a good leader, but I wanted to be. I wanted to be a force, an unrelenting power. I wanted the waters to quake and the earth to shift in my presence. I wanted the humans to fear me, the Cursed Beings to dread me. Wanted—so *badly*—but wasn't.

I feared I would never be. And then it would be too late.

CHAPTER FOURTEEN

GRAYSON

APRIL 3 – AFTERNOON

THE SUN WAS MAKING ME TIRED. THE WAY IT FILTERED through the oak tree's leaves and landed on my open sketchbook, leaving splashes of light on my scribbles. Its soft heat sank into my clothes and nestled against my skin. I could feel my eyelids growing heavy, my lashes drifting down, down, down. My grip on the pencil slackened, my chin drooping toward my chest. Sleep reached out to me, and I stretched my fingertips to meet it—

Thwack!

I flinched, my eyes snapping open in time to watch a pebble tumble down my arm and into the grass. Little burning *pings* scattered along my skin underneath my rolled-up sleeve.

"Oy. No sleeping on the job." Jasper was propped up on an elbow, his bad leg cocked awkwardly over the other. "You're supposed to be sketching me," he said around a lazy grin.

I brushed off the trail of dust left behind on my shirt and shot Jasper a scowl. "I never actually agreed to sketch you."

Jasper grunted and flopped back to the ground, tucking his hands behind his head. "I'll bet my entire allowance that drawing me is far more entertaining than those plants you like doodling." He reached out haphazardly and plucked a long strand of straw grass, tucking it neatly between his teeth. Using his tongue to swivel it back and forth like a little straw flag, Jasper stared up at the tree that loomed above us. "Good memories here."

I scoffed, wiping hunks of eraser from my notes. I had the eyes right, but I was struggling with the mouth. "You mean the time you broke your femur in a million spots because you decided to climb a tree you had no business climbing?"

Jasper snorted. "No. I mean the time you barfed and fainted at the sight of my bone sticking out of my bloody leg."

"It's the same memory, doofus."

Jasper inspected the chewed end of the straw grass before popping it back into his mouth. "The way I remember it is better."

I sighed, leaning my head against the tree's bark and staring up at the branches. I always wondered if Jasper's leg would have healed better had I been able to get help instead of panicking at the sight of blood, like I always did. I wondered if he blamed his awkward limp on me.

Thwack!

Another stone pelted me.

"Will you stop that?" I growled, rubbing at the increasingly tender spot on my arm.

Jasper laughed, settling back on the ground. "You need to work on your reflexes."

"If I get a bruise, I'm blaming you."

"If you get a bruise, it means my marksmanship is top-notch, and I'll take it as a compliment."

I rolled my eyes. "You would."

Jasper inhaled deeply, his slender chest puffing out. After a heartbeat of blessed silence, he cocked his head toward me. "Hey, where did you go after Mr. Grieves's dazzling speech? I couldn't find you anywhere."

I squinted at the sketchbook. I wasn't getting the hair right either. At this point, I was about ready to give up. "If I recall correctly, *you* abandoned *me* after the speech." I added a couple more strands before giving a solid side-eye at Jasper. "To find a girl just *dying* to dance with you?"

Jasper returned his attention to the branches overhead. "Speaking of dancing, I'm going to cut a rug around that comment and pretend you didn't say it."

"So, you didn't find a dancing partner, then."

"Some First Festival, hey?" Jasper responded with robust enthusiasm, ignoring my jab.

I clucked my tongue and looked back at my sketch. "The best."

"Okay," Jasper said, "I know you're just saying that to get me to stop talking, but I really think it *was*!"

"How many have you been to? Like, five?"

Jasper propped himself onto his elbows to frown at me. "Definitely more than you. Come on, Grays, it was fun! The music, the fireworks, the drinks, the dancing!" When I didn't reply, he reached forward and jostled my arm. "Why are you so sour about it? Didn't you have a good time?"

I tapped the pencil against my lips and rolled my head to the side. "Let me think. There's the fact that you bailed on driving me—"

"It was a war zone at my house!" Jasper quickly countered.

"So I had to travel with Pastor Kline," I continued. "I got jelly on my cheek, which you didn't tell me about. Who knows how long it was on there for and how many people saw it." I paused to see if Jasper had a rebuttal. He didn't. "And I unintentionally—yet gravely—dishonored your sister by not dancing with her." I set the pencil down and raised my eyebrows. "I don't think I've left anything out."

Jasper grimaced. "I did hear that some poor soul nearly fainted at the sight of red paint."

"Oh, yes, that too. Add that to the list."

Jasper groaned, rolling his head with such an exaggerated force that his hair swooped around like a ginger wave. "Things will get better. After the Symbolic Sign-In, no one is going to think about what a mess you were at the First Festival. Everything will change. Trust me."

I let out a snort of laughter. "How would you know that? You've never participated in the Sign-In."

Jasper's face grew solemn as he pointed to his chest. "Because I can feel it. In my bones."

"That's your heart."

Jasper had just opened his mouth to debunk my anatomy lesson when his head whipped to the side, his eyes on the dirt road just beyond the weeds and wooden fence beside us. "Ah!" he said, offering me a sly smile. "Speak of her, and the dishonored sister shall appear."

All the air left my lungs as I followed Jasper's line of vision to the road. I would have welcomed seeing Mr. Grieves adventuring through the country-side instead of Holly. Maybe even Mr. Brightly. Maybe even my pa. I prayed Jasper's eyes were playing tricks on him.

But there she was, her braided copper hair sun-drenched, her freckled cheeks rosy from the walk, her green plaid skirts billowing with her strides.

Holly was clutching several books to her chest, her chin tucked low to ward off the ever-present island breeze.

I sank lower to the ground, the tree bark digging into my back as I fought to become invisible. *I'm not here.*

Holly was nearly past the tree, her footsteps small and hurried.

Don't look this way. Please don't look this way.

She was at the point in the road where it took a lazy bend to the left, winding around sloping green hills of clover. A few more steps and she would be gone.

And then Jasper ruined everything.

"Hello, sister of mine!" he called out, waving wildly to get Holly's attention.

Holly stuttered to a stop. She spun on her heel, her eyes darting left and right until they landed on the tree, and us underneath it.

Jasper continued to wave, and it took everything in my power not to smack his arm into stillness. "How was the library today? Is Mrs. Humphries still positively irate with us?"

Holly didn't say anything, but I could see her arms tighten around her books, her face becoming a mask of stone. Her gaze landed on me and stayed there.

I reluctantly straightened from my piss-poor hiding spot, lifting my hand in a small wave. "Hi, Holly."

Holly's mouth twitched into something between a frown and a snarl. She pointed her nose into the air, let out a huff, and snapped forward. Her back was spear straight as she marched down the road with renewed vigor. It was the biggest *screw you* move I've seen in a while.

Jasper watched his sister's retreating form and whistled. "Ooh, someone's in trouble."

I rubbed the back of my neck, sighing. "I thought you said she could never be mad at me!"

Jasper snorted, shaking his head. "Mad? No. In trouble? Absolutely."

"What's the difference?"

Jasper leaned over and planted a hand on my shoulder. "A great deal of difference when it comes to girls, Grayson Shaw." He gave me a squeeze before pulling away with a satisfied exhale. "You'll understand one day."

Compelled by the guilt, I hopped to my feet and stumbled toward the road. "Holly, wait!"

Holly didn't stop, but she did slow down. I vaulted over the fence and jogged to her.

What do I say? What do I say? What do I say?

Holly's expression was enough to refreeze the ocean. I offered a small smile, hoping it would thaw her a bit. I was on dangerous ground; one misstep and it would cave in, swallowing me whole. "Some First Festival, hey?" I said, using Jasper's line.

It was the wrong thing to say. I swore I could hear the dirt road groan as cracks formed underfoot.

Holly stared at me, her hazelnut eyes narrowing slightly. "What about it?" she asked coolly.

"Oh, you know," I fumbled, "the music, the fireworks, the drinks, the dancing." *Dancing? Why would you say dancing?*

Holly's mouth dipped downward. "I wouldn't know about the dancing."

Honestly, if the ground decided to eat me alive, it would be less painful than this conversation. I tried again. "Well, what about the Symbolic Sign-In? Surely you must be excited for that?"

Holly inhaled slowly, like she was inflating so she could float away. "I'm not allowed to go."

I bit my lip. "The twins?" I guessed.

"Grayson Shaw," Holly cut me off abruptly. "Did you really come over here to remind me of my terrible time at the First Festival and the fact that I can't attend the Symbolic Sign-In, or is there something else you want to say to me?" When I didn't respond immediately, she shrugged tensely, still strangling her books against her chest. "Anything else? Anything at all?" Her shoulders rose higher. "A single word, perhaps?"

I may have drawn blood, I was biting my lip so hard. I subconsciously wiped at my mouth. A single word. A single word to melt the ice cloak Holly had wrapped around herself. It had to be a good one. I scoured my brain for ideas, my frantic gaze flitting from Holly's eyes, to her hair, to her shawl, to her books. I stilled, a *ding-ding-ding!* echoing through my head. Books. That was it! It was the one thing we had in common; we loved reading. I flashed her the brightest smile I could manage and pointed at her armful of books. "Nice."

Whatever word Holly was looking for, *nice* wasn't it. Holly's mouth dropped open as she looked to where I was pointing, then back at me. A flurry of emotions swept over her face, but most of them were of the angry sort.

And then I realized it looked like I was pointing at her chest, and not her collection of books.

Holly juggled the books into one arm and clasped her shawl tightly with the other, covering herself up. Her frigid expression had finally cracked, but in the worst way.

"Oh, jeez. Holly, that's not what I meant!" I stammered out, pointing vigorously at her chest again. "I meant nice as in . . . nice books! Not nice . . . you know."

Holly's lower lip trembled, and a tiny whimper slipped through her clenched teeth.

"Please, Holly. You have to believe me," I pushed hurriedly. "Nice books. I swear that's all I meant."

Holly's brows knitted, and if I didn't know better, I'd swear she was both angry about my poorly chosen words *and* that I didn't think she had nice breasts. Another soft whimper escaped.

The conversation had been torturous from the start, and like a rotten miracle, I'd made it worse. My mind was blank, struggling to find anything that would make everything better, and the ground still hadn't put me out of my misery. And in the midst of the mess, I realized that I'd been staring at Holly's chest the whole time. Again.

Panicked, I forced my eyes upward, but it was too late. Holly's face was as red as a sunbaked tomato, and she was clutching her shawl so tightly that her bony knuckles had gone white. Tears she was too stubborn to let fall clung to her thick eyelashes. Her eyes were wide, like she was willing herself not to blink. Holly pushed around me, knocking me back a step with her force.

"Holly!" I called after her, desperation making my voice crack.

Holly continued down the road, kicking up dust with the strength of her footsteps. When she was out of view, I hung my head dejectedly and wandered back to Jasper.

Jasper was lazily scouring my sketchbook, turning the pages without really looking at them. "Well, you certainly made a mess of things."

I hobbled over the rickety fence and snatched the book out of Jasper's hands. "Those are private!" I growled, needing to channel my annoyance at myself into something else.

Jasper rolled his eyes and sat up, leaving an indent of his body in the weeds. "Yes, Grayson, those plants you like to doodle—absolutely no one has ever seen them before!"

The plants smothering the first half of the sketchbook weren't what I was worried about him seeing. It was the sketch of the mermaid in the back. The one I was absolutely butchering.

Jasper sputtered out a heavy breath. "In any case, whatever it was you were trying to accomplish, I think it's safe to say that you failed miserably."

I faltered. "With my sketches, or your sister?"

Jasper gave me a sardonic look. "Think, Grayson. Think really hard."

I groaned, plopping onto the ground. "How was I supposed to know what *single word* she was looking for?"

Jasper laughed so hard that he had to clutch his stomach. "It's *sorry!*" he said between gasps of air. "Whatever you *think* the single word is, just keep in mind that it's actually *sorry*."

I covered my eyes with my hand. "Duly noted."

Jasper bopped my shoulder. "You're a hopeless thing, Grayson Shaw."

"Also duly noted."

There was a beat of silence, besides the occasional giggle from Jasper. I opened the sketchbook again, thumbing through the pages until I found my pencil stuck in the creases. Jasper watched me as I began to flip to the mermaid's unfinished portrait. Thinking better of it, I circled back to a sketch of a rhodiola rosea.

"What are you planning to do with it, anyway?" Jasper asked, gesturing to the book. "Sell it? Keep it from prying eyes forever?"

I began jotting notes underneath the cluster of flowers and thick, spiky leaves. "It's for me. When I find a plant with good medicinal properties, I need to know what it looks like when I'm foraging."

"My friend, the flora fairy." Jasper batted at my pencil. "Of all the hobbies you could have picked, you went with flowers."

I leaned away from Jasper. "Well, I'd like to make it more than a hobby."

Jasper's mouth went a little slack. I pressed the pencil into the paper harder than necessary. "I'd like to make a practice of it," I said reluctantly, like I was sharing a secret. "Become an ethnobotanist, study healing methods, maybe even pursue a life outside of the island. Mrs. Morris thinks I'm cut out for it."

Now it looked like I had slapped Jasper across the face. "I mean," I pushed, nearly tearing a hole through the paper, "you don't really want to stay at the docks your entire life, do you? Don't you have any long-term goals?"

I had asked a simple question, but it was like I had cast a curse on Jasper, his family, and his dog. "Uh, yeah, Grayson," he said haughtily. "It's called the Hunt."

I bit my tender lip. "But what about after that?"

"Well, then there's another Hunt the following year."

"And after that?"

"Jesus, Mary, and Joseph!" Jasper scoffed, clumsily rising to his feet. "What are you getting at, Grayson?"

I rose to meet him. "What are *you* getting at, Jasper?" I responded, matching my hostility to his. "Are you really telling me that you are *happy* to walk in circles? Just docks, Hunt, docks, Hunt until you die?"

Jasper stared at me for a second before an incredulous laugh slipped out of his mouth. He lifted his arms helplessly. "I *love* my life. Sure, it's not fancy, and the pay isn't great, and I'll probably live with my parents forever, but I love it." He let his hands fall, slapping at his sides. "And look, just because you hate your life here on Lethe doesn't mean you have to make fun of mine."

I ran my hands through my hair. "I don't hate my life, Jasper. Just . . . parts of it." I sighed, shaking my head. The fight within me was already dwindling. "It's just that there's more to life than the Hunt. I mean, don't you want to know what it's like on the mainland? Don't you want to see more than this island, and bloodshed, and mermaids?"

Jasper crossed his arms. I could tell he was fizzling out too. Our fights were like fireworks: bright and loud but quickly snuffed out. "I'm sure you'll send me a postcard," he huffed reluctantly. "When you become a famous ethno-whatever."

I smiled with relief. "Deal." Scooping up my sketchbook, I patted Jasper on the shoulder. "Come on, let's brainstorm more ways I've unintentionally tormented your sister."

As Jasper began prattling off more things I could add to my already-staggering list, I allowed my mind to drift. And for a split second, I could see it—my life outside of Lethe, outside of the Hunt. A lab with windows that reached the ceiling, sending dust-speckled sunlight scattering over the old wooden floorboards. There were shelves filled to the brim with medicinal herbs and plants of every shape and color and desks littered with papers and beakers and microscopes. There was research, and excitement, and discoveries. And there wasn't even a mention, or a thought, of mermaids.

But then I blinked, and the second had passed, and I was back beside Jasper, stuck on an island drenched in blood and hate.

And I knew that was all it was. A dream.

I wouldn't become a botanist. I wouldn't be leaving Lethe.

I was trapped.

I wondered if the mermaid was trapped too.

CHAPTER FIFTEEN

EVANORA

APRIL 3 – AFTERNOON

I'M NEVER GOING TO FIGURE THIS OUT," MAVI WHINED.

I watched as the orb of water Mavi had created collapsed in on itself, swallowing my light within it. The water sloshed into her hands, spilling over her splayed fingers before merging with the ocean surrounding us, succumbing to the ever-pulling undercurrent.

"Again," I pushed gently, cupping my hands together and placing them between us.

Mavi eyed me, biting her plump lip. I shook my hands in front of her face. "Come *on*, Mavi. Again."

"Ah, fine," she groaned.

Letting out a slow breath, Mavi dipped her chin and closed her eyes. After a heartbeat, I could hear the soft hum of her Gift singing within her, tangling itself through her bloodstream as it worked its way to her fingertips. She lifted her hands and began to swirl them around mine, moving in a graceful sphere. Each hand seemed to have a mind of its own, moving in opposite directions as they circled and swooped over mine, but they never slowed, never faltered. Drops of water began to pool at her fingers, pulled from the ocean, heeding the water wielder's call. They dripped off her nails, suspended in the space between us.

As her magic dangled over my hands, I forced my own Gift out of its slumber. Nerves straining, I slowly unfurled my fingers, revealing a fistful of light. It bounced off the hanging water droplets, ricocheting off them and scattering shattered light. My Gift begged to flicker out, to fizzle back to sleep. I grunted, willing it to stay put.

Opening her eyes, Mavi focused on my light with a grim expression. Furrowing her brow, she deftly scooped the water collecting between us and began to shape it around my hands. Her movements were fluid, a dance. "Into a cage," she breathed.

The water began to take form, shape-shifting around my open hands. It followed her movements, churning and dipping to become a wobbling globe.

I suppressed my grin. "Steady," I encouraged.

The water grew thick, the walls of her magical cage becoming more solid than liquid. My light burned brighter in response.

"Now!" Mavi cried.

In unison, I wrenched my hands out of the center as Mavi's hands stilled against the water's walls. My light hung in the middle of the orb, hovering in the prison Mavi had created. Her water shimmered, continuously coiling around my magic as it acted like the cage she had whispered into being. Our Gifts merged in perfect unity, light and water singing to each other, acting in a harmony that defied all laws of reality.

And then the magic collapsed.

My light was snuffed out as Mavi's water folded in on itself, sloshing between us like a mini current.

Mavi leaned away, groaning. "It's hopeless."

I shook out my hands, ridding them of the residual magic vibrating at the tips. "No, it's not! That orb lasted a great deal longer than the previous ones."

Mavi dipped her fingers into the sand, creating long divots in the grains. "I don't understand why we are even attempting this." She frowned at me, her golden eyes searching mine. "Don't the lanterns do a good-enough job?"

I nodded. "Yes, but no matter what I do, they always go out when daylight arrives." I leaned back on my hands, sighing. "I want to create something that is more sustainable, something I don't have to worry about tending to every night." I looked over my shoulder at the empty lanterns bordering the path beyond the seaweed forest. "What if I need to leave again, or I'm not able to return in time to light them? No . . ." I shook my head. "There has to be another way, a *better* way."

The wielder gnawed at her lip, deep crevices etching into her forehead. "But why would you want to leave again? Especially after what happened last time, with the net and the boy. Wasn't that traumatizing enough?"

I blinked at my friend, at the fading spots on her violet tail, at the anxiety flickering in her wide oval eyes. Mavi was so young. Her dorsal fin hadn't even fully formed yet. She didn't understand trauma or burdens. She didn't know how I could still feel the net constricting around me, or how I kept waking up in the middle of the night, convinced I was still stranded on that beach, lost and never finding my way back home. She didn't know how terrified I was that, for as long as I lived, the chance of it happening again would always linger. She didn't know. And I wanted to keep it that way.

I smiled softly, flicking her daintily pointed nose. "You're right. It was."

Mavi opened her mouth, then snapped it shut when Illeron appeared, pushing through the throngs of seaweed and drifting over to us, his mouth already curling into a deep frown.

I looked over at the warrior with a carefully neutral expression. "Gracing us with your presence? What an honor."

Illeron swam until he was hovering just above us, the end of his spear grazing the ocean floor near my tail. He moved his hand from his chest to his side in greeting, the movement forced but fluid.

I clucked my tongue, flopping onto my back next to Mavi. "I'm not doing it back."

The corner of Illeron's mouth quirked the slightest bit upward. "Ever the image of royalty."

"What do you want?"

Illeron gripped his spear tightly, averting his gaze to the sand. "I was hoping for your company."

My heart stilled. But only for a moment. I observed my long, pointed nails. "Mavi and I are busy."

He eyed my lazy stretch. "Clearly."

"Evanora," Mavi said, nudging my side, "go ahead. He's being polite."

I rolled my eyes, hoisting myself up onto my elbows. "Must I?"

Illeron stomped his spear against the ground impatiently, his long silver-and-crimson tail swishing. He bared his teeth, squeezed his eyes shut for a breath, and then grunted out, "Please."

I rose with a playful spin, grinning as I swam up to Illeron. I patted him on the shoulder as I swam by. "Well, since you asked so nicely."

I could hear Illeron groan but trail behind me. My grin grew larger. *"Good boy."*

"Quiet," Illeron growled.

I halted when we hit the edge of our border. Illeron came to a stop beside me, his sharply angled face pensive.

"Now," I said, reaching for one of the lampposts and twirling around it, "what's all this about? Did you come to tell me more ways I'm a terrible ruler? Perhaps offer a snide retort or two?"

I hadn't seen Illeron—or Jorah—since our last meeting in the throne room, when everyone had ultimately ganged up on me and my misgivings as a leader. My feelings of inadequacy remained, but so did the aggressive amount of embarrassment for the temper tantrum I'd unleashed about the crown. I was no better than a merling being denied the biggest oyster.

Illeron suddenly looked very interested in his spear. His fingers played with the twine holding the blade in place, his eyes fixed on the spear's jagged teeth.

"Illeron," I urged. "I'm returning to Mavi if you don't tell me what's going on."

Illeron's head shot up. "Don't."

I sighed, raising my arms.

Illeron pursed his lips together. "I felt like . . ." He closed his eyes, taking a slow breath. "I felt like I owed you an apology."

I lifted my eyebrows but said nothing. Illeron continued. "The last time I saw you, I said some things I should've kept to myself. They were hurtful and uncalled-for." He shrugged. "You deserve an apology. Happy?"

"Not really." When Illeron gawked at me, I nearly laughed. "Saying you owe me an apology isn't exactly the same as *giving* me one."

I could hear a growl creeping up Illeron's throat. He smoothed back his long silver-white hair, his widow's peak looking menacing on the tip of his forehead. He gritted his teeth, the muscles in his jaw tightening. "*Sorry.*"

I crossed my arms. "Out loud."

"Evanora—"

"Out. Loud."

Illeron *did* growl then. "Sorry."

I sighed heavily. "There. Was that so hard?"

"Exceptionally."

It looked like the entire process of apologizing was a painful thing for him. I looped around the lantern again. "So, do you take back what you said, then? Do you think I am capable of ruling?"

Illeron brushed his thumb against his lower lip thoughtfully. "I think you have the drive, and the spirit. But I also think you have a lot to learn." He watched me spin, and spin, and spin. "A lot."

I paused mid-loop to throw a hand over my forehead. "Oh, *gods*, and who out there shall *ever* teach me, a poor, pathetic, unlearned soul?"

Illeron made a face. "Don't look at me, Your Majesty. I'm a warrior, not a miracle worker."

I grinned, cutthroat. "Oh, don't be ridiculous, Illeron. If I wanted a miracle worker, I'd go to Jorah—that fish can make me disappear by simply opening his mouth."

The warrior chuckled, shifting closer. "If only your wisdom were as sharp as your wit. We would have found a way to end the Hunt centuries ago."

"Ah, if only."

Illeron's face softened. "Jorah is trying to help."

I scrunched up my nose. "*Trying*, key word."

"You need to cut him some slack. Since the death of your parents, the pod has been in a free fall." Illeron shook his head, sighing. "Jorah is attempting damage control, but . . ."

"But it's not enough," I finished for him quietly.

Illeron nodded. "It was a slow bleed when your parents reigned, but I'm afraid the wound is too deep now, and we don't have the resources to staunch the flow."

I nearly lost my grip on the lamppost. "You mean, there were issues even while Ammah and Appah were the pod's leaders?"

Illeron tossed his spear back and forth between his hands. "Most definitely. So, don't fill that pretty—albeit petite—brain of yours with thoughts that the problems occurred the second you stepped up to rule."

I cast a withering look the warrior's way. "I'll try not to."

Illeron laughed, flashing me his sharp canines. I felt a flutter in my stomach and looked away. "It's all such a headache," I said, letting go of the lamppost and floating next to Illeron. "I'm constantly under scrutiny. Every move I make is surely the *wrong* move, and every time I try to help, I end up making things worse." I covered my face with my hands. "I just wish my parents were still here."

Illeron's laughter faded. "I told you, I'm not a miracle worker," he said. "I don't have all the answers."

I groaned in reply, keeping my hands anchored to my face.

Illeron cleared his throat, and then his hand was pulling at one of mine, gently prying it off my face like a suctioned squid tentacle. He craned his neck to meet my averted gaze, his fingers still tangled with mine. "The one answer I have is this: You are not alone. You don't have to do *any* of this on your own."

"I can't lean on my pod." I shook my head, ashamed of the knot of emotion in my throat. "They'll think I'm weak."

I realized we were holding hands the same time Illeron did; we quickly pulled away from each other. My hand felt barren, my fingertips burning.

Illeron's gaze became fleeting. "I wasn't talking about the pod, Evanora." In the soft daylight, his eyes found mine again, and they said all the things his mouth and mind couldn't.

That was when the screaming started.

A burst of white-hot fear snaked through my insides. I flinched back. "What was that?"

The warrior was already gone, racing along the path. "It came from the Barrens!"

It happened again, a keening high-pitched wail. My mind snatched up the sound, echoing and distorting it.

I forced myself forward, pressing down the terror encroaching on my heart. I sped behind Illeron, following his sharp turns down the lava-rock path, his dips through the stretching seaweed. He was pulling ahead, leaving me in clouds of sand. I growled, willing myself to go faster, to fly in the undercurrent.

The path rounded a wide corner littered with boulders and scattered coral. I almost didn't have time to stop. Illeron was suddenly right in front of me, completely still.

The path continued its winding course, but the warrior had pulled away from it and was in a small clearing bordered by the lava-rock path on one side and a sharp cliff on the other. He was surrounded by merlings. The spots on their tails were vibrant against their pale scales. They clung to his hands, his spear, his fins, fearful cries filling their mouths. The panic emanating from them was palpable.

I skittered up beside Illeron. "What is it? What's wrong?" I panted, sharply scouring the area for signs of danger. No sharks, no giant squid, no signs of humans, only the desolate presence of the Barrens, looming from the cliff's edge beside us.

Illeron's eyes remained fixed on the trench, wide and unblinking. The merlings gripped him so tightly that his light skin was turning red, but it was like he hardly noticed them. It was like he was alone.

One of the merlings sniffled, letting go of Illeron to wipe his nose roughly. "We were only playing, Your Majesty."

My heart growled within me. I twisted around to see who had spoken. It was Andoras, one of the kingdom's younger water wielders. I lowered myself, taking Andoras's chin and claiming his attention. "What happened?"

Andoras's bright orange eyes darted away from mine, his dark blue tail squirming. "We were only *playing*," he tried again, his little voice wobbling with every word he forced out. "Playing battle." He began to cry again. "We didn't mean for anyone to get hurt, I swear!"

"Andoras," I said, trying to remain calm, "it's okay; you're not in trouble. But you need to tell me what happened."

Andoras's eyes shifted to the jagged edge of the cliff. "Some of the sirens wanted to play battle with us, but the training grounds weren't big enough, so we moved out here." He started to writhe underneath my grip. "We know we aren't supposed to be so close to the Barrens, but we were going to be careful."

My fins grew stiff. I took a slow breath, offering the merling a grim smile. "Go on," I encouraged.

Andoras whimpered, finally looking at me. "Well, Solandis was beating me, and the other merlings were taunting me about it . . . about a *girl* besting *me* at my *favorite* game . . . and I lost focus. My Gift rushed out, and I wielded poorly. I hit her, and . . ." Andoras's gaze trailed back to the cliff's edge, to where the Barrens lay, hungry and waiting.

My blood ran cold. Solandis. Trapped in the dark, alone, vulnerable. Likely dead the second she entered the Barrens. And if she wasn't, it wouldn't be long until she wished she were.

I released Andoras with a quiet hiss. "We must find her, Illeron. We must go into the Barrens." I turned to the warrior. "Illeron?"

Illeron was still frozen in place, and for a second, he looked no older than the merlings surrounding him. His face had grown impossibly pale, his lips drawn into a tight line that threatened to splinter. His hands, clutching his spear, were shaking.

Swallowing the nausea pooling in my mouth, I looked back to the Barrens. I had never been this close to them before; since the creation of the curse, it was forbidden to veer outside the lanterns' borders. I could hear the evil lurking within, scuttling within the shadows, a symphony of death and despair.

An anxious whine escaped Illeron's mouth.

"Illeron," I barked, grabbing his shoulders, "focus!"

The warrior blinked, and he was back. His grip on the spear tightened, but it was no longer a trembling thing. He sucked in a breath, his eyes finding mine. *"Thank you."*

I nodded, forcing a small smile onto my lips. "There is no time to waste. Illeron, I want you to wait here with the merlings." Illeron immediately opened his mouth to object, but I silenced him with a raised hand. "We cannot leave her in the dark. I will go."

Illeron bared his teeth. "You cannot ask me to do that."

"Would you rather go in there?" I asked, narrowing my eyes.

"What would Jorah say if you, the last remaining ruler, went down there and didn't come back?" Illeron's gaze flicked over my shoulder to the looming dark. "Evanora, it's just too dangerous."

"He doesn't have to know." I turned to the Barrens. "We'll be back before you can think of another thing to scold me about."

"Evanora," Illeron bit out, snatching my wrist before I swam out of reach. "Please." He swallowed hard, glancing at the merlings crowded around us. *"What if it's too late?"*

Anger flared in my chest. I wrenched my hand free. "I have to try!"

And before Illeron could try to stop me again, I dove for the Barrens, letting the darkness swallow me whole.

The canyon was far deeper than I expected. Even with the pulse of my nerves, the glow barely illuminated my surroundings. I could hardly make out my hand in front of my face. The heavy scent of sulfur choked me, stinging my eyes and making my nose itch. The icy grip of evil crept up my scales, curling around my heart, sinking into my bones. It wanted me—my flesh, my blood, my life. Whispers in the dark clawed at my mind, deafening and relentless.

I reached inward, clutching at the threads of my Gift. When I had a good grip, I pulled. My light pulsed around me, a shield of brilliance to combat the depthless dark. The shadows immediately shrank away with a hiss.

"Evanora?" Even in the confines of my mind, Illeron sounded worried.

My magic crackled. *"I'm all right."* I peered downward. The cliff's jagged side stretched leagues below me, and there was no sign of Solandis. *"The darkness seems to stretch forever. I need to go deeper."*

There was silence, and then: *"Be careful."*

Sifting through the dark, I eyed the algae-covered rock ledges jutting off the cliff wall. They were scattered, cascading down the face like bony fingers—small, but large enough to hold a merling. I opened my mouth, only to close it again, Solandis's name caught in my throat. If I was too loud, would the Cursed Beings hear me? Did they already know I was there? Were they looking for me?

My Gift sputtered out, locking me in the darkness's tight grip. *No!* I scrambled to collect the threads once more. The magic within me fizzled, then flared to life. I had nearly exhausted my Gift while playing around with Mavi. It wouldn't be long before my light extinguished completely and I wouldn't be able to draw it out.

Biting my lip, I pushed farther into the shadows, ignoring the growing pressure in my head, the swell of pain in my heart. I had to find her. I had to—

There was a sound.

At first, I thought it was the taunting whispers of the Cursed Beings, their low moans of pleasure upon finding me. But as I stilled in the water and held my breath, I realized it was something else entirely.

I closed my eyes, steadied my vicious heart, and listened.

A quiet, whimpering sob reached my ears.

Solandis.

My eyes flew open, a quiet gasp escaping with my ragged breath. The merling was close. I darted for the rock face, scraping my webbed hand against its sharp edges as I swam from lip to lip, begging for a glimpse of her.

And there she was, huddled on a slimy ledge, her head buried into her scales. Her arms were shaking violently as they clasped around her spotted fins, her long black hair cascading over her scrawny shoulders. She looked so small, so fragile, surrounded by the dark.

I swooped down to her. "Solandis!" I cried out quietly, slipping onto the ledge and folding my arms around her. "Solandis, I'm here!"

The merling jerked away from my touch with a yelp, nearly pushing me off the ledge. "Get away!"

I fought to regain my hold on her. "Solandis, it's me! It's Evanora!" She was being too loud. *I* was being too loud. I glanced into the shadows frantically before releasing Solandis's arms and grabbing her face. "Open your eyes!"

Solandis's eyes shot open, blinking against the harshness of my glow. She stopped fighting me, her heavy breaths slowing. She looked at me for a long, wild minute, like she wasn't altogether sure if I was an illusion or not. Her lip began to wobble. "Are you real?"

I nodded, gently brushing the hair out of her eyes. "Yes, little one. I'm real."

The merling cracked a smile, but it instantly vanished under the weight of her tears. "I'm so afraid," she sobbed, collapsing into me. "It was so dark. I was so alone."

I hummed softly, rocking Solandis in my arms as she cried. I pressed my cheek into her hair, my eyes drifting into the Barrens, searching for any lurking evil. "There now," I whispered, placing a kiss on the top of her head, "you're not alone anymore. You are safe." I waited until Solandis's whimpers quieted before pulling her up to face me. "You are very brave."

Solandis sniffled, shaking her head. "I don't feel very brave." She glanced upward at the cliff that loomed an eternity away. "I couldn't even make it back. I couldn't move. All I could think about was . . ." Her voice trailed off as she glanced into the ever-present shadows. "All I did was cry."

I forced a smile, taking her hands in mine. "Being down here all by yourself is scary."

Solandis frowned. "I don't think Andoras would cry."

I tipped her chin up. "He was crying the hardest out of *all* the merlings about you being down here."

"Really?"

"Really." My magic fluttered in my veins, a warning sign that it was ready to burn out. We were nearly out of time. I gave her hands a little shake. "Do you think you can keep being brave for me, little one?"

Solandis's hands went rigid in mine. "I think so." She huffed heavily, then nodded. "Yes, I can."

I smiled warmly. "It is time for us to go back home." I rose off the ledge, pulling Solandis with me. "I want you to keep hold of my hand, Solandis, and I want you to swim hard—as hard as you can. Don't stop, don't look behind you, and whatever you do, do not let go of my hand."

The merling nodded gravely.

The whispering had picked up. The second we were off the ledge, the darkness seemed to swarm us, hungry for a taste of our fear. Solandis did as I had commanded, her grip like iron in mine. But she was slow, her little tail flailing compared to my swift pumps. The cliff's edge wasn't getting any closer. It remained fixed above us, a taunting safe haven we couldn't seem to reach.

I could hear a deep, oozing hiss in my ear. I sucked in a breath, fighting against the terror welling inside me. "Faster, Solandis!"

The merling groaned at my side, already tired from the forceful exertion. But she kicked harder, her small body writhing with effort.

It felt like we were stuck, trapped in a nightmare that was never-ending. I clutched Solandis's hand, feeling the weight of her as I pulled her with me. "Faster!"

The hiss morphed into a low cackle, taunting, toying, *hunting*.

There was a piercing ache at the peduncle of my tail, the feeling of icy fingers slithering along my scales, shredding my fluke. The pain was blinding, nails sinking into my flesh, trying to claim purchase. I gritted my teeth, pushing against the pain, against the evil trying to hold me still. *Don't look back. Don't look back don't look back!*

My Gift strained, and the fragile threads slipped from my grasp. With a final flare of light, my magic burned out, and we were left in the shadows of the Barrens.

There was a shrieking wail, drenched in hunger.

Solandis and I burst above the cliff's ledge, surging from the depths of darkness and into the light. We tumbled into the sandy floor, skidding to a stop just before Illeron and the merlings.

There was a collective cry of shock, then a cacophony of chaos as the mermaids surrounded our limp bodies. Illeron dropped to the ocean floor and reached for me. "Evanora!" he croaked, shaking my shoulders. "Evanora, are you okay?"

I wasn't. I couldn't catch my breath, couldn't stop shaking, couldn't stop feeling evil's grip on me. And gods, the pain. Every part of me was cinched in agony. But I cracked my eyes open and offered Illeron a sly smile. "Never better."

I was still holding Solandis's hand like our lives depended on it. The merling was crying again, but it sounded like tears of relief. She, thankfully, was in one piece, with only a couple scrapes to show for her misadventure into the Barrens. Andoras was crouched beside her, sobbing profusely and spewing apology after apology.

I didn't want to look at my tail. The icy ache had turned into a blistering torture, one that I didn't have the strength to heal. Illeron's gaze dipped to the merlings, and I bit my lip, forcing myself to look.

Deep claw marks raked over my iridescent scales, flitting through the ripped edges of my delicate fins. The stench of rot and decay clung to the tears, along with a foul black ooze that burned. I inhaled sharply, shakily tucking my tail underneath me so the others couldn't see.

Illeron turned back to me. His grip softened on my arms. "Are you hurt?"

"Only my pride. I could've made our exit out of the Barrens a *little* more graceful, in my opinion."

"*Evanora.*"

"I'm fine, Illeron." I forced myself up, smiling through the deep ache settling into my bones. "See to it that the merlings get home safely. I'm going to rest here for a bit."

"You'll be all right?"

I laughed, pushing the warrior away. "I'm *fine. Go.*"

Illeron let out a deep sigh that he had clearly been holding in since I'd vanished into the Barrens. Still frowning, he reached forward and ran his fingers over the side of my face, gently caressing my cheek. He held my gaze firmly in his own as his fingers moved. "You're alive. That's all that matters."

When Illeron and the merlings left, I collapsed back onto the ocean floor and let the tears I'd been holding captive flow freely. Cursed Beings moving during the day. It was impossible.

Except . . . it wasn't.

The truth of the matter was, despite what we knew about the Cursed Beings, it wasn't enough. It would never be enough.

Our knowledge barely scratched the surface.

We were in the dark. Right where they wanted us.

CHAPTER SIXTEEN

GRAYSON

APRIL 4 – MORNING

THE BIG BLACK BARN WITH A BRICK ATTACHMENT AND A broken wooden fence gave off all the signs that it was closed. The door was locked, the dusty windows were shuttered, and there was no smoke billowing from the chimney.

I started with a polite knock, which turned into me calling out, "Excuse me, Mr. Craigsby, sir?" which then turned into me jiggling the handle with urgent enthusiasm. None gave me any sort of reaction.

Hands deep in my pockets, I glanced at the sign above the door.

Tully's Blacksmith and Farrier—open all hours, save for the Lord's Day.

All hours. Yeah, right.

Stifling a couple curse words, I resisted the urge to kick the door.

Penny's girth gall wasn't getting any better. And now she had a limp. It had taken an agonizingly long time to coax the stubborn Clydesdale into letting me look at the foot she was favoring. It had taken even longer to convince my pa to give her the break she desperately needed. Pa had been able to secure a ride to work with Pastor Kline, who'd promised he was as sober as Sunday service. And after digging through the pockets of all my pants and jackets, I'd been able to find enough money to replace Penny's shoe, which had grown loose and created a pressure point on her sole. I hadn't, however, been able to find enough loose change to buy her painkillers, which I suspected she needed more than the shoe.

Despite Penny not being on her best behavior, I managed to ease her aches with a salve and leg wrap. I had just enough time before work to race down the hill and plead my case to Mr. Craigsby. I'd pay with my chump change, offer free labor, even sell my soul to start a tab with the condition that I pay it back before the second coming of Christ—whichever he preferred. Penny was desperate, and so was I.

As I tried to peer through the shutters, I had a feeling my soul was my own for another day. I didn't feel very thankful about it though.

I huffed out a growl and gave into my urge, letting the tip of my boot connect with the wooden door with a satisfying *thump*.

"Please refrain from damaging my property, Mr. Shaw."

Stomping my foot back on the ground like it would destroy the evidence, I whipped my head around, hoping to see Mr. Craigsby's hunched form hobbling toward me. He could have been waving his gnarled walking stick at me in a threatening manner, and I still would have been ecstatic to see him.

But instead of Mr. Craigsby in his usual thick leather apron and rolled-up sleeves, absolutely smothered in dirt and grease, wearing his typical squinty-eyed scowl, it was Mr. Grieves. Mr. Grieves, who owned the building Mr. Craigsby worked in, along with the door I had just kicked. He was standing tall, walking in slow, strong strides that made his long gray cloak billow out behind him.

The gold cane in his gloved hand swung with his confident steps, which led me to believe that it was as much for show as his monocle—a bloody monocle, complete with gold wiring and everything!—was. His short blond hair was tucked neatly underneath his top hat. The only thing that looked like it could belong to Mr. Craigsby was the dark scowl marring his lips.

Mr. Grieves looked ready for church, not for a stroll through the muddy, stench-infested streets of Tully.

"Good morning, Mr. Grieves," I said, clumsily pulling my hand out of my pocket and thrusting it forward.

Mr. Grieves eyed my dirty hand for a painfully long moment before allowing his gaze to trail back up to mine. The scowl was still there. "I never took the Shaw boys to be the destructive sort," he said.

"Oh." My cheeks went stiflingly hot. "We aren't—weren't—I'm not," I stammered out.

Mr. Grieves's eyes flashed for a second, his mouth twitching at the corners. "Your boot print is still on the door." He waved his hand nonchalantly before resting it on the cane. "In any case, what are you doing out and about so early? It's dangerous to be alone, with the fretful disappearances and what have you."

I was in the middle of wondering if Mr. Grieves half expected me to get on my hands and knees to wipe the boot print off the door when the second part of his sentence reached my ears. I slowly put my hand back into my pocket, wondering why I'd ever want to shake hands with a man who cried fake tears for the missing victims. "I needed to speak to Mr. Craigsby."

"About?"

"My horse."

"Oh, dear." Mr. Grieves placed a hand delicately over his mouth. "Nothing dreadfully urgent, I hope."

I shook my head. "She needs a new shoe. And medicine for pain."

Mr. Grieves lowered his hand, revealing a smile. "Have you tried something other than pummeling the door with your feet?"

I was sorely tempted to show Mr. Grieves what *pummeling* actually meant. But that wouldn't help my shaky I'm-not-destructive stance. "What brings you to Tully, sir?" I asked instead.

Mr. Grieves raised an eyebrow, his icy-blue eyes twinkling with mock surprise. Like it was unthinkable that I'd ask. "Why, a morning stroll, of course! I do so enjoy early mornings in Tully. That, and I like to keep an eye on my busy bees." His gaze flicked over the empty street. "Make sure the businesses are running as they should."

A couple things ran through my mind. The first: Besides the blacksmith, no businesses were actually *open* and *running* at this time. The people of Tully weren't even out of bed, let alone being *busy bees*. The second: I really hoped he hadn't stopped by the butcher shop; it had turned out Pastor Kline was in the middle of nursing a hangover when Pa called. Pa had to wait for him to sober up with a good dose of self-confession.

And a morning stroll? The idea was laughable. Mr. Grieves sidestepping the potholes and sheep manure? Breathing in the briny seaweed air? Taking in the sights of the permanently closed shops and ramshackle homes that were long overdue for a roof job? It didn't add up.

And that was when I had my fourth thought: Either Mr. Grieves was a top-notch weirdo who truly did enjoy potholes and seaweed and poverty, or he was a liar.

I stared carefully at Mr. Grieves. Mr. Grieves stared carefully back at me. I was leaning toward liar.

Mr. Grieves suddenly smiled. His entire face shifted to match the radiance—his eyes, his cheeks, his eyebrows—until everything was in proper working order. It reminded me of a jigsaw puzzle, the pieces getting shoved and crammed into their appropriate spaces. "So, young Shaw, rumor on the wind is that I'll be seeing you at the Symbolic Sign-In tomorrow."

My stomach dipped. "That's right."

Mr. Grieves whistled. "Never thought I'd see the day, frankly!"

I tried to smile, but it felt an awful lot like a grimace. "Me neither."

"You'll see my son there." Mr. Grieves stood tall and puffed out his chest, his hands propped on the top of the cane he didn't need. "You know Ambrose, don't you?"

It took every effort not to roll my eyes. Who didn't know Ambrose? He was a self-absorbed rich kid who flaunted his birthright as much as his wealth. I was keenly aware of my own empty pockets whenever I saw him. Ambrose was everything I wasn't: confident, charming, tall. Muscles stacked on top of muscles, and no calluses to show for it. It made me wonder how he'd even built those muscles. He claimed his light blond hair, electric-blue eyes, and sharp cheekbones were the result of his ancestral lineage—not just good genetics. Either way, Ambrose knew he was handsome, and he made sure everyone else did too.

Mr. Grieves continued before I could come up with a reply that was neither snide nor catty. "He was born for the Hunt, you know. Like the very ritual was created for him."

"Except it wasn't," I said before I could stop myself. "It was made out of tragedy."

Mr. Grieves looked taken aback, but only for a moment; he raised a hand to his chest and let out a quick laugh. "Oh heavens, yes. Quite right you are." He shook his head. "What I'm saying is that Ambrose . . . He's gifted, you see. Talented in all aspects—swimming, fighting, spear handling. His net mending leaves a little to be desired, but . . ." He laughed again. "I believe this is the year he will win. I truly do."

Because you clearly need the victory pot. But even as I thought it, I knew that it wasn't about the money for the Grieveses. It was about the competition, the winning. They had to be the best, or nothing at all.

Mr. Grieves cleared his throat and pulled a gold pocket watch from his coat. He frowned at the gleaming face before tucking it back in. "Well, as lovely as it was to chat, Mr. Shaw, I best be off."

I nodded slowly. "To tend to your busy bees."

It was there, but only for a second—a flash in Mr. Grieves's eyes. Annoyance, unfiltered and red-hot, aimed solely at me. If it had lasted longer, I might've had time to feel the complete weight of that annoyance settling into my bones and curdling my insides. But then he blinked, and Mr. Grieves was smiling and tipping his hat to me, the puzzle pieces back in place. "Good day, Mr. Shaw."

As I turned back to the door, wondering if I really should try to buff out my footprint, Mr. Grieves called out, "Oh, Mr. Shaw!"

Sucking in a breath, I tensed my shoulders and faced the road, where Mr. Grieves stood by the broken fence bordering the yard. He was shaking his head and pinching the bridge of his nose. "I do so hope you're not planning on waiting for Mr. Craigsby?"

I shrugged stiffly. "Penny really needs a shoe."

"Well, you'll be waiting a while, I'm afraid." Mr. Grieves sighed mournfully. "Mr. Craigsby's in Fariid, you see, tending to my horses. He'll be gone most of the day, I gather."

A flicker of exasperation burrowed deep within me. A painfully useless conversation that could have been avoided had he told me that information up front. But Mr. Grieves didn't operate like that. He reveled in the withholding, the *sneaking*. I stuffed my hands into my pockets, hiding the clenched fists I'd formed. "Yes, I gather," I muttered.

I considered asking if Mr. Craigsby would return by sundown, but I didn't want to risk triggering another round of conversation. Instead, I forced a curt smile, nodded, and waited for him to saunter down the road before I headed in the opposite direction.

I sighed, dropping my head as I walked, kicking at any poor unsuspecting stone in my way. I didn't have time to go home, which was probably a good thing; I didn't want to tell Penny the bad news. But it was still too early to go to the docks.

As if in answer, I could feel it: The pull of the ocean. The press of salt on my skin. The whisper of wind in my hair.

I went to Hannigan's Cove.

The sky was a peach-and-strawberry sorbet with whipped-cream clouds hanging over my head. My eyes, however, were on the water.

The water sang softly at my feet, creeping closer each time, like it wanted just a taste of me. I made sure to place enough dry sand between me and the water's edge. A flush of pain filled my chest at the sight of the waves' foamy fingers.

I hadn't always been scared to death of the ocean. There was a time when I loved it, craved it, even. To feel its icy grip on my bones, the sand between my toes. To hear the pulse of life when I was just underneath the surface. In the silence, I could hear the ocean sharing its secrets and begging for mine.

I busied myself by picking flowers, then busied myself some more when I tripped and dropped them all. I tried to bury the ache in my heart, the burning that resided whenever I was near the water. The contradictory mixture of panic and craving that wanted to burst through my skin whenever I stared out into the ocean.

The fear hadn't always been there.

It started the day we lost Warrick.

I sucked in a shuddering breath, fighting the shiver crawling up my spine as I shoved the memory of my brother back into the darkest corners of my mind. Losing Warrick was the worst thing that could have happened to my family. It didn't just break us—it shattered us, scattering the pieces of our lives beyond reach. Some pieces were like glass shards, sharp and painful, but big enough to pick up and glue back together. The cracks remained, cutting us from time to time, but it was manageable. Others were too small, dust that glittered in the sunlight. Pa and I were the larger pieces. Ma was all glittering dust. Warrick had been her favorite, after all; of course it hit her the hardest.

As I rubbed my scarred wrists, I wondered, not for the first time, if Ma had ever wished it had been me who died that day.

The village was beginning to wake up. From my place on the beach, I could just make out the sounds of life cresting over the rolling hill behind me: wagons being pulled along the road, the occasional honk of an impatient car horn, the ringing of bells as doors swung open and shut.

But the ocean sang to me, asking me to stay, stay, *stay*.

So, with my feet planted in the sand and the water reaching for me in vain, I decided to stay.

Just for a moment longer.

CHAPTER SEVENTEEN

EVANORA

APRIL 4 – MORNING

THE WATERS WERE STILL DARK, BUT I COULDN'T WAIT around any longer. I had to get moving. Everything within me screamed to go, go, *go*.

The pod was still nestled in sleep's embrace by the time I tumbled into the city square and swam east, aiming for the island. Still, I remained quiet, my soft white glow the only evidence of my presence.

A stinging ache coursed through me with every pump of my tail. The Cursed Beings had done a lot more damage than I had originally anticipated, and after rescuing Solandis from the angry black void of the Barrens, I'd had no strength left to heal myself.

Hence my impromptu, likely foolish, definitely reckless trip to the surface.

I needed the sun to heal me. I needed to feel its warmth on my torn fins, its light on the black blight blistering along my scales. I needed the power of its golden rays to make me whole, to fix the things I was not capable of fixing on my own.

Hiding my wounds from prying eyes wasn't hard. I had barricaded myself in my room once I was able to scrape myself off the sandy floor. Jorah didn't visit, likely still perturbed from our last conversation. Mavi stopped by, asking if I wanted to practice our Gifts a little more; I pretended I was sleeping. And when Illeron knocked on my door, a gentle, hesitant rapping of his knuckles on algae-covered stone, I closed my eyes, held my breath, and tried not to think of how soft his touch had been on my cheek.

By the time night had crested our kingdom, I was in a wild state of pain. Nothing I did could subdue the blinding agony. I tried—and failed spectacularly—to heal myself. I used Mavi's precious ointments. I swam in circles. I tried to remain completely still. I prayed, and prayed, and prayed. Nothing worked.

I needed the sun.

I was diving underneath a stone arch drenched with sea fern when I heard it. A tiny, mournful squeak behind me, followed by a pulse that echoed in the water. Another squeak, and a ring of bubbles pummeled into me, nearly propelling me into an unhappy lionfish. The force behind the sound fluttered through my scales. I dug my hands into the rocky pockets of the archway, trying to stabilize myself as the noise met my ears once more, driving another wave of bubbles into me.

No. Not noise. A song.

I stilled, my tail swishing with apprehension. *A siren.*

Solandis, out of breath, rushed to catch up to me. The spots on her tail shimmered as she heaved to a stop. She clapped a hand over her mouth. "Did it work? Did my voice stop you?" Her words were muffled beneath her fingers, but that didn't stop her from talking. "Jorah said my siren song was getting better! He said the pulse I created was enough to stop a mermaid in their tracks, but I didn't believe him."

I remained frozen for a heavy second. "Solandis," I said carefully, tucking my tail away from her searching eyes, "what are you doing here?"

Solandis lowered her hand, only to stick it in her hair, wrapping an inky black strand around her finger. "I couldn't sleep." She looked away, as if ashamed for surviving her trip into the Barrens. "I saw you leaving home, and I was curious about where you were going." Her large eyes met mine, a whisper of delight glimmering in them. "Are you off on an adventure?"

Annoyance blossomed within me, but I stomped it out and forced a smile. "Yes. I am." I lowered my voice and looked around dramatically, checking for hungry ears and watchful eyes. "It's a big one."

Solandis gasped, then clapped her hands together. "How thrilling!"

I quickly shook my head. I needed to squelch her excitement, and fast. "No. It's dangerous." I hunched over until I was face-to-face with the merling. "It isn't safe for you to be here. You need to go home right now."

Solandis quickly deflated. "If it's dangerous, why are you going?" She hit me with a hard, challenging stare.

I had to give Solandis more credit. She carried a lot of intellect in that tiny body. "Because this adventure is for me, and only me," I said. "I promise I'll bring you along for the next one."

Solandis pondered, then nodded reluctantly. "All right. But you promise? The very next one?"

"The very next one." I straightened, looking behind the merling. "Would you like me to take you home?" I asked, hoping Solandis would refuse. Any second, the sun's rays would strike the water, and the ocean would wake up. I was running out of time.

Solandis shook her head. "No. I can go alone."

Relief shuddered through me, but I hid the emotion with a smile. "You are so brave! Pretty soon I won't be able to call you a merling anymore."

Solandis brightened, a delicate blush flitting to her cheeks. "And I'll lose my spots?"

I grinned. "Faster than any of the other merlings."

"Definitely faster than Andoras."

I laughed. "Most *definitely* faster." I placed my hands on Solandis's shoulders and swept her around until she was facing where we had come from. "Now go straight home. And don't tell anyone about my adventure, okay? It'll be our little secret."

Solandis fixed me with a solemn stare over her shoulder and nodded slowly. It was like the weight of our secret was going to pull her down to the ocean floor.

I waited until Solandis was out of my sight before I turned and rushed forward. I picked up my pace, gritting my teeth around the pain. Dealing with Solandis had put me behind schedule, but I couldn't fault her for her curiosity. I'd been the same way when I was her age. I still *was* that way. It was probably what made me such a poor leader.

The closer I got to the island, the more my resolve grew. A quick sunbath where the waters were warmer and the ice was already chipped away, then home. The Cursed Beings hummed, and I eyed the Barrens paralleling to my right, its shadows stretching out to me. I snarled at the darkness. There could be no room in my heart for fear.

The sun was just thinking about rising when I arrived. Pressing myself against a rigid rock wall, I peeked at the beach looming before me.

It was empty.

Scales tight, I inched closer to the surface. My entire body was a heartbeat, the pain singing in my nerves, my blood, my mind. I gave my head a quick shake, biting back the whimper on my tongue. Gods, how could anything hurt this bad? A single touch from the Cursed Beings had me going mad with agony. I loathed to think about what Braemos and Safra had experienced before their tragic end.

I surfaced. The cool morning air kissed my skin, and sea-foam licked my fingers. Thankfully, the sky was clear. Holding my breath, I closed my eyes, floated onto my back, and waited.

The sun rewarded me instantly. The moment it rose over the horizon, warmth bathed my body. Its rays soothed my scales, and I could feel them begin to glow. The areas the Cursed Beings had touched burned, but it was cleansing, not painful. The sun's light purified the damage, knitting the broken pieces back together. The black stains on my tail faded slowly.

I didn't know how long I floated in the ocean, rocked by the waves, but I never wanted to leave. I wanted to stay, bathed in the sun's warmth, until it healed not just my body, but my mind, my burdens, my responsibilities. Surely, if it could heal my wounds, it could erase all my troubles too.

A sudden splash near the shoreline—a sound that didn't belong to the waves. A mournful chirp, followed by frantic shuffling. Impulsively, I dove beneath the surface, straining to see the source. An animal, caught and struggling. But I was too far away; I couldn't see anything but seagrass. A bird, perhaps? A harbor seal?

I swam back toward the rocks, glancing at my tail. It looked better, though the pain still flickered in my nerves. Despite the pulling of my heart, I knew I couldn't help the poor animal yet. I had to stay focused. If it still needed saving after I was healed, I'd gladly free it.

I was about to resurface when the animal's cries went quiet. I perked up at the sudden silence, shifting around the rock wall and gazing at the beach.

My heart stopped.

A human was making their way down the sandy trail.

Fins bristling, I sidled around the wall, trying to get a better look. My gut told me to flee. My heart told me to stay.

The figure had nearly made it down the embankment when they stopped and crouched, their hands moving through the shrouds of weeds at their feet.

I stiffened, my adrenaline flaring within me. *Stay*, my heart whispered. *Stay*. I narrowed my eyes and crept closer.

The figure stood up, inspecting their hands, which were now full of something purple.

I fought back a gasp, clamping my hand over my mouth.

The figure was holding flowers. Purple flowers, like the one the boy had placed in my bag.

It was him. The boy with ocean eyes had returned.

My heart was a wild thing within me, and I was instantly greeted with a tugging in my chest, a humming in my bloodstream as I watched the boy creep along the sand. I pushed the feelings down and replaced them with rage.

That boy was the reason Jorah thought I was an unfit ruler.

That boy was the reason I appeared so weak to my pod.

The thoughts were irrational, but once I started thinking them, I couldn't stop.

That boy . . . That damned boy was to blame for everything.

Mermaids were gentle creatures. Killing wasn't in our nature. To draw even a drop of blood was considered a grave crime against our code—the code my parents had helped create after the tragedy of the Initial War. But in that moment, that cursed moment, I didn't want him to exist. I wanted to snuff his light from the world, eradicate his soul from our plane of existence. I wanted to kill him, feel his blood on my hands, watch the life drift from his endlessly blue eyes.

I knew it wouldn't stop the pod from thinking I was weak. It wouldn't stop Jorah from seeing me as a merling. But it would certainly make me feel better.

The boy tripped, dropping onto the sand, sending the flowers scattering. I could hear his panicked voice warble and stretch along the water as he raced to collect them before the wind could snatch them up.

Stay, my heart pleaded.

Kill! every other part of me roared.

Clutching the flowers to his chest, the boy straightened and stared out into the water. I grunted, dropping low, sending a cloud of sand into my face.

After a frenzied heartbeat, I dared another peek. The boy was no longer gazing at the ocean, but at the ground, as though he was searching for something. After pacing back and forth, he paused, nodded sharply, and gently placed the flowers down, just where the waves kissed the sand. I widened my eyes, curiosity blooming within me, as the boy dug his fingers into the sand next to the flowers, carving something I couldn't see.

My fins stiffened in anticipation, the sharp edges flicking. He was still too far away. If I tried to attack him now, I'd run the risk of getting stuck on the beach and ruining everything.

The boy straightened, planting his dirty hands on his hips as he admired his handiwork. As his eyes flicked over the surface of the water, my insides roiled. What was he doing? I looked at the flowers in their neat little pile and swallowed. Were those . . . for me?

I immediately shooed the thought away. It was way too presumptuous of me to think such a thing, not to mention pointless; the boy would be dead in a matter of seconds, and it wasn't like I could hold his cold, lifeless body and ask.

I licked my lips, beads of sweat dotting my clammy forehead. I needed him to get closer to the water. If he could take even a single step . . .

The boy's head jerked to the side, his attention snagged by something. His eyes darted back and forth until they landed on something to the far side of the beach, right where the waves broke. I watched from the safety of the water as the boy stumbled forward, hurrying until he was at the edge of the shoreline. Even with the distance, I could see the fear swimming in his eyes as he took a large breath, shook his hands in quick, flicking motions, and stomped into the water, not stopping until he was up to his knees.

This was my moment.

My blood was alive within me, thrashing and violent in my veins. Holding my breath, I crept closer, using the waves to propel me.

The boy bent down, thrusting his hands into the ocean.

I sprang forward, my hands gnarled into claws, my forearm fins rigid and ready to strike.

I was close. One more push of the waves and I'd be able to grab him.

I could hear the boy grunt with effort as he hoisted a seal out of the water. The words he spoke were soft and soothing as he fastened his grasp on the shrieking animal and the net it had become ensnared in. After looking around quickly, he began to tug at the ropes.

I swallowed my growl and dug my hands into the sand, fighting the current as I stuttered to a stop. *Now is your chance!* my thoughts roared, urging me forward.

But I couldn't move. I was transfixed as the boy carefully untangled the harbor seal from the net, removing the thick cords wrapped around its flippers and neck.

What are you doing? my thoughts continued.

I didn't know. I didn't know what I was doing. Every single part of me had gone numb.

Move! Kill!

And still, I watched.

Once the seal was free, the boy glanced over his shoulder a final time before submerging the creature into the water and releasing it. His ocean eyes were trained on the animal as it plunged into the waves, darting away from the beach. His gaze followed the seal as it sailed right by me, nearly clipping my cheek with its flipper.

And that was when he saw me, staring up at him from the sandy floor.

The boy stilled, his hands hanging in the water, his body still bent over, his face contorted in a mixture of fear and—surprisingly—curiosity.

He didn't move, and neither did I.

We stared at each other for an eternity.

CHAPTER EIGHTEEN

GRAYSON

APRIL 4 – MORNING

I COULDN'T SEEM TO MOVE. I FELT FROZEN IN PLACE, PINNED underneath the weight of the mermaid's intoxicating eyes.

My mind seemed to be the only thing working. It screamed at me to run, run, *run*, but my body was stuck in time, rendered immobile as the seconds turned into minutes.

The mermaid was the first to move. Slowly, she emerged from the water, peeking through the surface until just her head and shoulders were cresting the waves. She moved so gracefully, so fluidly, like she was part of the water.

The spell was broken, and I uncurled from my hunched form, my joints and spine cracking in protest as the pieces slipped back into their respective places.

I was careful to keep my eyes locked on hers.

My hands dripped at my sides, the waves ebbed and flowed at my knees, and the seagulls cried overhead.

And the mermaid spoke.

"Why did you free that seal?" she asked, her voice light as the air, carrying a hint of a melodic accent that sent my stomach fluttering.

I wasn't sure what surprised me more—the fact that the mermaid spoke English, or that her first words were about a seal. I scratched the back of my head, shrugging. "It was just an innocent creature."

The mermaid was silent, bobbing gently in the current. She cocked her head to the side, her winter-white hair cascading over her shoulder with the movement. "Is that why you freed me?"

"I . . ." I wasn't sure why I'd freed her. I had been trained all my life to hate mermaids, to hunt them. Not that I could tell her that. "I couldn't just leave you like that," I finally said. "It seemed wrong."

The mermaid's eyes narrowed. "I am hardly innocent," she said with a cool grin.

Her words sent a chill down my spine, slipping through my nerve endings and sparking my limbs.

The mermaid went on. "Do you care to know why I am here now?"

I staggered back onto the sand as the mermaid slinked forward, drawing closer to me, a predatory glow in her wild eyes. She paused just before me, resting her weight on her hands, her white tail swishing back and forth behind her. "I came here before the sun rose. I saw you on the beach, oblivious to my presence." Her eyes trailed to mine, cold and calculating, a smile playing at the corners of her lips. "I was going to kill you."

I swallowed, taking another small step back. "Are you still planning to?" I asked quietly.

The mermaid leaned closer still, looking up at me with those vibrant violet eyes. Then she turned away, shifting back into the water. "No," she breathed, looking down at the waves lapping at her scales.

I refrained from loosing a relieved sigh. "Why not?"

The mermaid seemed to consider my words. She tilted her chin up, taking me in with a careful side stare. "It seemed wrong."

A smile made its way onto my face, and it felt as welcome as it did foreign.

The mermaid gestured to the flowers several paces away with a dip of her head. "Are those for me?"

A heavy blush crept onto my cheeks. "Yes." I glanced at the pile of purple petals. "You looked like you enjoyed them the last time." Another wave of heat flooded my face as I stuck my hands into my pockets. "I've brought them to the shore every day since I last saw you."

The mermaid clucked her tongue, then ducked underneath the waves. I immediately ripped my hands out of my pockets and took a stiff step back, my eyes on the water. When the mermaid emerged, she was down the beach, in front of the flowers. Her face was alight with joy as she leaned forward and plucked the flowers from the sand, instantly bringing them to her nose and inhaling deeply. The gills on her neck worked with her breaths. I stood, fastened in place, and waited for the shudder of disgust to ripple through me, for the revulsion at the alienness of it all.

But my heart only began to beat harder, a pang in my convulsing stomach as the butterflies trapped within ached to get free.

She was so ridiculously beautiful.

The mermaid opened her eyes and flicked her stare to me, the flowers still pressed to her nose. "I do not think I can bring them back with me."

I ducked my head, trying to hide my disappointment. "Right." I sighed, stepping toward her. "I guess it would look rather strange if you came to kill me and ended up leaving here with flowers instead of my corpse."

The mermaid laughed, the sound like lilting music. It sent a jolt of electricity through me, vibrating on my skin.

"No." She shook her head. "Because they wouldn't survive in the water. Land plants rarely do."

It was becoming apparent that my cheeks would never stop burning. I allowed myself to laugh quietly. "Right," I said again.

The mermaid lowered the flowers and pointed at what I had drawn in the sand. "And what is that?" she asked.

Feeling bold—and a little stupid—I stepped closer, crouching next to the lines. The mermaid jerked away at my sudden movement but, to my delight, remained on the sand. "It spells *hello*. It's a greeting."

She gave me a dry look. "I know what greetings are."

The heat on my face shifted down my chest, down my stomach, until I was one giant inferno. *Can humans self-combust?* The mermaid turned her gaze to the horizon, and for a moment, panic gripped me. She was going to leave again. I wanted to keep her here, even just for a moment longer.

"What's your name?" I blurted, forcing the words out.

The mermaid slowly turned to assess me, raising a thin eyebrow, a coy smile on her lips. Everything about her seemed cold and analyzing—even her smile. "What is *your* name, human? Tell me, and perhaps, if I feel like it, I'll tell you mine."

I gulped hard, the butterflies straining inside me. "Grayson. Shaw."

The mermaid frowned. "Is it Grayson, or is it Shaw?"

I snorted, then quickly slapped a hand over my mouth, smothering the sound. "It's both, actually. Grayson Shaw. Shaw is my family name, and Grayson is what I was given at birth. My parents told me that when I was born, it was the coldest, grayest day of the year, so it only made sense to name me Grayson." I was babbling. And worse yet, I was babbling to a creature who was likely much smarter than I could ever hope to be.

The mermaid shifted in the sand, her tail snapping against the water. "Grayson Shaw," she repeated, like she was testing the words out, seeing how they felt in her mouth.

My heart punched against my rib cage at the sound of my name on her lips. "And yours?"

The mermaid pulled a lock of her hair over her shoulder and began to comb her fingers through it. I wondered briefly what it felt like. Did it feel like my coarse curls? Or like silk? I drove my hands into my pockets before the urge to reach out and touch her hair became nearly irresistible.

"My name is much too complicated for a human to articulate," she eventually said with a sniff.

I wondered if I should've been offended, but all my heart did was sputter at an unhealthy rhythm. "Well," I tried, "what would it sound like in my language?"

The mermaid stilled, her fingers lingering in her hair. With a small breath, she tucked the lock behind her delicately pointed ear. When she turned to face me, the scales dotting her cheeks shimmered like stardust. "Evanora," she finally whispered, her piercing eyes flitting to mine.

I inhaled sharply, my skin suddenly awash with goose bumps. I smiled hesitantly, nodding slowly. "It's really nice to meet you, Evanora. Officially."

The mermaid, Evanora, dipped her head solemnly. Still, I could see the faint joy there, glimmering behind her heavy stare. "It is nice to meet you, Grayson Shaw."

I wanted to tell her that she could simply call me Grayson. But, if I was being honest, I really liked the way she said my full name. Like it was precious, like she was savoring it.

There was a sudden crash of sound above us, followed by the stuttering honk of a car horn. I started at the invasion of noise, and the mermaid hissed, shrinking back. The town was officially up and in working order.

I glanced back at Evanora, worry forming thick creases in my face. "You should go."

Evanora pinned me with a sour look. "I can take care of myself," she replied hotly. Still, she slipped farther into the water, pushing herself until she was covered back up to her shoulders.

"If I'm seen with you, we will both be in trouble. So, please," I urged, sparing a quick glance back up the sandy embankment, "hurry back to your home."

The mermaid clearly didn't enjoy being told what to do. But she nodded sharply. "Very well."

As Evanora was about to dive, I spun and lunged toward the water. "Wait!"

Evanora faltered, turning back to look at me with a frown. The water danced at her shoulders, spinning within her hair, sliding down her ivory skin. She was like a gemstone breaching the water's surface. One that was not meant for human eyes.

But how desperately did I want to keep staring at her.

"Can I see you again?" I asked.

Evanora smiled, but it looked sad. "Thank you for the flowers, Grayson Shaw," she said quietly.

And then she was gone, ducking underneath the water and surging into the deep.

CHAPTER NINETEEN

EVANORA

APRIL 4 – MORNING

THERE WAS A LIGHT PRESSURE OF WARMTH IN THE CENTER of my core as I drifted away from the beach. I had been right.

The boy and I shared a bond, a curious and confusing connection that seemed to thread our hearts together. I didn't know what it was, or what it meant, or why it was even there. It just *was*, tickling my scales and burning my blood, singing a foreign melody I didn't know the words to.

"Grayson Shaw," I whispered into the deep, my lips curving into a secretive smile as I shared his name with the undercurrent, where no one could hear me. The words felt strange on my tongue, and I doubted they could be translated into my language. Still, I liked saying them.

And what was possibly more confusing than the bond that cinched our hearts together was the fact that I wanted to see him again.

Not to kill him.

To be with him.

Talk to him.

To smell the flowers he picked for me.

To look into his stormy eyes and drown.

I gave my head a shake, chuckling incredulously to myself. Confusing, indeed.

Not quite ready to trade in the sunlight for my dark kingdom, I swam along the surface, my dorsal fin breaching the waves. It was a risky move, but my tail still hurt, and I wanted to soak in the sun's rays for as long as I could. I dipped and turned, playing with the water, swooping when it plummeted, arching when it rose. I barrel-rolled and somersaulted, laughing like a merling as the waves gave chase.

I felt weightless, joyful, even. Maybe the sun really *had* taken away a portion of my problems.

But then I heard a shriek, and I realized I was wrong.

The sound was cloaked in a shroud of bubbles, a haunted song wrapped in terror.

I went still, my weight returning to me with a sickening *thud*.

It came again, quiet, mournful, awash with fear.

And pain. So much pain.

By the third time the sound reached my ears, I knew what it was and who it belonged to.

It was Solandis, singing her siren song.

It was similar to before, when she was trying to get my attention, trying to stop me in my tracks.

She was calling out to me again, singing for me.

And then I realized that she wasn't singing. She was screaming.

My blood turned to ice.

"Solandis?" I shrieked, whipping my head around frantically, trying to locate the merling. "Solandis, where are you?"

She sounded close, but in the wide expanse of the ocean, it was hard to know which direction the cries were coming from. They were distorted, echoing off every wave, every grain of sand. She was everywhere, and nowhere.

Another scream.

Another.

"I'm here!" I shouted, turning in a quick circle. "Where are you?"

There was no response, only the haunting wails of a lost merling, a *hurting* merling.

I turned back to face Lethe, my breath coming out in wild gasps.

The island. She had followed me to the island.

Choking back a sob, I surged forward, fighting against the current to make it back to the beach. The waves, once playful, were no longer a gentle, lilting thing. They pulled me back, shoved me aside, turning my sprint into a crawl.

Solandis. Foolish, stubborn, spitfire Solandis had followed me. She hadn't listened to me when I told her to return home. She hadn't listened when I told her it was dangerous. I swallowed around the fear lodged in my throat. Why hadn't she listened? She had followed me and become lost. I squeezed my eyes shut, willing my tail to move faster. Lost. That was all she was. Solandis was lost, and she was afraid.

But even as I thought it, flashes of nets, of spears, of greedy humans and their hungry hands assaulted my mind. I growled, thrusting the torturous images away, and swam faster.

Another scream. Closer this time.

I veered away from the beach, following the western bend of the island. Natural rock formations and sand became man-made walls of concrete and stone. I skimmed the ground, ignoring the growing ache in my tail, the jagged edges of broken wood and glass that bit into my belly.

On the tail end of the next cry, I could just make out faint sobbing words. ". . . me. Help me!"

"I'm coming, Solandis!" I cried, my voice cracking with desperation. "I'm coming!"

Ahead, the shoreline dipped inward, revealing three long wooden piers stretching into the ocean. Nets draped the edges, and empty buckets sat beside spears and butcher knives. Humans swarmed the middle pier, their shouts echoing across the water. They stomped and clapped, their excitement reeking of sweat and the sickly stench of bloodlust.

I looked beneath the dock and saw her.

Solandis.

She hung limp in a net, her small frame twisted in the mesh. She was silent, deathly still.

My heart stopped.

"Solandis!" I shrieked, racing forward.

The merling's eyes flicked to mine—*thank the gods, she's still alive!*—and she blinked slowly, like she couldn't believe that I was there, that I had found her. Like she had given up all hope of being saved. Slowly, she threaded her tiny arms through the net's holes, stretching her trembling fingers out to me. She opened her mouth, a hitching sob on her tongue.

And she screamed, a loud keening cry that sent the humans scuttling back, pressing their hands to their ears.

Time stretched. The distance between us seemed infinite, my frantic swimming erasing mere millimeters. I pushed myself harder, forcing aside any fear that I would be spotted, that I, too, would end up in a net. "I'm here," I cried, diving underneath the first pier. "I'm here!"

The merling began to thrash in her cage. She fought against the ropes pressed against her, the confines that made her small frame suddenly seem too large for the space she was taking up. The net cinched around her tighter, rubbing at her scales, marking her pale skin.

"Help!" she screeched, her voice stretched and raw. "Help me! Please!"

I ducked underneath the next dock, reaching for her. Solandis grabbed for my hand, sobbing as her fingers intertwined with mine. She pushed her face against the net, her large green eyes drenched with fear. "Get me out," she whined. "Get me out!"

"It's okay!" I whispered fiercely, giving her shaking hand a squeeze. "You're going to be okay, Solandis!"

The merling moaned, low, long, and feral. "Please," she pleaded.

"I won't let them take you, you hear me? I won't let them!" I ran my free hand over the net, the coarse fibers catching on my nails. There had to be a weak point, a frayed edge I could sink my teeth into, saw through with my razor-sharp fins.

"Please." Solandis convulsed violently; the net tightened its grip. "Please!"

I let out a growl, desperation clawing up my spine. The merling's mewling whimpers were daggers through my heart. I searched the net again with frantic vigor. A loose knot, an unraveling braid, something!

There was nothing.

The net bobbed downward. Solandis squeaked with fright, her grip on my hand growing painful. "It's okay!" I forced out, my voice catching. "You're okay." I bit down on the rope, only to rear back with a hiss as the barb hidden within the strands bit back. A cloud of blood bloomed in front of my face, the sharp metallic scent oozing from the cut on my lip and dribbling down my chin. Ignoring the stinging ache, I bit down again. And again. And again. The ropes, with their reinforced steel innards, refused to yield.

The net lurched upward, wrenching itself out of my mouth and yanking the merling with it.

It moved again, a steady rhythmic pulling. The bells jostled merrily with each condemning tug.

They were pulling up the net. Gods, they were going to take the merling!

My hands stilled. I could feel Solandis's raging heartbeat against my skin, her fever-hot despair burning through my scales. I looked at the merling, horror filling every inch of me. "I'm . . ." I swallowed a sob. "I'm so *sorry*."

Solandis gave a collapsed wail, writhing violently in her cage. "No!" she cried, straining against the ropes. "No! Please, no!"

"Oh, she's a feisty one!" a human crowed from above. "Got a lot of fight in 'er!"

The net heaved with enthusiasm. The merling's fingers began to slip out of my grip. I gave a broken cry and lunged forward, grabbing her hand with all the strength I carried. "I'm so sorry," I said again, tears flooding my vision. "I'm so *sorry*!"

"Don't let them take me!" Solandis shrieked, her voice rising to match her delirious panic. "Don't let them! Please, no!"

Her fingers ripped out of mine as the net jolted again, her small body yanked higher. The top of her head brushed the surface. In mere seconds, she would be wrenched from the water—out of reach.

Solandis shook her head frantically, her wild eyes darting to the looming dock above. A desperate sob clawed its way out of my throat as I reached for her hand again.

"Look at me!" I choked out. "Just keep looking at me, Solandis."

The merling whimpered, her eyes latching back on to me. She opened her mouth, but nothing came out: a silent plea meant not for my ears, but my heart. Her grip was already loosening.

"I'm right here, okay?" I forced a wobbly smile. "I'm right here. Just keep looking at me."

Solandis's quivering mouth slipped shut, but her eyes—her beautiful big green eyes—sank into mine with a gaping sorrow. Drowning in them, I made my smile grow. "Yes. Just like that. Just look at me," I whispered. "I'm here, little one. I'm here."

The merling's head broke above the waves. Then her shoulders. Then her chest.

Her eyes remained on mine until the humans began to yelp in victory as they hauled her body over the dock's edge.

I sucked in a shuddering breath, straining to see through the cracks in the wood.

Solandis fought against the gloved hands that pried at the ropes. She bit at the fingers as they circled around her scrawny arms and yanked her out of the net. She kicked at the feet that stomped on her fins, holding her in place. She howled, ferocious and rageful, her siren song pouring out of her, sending some of the humans skittering back, spitting curse words on the wind.

It wasn't enough.

A flash. Sunlight glinting on metal.

One of the humans—broad shouldered and grinning darkly—tossed a blade between his hands as he crouched beside her. He eyed the knife, then Solandis, his lips curling into a sneer. "Let's see ya try and sing yer way outta this!"

He dragged the blade against her throat.

Solandis's cries were cut off, replaced with a thick gurgling wheeze. Her body twitched, still fighting, not realizing it was slowly bleeding out, slowly dying.

I choked back a sob, pressing my hands tightly to my lips as blood began to seep between the wooden cracks and splash upon the water above my head. Fat drops that sank beneath the surface and slithered through the current like smoke before my eyes.

The humans retrieved their flimsy bravado and circled around the merling once more, laughing away their embarrassment as they grabbed heavy blades of their own. They pinned her spasming body, stepping on her arms and fluke. And the blades began to rain down in a flurry of hate and greed.

I squeezed my eyes shut, blocking out the images of them hacking the merling's body apart. The steady *thump* of their knives meeting their marks filled my ears, each one burned into my memory, a haunting echo to match my aching heart.

Thump. Thump. Thump.

They hacked and sawed, tearing into her tail, shaving off her scales, peeling away her hair. The steady trickle of blood through the cracks became a geyser, spraying the water with flecks of broken scales and shreds of silken fins.

Thump. Thump.

The merling gave a wet cough, and the sound shattered me. She was still alive. She was feeling every single vile thing the humans were doing. *Please just die*, I found myself praying. *Please just fade away so you don't have to experience any of this!*

Thump. Crack!

There was a sickening crunch, then a victorious cheer, and I forced my eyes open, blinking through my tears and the blood and the gore to look up at the dock again.

Solandis's head had been hacked off, attached to her body by a flimsy strand of skin. It was twisted almost all the way around, her hair covering most of her blood-drenched face. And through the curtain of hair, through the cracks of the wood, I could see her green eyes, wide, dull, unblinking, staring down at me. Her mouth was a cavernous opening, frozen in a scream that I swore I could hear.

I whimpered, reaching for Solandis, trying in vain to stroke her tearstained cheek. I had to leave. And I could not take the merling with me. I could not give her the burial she deserved. I could not pray over her. I could not send a blessing to chase her into the afterlife. No. I had to leave her to the humans, a trophy that they would boast about when they were tucked away in their warm homes, safe and unbothered by their vicious, bloodthirsty acts.

"I'm sorry," I moaned. "I'm so sorry."

A grunt above snapped my attention back to the dock. One of the humans grabbed her by the hair, tugging viciously until the last strands of skin ripped free. Her head came away, severed completely.

He held it high, triumphant, as blood sprayed in crimson arcs. His laughter clawed at my ears. And then his gaze shifted. He froze, his eyes narrowing as he peered through the cracks in the dock. He spotted the iridescence of my scales, glowing faintly beneath the water.

His finger rose, pointing.

It didn't matter.

By the time he managed to form words, I was gone.

CHAPTER TWENTY

GRAYSON

APRIL 5 – EVENING

THE COURTHOUSE WAS GETTING NOISIER BY THE SECOND. The solid oak double doors had been propped open, and more and more people were pouring in, filling the large space with loud voices, body heat, and predatory hormones. I leaned against the smooth wooden banister, rubbing my forehead. Whispers of a headache nipped at my temples. It would likely be a full-blown migraine by the end of the night.

It was April 5, the night of the Symbolic Sign-In at the courthouse. I didn't want to be there.

I sighed, pressing my fingers harder against my forehead as my gaze drifted to the vaulted ceiling. The mermaid murals swimming over the plaster were my favorite part of the courthouse. They glided along the timber beams, circled the chandeliers, and seemed almost alive, like they'd begin moving if they thought you weren't looking. Rumor had it that Mr. Grieves was raising pledges to paint over them. I hoped people would come to appreciate the beauty in art before it was too late. Lethe didn't seem to hold on to nice things for long. The mermaid statue in the city square of Fariid had already been reduced to rubble, leaving the fisherman sitting next to a pile of stone where once a mermaid had offered him a fish.

A hand tapped me on the shoulder, and I startled back, only to see Sybil Morris grinning up at me from two steps below. She was holding the arm of a younger man, who looked just about as pleased as I was to be there. "Young Shaw!" she exclaimed, knocking my shoulder one more time. "You made it to the Sign-In!"

"Nice to see you again, Mrs. Morris."

Mrs. Morris was swathed in a voluminous black cloak, its hood so large it threatened to swallow her whole. Her tiny arms peeked out from sleeves that billowed to the floor. As she shifted on her toes, the heavy fabric swished against the carpeted steps.

"Do you like it?" she asked when she caught my stare. "I'm part of the Sign-In. It's a contractual obligation that I wear it." She leaned in, cupping her mouth with a gloved hand, as if sharing a hushed secret. "But, if I'm being honest with you, the thing is hot, itchy, and desperately needs a wash."

Despite my tangled nerves, I laughed.

Mrs. Morris tugged on the young man's arm, drawing my attention to him. "You've met my Owen, haven't you?"

At the sound of his name, Owen offered me a polite smile. I nodded in return, though my mind was drawing a horrendous blank. I knew Mrs. Morris had two sons, but I had always thought the one in front of me was Tommy. And was it Owen who had a stutter? Or did he have asthma? The Morris brothers had been Warrick's friends, not mine.

"He's the oldest of the two," Mrs. Morris went on. She pulled Owen in for a tight side hug. "Go on, say *hi*, Owen."

"*Mom.*" Owen squirmed out of Mrs. Morris's grasp. "S-s-stop embarrassing me."

Owen had the stutter.

"Oh, ta!" Mrs. Morris clucked, rolling her eyes. She grinned at me. "This is Owen's *sixth* Hunt! My boy," she sighed, tugging Owen back under her arm, "growing so big and strong!"

"*Mom!*" Owen, a stocky young man towering over his mother by at least a foot, adjusted his newsboy cap, which had gone askew during the hug. He gave me a sheepish grin identical to hers. "Welcome to th-the Hunt," he said, his stutter softening the words.

I nodded distractedly, wondering if I knew someone else who had asthma. "Thank you."

Owen had gone on to fixing the tie around his neck. "I haven't s-s-seen you at a S-S-Sign-In before."

"This is my first."

Owen frowned, cupping a calloused hand over his stubbled chin. "Don't you have a problem with blood?"

I whipped my head to stare at Owen. "Excuse me?"

Owen put his hands up quickly. "My mistake. I must have you confused with s-so-someone else." He spotted someone in the atrium of the building, his cheeks instantly reddening as he lifted a hand in a shy wave. I thought to peer over the banister to see who had grabbed his attention but decided against it; I was still stuck on the topic of blood. Owen turned back to me. "Just enjoy t-tonight," he said, stepping out of Mrs. Morris's grasp and walking down the stairs. "It's all about us—th-the warriors."

Blood? What did he mean about blood? What exactly happened during the Sign-In?

Desperate to remove myself from the conversation, I made my excuses to Mrs. Morris and stumbled down the stairs. Every time my feet thudded against the plush steps, a needle of fear poked at my heart.

The courthouse was too hot, suffocating. My clothes were beginning to stick to my skin, the tie around my neck threatening to strangle me. I loosened the knot and pushed around people, frantic to reach the open doors for even just a taste of fresh air. Maybe I could slip out, just for a moment. *Maybe I could just disappear altogether.*

I knew the Symbolic Sign-In was a grand ceremony, but I hadn't realized how many people actually attended. It felt like all the people in Lethe were crammed into Fariid's courthouse, making the gargantuan building feel more like a dollhouse. Everyone was dressed nicely too, like they were off to church and not vowing to commit a multitude of murders. There were even children present. I swallowed the ball of bile that burned up my esophagus. *Starting the desensitization young.*

"Grayson Shaw, at a Sign-In?" a voice called over the rumbling crowd. It was followed by a scathing laugh. "Has hell finally frozen over?"

I halted in my tracks, spine stiffening. Turning in a slow circle, I found Ambrose Grieves sneering at me from his place in the center of the room. He was clad in Fariid's finest—a form-fitting tuxedo complete with tails and a gleaming navy bow tie to match the pocket square in his jacket—and despite the building's growing heat, I didn't see even a drop of sweat on him. His short blond hair was perfectly coifed back, shining from the light of the chandeliers above. His blue eyes were penetrating, sharp enough to slice me in two.

It looked like he wanted to.

I fought to keep my breathing steady. "Hey, Ambrose."

Ambrose tilted his head back, staring down his nose at me. "Decided to be a big boy and join the Hunt finally?"

I tucked my hands into my pockets, the picture of calm and collected when I felt anything but. "I just turned eighteen," I said. "I couldn't join before, even if I wanted to."

Ambrose's jaw clenched. "You could have bothered to show up to previous Sign-Ins, offer your support to the *real* heroes of Lethe. Why, even Rosemary has been to most of them," he said, gesturing to the petite girl hanging off his arm.

Rosemary Little giggled, the sound grating against my ears like nails on glass. With a coy flutter of her thick lashes, she twirled a curl of strawberry-blond hair around a gloved finger. Her smile carried the same smugness as Ambrose's, though she wore it more gracefully. Her forest-green evening gown swept the marble floor, shimmering like sunlit waves from the embedded jewels in her cinched corset. She was the picture of wealth and refinement—something Lethe could never claim as its own.

"It didn't seem necessary for me to be here," I said, glancing at the open doors again.

Ambrose snorted, and Rosemary giggled again. "Necessary? Don't embarrass yourself. You're a coward. That's why you never came."

I faltered, frowning. "I'm not."

"Yes, you are," Ambrose assured. "And if you aren't one now"—he lifted a finger in the air and wagged it slowly—"you will be later."

A hand clamped down on my shoulder, pulling me away from Ambrose and his riddles. I looked up to see Pa glowering at me. Despite his clean suit, the smell of blood clung to him, wafting with us as he pulled me farther into the courthouse and farther from escape. I had to resist the urge to lean away, trying to catch one last glimpse of the entrance.

"What are you doing, talking to the likes of him?" he asked.

I made a face. "Trust me, I didn't want to."

Pa pinched his lips together. "The Grieves family might be Lethe's biggest financial contributor, but they are *dangerous*." He jerked me to a stop, pulling me close as more guests shuffled by. "You can't trust them, you hear me?"

I opened my mouth, then promptly snapped it shut when the gentle chiming of bells began to sift through the crowd, hushing everyone into a reverent silence. I held my breath, listening as the jingling grew closer. They sounded like the ones I tied onto the fishing nets down at the docks. The ones to lure mermaids. In the vast courthouse, the bells echoed into the eerie stillness before getting swallowed by the shadows. A shiver raced up my spine, causing the hair on the back of my neck to stand on end.

"Right," Pa grunted, swiveling on his feet and taking my arm again. "It's about to start."

A deep unease rested against my shoulders, pressing me into the floor. "Wait, what?"

Pa pointed to the balcony. "Here they come."

My gaze followed his gesture, climbing to the balcony's edge, where a row of cloaked figures loomed, standing rigidly against the banister. Four wore deep red cloaks, five were draped in black, and one stood in the center, clad in gold.

The figures in red held large brass bowls, while those in black carried lanterns that glowed faintly with candlelight.

Without a word, they moved. The outermost figures began descending the twin staircases, their movements fluid and synchronized, their cloaks billowing as if they floated instead of walked. The faint jingling accompanying their steps came from bells tied to their wrists and ankles. The golden figure remained still until the others were halfway down the stairs, then began their own descent.

As the procession reached the bottom, the figures formed two parallel lines that arched gracefully through the foyer, their eerie coordination resembling a macabre dance. The golden-cloaked figure took the lead, guiding the group into the courtroom. I stood frozen, nausea bubbling in my stomach as the crowd parted wordlessly for the cloaked figures. The scent of copper— sharp and unmistakable—filled the air as they passed.

Pa yanked me aside, his grip firm. "Stay out of their way," he muttered.

The crowd moved as if under a spell, filing silently into the courtroom after the cloaked figures. My instincts screamed at me to resist, to plant my feet and refuse to follow, but before I could act, Pa was ushering me into a seat near the back.

The hooded figures assembled on the raised stage. The red ones took the front, brass bowls gleaming, while the black-cloaked figures stood behind them. The golden figure ascended the steps, turning to face the crowd from the center.

In unison, the black cloaks doused their lights, plunging the room into an oppressive darkness. The spell over the crowd broke, replaced by a low hum of anticipation.

"I have no idea what I'm doing," I mumbled, a swarm of nerves wrenching at my insides as I took my seat.

Pa's mouth twitched downward. "You'd have a better idea if you bothered to attend a few Sign-Ins." He sucked on his teeth for a second and spared the stage a quick glance before dipping his head and lowering his voice. "Look, you have nothing to worry about."

His words brought me absolutely no comfort.

"There is a small speech, then the hunters wishing to sign in are ushered to the front. We state our names, say a few lines, perform an act of loyalty, and then it's over."

I swore my heart stopped. "What do you mean, *an act of loyalty*?" My wide eyes darted to the stage. That was when I saw it.

A knife on the stairs. It rested atop a plump red cushion, and looked utterly menacing.

I had been burning up only moments earlier. Now I was certain I was going to freeze into a block of ice. I swiped at the cool sweat on my forehead. "Pa, Owen said something about blood." I licked my chapped lips. "What sort of *act of loyalty*?"

He wouldn't meet my wild gaze. "It's nothing. Really."

"*Pa!*"

Almost everyone was in their seats. The place was so packed that some had to resort to sitting on the balcony. Pa looked at the stage once more. "It's just a drop of blood. A pinprick. Hardly anything at all. You'll be fine."

A dry, incredulous laugh sputtered out of me. "No. Nope. I changed my mind. I can't do this." I shot out of my seat, my neck swiveling as I searched for the exit. "I need to go."

Pa snagged my wrist, halting my escape. His eyes were trained on the front of the room, but his voice was deep with warning. "You will not embarrass me, boy."

I couldn't catch my breath. I could feel a sea of eyes on me, watching, waiting for me to make a spectacle of myself, to prove that all Shaws really were crazy. Swallowing down a groan, I tumbled back into my seat. Pa made sure to keep hold of my wrist, just to be safe.

The cloaked figures began to ring their bells, remaining immobile save for their tied wrists. They began quietly, each chime sharp and poignant. With each drop of their wrists, the bells grew louder, and louder, until it was a cacophonic frenzy, shattering through the stillness, building the pressure in my chest. The gold cloak lifted their arms, and when they dropped them to their sides, the bells abruptly hushed.

The gold figure stared out at us, their hood turning from side to side as they assessed the sheep in their flock. "Brothers and sisters," they began, their voice deep, low, oozing command, "welcome to the Symbolic Sign-In."

I was expecting the thundering of applause, the bellowing of voices. Yet everyone remained quiet, leaning forward in their seats, tongue-tied in the stillness of the room and enamored by the man in gold.

The man continued, his voice steady yet heavy with accusation. "There was a time when Lethe was a peaceful island, a time when trust between humans and mermaids was pure, the balance strong. We had a symbiotic relationship—working together to make Lethe thrive. We protected the land, and they protected the waters. But over time, the islanders grew complacent."

He shook his head slowly, the movement causing his hood to sway like a pendulum. "We velveted our claws, trusted too deeply in the mermaids. And we paid for it with blood. Tragedy struck, again and again. Their hunger for us was insatiable. The mermaids took and took, until we had nothing left to give, until we had no choice but to fight back."

He paused, drawing a breath that seemed to carry the weight of history. "The Initial War. A week of unimaginable pain, bloodshed, and death. Humans rose victorious, and from that victory, the Hunt was born. Each year, we remember the Initial War. We perform the Hunt to reclaim what is ours, to avenge the souls stolen from us."

The man lifted his hands, palms outstretched to the gathered crowd. "Alfred Young. Cassandra Kent. Warrick Shaw. Theodore Wright."

As he spoke each name, one of the crimson-cloaked figures stepped forward, gripping their brass bowls tightly.

At the sound of Warrick's name, a shudder raced down my spine. Pa remained immobile next to me, but his grip on my arm tightened.

My eyes trailed over the four crimson figures, and I counted the bowls in their hands. "Only four names?" I asked quietly.

Pa nodded sharply.

"Haven't more people died?"

Pa gave an exasperated sigh. "These deaths are prominent."

I bit my lip. "Why?"

Another sigh. "Alfred Young was the first documented death from a mermaid attack and the very reason why the Initial War happened and the Hunt manifested. The rest were documented deaths during Hunting Month. Deaths that happen during the Hunt itself, or any other time during the year, don't count."

Harsh. "But—"

Pa glared at me. "Quiet!"

The gold cloak peered at us from his place on the stage. "Four names," he said, gesturing to the crimson cloaks behind him. "Four names to avenge. And so, I ask, who are you fighting for this Hunting Season?" He lifted his hands once more. "Rise, my brothers and sisters. Rise, those who wish to fight."

There was the clattering of chairs, the stomping of feet, until there were more people standing than sitting.

"Come forth, hunters," the golden cloak commanded with a ferocity that made my chest heave.

In silence, the standing members began teetering out of their rows and into the aisle. Pa had to yank on my wrist several times before I could make my body move. I followed behind him, my feet leaden. Once we were all tucked into a neat line, the Sign-In officially commenced. I peered over my pa's shoulder, trying to see who was up first.

Jasper loped up the stairs, an enthusiastic spring in his step. His bad leg caught on the last stair, and he lurched forward, nearly running into the golden-cloaked figure. He righted himself, throwing a bashful smile over his shoulder as the crowd chuckled lightly.

"A little too eager, aren't we?" Ambrose said from behind me, turning everyone's polite laughter into something a shade more sinister.

Jasper's smile instantly vanished, but the deep blush coating his pale cheeks remained. Snapping forward, he limped his way to the man in gold and retrieved the knife.

"What is your name?" the hooded man asked.

"Jasper Warren," Jasper said.

"Who are you fighting for?"

Jasper gave me and Pa a heavy, poignant look before announcing loudly, "Warrick Shaw."

The golden figure nodded solemnly. "And how will you fight for them?"

Jasper stood a little taller, holding his head high. "With my blood, and with their name on my last breath."

The cloaked man nodded once more, and Jasper took the knife to the red-cloaked figure holding the bowl dedicated for Warrick. Hovering his hand over the bowl, Jasper sliced the tip of his finger.

I turned away, squeezing my eyes shut.

In the stillness of the room, there was the gentle *plink* as Jasper's blood seeped from the cut on his finger and dropped into the bowl.

I opened my eyes as Jasper strode to the table and signed the roster. Dropping the pen, he pressed his finger onto the paper, a bloody period next to his name. When he was done, he turned and found me and Pa once more. With a great display of camaraderie, Jasper placed a hand over his heart and bowed his head before returning to his seat, hobbling a little less than he had been before.

The Sign-In continued.

Pa made sure to give me one last scorching glare before stomping up the stairs. He made quick work of going through the vow, declaring to fight for Warrick, and sending his blood into the bowl. He didn't even flinch when the knife pierced his finger. I could feel his eyes on me when he walked back down the stairs, all the way until he was back in his seat.

It was my turn.

"Next," the golden man called.

I couldn't move. Was I going into cardiac arrest? Could people my age die from that?

"Come forth, hunter," he tried again.

I was back to being soaked in sweat, ready to burn from the inside out.

The gold-cloaked man took a step in my direction. "Grayson!" he said, his voice quiet but commanding.

At the sound of my name, I snapped to attention. "Sorry," I managed to stutter out.

The hooded man ushered me up the stairs with a hand, but I was frozen in place. Maybe my legs really *had* turned to lead.

Ambrose snorted from behind me. "Can't wait all day, princess," he said, shouldering around me and taking the stairs two at a time.

God, I hated Ambrose. I hoped he got blood on his nice jacket.

As Ambrose took his place before the cloaked man, the crowd began to thrum with a quiet excitement. Lethe's golden child was always a sight to behold.

Ambrose breezed through his vows, his voice strong and arrogant. And when asked who he was fighting for, Ambrose smirked as he dragged the knife over his smooth palm. "Everyone," he boasted, walking from one end of the stage to the other, creating a trail of red as he allowed his blood to fall into each outstretched bowl. "Alfred . . . Cassandra . . . Warrick . . . Theodore. I'll fight for them all."

The crowd hummed with astonishment, at the *bravery* of this snide young man, but when I looked over my shoulder at Pa, he only rolled his eyes and scoffed. I mustered a wry grin.

The crowd hung on Ambrose's every movement as he sauntered back to his chair, wiping his palm clean with the navy pocket square from his suit. Rosemary leaned over and kissed him on the cheek. I stifled a groan and faced the stage.

It was my turn . . . again.

I couldn't see his face, but I had a feeling the golden-cloaked figure was trying to decide whether or not he'd have to drag me up the steps. I sucked in a breath and forced my legs to move. My knees felt unstable underneath me as I trudged up the stairs; one wrong move and they'd buckle. "Oh, God," I moaned under my breath as I took the stairs one at a time. "Oh God, oh God, oh *God*!"

I stood before the golden man. Was I going to pass out? The lights were too bright, swimming in my blurry eyes.

"What is your name?"

My throat threatened to close. "Grayson . . . Shaw."

"Who are you fighting for?"

"I'm . . ." I let out a slow, wavering breath. "I'm fighting for Warrick Shaw."

The cloaked figure nodded. "And how will you fight for them?"

I looked down at my hands, where I had been clenching and unclenching them at my sides. "With my blood."

The gold cloak stared at me from underneath his hood. "And?" he prompted.

"Oh." I cleared my throat. "And with their name on my last breath."

The man nodded, and I inched my way to the red-cloaked figure holding the brass bowl for Warrick. I'd made it about halfway when I realized that I had left the knife at the front of the stage and quickly scurried back to get it. Laughter fluttered to my ears as I picked up the bloodstained knife; I could've sworn I heard Pa groan. *So much for not embarrassing you.*

The handle was like fire in my hands, and I worried that my sweat would cause it to slip out of my grip. The bowl was a gaping mouth before me, dripping with crimson yet hungry for more. I swallowed a whimper, glancing up at the red cloak. The figure stared back from underneath their hood, pushing the bowl closer to me. Wordlessly, I lifted my shaking hand before the bowl, raising the knife in the other. But before I could press the cool blade to my fingertip, I shifted, offering the hilt to the figure in red.

The red cloak shook their head once. "No," they said softly. "You must offer your blood freely."

The crowd began to stir behind me. I winced apologetically. "I do offer it freely. I just don't think that I can do . . . it."

The crimson figure glanced over to the man in gold, only to look back at me, silently offering me the bowl once more.

I shook my head. "Please?" I pleaded, trying to ignore the rumbling voices emerging from the audience.

"Some people are still waiting here, Shaw."

I turned to see Peter Lyre shifting impatiently at the bottom of the stairs, his round cheeks full of air as he stamped his feet. Peter was friends with Ambrose. I didn't care for him either.

The gold cloak cleared his throat, pointing at one of the black-hooded figures standing in the background. With a nod of their head, the black cloak stepped forward, wordlessly taking the knife from my hand.

I wanted to breathe a sigh of relief, but the air was trapped in my lungs.

The black cloak gestured for my other hand, a groaning sigh escaping from underneath the hood. I glanced down and realized that I had tucked it behind my back, hiding it from the rusty blade. I could practically feel my pa's eyes burning through the back of my sweaty skull as I reluctantly pulled it out of hiding and held it out for the figure in the black cloak.

The blade came down. The whimper I had been holding captive seeped through my tightly clamped lips. I tried to pull my hand free before the pointed tip met my skin, but the black-cloaked figure held me in a viselike grip.

I clenched my eyes shut.

There was a sharp prick, then a burning afterthought, then nothing.

I loosed a shuddering breath, cracking my eyes open to see my hand still intact and in one piece. I managed a smile. "That wasn't so bad."

But then the blood began to bubble at the incision, oozing out of my skin and dripping down my hand.

Everything went dark. I moaned quietly, swaying on my feet, the ground suddenly quicksand. *Please, God, don't let me faint.*

The figure in the black cloak tilted my hand and gave it a rough shake, sending several drops of blood into the mouth of the brass bowl. Tedious transaction complete, they promptly let go and returned to their place in the shadows.

The edges of my consciousness pulled inward, trying to draw me into its promise of black emptiness. I willed my feet to move, holding my bleeding finger as far away from me as I possibly could. Stumbling to the desk, I jotted my name down. I nearly dropped the pen several times. As I pulled away, the black-cloaked figure sitting behind the desk reached for my bleeding finger. "Good job, dear!" the figure said, pulling up their hood and grinning at me.

I stared blankly at Mrs. Morris, wondering if I was going to vomit all over her. "I'm done?"

Mrs. Morris winked at me. "Almost! Just one last thing." She pulled her hood back into place and stamped my finger next to my name, smudging my blood against the page.

And just like that, it was over.

I was a part of the Hunt. In less than a month, I would be participating in a mass murder of mermaids.

The rest of the ceremony went by in a hushed blur. I could hardly pay attention. I sat slumped in my seat, trying to stay conscious, my fingertip throbbing with every anxious beat of my heart.

There was a voice, warbled and a thousand miles away, that suddenly boomed, "People of Lethe, may I present to you . . . your hunters!"

Pa took my arm, pulling my limp body upward as the crowd cheered for us.

All I heard was torture.

All I heard was death.

CHAPTER TWENTY-ONE

EVANORA

APRIL 5 – EVENING

THERE WERE MANY THINGS I COULDN'T STOP DOING.

I couldn't stop crying. My eyes ached with every blink, like brine had accumulated beneath my eyelids and scratched my corneas raw. When I thought I was done, another wave crested my bottom eyelids, pooling into my lashes before dripping down my cheeks, burning the entire way.

I couldn't stop picturing Solandis. Sweet, innocent, stubborn Solandis, who only wanted to go on an adventure with me. Me, her queen, her leader.

She was dead because of me.

Just like Safra.

Just like Braemos.

My mind was a damning thing, not showing me Solandis as she had been—the joyful, vibrant, beautiful merling she was—but as I had last seen her. Torn to shreds. Her scales wrenched from her body. Her fins hacked off. Her head in the hands of that ugly human.

Dead. Dead. Dead.

She would never grow old enough to lose her spots, never learn to fully hone her Gift. She would never play battle with her friends again, never sneak up on me again, never disobey the rules again.

She was gone, ripped from our world.

Because of me.

"Hush, now. Hush!" Jorah called out to the ever-frenzied pod.

We were all gathered in the throne room. At one time, our pod would have never been able to fully fit in there; they would've been strained at the walls, pressed against the pillars, streaming out the entrance and tumbling down to the square. Now, the several hundred left could fit neatly within the room with space to spare.

Jorah was failing at capturing their attention. I could feel his helpless eyes peeking over his frail shoulder at me, silently begging for assistance.

I stared blankly ahead, slumped on the throne, my tail draped over the shell-covered arm. The only indicators that I was even remotely present came from the occasional slow blink, and the hitching sob that fought to escape my chest every other minute.

I was listless, detached, unmoored. I wasn't suitable to be helping anyone.

Jorah let out a meek sigh and turned back to the roaring crowd, lifting his hands up in an attempt at silencing them. "Come now," he tried again. "We cannot carry a conversation like this."

The polite request fell on deaf ears. With everyone talking at once, I could only hear snippets of the pod's frantic cries.

"They are coming after our merlings now—"

"This shall be the end of us—"

"Bloodthirsty *monsters*—"

"Enough!" Illeron thundered from behind me, slamming his spear onto the stone floor for good measure. "For the gods' sake, let the mermaid speak."

The pod's energy fizzled out, leaving only a handful of disgruntled outbursts and a fistful of tears.

Jorah's shoulders relaxed, and he lowered his hands. "That's better," he murmured. "Now, I know you are all upset. You have every right to be. Solandis didn't deserve what happened to her. Such a dreadful accident."

I could feel Illeron tense behind me. My own fins went razor-sharp. "It wasn't an *accident*," I said quietly. Jorah turned to look at me as I slowly straightened from my slumped state. "They murdered her, Jorah. In cold blood. They saw the spots on her tail, and they didn't *care*."

Jorah swallowed audibly. "Of course, Your Majesty." He shook his head. "I only meant that—"

"Meant what, exactly?" I asked roughly. "That they didn't mean to? That they were merciful?" I laughed coolly. "They butchered her, sliced her tail, ripped off her head. They plucked her scales. One by one."

The pod began to murmur, looking around as the discomfort tightened like a squid's suctioned grip. The crying, soft at first, grew louder.

Jorah narrowed his eyes at me. "Your Majesty, I think that's quite enough."

"The humans took. Their. Time." I spoke slowly, enunciating each word. "They caught her. And they killed her. And make no mistake: It was *not* an accident. They did it because they could; the Hunt is just a formality. They take what they want *when* they want it." I leaned forward, my fingernails digging into the throne's armrest as I leveled the pod with a glare. "They took Solandis because she was weak. We are *all* weak."

"Evanora!" Jorah shouted, his voice echoing off the domed ceiling.

I didn't know what shocked the pod more—the fact that Jorah had addressed me informally or the brutal truth my words held.

"She has a point, Jorah," Illeron said hurriedly, sweeping forward until he was next to the throne. "Though"—he looked down at me with a grimace—"I suggest she get to it quickly."

I blinked, staring up at the warrior. Illeron had been the one to find me after Solandis, swimming through the kingdom in a daze, and had been kind enough to let me break apart in his arms. Looking at him was hard; it made me feel off-kilter. There had been a softness in the way he cradled me, a gentleness I didn't recognize when he caressed my hair. But he was glowering at me now, and any traces of that side of him were gone.

Illeron's grip on the spear tightened. *"You* do *have a point, don't you?"*

I set my jaw and gave the smallest nod. Illeron exhaled softly and drifted back to his place behind the throne. Pushing aside my nerves, I rose fully, my voice barely above a whisper.

"I'm tired," I said, crossing my arms. "I'm tired of being weak. Tired of living in fear, never knowing when they'll strike again. Tired of wondering who will be next." My gaze settled on Jorah. "I'm tired of scavenging in the dark, watching our resources vanish, watching *us* vanish. I refuse to see another mermaid succumb to fin rot, bloat, or Dark Madness—not when there's something we can do."

Jorah, who had been absently picking at his blistered elbow, paused to shrug. "So, what's your plan?" he asked, his tone weary.

My pulse thundered in my ears, heat coursing through me. Fear had no place now. I lifted my chin. "We fight back."

Laughter broke out from the back of the room. I sent a frosty glare in that direction, silencing it at once.

"I'm sorry," Jorah sputtered, shaking his head. "You want us to do *what*?"

"We fight back," I repeated, my voice steady. "It's time to stand our ground, to end the Hunt once and for all."

Silence fell, like the calm before a storm. Then chaos erupted—voices clashing, some high-pitched and frantic, others booming with outrage.

"But we are *peaceful* creatures—"

"We've never fought back—"

"Your parents would be devastated—"

"What would our ancestors think—"

It might have gone on for a minute, or an hour, or several infinities. It was hard to know when the voices finally tapered off. I didn't realize that I had closed my eyes until I felt a hand on my shoulder, squeezing it lightly. I cracked them open to see Illeron looking at me, a flash of concern in his sharp features.

"Keep going," he encouraged in my mind.

I inhaled sharply and forced myself to relax. Illeron removed his hand but stayed by my side—an act of unity, even if it was just the two of us.

"Listen," I called out, staring hard at the pod. "Many lifetimes ago, the humans drew our blood, and we drew theirs. That's how the curse came to be, is it not?" I raised my arms, laughing incredulously. "How is it that they still continue to fight us, and we've crept into the dark, afraid?"

Jorah swept forward, his teeth bared. "It's not that simple."

"It *is* that simple!" I pushed back. "What we have done in the past isn't *working*, Jorah. You've seen our numbers dwindle. Every year our pod grows smaller and smaller. If we continue on like this, I can assure you that our time in this world will be finite." I scanned the pod, trying to meet everyone's gaze, to see if my spark had caught fire. "We must make a stand. Before it's too late."

Jorah lifted a hand, silencing me. "It cannot be done, Your Majesty." As I went to speak again, he jutted his hand forward, stopping my words in their tracks. "How your parents reigned, how they led the pod, it *worked* for us."

I shook my head, resisting the urge to swat his hand away. "It was flawed!" I laughed. "So very flawed!" I cocked my head to the side, studying my advisor carefully. "How can you not see that?"

Jorah folded his arms. "The only thing I see here is a little girl who is trying to eradicate her entire pod. You might as well ask us to swim through the Barrens."

I raised an eyebrow. I refused to let him see how his words had bitten through my scales. "Is that an option?"

Jorah slumped forward, pinching the bridge of his slim nose with a sigh. "This conversation is over. It's not happening."

I growled, running my hands through my hair, pulling the ends until my scalp burned. "But, I—"

"It's *over*, Evanora," Jorah interrupted firmly. He turned to the pod. "Return to your homes. When your queen has collected herself, we will address Solandis and give her the proper ceremony she deserves. And we *won't* be discussing any foolhardy notion of *fighting back*." When the pod continued to loiter in the throne room, Jorah grunted and flicked his arms out in a shooing motion. "Go on, now. Go home."

As the pod slowly began to disperse, many with a final concerned look over their shoulders, Jorah faced me with a glower. "I am beyond disappointed in you."

"Well," I said inwardly, *"the feeling is mutual."*

Jorah's lip curled back, but he focused his sneer on Illeron. "And you," he seethed. "I expected more out of you."

Illeron straightened, tipping his chin up, his gaze directly ahead. "My duty is to serve the leader of this pod."

"Your duty," Jorah snarled, "is to *protect* this pod. Not send them out to slaughter."

"Oh, stop it, you soul-stealing sea urchin!" I said, swimming in front of the warrior. "Illeron had nothing to do with this. Focus your temper tantrum on me."

Jorah pursed his thin lips, the corners sagging dangerously low. "Gods, there you go again." He looked at Illeron. "You. Out. Now."

Illeron tried to push around me. "I really think—"

"Out!" Jorah bellowed, pointing to the empty halls behind the throne.

I let out a low breath and looked over my shoulder. "I'm fine, Illeron," I said quietly, my eyes flitting to his hesitantly.

The warrior relented, offering us both a curt nod before sailing out of the room.

Jorah faced me, his mouth still contorted in that disappointed frown. "I just don't understand you, Evanora. When will you stop acting like you have spots on your tail and start acting like the leader your parents raised you to be?" As if his outburst exhausted him, Jorah suddenly collapsed to the side, clutching the throne for support. His thinning gray hair drifted into his eyes, but he didn't look like he had the strength to push it away. I could see his arms shaking as they hung on to the throne, like one wrong move and he would float away. Catching my stare, Jorah cleared his throat and hesitantly pushed away from the transparent backrest, his fingers hovering along the blue-tinged sweeping glass tips. "Go light the lanterns," he murmured, his voice frail. "When you are ready to have an adult conversation, come find me."

Jorah's hand returned to his aching elbow as he swayed out of the room. In that moment, he looked old, tired, and in pain, and I hated how much my heart went out to him. Once a healer, always a healer.

But, according to Jorah, apparently not a leader.

T HE GARDEN WASN'T OFFERING ME ANY OF ITS USUAL COMFORTS.
It seemed darker than usual, colder, lonelier. The Barrens seemed closer, the voices trapped within the void louder. Not even the octopus came to see me.

My vision swam, and I blinked away the onslaught of tears. Gods, crying again. Not just for Solandis this time though. The tears felt hot, tinged with frustration. For not being seen, for not being heard.

For being treated like a merling.

Someone was approaching. I could feel them rather than hear them—poking around with their mind-bending Gift, inwardly trying to decipher my location. When they zeroed in on me, I lashed out, as quick and hard as my thoughts would allow. *"Don't waste your time, you old, rotting blowfish! I'm not ready to talk to you yet."*

The mermaid who emerged through the surrounding reeds wasn't Jorah, however. It was Illeron, wincing as he rubbed his temples. "It's just me," he muttered, giving his head a shake. "Goodness, who taught you such language?"

I groaned, sinking to the floor on my belly, resting my head on my arms. "You, probably."

Illeron chuckled as he took a seat next to me. His silver-and-crimson tail was a stark contrast to my glowing white one. His fluke jostled mine. "That was some meeting," he said carefully.

I groaned again, turning my head into the sand and squeezing my eyes shut. "I just wish Jorah could see things my way, if even for a second." I paused for a beat before uncovering my face and offering Illeron a small smile. "Thank you for supporting me, even if it was for pity's sake."

Illeron looked startled. "I *do* support you, Evanora."

When I didn't say anything, the warrior continued. "Jorah isn't the leader of this pod. *You* are." He frowned, his sharp teeth flashing. "Why do you let him have the final say?"

I propped myself up on my elbows. "Because he's right?" I shrugged, watching my fingers as they dipped into the sand. "I don't know what I'm doing. He's been doing this a lot longer than I have. He knows things that are going to take me years upon years to learn."

Illeron leaned forward, trying to meet my eyes. "He's also old. And scared. And no, he's not right. Not about this, anyway." He reached forward, tilting my chin up. "I saw the fire in your eyes tonight, Evanora," he breathed. "And I saw it in a great many of the mermaids in your pod. Many *want* to fight."

I held his gaze for as long as I dared. My heart was pounding, my blood singing. Eventually, I jerked my chin out of his grip. "How can you be so sure?"

Illeron leaned away, resting his back against a boulder. "Would *because* be a good-enough answer?"

"Not in the slightest."

Illeron sighed, running a hand through his hair. "Jorah may know many things, but he doesn't know everything. Our pod needs a leader. They need to make a stand. They need *you*." He chewed on his lip thoughtfully. "Whether they want to admit it or not, our numbers are dwindling. Sooner or later, we will go the way of the leviathan and become wholly extinct. It may not be this year, or the next. But it *will* happen." Illeron shrugged. "Jorah has his head in the sand if he doesn't see that."

I waited for my breathing to steady. Illeron was right. I knew it in my core, had known it all along. Everything within me felt alive, screaming, *Yes, yes, yes.*

"So," I whispered, "what do we do?"

Illeron grinned wickedly at me. "We fight back."

"Yes, I know that," I said, rolling my eyes. "But how?"

"Well . . ." Illeron pushed himself off the boulder and began to pace in the circular garden. "Surely there must be some tricks up your fins, some secrets to dredge from the dark."

I didn't want to admit that I hadn't put much thought into it. In fact, I hadn't gone any further than *we must fight back.*

"You have nothing," Illeron guessed.

"Oh, just hush for a moment and let me think." I rose from the ground and swam, my fingers grazing each smooth boulder I passed. In circles I went, hoping that with each loop an idea would spark. But all I could think of was Solandis. And with the merling came the embarrassment of the meeting in the throne room, the fear emanating from the pod, the disappointment in Jorah's eyes.

Eyes.

Blue eyes. Like the ocean. Like a storm.

Grayson Shaw.

The boy. *Yes*, that could *work*.

My swimming ended so abruptly that Illeron nearly bumped into me. The warrior righted himself and scowled at me, but the look was immediately wiped clean from his face when he saw the glow that had captured me from head to tail. "Do you have an idea?" he asked tentatively.

I nodded, trying to suppress the smile on my face and the guilt in my gut. "I have an idea," I agreed, "but trust me when I say that you are *not* going to like it."

CHAPTER TWENTY-TWO

GRAYSON

APRIL 6 – MORNING

IT WAS HAPPENING AGAIN.

I was trapped in a cycle. The waves crashing onto me, my ma's fingers digging into my neck, my voice broken to pieces by the rain. I wanted to fight back, to push her off me, but I was too weak, too disoriented. The water kept coming, a tsunami on top of me, penetrating my eyes, my nose, my mouth. I was dying, and Ma didn't care. In fact, she was smiling. At my pain, my fear, my impending demise.

I grabbed for her hands, but my grip kept slipping. I peered at my fingers from my water casket. Every single one of them was bleeding, large gashes racing along my fingertips, snaking down to my palms. My blood wrapped around my torn wrists, mixing with the water in clouds of crimson.

A voice sifted into my ears, as dark and ominous as the shadows reaching for me from the depths of the ocean. It slithered into my subconscious, cracked and brittle and oozing with an evil so black that it could have drowned out the sun.

The one, it breathed into me, broken glass shards dragging along my skin. *The one who was promised!*

I shuddered out of sleep as Pa shook my shoulder roughly. Bolting upright, I gasped for air, my lungs starving for it. Pa took a strong step back, his brow creased as he watched me collect myself. I must've been a sight to see—

panting and sweaty and delusional with panic. I swallowed around the lump in my throat, pushing my slick hair out of my eyes. "What is it?" I croaked.

Pa stared at me for a hard moment, at my soaked bedsheets, at the hand I had over my pounding heart, before he turned away. "Come outside. Now."

I blinked, looking out the window, at the soft grays bleeding into my room. "It's barely even dawn."

"Doesn't matter. Hurry."

The air was cool on my damp skin as I stepped outside, the ground crunching with hints of frost. I fumbled into my flannel jacket, fighting off the shiver that pinched my back.

My pa stood by the barn, arms crossed, his face carved into that particular breed of unreadable. I jogged toward him, rubbing life back into my cold hands. Beside him lay bales of hay, long wooden rods propped against them, and an axe wedged into a chopping block.

My finger throbbed at the memory of the blade's bite from the night before. A scab had sealed it over, but the thought still turned my stomach. Was this setup some kind of punishment for nearly causing a scene at the Sign-In? Had he dragged everything out just so I could haul it back into the barn?

Pa's gaze tracked me, sharp and steady, as I approached. The silence between us stretched. I rubbed my thumb over the tender spot on my finger, a little queasy. If he offered me another chance to opt out of the Hunt, I was certain I'd take it.

Penny nickered softly in the barn, breaking the stillness. Pa spoke just as I opened my mouth.

"About last night, Grayson—"

"Pa, I—"

We both stopped, chuckling awkwardly at our eagerness. I rubbed the back of my neck, breaking eye contact. "You go first."

Pa nodded sharply. "About last night," he started again, "I just wanted to say how proud I am of you."

I froze, my heart clumsily skipping a beat. *What?*

"I know that it wasn't easy for you, going in front of all those people and . . . you know." His face crinkled, and I realized he was trying to smile. "You were nervous, and you did it anyway, and I'm proud of you."

I should have gone first. I shrugged, but the movement was stiff. "It wasn't that bad." Pa raised an eyebrow, and I sighed, slumping. "Okay, maybe it was. But at least I didn't immediately faint." I looked down at my finger. "So . . . I didn't embarrass you?"

"Oh no, you did," Pa said matter-of-factly. "We were the laughingstock of the entire ceremony."

I grimaced. "Perfect."

Pa unfolded his arms, letting his hands slap his sides heavily. "But it doesn't matter. You did something you didn't think you could do, and that triumphs over any silly embarrassment I feel." He cleared his throat, nodding. "Right. What were you going to say?"

I gripped my finger tightly, the scab pulsating. "I . . ." I sighed, turning away. I couldn't look at my pa when I said it. "I don't know if I can do this."

Pa snorted. The sound made me look back hesitantly. I was expecting rage, earthquakes of anger. Not a *laugh*.

"Sure you can!" he said, reaching for a bale of hay and picking it up like it weighed less than paper. "With some proper training, you'll be fighting like the best of them. It'll feel as natural as breathing. And training," he grunted, tossing the hay in my direction, "starts now."

I jolted to the side, avoiding the hay bale careening toward me. It tumbled into the dirt by my feet in a cloud of dust. I glanced at my pa with a frown. "Was I supposed to . . . ?"

"Catch it, yeah." Pa inhaled sharply, shaking his head. "No matter. Pick it up. Training starts now."

Pa hefted another bale of hay over his shoulder. He looked more jovial than he had in months, more alive, with a spring in his step as he marched to the back of the barn. Stifling a groan, I reluctantly picked up the block of hay at my feet, struggling to keep a firm hold of it. "Can't wait."

I WAS CONFIDENT THAT MY FINGERS WERE EXPERIENCING A PREDE-ceased rigor mortis. They cracked and seized whenever I tried to flex them, the hot welts and red blisters coating my palms threatening to ooze open with the slightest movement. The net I was supposed to be mending was at my feet, ignored and untouched since I got to the docks an hour ago. Even the thought of bending over to collect it was agonizing.

A hand slapped my shoulder, sending a spurt of pain rippling down my ribs. "Hey, champ!" Jasper chirped, a lazy grin on his face as he waltzed by me.

I groaned in response, envious of how pain-free his steps looked—limp and all.

Jasper walked to the end of the dock, assessing the rows of nets strewn into the water. "Let me guess—training has started?"

I groaned again, slowly opening and closing my hands. "How could you *possibly* tell?"

"Psychic, I think." Jasper pulled an apple from his pocket and swiped it haphazardly against his jacket. He eyed the dull red skin before taking a hearty bite. "You were ridiculous last night, by the way," he said, sending bits of apple everywhere.

"You were no better; you nearly fell on your face trying to get up the stairs."

Jasper shrugged. "Fair enough." He offered his half-eaten apple to me. I grimaced and shook my head. He shrugged again and took another bite. "Did you wait until you were home to faint?"

Heat rushed to my cheeks. "*No.*" A smile curled at the corners of my lips as I gave Jasper a side-eyed stare. "I fainted on the way home."

Jasper nearly spat out his apple. "No way!"

"Honest to God," I said, placing a hand over my heart despite my body screaming at the movement. "Pa nearly had to carry me into the house."

Jasper slapped a hand against his bad leg, crowing with laughter. "Wish I could've seen that."

"Trust me—it wasn't pretty."

"Cripes," Jasper wheezed, wiping his eyes. "You sure are a lost cause, Grayson Shaw. How are you going to handle the challenges if you can barely take a finger prick?"

I blanched. "I haven't really thought that far ahead, to be honest. I'm sort of making it up as I go." I shifted, trying to loosen the knot pinching my stomach. "It's still the same three, right?"

Jasper exhaled loudly, his lips flapping. "Net building. Swimming. Combat." As he spoke, he counted off his fingers. "One challenge every five days."

I bit my lip. "Well, I can build a net with my eyes closed, and after this morning, I'm more than confident that Pa will be able to whip me into shape in time for combat."

"But swimming?" Jasper whistled. "You might be in trouble there."

More accurately, I was screwed. "Like I said, I'm making it up as I go."

Jasper shook his head. "That sort of attitude won't get you betted on."

I rolled my eyes. "Betting on hunters is nothing more than a waste of money. We should be putting that money toward keeping our shops open, getting food on tables."

"Oh, I'm sorry, *Pastor Kline*," Jasper scoffed, tossing his apple into the water. "I didn't know you'd be gracing the docks today."

I snorted, tentatively reaching for the net bundled at my feet. "The betting is meant to motivate the hunters into working harder, putting on a better show for the nonparticipating members. That's all it is, Jasper. A show." *A show that ends with death and bloody water.*

"Uh, yeah," Jasper replied, dubious. "And the best showman gets half of the money that was betted on him. Seriously . . ." He gawked at me. "*Are* you Pastor Kline?"

"That's not Pastor Kline."

Jasper and I looked up to see Ambrose striding along the boardwalk, Rosemary tangled in his arm, Peter Lyre and Tommy Morris trailing closely behind. Ambrose looked down his nose at us, running a hand through his gelled-back hair, his smile sharp enough to cut. "Pastor Kline did *far* better at the Symbolic Sign-In."

Peter sniggered, elbowing Tommy in the ribs. "Yeah," he sniffed, "at least Pastor Kline didn't faint."

"Hey now!" Jasper barked, taking a lurching step forward. "Grayson did no such thing, you pig-nosed liar."

Peter's hand fluttered to his squashed nose, his splotchy cheeks puffing out with trapped hot air. "My nose is *fine*!"

I tugged sharply on the hem of Jasper's coat. "Settle down," I said quietly.

Jasper swatted my hand away, then pressed his thumb against the tip of his pale nose, smushing it upward. He squealed loudly like a pig.

If Peter tried holding any more air in his cheeks, he was going to float away. To make matters worse, the pudginess clinging to his midsection made him look particularly balloonesque.

Tommy ducked his head, looking like he was trying to hide a smile. He pushed up his glasses, offering me a quick glance from underneath his blond bangs. "*United, we stand as strong as giants. Divided, we are no better than the dirt the giants stand upon,*" he muttered.

Ambrose rolled his eyes. "I'm not in the mood for one of your book quotes, Morris. Try again, in English."

Tommy pinched his lips together, deflated. "Being hunters means we are all on the same side. We should be playing nice with one another," he said flatly.

Ambrose looked over his shoulder, pinning Tommy with a sour glare. Tommy went back to observing the book in his hands.

Rosemary wriggled at Ambrose's side, clutching him tightly with one hand while the other hiked up her deep blue skirts so they wouldn't drag on the slick boardwalk. "Surely there's nothing wrong with some friendly competition," she commented, eyeing the buckets of chum lining the stone stairs leading to the docks.

Ambrose twisted back, tugging Rosemary close. "The voice of reason," he said, tucking a delicate curl behind her ear and planting a kiss on her carefully rouged cheek. "That's why I keep you around."

Peter stopped protecting his nose long enough to snort. "That's not the *only* reason, is it?"

Rosemary squeaked her protests as Ambrose let out a playful growl and dipped her for an onslaught of kisses, but she didn't truly seem all that bothered by them.

Jasper groaned with disgust, shielding his eyes dramatically. "Oh, please." He waved a hand at the group. "You all make me sick. Get out of here before I puke."

I widened my eyes at Ambrose. "It's the projectile sort."

Ambrose pulled away from Rosemary to frown at us. "Grow up, Warren."

Jasper placed his hands over his stomach and heaved. "Oh, jeez," he moaned. "Here it comes!" He retched violently, his entire body spasming.

"Seriously." I leaned away, giving Jasper a wide berth. "He's not joking."

"I'm really not," Jasper grunted, heaving again.

Ambrose took a step back, pulling Rosemary with him. He was clearly torn between wanting to wait around to call our bluff and fleeing the docks so he didn't get puke on his shiny black shoes. He smoothed the front of his wool jacket, his mouth twisted into a snarl. "Let's get out of here," he finally grumbled, shouldering through Tommy and Peter and stomping down the boardwalk.

I leaned forward, watching as the group cleared the boardwalk's lazy curve against the island. When I could no longer see them, I sighed, slumping back into my seat. "They're gone."

Jasper abruptly stopped making horrific sounds and wiped his mouth. "About time. Any longer and I actually might've hurled."

I chuckled, shaking my head. "You're disgusting."

Jasper batted his eyelashes at me, grinning. "Only for you."

I pushed Jasper away. "So, you're allowed to make fun of me, but Ambrose and his gang can't?"

Jasper scrunched his face. "Of course! He isn't your best friend! Poking fun is *my* job, not his."

My gaze trailed back to my hands, curled up and useless in my lap. In the sudden excitement, I had nearly forgotten about how much they hurt.

"Hey," Jasper said, patting my shoulder gently. "It'll get easier."

I swallowed, forcing a smile. "Let's hope so."

Jasper brightened, my own personal ray of blinding sunshine. "I'll bet you won't even notice the pain when you make your first kill."

The world went quiet.

My first kill.

A mermaid, stuck at the end of my hunting knife.

A mermaid like Evanora.

It was all I could think about during my lesson with Pa that morning. But I had a feeling that sinking my blade into living, squirming flesh would feel a lot different than a bale of hay. Feeling someone else's warm blood on my hands as their life drained away.

I didn't know if Jasper was still talking. I slowly stood from my chair, wobbling to catch my balance as the pier shifted beneath me. I swayed from the docks, my knees quaking and buckling with each feeble step. I walked up the stairs, past the boardwalk, and up the dirt road, until the salt-kissed breeze and ocean waves were a whisper at my back.

And when I was alone, surrounded by wildflowers and weeds, I vomited until there was nothing left to bring up.

CHAPTER TWENTY-THREE

EVANORA

APRIL 6 – AFTERNOON

IT WAS HARD TO PRAY WHEN WAR AND BLOODSHED WERE ON the mind.

I had been in the garden all day, trying to get in touch with my ancestors and the gods of the waters. I was dead set on the plan Illeron and I had come up with, but I wanted to make sure I had the ancestors' blessing. But despite having been there for hours, I felt I was no closer to gaining the enlightenment I had set out to find. I was, however, beginning to hate the garden.

My mind strayed from prayer to darker things. Thoughts of pleasing the gods twisted into doubts about whether I could truly follow through with the plan. Well-wishes to the ancestors curdled into anxiety about Grayson. Would he fall for any of it?

And then there was the plan itself.

First and foremost: fooling Grayson Shaw. The boy was enchanted by me; I could most certainly use that to my advantage. He had a soft heart, the kind that made manipulation easy. His naivety would serve our cause well. Grayson was a wealth of knowledge, and any insight into the Hunt would be invaluable. I didn't know much about how humans prepared for the Hunt, but Grayson surely did. And when his usefulness ran out, so too would his life on earth.

Secondly: Illeron would quietly rally the troops—only those willing to fight, of course. However, according to Illeron, a great many wanted to spill blood. And not just the warriors, but the water wielders, mind benders, and sirens too.

Thirdly, and ridiculously crucial: Jorah could *not* find out. Would he be devastated if he knew what we were doing behind his back? Absolutely. Would he attempt to put a stop to it? Without question.

I grunted, squeezing my eyes shut, willing my breathing to slow. "Prayer. Concentrate."

The ancestors whispered to my restless mind as I lay on the sand, my fingers threading through the seagrass. My magic hummed faintly against the blades, light glowing at my fingertips. I inhaled deeply, trying to quiet the noise in my head. The ancestors' voices shimmered in my mind like silk on glass, shifting between planes and time. I could always feel them there. Understanding them, however, was another ordeal entirely. Half the time, their murmurs were unintelligible, like the black speech of the Barrens.

He is the key.

And sometimes, they spoke in riddles, which was just as infuriating.

I turned my head to the side, trying to home in on the wandering voices. "Who is?"

The key to unlocking your powers.

My fingers froze at my sides. "My Gift?"

Yes, my ancestors breathed.

So, that was why my magic sputtered and choked in times of need. It wasn't fully formed yet. I knitted my delicate brow. Or maybe it was fully formed but just . . . stuck, out of reach. And I needed to find out how to reach it. "Who will help me retrieve my powers?"

The voices hushed, and I strained in the stillness to listen. The undercurrent rippled against me, tugging at my tail, fluttering in my hair.

Grayson Shaw.

My eyes snapped open. "The boy?" I coughed out, bolting upright, startling a bloom of jellyfish drifting by.

Yes, my ancestors whispered. *He plays a crucial role. The ending of your story is unwritten. He will help you fill in the empty spaces.*

I bit my lip, slipping back to the ocean floor. "So, I was right. About the connection I feel with him. There is something that ties us together." I dug deeper into the sand. "Running into him was a promised fate."

Yes.

This wasn't the sort of enlightenment I'd been hoping to find. "He cannot be," I argued, shutting my eyes tighter. "Surely this must be a mistake."

The power of three.

"The power of three? What in Poseidon's waters does that mean?"

Find him, my ancestors willed, their voices growing distant. *Find him. He is the key.*

The waters went still.

I scrunched my face, focusing on the silence. "So, you toss me a cryptic message and then vanish?" I exhaled sharply. "What do you mean, *key*? And *power of three*? And how is a mere human going to help me with my Gifts?" I paused, my heart beating heavily. "Hello?"

I was met with nothing.

I growled, thudding my head against the sandy floor. "Great," I moaned, draping an arm over my eyes. I replayed the message my ancestors had whispered to me. Over and over, yet I was no closer to deciphering it. What did any of it mean?

Each mermaid possessed a Gift, a certain magic that they could harness and master. And while the pod received a single Gift, members of royalty were blessed with two. Ammah was both a light bringer and a siren. My appah was a healer and a mind bender.

I was a light bringer and a healer, and I was good at neither.

There was no such thing as a mermaid possessing more than two Gifts. It was already a miracle that royalty received two. Anything else was unheard-of, laughable, even.

I shook my head, pinching my lips together tightly. It didn't matter. It didn't matter what my ancestors wanted me to do. I had a plan in place, and I would not be allowing myself to get close enough to Grayson Shaw to find out what nonsense my ancestors meant. *No,* I refused firmly, *I will not falter. I don't care what any of it means. I will not fail. I'll figure out another way to unlock my powers. Key and power of three be damned.*

There was a light thump against my stomach, a suctioning pull on my bare skin.

"I'm trying to pray, you know," I muttered.

The pale octopus stared at me with its endless eyes, patting my cheek with its skinny arm.

I giggled, plucking it off my stomach. "Oh, you."

The darkness shifted beside me, murmuring within the Barrens. I looked around the octopus, gazing into the murky dark, a deep unease curdling in my blood. The Cursed Beings groaned at me, their whispered words slithering along my skin, pricking at my scales. I couldn't hear them when I was focused on my prayers, but now that they had my attention, they were louder than ever, keen to sink their claws into me like they had when I was in the belly of the Barrens.

"Evanora," a voice rang in my mind, startling me back to reality.

I blinked, breaking my staring contest with the Barrens. The darkness within seemed to mourn my lost attention.

"Evanora?"

At first, I thought it was the ancestors returning to give me more riddles. But as I listened harder, I realized that the crisp voice echoing through me was Illeron. A spark of surprise tingled through my fins.

"I know you can hear me."

I sank back into the sand. *"Go away. I'm praying."*

I could practically hear Illeron's snide laughter. *"Sure you are. Come over to the weaponry."*

Grumbling, I rose from the ocean floor and scurried out of the garden.

The weaponry was empty save for Illeron, pacing around the cylindrical room, his gaze on the large gaping windows and the training grounds beyond them. A thin smile curled on his lips when I burst through the open door. He dipped his head sarcastically. "Majesty."

My heart thudded painfully when his crimson eyes met mine. Illeron wasn't wearing his usual armor, and the sight of him bare chested and exposed was . . . unsettling—but not at all in a bad way.

"What has you so desperately wanting my attention?" I huffed, smoothing out my hair.

Illeron looked at the spears to his side, all in a neat row, their blades glinting in the filtered sun. "Since your plan involves conspiring with our enemies, I figured it would be in your best interest to learn some fighting skills in case you found yourself tangled with the Grim Reaper."

I rolled my eyes, crossing my arms against my chest. "Must you be so dramatic?" I shrugged, eyeing the hungry-looking weapons. "Besides, lessons from you aren't necessary. I can defend myself."

Illeron laughed, rolling his shoulders out and stretching his arms. "Trust me, I don't want to train you any more than you want to learn."

"And yet"—I waved my arms at the empty weaponry—"here we are."

Illeron shook his arms loose, his long, red-tipped fins following after the movements. "Humans are monsters. Even that *harmless boy* of yours." His gaze darkened. "They are wild and unpredictable and aren't afraid to stoop to hellish lows in order to win. You need more than your wits and fins."

I flashed a sharp grin at him. "I told you that I can defend myself."

The words hadn't even left my mouth. In an instant, Illeron was behind me, pinning my body against his, a knife I hadn't even realized he had pressed to my throat.

Illeron smirked, his breath on my ear. "Can you now?" His body was rigid, taut with muscles I hadn't known were there. His fingers sidled along my neck, tilting my chin up, giving his blade more access.

I hissed, stiffening in his grip. "Let go of me."

Illeron dipped his head low. His words vibrated against my soft skin when he spoke in a whisper. "If you're so convinced you don't need help, get yourself out."

My blood raged within me, but only part of it was from anger. He was so *close*. With a growl, I let my magic flood my system, humming through my veins and sputtering out of my scales in a flash of crackling light. With a grunt, Illeron let go, covering his eyes with his hands from the brightness that emanated from me. I heaved in a breath and clutched at my throat, the memory of the blade still imprinted on my skin.

Illeron bared his teeth, blinking rapidly as he slowly lowered his hands. "We both know your magic is powerful, but there is a limit. Sooner or later, you always exhaust your reserves and are left with nothing. You need to learn other skills in case that should happen."

The ancestors' voices fluttered through my mind uninvited. *The key to unlocking your powers.*

Illeron squinted at me, confusion flickering along the twitch in his jaw. I brushed the thoughts aside before he could hear them again. "If I let you teach me one lesson, would you be satisfied?"

Illeron cocked his head to the side. "Exceedingly."

"Great," I said flatly.

"Great." Illeron crossed his arms and nodded to the rack of spears next to the door. "Grab one."

I gawked at him, my fins drooping. "Now?"

Illeron smiled thinly. "We have entered Hunting Month. The humans are officially preparing for the arrival of the Hunt on May 1. We must prepare as well."

With a hearty pout, I grabbed the spear closest to me. The thing felt heavy in my hands, the shaft cool and smooth in my palms. I frowned at the bone-carved blade erupting from the end, running my fingers along the jagged teeth. "It's blunted."

Illeron grabbed a spear of his own and tossed it from one hand to the other. "I teach merlings. Can you imagine if I armed them with actual weapons?"

I cringed, my grip tightening on the spear. "Sounds messy."

"Indeed." Illeron's mouth drooped. "You're holding it all wrong."

I glanced down at my hands clutching the middle of the shaft. "Ah," I sighed, smiling brightly at Illeron, "ever the conversationalist."

Illeron grunted, swooping toward me. He pried my fingers loose and separated my hands, guiding them down the shaft. "You want your hands to be farther apart. You won't get any power behind your swings if you keep them locked together." His hands folded over mine, pressing tightly; the smooth wood caressed my skin as the heat of his fingers blended into my own. "And you want to have a firm grip, but nothing too tight. You want to be able to shift your hands quickly if you need to."

I nodded, concentrating on my hand placements and not on Illeron's fingers tangling with mine. I kept my eyes on my hands despite feeling his gaze on me, warming my insides.

Illeron leaned away, assessing me. "Better. But take care to keep your arms up." He pushed the spear upward so that it was crossing my chest. "Your spear will serve as both an attacking tool and a defending one. You won't be able to block a blow if it's lowered."

My muscles twinged as I tensed my arms, my tail fighting to keep me upright. "I'm already tired."

Illeron grinned. "And we've only just begun. Now, strike."

I gave a stuttering laugh. "At you?"

Illeron's grin went lopsided. "Afraid you'll hurt me?"

With a growl, I poked the spear forward. Illeron avoided it with ease, twisting his torso as the spear's tip sailed by.

"Well," he said, watching as I straightened, "that was fairly terrible."

I rolled my eyes. "I certainly hope you don't talk to the merlings like this."

Illeron brushed up next to me, taking his spear in both hands. "I know it feels clunky right now, but you need to picture the spear as an extension of your arm. It moves when you move, stops when you stop. Strikes when you want to strike." He sucked in a breath, then shot forward. The spear darted through the water, an eel seeking prey. Illeron pulled it back just as quickly. The entire attack was over in less than a second.

I blinked, my jaw threatening to hinge open. Adjusting my grip on the spear, I dipped my chin, held my breath, and tried again.

Illeron nodded. "Better. Again."

I gritted my teeth. My muscles were already sore, my fingers cramping from gripping the spear. But I did it. Again, and again, and again, I struck imaginary foes in the water.

Illeron circled me, watching my form. He tapped my elbow gently. "More rigid here. You keep slackening at the end of your attack. You lose spears that way." He looped around me again. "Good. That's good."

He sounded . . . breathless. Even though I was the one doing all the work.

Illeron swam in front of me as I withdrew my spear from another imaginary enemy. His pale cheeks were tinted in a dusty rose as he lowered his gaze, pointing to his stomach. "Tighten here. Your core is where a lot of your strength will come from."

My shoulders were beginning to seize. I paused, letting my head roll back. "There are too many things to remember."

Illeron's eyes met mine. "Sounds like you might need another lesson."

I raised an eyebrow. "I thought you didn't want to teach me."

"I don't." Illeron took my spear and placed it back on the rack. "But you have a lot to learn, as it turns out."

I scoffed but instantly appreciated the weightlessness of not holding the weapon. I sank to the floor, flexing my hands, groaning as they cracked and cramped. "I guess I do," I replied softly.

Illeron nestled beside me, clucking his tongue at my tender palms. "It gets better," he said, showing me his callused hands. "Eventually it stops hurting."

My fingers began to glow as my Gift flowed through me. I offered Illeron a coy smile as I rubbed at my arms and shoulders, my magic finding the knots and tension hidden there.

Illeron shook his head, chuckling under his breath. "Show-off."

I wiggled my arms and clenched my fists. The memory of pain was still there, but a mere whisper of what it had once been. And thankfully, it hadn't sputtered out in front of Illeron. That would have been embarrassing.

The power of three. The key.

I could feel Illeron's eyes on me, deep and questioning. I bit my lip, forcing the echo of my ancestors' words out of my mind and into the still waters.

The warrior chuckled. "You're shutting me out."

"Am I?" I asked flippantly.

Illeron stared at me for a moment longer before relenting. "You don't have to, you know."

"Oh, please," I scoffed. "I have a lot of boring royal thoughts on my mind. Trust me, I'm saving you from the suffering of it all."

Illeron didn't say anything for a breath, but I could feel him stiffen beside me. "Solandis," he uttered quietly.

My heart thundered to a stop. I hadn't been thinking about Solandis, but suddenly, I was sick with grief about it. It was like a weight on my chest, squeezing my insides so tightly that I could barely inhale. How had I forgotten about her? I should have been praying in the garden for *her*, not my revenge plan.

"I failed her," I admitted quietly.

Illeron shook his head. "You didn't know she was going to follow you."

"Sometimes I wish I were a mind bender. Then I would have known."

Illeron shrugged, bumping his shoulder into mine. "Well, then you wouldn't be you."

"That might be the kindest thing you've ever said to me."

Illeron rolled his eyes. "Don't read too much into it, Your Majesty." He leaned his head against the stone shelf behind us, his eyes drifting to the domed ceiling looming above. "So, you think you'll be able to do it? Follow through with the plan?"

I waved a hand dismissively. "You mean the plan to bring down mankind, put an end to the Hunt, and eliminate the threat of our extinction?"

Illeron chuckled under his breath. "Just that, yes."

I clasped my hands together, leaning my head back too. "I don't really have a choice. Times are changing. The humans are fighting harder, dirtier." I could feel my throat tighten, my words beginning to wobble. "We are being picked off, one by one. I just . . ." I sighed, running a hand through my hair and pulling several strands over my shoulder. "I just don't see any other way of handling this."

Illeron's jaw tightened, his sharp cheekbones nearly popping out of his skin. His face set with determination, he leaned forward, placing his hand on the floor between us. "Let me do it."

I gave a choked laugh, avoiding his gaze. "Do what?"

"Everything. Let me go see your Shaw boy. Let me put myself in danger instead of you. Let *me* be your eyes, your hands, your ears." He loosed a breath. "There's no need for you to carry all this weight alone."

I busied myself with my hair, fingering through the silken white locks. "Illeron, be serious."

"I *am* being serious." Illeron scooted closer to me, his tail swishing against mine. "If drawing their blood is what you wish to do, then have me do it."

"That's not your job."

He laughed. "Evanora, I'm a warrior. That is quite literally my main job."

I swatted the water dismissively. "Your job is to protect the pod, keep them safe. You are needed here, above all else. Rallying the pod, teaching them to fight, until it is time to go to the surface. Besides . . ." I let out a heavy breath. "Grayson Shaw already knows me. For you to meet with him instead could really set us back. And let's be honest, I don't see him warming up to you. As charming as you are."

"I want to help," he pushed. "And yes, I think you'll be able to handle the majority of the plan on your own, but when it comes to killing . . ." Illeron narrowed his eyes, a silent challenge. "Do you really think you'll have what it takes?"

"I don't need help killing Grayson Shaw."

Illeron shook his head, pushing his silvery-white strands behind his ears. "Evanora, I could kill a human in a heartbeat. I was born to fight, and I'm not afraid to go against the code your parents created. But you—" He winced. "I worry you would hesitate. You have too much love in your blood."

He was right, but that was beside the point. I fought to keep my voice even. "I may have love in my veins, but none of it belongs to humans." I slapped my hand against the stone floor. "None. The plan is to win Grayson over. I will do just that. And when his use to us is over and it is time to take his life?" I shrugged. "I will do that too."

Illeron cocked his head to the side, his lip pulling up to reveal his sharp teeth. "Are you so sure?"

My Gift crackled and burst like an electrical current seeking a grounding source. But Illeron did not yield. He continued to stare at me, a quiet rage in his steely gaze. I could feel him attempting to penetrate my mind, see into my thoughts, witness my secrets. With a hiss, I sent my magic inward, creating an impenetrable force inside myself. The action seemed to cause him physical discomfort, and he flinched away, breaking our staring contest.

I rose, pushing off the wall. "Thank you for the lesson, but we are done here," I snapped, turning for the exit.

I didn't have to look back to know Illeron's eyes were on me the entire time.

CHAPTER TWENTY-FOUR

GRAYSON

APRIL 7 – AFTERNOON

HOLLY DIDN'T LOOK THRILLED TO SEE ME. HER SMILE instantly fell when she opened the door and found me huddled at the top of the stairs. Crossing her arms, she let out a huff of air and leaned against the wooden doorframe. "Jasper isn't here," she said by way of greeting.

"I know," I said quickly. "I came to see you."

Holly scoffed, but she choked on the end of it when she saw the bunch of flowers I produced from behind my back. "Daisies!" she squealed, her eyes wide as she took in the splashes of white and yellow. "They're my—"

"Your favorite," I chimed in, handing the bouquet to her. "We have an entire field of them behind the house. I saw them and thought of you." I'd also seen a great many purple flowers that made me think of Evanora. I couldn't bring myself to pick those ones.

"You remembered." Holly held the flowers to her chest like they were her most prized possession. She smelled them briefly, her eyes flitting to mine. "So, what's the occasion?"

Uninvited heat brushed against my cheeks. "An apology." I winced, looking away. "I'm sorry for how I acted at the First Festival. I have two left feet, you see, but I . . ." I sighed, running my hands down my face. "I should have danced with you. I'm sorry that I made you mad."

Holly bit her lip, her fingers gliding along the silk petals. "And?"

I cringed, ducking my head. "And I'm sorry for making a complete ass of myself when you were walking home. I'm carrying enough shame and embarrassment for the both of us, I think."

Holly considered my words, but only for a brief moment. She grinned up at me from over the flowers. "I could never be mad at you, Grayson Shaw."

So I've been told. I shoved my hands into my pockets, offering a lopsided smile. "Well, that's a relief."

"Do you want to stay for a cup of tea?" Holly stepped away from the door, holding it open with her back. "The kettle's nearly finished heating."

I wanted to say no, but the second I opened my mouth, I could hear the slow and steady scream of boiling water in the kitchen tucked around the corner. Holly turned and rushed down the hall, leaving me alone at the entrance. "Close the door behind you!" she called over her shoulder before disappearing into the kitchen.

Restraining a sigh, I quietly clicked the door shut and followed Holly. I had never been to the Warren house when Jasper wasn't there. Being alone with Holly seemed like dangerous territory.

I rounded the corner, finding Holly scurrying around the cramped kitchen. In the time it had taken me to get there, she had already placed the flowers in a cup of water, pulled the kettle off the stove, and stuffed wads of loose-leaf tea into two mugs.

"Do you like milk in your tea?" she asked, looking at me through the curtain of hair that had fallen over her shoulder.

Giving my hands something to do, I removed my newsboy cap and began scrunching up the fabric. "Just plain, thanks."

Holly gestured to the large round table planted in the center of the room. "Have a seat."

I settled into one of the wooden chairs; it wobbled underneath my weight.

"Jasper made that one."

I realized Holly was talking about the chair. "Is that why it's so"—I shifted, tipping the chair back and forth on its uneven legs—"immaculately perfect?"

Holly giggled, sitting across from me and pushing a mug in my direction. She leaned back in her chair. "Is it weird? Being here without Jasper?"

It was, but I shook my head. "No," I lied, warming my hands on the steaming mug. "I mean, you're my friend too, right?"

Holly suddenly became fixated on her tea, but I could see a dash of color on her freckled cheeks, a whisper of a smile on her lips. She took a sip from her mug. The clock in the living room ticked away a handful of long, long seconds.

"How's training going?" she asked, setting her mug back down. "Jasper told me Mr. Shaw is really whipping you into shape."

"He's definitely trying to." I slouched back into the chair. "I don't think he knows the difference between *training* and *torture*."

Holly tapped her fingers against the ceramic mug. "Don't you have a salve or ointment for that?"

I began to nod but stopped when a muscle in my neck twinged in protest. "Nothing strong enough to make me forget I'm one giant bruise," I said, rubbing my neck.

Holly bit her lip, then reached forward and poked me in the arm. I squawked and toppled back in the chair, sending the uneven legs skittering. "Rude!" I cried, rubbing my arm. "So very, very rude!"

"You need to toughen up!" Holly said between spurts of laughter and snorts.

"You need to take pity on me and my fragile state."

Holly went in for another poke. I swatted her away. "Well," she said, smirking, "Mr. Shaw certainly has his work cut out for him." She eyed me thoroughly. "And so do you."

I wilted in the chair, groaning. "The gospel truth."

Holly sipped her tea. I stared at mine. A silence fell over us, and with it, the puzzling tension that seemed to follow me and Holly whenever we were alone—one that I desperately ignored but Holly seemed to thrive in. Even now, across the table, she was beaming at me, a sunflower pointed toward her sun.

As the clock chimed the hour, I spoke. "I really should be—"

"Would you like to stay for dinner?" Holly asked before I could finish my sentence. She stood up hurriedly, wrapping her deep green shawl over her bony shoulders. "Ma and the twins should be home with the ingredients soon. We're having stew tonight."

My heart tumbled at her eagerness. I rose carefully out of the rickety chair. "I wish I could, but I was actually making my way down to Maude."

Holly attempted to hide her disappointment, but I saw right through it. "That's quite the walk."

"It's only an hour or so. Maybe two." I winced. "Maybe three. Is it weird that even *thinking* about walking is painful?"

Holly's mouth quirked to the side. An almost smile. "I thought you weren't allowed to visit your ma."

Annoyance festered. I buried it with a grin. "Pa doesn't have to know; I'll be there and back before he gets home, and he'll be none the wiser."

The truth of the matter was, I was officially eighteen. Which meant I didn't need Pa's approval to visit Ma anymore. But I was still too scared to let him know of my decisions; better to ask for forgiveness later than permission—and likely rejection—first.

But I had to see her. I hadn't laid eyes on her since she was carted away in a strapped jacket in the back of Rose Hill's van. I had to replace that cursed image with a new one—and hopefully something more pleasant.

Holly walked me to the front door, her steps as sharp and curt as her mood. "I never took you for a rebel, Grayson Shaw," she said, her voice light but her eyes carrying daggers.

"Neither did I." I chuckled, taking the stairs gingerly. "Maybe the Hunt is forcing it out of me."

Holly tilted her head, letting it rest on the doorframe. "It doesn't suit you."

"What doesn't?"

"Rebellion."

I nearly tripped on the last step. When I caught my balance and looked at the door, it was already closed.

STERILE. COLD. ISOLATED. THOSE WERE THE FIRST THINGS I thought of when I entered Rose Hill Asylum.

Also, white. There was a lot of white.

The asylum in Maude took its name from the labyrinthine courtyard sprawling behind the building, perched precariously on the cliffside. Thick walls of rosebushes, wild and untamed, twisted like serpents through the grounds. On sunny days, patients were permitted outside to tend to the flowers. Either Maude seldom saw sunshine, or its inhabitants had no affection for roses, as the bushes seemed to be thriving in death.

The building itself was an old abandoned castle. Built in a square with jagged watchtowers at every corner, the crumbling gray stone walls were dotted with tiny windows that looked like a thousand eyes staring at me through their barred eyelids. Rumor had it that the Grieveses had wanted to purchase the castle to live in, just to be able to say they lived in a castle. Royalty demands royalty. Ultimately, the deal fell through because royalty doesn't live in Maude. No one does, if they can help it.

Inside, the castle bore the sterile, joyless hallmarks of a repurposed hospital. Banquet halls had become dining rooms. Ballrooms were now activity spaces. Even the former torture chambers had been softened into bathing rooms. The endless expanse of white—walls, hospital gowns, nurse uniforms—was broken only by paintings of fields bursting with wildflowers, cascading waterfalls, or rugged cliffs. The dreary splashes of color felt more like a mockery than an invitation to hope.

I had only been in Ma's room for five minutes, and in that blink of time, I'd put the wildflowers I had picked for her in the plastic vase on the round table bolted to the middle of the room, made the small, child-sized bed wedged against the wall, and tidied up the shelf stuffed with various paperback books and plastic figurines. No hard edges, no sharp teeth. Everything about Rose Hill was soft, safe, and wrung dry of all personality. Ma wouldn't be caught dead with such lackluster things. If it wasn't made out of porcelain or silk, it wasn't worth it.

I spent another ten minutes standing idly by the door, wondering what to say to the woman who had raised me—and who had tried to kill me. I'd already gone through the talking points I had carefully collected on my walk over. I kept my voice cheerful and tossed questions her way, only to watch them spill onto the ground in a puddle of words and question marks, her silence loud enough to fill the empty room until it was cramped.

Fifteen minutes gone, and she had yet to acknowledge me. Pa was right: She was nothing but a shadow, a whisper that couldn't reach my ears.

My heart twisted with a sordid mixture of pain and love for the woman sitting in front of the rain-stained window. She was gazing through the barred glass, but her eyes were glazed over, staring at nothing. Her thin, sinewed hands were clasped in her lap, getting lost in the folds of her wrinkled white skirt. Her shoulders, thin and bony, were strained to straightness, her dark blond hair clumped into a braid that slung around her taut neck.

I wondered if I was allowed to brush her hair, or if she would even let me. When Ma had lived with us in Tully, I had been convinced that her pride and joy had been chopped into two pieces: Warrick, and her hair. My ma *loved* her hair. It was always shining and carefully curled, not one strand out of place. Now her hair was dull, greasy, and horrendously matted. Did she know? Did she even care?

I glanced at the door, knowing that a single knock would signal the nurse hovering outside to let me out. But as I raised my hand to the steel door, I paused.

"I met someone. A girl," I said, peering over my shoulder to Ma. Besides a slow blink, she gave me no reaction, no indication that she had even heard me. I turned away from the door, biting my bottom lip. "She's really pretty. I think you'd like her."

My mind was a feast of thoughts, seasoned with a hardy dose of warning. I shouldn't talk about Evanora. I shouldn't be talking about mermaids, period. I had to be careful. I was treading on dangerous ground. Even if Ma wasn't listening to me, someone outside the door might be. But the problem with thinking about Evanora was that once the tap was turned on, it was hard to turn it off. In fact, in most cases the tap broke.

I crossed my arms, feeling a light blush prickling my cheeks. "She's not from here. Well, no . . ." I shrugged. "I guess she is. When we first met, I thought she hated me. She was cold and cruel, if I'm being truthful." I smiled bashfully. "But I think she's warming up to me now. She doesn't look at me like I'm a meal, anyway."

What was I saying? I needed to stop talking, *now*.

"Whenever I see her, God, my heart just . . ." I clutched my chest tightly, scrunching up my shirt. "Was it like that for you and Pa?" I snorted, shaking my head. "What am I saying? Of course it was! Everything about her is breathtaking. Her smile, her eyes, her name." I leaned against the door, my head thudding against the steel. "Evanora," I breathed, her name escaping my lips in a sigh. "Isn't that a pretty name?"

It was barely noticeable. I had actually almost missed it.

Out of the corner of my eye, I saw Ma turn her head in the direction of my voice. The movement was slow, grating, like the muscles in her neck had forgotten how to function. They twitched and quivered beneath her dry skin, tripping over sinew, colliding into throbbing arteries. The jarring movement seemed to take effort, and a low, rasping breath squeezed out of her lungs.

I took a timid step forward. "Ma?"

"That's a mermaid's name," Ma wheezed, her voice low, the words getting caught in her dry throat.

Her words replaced all my blood with ice shards. "It's not," I lied.

Ma turned back to stare out the window, the movement just as slow and unsettling as the first time. Her hands fluttered from her lap to the chair's armrests, where she gripped the plastic so hard her knuckles popped. She began to speak again, but her voice was brittle from lack of use, and the words cracked the second they left her mouth. "*They come out . . . at night. They'll give . . . you a fright. If you choose to swim . . . in the dark.*"

I furrowed my brow, forcing another step out of my legs. "What was that?"

Ma continued as if she hadn't heard me. "*You shall become . . . become . . .*"

I realized I wasn't breathing. I carefully filled my lungs. "Become *what*, Ma?"

Her words picked up speed, urgency threading itself into them. "*They'll pull you down. Down. Down!*"

I stopped just behind her chair. It felt like my heart had wedged itself into my ears, its droning drum muffling. "That's the old nursery rhyme you taught me, right? 'The Barrens' Lullaby'?" I forced a gentle chuckle. "I think you're getting the verses mixed up."

Ma's voice rose, a panicked hysteria causing the walls to quake, the wildflowers to shudder. "*If you hear whispers, it is already too late! Follow death down and accept your fate! Your fate!*"

The laughter died in my throat. I hadn't heard that verse before. "Ma, please." I spared a glance at the door. "The nurses will hear you."

"*Your fate!*" she screamed. Spittle flew off her chapped lips. Her sunken blue eyes were wild as they stared ahead, burning into the window. Her entire body was shaking, her knobby knees clacking together, her elbows digging into the chair. "*Your fate!*"

"Ma!" I begged, placing a hand on her shoulder.

Ma whirled around in her chair. Her face was misshapen, an ugly snarl on her lips, every crease and wrinkle a dotted line of hate. "It should have been you!"

I had no time to react.

In an instant, my ma was out of the chair and flinging herself at me.

All the air rushed out of my lungs as she collided with me, knocking me into the unmoving table before tumbling to the floor in a heap of flailing arms, biting teeth, and feral shrieks. I scrambled back, struggling to free myself from her rageful grip, but Ma was surprisingly strong as she clambered on top of me, pinning me in place. Wedged between the table and her abandoned chair, I had nowhere to go as her fists began to connect with any part of me they could purchase. Her nails ripped into my clothes, desperate for skin, for blood, *my* blood. Her teeth gnashed as she screamed, and screamed, and screamed.

I realized that I was screaming too.

"It should have been you!" she howled into my face. "It should have been *you*!"

I squeezed my eyes shut, covering my head with my arms in a feeble attempt to fend off her rabid attack. This wasn't happening. This *couldn't* be happening.

There was the screech of a dead bolt sliding out of place, the sound of the steel door connecting with the stone wall, the stomping of feet. A vicious eternity later, the room became cramped as nurses in starched white uniforms hurried around us. The cutthroat shrieks were penetrated by shouts to "move" and "get him out of here" and "get her on the bed" and "grab the syringe."

Three nurses began to grapple with Ma, taking hold of her writhing limbs and prying her off me. Strong hands slipped underneath my arms and yanked me back, pulling me out of harm's reach.

With a burst of energy, my ma surged forward, flailing to get another piece of me.

A sharp, searing pain bit at my cheek, lighting my entire face on fire. I flinched away, nearly causing the nurse behind me to trip. He recovered and continued pulling me up and toward the yawning door.

The nurses managed to successfully wrangle Ma onto the bed. Her legs were already buckled into the straps attached to the bed frame, and one of the nurses was hiking up her wrinkled gown, exposing her pale pencil-thin thigh to the syringe in her hand. The needle oozed with a cloudy white mixture, the bevel sharp with the promise of pain and peace.

"Hold her arms!" the nurse directed as she gripped Ma's trembling leg and pointed the needle down.

"Please," I croaked, trying to push around the closing door. "Don't hurt her!"

The nurse hauled me back and closed the door, locking the chaos inside. I panted, leaning back into the door as my ma's frantic cries dwindled into primal moans. My entire body was slick with sweat, but it felt like kerosene. One open flame and I'd combust. I couldn't stop shaking, couldn't stop hearing Ma's screams echoing through my mind.

It should have been you!

The nurse slid the dead bolt into place before giving me a heavy look. He whistled, crossing his thick arms. "Looks like she got you good."

I flopped my head to the side, letting it thud against the cool steel. "What?"

The nurse pointed at my cheek.

Numbly, I brought my hand to my face.

My fingertips came back warm, wet, and bloody.

A moan oozed out of my mouth. Hand still in front of my face, I raised a blank stare to the nurse. "Oh."

And then the world went dark.

SIGHT WASN'T THE FIRST THING THAT CAME BACK TO ME.
It was the smell of salt tangling with the air, the sound of sheep playing in their overgrown fields, the feel of cool wood digging into my spine. My limp body jostled and swayed as wheels crunched on dirt and slammed into potholes. Moving. I was moving. One minute, I was visiting Ma in Maude. The next . . .

A quiet groan escaped my lips as I cracked my eyes open. The brightness of the sun nearly had me shutting them again. The clouds that had been hoarding the horizon were now gone, and I was ferociously bitter about it. Forcing myself up, I blinked, trying to make sense of where I was. Lush green fields full of wildflowers and livestock surrounded me, each paddock bordered with crumbling rock walls that stretched over the rolling hills. I could hear the whisper of the ocean to my left, though I couldn't see it.

Behind me, Maude's lights were beginning to flicker at the promise of an approaching night, and the sharp mountains beyond observed quietly. Up ahead was the outline of Tully, the faint crawl of the hill and the glowing lanterns from the docks. At least, I assumed it was Tully; Pa and Pastor Kline were sitting at the front of the wagon, obscuring my view.

At the sound of my grumbling, Pa spared me a glance over his shoulder, a well-placed frown on his lips. "Took you long enough to wake up."

I grimaced, stiffly raising my hand to my cheek. Puffy gauze was taped to my skin. I could feel my heartbeat underneath the scratchy fabric, the hardened edges of dried blood. I pulled my hand away, holding my breath as I twisted it back and forth. Dirty, callused, but no blood. Someone had not only taken the time to bandage me up, but they'd also washed my hands of any sordid reminders.

I had a feeling it wasn't my pa.

Shame flooded my veins. Not only had Pa found out about my failed visit to Ma, but he'd had to rescue me from it. Exhaling, I leaned back on my hands. "I'm torn between saying *thank you* and *I'm sorry*. Which would you prefer to hear?"

When Pa said nothing, I pressed on. "Both? Neither?" I slouched forward, clasping my hands together and forcing a soft laugh. "Would you prefer me to just stop talking?"

Pastor Kline offered a meek smile over his shoulder. "I personally think an apology would be a great start."

Pa shifted violently in his seat to look at me, his face as dark as a storm. "I'd prefer to have a son who *listens.*"

"I *do* listen."

"No," he seethed, "you don't." He rubbed his forehead. "How many times did I tell you to not go see her, Grayson? How many times?"

I sighed, wilting until my back was against the wagon's wall. "More than you should have."

"Obviously not. What were you thinking?"

It was a trick question. "I wasn't thinking," I said, staring down at my hands.

"That's right! You weren't! You were careless and irresponsible. You could have been killed." Pa pointed at my face. "You're lucky that was the only gift she gave you."

My cheek burned at the memory of Ma's nails sinking into my flesh. I resisted the urge to touch the bandage again. "I just wanted to see her."

But, if I was being honest, I wished I hadn't.

It should have been you!

"Grayson," Pa said, his voice all stone and steel. "She is a *shell* of what she once was. It will do you no good to think of her as anything else." He shifted to look at me. "She hasn't been your mother for a long, long time."

The words stung more than my cheek, and I couldn't help but flinch from the impact of them.

Pastor Kline cleared his throat, looking dreadfully uncomfortable. He urged his horse onward, his fingers toying with the reins. Really, it looked like he was simply giving them something to do so he didn't grab for the flask in his coat pocket.

Pa softened, leaning back and placing a hand on my knee. "I hope you learned something today."

"Yeah," I said, gingerly wiping my nose with my sleeve. "I need to work on my reflexes. Maybe practice some ducking and weaving."

With a sigh, Pa reached over and pulled the reins out of Pastor Kline's shaking hands. He forced the horse to a disgruntled halt. "Out."

I jerked my chin up. "What?"

"Out of the wagon. Now."

I rose to my feet and clambered over the side of the wagon, sidestepping loose boards and rusted buckets. When I landed on the ground, I turned to Pa and raised my arms. "Now what?"

Pa placed the reins back in Pastor Kline's hands. "Now you're going to go home."

I frowned, gripping the wagon and swinging my leg up.

"No," Pa said sternly with a shake of his head. "On foot."

I gawked at him, not believing him enough to let go of the wagon. "On foot?"

"I hardly think that's necessary—" Pastor Kline started to say, but he was quick to stop when my pa gave him a sour look.

Pa nodded. "If you insist on making jokes about training during a serious conversation, then you can train."

"I was trying to lighten the mood!"

"You aren't Jasper." Pa stared pointedly at my iron grip. "Let go."

Laughing incredulously, I ripped my hands away from the wagon's wooden side, glancing at Tully's faint outline. "But the village is miles away still."

Pa offered me a hard smile. "Yes, and I expect you to be home in less than an hour." He motioned to Pastor Kline, who reluctantly clucked his tongue and snapped the reins. "Best get running."

Feeling helpless and hateful, I watched as Pa, Pastor Kline, and the wagon left me behind in a flurry of dust. Within minutes, I was alone, with only a handful of curious sheep for company. The sun was stretching its rays for the horizon and the mass of clouds forming there, a soft blanket welcoming the promise of slumber. If I didn't hurry, the sun would be off to bed before I even made it to my front door.

With my aching bones, racing thoughts, and throbbing cheek, I began to jog in the direction of home, burying my resentment for Lethe, for my pa, and for the Hunt.

CHAPTER TWENTY-FIVE

GRAYSON

APRIL 7 – EVENING

I COULDN'T CATCH MY BREATH.

I didn't know how long I stood outside, staring at my house. It could have been two minutes, five, thirty, an hour. There was movement in the kitchen, the faint glow from the fire casting dancing shadows on the wall. Pa was still up, waiting for me to return home after my run of shame. He was likely stewing, already preparing to bite my head off for taking longer than an hour. Much, much longer.

I turned away from the house. I was exhausted and drowning in sweat, and my cheek was throbbing like it had its very own heartbeat. The last thing I wanted to do was go into the house and have an I-do-this-to-you-because-I-love-you talk. Not that my pa would put it so eloquently. In his version, I imagine there would be a lot more head shaking, fist clenching, and beard rubbing. The man wouldn't know soft and gentle if it bit him on the ass.

My feet hurt. I could feel blisters forming from where bony prominences had rubbed against threadbare socks. But I let them lead me down the hill. Pa could wait a little while longer.

Before I knew it, my feet had brought me to my and Evanora's beach. My heart spasmed at the thought. I had only seen her there three times, yet my brain had confidently claimed the beach as ours. How delightfully terrifying. Still, I didn't feel like correcting myself and calling it Hannigan's Cove.

Our beach had occupants.

Down in the corner, where sand met the rocky cove, sat Ambrose, Peter, Owen, Tommy, and surprisingly, Sebastian Brightly. They were scattered around a fire, all their shoes discarded in a pile, their trousers rolled up to their knees, like it was a hot summer day and not spring crawling away from winter's grip. There was a crate next to the rumbling flames, the contents glinting merrily.

Tommy was sitting off to the side, close enough to the group to be involved, but far enough away to suggest he didn't want to be. His nose was in a book, but with the fire being his only source of light, I doubted he could even see the words. Owen was huddled next to Sebastian, a knitted blanket sprawled over their shoulders as they played a game that involved pressing their palms together and slapping the tops of each other's hands. Peter was the only one not wearing a shirt. His gut spilled over the top of his trousers, and his suspenders dug into his soft shoulders.

Ambrose, the leader of the pack, was leaning against the cove wall, his arms crossed, his face a calculated mixture of amused and bored.

I turned to head back up the embankment. I didn't want to face Pa, but I didn't want to face Ambrose more. But just as my knees braced themselves for the incline, I heard my name being called out.

"Grayson!"

I reluctantly turned to see Owen waving at me. I slowly lifted my hand and waved back. He ushered me closer. "Come on over!"

"Yeah," Peter crowed. "The water's warm!" He slapped his naked belly on the word *warm*.

I dropped my hand, my gaze darting to the embankment. Ambrose chuckled as he pushed himself off the rock wall and joined the others around the fire. "Grayson doesn't want to hang out with *us*," he said, sitting next to the crate. "He doesn't have good taste in friends. Plus, we don't smell like fish."

"Oh, st-stop it," Owen said, throwing Ambrose a dirty look before reaching into the crate and pulling out a glass bottle. He held it out in my direction. "He's only t-teasing. St-st-stay for a bit. We have refreshments."

I'd sooner eat sand. But my feet were roaring at me, begging for a break. I hobbled down the slope and made my way to the fire. The second I touched the sandy floor, I heard it.

A soft whispering.

I glanced at the boys by the fire. None of them were talking. Yet the whispering persisted, a low, groaning sort of sound that fluttered in and out of my ears. I looked around the beach for more people, only to find it abandoned of life. My eyes trailed to the waves. They crested and lurched on the sand, hungry for the solidness of the earth. And with each swipe at the beach, they hummed like a living being. They hummed for me.

"I say!" Sebastian gasped, pointing at my cheek, snapping me back to reality. "What on earth happened to you?"

His posh accent belonged in Lethe about as much as vinegar belonged in tea and was a dead giveaway that he wasn't from here. It was nothing like his uncle's. Where Mr. Brightly liked to cut corners and rip off a couple letters from the words he spoke, Sebastian seemed to enjoy enunciating each one in his gentle, floral tone.

My hand drifted to the crusty bandage on my cheek. "Just an accident at the docks."

"Looks painful," Tommy muttered, his eyes meeting mine from over the top of his book.

"Don't you have a salve for that or something?" Ambrose asked, his words, while accurate, meant to sting.

"I haven't been home yet." I sat carefully next to the fire, wedged between the crate and Ambrose. "I went for a jog."

Sebastian's amber eyes went wide, his smooth hand clutching the silk cravat around his throat. "For *fun*?"

Owen snickered, lightly bumping Sebastian's shoulder with his own. "For the . . . the *Hunt*, S-S-Sebastian."

Tommy coughed, turning a page in his book. Maybe he *could* read in the dark. "I'm not sure anyone runs for fun. Peter certainly doesn't."

Peter, who had been busy adjusting his suspenders, froze. "Are you calling me fat?"

Tommy coughed again, hard enough that his metal-framed glasses nearly slipped off his delicate nose. He sniffed, putting his book down and riffling through his trouser pocket. Pulling out a pipe, he gently knocked the bowl against the rock wall, emptying out the chamber of its ash and residue. "Do you?" he asked as he began stuffing it with bits of dried green clumps.

Peter frowned. "No. But neither do you."

Tommy struck a match and brought the pipe to his lips. Taking a long inhale, he held his breath for a handful of seconds before letting it out in a thin wisp of smoke. "My reason doesn't involve laziness."

Peter rolled his eyes. The movement seemed to make him dizzy; it took him a couple staggering steps to catch his balance. "Yeah, yeah. Shit lungs. We know."

I leaned forward, daring the flames to lick at my fingers as I held them out for warmth. So, it was Tommy who had asthma.

Owen reached around Ambrose, offering me an emerald bottle. "Do you like beer? Peter st-stole it from his pa's brewery up in Fariid."

I was about to decline when Ambrose snorted. "This delicate flower doesn't drink. One sip and he'll faint!"

I reached for the bottle. The glass was cool in my hands. I fumbled with the cap, its metal teeth digging into my palm.

Peter lurched forward. "I got it." Without giving me a chance to reply, Peter yanked the bottle out of my hands, placed the jagged cap between his teeth, and ripped it off. Spitting the cap onto the sand, he handed the bottle back to me.

I held the bottle gingerly, eyeing the slobber coating the neck of the glass. "Thank you."

Peter belched, the tangy smell matching the cloud of yeast floating around his head.

"So, *the Hunt*," Sebastian said, wiggling his fingers playfully. "It's quite the spectacle, I'm told."

"Oh, sure," Ambrose said. "Bravery and bloodshed and all that."

Owen rolled his eyes. "Ambrose's just playing t-t-t-tough. He loves th-the Hunt."

"Damn straight," Ambrose said, lifting his bottle into the air to toast himself before tilting it to his lips.

"It's *barbaric*," Sebastian said incredulously.

"It's *necessary*," Tommy said, taking another drag from his pipe. "Gingham said it best: *A bird catches fish—not because it delights in killing, but because it needs to feed. A death to support life, a cutthroat necessity.*" He lifted his book for us to see the worn green cover. "Call the Hunt any name you want, but it's a staple for Lethe."

"What," Sebastian said, "to maintain oath and order?"

"No," Tommy said, shaking his head. "To keep Lethe alive." Lungs back in working order, he snuffed out the pipe. "Lethe's money doesn't come from the Hunt. It comes in afterward."

"Ah," Sebastian said, tapping his bronze forehead. "Tourism. Uncle Graham mentioned that, but I don't understand half of what that crotchety old man says."

Ambrose nodded. "Once the Hunt is over, the ferry terminal opens back up, and in come the tourists."

I wiped at the lip of the beer bottle with my sleeve and took a tentative sip. Warm liquid that tasted like dirty socks slipped down my throat. I forced myself to swallow. "Are they hoping to see mermaids?" I asked.

Peter laughed, then belched again. Tommy shook his head. "Maybe once, a long time ago. Now they are hoping to see the spoils," he said.

Sebastian gulped loudly and began rubbing his neck again. "Excuse me, what do you mean by *spoils*?"

"You know. Mermaid s-sp-spoils." Owen pinned Sebastian with a mischievous grin. "Mermaid hair for wigs, fins for medicinal powders, s-sc-scales for makeup." He reached over and pinched Sebastian's cheek, and Sebastian slapped him away with a giggle. "The t-t-tourists love what we procure from mermaids. Having a s-s-successful Hunt means having a . . . successful t-tourist season."

"I'm sorry," Sebastian said, suddenly looking pale, "but I maintain my previous statement: Barbaric. The lot of you."

Ambrose's gaze flicked to mine, sharp and analyzing. His mouth twitched into a cutthroat grin. "Think you can handle it, Shaw?"

Sebastian pointed a finger at me. "Is this your first Hunt?"

I swallowed hard and nodded. I hadn't realized that I had actually finished the beer in my hand until Owen was handing me another. Peter rushed forward to help me with the lid, but I held up a hand. "I got it, thanks."

Peter lifted his hands into the air and hooted. "One of us! One of us!"

Ambrose clapped me on the back, a little harder than he needed to. "Little Grayson here is going to give us a run for our money, aren't you?"

I shifted away from Ambrose's reach. "Just because my pa is one of the best hunters on Lethe doesn't mean I'm going to be his mirror image." I took another sip of beer. "I like to faint, remember?" The beer was warming my empty stomach, softening the edges of the pain loitering on my cheek. I took another drink. Maybe it'd help block out the ominous whispers coming from the ocean waves. Even above the crackling fire, they were reaching my prickling ears, a soft lullaby that felt like down feathers hiding razor blades underneath.

Ambrose scoffed, shaking his head. "That's not how you drink beer. Here," he said, gripping the end of my bottle and tipping it so far up that it was nearly hitting my nose, "let me help."

I managed to catch most of the bottle's contents in my mouth before my throat closed up, causing me to sputter. The remainder of beer sloshed down my chin and onto my shirt, staining it with thick brown splotches. Sebastian gasped. Owen groaned. Peter snorted. And Tommy simply turned another page in his book.

"Yikes." Ambrose laughed, wiping his hands on his pants. "Can't hold your liquor, can you?"

I swiped my chin with my sleeve. My blood was thick and hot as it pumped anger through every inch of me. I felt sluggish and heavy with it. "About as much as you can."

Ambrose said, "What?" at the same time I yanked Owen's beer out of his hand and poured it over Ambrose's head.

I would have wrung that bottle dry if I could. I wanted every last drop to mix with his perfectly coifed hair.

Ambrose had the decency to wait until I had set the empty bottle down before he moved. Swift as the waves, he stood and lunged for me. I squawked and tried to wrestle myself free, but Ambrose's grip held firm as he pulled me toward the ocean's greedy hands.

"Wait!" I cried, struggling harder. "Stop!"

Ambrose ignored my pleas and continued dragging me to the water's edge.

The whispers had grown louder, singing to my panicked blood, my frenzied breathing.

Flashes of Ma's hands holding me down, pinching around my neck, of water surging into my mouth, my nose, my eyes. "Stop!"

"Don't be such a pansy bitch," Ambrose growled, swinging me forward until my boots connected with the receding waves. "It's only water."

It was death. It was a monster. It was—

The whispers were in my ears, pushing against my eardrums, needling into my brain.

A hoarse yelp escaped my clenched teeth as a wave jostled against my knees, soaking through my trousers, my thin socks, pooling in my boots.

And Ambrose let go.

I slammed into the wet sand just as another wave pushed upward. It splashed into my face, and all I could hear were hungry moans, starving for a piece of me.

Ambrose's laugh was loud and mean as I scurried out, tripping over my numb feet as I fought to put distance between myself and the water. Coarse sand bit into the soft flesh underneath my fingernails when my feet failed me once . . . twice . . . before finally finding the flimsy strength to stand. My bones felt brittle, one wrong move and they'd all splinter apart.

"N-n-not funny, Ambrose," Owen groaned as I stomped around the fire, aiming for the embankment, not daring to take my eyes off the sandy slope.

"My bad." Ambrose chuckled from behind me. "But for someone participating in the Hunt, it seems a bit ironic that you are so deathly afraid of water."

I'm not afraid of water, I wanted to say, but there was a sob lodged in my throat, and I was confident that if I tried to speak, it would come out too.

"It's going to be a downright riot when we have to do the swimming challenge," Ambrose went on, his words digging into the base of my spine.

"Ambrose," Tommy sighed, "*enough*."

"Fine, fine," Ambrose relented, and from the corner of my eye, I saw him sit back down by the fire and pull out another beer. "Just trying to have some fun."

Fun. His version of fun was violent, malicious, and cruel. That was fun? What did he do when he was angry, or hurt, or embarrassed?

The monsters weren't just out in the ocean. Sometimes they sat right next to you.

I SMELLED OF BEER AND PANIC, AND I HATED MYSELF FOR IT.

I couldn't go home. Pa would be furious if he saw the state I was in. Soaking wet, alcohol on my breath, my brain replaced by a cotton ball. I was a walking disaster—if you could call what I was doing *walking*. It was swaying, staggering, and tripping over my own two feet, at best. Those two beers had packed a punch on my empty gut.

The beach I had shared with Evanora was now sullied. I slumped against a tree halfway up the hill to my house. I stared at the dirt road as it zigzagged in my crooked vision. Two paths became one, then became two. "Maybe I'll find another beach," I said, my words jumbled and slurred. "Maybe she'll find me there."

I drifted off the road, stumbling through the rough terrain, slouching over fences, tripping onto forgotten deer trails. The base of Howler's Hill was slowly getting eaten away by the waterfall, eroding the black basalt columns until it was bending inward in a crescent shape. There was a walking path behind the waterfall now, all bright green moss and dangerously slippery rocks. The waterfall emptied into a circular pool of large broken chunks of basalt, which fed tiny tide pools, before eventually trailing into the ocean. Deep aqua water collided with the ocean's churning grays, which swallowed it up, constantly wanting more. It wasn't much of a beach, just a patch of scratchy sand and basalt column shards surrounded by wildflowers and weeds.

But it was the best I could do. If Evanora wanted to find me, I would be there.

I picked a bunch of purple flowers on my way down to the waterfall, but one slip on an algae-covered rock had me dropping them all. When I bent to pick them up, I found myself somersaulting down the last few steps clinging to the cliffside and landing flat on my back by the water's edge. Staring up at the night sky, I caught my breath, grateful the alcohol was dulling the pain I'd certainly feel tomorrow. The stars blinked at me, shimmering with secrets from a thousand years ago. What did Evanora look like at night, with the moonlight tangled in her hair and the stars dancing across her glowing skin? My breathing slowed, but my heart remained a wild thing, beating fiercely inside me.

I closed my eyes and whispered her name to the stars, adding my secret to theirs.

With the roar of the waterfall, the whispers were nearly nonexistent.

Nearly.

CHAPTER TWENTY-SIX

EVANORA

APRIL 8 – MORNING

I COULDN'T WAIT ANY LONGER.

Before the sun awoke from its slumber, before the water stirred with the sweeping of ships, before the pod could rise from their seaweed beds, I was gone.

I had wanted to leave earlier. But since Solandis's death, the pod had been on high alert. There had been curfews put into place, perimeters were checked and rechecked, borders had been adjusted, and Jorah wouldn't let me out of his sight—not that we were on speaking terms. The old fish would barely look at me. Which suited me just fine; the less he prodded into my life, the less likely he would find out about my and Illeron's scheming.

I had to wait for the sand to settle, for scales to soften, before I could make my move.

I only hoped that Grayson hadn't forgotten about me.

The concept was highly unlikely. But still, it filled my heart with apprehension. The last time I had seen him, I hadn't exactly promised to meet him again. If the boy with stormy eyes stopped going to the beach, our plan would be for naught. We would have no inside access, no way of obtaining hints about the Hunt, no way of tearing the organization down from the inside out. We would have nothing.

Everything was riding on Grayson Shaw.

I shouldn't have been disappointed when I discovered that the beach where Grayson and I had first met was empty. There were the smoking remnants of a fire, abandoned glass bottles littering the ground, and old footprints stomped into the sand, but nothing more. No purple flowers, no wandering boy searching the waves, nothing.

I crept along the water's edge, spanning one end of the beach's mouth to the other. There were hints of him on the wind, clips of his scent mixed with others. He had been here recently. I considered waiting for him. He *did* seem fond of this beach; perhaps he would come back.

I'd never been the patient sort.

My gut was telling me to go west. I followed the gentle tugging that seemed to pull me along the edge of the island. With the eastern coastline came black-sand beaches, stunning underwater cave systems, and cliffsides boasting natural rock arches that rocketed out of the ocean like a giant's legs. Going east also led to Lethe's largest populated area and the ferry terminal, which always reeked of oil and machines and humans. I never liked going east if I could help it. I hoped that Grayson Shaw wasn't from there.

The island jutted out like little fingers reaching for the waves, rows of wooden piers connected to Tully's local fishery.

The place where everything had fallen apart. Where Solandis had died.

My heart a wild thing within me, I sank low to the ground, my belly scraping along the sand. I kept my eyes ahead. If I spotted pieces of the merling, decaying bits of flesh or shimmering green scales, I wasn't sure my resolve would hold. I couldn't abandon the plan so early on. I *had* to push forward, both for the pod and for myself.

The coastline swept inward, showcasing an empty bay smothered with sea urchins. Scattered along the ocean floor were broken bits of glass, planks of wood, and even the ragged remains of a sail. I narrowly avoided a crumbling rudder that was leaning against a large spindly wheel.

There was a whale carcass nestled where sand met water, and by the smell of it, the poor gentle giant had been dead for a while. Its rubbery skin was crawling with crabs and bugs, and a few seagulls circled overhead, screaming for just a taste. Dried blood drenched the creature's mouth. Its bloated belly looked fit to burst. It stank of death, of darkness. Of the Cursed Beings.

I pushed on, trying not to grow desperate.

The island jutted out once more. I wound myself around the curving bend, the blood pulsing in my veins, the tugging in my soul growing more insistent.

I was getting closer. I had to be.

A warbled sound met my ears. It was like crashing thunder, hard and fast as it collided with the water. Zeroing in on the noise, I followed it, a mixture of curiosity and fear pushing me forward.

The roaring grew louder. It was a constant, heavy sound, and nearly drowned out my thoughts with its persistence.

I dipped inland, and I saw it. The strangest thing.

Water falling from the sky.

It wasn't rain. I knew that much. Rain was scattered all over, coating everything, everywhere, all at once. And rain always came to an end. This water was pinpointed to one location, where it fell in a continuous, steady stream, so loud that it was nearly deafening. And it didn't stop. The water slipped off the rocky cliffside and poured into multiple pools bordered by black stones before it melted into the ocean.

I was watching the miracle, marveling at the mechanics of water crashing onto the earth without rest, when I heard another sound.

A low, heavy groan.

My heart seized, my scales growing tight with dread. Sinking lower, I eyed the rocky shoreline, trying to spot who, or what, had emitted the sound.

My eyes fell onto a boy, crumpled into a heap, discarded on the shore. The tide was working its way inward, and water lapped at his ankles. But the boy didn't stir save for the occasional worried moan that slipped from his slackened lips and the rise and fall of his chest.

I was too far away to get a good visual. But I didn't need to.

My heart knew. It was singing at the sight of him.

It was Grayson Shaw. I had found him.

The tugging in my chest was nearly impossible to ignore. Making sure no one else was around, I swam closer, breaking through the water's edge and drifting to the shore.

Grayson appeared to be asleep. Bunches of wilted flowers lay strewn around him like a glowing aura. His chaotic brown curls were tangled and covered in sand. A dirty piece of fabric covered his cheek, hiding the birthmarks and freckles that resembled scattered constellations. His eyes were closed, but knowing the raging blue ocean orbs that were hiding underneath his fluttering eyelids was enough to send my stomach tumbling, my tail twitching, my fins shuddering. He looked so peaceful. I almost didn't want to wake him.

Almost.

Pulling myself out of the water, I reached out a trembling hand, and touched him.

CHAPTER TWENTY-SEVEN

GRAYSON

APRIL 8 - MORNING

SOMETHING—NO, *SOMEONE*—WAS TOUCHING ME.
I stirred with a groan, opening my eyes one at a time. They felt raw, scratching against my eyelids with every sluggish blink. It was like sandpaper. *No*, I corrected, rubbing my eyes like it would cure my blurry vision, *just sand.* Sand everywhere.

When I forced both eyes to open and *stay* open, they landed directly on the mermaid before me. Her long fingers were curled against my ankle, her skin shimmering in the sunlight like a thousand bursting diamonds. Her eyes, large and violet, were trained on me, and while her face was still with caution, a gentle smile tugged at the corners of her mouth.

"Evanora!" I gasped, straining to sit up on my elbows. "You found me."

The mermaid said nothing. She didn't breathe, didn't blink, didn't move. Her hair slipped off her shoulder, pooling against her bare chest like a waterfall of white silk.

I gave my head a rough shake, causing a spark of pain in my cheek as I attempted to rid myself of the sleep still clinging to me. "I waited for you. At the beach. But there were others. It wasn't safe."

Evanora's eyes danced, the colors shifting to amethysts and orchids. The smile still pressed to her lips grew.

My heart was thundering, and I found myself having to look away from her hypnotic stare before I spoke again. "I can't deny that I'm happy to see you."

I almost didn't feel it at first, the tightening of Evanora's grip on my ankle. But then her pointed nails pressed against my skin, *into* my skin. Her smile had grown large, too large for her sharply angled face. Her lips were pulled back to show her white teeth, her daggerlike canines, the stream of saliva bubbling on her gums. It didn't look natural, the way the smile hung on the lower half of her face. Eerie and sinister, like a fixed grin you'd see on a doll.

"Are you . . ." I licked my lips, forcing my eyes to hers. "Are you happy to see me too?"

There was nothing, and then Evanora was surging forward, hauling me down by my ankle and climbing up my body. She howled as she moved, the saliva now dripping down her chin, turning into thick blood as it dribbled onto me.

I yelped as she pinned me under her monstrous, impossible weight. Her tail slapped behind her as she scrambled up the length of me. Her clawlike hands were on my chest, my shoulders, my throat, her razor-sharp fin pressed to my jaw. She pushed her face down to mine, her hot breath carrying hints of blood and fish.

We were eye to eye.

I couldn't move, couldn't speak.

"It should have been you!" she screamed before raising her arm and bringing her forearm fin against my throat, slashing it in two.

I awoke with a gasp, lurching upward and clutching at my intact neck. A dream. It seemed so obvious now that it was a dream. But it had felt so real.

Keeping my hands locked around my neck, I grappled to understand where I was. My eyes darted from spot to spot, trying to make sense of it all.

The waterfall to my right, thundering merrily and ignoring my distress.

The dirt trail behind me, scattered with dead purple flowers.

The ocean before me, foam-crested waves licking through my pants.

And a mermaid to my left, gazing at me with those doe-like eyes, her hand resting carefully on my leg.

I gave a hoarse cry and shuffled back, yanking my leg out of Evanora's reach. The mermaid flinched at my sudden movement, pushing herself back into the coaxing waves until just her chest, shoulders, and head were protruding. The water seemed to swirl and quiver around her, like every inch of her was vibrating. I could see her tail swish and churn in the sand; she was ready to swim to safety in an instant.

We stared at each other for a handful of heartbeats. Mine was raging so loud that I was certain she could hear it.

Was *this* real? Or was I still dreaming?

Evanora's shoulders slumped, and she turned away. "This was a mistake," she murmured. "I shouldn't have come."

Evanora's words chilled me to the bone, and the thought of her leaving scared me more than any silly dream.

"Wait!" I called out, causing the mermaid to stop. When she looked over her shoulder at me, her chin dipping low to rest on her naked skin, I realized she was giving me a chance to speak. But no words came to mind. In fact, *nothing* was coming to mind. God, my head hurt. I hadn't realized a couple beers could be so potent. What had Peter's pa put in those bottles?

I squeezed my eyes shut and gripped the side of my head. "Are you real?" When Evanora didn't say anything, I cracked an eye open to grimace at her. "Are you real, or am I still asleep?"

Evanora raised a thin eyebrow. She was frowning, but her eyes were shining. "What answer would you like me to give you?"

I chuckled helplessly, dropping my hand. "I want you to be real," I admitted quietly.

Evanora remained silent for a moment before turning to face me. It was the smallest gesture, but I could have sobbed for joy at the sight of it. "Then I am real," she said.

And just like that, I felt it again, that insistent tugging in my chest, the one that tangled itself around my blood and whispered, *Important. This is important.* I looked at Evanora, and the connection strained, like my heart was trying to beat through my rib cage to get closer to the source.

I sat up and folded my cold, wet legs underneath me. "I thought I'd never see you again."

Evanora's mouth parted slightly, and she dropped her eyes to the foam accumulating on the rocky beach. "So did I," she whispered, like she was sharing a secret, or a deep-seated fear.

Unable to help it, I scooted closer to the water's edge. I wanted her to look at me again. "You aren't afraid of me?" I asked.

Evanora's gaze flicked to mine, and it nearly knocked the air out of my lungs. "You aren't afraid of *me*?" she countered.

I felt like everything hinged on my answer, like the world was holding its breath for me. Luckily, my heart knew the words before I had to put much thought into it. Careful to maintain eye contact, I slowly shook my head. "No." I sighed, leaning back onto my hands. "And I know I'm probably foolish because of it."

Evanora bit her lip, pinning the smile that rose to greet my words. "As am I, Grayson Shaw."

She remembered my name. Granted, her memory was likely immaculate and eternal. Still, hearing her say it made my stomach twist into knots that weren't entirely unpleasant.

Evanora slung her hair over her shoulder and began to curl it into one giant bunch. "In truth," she said, her stare drifting to the waterfall, "I couldn't stop thinking about you."

Was my heart going to give out on me? It certainly felt like it was skipping an unhealthy number of beats. "I couldn't either," I said, earning another heavy, undiluted stare from the mermaid. "I can't explain it. Something about you, about this feeling whenever I think about you, is so . . ." I trailed off. So *what*, exactly? Hypnotic? Mesmerizing? Intoxicating?

Important, my heart whispered.

Content with her hair, Evanora dropped her hands until they hovered just above the water's surface. They moved with the curve and caress of the waves, like she was dancing with it. The water pulsed and shifted, like it was aching to reach out and touch her. Her silken forearm fins dipped into the foamy waves, long and flowing with the tide. And for the first time, I looked at her. Like, *really* looked at her.

For starters, she wasn't exactly naked. I had always been careful to keep my eye level trained on the mermaid from the shoulders up, but looking at her now, I realized I didn't really need to. Where her breasts were, there were scales. Shimmering iridescent teardrops of all sizes danced from Evanora's hips, up and over her chest, before swirling farther up still; they dotted her shoulders, speckled her neck, and gleamed on her cheeks. She was a thousand mirror shards collected into a masterpiece.

And for the umpteenth time, I wondered how anyone could kill such a magnificent creature.

"What caused you to panic before?" Evanora asked.

I forced my eyes to the water. I wished she had asked me anything but that. "It was just a bad dream. I get them from time to time."

Evanora's hands went still; the water leapt up and splashed her fingertips. "Dream?"

"Yeah," I said slowly. "You know, when you're asleep?" I ran a hand through my hair, causing chunks of dried sand to tumble out. "Your mind creates stories."

Evanora's face lit up. "Oh! We call those visions. They are very precious to us."

Why was I blushing? I covered my burning cheek with my hand. "Even the bad ones?"

Evanora fixed me with a heavy stare. "*Especially* the bad ones. The ancestors send us the visions as a way to guide us. They are very wise, our ancestors."

Before I could even process the mermaid's words, she was on to the next subject. "And what's that?"

I looked to where she was pointing. "A waterfall."

Evanora stared at it. "I've never seen so much water falling in the same spot at the same time."

She was looking at it like it was a miracle. To a creature reliant on water, I guessed it was. She gazed at the waterfall, but I couldn't stop looking at her. "So beautiful." My mouth uttered the words before my brain had the half-decent thought of locking them away.

"What is?"

You. My sluggish brain finally caught up, snatching the word before it had a chance to escape off my tongue. "The waterfall," I managed to stammer out instead.

Evanora remained transfixed by the waterfall, but I could see the corner of her lips pull upward, a secret smile just for me. "What happened to your cheek?" she asked, her gaze drifting to me, smooth as oil on water.

My hand fluttered self-consciously to the crusty bandage. I was about to tell same lie I had told the boys at the beach, then decided against it. "I was struck." I blinked slowly, stifling the sudden nausea that came with the memory of Ma's fingernails digging into my skin, her feral shrieks ricocheting in my eardrums. When I opened my eyes, Evanora was right in front of me, studying me sharply.

She was so close. We shared the same breath.

Her attention was a force. I could feel the weight of it pushing against my skin, my muscles, my bones. Her eyes bored into me, *through* me, and I was certain I would collapse under the pressure of it all.

I inhaled sharply but kept still. "It was an accident." At least, I *hoped* it was.

Evanora's eyes were deadly. Large violet orbs with flecks of gold, like stardust trapped in an aurora borealis. Her diamond-shaped pupils dilated, pulsing against the endless purple galaxy. Widening, narrowing, widening, narrowing. It was hypnotic. I found myself drowning in them, too entranced to come up for air.

Evanora, done with her investigation, leaned back onto her hands. The space between us grew like a gaping mouth. "Did you deserve it?"

I found myself aching to close the space Evanora had created. "I'd like to think not," I said, smiling sheepishly. "But I have been known to have a way with words, in the worst possible sense."

The mermaid bit her lip, then reached for me.

Her fingers were cool against my cheek as she gently pried the bandage free. The tape clung feebly to my sweaty skin before losing its grip altogether, hauling the bloody gauze with it. The air kissed my naked cheek softly, crisp and refreshing against my sweltering skin. A shiver raced down my spine, but I wasn't sure if it was from the breeze, Evanora's touch, or the bloody bandage she was now holding. I closed my eyes.

"Please." I licked my lips, hating how weak I sounded, how my voice came out warbled and clipped. "Can you get rid of it?"

When Evanora didn't say anything, I cracked an eye open, my gaze taking a wide berth away from her hands until I found her face. "The bandage. I don't want to see it."

Evanora widened her eyes, then silently slipped into the water, submerging herself completely. I tried to follow her glow as she skirted out of view but decided to focus on more pressing matters, like breathing—and why my lungs weren't doing it.

One second passed, then two, then three. By the tenth second, I had concluded that I could breathe but that Evanora had left, likely put off by the lack of testosterone and masculinity oozing out of my pores.

Now that the gauze was off, my cheek was immediately itchy. I rubbed at the tender skin, groaning at the water as it fell unceremoniously onto the mermaid-free shore. "Stupid, stupid, stupid," I muttered.

"What does that mean?"

I looked up to see Evanora eyeing me curiously from her spot in the foamy waves. I dropped my hand and straightened, not bothering to hide the huge grin that bombarded my face. "What?"

Evanora's mouth pinched to the side, her hands—bandage-free, thank God—pulling at a lock of her hair. "Stupid. What does that mean?"

"Oh." I laughed. It sounded an awful lot like a donkey braying. "It means . . . dumb, foolish, ridiculous."

Evanora crept back up the beach, pulling herself onto the sand. Her tail flopped against me, the glistening snow-white fluke draping over my pants. "Should I be offended?" She huffed, bringing her shoulders up to her ears. "You were saying it over and over."

I laughed again. Thankfully, it sounded a little more normal. "Oh, no. I wasn't calling *you* stupid. I was calling *myself* stupid." Unable to help it, I jostled my foot, watching as Evanora's scales glittered as the sun kissed them at all angles. "I was worried I had scared you off."

It was Evanora's turn to laugh. Like chimes on a windy day. I could listen to her laugh for hours.

"A little blood doesn't scare me, Grayson Shaw."

I blew out a breath, shaking my head. "It scares *me*."

Evanora watched me from underneath her thick lashes. "Yes," she said demurely, "I can see that."

I bit my lip, tilting my face up. "Well? What do you think? Will I live?"

Her fingers were on me again, lightly gripping my chin, swiveling my head back and forth, inspecting my tattered cheek with the utmost scrutiny. My skin felt warm against her winter touch, a fire to her ice. She traced the scratches with her other hand, and I shivered again at the burst of electricity trailing after her fingers.

I flicked my eyes away, self-conscious, embarrassed, yet hoping she wouldn't let go.

After a rabid heartbeat, she clucked her tongue and released me. "You'll live," she declared, leaning in until her forehead nearly touched mine. "But just barely," she whispered, a teasing laugh following her words.

I swallowed hard, certain it was audible. Evanora began to pull away, turning her attention back to the waterfall, and I needed her.

To look at me.

To talk to me.

To touch me again.

With every fiber of my being, God, I needed her to do *something*. Which meant *I* needed to do something.

"How did you find me?" I blurted.

Evanora's face snapped back in my direction. The movement was so sudden that I nearly startled back. Her mouth pinched to the side, and she opened it once, only to close it again. Her eyes trailed to the water. "I just followed a feeling," she eventually said.

The connection that seemed to tether us together strained at her words. Could she feel it too?

Crazy. I was being *crazy*. I had to calm down. If I wasn't careful, Pa would lock me up with my ma faster than I could say *mermaid*.

Oh my God. Pa.

I looked at the sun wildly, then instantly regretted it. What time was it? I had fallen asleep on the beach. Pa hadn't seen me since he'd abandoned me on the side of the road. I could only imagine the state he was in. I leapt to my feet, earning an alarmed hiss from Evanora. I brought my hands up in a silent apology. "I overslept," I said, as if she would understand completely. "Pa must be worried sick about me."

Evanora's face relaxed, smothering her snarl. She cocked her head to the side, curiosity giving her sharp features a youthful glow. "Who is Pa?"

I patted out the wrinkles in my clothes and tried to smooth out my frizzy curls. The wrinkles didn't budge, but another hearty amount of sand sifted from my hair. Trying to look presentable was hopeless. "Pa," I said again. "My father."

Evanora's face morphed into recognition. "Why would your pa be worried about you? Are you not fully grown?"

Unable to help it, I let out a snort of laughter. "I am," I said, nodding. "But I still live with him. He was expecting me home last night, and I didn't show up. I'm . . ." I sighed, dropping my head. "I'm all he really has now. To not return home . . . He's going to assume the worst. He must be a wreck right now."

Evanora's shoulders drooped. "And you must leave. To ease his stress."

"I don't want to." I groaned, rubbing at the back of my neck. "You only just arrived."

A smile curled a corner of Evanora's lips. "It seems that whenever we meet, one of us is quick to run away again. Perhaps it's the world telling us we are fated to remain separated."

"No!" I said, a little too quickly. Evanora eyed me silently, her delicate eyebrows raised. I knew what I was about to say carried a lot of weight, so much so that I had to sit back down. "I would very much like to spend more time with you," I said earnestly.

Evanora slid closer to the shore. Her hands went back to dancing above the water, but as her fingers fluttered and coiled around the waves, I realized they were moving closer to me. I held my breath as her fingers slowly left the water's edge and landed hesitantly on my knee. "As do I."

Something in my chest shifted, and I knew I would drain the ocean, move mountains, and handpick every star in the sky just to see Evanora again. "I have an idea," I said, standing.

Evanora's eyes were on me as I moved around the rocky pools, peering into each one until I found what I was looking for. I had spotted it years ago, long forgotten and abandoned. I hadn't thought much of it until now. Taking a deep breath, I climbed onto one of the slick boulders, my knees popping as I moved. The waterfall's steady roar echoed behind me, its mist brushing against my back. I rolled up my sleeves, stealing a quick glance at Evanora. "Don't be afraid."

Before the mermaid could respond, I plunged my hands into the swirling pool, my fingers tangling in shards of basalt, sand, and thick strands of rope.

Evanora recoiled with a hiss when I pulled out the net. "It's okay! It's okay," I hurriedly reassured her, hoisting the net higher until I could hear the familiar jingling. I tugged on the loose string of bells; the row slipped off the old net with ease. I made sure to keep careful eye contact with the mermaid as I dropped the net back into the pool, holding only the bells.

Evanora remained tense, but she didn't move as I approached, holding out the bells like a gift. She took them, turning the strand over in her hands, eyeing the algae-covered brass as though it might bite her. Her violet eyes met mine, uncertainty clouding her gaze.

I laughed, taking the strand back. "You ring them." I jostled the bells, producing a waterlogged jingle.

Evanora flinched at the sound, her fins twitching. She snatched the bells out of my grip, her gills flaring. "I know that!" she snapped. She paused for a heartbeat before mimicking my movement, flicking her wrist and sending a vibration through the bells. They clinked and teetered against one another, chiming heartily.

"It's a form of music," I explained as she rang the strand again.

Evanora fingered the bells, her eyes trailing to where I had discarded the net. "It sounds like capture."

A swell of guilt threatened to squeeze my lungs into oblivion. "I guess it would," I said, ducking my head. Eyeing the end of the strand dangling from Evanora's hands, I plucked it up timidly, my fingers skimming the smooth scales of her tail. "Can these bells be different?"

Evanora cocked her head to the side, her mouth pulled into a frown.

I twisted the strand, gently taking the bells. "These can sound like freedom, like a chance for us to see each other again."

Evanora's frown loosened. "How?"

I thought for a moment, then shook the bells. Not haphazardly, like an excited child during Christmas caroling, but strategically, systematically.

Three solid shakes, then a pause for five seconds, then three more shakes. I repeated the process.

"What are you doing?" Evanora asked, a lilting giggle snagging her words. "You're acting possessed."

"I'm creating our signal." I handed her the strand. "If you ring it how I just did, I'll know it's you." I gestured to the bells. "Now you try."

Evanora gave another laugh, then repeated my ringing pattern. On the last chorus of jingling, she dropped the bells onto her lap, staring at them in confusion. "I don't understand. I may ring them, but how will you hear them?"

I grinned. "That's the easiest part. I live up there"—I pointed to the dirt trail behind me—"just beyond the forest at the top of the cliff. The sound carries surprisingly well. I'll be able to hear them, I promise."

Evanora stared at the path sidling along the mountain wall. She then looked at my legs, as if she suddenly remembered that I was human and she was not. I had never been self-conscious of my legs until that moment, when her eyes were on me, on the thing that made us so, so different.

"And will you remain within earshot of the bells at all times?" she asked.

I shook my head. "We should only meet when there is less of a chance to get caught. Morning or sunset. It'll be safer for you, and I'll have a better chance at sneaking out of the house." I drove a finger into the ground. "And we meet *only* at this beach. Anywhere else is just too risky."

Evanora's fingers slid along the brass bells. I never knew I could be so jealous of an inanimate object. I tried to rub the blush off my face, failed miserably, and stood.

"I really need to go," I said, looking over my shoulder. "Pa's likely throwing a fit."

When I looked back at Evanora, she was unsuccessfully masking her disappointment. "Very well," she said. She leaned forward, wedging the strand of bells between two large rocks.

I clasped my hands together and pressed them to my lips, throwing up a silent prayer before speaking. "Does that mean you'll come back?"

Evanora made sure the bells weren't going anywhere before she flicked a look over her shoulder, a grin morphing her lips into a coy, playful thing. She waited a painfully long time before replying, her voice low, sweet, and luring, "Perhaps."

I stifled a laugh and shrugged, my hands slapping against my sides. "I'll take what I can get."

I had a feeling, though, that it would never be enough.

Evanora pushed off the sand and floated into deeper waters. "Until next time, Grayson Shaw."

I took a step back, unwilling to sever the moment just yet. If I blinked, if I breathed, I knew it would be over. "Until next time."

Evanora allowed the waves to consume her. I could have sworn she waited until the last possible second to fully submerge. Her eyes never slipped away from mine.

My body ached, my breaths were ragged, and my mind was as loud as the waterfall.

But my heart . . . God, my heart was singing.

CHAPTER TWENTY-EIGHT

EVANORA

APRIL 8 – MORNING

DON'T FEEL GUILTY. DON'T FEEL GUILTY. THOSE WERE the words I repeated to myself the entire way home.

I was feeling incredibly guilty.

But I was also feeling something else, something far more troubling than a little guilt.

I felt light.

Lighter than sea-foam. Lighter than air.

I knew it. I just *knew* it.

With every thrum of my heartbeat, with every scale on my body, with every pulse of my Gift, I knew there was something different about Grayson Shaw. Something good, something *pure*, something that connected us.

I didn't understand it, but deep in my heart, I knew that Grayson Shaw had *everything* to do with the magic that sang within me.

And I was absolutely enraged about it.

Learning more about Grayson Shaw and how he fit in with my Gift didn't matter. None of it mattered.

The key, my ancestors whispered as I neared the edges of my kingdom.

I blocked them out, ignoring the pull of my heart that came with their words.

The plan was the only thing that mattered.

Not Grayson. Not the connection. And certainly not how he made my insides squeeze whenever he looked at me.

Like I was a precious jewel.

Mavi and Illeron were waiting for me in the empty weaponry. Mavi, who was the first mermaid Illeron had contacted when our scheming began, rushed forward, her deep golden eyes wide and her hands clasped tightly together at her chest. "So?" she asked breathlessly. "How did it go?"

Illeron hung back, his arms crossed against his chest, his teeth worrying at his bottom lip. "Well, she has all her scales and fins and doesn't reek of fear, so obviously, it went better than I was expecting."

I rolled my eyes at the warrior. "Always have a way with words, don't you?"

Illeron nodded his head in a silent and all-too-mocking thank-you.

I looked at Mavi and pasted on a smile. "It went fine. Better than fine. We have a plan in place to be able to meet up more often." I shrugged, the movement stiff. "And it was his idea. I didn't even have to encourage it."

The wielder bobbed up and down excitedly, a poorly restrained squeal exiting her lips. She reached forward and grabbed my hands. "That's amazing! And?" She shook my hands fervently. "Did he tell you anything? Spill any secrets?"

Illeron let out a short chuckle. "Calm down, merling. They've only officially met once. Evanora knows better than to push the boy too quickly without laying down the basic building blocks of trust." He stopped. "Oh, gods, at least I hope she does. Do you?"

Mavi pouted, throwing a glare at the warrior from over her shoulder. "Don't call me a merling!"

"You still have spots."

"Only just!" Mavi turned back to me, her tail flicking self-consciously. "They're fading, aren't they?"

Breaking free from Mavi's grip, I lifted my hands in an effort to stop the bickering. "You two are exhausting. Yes, Mavi"—I pointed at her vibrant purple tail—"your spots are fading. And *yes*, Illeron"—I scowled at the warrior—"I *do* know better." I exhaled heavily. "Did Jorah ask about me today? Was he suspicious?"

Illeron shook his head. "I kept a close eye on him. He spent most of his time visiting with members of the pod and praying in the garden."

"Oh, enough about that old fish." Mavi blew a raspberry. "Tell us how the meeting went!" She looped her arm through mine. "We want to hear all about it."

Illeron frowned. "Speak for yourself."

I forced a laugh and uncoiled myself from Mavi. "To be honest, I'm actually rather tired. I think I'm going to go sleep for an eternity or two, then light the lanterns."

Mavi's face fell, but she gave her head a quick shake. When she looked at me again, she was grinning. "Being a master manipulator must be exhausting. Go get your rest. We can talk more later, perhaps practice combining our Gifts again." She spun and swam for the door, squealing as she went. "This is all so dangerously thrilling!"

I stared after Mavi, feeling bad that my excitement didn't match hers. It should've matched hers. If anything, I should have been *more* excited.

"I wasn't serious before."

I crossed my arms and turned to look at Illeron. "What?"

"About you returning all battered and afraid. I knew you'd be fine."

I cocked my head to the side. "Considering what you said to me during our sparring lesson, I find that hard to believe."

Illeron winced, his gaze fleeting. I clucked my tongue and swam forward, erasing some of the distance separating us. "There are some things I need to do on my own. Whether you like it or not. Whether you think I can do them or not."

Illeron dropped his head, his jaw tight. "I do think you have what it takes," he said quietly. "It's just . . ." He sighed, his eyes meeting mine. "It's a hard thing for me to admit."

I smiled, reaching forward and flicking him on the nose. "It's because you're too proud."

Illeron grabbed my wrist as I pulled away. His grip was strong but kind. "It's because I'm worried you won't need me."

His words were a tidal wave, splashing into me, pinning me in place. "Of course I need you," I protested.

How could he think such a thing? Solandis was the catalyst, the piece that had started it all, but Illeron was the driving force. He was the very reason I was risking everything by going to the beach to see Grayson. He was the one collecting the mermaids willing to fight, the one teaching them to be fearless warriors. Not need him? The thought was ridiculous.

I tried to pull away, but Illeron's grip was resolute. His eyes flashed, and there I was, frozen again. "Not where it truly counts."

I opened my mouth to speak, but Illeron shook his head, a quiet sigh on his tongue as he released me from his grip.

"Go rest, then light the lanterns," he said, drifting to the shelves of discarded bone knives and spearheads. "Can't have you slipping up with your duties, otherwise Jorah *will* get suspicious."

I allowed myself to hover in place for a handful of seconds more before leaving. The conversation was far from over; the water felt heavy between us, thick with words left unsaid and emotions too small and precious to relinquish. But Illeron was right—I needed to continue on as though things were fine.

I BEGAN TO LIGHT THE LANTERNS BEFORE DARKNESS SETTLED INTO the bones of the city. As I breathed life into each one, I found myself thinking of Grayson Shaw.

I also found myself smiling.

Sure, he was young; I had no doubt lived countless lives before he was even conceived. But there was a boyish charm about him, an excited innocence he radiated. I rather enjoyed the way his eyes twinkled when he was pleased, and the crinkle in his nose just before he laughed. And the fact that he hated the sight of blood sent a pleasant shiver down my spine. A human, afraid of blood? That *had* to be a first.

The key, my ancestors whispered in the undercurrent. *The power of three.*

My smile vanished. I sparked a lantern a little harder than I needed to; it flared brightly for a heartbeat, the glass containing it creaking from the heat, before it settled into a warm glow.

I couldn't think of Grayson like that. I couldn't think of Grayson at *all*. Even though my heart ached for the truth, to know what my ancestors meant with their riddles, I knew that my powers would suffice for now. They had to. And in the end, if we were successful in overthrowing the Hunt, my powers would cease to even matter.

Still, the part of me that wanted to know, wanted to know *really* badly.

I stopped at the last lantern. It rested on the very edge of our city, on the precipice of safe and unpredictable. I looked into the unnatural darkness of the Barrens.

And I heard it.

I heard *them*.

Come closer, the cavernous mouth of the Barrens whispered.

A cool tendril of fear snaked its way up my scales before settling into my veins like ice. There was a pressure on my chest as I squinted hard at the dark.

"Hello?" I called out, hoping in vain that it was a bender merling trying to spook me.

There was nothing, only the eerie stillness that lived within the Barrens, the smell of decay and sulfur.

I shook my head. "I'm being foolish," I mumbled, turning away. "Or, as Grayson Shaw would put it—stupid. I'm being stupid."

Closer, I heard the darkness say.

I whipped around, facing the Barrens. I was fairly certain my heart had stopped beating.

The Cursed Beings were speaking to me.

And I could *understand* them.

Before I knew it, I was inching toward the underwater cliff, my forearm fins flexed with nerves.

Come, the Cursed Beings breathed. *Come see what secrets we hold.*

My fins brushed the edge of the drop-off, and I peered into the utter blackness of the Barrens. Illeron had been right—the closer you were to the dark void, the more you could hear them. It had always been jumbled nonsense before, a chorus of voices overlapping with not a single one breaking free to make sense.

But that was during the day, when I was a healthy distance away from the Barrens. Even when I'd had to enter the endless dark to find Solandis, I could hear the Cursed Beings, but I couldn't understand them.

But now I could. And they were talking to me.

Queen Evanora, the darkness crooned. *We know what it is you desire.*

A shudder rippled through me. The pressure in my chest was getting worse. Despite the alarms blaring within my mind, I found myself unmoving. I wasn't entering the Barrens, but I wasn't deserting it either. "I'm sure many know what I desire."

There was a grating sound, like nails on stone, and I realized it was the Cursed Beings laughing. I refused to show my fear to the evil lurking within the shadows. "You can try to guess, if you'd like," I said, careful to keep my voice strong and unyielding.

Oh, the Cursed Beings sighed, *we don't need to guess.*

The voices began to overlap again, excited at having my attention, but I could still make out their words.

You wish for the flourishing of your pod.
You wish for the end of the Hunt.
You wish for your powers to grow.
You wish to be worthy of the crown.

I rolled my eyes, but the nonchalant movement took effort. "Those are hardly secrets; I talk about those things every day." I grinned at the depths, cutthroat. "Surely you can do better than that."

There was silence, and then: *You wish to know how your ammah died.*

I couldn't breathe. "My ammah?" I ventured.

Oh, yes, the darkness moaned. *You know your appah died at the hands of a bloodthirsty human, but the great Nereida? You don't know why she left the city borders one day and failed to return. And it eats you alive. Every. Single. Day.*

I bit my lip, the flimsy facade of bravery crumbling. "What happened?" I asked, my voice barely audible.

But the Cursed Beings heard. They laughed again, the sound causing me to cringe away as if I'd been struck. It sounded so close, like they were right next to me, breathing down my neck, whispering into my ear. *Come closer, and we'll tell you.*

It was a trap. They were trying to lure me into the Barrens, to fall into their shadow. And I'd be lying if I said it didn't almost work. It took all of my strength to pull myself away from the cliff's edge, every piece of willpower to turn my back to the Cursed Beings. "That won't work on me," I said. "I know better than to trust you."

More silence. *Pity,* the voices hummed. *We thought you'd be stronger.*

"Well"—I swept farther away—"I'm sorry to disappoint you."

You'll come back, the Cursed Beings promised. *Whether you wish for it or not, you'll seek the darkness again. Next time, you won't be able to resist. And it will end in agony.*

I swiveled back to face the abyss, my movement so fast that I sent up a cloud of sand. "I'm not afraid of you," I growled, trying to convince both myself and the Cursed Beings.

The evil within the Barrens laughed again. *You should be,* they whispered, fading into the blackened void. *You will be.*

CHAPTER TWENTY-NINE

GRAYSON

APRIL 8 – MORNING

THE WALK HOME WAS A BLUR. I WAS FAIRLY CERTAIN I LEV-itated the entire way.

There was something about Evanora. I *knew* there was something about her. And it wasn't the startlingly obvious fact that she was a mermaid—it went *so much deeper* than that. The connection between us . . . It felt infinite, ancient, timeless. Two souls trapped in two different worlds, destined for a single purpose.

I wasn't sure what that purpose was, but I was nearly delirious in my ambition to find out. I felt it in my lungs, in the air I breathed, in my heart, in the blood it pumped. An infinite loop, an unending song, a chorus of *Evanora, Evanora, Evanora.*

I knew exactly what I would do first when I got home: I was going to open my bedroom window. I'd only leave to eat or work. Nothing else mattered. There was nothing else. Only Evanora.

Pa had other plans. As I stumbled up the dirt path to our front steps, he barreled through the door, his rage a hurricane that hit me head-on. His face was a grotesque mask—creases like craters, brow furrowed, lips curled in a snarl that trapped his bared teeth.

"Where in God's name have you been?" he bellowed, his voice slamming into me, knocking the wind out of my good mood.

I shrank against his shadow, a flower wilting in the dark. "I was—"

"Do you know how worried I was, boy? How *bloody* worried I was when you didn't come home?" Thick flecks of spittle shot from Pa's mouth as he bit out the words. His eyes were so wide that I could see the glossy white circling his entire dark irises. "I was sick with it. Sick with fear that my son was in trouble." He ran his hands through his hair, pulling several of the coarse strands from the leather tie holding them together. Pa turned away from me, shaking his balled-up fists like he was getting ready to strike. Strike *what*, I didn't know. "I checked in with the Warrens, searched the docks." He choked out a humorless laugh. "I even went to Rose Hill to see if you had crawled your way back there."

Nerves bristling, I forced myself to stand tall. "I went for a jog, just like you commanded."

Pa whirled back to face me. The veins were bulging in his neck, threatening to burst through the skin with every pounding throb. "Yes. Jog *home*. It shouldn't have taken you all damn night."

I shrugged stiffly. "Well, I'm slow."

Pa began to pace, wringing his hands together. The callused skin looked red and chapped, like he had been doing the same repetitive motion all night. "I was about to check the beaches." His voice was so low that I had to strain to hear it. "Do you understand me? I was about to check the beaches, Grayson." His shoulders started to shake; the pillar was crumbling. "After Warrick, I—" He shook his head viciously, a mournful growl on his tongue. "I was beginning to assume the worst."

I could feel myself deflating. I sighed, pinching the bridge of my nose. "I'm *fine*, Pa."

Pa's pacing came to an abrupt halt. He was in front of me once more, his hands gripping the sides of my arms. He gave me a rough shake that sent my bones rattling. "Do you want to end up like him? Do you?" He was shouting again, so loud it sent my eardrums ringing.

I opened my mouth to speak, but Pa's arms were around me, pulling me into a firm hug, his face buried in the crook of my neck, his breath shaking with emotion. I froze, unsure how to react. Pa . . . hugging me? He never did that—not even after Warrick died, or when Ma was sent to Rose Hill. It was like he was allergic to affection.

His grip tightened, and I could feel his heart pounding against my chest. "You're all I've got," he whispered, and a chill ran up my spine. "Don't you know that?"

When I found my voice, it was a feeble thing. "I'm sorry, Pa."

He held me for a moment longer before clearing his throat and wrenching himself free, as though *I* were the one holding *him* hostage in the embrace. "Right." He sniffed, wiped his eyes with the back of his hand, and fixed me with a glare. "Don't pull a stunt like that again, you hear me?"

I nodded, looking at the father figure I was more familiar with—blisteringly cold, ruthlessly hostile, and scared to love.

Penny whickered in the barn. Pa frowned at the sky. I stared at my feet.

"Right," Pa said again, turning his frown to me. "I was expected at the shop over an hour ago." He said it as though him being tardy was my fault, which I felt was both harsh and fair.

"Sorry," I said again.

Pa shook his head. "No matter. Do you still have that box of mangled nets?"

"It's in the loft. Why?"

Pa nodded. "Pull it out. We can work on them tonight when I return."

I was about to ask what on earth we needed a bunch of destroyed nets for.

And then I remembered.

For the Hunt.

For killing mermaids.

Mermaids like Evanora.

"OH, FOR THE LOVE OF JOB!"

I looked up in time to see the net gauge slip from Jasper's hands for the umpteenth time that afternoon. Despite the first challenge being only a couple days away, Jasper's attempts at crafting a net were as good as the day I had taught him how—which was a long time ago. He had been going at it all morning and was still fumbling with the initial row of knots.

Jasper stiffly shuffled his bad leg to the side and leaned down to grab the net gauge. In the process, he dropped the netting needle, then the shears, then the poor excuse for a net. "For the sake of Pete!"

"Here," I said, dropping my own net and hopping off the bench to retrieve his items. "Before you go and name all the people in the Bible."

Jasper sat up with a huff, his frizzy ginger locks splaying like wispy fingers. He frowned at the instruments I placed back into his hands. "Bath time with the twins is easier."

I smirked, dusting off my pants and perching back onto the bench. "It's really not that bad," I said, gesturing to his net.

Jasper raised his row of straggly knots. "I beg to differ." He sighed, tossing the net next to his feet. "I'll never get the hang of it. But it doesn't matter. I'll win the crowd over with my charm." He flashed me a smile. "Show them what I'm capable of."

I tried not to stare at Jasper's bad leg, the awkward angle it seemed to permanently be stuck in. How was he going to swim? Or fight? I focused on the net in my hands instead and began looping the rope around the net gauge. "You should just focus on the challenges, not making a good first impression." *You should focus on trying to make it out alive.*

Jasper groaned, leaning his head back as he rolled his eyes at the sky. "That's a loser's attitude." He drooped forward and fumbled with his net and tools. "Don't you want to do well on the Night of the Betting?"

"Not really."

Jasper scoffed. "Well, that makes you the first." He peeked at my hands, then copied my movements. "Slow down."

I looked up. "What?"

"Slow down." Jasper pointed at my hands. "How am I supposed to cheat off you if you're moving at lightning speeds?"

"We aren't in school anymore, Jasper. I don't think this qualifies as cheating."

The net gauge slipped again. Jasper looked like he was about to throw the net into the water. I slowed down.

"You don't have enough tension." I brought my hands forward, showing Jasper as I wrapped the rope around the gauge. "You need to keep it taut right up until you make the knot. Pinch it with your finger here," I said, trapping the rope at the top of the net gauge with my index finger. "Create a loop over your hand—"

Jasper struggled to keep up. "Why does yours look so different?"

"Because I'm left-handed," I said, trying to keep my impatience at bay. "Just do what I'm doing, but with your right hand." I waited for Jasper to catch up. "Now you need to thread your netting needle just above your pinched finger. Underneath the first two lines of rope, and over the last one." I pulled on the netting needle, cinching the newly formed knot tightly. "You need to keep the net gauge in place until the very end . . ." My sentence trailed off as I saw the net gauge on Jasper's lap and a gaping hole in his net. "Otherwise, the hole won't match the others."

Jasper winced, ducking his head. "Show me again?"

I pinched my lips together. "Absolutely not."

"Hello, there!" a voice called from the boardwalk.

Sebastian Brightly glided along the walkway, his silver cane thumping against the rotting boards. He wore a large top hat with a green fabric trim that matched the silk handkerchief poking out of his suit pocket. His hands were gloved, his shoes shiny. He looked completely out of place.

I lifted a hand slowly when I realized he was speaking to Jasper and me—or rather, just me. "Afternoon."

Sebastian stopped where the boardwalk met the crumbling steps leading to the piers. He positioned both his hands on the top of his cane and stared down at us. "How's that hangover of yours?"

Jasper, who had gone back to meddling with his net at the sight of Sebastian, reared his head to gawk at me. My face began to burn from the heat of his stare. "Not as bad as yours, I'd wager."

Sebastian lifted a hand to his chest, his fingers flitting like butterfly wings. "Quite so. I hate to admit it, but I only just got out of bed a little over an hour ago. Shameful. A waste of a perfectly fine day."

Jasper snorted, returning to his net. "Yeah. *Shameful*," he muttered, mocking Sebastian's accent.

Sebastian shot Jasper a look before pelting me with a smile. "No jogging for you today, I take it?"

I shook my head, sheepish. "No, not today. I don't think my stomach could handle the turbulence."

Sebastian laughed a crisp, jaunty tune. "How dreadful! And your head?"

"Like I've been smacked with a hammer."

"Positively ghastly," Sebastian agreed, even though he resembled the picture of perfect health. "Remind me to never accept alcohol of any kind from Peter again."

"As long as you remind me of the very same thing," I countered.

Sebastian nodded. "Deal." He pulled a delicate-looking watch from his pocket, the silver chain catching in the light. "I best be off. Uncle wished to see me this morning, and I'm"—Sebastian glanced at the watch again—"officially late." He sucked in a breath. "Staying in that man's good graces is difficult at the best of times. I doubt my tardiness will help my case."

Jasper looked up from his net, which was coiled around his fingers like he was attempting to create Jacob's ladder. "Don't take off your shoes. Bad things have been known to happen to abandoned shoes at the docks." He leaned forward, as if sharing a secret. "I heard some scumbag around here fills them with fish guts!" he said in a stage whisper, his eyes wide with shock. "The horror!"

Sebastian glowered at Jasper, who smiled innocently back at him. "I'll make sure to keep my shoes on my feet, Mr. Warren."

Jasper offered Sebastian a thumbs-up. "Smart man."

Sebastian literally *harrumphed* and walked away, swinging his cane with newfound purpose. I waited until he was out of earshot before frowning at Jasper. "What was that all about?"

Jasper's mouth dropped open. "*What was that all about?*" He pointed at me. "What was *that* all about?"

I faltered. "What?"

"Oh," he scoffed, shaking his head. "I think you very well know what."

I glanced down at my hands. "I was just being nice. You should try it sometime."

"Right. Having drinks with the most spoiled brat alive is you just *being nice.*" Jasper's brow creased. "And for your information, warning him about taking off his shoes *was* me being nice." Jasper picked at a weakening knot in his net before casting another scorching look my way. "What were you doing drinking Peter Lyre's alcohol anyway? Are you trying to fraternize with the enemy?"

I bit back a laugh. "The enemy?"

Jasper nodded his head vehemently. "Yes, Grayson, the *enemy.* You know who Peter hangs out with. Sebastian, Owen, Ambrose." He spat out the last name like it was poison. "The Hunt makes enemies out of all of us; *no one* is safe. Trying to get ahead by teaming up with those guys is a bad move, and you better not come crying to me, your *best friend*, if they turn around and kick you out of their gang."

There was no talking sense into Jasper. I wanted to tell him that, by his reasoning, *he* was *also* my enemy. But I also wanted him to stop talking about the Hunt. I leaned forward and placed a hand on his knee. It was practically vibrating as jealousy radiated off him. "I'm sorry."

Jasper sniffed, tilting his nose into the air. "Good."

"I'll make sure to invite you next time."

"You better."

Satisfied, Jasper returned to his rat's nest of rope. I stood, stretching out my stiff back. I hadn't been lying; I felt like absolute death. The gruesome jog, not to mention sleeping on the rocky beach, had left me feeling pains in places I hadn't known existed. I hobbled down the dock, kicking life back into my legs and swinging the ache out of my joints. The seagulls cried out overhead, begging for scraps. I wanted to tell them that Mr. Brightly didn't give anything away for free.

The waves lapped at the dock's wooden legs, a gentle *shushing* sound mingling with the ocean breeze. I closed my eyes and tilted my face to the sky, where the sun rewarded me with its warmth. The wind stroked my cheeks, and I was reminded of Evanora's fingers reaching for me, tracing my skin with her icy touch. I sighed, my shoulders relaxing despite other, deeper parts of me tensing up. I had seen her just a few hours ago, yet I was desperate to meet with her again. When would I hear the bells? Tonight? Tomorrow? Never? I groaned, pushing the palms of my hands into my eyes, not stopping until I saw stars.

Grayson Shaw, I thought, *you truly* are *hopeless.*

CHAPTER THIRTY

EVANORA

APRIL 9 – EVENING

MY MIND WAS ALIVE WITH THOUGHTS AS I SWAM for the beach.

Would Grayson Shaw hear the bells?

Was I swimming into a trap?

Would the plan even work?

I created an answer for each of the questions the nagging voice in my head brought up.

Yes. The boy had told me he would hear the bells. I just had to ring them like he had shown me.

No. I was not swimming into a trap. I highly doubted Grayson had the capacity to do something so malicious.

Yes. *Yes.* The plan *would* work. Because it had to. Because there was no other choice.

It was nearly dusk. The sun was in the process of creating a fantastic sunset against the horizon, full of ruby reds and deep burnt oranges. The way the colors played in the ocean's waves was almost dreamlike.

The beach was as beautiful as the last time I had seen it. The waterfall was a turbulent force, careening off the cliffside before slamming into the rock pools below, creating walls of rainbow mist and whirlpools of foam and sediment. I wished I could crawl over the sharp boulders to feel the full power of it. But then I remembered the discarded net in there and decided against it.

And the flowers. The entire embankment was nearly overrun with splotches of yellow, sprigs of white, and splashes of purple. I had failed to see them before. The way they swept up to the wooden steps hugging the cliffside, scooping widely where the beach had carved itself out. I wanted to touch the velvet petals, but they were just out of my reach.

Instead, I went for the bells. My fingers slipped along the slimy brass as I placed the row of bells on my lap. My heart was thundering. I held a hand in front of my face, watching as my fingers twitched and trembled. And then a terrible realization hit me.

I was excited.

I shook my hand out viciously and grabbed the bells with conviction. *Yes,* I told myself, *I am excited. At getting closer to the boy, at learning his secrets, at warming the temperature between us.*

Still, my heart was a beast. And I didn't need it or the nagging thoughts to tell me that the temperature between me and Grayson Shaw was already stifling.

I rang the bells.

It took several tries in the silent dusk before I heard hurried footsteps. The sound traveled, and I couldn't see who they belonged to. A burst of white-hot fear leapt through me, the alarm of *trap, trap, trap* echoing through my subconscious. I dropped the bells and ducked behind one of the boulders outlining the rock pools. Sinking low to the ground, I tucked my tail between my arms and waited.

There was nothing, and then, pensively: "Evanora?"

The straining in my chest at the sound of his voice was a ghastly, treacherous thing, and I hated myself for it. Hesitantly, I peeked over the boulder.

And there he was.

Grayson Shaw stood at the water's edge, hands on his knees, looking breathless and adorably disheveled. At the sight of me, the boy straightened, his entire face morphing into a look of pure, unfiltered joy.

And I realized my face was doing the same thing.

The plan, I recited as I crept up to the beach. *Remember the plan. Remember why you are here.*

The key, my ancestors whispered back. *The key, the power of three, the power—*

Grayson lowered himself slowly to the ground, folding his legs underneath him. He smoothed out his frazzled curls, his eyes not leaving mine. "Hi," he said around a lopsided smile.

Gods, was it possible that the connection tethering us together had gotten tighter? I felt like I couldn't breathe, and I wished my heart would calm down to an acceptable rhythm. I dared a quick glance at my fingers. They were *still* shaking. I pushed them underneath the water, away from prying eyes.

"Hello." I rested my back against one of the boulders closest to the beach. The night air rippled along my torso like chilly love bites, sending shivers down my submerged tail. "It's good to see you," I breathed, blinking up at the boy.

A blush crept along Grayson's face, and my insides did something violent. "I didn't know if you were going to come back," he said quietly, his fingers digging holes into the sand.

I giggled and leaned forward, resting a hand on his. "I wanted to come."

Two things occurred to me. The first: I wasn't lying. The second: I didn't *have* to touch Grayson to convince him; my words would have been enough.

But I wanted to. To feel the remnants of sunlight on his skin, the heartbeat underneath. I needed to.

The boy's fingers stilled underneath mine, and he shuddered. I had a suspicion that he craved the contact almost as much as I did.

I withdrew, leaning back against the boulder. "We planned it, did we not?"

Grayson, still staring down at his now-empty hand, gave his head a quick shake. "Yes," he agreed, peering up at me from underneath his brown curls. "That's true."

I knitted my brow. Grayson had been a lot more talkative the last time I saw him. He'd practically babbled. Now the words seemed to get stuck on his tongue, like he had to force them out. Was he nervous? Did *I* make him nervous? "How was your pa?"

Grayson looked at me, confusion riddling his face before the memory of our last conversation broke through. "Oh! I was right; he was a wreck." He chuckled sordidly. "He made me haul all the broken nets from the barn and mend them as punishment." He gazed at his hands, opening and closing them slowly. "I'm surprised my hands are still working."

My fins flared at the mention of *nets*. "That seems cruel."

Grayson shook his head, smirking as he placed his hands back into his lap. "It's just how he functions. He's trying to prepare me for the first challenge."

I went still, my blood singing within me. My ears felt like they were on fire, and I found myself pushing my hair behind them, making sure they were okay. "Challenge?"

The boy nodded, letting out a puff of air that sent his shoulders drooping. "It's tomorrow." He leaned back, his fingers running through a wad of flowers. Glancing at me quickly, he began to pluck them out, one by one, until he had a hefty clump.

Unable to help it, I scooted closer to the shoreline. "What sort of challenge?" I asked, trying not to sound too eager.

Grayson spared me a look, his fingers slowing. His jaw had gone tight, his stormy eyes wary. "I don't know if we should talk about it."

I forced a smile, cocking my head to the side. "Why not?"

The boy winced, focusing on the flowers in his lap. "Because it's about . . . You know."

The mention of the Hunt hit me like a wave, but relief blossomed inside. He wasn't suspicious of me. He just didn't want to hurt my feelings. I shook my head and leaned forward, meeting his averted gaze. "The Hunt doesn't scare me, Grayson Shaw."

"It should," he said forcefully, his glare hard with self-loathing. "It really, really should." His energy seemed to drain away as he slumped, gazing at the flowers in his lap. "It scares me," he admitted quietly.

The sun dipped lower in the sky. I sighed gently. I couldn't pressure the boy; there was a chance my vigor would frighten him. I lowered myself onto my forearms, the sand sticking to my fins. Peeking up at him through my eyelashes, I plucked a flower from his lap and twisted the stem between my fingers. "Please tell me?" I asked, bringing the flower to my nose and inhaling.

Grayson watched me for a long, heavy moment. His cheeks flushed crimson, and after what felt like an eternity, he began to busy himself with the flowers again, weaving the stems together. He started with purple, then alternated to white. "Tomorrow morning, the hunters will meet on the beach to practice their net-building skills," he said in a low voice, like he was sharing a secret. "We'll get a bunch of supplies, and within a time limit, we have to create a net from scratch." He picked up a purple flower, then discarded it, grabbing another.

My heart went back to racing. "That sounds stressful."

Grayson chuckled and shook his head. "Not really. It's a skill I actually possess." His eyes darted to mine, and I could have sworn I saw a swell of sadness. "Can I have that?"

I handed the boy the white flower I had been playing with, and he threaded it into the others. "What happens to the nets afterward?"

"When the challenge is done, we leave the nets out for onlookers to view." Grayson shrugged. "They are collected the following morning." He squared me with a sardonic look. "I don't know why they wait though. Several have been stolen in the past."

I was holding my breath. I let it out carefully. "They aren't guarded," I guessed.

Grayson clucked his tongue. "Hunters are celebrities around here. I think the thieves believe the nets will bring them luck or something."

This was big. This was *huge*. This was exactly the sort of information I needed to collect. Everything within me *screamed* to flee home, tell Illeron and the others, and revel in the victory of today. I had gotten what I came for, and I had to go.

And yet I remained where I was on the beach.

Grayson sighed happily and held out the flowers for me to see. They were tangled in one another, a dotted ring of purples and whites. A neat little circle of wild beauty.

I found myself smiling. "It's lovely."

The boy leaned forward, his hands outstretched for me.

I froze, torn between wanting to hiss and strike out and seeing what would happen.

Grayson smiled softly. "It's all right," he whispered, placing the flowers onto my head. He leaned back, studying me. "It's lovelier on you."

I blinked, breaking free from my statue state. I brought my hand up to touch the delicate flowers. Warm velvet, a floral symphony of smells. "A crown?" I asked hesitantly.

The boy nodded. "When I was little, Ma and I would make them all the time. We would sneak out after dinner and have competitions on who could make the best one." He looked down at his hands, flexing them. "I didn't realize I still knew how to make them." When he looked back at me, he was still smiling, but he seemed . . . smaller, sadder.

I slowly lowered my hand. "That is a beautiful memory."

Grayson shrugged stiffly. "She always won," he said wryly. "She always picked the biggest flowers, the brightest colors. Mine fell apart more often than not." He eyed the floral arrangement on my head and sighed. "If she were here and made you one, you wouldn't give my crown a second glance."

I shook my head carefully. "I do not believe that, not even for a moment."

Unable to help it, I went back to playing with the flowers. "I would still wear this one because *you* made it for me, Grayson Shaw."

The boy blushed, and he shrugged again. His deep blue eyes tore away from mine, wandering to the looming waves and the setting sun.

I bit my lip, my heart flopping. And my mouth was moving before I even had a chance to gather my thoughts. I didn't know why. Perhaps it was because Grayson had shared something with me, an intimate memory that made him sad. Perhaps it was because I wanted him to look at me again.

"I have a crown. It is the only thing I have left of my ammah." Grayson looked at me, and I had to remember how to speak, how to breathe. "It was hers before she inexplicably vanished from our lives."

The boy furrowed his brow, the muscles in his jaw tightening. "I'm so sorry," he murmured. "You must treasure it dearly."

I offered a small smile. "It is a beautiful thing, full of gemstones and shells. A symbol of power, grace, and wisdom." And it was collecting algae in my room, abandoned—but far from forgotten.

Grayson's mouth quirked. "Yet you are sitting here, wearing scraps of flowers."

I pulled my tail up and clasped my arms around it. "I don't deserve to wear Ammah's crown yet." I flicked my fluke, the silk fins brushing the boy's leg. "Your crown will do just fine for now."

To my relief, the boy nodded. He didn't try to convince me to put on Nereida's crown, to bear the weight of it, to pretend to be something I wasn't. I could be the mermaid in the flower crown for a moment longer.

Grayson inhaled deeply, and when he spoke again, his words were soft, his cheeks red. "I should like to see you in that crown sometime. When you are ready to wear it."

The connection in my chest sang. "I would like that too," I whispered.

Grayson held my stare for as long as he dared before rubbing his face and clearing his throat. He glanced at the stairs behind him with a sigh. "I suppose I should be heading back home," he mumbled, looking back at me bashfully. "I have to get up rather early tomorrow."

My lips pinched to the side. "Worried your pa might panic again?"

Grayson laughed quietly, but the mirth failed to reach his eyes.

And then I remembered.

The challenge. The nets.

For the Hunt that I had claimed not to be afraid of.

In that moment, as Grayson's troubled eyes met mine, I believed without a doubt that we were thinking the same thing.

What we were doing was wrong.

With a shy chuckle, I reached up and took off the flowers. "Thank you for letting me wear this."

The boy quickly shook his head, forcing the wreath back into my hands. "Keep it." He smiled, and my heart fluttered at the sincerity of it. "I wouldn't look good in a crown, anyway."

Pleasure warming my insides, I placed the flowers back onto my head.

Grayson's mouth wobbled, his eyes dancing. I narrowed my eyes. "What's wrong?"

"Nothing," he said quickly. But he was snickering now, a cute little snorting sound he was clearly embarrassed about making.

I frowned. "Tell me this instant."

"It's just . . ." Grayson covered his mouth until the snorting sound ceased. "It's a little crooked."

It was my turn to blush. "Oh."

Still smiling that lopsided smile, Grayson reached up and pushed on the crown until it was perched perfectly in place. His fingers twitched as he withdrew them.

But then he stopped.

His fingers hung in the air next to my head, his blue eyes fixed on mine.

After a brief infinity, his hand moved again. Warm fingers grazed my cheek as he gently pushed a strand of hair behind my ear. And as Grayson slowly, painfully pulled away, his thumb caressed the tip of my ear. Tentative, purposeful.

So very, *very* wrong.

It was like I had been struck with a bolt of lightning, and a surge of electricity was coursing through me, bursting out of my veins, breaking through my scales.

The tether around my heart strained to be loosened.

The way Grayson Shaw was staring at me, I wondered if he felt the same way.

"I'll see you again?" Grayson asked quietly.

I nodded dumbly, at a complete loss for words.

Grayson beamed as he stood. "Good." He looked down at me, tilting his head to the side. "Until next time, Evanora."

"Until next time," I uttered automatically.

The boy wandered back up the steps. When he was out of view, I made sure the bells were back in their hiding spot before I left.

I had been touched before. I was no stranger to the comfort of contact. But it had never felt like that.

When Grayson Shaw touched me, it was like all the ice in my heavily guarded soul had dissolved, leaving not a single icicle behind.

What was left was a scorching fire. And it was setting me ablaze from the inside out.

CHAPTER THIRTY-ONE

GRAYSON

APRIL 10 – MORNING

"Don't be nervous."

"I'm not nervous."

"Well, stop fidgeting, then."

I shoved my hands into my pockets, eyeing the growing crowd. I was surprised by the number of people pressing up against the rope barrier, scanning the hunters with hungry eyes. I felt like an ant stuck under a microscope. "I feel ridiculous."

Pa glanced at me. "You're wearing the official hunter uniform. Wipe that scowl off your face and wear it with pride."

The large leather belt around my waist was cinched too tight, and the white fabric bands wrapped around my arms kept slipping down to my wrists. At least the shirt was loose and sleeveless, and the pants had a drawstring that bunched the fabric at my knees. It was going to be a hot day.

Net building, as a whole, was a rather boring activity to watch; there was no speaking and no fast-paced action, and the only blood you might see was if a clumsy participant mishandled the barbed wire. The challenge would be three hours of hunters bent over their spots in the sand, feeling the heat of the spring sun beat down on their hunched backs as they played around with a heap of materials until they held something that resembled a net.

Talk about a wild time.

The hunters had been told to arrive at Fariid's main beach early, but I was pretty sure some eager spectators had beaten us there. They watched us with poorly subdued excitement as we signed in at the table tucked beneath the Fariid boardwalk. They pointed and whispered while we were herded onto the black sand where our piles of materials waited. Shouts of encouragement rang out for their favorite hunters, though their words were snatched away by the wind, shredded by the seagulls above.

The air felt charged, an electric tension tugging at my already-fraying nerves, ready to snap. I didn't want to be on this beach.

Fariid's beach *was* beautiful, with its sun-bleached boardwalk lined with shops selling crab legs and jewelry and its shimmering black sands forming a crescent before meeting the water's edge, combed smooth every morning. Even the water here was nicer than the usual gray of the Balafor, replaced by the bright aqua waves of the Floria Sea, foam kissed at the tips. The air smelled cleaner too, with no fishery or butchery scents lurking nearby. By all rights, Fariid's Black Sands Beach was the nicest I'd ever set foot on.

But I didn't want to be on this beach.

Pa jostled my arm. "You might not be nervous, but your friend sure is."

I lifted my head and squinted down the row.

Jasper looked like he was about to be sick. He was staring down at his supplies, sweat plastering his frizzy ginger hair against his pale forehead. His fingers twitched at his sides, like he was going through the motions, attempting one last effort to memorize the steps it took to build a net. He caught my stare and gave me a pained smile. I offered a thumbs-up in return. Jasper swallowed, nodded, and looked back down at his materials, his fingers twitching again.

"I'll bet you three dollars he throws up before we even get started."

I frowned at Pa. "That's rude."

Pa chuckled under his breath. "Not a gambling man?"

I peeked over at Jasper, who was burping into his hands, his eyes glossy and wide as he fought to keep his stomach contents in their place. "Not when it's obvious I'm going to lose."

"Spoilsport."

When the last of the hunters had signed in, Mayor McCoy rose from his spot by the table. He hobbled toward the beach's entrance, where cobblestone met sand. Dressed in his Sunday best—brown tweed suit, yellow tie, and matching handkerchief—he climbed the steps and clapped his hands to gain the crowd's attention.

"Ladies and gentlemen," he called, his nasally voice cracking under the strain of the volume. "It is my utmost honor to welcome you to this year's first Hunting Month challenge!"

The crowd erupted in cheers, whoops, and shouts. Feet stomped, hands clapped, and scarves waved in the air. I scanned the crowd, looking for familiar faces.

Cramped beneath the boardwalk's wooden legs were the Warrens. I could just make out Holly's solemn face as she juggled one of the twins on her hip, oblivious to the child yanking on her hair. Farther up the roped section was Sebastian, cupping his hand around his mouth to hoot as he waved his silken handkerchief in the air. Seeing him threw me off—after all his talk about us being barbarians, he'd still decided to show up? Mrs. Morris bounced beside Sebastian, linking arms with him, nearly throwing him off-balance. Ever the gentleman, he just laughed and joined in on the bouncing.

Rosemary Little was there too, but I only glanced long enough to know she'd picked the best spot to watch Ambrose. She was wearing a dress that was decidedly not beach appropriate. It would take ages to get the sand out of all those colorful layers.

I felt like I was on fire—not from the unseasonably warm morning, or from the stupid uniform, but from the weight of a pair of eyes boring into me. I'd felt it the moment I stepped onto the black sand, and the pressure of that gaze was becoming impossible to ignore. The hair on the back of my neck stood at attention, my skin prickling. I glanced up and found Ambrose glaring daggers at me from several rows ahead. His eyes held wicked secrets—secrets I had no interest in learning. He grinned, but I didn't return it.

Mayor McCoy soothed the rumbling crowd with a wave of his hand. "Yes, yes, we are all very excited to get this challenge underway." He eyed the crowd over his large, bulbous nose, his beady eyes twinkling. "As you know, every year we have our brave hunters compete in three separate challenges leading up to the Hunt. The first"—he gestured to us on the beach—"is the great net building. It is a test of strength, strategy, and endurance. It might not be the most physically taxing, but rest assured, it is not meant to be." He placed a finger to his head, tapping on his dried scalp. "It is a game, you see. A *mental* game. Who can build the best net in the allotted time? Who can build the largest, the strongest, the most durable, without sacrificing weight? Those, my good people, are the things our great judges will be looking for." Mayor McCoy waved at the two men by the desk.

As one, the audience and the hunters shifted to stare at the men. One of them was Mr. Brightly. He stood with his thick arms crossed against his chest, his belly sagging over the front of his trousers, a black pipe sticking out of his mouth. The other man, reedlike Mr. Krieg, awkwardly shuffled from foot to foot, scratching his blond beard, his eyes on the sand.

"These two men are Lethe's best net builders and therefore won't be participating in today's challenge," Mayor McCoy went on, chuckling. "We don't want them to have that sort of advantage, after all. Instead, Mr. Brightly and Mr. Crogg will be judging the nets our fine hunters create."

Mr. Krieg looked up, grimacing. "It's Krieg."

Mr. Brightly elbowed Mr. Krieg, and the man looked back down at the sand, his hands moving from his thin beard to the newsboy cap on his head. "It's Krieg," he mumbled again, more to himself than anything. "Bloody fool got my name wrong."

Mayor McCoy pointed at the board above the table. "Once the challenge is complete and the assessments are done, the judges will decide which hunters flourished in today's test, and which ones floundered. The most dominant of the hunters will be placed on the board for your viewing pleasure. As the challenges go on, the names may shift or drop off completely. Now"—he wagged a finger at the crowd, a conniving grin on his face—"I know some of you aren't of the betting sort, but those who *are* . . ." He raised his bushy eyebrows. "You'll want to keep your eye on this board. When it comes to the Night of the Betting, this board will help you decide who to put your money on; it'll give you a clear view of who is most likely going to win the Hunt. Picking someone from the top three, I'd say your chances are pretty good. Choose someone from the bottom rung, and you might just find yourself with empty pockets."

I could hear a hunter behind me stamp his feet impatiently. "Come on," he growled. "Let's get *on* with it."

I peeked over my shoulder to see Peter locking his fingers together and stretching until each and every one of them cracked. Tommy, who was standing next to him, glanced up from his supplies and frowned. "Eager to lose?" he asked, pushing up his glasses.

Peter rolled his eyes and snorted, leaning from side to side with his arms over his head. "Eager to kick your ass, you mean."

Owen shot a glare in their direction. "Both of you, hush." His eyes stayed on Peter a second longer, annoyance fluttering through them. "Peter, for God's s-s-sake, we are making *n-n-nets*, not running a race."

Peter had gone on to bending over in a sad attempt at touching his toes. "Gotta limber up." The movement seemed to knock the breath out of him, however, and he quickly stopped.

There it was again. Those burning eyes on me. I found Ambrose amidst the sea of hunters. He was locked on to me, staring at me with such a ferocity that it made my insides quake. I narrowed my eyes and ground my teeth together.

"Now," Mayor McCoy continued, breaking my staring contest with Ambrose, "the hunters have three hours to create a net using the provided tools at their feet. They have all the essentials: ropes of various lengths and thickness, twine, barbed wire, bells, shears, and other weaving materials, such as flax, wheat, and grass. Three hours to build a net from scratch." He turned, staring at us with a raised eyebrow. "Do you have what it takes?"

"Don't be nervous," Pa said again under his breath.

"I'm *not* nervous." I glanced up at him. "Are *you* nervous?"

Pa grunted, folding his arms against his chest, staring ahead. "Just remember the tricks I showed you, and you'll be fine."

I dipped my chin into my chest, stifling a snort. "How could I forget?"

Every spare chance we had together had been dedicated to fixing the busted-up nets in our loft. Pa would assess the nets I had mended, then tear them apart and force me to put them back together. Over and over again, until it was muscle memory, until I could do it with my eyes closed.

The net-building test didn't scare me. The other challenges did.

I held my breath as Mayor McCoy nodded to Mr. Brightly, who grunted and reached for the pistol on the desk. The crowd watched in hushed wonder as Mr. Brightly squinted at the sky and raised his arm, the muzzle reaching for the clouds.

Time slowed.

Everything went quiet. There wasn't the crashing of waves, the screeching of seagulls. There was only the thunder of blood in my ears.

The *crack* of the firearm tore through the beach, and in an instant, the hunters were on their knees, sorting through their materials. The audience began to scream, offering their support from the sidelines.

I gave my head a rough shake, suddenly feeling dizzy. I had to focus. Three hours was *not* a lot of time to create a net. I was about to drop to the sandy floor when something caught my eye.

No. Not something. Someone.

Ambrose was still standing too.

And he was still looking at me.

I could feel a growl rise up my throat as I glowered at him. What could he possibly want? Was it a scare tactic? Was it meant to be intimidating?

If it was, I hated that it was working.

Ambrose's eyes gleamed with the spring sun as they dipped from my face, down to my supplies, and then back up to me. The toying grin never left his lips, the wicked evil carved into his features. I could feel the color drain from my face, and Ambrose's smile grew. Then, without another sparing glance, he turned and settled onto the sand with the grace of a predator. Like it wasn't a challenge, but a game.

My growl was replaced with the sudden surge of bile. Heart thudding, I collapsed to the ground, my eyes viciously tearing through my materials. Everything looked in order. The pile of rope, the coil of barbs, the row of bells, the shears—

I sucked in a breath, my heart coming to a tremendous stop.

The shears were gone.

In their place was a folded-up piece of paper.

No.

With shaking fingers, I plucked up the note nestled neatly in the sand. My blood burned within me as I unfolded it and took in the words.

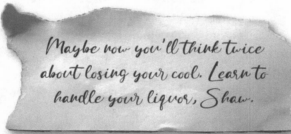

Maybe now you'll think twice about losing your cool. Learn to handle your liquor, Shaw.

My vision began to swim. The note slipped from my fingers, gliding back to the sand.

No!

My entire body was shaking as rage surged through it. Blind, red-hot rage.

Pa was on the ground. He had already divided up his supplies and was working on driving the bolt into the ground to anchor his rope. He paused long enough to shoot a concerned glance my way. "What's wrong?" he asked gruffly. Sweat was already beading his forehead.

Gritting my teeth, I grabbed the note and stuffed it into my pocket. "Nothing," I snarled.

I let my anger fuel me, guiding my hands as I raced to collect my frazzled bearings. Shoving in the anchor, I ran my fingers along the thick wads of rope. Without the shears, I wouldn't be able to cut the rope or the barbed wire. I bit my lip, my eyes drifting to the other supplies. I had to use the length to my advantage. Shaking out my fingers, I loosed a breath and set to work.

The sounds of the world faded into a hum as I found my rhythm. I worked as one possessed. It hadn't been about beating anyone before. Going into the challenge, my mentality was to simply keep my head down, work hard, and hope I didn't prick myself on the barbed wire.

Not anymore.

I wanted to win.

I wanted to beat Ambrose and wipe that smug smile off his face.

I needed to.

I couldn't do my standard diamond-shaped fishing net; the length of the ropes wouldn't allow me to. I had to do something larger. I grabbed another bolt and drove it into the ground, parallel with the other anchor, then snatched three of the longest pieces of rope and began braiding them together. I cinched it tight and wedged it into the anchors, giving the ends a couple yanks to see if it would budge.

Curious eyes were on me as I looped and knotted the shorter ropes onto the braid, pulling them down like tendrils of hair. I used my hand to gauge the distance, grabbed another long rope, and began tearing at the fibers. I formed a hole between the strands just big enough to fit, then pulled it through the vertical ropes, pushing it up until it was about a hand's width from the braid. I tied it in place with a small piece of flax. Over and over, I separated the rope and pushed it up the strands. When I'd threaded it through all of them, I removed the flax and double knotted it.

Sweat ran down my neck, pooling at my back. My hands burned, raw from the fibers. By the time I was on the third rope, my shoulders were seizing, but I pressed on. I couldn't embarrass myself—or Pa—by giving up. I *wouldn't*.

Mayor McCoy jubilantly called out the halfway mark, but his words were a million miles away.

I only had one strand left to push up the vertical pieces. I hadn't even started working with the ridiculously long coil of barbed wire, not to mention the rows of bells.

I felt the rise of fear and quickly snuffed it out. *I do not have time to panic.* I didn't even have time to think.

It was just me and the damned net.

Blisters rose to the surface of my fingertips, filled, then burst rather unceremoniously. The pain was a flicker compared to the commotion happening in my back.

I kept working.

When the last strand was knotted, I grabbed the ends of the braided rope and bordered the net, weaving the loose ends into the braid and double knotting them. I exhaled sharply, sitting back on my heels. My entire body screamed in protest. Soaked in sweat, my scratched cheek burned with it. I stole a glance at the bells and barbed wire. Impulsively, I grabbed them and the flax, praying my body could hold up long enough to finish.

Using the flax, I attached the bells to every fourth knot in the net, winding the plant around the ropes and ripping off the excess with my teeth. A bristle of worry crept through my veins. Twine would have been a better choice, but I didn't think my teeth were up for the challenge. When the bells were on, I reluctantly grabbed the barbed wire.

"Thirty more minutes, hunters!" Mayor McCoy announced excitedly.

I had actually forgotten about him.

The barbed wire was the real challenge. It was twice the length of the rope. Biting my lip, I worked at unspooling it, careful to avoid the sharp barbs. Once freed, I began looping it around the net, starting at the top of the braid. I ran it along the border, then started weaving it through the strands, avoiding the bells, crisscrossing it until the whole thing became a chain-mail death trap.

It wasn't pretty. And I wasn't envious of the person who would have to carry it; the beast was going to be heavy.

But it was done.

And it would surely kill any mermaid who swam into its taunting grasp.

"Annnnnd," Mayor McCoy said, dragging out the word as he eyed his pocket watch, "that's time!" He looked up, but his eager smile was quick to fade when he saw the hunters still working away. Shoulders slumping, he turned to Mr. Brightly. "Mr. Brightly, if you please," he muttered, gesturing to the beach.

Mr. Brightly stared at the mayor for a heavy second before letting out a grunt. Planting his hands on his hips, he inhaled deeply. "Oy! Mayor says ya done! Hands down, hunters!"

The beach went still. The crowd, which had lost its thunder about thirty minutes into the challenge, picked up where it had left off, screaming loudly and clapping. Out of the corner of my eye, I saw Peter stomping around, collecting high fives from a few willing hunters. At some point, he'd removed his shirt, his chest glowing in the sunlight. I saw Jasper wiping his mouth, waving at his family, desperately trying to kick sand onto a pile of vomit. Ambrose was blowing kisses to Rosemary, who giggled and swatted them away with her gloved hand.

I couldn't catch my breath. My shaking had stopped as soon as I got to work, but it had come back with a vengeance, and I was worried my knees would give out. I looked at my hands and wished I hadn't. They were absolutely shredded. Large angry red craters of torn blisters on my palms. Deep scratches on my fingertips. It was a miracle there wasn't any blood.

Pa slapped me on the back, bringing me out of my daze. I could smell his sweat as he pulled me into a hug. "Well done," he said, smiling at the crowd. His smile quickly transitioned into a quizzical look when his eyes fell on my net. "Good grief, look at the size of that thing."

My cheeks flushed, and I glared sourly at my creation. "Well, I figured, go big or go home, you know?"

"*Big* is a polite word for it. The thing is massive." Pa raised his eyebrows worriedly, his mouth in a pensive line. "You'll be docked points for weight."

I snorted, rolling my head to the side so it rested on the edge of my pa's rigid shoulder. "Honestly, I'm just glad it's over."

The judges wasted no time. Donning their thick gloves, Mr. Brightly and Mr. Krieg started at the first line of hunters, talking quietly amongst themselves as they picked up each net and assessed it with eagle eyes. They tugged on the ropes, jostled the bells, and took turns throwing it as far as their arms would let them. Then out came the notepads and pens, and after a handful of furious scribbles, they moved on to the next hunter.

They seemed especially pleased with Mr. Grieves's neat diamond-shaped rows, the tautness of his knots. They got to Ambrose, and I could hear Mr. Krieg murmur, "With a father like Silas, you know it's going to be good."

They picked up Ambrose's net, and a bell promptly fell off. Then another. And another.

I had to suppress a laugh, but God, I wanted to let it out. Too bad I was so damn polite.

Both Mr. Brightly and Mr. Krieg stared down at the bells, then at Ambrose, who looked like he was about to have an aneurysm. Wordlessly, they continued their assessment, made their notes, and then carried on, shaking their heads the entire time.

"Shame," Pa muttered, and a choked giggle squeezed by my clenched teeth. I slapped a hand over my mouth, but it was too late. Ambrose's eyes cut over to me, drenched in a hardy dose of hate.

I cleared my throat and turned my attention to the judges.

They neared the end of the row and started on the next. The Morris brothers presented perfectly average nets. Their holes were a bit too big, and some of the barbed wire came loose with the final toss, but at least no bells fell off.

Pa's net seemed to catch the judge's interest. They poked and prodded, but the knots and bells didn't budge. Mr. Krieg hefted the ropes and nodded approvingly. "It's a good weight and sturdy enough to withstand turbulent waters."

Rowan Shaw, not knowing how to accept flattery, grunted with a curt nod.

"Heaven almighty," Mr. Brightly coughed out when he came to mine. "Ya could fit three or four mermaids in that thing an' still have room to spare."

I grimaced as Mr. Krieg tried in vain to pick up the net, the blood vessels in his neck bulging with the strain. With Mr. Brightly's help, they managed to lift it off the ground, but casually throwing it was out of the question. They dropped it into a heap and caught their breath. Mr. Brightly eyed me warily. "Just what were ya thinkin', makin' a net like that?"

I bit my lip, feeling Ambrose's heavy stare back on me. "It was a challenge," I said, standing as tall as I could and lifting my chin. "I wanted to challenge myself."

Mr. Brightly stared at me for a long second. The corner of his mouth twitched, and I realized he was smiling at me. "Aye, that ya did."

Mr. Krieg worried at his beard. "Can you imagine this thing in the water? It'll be downright lethal! A regular killing machine."

Jasper's net was deplorable. The second they lifted it up, almost every knot loosened, the bells began to tumble off, and the barbed wire released its grip from the rope. Mr. Brightly watched as Mr. Krieg gently lowered the net back to the ground, narrowly avoiding the barbs as they sprang toward his face. "For Pete's sake, boy!" he growled, spitting on the ground next to the heap of ropes and bells. "You've been workin' at my docks for years! Just what do I pay ya for?"

Jasper, red as a tomato, smiled meekly. "My charming personality?" He looked like he was about to be sick again. Thankfully, the judges moved on before they did any more damage, to both Jasper and his poor excuse for a net.

When the judges were done, they marched back to the board, bickering back and forth about the nets and who deserved to be first. The hunters were hot on their heels, eager to see the outcome of their hard work. I trailed behind Pa, collecting a disgruntled Jasper on my way to the boardwalk.

"I'm declaring a miscarriage of justice!" he cried as he hobbled beside me.

"Jasper, your net was literally falling apart in their hands."

Jasper groaned, shoving his frizzy hair out of his eyes. "They just didn't know how to pick it up properly."

I smirked. "The best net builders on Lethe didn't know how to pick up your net properly?"

Jasper glared at me, giving me a shove. "At least they were *able* to pick mine up."

"That's hardly a strong argument."

We arrived at the scoreboard, where several names had already been jotted down. Jasper was practically buzzing beside me. I held my breath, my gaze tentatively trailing down the written names.

Silas Grieves.

Rowan Shaw.

Gregory Malbourne.

Sam Strange.

Grayson Shaw.

Fifth. I was in fifth place. All the air left my lungs, and my heart twitched painfully within me. I felt like I was in a vise, getting squeezed into a cube, until I was dust. And then I realized it was my pa, clenching me tightly against him.

"That's my boy!" he crowed. "Fifth place! Praise be."

It was too soon to celebrate. I hurriedly scanned the names as they were written, eating up each one. My heart was in my throat, and for a horrible second, I thought *I* was going to be sick.

Until I got to it.

Ambrose Grieves, written neatly in the tenth-place slot.

Tenth. Place.

I had beaten him. And not by just a little, but by a lot!

I turned and rushed back into Pa's arms, the blood exploding in my veins, pounding in my ears, singing through every fiber of my body.

I beat him. I beat him. I beat him!

Pa laughed and slapped me on the back, pulling away just enough so he could clutch the sides of my face. "My son! A true hunter!"

The mirth welling up within me immediately fizzled out, and—

Holy shit, I really am *going to be sick.*

"I'm at the bottom!" Jasper exclaimed next to me.

I was grateful for the distraction. I extracted myself from Pa's grip and turned to look back at the board. There Jasper was, in big, blocky letters, nearly dangling off the end. I patted him on the back, shaking my head. "Hey, at least you aren't in—"

"*Last place?*" Peter roared, stomping through the hunters to get a better look at the board. "What do you mean by that garbage?"

Mr. Krieg set the chalk down and dusted off his hands. "What I mean is that you are in last place, Mr. Lyre. You failed to complete the challenge; your net was only half done."

Peter scoffed and stamped his foot, causing his belly to jiggle. "This is a load of baloney! I demand a recheck!"

Mr. Brightly, who had tucked himself behind the desk, stood up and slammed his hands onto the wooden tabletop, sending the chalk flying. "Christ on a cracker! If we put ya in last place, it means yer in last place! And put yer shirt back on; this ain't no peep show!"

Peter jutted out his lower lip, his fists shaking at his sides, before he turned and stormed back to his discarded shirt, mumbling colorful obscenities the entire way.

Jasper whistled beside me. "Fifth place." He punched me on the shoulder as an act of approval. "How's the view from up there?"

I shrugged. "It's a little hard to see all you peasants, I suppose."

Jasper guffawed. "The victory has gone straight to your head."

"Don't worry, I'm sure the next challenge will knock me down a peg or two."

Jasper nodded heartily. "And that will be my time to shine!" He puffed out his chest, grinning at me. "I'll teach them for putting me near the bottom of the list." He anchored an arm around my shoulder and waved his other hand theatrically in the air. "I can see it now: Jasper Warren, top-tier swimmer."

I tried not to stare at his bad leg. "Just remember to drag my lifeless body back to shore before the tide takes me."

Jasper laughed. "You're so dramatic."

I didn't think I was being dramatic. I didn't think I was even joking. I was fairly certain the next challenge would claim my life, if the water had any say in the matter. And lately, it always did.

There was an outburst of voices. Jasper's words fluttered into the ether, becoming a white noise as I looked around to find the source of the sudden volume.

I wasn't surprised when my gaze landed on Ambrose and Mr. Brightly. Mr. Brightly stood with his arms crossed over his round chest, shaking his head as Ambrose gnashed his teeth, speaking with such intensity that spit flew from his mouth. As his voice reached a crescendo, Ambrose pointed viciously in my direction, his finger aimed directly at me. I couldn't make out his words, but I didn't need to.

Ambrose was downright pissed that I had placed higher than him. Despite his trickery, despite his *cheating*, I'd beaten him. I would be lying if I said the sight didn't give me a sick pleasure that warmed my insides.

What *did* surprise me was when Mr. Grieves strode toward Ambrose and clamped a hand onto his shoulder, effectively ending the high-pitched rant. Ambrose looked like he had a great deal more to say but reluctantly allowed his father to pull him away from Mr. Brightly's orbit. Ambrose was above mumbling curse words under his breath, but his eyes said everything his lips didn't as they bored into me, tearing me in two.

Refusing to falter, I smiled and waved.

Ambrose shoved his way through the crowd, avoiding outstretched hands and enthusiastic congratulations, before wrenching the car door from his chauffeur's hands and slamming it shut behind him. He was inside for no more than ten seconds before it became clear he'd forgotten something. Red-faced and seething, Ambrose jerked the door back open and yelled at Rosemary. The poor girl whimpered, fanning her face, before picking up her skirt's voluminous layers and hurrying for the car, her strawberry-blond curls bouncing with every step.

Mr. Grieves was the last one to enter the vehicle. He stood tall, his steel eyes scanning the crowd. Until they landed on me.

My heart skipped a handful of beats.

Mr. Grieves held my gaze for a heavy second. I didn't know what to do with the attention. Avert my eyes? Bow? I didn't want him staring at me. I didn't like it.

As if reading my thoughts, Mr. Grieves quirked his mouth to the side in the smallest of smiles. He narrowed his eyes, appraising me with the utmost scrutiny. Nodding in approval, Mr. Grieves ducked into his car.

And just like that, the moment was gone. I was back on the beach, surrounded by hunters and a screaming audience.

Jasper's voice rushed back into my ears. "I can do a strong doggy paddle too."

"What?" I asked distractedly.

Jasper looked wounded. "I was telling you about my strategy for the next challenge. Have you not been paying attention?"

I winced. "You know me; my head is always in the clouds."

Jasper's mouth puckered like he had tasted something sour. "You are hopeless. It's a wonder you made it this far in life."

"A real miracle."

Pa, who had gone on to shake some hands and compare blisters and rope burns, strode back over to us. "I think we should celebrate," he announced, planting his hands on his hips. "I'll bet I can convince Pastor Kline to sit tight while we go to the Silver Fox for a treat."

I frowned. "With what money?"

Pa's eyes twinkled as he pointedly looked at Jasper and the flecks of vomit stuck to the corners of his mouth. "With the money from the bet you lost."

I widened my eyes, my mouth threatening to drop open. "I never actually agreed to that bet."

Pa smirked. "Really? I could have sworn you did."

I shook my head. "In all honesty, Pa, I'm pretty tired. I really wouldn't mind going home so I can bury my hands in some ice and then sleep for a couple eternities, or something."

Jasper, who had been wiping at his mouth, perked up. "I'll go to the Silver Fox with you, Mr. Shaw!"

Pa glowered at Jasper. "You're too young."

Jasper's face contorted in confusion. "But I'm older than Grayson."

"Did I say young? I meant mature. You're not mature enough."

Jasper scowled and went back to wiping his mouth.

I grimaced. "I can walk home if you'd like to stay in Fariid?"

Pa shook his head. "No, you're right; we should be heading back." He rubbed my head enthusiastically, sending my curls flying. "We can celebrate another time."

Pa left to find Pastor Kline, who was likely already drinking himself silly somewhere.

I wasn't lying. I really did want to get home and do something about my hands. They were killing me. With every heartbeat, a fresh wave of scratching pain coursed through them, from the tips of my sliced fingers to the ends of my swollen wrists. And my *back*; it was a wonder I was even standing.

But more than that, I really wanted to get home and be in my room.
With the door closed.
With the window open.
Waiting for bells.

CHAPTER THIRTY-TWO

EVANORA

APRIL 10 – EVENING

WHEN ILLERON FOUND ME IN THE THRONE ROOM, I was a ball of nerves.

He had encouraged me to try to rest before we set off for the island, but I couldn't. My mind was too alive and frantic. So, I did the opposite.

I lit the lanterns, making sure to give the Barrens a wide berth.

I visited the garden and sent off my prayers to the ancestors.

I tended to the sick, healing fin rot when my Gift let me and providing salves and promises of sneaking off to sunbathe when it didn't.

I tried not to think about Grayson the entire time.

When Illeron told me it was time to go, my eyes flitted to the extra spear in his hand.

"Don't," the warrior warned.

"Don't *what*?"

"Try to convince me not to go with you. It's not going to happen."

I frowned. "The thought hadn't even crossed my mind."

Illeron scoffed. "It's fairly bold of you to lie to a mind bender." He handed me the spear; the staff was cool and slick in my hands. "I need to go with you to keep you on track. Amongst other things, like keeping you safe. Minor details."

My head jerked up, my white hair wafting away from my face. "Keep me on track? What's that supposed to mean?"

Illeron cocked his head to the side, his lips pulling upward in a crooked smile. "Remind me—why do we need to visit Grayson Shaw tonight?"

I felt my cheeks flush, and I looked back down at the spear, which I had begun to clutch a bit too tightly. "I might've forgotten to ask where the nets were being held."

"Right."

"But at least I found out about the nets in the first place."

Illeron leveled me with a heavy look. "If you are looking for praise, I suggest you find it elsewhere. I'm sure Mavi would be more than happy to provide a boost to your ego."

I growled and pushed away from the dais, making sure to swat Illeron with my tail as I passed. "Come," I commanded, exiting the throne room. "We are losing time."

Illeron chuckled under his breath. "After you, Your Majesty."

The waters were growing dark as we neared the kingdom's border. The lanterns hummed with magic as we passed, glowing with my light trapped within them. I was pleasantly surprised to see that the few I had combined with Mavi's Gift were flourishing; not one had sputtered out. My heart thrummed with happiness. But when Illeron suddenly swept in front of me, placing an arm out to hold me back, all traces of joy vanished. His jaw was tightly clenched, his brow low over his eyes. His outstretched arm was taut against my stomach, his rigid fins careful to not touch me.

"*Don't panic,*" he said in my mind.

I opened my mouth to question the warrior, but when I caught sight of what he had spotted, I snapped it shut so hard that I nearly bit my lip.

A lone mermaid, swimming amongst the seaweed forest. They weaved through the long plants, pausing at every turn to look up at the lanterns.

Jorah.

I sucked in a shuddering breath, guilt turning my blood to ice. "*He knows,*" I thought, casting a worried glance Illeron's way. "*He knows, and he is here to stop us.*"

Illeron dropped his arm. "*Steady now. We don't know why he is here. If he questions us, we will say we were sparring and then decided to do a final perimeter check together.*"

I frowned at the warrior, squeezing my spear tightly. "*He will hardly believe that. He knows I can't stand the sight of you.*"

Illeron shot me a hard look, only to roll his eyes when he saw the hint of a smile on my lips. *"Neptune spear me, I swear the last words you utter on your dying breath will be a sarcastic comment."*

Slowly, we approached the advisor. Jorah seemed entranced by the lanterns, staring at them with fervent wonder. The light cast shadows on his gaunt face, exacerbating his hollowed-out cheeks, his sunken eyes, and the sickly pale scales on his nose and jaw. He was sick, I knew that, but in that moment, he looked like death reincarnate.

I stretched out a tentative hand, willing my fingers to cease their shaking as I placed them gently on his shoulder. "Jorah?" I asked in a quiet, careful tone.

I didn't know what I was expecting. Maybe for Jorah to whirl around, startled at our sudden appearance. Maybe for him to immediately begin interrogating us with a ferocity that made me admit to everything. Both of those seemed horrendously plausible.

But Jorah did neither. Instead, he blinked slowly, tearing his gaze away from the lanterns, his eyes bleary and unfocused as they landed on me. His mouth hung open slightly, and I could see bits of fish flesh stuck between his teeth. He smelled of rot, hot and wretched.

"Jorah," I said again, more commanding, willing him to concentrate.

My advisor blinked again, and finally, he saw me. He let out a gasp, reeling back. "Your Grace!" he exclaimed, his eyes growing wide as they swept over me. "What are you doing out at this hour?"

I glanced at Illeron, praying that both my heart and my mind wouldn't give me away. "We were just—"

"Oh, this will simply not do!" Jorah pressed on, shaking his head quickly, his face crumbling with concern. "Your parents must be worried sick about you. You must hurry to bed at once!"

My breath caught in my throat. "My parents?" I managed to squeak out.

Jorah ran his hands over his face. I could see the scales pull and crack at his rough touch. "They will surely have my head for this. Little Evie, out for a night swim. Poseidon drown us all."

Swallowing hard, I looked at Illeron again, but there was nothing the warrior could do to help. The signs of Dark Madness were undeniable. With all the sores on his body, I should have known that delusions were just around the corner for him. Gods, why did he never let me heal him? We could have gotten on top of his wounds, bought ourselves more time.

In Jorah's eyes, I was a merling again, spots and all, and my parents were very much alive. He was deranged, trapped in the past, grasping at mere memories. It was a cruel twist, and the knife doing the damage was wickedly sharp. "Jorah . . ." I sighed gently. "My parents—"

Illeron placed a hand on my elbow, his nails digging into my flesh. *"Stop,"* he said. *"Go along with it."*

I spared a glance over my shoulder at the warrior, worry sending deep creases along my forehead.

"Don't fret, little Evie," Jorah said, giving me a knowing smile as he touched a finger to his lips. "I won't tell them if you won't! That way, we can both be spared from their wrath."

I forced a wobbly smile and nodded. It was for the best, I decided, that I didn't break the moment and confuse Jorah further. "Thank you."

My advisor rubbed at his elbow, and a thick wad of scales and skin scraped off. His eyes traveled back up to the lantern, oblivious to the dark blood seeping from the wound. "Such a beautiful power, isn't it? Your am-mah . . ." He sucked in a reverent breath. "She truly is a wonder to behold."

My eyes pinched, threatening tears, and I found myself blinking up at the lantern I had lit earlier that day. "She really is."

When I was younger, I would trail after Ammah as she lit the lanterns, praying over each one. She took such care, treating each lantern as if it were the most important one of all. I was always quick to grow bored, eager to run off and play or sneak into the garden. As she worked, Ammah would explain the lanterns' purpose: how they protected us, and how soon it would be my job to light and care for them. I rarely listened, believing, with the certainty of youth, that Nereida would live forever.

Now I would give just about anything for those late-evening swims, to hear Ammah breathe life into each lantern, to listen to her whisper positive affirmations to them. A part of me wanted to be trapped in the past, like Jorah.

He shook his head, snapping me back to the present. "But enough about that. Off to bed with you. Don't want a Cursed Being to gobble you up for a midnight snack!"

I forced a laugh, wiping my eyes quickly and nodding. "Yes, of course," I agreed. "Please follow your own advice and do the same."

I turned to leave, but my heart wailed within me, begging me to hold on to the precious moment a second longer. I swam back to Jorah and hugged him fiercely, burying my face into the crook of his neck. I tried to avoid the angry red sores, but there were too many to count.

Jorah let out an "oof!" but laughed as he wrapped his thin arms around me.

"Thank you," I whispered, pulling away. "For taking such good care of me."

Jorah smiled, reaching forward and tapping me lightly on the nose. "Always, little Evie."

As I turned, my stomach in knots, I could have sworn I saw a gentle flicker of recognition flutter over Jorah's face, but it failed to land.

He went back to staring at the lantern, the thin milky-white film returning to his eyes.

Illeron and I swam in silence. When the city was long behind us and the glow of the island was just beyond our reach, the warrior broke the stillness. "Do you wish to talk about it?"

"No," I said curtly.

Did I want to talk about how my advisor was slowly losing the battle against the darkness? How he was riddled with sores and refused to let me heal them? How he was losing his eyesight and his mind and was growing delusional? Was this the first time he'd fallen back in time? The second? The twentieth? I couldn't be sure. But I knew for certain that I absolutely didn't want to talk about it.

There was silence, and then: *"Do you wish to think about it, then?"*

I softened, looking at Illeron with a sad smile. "I can't think about anything but the plan right now. The plan is all that matters. I can fix Jorah when we are done."

I T WAS NEARLY NIGHTFALL BY THE TIME WE ARRIVED AT THE BEACH. Seeing Jorah had set us back; returning home after our mission was no longer an option. We would have to remain at the island for the night. The only glimmer of hope we had was in the moon—it was plump in the night sky, shedding its light unabashedly on the water like the entire world was a stage and the moon was the main act. The Cursed Beings didn't like coming out to play when the moon was at its fullest, and the chance of them attempting to eat us tonight was slim.

Not completely absent, but slim.

I waited for Illeron to hide—much to his disdain—and tucked my spear next to him. "I won't be long!" I said, a little breathlessly. I couldn't stop the excitement from creeping into my words.

Illeron narrowed his eyes at me. "I know you won't; I'll make sure of that."

I waved my hand dismissively. "Oh, hush now."

Illeron glanced down at the spears, and I didn't have to be a mind bender to know what he was thinking.

I was now unarmed, and I was approaching the beach alone.

Before he could drown me in his worry, I pushed away from the boulder he was tucked behind, making sure to toss a nonchalant grin over my shoulder for his pleasure.

I skirted along the island's edge, keeping low until the ground began to tilt up and the coarse sand became littered with smooth pebbles and basalt shards. I broke through the surface, letting the waves push me to shore. The beach was empty. I scooted up to the boulders circling the churning pools and pressed myself against them, allowing their chill to seep into my naked skin. The cold felt different on the surface, more tangible, visceral—not at all like the constant icy grip of the water. I hated how much I was beginning to like it.

Fishing the bells from the rock pool, I held them above the water's grasp and rang them like Grayson had shown me. I held my breath, straining to hear above the crashing of the waterfall, the rumble of the waves, the ripple of the wind in the surrounding wildflowers. I rang them again, putting more force into the action.

"No-show?" Illeron asked from his hiding spot.

A mixture of fear and annoyance blistered my insides. Grayson would hear the bells. He had to. I was about to ring them again when I felt it.

A snapping in my chest as the thread that connected me and Grayson together went taut.

I did a poor job at stifling my grin as footsteps reached my prickling ears. *"He is here."*

"Joy."

Grayson stumbled down the hill, clearly torn between keeping an eye on his clumsy footing and staring at me. He leapt off the last three steps and tripped to the water's edge, breathless and ruffled, his face a beacon of delight. "You didn't run away this time," he said quietly, sitting down and pulling his knees to his chest.

I shoved the bells back into their designated spot. "I can tell it's you."

Grayson's hand went for his chest, and he gripped the fabric of his shirt, above his heart. "How?"

I cocked my head to the side, allowing a hint of a smile to grace my lips. "Your thunderous footsteps, of course. I'd recognize those heavy sounds anywhere now."

Grayson widened his eyes, and he let out a burst of laughter. "Oh my God, is it that bad?"

I giggled, tucking a strand of hair behind my ear. "You're as loud as a mating sperm whale!"

Grayson rubbed his neck, and I caught a dash of red in the moonlight. "That paints a very graphic image."

I patted his knee. "You're welcome."

Seemingly without thought, Grayson slipped his hand underneath mine and threaded our fingers together. He moved so smoothly, like the action of holding my hand was purely natural, strictly instinctual. It looked like he had thought about it for a long, long time.

I couldn't stop the shuddering breath that made my lungs threaten to collapse.

His hand in mine. It felt good. It felt *right*.

Grayson's callused skin was warm against my cool touch. I could feel his erratic heartbeat in his fingertips as he ran his thumb against the tiny scales dotting the inside of my wrist. Grayson's eyes had been on our hands from the second he had laced them together, but when they flitted to mine . . .

The entire world could have crumbled. The ocean could have dried up. The mountains could have quaked and trembled into dust. And I wouldn't have noticed.

Grayson Shaw's eyes were burning with a raw hunger that mirrored the ache in my chest. A dazzling hurricane of desire, intent on destroying the thimble of composure I had within me. With a single look, I felt the string tethering my heart cinch so tight that I feared it would stop the poor thing from beating altogether. The tension was thick and hot and sent wave after wave of tingles down my tail. I could feel it building, heaving and tremulous, ready to burst through my scales.

It was ecstasy. It was terrifying.

I swallowed hard and forced myself to look away. I was on fire, I was certain of it. It took everything within me not to look for smoke or scorch marks. I focused on our hands instead. My smooth, nearly translucent skin next to his shredded—

Wait, shredded?

I frowned, unclasping our hands and pulling his up to my face so I could inspect it. Grayson jerked forward with the movement, a startled chuckle on his tongue.

"Your poor hands," I whispered, tracing my fingers lightly along the broken blisters and deep scratches.

I could see—and feel—a shiver ripple through the boy's body. "We had our first challenge today," he said, trying not to wince as I continued to prod at him.

"Net building," I said, lowering his hand down to my lap and keeping it there.

Grayson grinned at me, obviously pleased. "You remembered."

I scoffed delicately. "Yes, well, I'm not *that* senile. Though"—I sniffed, pointing my nose into the air—"by your age standards, I'm sure I am considered elderly. You humans age so peculiarly."

Grayson's mouth pinched to the side. "Wait, how old *are* you?"

"A lady never gives that information away. Frankly, it's rude of you to even ask."

"I'm sorry," Grayson said with a laugh, clearly not sorry at all.

I tried to bite back a smile. I went back to tracing his hand.

I had an idea. A deliciously wicked idea that Illeron would scold me about later. "Can I try something?" I asked quietly.

Grayson went still, his complexion growing pale.

I rolled my eyes. "Calm down. It shouldn't hurt. Much."

The boy's eyebrows spiked up to his hairline. "Should I be worried?" he asked carefully.

I shook my head, then shrugged. "Probably not?" I took his hands and held them firmly. "Is that a *yes* or *no*?"

"It's a very reluctant *yes*."

I grinned. Before Grayson could take his answer back, I closed my eyes, took a deep breath, and unfurled the strings holding my Gift in place. I plucked at the threads hesitantly, praying inwardly that the magic would flow freely. I had used quite a bit of it earlier today, and the idea of it sputtering out in front of Grayson was an all-too-real possibility that would be devastatingly embarrassing. Not that he would know what was happening. He'd never seen magic before, after all. I could be a downright failure and he would still be amazed.

But I didn't want to be a failure. I wanted to be spectacular.

I scrunched up my face and focused harder on my energy. I was certain I looked ridiculous, but I couldn't waste any time thinking about it. And then the strangest thing happened.

I barely had to call upon my Gift. In fact, I hadn't; I'd merely pulled on the strings and thought about reaching into my reserves and coaxing it out of its slumber, and suddenly, it was there, pooling within me, ready to surge through my veins and out my fingertips. I could feel it warm my insides as the familiar hum vibrated through me, a scattered light sending my scales glowing.

I held my breath, focusing on harnessing the Gift until it was flooding my hands. It was almost difficult to control, the amount of it, the power of it. It craved a release, the tension behind it palpable.

I opened my eyes, found Grayson's uncertain ones, and smiled warmly.

With barely a whisper of a command, the magic pulsed forward, encompassing the boy's hands in a blinding light. Grayson yelped and tried to yank his hands away, but I held on to him firmly, keeping him still until he was wholly enveloped by the Gift. The magic hummed and crackled as it rushed over Grayson's hands, binding his broken flesh, soothing his rope burns, peeling off the scabs and replacing them with fresh skin. It was steadfast, unrelenting, hell-bent on eradicating the pain until it was a distant memory.

There was no flickering, no snuffing out. Nothing. Just pure, unfiltered magic.

I pulled on the edges of my Gift, willing it away from Grayson's hands and back into mine. When it was safely nestled within me, I began to cinch up the strings again, feeling a fluttering pleasure in my chest as the magic strained against them, fighting to be released again. I had never felt so powerful before, so unstoppable.

Was it because of Grayson?

Fingers still tingling, I bit my lip and glanced at the boy. I felt weightless, unmoored. Suddenly, his opinion was the most important thing that mattered.

"Well?" I asked hesitantly.

Grayson was looking at his hands, turning them back and forth, his eyes wide, his mouth agape. "How . . ." he croaked, coughed, and cleared his throat. "How did you do that?" he managed to ask in a thick, strained voice.

I shrugged gently, tossing him a whimsical smile. "Magic."

Grayson's eyes darted to mine, his expression frustratingly unreadable.

My smile faltered. "Do you not believe me?"

Grayson shook his head with enough force that it nearly sent him off-kilter. "It's not that." He exhaled a heavy breath and sat up straight. "Magic," he said, testing out the word in his mouth. "I just witnessed magic."

I nodded slowly, my smile returning. "Yes."

Grayson whipped his head to me, his face glowing with excitement. He let out a gasp of laughter. "Magic! Real live magic!" He put his hands to his head, his fingers digging into his wild curls. "That was incredible! *You're* incredible!"

My cheeks began to burn at his praise, but the feeling wasn't necessarily unpleasant. The boy's enthusiasm was contagious, and I found myself laughing along with him.

My laughter was cut abruptly short when Grayson pounced forward, leaning on his hands, his face right in front of mine. "Can I see it again?"

I held my breath and gave the boy a once-over, trying in vain to not think about how close he was. "Are you still injured?"

Grayson sulked heartily. "No," he sighed, pulling back. "I actually feel better than I have all week." He sounded so disappointed as he stretched his arms and craned his neck, hoping in vain to find a crick or cramp. "But that . . ." He whistled, leaning back on his hands. "That sure was amazing. Can all mermaids do that?"

A seed of sadness planted itself in my gut. "All mermaids possess a Gift," I said, agreeing. "But I am the last healer."

Grayson immediately sobered up. "That must be a lot of pressure."

The boy's words unlocked something within me, and my heart began to beat in a frenzy. *He understands me*, I thought. *He gets it*. The relief was nearly intoxicating.

"Yes," I said quietly. "The last healer, and the last leader. The pod looks to me for support, for all their wounds and troubles. I worry that I will give them everything I have, until I am nothing but a dried-up husk, and it still won't be enough."

Grayson said nothing for a beat, only clucked his tongue and reached forward, placing a hand on my tail. "I'm so sorry," he eventually whispered, his heart in his throat, in his eyes, and I believed him. Truly, without a doubt, I believed that he ached with a comprehending that no one else seemed to grasp.

No matter how much I pleaded, how much I begged, there was always a part of them that assumed I was a queen, a leader, and therefore, I could handle it. They never looked close enough to see the cracks riddling my scales, the crevices and fissures following my veins. One more problem and I'd shatter completely.

"If it comforts you any," the boy continued, "I know what you mean." He chuckled wryly. "Not about the magic, obviously, but about feeling the weight of everyone's expectations. My pa . . ." Grayson sighed, rubbing his forehead. "I'm all he has, and some days it feels like he has put all his hopes and dreams on me, not realizing how heavy those things really are. I'm so worried that one day I'll let him down." He shrugged, frowning. "Well, I *know* I've already let him down in countless ways, but . . . you know . . . in a way that's irreversible. And I won't be able to fix it."

A feverish shiver raced up my spine. "We are simply supposed to be perfect," I said in a low whisper.

Grayson nodded. "And nothing short of it."

Silence began to settle into the bones of the night. I could feel the boy's eyes on me, waiting to see if I'd tear down more of my walls. Part of me wanted to. Gods, part of me wanted to so *badly*. But I had already overshared, avoiding the real reason behind my visit long enough. I blinked rapidly, letting out a quick laugh as I shook my head. "Enough about me," I said, waving my hand, hoping it would erase the pain burdening Grayson's face. "Tell me about your day. How did the first challenge fare?"

Grayson stared long and hard at me for a moment more before he reluctantly relented. "Pretty well, if I'm being honest," he admitted, trying—and failing—to not beam with pride. "Out of all the hunters, my net was fifth best."

I gasped, clapping my hands together. "That's superb! You must be pleased."

Grayson shrugged, ducking his head, but I could tell he was. I steadied my breathing. This was it. Now was my chance. I glanced down at the foam starting to accumulate around my fluke and gently dipped my fingers into it, watching as the bubbles popped. "Are you worried someone might steal it?" I asked, keeping my voice even. "Being one of the better nets?"

Grayson snorted. "No." He gave me a wry smile. "The beast is much too heavy for anyone to carry. And even if someone was brave enough to try, Black Sands Beach in Fariid is sandwiched between the bustling boardwalk and the town center; they would get caught for sure."

My skin began to itch. *"Black Sands Beach,"* I thought, glancing nonchalantly over my shoulder to the water, where I knew Illeron was waiting with prickling nerves. *"Fariid."*

"Good," Illeron replied, and I could practically hear his sigh of relief. *"That's good. We have what we need. Let's go."*

I chewed on my lip, glowering at the water. *"Not yet."*

"Evanora," Illeron said, the impatience evident.

"Not. Yet." I turned back to Grayson. "Surely Fariid isn't busy at all hours," I coaxed gently. "Night seems like the perfect time to commit such a crime."

Grayson considered with a slow nod, then went back to shaking his head. "I don't think so. The other nets, maybe. But not mine."

I lifted my hand, inspecting the foam on my fingers. It shimmered in the moonlight. I grinned coyly, reaching forward and dotting the tip of Grayson's nose with it. "You called it the first challenge," I said as the boy laughed and wiped at the foam. "Will there be more?"

Grayson's hands went from cleaning his nose to running down his entire face, a long, drawn-out groan escaping through his fingers. "Yes," he moaned. "It's going to be awful."

I shifted my facial features to match Grayson's, making sure to mask my delight with concern. "Worse than destroying your hands on ropes and barbs?"

Grayson nodded emphatically. "Much, much worse," he said, finally pulling his hands away. "We have two more challenges. Swimming is in five days, combat in ten." He shrugged defeatedly, stuffing his hands into his lap. "I can fake my way around combat, but swimming? I'm pretty sure I'm going to die." Grayson laughed, but he had grown pale, and the mirth was weak.

I pursed my lips to the side and raised a single eyebrow. "Why are you so afraid of the water, Grayson Shaw?"

It wasn't a question that would benefit me or the plan. But I wanted to know.

Because the boy understood me so well, and I wanted to understand him too. I wanted to help.

Grayson opened his mouth, but his words were cut short when a mighty splash erupted from the water. The boy was immediately on his feet, his hands on the hilt of his knife, his eyes scanning the ocean for signs of danger. His fingers trembled as they danced along the handle, his eyes narrowed as they darted back and forth. His throat bobbed as he swallowed hard. "What was that?" he asked, his voice quivering with poorly concealed fear.

I fought against rolling my eyes. *A pesky mermaid*, I thought. "Just the waves," I breathed, keeping my voice soft as I reached a hand up and brushed my fingers against his. "Only the waves."

"I'll do it again," Illeron warned from his hiding place. *"Let's go."*

I almost turned to scowl at the crashing ocean, knowing the warrior would be able to feel the heated wrath of it despite the distance. But something about Grayson held me still. The fragility of him, the vulnerability. He was afraid. I could see it in his eyes, hear it in his shuddering breath, feel it in his twitching fingers. Truly, truly afraid.

It took a second, but Grayson slowly let his fingers tangle with mine. He stood there, his eyes on the dark waters, but his body was anchored to the shore, to me. He shook his head. "I should go," he whispered, tearing his eyes away from the murky black to look at me. "It's late."

I attempted to hide my disappointment—my very real, very damning disappointment—but judging the look on Grayson's face, I failed spectacularly. The boy chuckled under his breath and crouched, not letting go of my fingers.

"Until next time?" he asked shyly, his eyes burrowing into mine with such earnestness that I found myself frozen, trapped in those stormy blues, drowning.

I forced a smile and nodded. "Until next time, Grayson Shaw. And not a second later."

The boy's mouth quirked, and he leaned forward. Not to caress me like I dared to want—like my heart craved—but to skim his free hand in the water's edge, collecting a dollop of foam. Quick as lightning, he poked my pointed nose, covering the tip with it.

"Bye," he whispered as he stood, taking small steps back, his eyes never leaving mine.

He didn't let go of my hand until he absolutely had to.

The second the boy was out of view, I felt a rush of water at my back, the heat behind a pair of scathing ruby-red eyes.

Illeron said nothing, allowing me to gaze up at the steps a little longer, to hold on to the image of the boy, to replay his words in my mind. Until my heartbeat resumed its natural rhythm, and my breathing slowed, and my fingers stopped aching for Grayson's touch.

Until the threads connecting me to the boy loosened the slightest bit, allowing a minuscule reprieve.

"What are you doing, Evanora?" Illeron finally asked, his voice low and dark.

I knew what he was asking. I knew there was a right way to answer him, and a wrong way. I wiped the foam off my nose and forced myself to look over my shoulder at the warrior. "I'm getting information," I said carefully, hardening my features. "I'm following through with the plan. *Our* plan."

Illeron's eyes were deadly as they slowly dripped from mine to the wooden steps sidling the cliff, then back to me. "I hope," he sighed quietly, turning away, "that's all you're doing."

CHAPTER THIRTY-THREE

GRAYSON

APRIL 10 – EVENING

COULDN'T STOP STARING AT MY HANDS.

I was in bed, hands above my face, turning them back and forth. I tried to remember where the blisters and rope burns had been, but besides the calluses, there was no trace of the challenge from earlier that day. I exhaled sharply, dropping my hands to my chest, feeling my heart thrum against its cage.

Evanora's touch had been like cool silk. I kept expecting it to be wet, almost slimy, but it wasn't. Her skin held the ocean's kiss, a whisper of shimmering jewels hidden beneath the sand. It wasn't coarse like mine. Her sparkling scales were soft, and the webbing between her fingers felt like satin. I pressed my hands together, watching my fingers intertwine.

Every time I saw her, I could feel the connection between us tightening. It was perplexing—I had no idea why it was there or why it was with her. And each time I left the beach, the thread binding my heart would loosen slightly, but it never completely gave way. I could always feel it, constricting my heartbeats, stifling my blood.

Did Evanora feel the same way?

I sat up in bed, determination swirling within me. I wanted to give her something, something to show her that I *saw* her, I *understood* her. Even if we never talked about the connection between us, I wanted to show her that I felt it and all the light and life it possessed.

But it needed to be something that wouldn't break if you so much as looked at it the wrong way, something sturdier than flowers. Something as strong as the bond that tethered us, linking us together.

I scanned the room, eyes drifting to the bookshelf Warrick and I had shared. A small wooden box atop a pile of books caught my attention.

"That might work," I murmured, pushing myself off the bed and heading toward the shelf.

The box was simple, fitting comfortably in my hands. Dark walnut stained the wood, and a swirl of natural grain formed a heart on the lid. A small golden clasp kept it shut. I flicked the latch and eased the lid open, the side hinges squeaking in protest. It had been a long time since I'd dared to look inside. As the box opened, a ballerina popped up, spinning lazily in a pirouette. She was a little lopsided and missing an arm. Quiet, haunting music filled the room—a tinny, out-of-tune melody. The box had belonged to Ma. When I was younger, she would set the ballerina free and hum the melody as she tucked me and Warrick into bed, scratching our backs until we fell asleep.

I didn't think I could bear parting with the music box, but the thing inside it was fair game. I carefully plucked out the silver bracelet nestled in the box's velvet lining. I ran my finger along the engraved Orion's Belt pattern, resisting the urge to touch my cheek, where my freckles created their own little constellation. The octopus charm caught in the bedroom's dim candlelight, glinting as it twisted on its silver hoop.

The bracelet I'd bought Ma, the one I'd never be able to give her. The patients at Rose Hill weren't allowed to have nice things. But Evanora . . . I sucked in a breath, folding my fingers around the bracelet as I looked out the open window. I had a feeling it would look amazing on her dainty wrist. It was the perfect gift for the perfectly unusual creature.

Nodding my head approvingly, I placed the bracelet on the desk and turned back to my bed. I would give it to her the next time I saw her.

The one who was promised . . .

I froze, one foot on the floor, the other up on my bed. The hair on the back of my neck rose as a cool breeze fluttered through the room. My heart thumped loudly in the pit of my stomach. *What was that?*

The one who was promised. Here.

Alone in my room, in the dead of night, when the rest of Lethe was asleep, it sounded like voices. A lot of voices mixing into one.

And they were talking to me.

Here. Here. Here.

I slowly craned my neck from side to side, surveying the room with wide eyes, afraid of what I might see. The candle flickered, casting long shadows onto the walls. I was alone. I had been all evening. So . . .

Where were the voices coming from?

I pushed off the bed, standing rigidly.

Here, here, here, the voices whispered again. They sounded thick, drenched in water, bubbling and gurgling as each voice fought to be heard over the others.

I swallowed hard, my gaze pulling to the open window. I took a shaky step forward, gripping the edges of the desk to steady myself. Holding my breath, I leaned forward, peering out the window.

Here, here, here! the voices cried, growing chaotic as they grappled for my attention.

My eyes drifted to the dark ring circling the island. The place where even the moonlight didn't dare touch. It was a black hole amidst the gleaming waves, a vortex swallowing all light and life from the ocean. The Barrens, dark and ominous and deadly.

HERE!

My bedroom door opened abruptly, crashing into the wall with a loud *crack!* I yelped and whirled around, stumbling back into my desk, sending jars clattering and notebooks flailing.

Pa stood at the threshold of my room, looking nearly as startled as I was.

"God, Pa!" I choked out, quickly turning to my desk and righting all the fallen jars before their juices spilled everywhere. I hoped he didn't see the sweat on my brow, the fear dancing in my eyes. "Can't you knock?"

Pa's face scrunched together, and he gently ran a hand through his hair, uncharacteristically out of its typical topknot and falling down to his shoulders. He took a step into the room. "It's a bit chilly," he said, ignoring my request. "You should shut the window."

My head shot up, and I nearly dropped one of the jars. "No!" I said, a bit too forcefully. My cheeks went warm, and I shook my head, avoiding Pa's hard stare. "I like the night air. It helps me sleep."

Pa narrowed his eyes, his mouth set in a thin line. He continued to make his way into the room. I looked down at my hands. Evanora's sketched eyes peeked out between my splayed fingers. Stifling a gasp, I slammed the journal shut, forcing out a weak chuckle when my pa frowned at me. I cleared my throat and leaned against the desk, folding my arms against my chest and trying to appear as nonchalant as I possibly could despite my insides turning mushy. "Is there a reason why you barged into my room with such vigor?"

Pa, who was running a hand over Ma's music box, stopped, his shoulders hunching. "There is," he said quietly, his voice suddenly low.

I took a long, slow breath. Had he heard the voices too? I swallowed around the lump in my throat. Had he seen the sketch of Evanora? I shrugged, the movement stiff. "What is it, then?"

Pa looked at the bookshelf a moment longer before he turned to face me, his eyes downcast, his lips dipping low, a light coating of blush—wait, *blush*?—splotching his cheeks. "My hands are hurting, you see," he mumbled. "I was hoping you'd have something for them. An ointment or salve, maybe."

My mouth dropped open, but I quickly smothered it with a fist. My eyes shifted to Pa's hands, where he was cradling them delicately against his stomach. "Your hands?" I asked, not sure if I'd heard him right.

Pa ducked his head, nodding sheepishly. "With the shape they're in, I can't even do my damned hair." He sighed, his dark eyes darting to mine. "I think I went a bit too hard at the challenge today."

I loosed something between a breath of relief and a laugh. "Well, that's what you get for coming in top five."

Pa growled, but the sound was burdened with embarrassment. "Do you have something or not?"

Still snickering, I turned and grabbed a couple jars from my desk. One was oil with flecks of dried leaves in it. The other was a thick salve with crushed white and yellow petals mixed in. "These should do the trick," I said, tucking them into the crook of Pa's arm. "Comfrey," I said, nodding to the oily jar, "and a mix of yarrow and calendula," I said, gesturing to the other. "Wash your hands first, then slather these on. The salve in the morning, the oil before bed. And make sure you wrap your hands in clean bandages afterward." I nodded, inspecting the jars Pa was cradling. "You'll be right as rain before the next challenge."

My pa held the jars like they were the most precious things he'd ever seen. "What would I do without you?" He glanced at me, at the hands I had casually tucked behind my back. "Well, how are you feeling?" He chuckled, shaking his head. "With a net like yours, your hands must be minced meat."

I grimaced. "That's gross."

"Let me see them," Pa prodded, lighting up. "Let's compare battle wounds."

I quickly shook my head, refraining from taking a step back and running into my desk again. I couldn't let him see my hands in all their healed glory.

"Honestly, Pa, I'm really tired. You caught me right when I was about to go to bed."

For the second time that day, I could see disappointment creep along Pa's face, hardening his features back into their usual stone. "Right," he said gruffly, turning away. "Get your rest. We'll resume training in the morning."

"But . . ." I stammered out, pushing off the desk. "But your hands, Pa. You need to let them heal a bit."

Pa looked at me from over his shoulder. "If your hands are up for the challenge, then so are mine."

I stared at him for a beat. He was suspicious. He knew something was up. I managed a small smile. "Tomorrow morning, then." I cocked my head to the side, forcing the smile to grow. "Hope you can keep up," I added, trying to erase some of the tension.

Pa nodded curtly. He left the room with a grunt, taking a bit more care in closing the door than he had with opening it.

I sighed heavily, turning in a small circle in the center of my room. I made a mental note to wrap my hands in bandages to ease my pa's suspicions, but it wasn't long before I found myself staring at the window again, listening for the voices.

There was nothing, only the distant crashing of waves and the ever-flowing thunder of the waterfall.

Had I imagined them? Sure, I felt the gentle, coaxing pull of the ocean all the time, lulling me with its hypnotic embrace. But this . . .

A shudder ripped through me. This was definitely different. It was visceral, ancient, a thousand years' worth of voices trapped into one. It was dark and sinister, nothing like the tender whispers of the water.

There were two options to consider. The first: I was taking after Ma and slowly going crazy. It was terrifying and absolutely plausible. The second: I could hear the voices in my head, my heart, and outside of my body, all weaving together until it was a symphony of ominous chaos. And it was very, very real.

CHAPTER THIRTY-FOUR

EVANORA

APRIL 10 – EVENING

W E SHOULD TURN AROUND."

"We should keep *going*." I shot Illeron a hard look. "*Silently.*"

Illeron didn't say anything for a beat, but I could see the skin around his eyes tighten, his jaw clenching. "It's too dark," he said in a low growl, glancing at the shadows surrounding us. "I can hear them."

I shook my head, forcing myself to swim faster. I could hear the Cursed Beings too, their incessant whisperings despite being miles from the Barrens. They were out tonight, hunting. I fought against the shiver that rolled over my scales and tightened my grip on the spear. "The moon will protect us. And if we stay close to shore, we should be fine. The Cursed Beings never venture this far inland."

Illeron's mouth dipped, and I saw the flash of his sharp teeth. "How could you possibly know that?"

I shrugged. "Well," I sighed, flipping around so I was swimming on my back, "for starters, if I was wrong, we would know it, because we'd be dead already."

Illeron rolled his eyes, but the tension drifted from his face—not completely, but enough. "What a charming thought."

I grinned cheekily and spun around, tossing one last furtive glance at the plump moon as I did. "We'll be fine," I promised. "We'll be in and out before they even get a chance to catch our scent."

"Again, with the charm."

"What can I say? I'm a delight."

Pebbly beige beaches on the western side slowly turned into black shale on the southern point, which then gave way to the glimmering onyx shores of the east. Churning gray waves shifted to that of sapphire and turquoise. The town's lights lining the boardwalk danced on the calm surface, and the distant sounds of drunken laughter wavered in the breeze. Music crept through the streets, becoming distorted as it ricocheted off brick buildings and squeezed through narrow alleys. The air was heavy with an assault of smells. Roasted fish. Chemicals. Oil. I could feel the telltale signs of a headache.

Even at night, Fariid was alive. The beach, thankfully, was empty.

I poked the tip of my head out of the water, scanning Black Sands Beach. Littering the shore, just as Grayson had promised, were the nets. A *lot* of nets. I bit back my grin and submerged, turning to Illeron. I was nearly giddy with my excitement. "They're all there," I said breathlessly. "Just like he said."

The warrior cocked his head to the side, rubbing his thumb thoughtfully over his bottom lip. "Perhaps your boy is good for something," he allowed begrudgingly.

I was about to push for the surface again when Illeron caught my arm, pulling me back down to him. I gave him a questioning look. Illeron loosened his grip but didn't let go completely. "So?" he asked.

I raised my eyebrows. "So . . . ?"

Illeron scoffed. "So, now what?"

I hefted my spear. "When I was trapped in the net, Grayson Shaw set me free. He shredded the entire thing in a matter of minutes." I shook my head. "He was using a knife, but I am certain we will be able to inflict the same sort of damage with these spears." I looked up at the surface in the direction of the beach. "We can't take the nets anywhere; it would be nearly impossible to move so many, not to mention dangerous for us. But to leave them behind as scraps? Well, that would be just a tragic misfortune, wouldn't it?" I pouted innocently.

"It would certainly send a message." Illeron crossed his arms against his chest. "Go on."

I nodded. "We will work separately, tearing apart the nets just enough so that they are useless. We start at the ones closest to us, then work our way up the beach. It's high tide, so let's use that to our advantage." I tossed the spear between my hands, the weapon becoming suspended in the weightlessness of the water. "How's that for a plan?"

Illeron stared hard at me for a long second before sighing, his armored shoulders drooping. "Well . . . at least it's a plan."

Together, we rose above the surface. The beach was still empty. We could hear voices, but they were locked behind closed doors, muffled by the clinking of mugs and the slamming of fists on tables. Wordlessly, we crept forward, our tails undulating silently in the water, careful not to create a single splash. The waves, a gracious transport, carried us to the first row of nets.

Nerves taut, fins rigid, I glanced around one last time before reaching out with a shaking hand, fingers wrapping around a cold, wet net. The bells jingled tiredly, the barb glinting in the moonlight. Illeron watched, holding his breath, as I aimed the spear between the rope's fibers.

A memory of being trapped in the net fluttered through my mind, uninvited and laced with fear. I shoved it aside, but blood-soaked images of Solandis wrapped in her own roped cage followed. I shook my head roughly, dispelling the memories. I was no longer inside the net. I was outside it, and what I had to do would prevent any mermaid from suffering the same fate as the merling.

Grayson had known exactly what to do to free me. If I could just replicate his steps . . .

The tip twitched and jostled before sinking its teeth into the rope, burying itself into the strands. I wedged the spear in hard and began to turn it, creating a big-enough hole to stick my fingers into. Exhaling sharply, I removed the spear and tossed it into the sand, staring hard at the hole I had created. Sparing a single look at Illeron, I stuck my fingers into the loosened fibers and began to pull.

It worked.

The ropes groaned against my straining and began to give way, snapping under the pressure of my fingers. I gasped with relief and pulled harder. When the hole was large enough for a head and shoulders to fit through, I began to make another one, confidence sending my hands still, my breathing controlled. I looked at Illeron. *Just like that,* I thought, nodding tersely.

Illeron watched my hands work for a moment longer, his entire face tight with concentration, before pushing away and grabbing a net for himself.

We worked in silence, poking as many holes as we dared into the nets before discarding them and grabbing another. I willed my fingers to work faster, careful to keep my thoughts calm and positive despite the number of nets that loomed before us. There were so many. Would we get through all of them in time? My mind said, *No*. My heart said, *We must*.

Illeron was quick to catch on, and he blazed a trail, leaving me several rows back. I could feel his eyes on me as he pulled himself farther up the beach. *"Try to keep up, Your Majesty."* In the deep dark night, I saw a flash of a grin.

My heart spasmed, and I felt my own mouth twitch. *"Just focus on your nets, warrior."*

Illeron chuckled quietly, turning his attention back to the ropes.

When I reached the second row, I froze. Before me lay a massive net. The bordering ropes twisted into one giant braid, and several bells winked in the moonlight, daring me to lift it quietly. The structure was different, with thick squares knotted in place instead of neat diamonds. It was heavy—I could barely lift the edge onto my lap. As I tried to grab the border, I hissed and pulled away. Barbs were woven into every strand, making it almost impossible to access.

Illeron crawled next to me, panting lightly with the effort. His eyes dragged along the giant net, his mouth tightening. "It's his," he guessed. "Grayson's."

Not trusting my voice, I nodded, cradling my finger where the barb had burrowed in with purpose.

Illeron continued to stare hard at the beast of rope and barbed wire and bells. "Can you destroy it?"

I nodded again, but my mind gave me away. *"I don't think so."*

Illeron sighed heavily, then nudged me with his elbow. "Lucky for you, I don't share the same attitude." He jerked his chin, gesturing to the surrounding nets. "Keep working. I'll catch up."

My heart swelled, grateful. I pushed away, trying not to wince as the warrior grunted, the sound of his spear digging into the rope reaching my ears. It had to be done. I couldn't be sentimental over something just because the boy had made it—especially when that very thing looked like it wanted to bury me in its needlelike teeth and eat me, jingling merrily as it did.

I grabbed another net and attacked it with vigor.

There was a scream, a long keening wail drenched in terror. It sailed through the surrounding alleys, shattering the silence.

Fingers seizing, my head shot up as ice filled my veins. I caught Illeron's alarmed look as the screaming ascended into a high-pitched cry.

And as quickly as it had pierced the night, it was over, leaving behind only the remnants of an echo tumbling off the buildings. The fear that had been clinging to the frantic sound hung in the air, thick and nauseating, before it, too, dissipated.

I looked at Illeron, swallowing. *"Hurry,"* I pleaded inwardly. *"We must hurry."*

I didn't want to think about the scream, about what had caused it, about who had made such a mortifying sound. All I could think about were the nets, about destroying them so we could go back home, far away from this ominous and evil place.

I forced myself to move. As quickly as my fingers would let me, as hard as my spear would go. Like that scream was a warning, and it was only a matter of time before I'd be next, making the same sound. Net after net, I worked ceaselessly. Even when my hands began to cramp, and the barbs began to bite back. Even when the clinking of bells sent my skin crawling.

I wasn't sure how much time had passed, but when I finally allowed myself a break, I was astounded to see how far we had come. We were on the second-to-last row of nets, a trail of destruction in our wake. The water was far behind, and the tide had receded. The moon hung low in a sky of shifting blues and ashy grays. Our hands were raw, our claws chipped. Even the webbing between my fingers pricked with slivers. Blood seeped from our skin, trapped between scales. I leaned back on my burning hands and surveyed the last row of nets lying just before the stone walkway separating the sand from solid ground.

Reading my thoughts, Illeron let out a low growl. "Evanora," he said, attempting a slow shuffle toward me, "we've done enough. It's time to leave."

"There is still an entire row of nets left."

"It's too dangerous!"

I shook my head and began hoisting myself through the sand. "We've already come this far." I gritted my teeth, ignoring the sting as sand burrowed into my wounds. "Keep working on this row. I'll start on the last one."

"Evanora," Illeron pleaded. "Please."

I kept moving, my arms trembling with fatigue as I wriggled my tail. I was sure I was the picture of poise and grace and not at all pathetic looking. "You can scold me about this later. Keep working."

I heard Illeron huff, then the sound of bells as he grabbed another net. I allowed a minuscule amount of hope to warm my heart. *We can do this*, I thought, reaching for a pile of rope. *We are so close!*

My scales had grown dry and scratchy hours ago, the gills on my neck crusty. Every breath I took was an effort, hitching in my lungs, scraping my insides like glass shards. A mermaid could be on dry land for short lengths of time, and I had a feeling my time limit had long expired. I desperately needed to go back into the water, to replenish my reserves. I eyed the last three nets as the waves called out to me. Their gentle sloshing was like music, but I shook my head, fighting against the urge to turn and scuttle back into its melodious embrace. To leave now was to give up, and I was too stubborn. And stupid. I was much too stupid to give up.

By the time I was reaching for the last net, I was nearly delirious with excitement. My breath was coming out in heavy choked pants, and my fingers could barely grip the thick rope. Holding on to the spear was a joke, and I was resorting more and more to using my teeth to pry the threads loose. I yanked open one hole and set out to make another. *Last one*, I chanted, sparing a precious second to wipe a mixture of blood and drool from my chin. *Last one!*

I was so focused on the net that I didn't hear the footsteps.

There was a sudden blinding light. I hissed and threw up a hand to cover my eyes, shrinking away from the brilliance. The movement was so hasty that I snagged my finger on a barb, the metal digging into the tip and dragging all the way to my webbing. The pain was muffled, not even registering.

"Mermaid!" a voice slurred from the stone steps. "Oy! There's a mermaid down 'ere!"

Baring my teeth, I lowered my hand enough to see the silhouette of a man swaying by the stone steps, holding a circular device in his shaking hand that was the source of the illumination. He had it trained on me with a laser focus, and once again, I found myself trapped, this time in a cage of light.

Illeron was already in the water. "Evanora," he cried. "Hurry!"

The man lurched forward and stumbled down the stairs, belching and grunting with each step. "Mermaiiiiiid," he sang, giggling as he tripped on the last one. "Come herrrrrre, little mermaid!"

Fear spiked in my bloodstream, sending wave after wave of adrenaline with it. I looked down at the net in my lap. I had only put one hole in it. It was still lethal and more than capable of doing its job. With a growl, I brought it to my lips and began tugging on the ropes with all the energy I could muster.

"Evanora!" Illeron screamed, his voice cracking with dread.

Out of the corner of my eye, I could see the warrior crawling up the beach to me, leaving the safety of the water behind. He would never reach me in time. The net slipped from my fingers, and I grabbed for it again.

The man staggered, struggling to find his balance as hard stone gave way to sand. "Mermaid!" he slurred, pushing greasy hair out of his eyes. "What's an ugly thing like you doin' out 'ere?" He tripped, falling to his knees, sending up a spray of sand. The light source flew from his hand, its beam spiraling before crashing onto the beach and blinking out. "Christ Almighty!" he groaned, pulling himself up slowly. "Look what ya made me do, hey?" He looked down at his trousers. "Got holes in me good Sunday pants!" Rolling up his sleeves, he began stomping toward me with renewed vigor. "Oh, you'll pay for that. I'll make a necklace outta yer scales!"

A piece of barb nicked the corner of my mouth, but I didn't let go. With a feral roar, I ripped at the ropes. There was a great tearing sound, and the net went slack. Hissing, I dropped it and began dragging myself toward the shoreline, straining against the sand. The sea seemed impossibly far away. I was exhausted—beyond exhausted—but I couldn't stop. I couldn't end up like Solandis. *Think of the pod*, I commanded. *You need to be there for your pod!*

Illeron stopped at the sight of my hurried crawl and began to wriggle back into the water, his eyes never leaving me. His face was cinched tightly with fear, his fins rigid. "Come on," he moaned, slapping the water with his fluke. "Come on!"

I didn't have to look back to know that the man was running. He was running, and even in his drunken state, he was catching up.

I scraped my way to the water's edge, ignoring the pain radiating down my front as the sand scrubbed me raw. Illeron reached for me, his lips pulled back in a snarl, a growl on his tongue.

There was a hand on my tail, thick and hot and sweaty.

"Gotcha!" the man cackled loudly.

I didn't give him a second to revel in his victory. With a shriek, I twisted around, the movement quick and fluid. I grabbed a fistful of sand as I turned, and I flung it into the man's smug face.

The man sputtered, eyes squeezing shut in a delayed reaction. He let go and began wiping his face, cursing under his breath between spitting. "You bitch," he howled. "You stupid fish devil!"

The second my tail was free, I whipped it back and snapped it as hard as I could, connecting the fluke with the side of his head. The man's neck cracked sideways, and he crumpled face-first into the sand with a muffled groan.

He didn't look like he was getting up anytime soon, but I wasted no time closing the distance between me and freedom. Grabbing Illeron's hand, I used my momentum to pull us both into the water.

The sea gripped me as I sank into it, the water like nectar on my wounds. It soothed my burning lungs as I breathed it in, soaking me from the inside out. In a matter of seconds, my scales softened, my fins plumped and flared, and my muscles relaxed.

We raced away from Fariid. And the entire time we swam, all I could think about was that man's hand on my tail and how it had felt nothing like Grayson's.

We didn't stop swimming until we reached Tully's beach, where the sleepy village lacked any sign of nightlife. We tucked ourselves next to the rocky cove, sinking to the sandy floor, gasping. Sitting close, shoulders brushing, fins tangling, we looked around, wild-eyed, waiting for footsteps, voices, or nets.

But nothing came.

It was just me, Illeron, and the ocean.

I looked at him, and unexpectedly, I began to laugh. It started small, a light snicker that grew until it erupted into an unladylike guffaw, tears in my eyes as I hugged my aching sides. Once it started, I couldn't stop. Illeron stared, horrified, until his chiseled mask cracked, little hairline fractures streaking his face, then shattering entirely. He began to laugh too.

I didn't know how long we sat there, cackling like lunatics. It felt good—like a release, a weight lifted from my chest. I was buoyant, weightless, free. Our first mission had been a complete success. I could've cried with relief.

Illeron stopped laughing first. He was looking at me, smiling gently, the moonlight making his crimson eyes dance. He reached forward tentatively and brushed a strand of hair out of my face. The movement must've hurt—his fingers were torn up, worse than mine—but the only shift in his face was the blush that rose to his sharp cheekbones, and the way his eyes darted from mine to my lips. When the hair was tucked behind my ear, the warrior didn't pull away. Instead, he cupped his hand to the side of my face, caressing my cheek with his thumb.

I forced myself to swallow the rest of my mirth. I could hear a low but mighty sound, a pulsing rush in my ears, and I realized it was my racing heartbeat.

I closed my eyes with a sigh and leaned into his touch.

And I found myself thinking about Grayson Shaw.

I pulled away, clearing my throat. "We should rest here for the remainder of the night," I said, hating how my voice quivered. "It's too dangerous to swim back home now." I nodded, more to reassure myself than Illeron. "The lanterns are lit; the pod will be safe."

I couldn't meet his hungry, searching gaze. It felt like an eternity, but eventually, the warrior let out a long breath and leaned back against the rocky cove. "That's my line, Your Majesty."

I smirked. "Oh, hush." I lifted my aching hands and ran them over my body, allowing my Gift to rise to the surface, healing the wounds it came across. Within seconds, it began to sputter and crackle, spasming as I reached the dredges of my reserves. I frowned as the light faded from my fingertips rather unceremoniously. "Well, that's pathetic."

Illeron chuckled, rolling his head to the side and raising a dark eyebrow at me. "What did you expect? You're exhausted." He sighed, shrugging. "No one can fault you for that."

I bit my lip, nodding. Still, when I was healing Grayson, my magic had felt bottomless, without end. I could barely control it; it had ached to be released. And now? I could hardly call it out of its slumber. I flicked my fingers and loosened up my wrists, as if that was where the problem was.

When I reached for Illeron, the warrior pulled his hands away, shaking his head. I looked down at my hands, wounded by his distance. "Don't you want me to at least try?"

"No," Illeron breathed. "I want to remember this night. I want the pain to be a reminder of how hard we worked, how we won." He looked at me, a smirk on his lips. "How you bested a man without a weapon."

I rolled my eyes and snorted. "The man was clearly drunk."

"Still." Illeron kept his gaze locked on mine. "I'll never forget the way you smacked him with your tail." He laughed gently. "You are brave—braver than you know, little Evie."

I smiled, then poked him hard in the chest. "Call me that again and I'll feed you to the Cursed Beings."

"Oh, I don't know," Illeron said, shrugging. "I think it rather suits you."

I poked him again.

"You're going to bruise me if you keep doing that." Somewhere along the way, Illeron's voice had grown heavy and thick.

"Well," I said, going in for another poke, "you can use that pain as a reminder too."

Illeron caught my hand swiftly, and I realized he had been *letting* me poke him. His eyes not leaving mine, the warrior brought my hand up to his face. I held my breath as he brushed his lips against my knuckles. I felt him inhale deeply as he closed his eyes.

I swallowed hard. "Illeron?" I asked hesitantly, my voice catching.

The warrior chuckled lightly. I could feel the vibration of it on my fingers. "I was worried," he said quietly, flicking his eyes to mine. "So worried I was going to lose you back there."

I opened my mouth, closed it, and then opened it again. The way he was looking at me was stirring something deep inside me. It warmed my scales, drenched my fluke in fire. It wasn't uncomfortable, or unpleasant, but I still didn't know if I liked it or not. I wondered if Illeron could feel the heat radiating off me. The way he squeezed my hand, I was guessing he could.

"Illeron?" I asked again, my warbling voice giving my nerves away.

Illeron slowly lowered my hand. But he didn't let go, and I didn't pull away. "Get some sleep," he said, turning his attention to the surrounding water. "I'll keep watch."

We sat in silence. The moonlight shimmered on the surface, fluttering through the darkness in dull patches. A school of fish swam by us lazily. The Cursed Beings whispered and moaned.

And Illeron held my hand.

I was far, far from sleep.

CHAPTER THIRTY-FIVE

GRAYSON

APRIL 11 – MORNING

NO ONE WAS AT THE DOCKS.

I stood on the pier, turning in a slow circle. It was dead silent. Nets were scattered on the walkway, waiting to be cast. The ships rocked gently in the waves, their captains nowhere in sight. Mr. Brightly's office light was off, no smoke billowing from the chimney. The fishery felt deserted, with me as the only occupant.

I pulled out my pocket watch, tapping the cracked glass. A few shakes, and the hands began moving again. Not early, not late. I tucked it away and scanned the empty space, frowning.

A lone seagull landed on a dock beam, squawking as it eyed a stray piece of chum. Two occupants now. "Where is everyone?" I asked it.

The bird ignored me, boldly jumping off the beam and hopping to the meat, chirping its victory as it gobbled up its prize. Beak smeared with fish guts, the seagull flew away, and I was back to being alone.

I was about to leave when I heard heavy hooves, quick and frantic. Pa and Pastor Kline came into view, tearing down the road at a pace that clearly made the pastor uncomfortable. Pa was gripping the reins. Pastor Kline clutched his hat, cloak billowing in the wind.

As they rounded the corner, Pa yelled, "Whoa!" The horse skidded to a halt, dust flying up. It chuffed and wheezed, slick with sweat.

I rushed off the dock, running up the boardwalk steps two at a time. "What's going on?" I asked, panic rising in my chest. "Is it Ma? Is she okay?"

Pastor Kline licked his dry lips and started to speak, but Pa cut him off. "It's the nets," he said gruffly, motioning for me to hop in. "Something's happened to them. We're going to Fariid."

I looked at the empty docks behind me. "But Mr. Brightly—"

"Mr. Brightly is in Fariid too," Pa barked. "If he's going to give you a hard time about not being at work, then he'd better look in the mirror while he's doing the scolding."

I didn't need any more convincing. I hoisted myself into the wagon bed. Pastor Kline gulped audibly and reached for the reins, but Pa was faster, and with a quick flick of his wrists, we were off again, racing out of the dirt and onto the road.

I was certain we made it to Black Sands Beach in record time, and I supremely hoped that Pastor Kline would reward his horse for its hard work. I was thankful they hadn't decided to take Penny.

I could hear the voices of outrage before I saw who they belonged to, long cries rising and falling with the waves. Despite the early morning, the beach was crowded. And every single one of its inhabitants was angry.

"Lord have mercy," Pastor Kline uttered as he gazed at the frenzied mass.

I leapt from the wagon before it even stopped, my heart in my throat as I ran down the stone steps to the beach. The crowd was facing the water. Some were staring down, others looking wildly around, eyes wide with rage. Some mouths were clenched, others bared teeth. In the distance, someone wailed.

I spotted Mr. Brightly arguing with Mr. Krieg, pointing at the ground, spittle flying from his lips. Mr. Krieg wiped his face and listened politely.

My stomach flipped with nerves. *What is going on?* I put my head down and shouldered my way to the front of the crowd, mumbling excuses and apologies as I fought to get around pointy elbows and stomping feet.

I tripped to the front, and there were the nets.

Pieces of them, anyway.

Every single one of them was destroyed. Bells and barbed wire were strewn everywhere, threads of rope trampled into the sand. Not a single net was left unscathed; each had a terribly fatal marring. I sucked in a sharp breath, electric shocks tingling down my arms and legs. All our hard work, utterly demolished.

"Who would do this?" I heard someone cry, and I looked over my shoulder to see Peter stomping around, facing off with anyone who dared to look him in the eye. "Was it you? You? Come on, you cowards! Show your face!"

Owen, who was standing next to Sebastian and Tommy, stepped forward, pinching the bridge of his nose. "Calm down, Lyre. N-n-none of us did it," he said, exasperated.

Peter, red-faced and indignant, jutted out his lower lip and trudged toward one of the benches lining the walkway. He sat down with a huff, slouching in his seat with his arms crossed against his wide chest. He had stopped accusing people, but his eyes were on the prowl, watching the crowd carefully.

"I know who did it!" a voice cried, loud and hoarse. "It was them evil mermaids, them *devil* mermaids! That's who did it!"

That was when I noticed the policemen—two of them, stout hats, shiny boots, and long navy jackets—struggling to drag a large man off the beach. He was easily six feet tall, wild-eyed, kicking and growling. The officers looked tired as they tried to haul him away, and judging by their pinched expressions, the man reeked. His hair was matted to his forehead, sand and dried blood coating his face.

"Mermaids!" he crowed, throwing his head back, his body arching away from the policemen. "I swear it!"

"Oh, shut up, Otis," one of the policemen barked.

Mayor McCoy and Mr. Grieves were walking down the stone steps to the beach, their expressions dark and somber. They stopped in front of the policemen doing a poor job of wrangling the man called Otis. Mayor McCoy glowered at him, then sighed heavily, shaking his head. "What seems to be the problem, Officer Crowley?"

Officer Crowley, the older, shorter, and crankier policeman, raised a thick black eyebrow. "Besides the nets? The usual." He jerked his chin toward Otis, his handlebar mustache twitching. "This one keeps spouting off that mermaids ruined the nets. We found him on the beach, passed out in a heap and reeking of booze, surrounded by the carnage, and a spear."

Otis wrenched away from the policemen's firm grip. "It's true! All of it!"

Officer Crowley growled, gripping Otis with one hand and smacking him over the head with the other. "Enough of that gibberish, I say!"

The other officer, tall as a string bean and with a youthful glow still attached to his clean-shaven face, yanked Otis closer to the stairs. "You probably just imagined it, Otis," he said, his voice softer, not yet doused with cynicism. "Right before you fell asleep."

Otis pulled away so he could look the taller officer in the eye. "You know me, Marley. Don'tcha? You know I wouldn't make this up! I might've been drunk as a skunk last night, but I'm sober as a breastfed baby right now!"

Officer Marley frowned. "That doesn't make sense."

Mayor McCoy shook his head and scoffed. "Oh, please. Enough!" He waved a hand to the stairs and the awaiting prison wagon. "Take him away. I can't stand the smell of him, and we have other pressing matters to address."

The officers seemed glad to get on their way, ignoring Otis's cries to be heard as they hauled him up the steps, having to catch him several times as he stumbled. They managed to get him locked behind the prison wagon's large caged doors, though that, too, had them struggling. By the time they crawled up the front of the wagon, both policemen were out of breath and sweating.

Several people beside me shook their heads and snickered under their breath. "Mermaids? Yeah, right," one whispered, elbowing the person next to him. "And I'm the richest man in all of Lethe."

"Mermaids can't do this," the other replied, rubbing his ribs where the elbow had connected. "They're just a bunch of dumb animals."

I bit my lip, turning away to look at the nets again. My stomach churned, and my body couldn't decide whether it was too hot or too cold. So I stood there, covered in sweat and shivering, wondering if there was a speck of truth to the drunkard's words.

Because I knew a mermaid, had seen the fire in her eyes, felt the strength in her touch, heard the feral howls on her tongue. And I had a feeling that she was more than capable of such destruction.

But . . . would Evanora truly do something like this?

I sighed quietly, rubbing the back of my neck. She *had* left in an awful hurry last night. I furrowed my brow. *No*, I remembered. *I'm the one who left. We were talking, and I—*

The sudden splashing. The fear that had swallowed me whole. I remembered wanting to flee. But the look in Evanora's eyes . . .

She didn't look scared. She looked . . . annoyed.

A high-pitched cry yanked my attention back. A woman raced down the stairs, pulling up her dress to keep from tripping. She was pale, with dark circles under her eyes, her long brown hair escaping the crooked bonnet atop her head. She scanned the crowd before spotting Mayor McCoy. With a frantic shriek, she rushed toward him. "Mayor McCoy! My daughter! We must find my daughter!"

Mayor McCoy released a long, drawn-out sigh, hardly glancing in the woman's direction. "Not now, Mrs. Abbott."

The woman, Mrs. Abbott, crumpled to his feet, her shoulders convulsing with heart-wrenching sobs as she reached for the mayor's leg. "Please, Mayor McCoy! My April is missing. She's been gone since last night." Mrs. Abbott could barely force the words out, her voice catching on every single syllable. "You know how she gets at nighttime!"

Mayor McCoy rolled his eyes and looked at Mr. Grieves. "Oh, yes," he mumbled, twirling a finger around his head and mouthing the word *crazy*.

April Abbott. I knew her. She'd been a bright, cheerful girl at school. Despite being blind, she could name every boy by their footsteps. Then the rumors started—voices, visions, and her obsession with the water. Soon enough, she was carted off to Rose Hill, and when she returned, something in her was gone. Her smile was missing, her skin had lost its color, and she withdrew from the world. She stopped caring about things like footsteps.

"Please!" Mrs. Abbott bawled, her hands digging into the mayor's leg. "You have to help me find her!"

Mayor McCoy shook her off with a ferocious tug of his foot. "Please, Mrs. Abbott! Can't you see we're busy?"

Mrs. Abbott dropped her head to the sand, sobbing. "But my girl," she moaned. "My poor April! She must be so scared, so frightened!"

Mayor McCoy looked like he wanted to kick the downed woman. Mr. Grieves stepped in. "Mayor McCoy!" he admonished, crouching to the ground and placing a hand on Mrs. Abbott's shaking back. "Can't you see Mrs. Abbott is in distress?"

Mayor McCoy pursed his lips, a blush rising up his thin cheeks. "Well, yes," he ground out between clenched teeth. "But—"

"There, there," Mr. Grieves tutted, coaxing Mrs. Abbott off the ground and wrapping an arm around her. "All will be well." He shucked off his coat and placed it around Mrs. Abbott's shoulders. His eyes darted up the steps to his chauffeur. "Beaton, start the car."

Mayor McCoy's mouth dropped open. "You're leaving?" he asked incredulously. He swept a hand at the beach. "But the nets!"

Mr. Grieves frowned at the mayor. "Shame on you, Mayor McCoy. Truly. Shame!"

Mayor McCoy promptly shut his mouth, his cheeks growing even redder.

"There, there," Mr. Grieves said again, gently leading the crying woman away from the beach. "We shall find your precious April, Mrs. Abbott. Mark my words. We shall find her."

Mrs. Abbott nodded in between hiccupping breaths and allowed Mr. Grieves to steer her away from the watchful eyes.

The second she was tucked away inside the car, the pair next to me began to curse. "Another one missing?" the first one gasped, shaking his head. "First Harland, and now April? Is anyone safe?"

"Those bloody mermaids," the other replied. "They may not be smart enough to rip apart nets, but they know a thing or two about ripping apart humans!"

"Curse those godforsaken creatures!" the first one spat. "The Hunt can't come soon enough."

My stomach somersaulted, hot and anxious to spill its contents. I gripped my waist, digging my fingers in until my knuckles popped. *Please*, I prayed silently. *Please don't let it be her who did this.*

Another horse and buggy pulled up to the beach. Jasper toppled over the edge and hobbled up to me, looking like he had just rolled out of bed moments before. The hair on one side of his head was pressed flat while the other stuck out at odd angles. Dried drool caked on one of his cheeks, he was attempting to tuck his nightshirt into his pants, one of his suspenders drooping at his waist.

"Hey!" he said breathlessly. "What'd I miss?"

I SAT AT MY DESK, SLOUCHED OVER AND CRADLING MY HEAD IN THE crook of my arm. I flicked my pencil up the slanted tabletop, watching listlessly as it rolled up the wood, then back down to my fingers. The cool evening breeze tickled my neck, trying in vain to wedge its icy fingertips down the collar of my shirt.

What a day.

What a horrible, absolutely terrible day.

I couldn't get the image of the wrecked nets out of my mind, the look on Mrs. Abbott's tearstained face as she wailed about her missing daughter.

I didn't want to believe that it was all a mermaid's doing.

I especially didn't want to believe that that mermaid was Evanora.

The pencil tumbled off the desk, and my eyes flicked to the unfinished sketch of Evanora. The truth was, I didn't know her. I didn't know *anything* about her. And it terrified me.

Was Evanora really a monster? Did I have it all wrong?

No. I shook my head, sitting upright. No, I refused to believe that. The next time I saw her, I'd ask for—no, *demand*—the truth. No matter how ugly. I needed to know if she was behind the horrendous events in Fariid.

Sighing, I slouched forward again. *But would I know if she's telling the truth?*

The connection tethering my heart to hers whispered *yes*, but the alarms in my mind screamed that I was a gullible boy with a head full of sand. All Evanora would have to do is bat her long white eyelashes and pout her full, pale lips, and I'd melt like the putty I was.

Groaning, I covered my face with my hands. "Hopeless," I mumbled. "Hopeless and stupid."

The bells began to ring.

CHAPTER THIRTY-SIX

EVANORA

APRIL 11 – EVENING

GRAYSON WALKED DOWN THE HILL, AND I KNEW SOMEthing was wrong.

He didn't race down the stairs, his feet barely grazing the ground. He didn't beam at me, his face lighting up like the sun was lit within it. He simply walked down the wooden steps, one hand on the cliff wall, the other clasping the metal handrail, his eyes cast down on the path ahead.

The connection squeezed, and Grayson Shaw stumbled to a near halt, his hand going up to his chest. His eyes flicked hesitantly to mine, and it was like the ocean had swallowed me whole.

Ah, I thought, *so you can feel it too.*

Music flowed within me, my power pulsing beneath my skin.

The key, my ancestors crooned. *The key!*

I wanted to laugh, splash in the water, dance until I was dizzy. I wanted to let my Gift burn and burn until the night shone as brightly as the day. The boy could feel the thing tethering my heart to his, the thread that pulled us into orbit with each other. But in that moment, he didn't look very happy about it.

Grayson finished making his way down the steps and curved around the rock pools, his footsteps silent and slow in the sand.

"Hello," I whispered, scooting farther onto the shore.

"Hi," the boy replied, sitting down a healthy distance away from me.

Burying my disappointment underneath a smile, I leaned forward, sliding my hand along the sand, my fingertips nearly brushing his. "I'm happy to see you."

Grayson swallowed, his eyes not quite meeting mine. "Yeah."

The smile grew stiff, but I took great care to keep it in place. "Is something the matter?" I asked, closing the distance and gently taking his hand in mine.

The boy jerked away as though I had burned him. The sudden movement sent me lurching backward, tail skimming the water's surface as a hiss escaped my lips.

"I'm sorry!" Grayson blurted. "I didn't mean to scare you." He dropped his head, his shoulders sagging. "Today just wasn't a good day."

I tried to smooth the rigid fins at my sides, but they only trembled in response. I focused on my hair instead, combing the strands through my fingers. "Do you want to talk about it?" I asked, keeping my voice light, though my heart thudded like a drum in my chest.

Grayson sighed again, rubbing his face with a hand that shook. His expression contorted as though each breath pained him. I suspected I knew why.

When the boy didn't say anything, just sat there with his head in his hands, I forced out a chuckle and leaned back, staring up at the darkening sky as the water lapped at my waist. "Fine," I said. "I enjoy silence too."

We sat there for a time, Grayson looking into his hands, me looking into the approaching night. Both searching for answers, for words to fill the tense silence, and both coming up with nothing. Eventually, Grayson groaned, and I really did wonder if he was in pain.

"It was the nets," he finally mumbled, his words getting stuck between his fingers.

My ears pricked. My heart roared. My scales bristled. "The nets . . ." I feigned confusion, scrunching up my face in thought. "You mean, from the challenge?"

Grayson groaned again, long and low. He nodded, slowly lifting his face and meeting my eyes. He studied me for a heavy moment before talking. "They were destroyed."

I gasped sharply. "Destroyed?"

The boy's mouth dipped into a frown as his stare hardened. "All of them."

I shook my head, clucking my tongue in sympathy. "Why, that's dreadful."

"It is," Grayson agreed. "Whoever did it knew to go at night, when they weren't being watched."

Biting my lip, I pushed forward until I was mostly out of the water again. I placed a hand gently on Grayson's knee, hoping he couldn't feel how hard it was shaking. "All that hard work," I said sadly. "I'm so sorry."

Grayson's eyes dropped to my hand, looking like he wasn't sure whether he enjoyed having it on his leg or not. When he spoke, his voice was a dark and dangerous thing. "Was it you?"

My body went rigid. My blood roared in my ears, muffling the world. "Excuse me?"

His gaze was sharp, slicing through me. "Was it you?" he asked again, the fury building in his voice like a quiet storm.

I glared at him. "I can't believe you'd ask such a thing," I said coldly, pulling away.

But Grayson's hand was suddenly on mine, holding it in place, his nails digging into my skin. "Evanora," he growled, "you knew about the nets. You asked me about them, and—" He broke off, laughing bitterly, raking a hand through his hair. "God. I gave you everything. Willingly."

I yanked my hand, but Grayson held fast. "The whole island knows about the nets, Grayson! So what if I was curious? Does that really make me a suspect?" My voice was sharp now, my fins catching the fading sunlight as I shrugged stiffly. "Just because I asked you some questions?"

Grayson's jaw tightened. "It seems a little coincidental, yes."

I rolled my eyes. "Oh, please!" I bared my teeth at the boy; he flinched but didn't release me. "Grayson, has it not crossed your mind that I was *trapped* in one of those nets not that long ago? The thought of it still sends shudders down my spine. I can barely think about nets, let alone being on a beach *surrounded* by them." I shook my head. "You saw my struggle, saw that I couldn't get out. You knew I would die if you didn't step in to help."

The boy faltered, his grip loosening. "I guess . . ."

A blaze of meek victory swelled within me. *He's softening.* I leaned forward, tucking a finger underneath the boy's chin. I tilted his face up, forcing his eyes to catch mine. "Do you truly believe that it was me?" I asked quietly, my voice lilting and melodic.

Grayson held my gaze for a firm moment before crumbling completely, his body sagging with defeat. "It's not just about the nets," he whispered, turning away, my fingers slipping along his jaw. "Someone went missing too. A girl."

My heart skipped a beat. *Well*, I thought, *I wasn't expecting that.* "Missing? What do you mean, *missing*?"

Grayson shook his head and finally let go of my hand. "Her name was April. She wasn't the first one to go missing this Hunting Season."

The second he uttered the words, I remembered.

The scream, drenched in fear.

Then silence.

"She was the kindest person." The boy's mouth tightened, and he swallowed hard. "She didn't have a bad bone in her body. She didn't deserve to go missing."

"Grayson, I'm so sorry," I said, meaning it. "When the light within one's soul is snuffed out at the hands of another . . ." I inhaled slowly, my mind flitting to Solandis. "It is simply the most irrevocable sin."

Grayson inhaled sharply and looked at me again, the fire in his eyes extinguished. "It wasn't you?"

I shook my head emphatically. "I swear it."

Grayson winced, and he gently took my hand in his. "It was cruel of me to even suggest it."

I hummed quietly, running my thumb lightly against his skin. "I don't think you possess a single cruel trait, Grayson Shaw. Truly." I flipped his hand over and began tracing my nails along his palm. Grayson let out a quiet, shuddering breath, closing his eyes as he tilted his head back.

And there it was again. The thread, pulsing with my heartbeat, stronger than ever. I welcomed its viselike embrace. "When I last saw you, you spoke of your great fear of the water," I murmured softly. "Why?"

Grayson's face remained upturned, but his mouth became pinched. "Water and I don't exactly get along."

I allowed my fingers to venture farther, dancing toward his wrist. The boy stiffened slightly, and I brought my fingers back to his palm. "I've seen you in water before. You looked like you got along just fine."

Grayson shook his head, letting his chin drop so he could crack an eye open at me. "Only when I've subconsciously reacted to something, and only up to my knees. Anything deeper, and I panic."

I batted my eyelashes and grinned coyly. "Subconsciously reacted . . . like when you saved that seal."

The boy laughed, opening both eyes so he could drink all of me in. "Like when I saved *you*."

I aimed for his wrist again. When I pushed against his shirtsleeve, Grayson placed his hand on mine, stilling my movements. "I truly don't know how I'll get through the next challenge alive," he admitted quietly, a flicker of fear whispering across his face.

I bit my lip, my tail twitching with a sudden influx of nerves. The subject of the Hunt seemed like precarious ground to be standing on; we had barely made it through our last conversation unscathed. I wouldn't push my luck on it. Not tonight. There was always tomorrow, when the wounds left behind by our words had time to heal. "You told me that the next challenge was five days away," I countered. "That should give you some time to prepare."

"Four days now." Grayson sighed, staring up at the distant glimmer of emerging stars. "Practically three. It's just not possible to learn how to swim in that time."

"I can help." The words were out of my mouth before I had a chance to actually think them through.

Grayson raised an eyebrow. "Help me? How?" As he spoke, he looked pointedly at my tail swishing beneath the waves, then to his legs tucked underneath him.

I blinked. "Well," I said slowly, my mind working furiously, "I might not have legs, but I know a thing or two when it comes to the water. Now, is it the physical act of swimming that has you paralyzed by fear, or the water itself?"

Grayson paled, his eyes flicking warily to the mass of water surrounding the island. I could see beads of sweat dot his forehead. His hand had grown clammy in mine. "It's the water, I think," he said shakily, swallowing hard. "Just the water. I used to swim as a boy. I think . . ." He swallowed again. "I think I could still do it if I had to."

I shook my head, a gentle smile on my lips. "There is nothing *just* about the water, Grayson Shaw. You have every right to be scared. But"—I held up a finger—"you also have me. I can show you how to harness that fear into something else, show you the true power behind such an emotion." I lowered my voice and leaned in, my hair spilling over my shoulders. "I can show you that there is beauty to be found as well, wonders beyond your wildest imagination."

Grayson slowly turned to me, his eyes dragging over my face, to my neck, to the hair draped over my shoulders. His breath hitched, and with trembling fingers, he reached forward and tucked the hair behind my pointed ear. "I have no doubt in that," he uttered, his hand sliding down my neck, caressing my glowing skin, his thumb catching on my collarbone.

It was my turn to forget how to breathe. I could feel my gills flare, and Grayson stared at them with wonder, his eyes drinking in the otherworldly nature that I was. His touch was like fire on my icy skin, and it warmed me all the way down to my tail. I found myself leaning into his touch, craving it, tendrils of desire swirling inside me like intoxicating smoke.

Grayson smiled crookedly, his constellation of freckles shifting on his cheeks. "You could do that for free—no swimming lesson required."

I erupted with laughter, sudden and ferocious in its mirth. I tilted my head back and let it run free, surprised at the happiness fluttering in my veins. It didn't seem possible that a human boy could make me feel such an abundance of it. "Oh no," I said between gasping breaths, "I'm helping you."

Grayson deflated slightly. "All right," he grumbled. "But I'm not going to be a good sport about it."

"I wouldn't have it any other way."

"And I'll probably argue and make excuses the entire time."

"I should hope so."

"And—"

I pressed my fingers to Grayson's lips. The boy's eyes widened, his breath stuttering against my fingers, his smooth lips quivering.

It should have been enough. To experience the boy's touch, to feel his excitement with every fervent heartbeat, to hear his poorly concealed pleasure as his breath came out in shallow pants. His lips pressed against my fingers, his stormy eyes hypnotic, pulling me in.

It wasn't enough. I wanted more.

I leaned in and pressed my forehead to his. Grayson's skin was soft and cool against my own, practically milky white with the reflection of my glow. "Meet me here," I whispered, grinning as my light danced in his eyes. "Tomorrow. At sunrise."

Grayson nodded shakily, seemingly forgetting all about his fear of water.

I brought my lips to his ear. I gave a lilting giggle, and Grayson's entire body spasmed with nerves. "Until next time?"

Grayson nodded again. "Until next time," he croaked, muffled by my fingers.

I dared myself to stay there a second longer, holding on to the moment until the last of the daylight faded. I closed my eyes and sighed lightly, my breath warm against Grayson's curly hair. "Goodbye, Grayson Shaw."

When the sun was gone, so was I.

But even as I traveled home, racing against time, I could still feel Grayson's breath on my fingertips, still feel the hunger radiating off him as his mouth touched my skin.

And I wondered, briefly, what it would have felt like to press my lips against his, instead of my fingers.

My Gift burst from its cage.

It erupted from me, clawing through my skin, lighting the path ahead and stretching far beyond it. I could see the crumbling archways leading to the kingdom, the white stone walkways winding through the seaweed forest, the distant towers of the palace piercing the dark waters. The magic surged and pulsed, alive in its own right, reaching into the darkness with glowing fingers, banishing the shadows. My entire body hummed with it, and my blood sang in rhythm. It was alive. It demanded more.

I gasped and stuttered to a halt, pressing my hands to my stomach, willing the Gift to subside. It was a wild animal, hell-bent on not being tamed. It reached into its reserves and took out handfuls of more magic. My Gift pulsed again, rocking me back as another wave of light crashed forward. *More*, it seemed to cry. *More!*

I gritted my teeth, breathless, my hair scattering against my face as I watched the reaches of my light stretch farther than I'd ever seen it. I could see the entire city, the entire kingdom. I looked over my shoulder and could see the edges of the island. I was a beacon in the night, and I was exposed. I shoved my hair out of my face and closed my eyes, focusing on my Gift and calling it home.

It took everything I had, but after what felt like an eternity, the magic slowly collapsed, pooling reluctantly into my hands before slipping beneath my scales. I hurriedly tucked it back into place, scanning my surroundings for any prying eyes. A swarm of jellyfish glided by, a lone porpoise danced past, and a pair of seahorses darted by in a blur, but nothing more.

Darkness pressed in once again. I exhaled deeply, holding a hand against my chest, willing my heart to slow. "All right," I muttered, shaking my head quickly. "No more thoughts of kissing."

My blood still burned with it, racing through my veins like it was on fire. All that magic with a mere thought of the boy. As I slowly continued home, I couldn't help but wonder if there was an ounce of truth to my ancestors' incessant messages.

Maybe he really *was* the key.

CHAPTER THIRTY-SEVEN

GRAYSON

APRIL 12 – MORNING

THE OCEAN WASN'T INTERESTED IN MY SWIMMING lesson. It wasn't interested in anything other than building waves larger than me, creating hidden pockets of riptides, and spewing large wads of foam onto the shore.

I stood there, hands deep in my pockets, my face tucked into the upturned collar of my flannel jacket, warding off the biting wind.

Evanora didn't *really* intend to take me out in this, did she?

I yawned and gave my head a rough shake. I had barely slept—partly because I couldn't stop thinking of Evanora's fingers on my lips, her forehead against mine, her mouth pressed against my ear. Every single time I nearly drifted off, the memory of her breath tickling my neck would send me bolting upright, heat pooling in places that left me both excited and ashamed.

Then there were the voices coming from the window. They had managed to needle their way into my dreams. They called out to me, taunted me, sang their water lullaby, promising relief if I just sought them out. And when I wasn't dreaming about the voices, I was dreaming about Ma, her fingers around my throat, the force behind her thin, sinewy arms as she thrust me deep, deep, deep under the ocean's waves.

Hardly any sleep under my belt, and I was expected to swim in a body of water that looked like it didn't want me anywhere near it. The feeling was mutual.

My fingers brushed against the cool metal bracelet tucked away in my pocket. I wanted to give it to Evanora today. After yesterday, it almost seemed necessary.

But . . . when?

While I was drowning? Or begging to be returned to shore? In the middle of showing her how much of a man I was?

I sighed, dropping my head. *This is going to be awful.*

The sun was just barely peeking over the horizon when I spotted the rowboat skirting the island's edge. A pang of worry clenched my gut; the water was unpredictable, and even anchored boats weren't safe sometimes. I swallowed hard, eyes tracking the boat's erratic course. How was *I* going to stay safe?

The waves tossed the boat like a toy, slamming it side to side. The oars clattered, water sloshed over the edge, and the bow nose-dived before being thrust back up by another wave. It careened toward the shore, but just as it was about to bottom out, it stopped. I watched, puzzled, as it hovered in place, unbothered by the thrashing waves. Then I saw the rope tied to the bow eye, dragging behind the boat, vibrating with the water's pull. The boat groaned, still unmoving. It was stuck.

Which meant I'd probably have to free it. That, or wait for someone to come stomping around the beach in hopes of finding it. Both options weren't great.

I looked at the boat, the bow eye, and then at the rope. I followed the rope's length into the water.

And found two large violet eyes staring back at me.

I yelped and startled back, tripping over my own feet and crashing to the ground.

Evanora slowly emerged from the waves. The water droplets clung to her skin, glistening like jewels on her iridescent scales. Her laughter was like music. "Did I frighten you?"

I waited for my heartbeat to slow before standing, knocking the sand off my pants. "If I said no, would you believe me?"

The mermaid raised an eyebrow and cocked her head to the side, looking more like the wild creature she was. "Likely not."

I smirked, my eyes drifting to the boat. "Who does that boat belong to?"

Evanora shrugged and pulled the rowboat to shore. "Someone who doesn't need it right now."

The boat crashed into the beach with surprising force. Not for the first time, I marveled at the mermaid's strength. She'd been able to pull the boat through tumultuous waters all the way to our beach. She wasn't even breathing hard. Evanora remained in the water, hovering next to the boat, her fingers tapping along the wooden siding. She looked purposefully at the boat, then at me, her mouth catching the smallest of smiles.

And then it occurred to me. She expected me to get *in* it.

My feet began to move on their own, backing away from the water's edge with slow, shaky steps. "I can't," I managed to stutter out, shaking my head quickly. "I can't get in there."

Evanora's fingers stilled. "Yes, you can," she said calmly.

I shook my head harder, holding my hands up as if I could ward off her assurance. "No. There's no way."

Evanora rested her head against the boat's side, her eyes following my slow retreat. "Grayson, it's just a boat."

"It's not!" I choked out, my words becoming thick with emotion. "It's—"

It was a monster. It was death.

It was Warrick, casting me one last terrified glance before his boat split in two, the pieces—and him—getting sucked under.

The mermaid reached out her hand to me, her palm upturned and inviting. "It's just a boat," she crooned soothingly. "It can't hurt you. I won't let it."

I forced my feet to stop, focusing on her hand instead of my gasps for air and the pain in my chest. "What if I fall in?" I whispered.

"Then I'll save you."

"What if the boat breaks?"

"It won't." Evanora stretched her hand farther. "I promise, Grayson. I won't let anything bad happen to you. I'll protect you."

I bit my lip, the sharp ache grounding me. I took a timid step forward, then another, keeping my eyes trained on her hand. My shaking fingers fluttered against hers, and I let Evanora guide me to the boat. Her grip was patient, not yanking and tugging, letting me go at my snail's pace. Sucking in a breath, I gripped the wooden gunwale, praying that my knees wouldn't give out as I hoisted one wobbly leg over the edge at a time. Collapsing onto the middle thwart, I grasped the gunwale until I was certain I'd get splinters. I looked at the mermaid. "It won't break?"

Evanora held my gaze and shook her head gently. "It won't break."

I held my breath for a beat, then nodded tersely. Evanora made a soft humming sound of encouragement, her face smooth and serene.

And then, before I could change my mind, she grabbed the rope and began pulling the boat away from solid ground.

I was instantly nauseated. It roiled inside me, as ferocious as the waves colliding with the boat. Evanora pulled me along in swift, confident movements, but it felt like the ocean was fighting her, doing all it could to make her drop the rope, to set me adrift. I groaned and squeezed my eyes shut, trying not to cry out every time a spray of water hit my face or the boat jerked uneasily. I couldn't stop shaking. My jaw ached from it, and I wondered how worried I had to be about cracking a tooth. My fingers dug into the boat's edge. Everything within me was alive and on alarm.

Evanora kept pulling, and I kept trying not to vomit.

It took me a while to notice the change. I was so focused on keeping my rapidly approaching panic attack at bay that I didn't notice how the waves had shifted from wreaking havoc on the boat to rolling gently alongside it. I cracked an eye open. Evanora had taken the boat farther up north, around the shoulder of Howler's Hill and into a neighboring bay, where the ocean was decidedly calmer and the wind not as nasty on my face.

Evanora pulled the boat into the center of the bay, where the water was most still. She turned onto her back, the rope going slack in her hands as she peered up at me, her large eyes twinkling. My stomach dropped, and I clutched the gunwale harder. "Please don't make me get out," I moaned.

Evanora giggled and shook her head. "Not today."

I heaved a massive sigh of relief, my shoulders drooping. "Thank God."

Evanora's tail worked furiously underneath her, but her upper body remained still and graceful as she began to run her hands along the water's calm surface. "Swimming," she said, her fingers dipping in and out, "isn't just about being in the water. It is about feeling it, understanding it, knowing what it wants."

It wants me, I thought, a knot forming in my throat. *It only had a taste of me before, but now it wants all of me. It wants to swallow me whole.*

"Feel the waves," Evanora went on, swimming around the boat, pulling it in a slow circle. "How they rock the boat. Hear how they sing as they connect with the wood."

All I could feel was my ma's hands around my throat. All I could hear was Warrick's panicked gasp as he took his last breath. I let out a shuddering exhale and closed my eyes, biting my lip to keep it from wobbling.

The boat lurched to the side, then went still. I opened my eyes to see Evanora leaning over the bow, her hands on the front thwart, her tail draped over the boat's edge. She was inspecting me closely, a frown on her lips. She lifted a hand and hesitantly poked my cheek. "What's that?"

I blinked, and felt it. The sting beneath my eyelids. The hot tears sticking to my eyelashes. The cool trail they left on my windburned skin. My hands wandered to my face, and I quickly wiped my cheeks, suddenly self-conscious. "Tears," I mumbled, a thick, barking laugh escaping. "I'm crying."

The mermaid's face lit up, and she drew closer. "This is what they look like?"

I wanted to shy away from her sudden advance, but that would've meant moving. In the boat. On the ocean. "Have you never cried before?"

Evanora grabbed my hands and pulled them away from my face, her eyes wide. She studied the tears as they continued to fall. "Oh yes," she breathed. "Many times. But being underwater, tears are felt more than seen." She brushed my cheek gently and caught one on her finger, holding it up at eye level, watching as the sun reflected off it. "They are rather beautiful."

I gave a snort. "I'm pretty sure you are the only one who thinks that."

Evanora sighed and sank deeper into the boat, lying perpendicular on the wooden floor. Her tail hung over the gunwale, the fluke lazily swishing, hardly making a ripple. She rested her head against the boat's inner wall, her eyes fixed on the sky. "I think beauty can be found in everything," she said, her gaze lost in the clouds. "You just need to know how to look for it."

She drew her hands to her chest, exhaled lightly, and closed her eyes. She looked so peaceful. I couldn't help but agree—beauty was everywhere. And I was staring at the epitome of it. With a grunt, I lowered myself from the thwart, arms shaking, and clambered to the bottom of the boat beside her. I placed my head near hers, panting with the effort. I wasn't brave enough to dangle my legs over the edge like Evanora, so I kept them bunched up, my shoes pressed against the boat's wall, knees nearly touching my chest.

The only change in Evanora's features was the gentle curving of the corner of her lip. She sighed happily, opening her eyes as she turned her face to mine.

We shared the same breath, the same fervent heartbeat, as we stared at each other. I was certain time had stopped, and I wouldn't have minded if it never started up again. The sun was just beginning to tease the sky with color, burning pinks and reds melting into oranges. It rippled along the water's glass surface, bouncing off the cliff walls and rock overhang.

Nothing compared to the color of Evanora's eyes. I held my breath, getting sucked into the swarm of violets and amethysts, the flecks of gold you could just make out if you looked hard enough. Evanora's eyes were the sort that you could spend your entire lifetime searching, and just when you thought you had memorized every piece, every shadow, every color, there would be something new to admire.

The mermaid turned away, and I felt a swell of longing like a punch to the gut. I exhaled heavily and forced myself to look upward, though the sky was not nearly as exciting.

"I will not ask about the tears," Evanora said quietly. "Not unless you wish to talk about them."

I didn't. I really, really didn't. I'd been reliving the memory of his death since the second I saw that boat. No one knew the full story. No one but me. And yet . . .

Something about the mermaid was so calming, so *damn* coaxing, I found my mouth moving before my brain had a chance to catch up.

"I had a brother once," I started, clearing my throat of the emotion that had wedged itself there. "Warrick."

"Warrick," Evanora repeated softly. "It's a lovely name."

I nodded. "It means *leader who defends.* It suited him." I swallowed hard. "One night, he crept out of the house. We shared the same room, and he wasn't exactly the quietest. When he saw that he had woken me up . . ." I inhaled slowly, my body growing rigid. "He didn't ask me to stay behind, but I should have known better. I shouldn't have followed him."

A wave rocked the boat, and my hand shot out to grab Evanora's. She clasped it willingly, squeezing gently, and I waited for the boat to steady before continuing. "I was young. Foolish. I chased after him. He went down to the beach . . . our beach. There was a rowboat, and even though it was illegal to be out at night, he shoved it into the water." I stopped to laugh—a strangled, high-pitched sound. "He didn't even think twice. It was like he couldn't wait to be out there." I shook my head. "I watched from the steps as he paddled out. He was waiting for a mermaid."

Evanora's head jerked in my direction. "A mermaid? Really?"

I nodded. "Sometimes I wonder how they met, how long they kept their relationship a secret, how long it took for them to fall in love." I chewed on my lip, thinking back to the kiss I was never meant to witness, the heavy breaths and soft sighs that reached my ears. "I have no doubt that they were in love," I whispered.

Out of the corner of my eye, I could see Evanora's face flush. "What happened?" she asked.

The clouds overhead darkened, matching my mood. "Warrick had barely been in that boat for five minutes when the water . . . It came *alive*, Evanora. I've never seen anything like it. One second, calm. The next, ferocious. Like it wanted what was inside that boat—not caring that it was my brother. There was a sickening crack, the sound of wood splitting. The mermaid fled, leaving him alone." A whimper escaped my throat, and Evanora squeezed my hand tighter. "Warrick must've been so scared. I called out to him. I just wanted him back on shore. I wanted him out of the water." I whimpered again. "But I couldn't stop him from being pulled under."

Evanora's free hand was on my face, and I realized that she was wiping away the newly formed tears dripping down my cheeks. "You don't need to tell me the rest."

"No," I choked out, shaking my head viciously. "No, I want to. I *need* to. Someone needs to hear this. Someone who will believe me."

Evanora continued to stroke my cheek. She nodded gently, encouraging me to go on. "Warrick must've been so *scared*," I continued, my voice quavering. "But he still found the strength to *smile* at me, Evanora. Even as his boat was wrenched underneath the thrashing waves, even though his face was cloaked in fear, he *smiled* at me." I covered my eyes with my hand, squeezing out the remaining tears. "It was his way of telling me that it was okay, *he* was okay. Even when he knew he was about to die, Warrick was trying to look out for me." I stifled a mournful laugh. "A true leader."

"Oh, Grayson," Evanora whispered, her hand drifting away from my face, landing gently over my pounding heart.

I shook my head. "When the boat capsized . . . sucked under the water in a single pull, I screamed. God, I screamed until my voice was hoarse, until tears poured down my cheeks. But not even my desperate pleas brought Warrick back to the surface. Not even pieces of his boat emerged."

When my parents found me slumped on the steps the next morning, I was nearly delirious in my anguish. As they wrapped me in blankets and carried me back to the house, the only words I could croak out were, "Warrick . . . Mermaids . . . The water . . . The water!" Over and over again. I couldn't stop myself. I felt like a broken record skipping over the most important parts of the song, only able to give snippets of the melody.

Evanora bit her wobbling lip. "I'm so sorry," she uttered. "I can't imagine what that must have felt like for you. So young. So alone."

I barely heard her. My mind was replaying the image of Warrick's death on a torturous loop. "It's been eight years since he was stolen from us. I was only ten when it happened . . . a mere boy." I knitted my brows together, baring my teeth as the memory flashed again. "I might've been young, but I know that mermaids didn't kill him. Even though it's what everyone else thinks, I refuse to believe it."

I felt Evanora's body stiffen against mine. She turned to me, her face solemn and dark. "There are things out there," she whispered, "far worse than the Hunt, Grayson Shaw."

I swallowed hard. "Like what?"

Evanora didn't answer. With a low groan, she rose from her space beside me, her eyes growing distant as she gazed at the sunrise. "We should go back," she said, tension lacing her words.

I opened my mouth, only to snap it shut. Disappointment snuffed out the embers of grief in my chest. I wanted her to talk, to tell me what was going on in her mind, what demons she was fighting so fervently that she couldn't—or wouldn't—elaborate. Worse than the Hunt? What could be worse than the Hunt? What had her so scared that she couldn't talk to me?

Deep in my heart, I couldn't shake the feeling that I knew what it was. It was the very same thing that plagued my mind whenever the days grew dark and the ocean went quiet.

I knew what she was scared of. I'd heard them before.

The voices in the water.

The boat began to tip and jostle as Evanora shuffled over to the edge. I bolted upright, my hands shooting out to the gunwale. "Don't get out!" I begged.

The mermaid paused, looking over her shoulder at me with a raised eyebrow. "As much as I'd love to spend the entire day here with you, I really must be getting back. The pod will be wondering where I've been."

I nodded shakily, growing dizzy as the boat heaved from side to side. "I know," I said, willing my voice to level out. "Just please . . ." I closed my eyes, wincing. "Don't get out of the boat."

Evanora laughed, but I knew it wasn't at me and my ever-present fear. It was a far gentler thing—and far more dangerous for my heart. "Then how do you propose we get back to the beach?"

I bit my lip, reluctantly opening my eyes. "I'll . . . I'll row us to shore."

Evanora watched me carefully as I fumbled with the oars, seating them into the rowlocks with twitching fingers. It took some time; whenever I got one in place, the other would slip out. And when I got them both in position, I was shaking so hard I nearly pushed them out the other side of the metal rings.

The mermaid remained silent as I began to work the oar tips in the water, fiddling with the length and movement until I found a rhythm that resembled a pathetic row.

It wasn't smooth. It wasn't graceful. There were a handful of times when I sent the boat in circles and twice when I dropped one of the oars into the water, forcing Evanora to stretch out her tail to retrieve it. The ocean fought me the entire time, one stroke forward erased with four paces back.

I wasn't sure how long it took me to get back to the beach, but when the boat bottomed out against the shore, I could have wept with relief. I crawled out and collapsed onto the ground, a panting, sweating, shaking mess. I flipped onto my back and stared at my hands, at the blisters dotting my palms. Heaving a sputtering breath, I let my hands flop listlessly against my chest.

I was exhausted, drained of all energy.

And I felt . . . incredible.

That was all me. *I* brought us back to shore. It wasn't Evanora, it wasn't the ocean's good behavior. It was *me*.

Evanora chuckled and pulled up beside me, staring down at me with a huge grin. She blocked out the sun, the rays peeking out from behind her, basking her in a warm glow.

"Well done," she said, wiping the hair away from my sweaty forehead. "That was amazing."

I coughed out a laugh, her praise sending heat into my cheeks. "Hardly."

Evanora shook her head. "You accomplished something incredible today. You have a great and terrible fear of the water, yet you went out on a boat *and* paddled us back to shore. You were very brave."

"I'm practically a sailor."

Evanora laughed, cocking her head to the side. "Practically."

Something was digging into me. I grunted and readjusted, but it still pressed awkwardly against my rib cage. I sat up with a groan and dug into my pocket. The bracelet tumbled into my palm, warm and moist from a couple rogue waves. My heart began to pound, and I wondered if Evanora could hear it. I glanced at her, at her soft eyes, her toying smile, at the rosiness in her pale cheeks. Everything inside me began to sing as the link between us cinched tighter. "I have something for you," I stammered out.

Evanora's mouth parted. "For me? Why?"

I shrugged, forcing a crooked smile onto my lips. I was pretty sure it looked like a wince. God, why was I *so bad* at this? "Because you deserve more than just flowers."

Evanora softened. "I like the flowers, Grayson Shaw."

"But they won't survive where you live." I shook my head, my heart beating harder. "I wanted to get you something that could be both on land, and in the ocean. Something that will remind you of me." I bit my lip, unable to look the mermaid in the eyes. "Maybe . . . I don't know . . . It'll feel like I'm always there with you . . . like such a thing could be possible for us."

I opened my hand, revealing the bracelet. The charm winked in the sunlight, dancing on its metal link. Evanora gasped, placing a hand to her mouth. I blushed, ducking my head.

"It's not much," I admitted. "It's okay if you don't like it."

Evanora shook her head rapidly, her eyes not leaving the bracelet. "It's beautiful." She tore her gaze away from it and looked at me, lowering her hand so I could see her grin. "Can I?" she asked, her fingers reaching for it.

I nodded, and in the blink of an eye, Evanora snatched up the piece of jewelry, bringing it up to her face, watching the way the sun reflected off the silver surface. "I've never received a gift like this before!" she said, her voice brimming with glee. Her eyes landed on the engraved Orion's Belt constellation on the inside, and she stopped, flicking her attention to my cheek. Biting back her smile, she reached forward and stroked the freckles dotting my face, my very own collection of stars.

My cheeks grew impossibly hotter. Melting was a sudden and very real threat.

The mermaid looked at the bracelet again, and her smile slipped into the smallest of frowns. She looked at her body, and the frown morphed into a scowl. She touched her pointed ears, then her slim neck, then the fins on her arms. She let out a frustrated chuckle. "I don't think I know where this is supposed to go."

I swallowed my laughter. "May I?" I asked, holding out my hand for the jewelry.

Evanora watched as I slid it over her slender hand until it hung off her wrist. "Here," I uttered. "It goes here."

Evanora lifted her arm, twisting her wrist back and forth, watching with delight as the bracelet danced with her movement. "Yes, well." She cleared her throat. "It's rather obvious, now that it's there."

I sat back, admiring Evanora as she admired the bracelet. "It looks perfect on you—"

Evanora leaned forward, her lips crashing against my cheek, where my tears had left a salty trail. She lingered there, lips pressed against my skin, her touch like ice against my sweltering heat. She pulled back, beaming at me. "I love it," she whispered. "Thank you."

I could still feel the pressure of her kiss on my skin long after the mermaid wriggled off the beach and tore through the water like a shot of light. I pressed my hand to my cheek, where her lips had been, then brought my fingers to my lips, closed my eyes, and prayed, not for the first time, that God would allow me to see her again.

CHAPTER THIRTY-EIGHT

EVANORA

APRIL 12 – AFTERNOON

I TWISTED MY WRIST. THE BRACELET FLOWED WITH THE MOVE-ment. I tilted my wrist again. The octopus charm glinted in the dim light filtering through my bedroom window. Over and over, I moved my arm, watching the bracelet with a smile on my face.

I hadn't moved from my bed since returning from the island. I couldn't stop looking at the bracelet. Such a simple thing, yet it brought me an immense amount of joy.

I bit my lip, trying to stifle the smile that was starting to hurt my cheeks. I couldn't remember the last time I'd felt so . . . good. My body ached with it, sang with it. For the first time in a long time, I was happy. Good and truly happy. It almost felt foreign.

I paused, my eyes flicking to the crown sitting atop the table next to my bed. A pang of longing piled in my veins, threatening to push out all the blood to make more space for the emotion. Reluctantly, I lowered my arm, my fingers dancing along the iridescent worm-snail shells spiking up, giving the crown a regal height. A large white scallop shell sat in the center surrounded by crystals, with strands of pearls draping elegantly underneath on silver chains. Glittering gems filled in the spaces between the shells, with a single moonstone dangling just below the middle.

It was such a beautiful, daunting piece of jewelry. I had only worn it once: the day Appah died and I was officially named both queen and leader of the pod. The thing was terribly heavy. I didn't know how Ammah had worn it all those years—and made it look effortless.

I wondered if I'd ever put it on again.

"Evanora."

The voice came from behind me, near the doorway. I let out a surprised hiss and whipped around, fins rigid and teeth bared.

Illeron hovered at the entrance of my room. He was gripping his spear hard, eyes narrowed as he studied me. "What are you doing?" he asked, his silver-and-crimson tail flicking agitatedly.

I looked at the crown, then at the bracelet, then back at the warrior. "Nothing, why?" I asked, rising from the bed cautiously.

Illeron clucked his tongue. "Because we are all waiting for you at the weaponry."

My happiness was immediately squashed. "The weaponry?"

"Yes," Illeron sighed, letting his neck go slack as he stared up at the ceiling. "The gathering of water wielders that you requested. The gathering you are currently missing. And making *me* miss, mind you. Because you're doing . . ." Illeron's words tapered off as he rocked his head to the side, fixing me with a glare.

"Nothing."

"Right. Nothing." His eyes flicked to the bracelet, and his lip curled into a sneer. "What is that?"

"Curious," I huffed, swimming for the bedroom door. "A lot of questions from someone who insists we are needed at the weaponry. If I didn't know any better, I'd say you were trying to make me even more late."

Illeron caught my arm as I tried to pass. He brought my wrist up to eye level, his face turning to stone as he peered at the silver band. He recoiled with a scoff. "It still smells of the island," he seethed, turning his dark look to me. "*He* gave this to you, didn't he?"

I wrenched my arm free, a kernel of anger wedging itself in my stomach. "So what if he did? Why does it concern you?"

"It concerns me," Illeron hissed, "because it's not just *your* life you're playing with, Your Majesty."

My blood sparked, my magic pressing against its confines. "I *know* that."

Illeron swam forward, pushing his face close to mine. He was breathing hard, his jaw twitching with poorly restrained anger. "Then *act* like it."

I fought against the desire to push away. I wouldn't give him the satisfaction of scaring me. Instead, I squared my shoulders, lifted my chin, and held up my wrist. "Don't you understand? This gift means our plan is *working*, Illeron. It means all our scheming, all our manipulation, is *working*. I have the boy nestled deep in my scales, and he is too infatuated to notice." I laughed coolly, turning away. "Or are you too jealous to realize that?"

A half-truth. Illeron could never know how much I delighted in wearing that bracelet, how my heart burned with joy at the memory of Grayson giving it to me.

The warrior's eyes widened, his mouth growing the slightest bit slack. "You mean—"

"Yes," I growled. "It's all going according to plan. Soften your fins, Illeron, and believe in me like you claim to do."

The warrior looked down at his flared fins, and with a grunt, he unclenched his fists. "I'm just worried about you," he uttered, moving in closer. He cocked his head, his fingers sidling along my chin. "I fear you are so deep that you can no longer see the surface. That boy . . ." He sucked in a breath. "You might have him wrapped around your finger, but I fear his grip on you is just as deadly."

I leaned away from his touch, the taste of something unfamiliar on my tongue, something hot and bitter. I didn't care for it at all. "You don't need to stress about me. That's not your job."

Illeron pulled his hand back reluctantly, frustration flickering along the cracks of his smile. "I cannot help it if I care about you."

I started, my body growing stiff. Illeron, too, seemed surprised at the words that tumbled out of his mouth. He chuckled hoarsely, running a hand over his face. "Forget I said anything."

Easier said than done.

As Illeron's eyes lingered on mine for a heavy second, his hand twitching at his side like he was physically holding back from touching me again, I realized what the taste was.

Disappointment.

I COULDN'T SLEEP.

I was certain that if the lack of rest didn't drive me mad, the chaos writhing in my mind would.

The meeting had gone as well as could be expected. When Illeron and I arrived, a league of water wielders were waiting for us. By the time we were finished, only a handful remained. Illeron reminded me that not everyone was willing to fight. Still, I expected more. Even Mavi, the meekest mermaid I knew, had stayed behind, though I had a feeling it was simply in solidarity and not for the thrill of violence.

I couldn't be greedy, I supposed.

Once the gathering had concluded, I had the wielders practice. They created whirlpools, riptides, and blasts strong enough to throw the mightiest swimmer off-kilter. And that was without using the waves. When we reached the surface, they would be able to summon waves powerful enough to swallow the hunters whole and stir enough foam to choke the island. As I watched them work, hope flickered in my heart.

Our plan would work. Just like it had with the nets. There was no stopping us.

A hand gripped my shoulder, shaking me violently.

My eyes shot open, and I found myself staring into Jorah's milky, feverish ones.

"Hurry, Your Majesty," he cried. "Hurry!"

His grip on my arm tightened, his thick nails puncturing my delicate skin. I sat up quickly, my fins immediately at the ready. "What is it?" I demanded. "What's wrong?"

Jorah shook his head rapidly, spittle clinging to his chapped lips as he panted. "Hurry!" he repeated, and without another word, he let go of me and raced out of the room.

I was up and moving in an instant, swimming as fast as my tail would take me. "Wait, Jorah!" I called out as I lost track of him behind one room, then another.

It was happening again. Gods, the poor old fish was stuck in another delusion, and this one didn't seem as nice as the last one I'd found him in. His time was running out. Sooner or later, the darkness would take hold of him completely.

Jorah was moving fast, *too* fast, like he was possessed. I shot into the throne room just in time to see him sailing out of it, swimming down the steps and into the city square.

"Jorah!" I cried.

My advisor ignored me, tearing through the city, twisting his body and taking sharp turns. He undulated with a frantic grace that no longer belonged to him. I couldn't give up; Jorah was in too dangerous a state for me to leave him alone. I gritted my teeth and pushed my body faster, ignoring the sudden splint of pain in my side, the burning in my lungs.

The distance between us slowly began to erase. I reached out my fingers, straining to get a piece of Jorah, seize any part of him to slow his speed. His fluke was a blur before my eyes. If I tried to grab it, I was at risk of hurting both myself and him. Seaweed whipped by, slapping my cheeks as Jorah took me farther and farther away from the kingdom. I spared a precious second to glance at the ground. The white stone walkway raced beneath us. If it weren't for the walkway or the lanterns running alongside it, there would be no way of knowing where we were.

"Jorah," I attempted inwardly, *"where are you taking me?"*

But he didn't respond. I could hear frenzied mumbling, but the water tore the words out of his mouth before they could reach me. Jorah's head jerked up, and, impossibly, he picked up speed, veering right.

Toward the lanterns.

Past the lanterns.

Straight for the Barrens.

"Jorah!" I shrieked, lunging forward and snagging his arm.

An entire layer of skin and scales sloughed off.

Still, I held on, burying the surge of nausea bursting up my throat. Jorah screamed and tried to rip free, his bloodshot eyes wide and wild as he gazed into the black abyss.

"Jorah," I pleaded, tightening my grip around his bloodied arm. "Jorah, please *stop*!"

"They're here!" he bellowed, pulling me toward the cliff's edge. "Here! We have to hurry!"

"Jorah, it is only us. We are alone!"

Jorah shook his head viciously, grinding his teeth together. "Not out here." He pointed with his free hand to the darkness. "*Here!* In the Barrens!"

My blood ran cold. I grabbed my advisor by the shoulders and forced him to face me. I gave him a harsh shake. "Jorah," I said, keeping my voice calm. "Who is in the Barrens?"

Was it another merling? Had another mermaid succumbed to Dark Madness?

Jorah moaned, deep and guttural. He dove for the cliff's edge again. "Your parents, Evie!"

I tasted the sharp metallic bite of blood. Red wisps floated before my eyes before dissolving away. I had sliced my lip with my sharp teeth. My nausea lurched upward again.

"Jorah," I forced out, "my parents are dead."

"No! They're trapped down there. They need our help!" He was growing stronger, waves of adrenaline crashing through him, giving him an other-worldly strength. I wasn't sure how much longer I could hold on to him.

I grunted, adjusting my hold on the flailing mermaid. "Jorah," I tried again, "my parents are *dead*. They've both been gone for over a year now. You *know* this! Try to remember!"

"I can hear them!" he wailed, squirming and writhing with delirium. "They're screaming out for us! Can't you hear them? They're in pain, Evie!"

Jorah's blood was acting as a lubricant. One more tug and he would be out of my grip and sailing into the darkness, straight for his doom. I was being too gentle. I didn't have the time to try to not hurt his feelings. A hiss curled around my tongue. I opened my mouth—

And then I heard it.

Voices I never thought I'd hear again.

My grip on Jorah slackened as my head rang out with the cries of Rainos and Nereida.

"Evie, save us!" my appah cried, terror dripping off his words.

"They're hurting us, Evanora!" Ammah screamed, a sob caught in her throat.

"It burns!" Appah bellowed.

"Evie, do something!" my ammah begged.

Tears flooded my vision. Gods, it sounded just like them. My heart raged against its cage, fighting to get out, to follow the voices. Was it really them? Were they truly down there?

My scales itched. Jorah pulled harder, and I realized that I was letting him. The distance between us and the darkness closed, bit by bit, as Jorah led me to it.

No. I squeezed my eyes shut, giving my head a rough shake. *No. Evanora, your appah died a year ago. He bled to death in your arms. You watched the light leave his eyes. You buried him.*

As if in response, Appah's voice drifted up the cliff's wall. *"I'm down here, Evanora! Please!"*

And you don't know what happened to Ammah, but you know she isn't down there either, I forced myself to continue, ignoring the voices ringing in the void.

"Evanora, please!" Ammah moaned. *"Don't be so cruel. It's me, Nereida!"*

My heart still burned, but the pace had settled. Head clearer, I opened my eyes, turning to Jorah. "My parents are dead. What we are hearing right now is an illusion put on by the Cursed Beings. Open your eyes, Jorah. Truly listen."

All the fire had gone out of my advisor. He no longer fought against my grasp, but he was still looking longingly into the dark. "No," he whispered, pulling away weakly. "It's them. I swear it's them!"

"Listen to your advisor, Evie," Appah, who really didn't sound like Appah anymore, but a bunch of voices mixing into one, commanded.

"He is wise and wise and wise!" Ammah, another chorus of voices, crooned.

So very wise, the mass spoke together, erasing my parents' voices completely with their deep and feral tones.

Join us!

Join us!

JOIN US!

"Enough!" I shouted.

My Gift pounced, bathing me and Jorah in a bright and blinding light. Crackling and electric, it swelled in the dark, stretching its fingers deep into the Barrens, surging forward to erase the shadows.

Jorah let out a yelp.

The darkness hissed, shrinking away.

I sucked in a breath and pulled the magic back in. Panting, I bared my teeth at the Barrens. "I'm done with your games. We both are."

The shadows were slow to come back, and the voices went quiet. I hauled Jorah away from the Barrens, dragging him the last couple lengths until we were in the safety of the lanterns' glow. With a groan, I set us both onto the walkway, falling back onto my hands as I fought to catch my breath. My mind swam with the voices of my parents. I knew what I'd heard in the Barrens was fake, but I also knew it would haunt me forever.

"They sounded so . . . real," Jorah uttered beside me, rubbing at his bleeding arms as he stared into the abyss.

I forced a small laugh, flopping onto my back and staring up at the lanterns. "Don't beat yourself up about it. I nearly fell for them too."

Jorah inhaled shakily, his gills barely moving. "I almost killed you."

"You also almost killed yourself." It was getting out of hand. I needed to talk to Illeron about finding a warrior to watch out for Jorah, if this stunt was any indication of what the future held. One of these times, he would slip into a delusion, and one of these times, he wouldn't wake me up in the middle of the night to join him in it. I needed someone with him at all times when I couldn't be.

"No." Jorah shrugged numbly. "The pod can get by without me. They will crumble without you."

I rolled my eyes. "I wouldn't be so sure."

Jorah's thumb caught on a loose scale, and he snarled quietly as it peeled back.

I propped myself up on my elbows, my face tightening with worry. "Jorah," I said softly, placing my hand tentatively on his shoulder. "Please let me heal you."

My advisor, still staring out into the Barrens, shook his head. "I'm fine."

I scooted closer, my fingers already glowing. "At least let me try." I tried to make my tone light, carefree, even though every part of me felt heavy with exhaustion. "It can be like practice. You are always telling me to practice."

The corner of Jorah's mouth tilted up, but the mirth failed to reach his eyes. "There's no need to heal me, Evanora."

I couldn't help it. My gaze flicked down his neck, where thick green pus oozed from his gills; to his arms, scratched raw and riddled with angry blisters; to his fingers, where several of his nails were missing, the nail beds red and swollen. Missing scales dotted his tail, and deep tears fissured the fins on his hips and near his fluke. His belly was round with bloat, but his ribs right above it stuck out with aggressive force.

Jorah was withering away to nothing, dying before my eyes. And he was forcing me to watch every agonizing moment.

I clenched my jaw, resolve burning through me. Craning my neck so I could look into his bloodshot eyes, I growled, "Stop being so proud for a second in your life and use that brilliant mind my appah hired you for. There is still time to help you!"

His shoulders sagged, and he looked at me with such a fragile smile that it nearly cleaved my heart in two. "I think," he whispered, barely audible, "my time has long run out, Your Majesty. Don't bother wasting your Gift on me." Jorah's eyes sluggishly drifted back to the Barrens, a shudder rippling up his protruding spine. "I'm already dead."

CHAPTER THIRTY-NINE

GRAYSON

APRIL 12 - AFTERNOON

BACK FOR MORE?"

I had been looking at my feet. The ground felt wrong, like the waterlogged grass was attempting to wrap around my boots and hold me in place. I turned my attention from my feet to the nurse standing off to the side. Besides the mud coating the hems of his pants, his white uniform was immaculate. His sleeves were rolled up, a box of cigarettes wedged into one of the folds. He had one dangling from his mouth, the cherry ember bright. As he blew out a puff of thick smoke, his tired eyes drifting from me to the rosebushes, he looked less like a nurse and more like a bored relative, waiting for visiting hours to end.

My fingers twitched at my sides, a nervous flutter in my stomach. "Excuse me?"

The nurse grinned, pulling a hand from his pocket to drag it slowly against his cheek. Instinctively, my own fingers went to mine, where the scab had only just recently crumbled off, leaving shiny pink skin underneath.

"Looks like it healed well enough," he commented, taking another long pull from his cigarette. "I thought you'd need stitches."

The very idea of a needle poking through my skin was enough to make me break out in a cold sweat. "I was told Persephone Shaw was out here?" I asked, trying to tilt the subject in a different direction. I didn't want to talk about my last visit at Rose Hill, not when I was on the cusp of another one. One that could either go smoothly, or devastatingly. It all depended on Ma's mood, which, ironically, wasn't dependable at all.

The nurse nodded, gesturing with a flick of his neck to the hedges. "Just over there, picking away at the deadheads." He chuckled around his cigarette. "It's going to take her a while; I don't think she's noticed that the whole thing is dead."

My feet wouldn't budge. I swallowed. Hard. "Is she . . . ?"

The nurse barked out a laugh. "Don't worry, lad. She appears to be in good spirits today. But just in case"—he leaned in and cupped a hand around his mouth, speaking in a low and conspiratorial whisper—"we clipped her nails. You never know with that one."

His breath smelled of bitter coffee and ashtray. I grimaced and pulled away, mustering a weak, "Thank you," before willing my legs to work. When had they become lead?

The nurse placed a thick hand on my shoulder before I could get very far. "I'm not going anywhere either." His dark eyes glimmered. "If you need me, just scream."

Just . . . scream.

I walked along the stone path. Thick rosebush walls, speckled with dead flowers, bordered the garden in a square. Tall spruce trees loomed at every corner, as if watching over the patients who dared enter. Four entrances, outlined by trellises smothered in dead vines, marked each quarter of the garden. The smooth white stones of the walkway were quickly buried under fallen petals and leaves, which stained them a mottled brown.

The garden inside was just as dead—hedges half the height of the bordering walls, running along the path until it ended in a circular opening. In the center, a bird fountain sat, full of stale water and leaves. Wooden benches with curved metal frames lined the circle's edge.

It must've been beautiful once. Before they'd stopped caring.

I followed the trail of deadheads, heart in my throat as I kept my eyes to the ground. Leaves crunched under my feet, breaking into tiny pieces for the wind to try to inhale. As I drew closer to the garden's center, I could hear the steady rip and tear of dead things being discarded. I sucked in a breath, said a prayer to any god who was listening, and rounded the final corner.

And there she was.

The wind picked up, howling through the rosebushes, rattling the barbed branches. Dead petals swirled around Ma's wheelchair, pelting her white loafers. The pale blue blanket on her lap tried to tear free in the gusts, but she clamped a hand on it, the other working at the rosebush. Her long blond hair, still matted, had been pulled back into a braid and tied with a blue ribbon. She wore a soft yellow dress with long sleeves and a frayed lace collar cinched tightly at her neck.

Tears pricked my eyes, and I couldn't blame it on the wind.

Persephone looked more like my mother than the ghost I had grown accustomed to.

I had forgotten.

I cleared my throat and took a step forward. "Ma."

Ma's shoulders tightened at the sound of my voice. Her hand stilled against the flowers, and slowly, she turned her head, looking over her shoulder at me, her eyes wide, her mouth in a pensive line.

I held my breath. This was uncharted territory. She would either be happy to see me, or curse me out of the garden. Considering how our last interaction had gone, I was leaning toward the latter. I couldn't remember the last time Ma had actually been glad about my existence. The scars on my wrist began to burn.

But then my ma's mouth broke into the most beautiful smile I'd ever seen. Her hands reached out for me, her fingers practically vibrating. "My son!" she cried, trying to lean farther back in her chair to get a better look at me. "Oh, my precious boy!"

My stomach did a somersault, a move my heart instantly tried to replicate.

Ma flicked her fingers at me. "Well, don't be shy! Come closer. Closer!"

I stepped forward hesitantly. This was *not* what I was expecting. Ma glowed as she reached for one of my hands. She brought it to her face, pressing it against her pale cheek. She closed her eyes briefly, sighing. I could feel the pressure of her cheekbone against the palm of my hand. She had always been thin, but not *this* thin. She opened her eyes and stared up at me, her mouth turned upward in a wistful smile. "I've missed you."

My eyebrows shot up into my hairline. "Really?"

Ma let out a laugh. Keeping my hand against her face, she reached up and pinched my cheek. I nearly flinched back as her fingers grazed the tender skin where she had marked me. "Of course, silly boy. How could a mother not miss her child?" She pouted, batting her long eyelashes at me. "Why did you wait so long to see me?"

"I . . . I tried—"

"Oh." Ma waved her hand dismissively. "It doesn't matter right now. All that matters is that you're here, and I'm here, and—" She gasped, clutching my hand tightly. "Wait, shouldn't you be at work?"

I shook my head, feeling the taut knots of my nerves slowly begin to unravel. "Day off today. I'm going to see Jasper and Holly later."

Ma gave me a quizzical look. "Whatever happened to the Morris brothers? Owen and Tommy."

I shrugged. "I see them too. From time to time."

Ma knitted her brows together but nodded. "They were your closest friends growing up, but I do so like that Holly girl." She gave me a knowing smile. "I always thought she was a good match for your brother."

I faltered, and the knots recoiled. "Really?" The idea of Holly and Warrick being together sent my stomach curdling—not with jealousy, but with the unusualness of it. Holly was only sixteen, two years younger than me. She barely knew Warrick before he died. "I never really considered it," I said quickly when I caught my ma's searching stare.

Ma smirked, her fingers going back to the rosebushes. "I have an eye for these things, love," she said, twisting a rotten bud off with a sharp *crick*. "I know a good match when I see it."

I smiled, watching as she plucked at another deadhead. "I wouldn't doubt it, considering you and Pa."

Ma scoffed, throwing the handful of dead flowers to the ground with vigor. "Ah, yes. When *is* your pa ever going to visit me?" She sniffed, surveying her clipped nails. "He sure is taking his sweet time breaking me free from this place."

I chewed my lip. My nerves were back to being fully cinched up. Something didn't feel right, but I couldn't quite place my finger on it. The epiphany was just out of reach while I continued to rake my brain and struggle. "He's just a bit reluctant. He'll come around, I'm sure."

Ma rolled her eyes, which began to well with tears. "I'm tired of being locked away here. I want to come home."

I sighed heavily, clasping my ma's hands in my own. "I want that too," I said softly.

Ma held my gaze firmly before groaning and withering away like a wilted flower. Her lower lip began to tremble, and she blinked rapidly, letting out a quick gasping laugh as she swiped at her face. "Don't look at me," she teased in a quivering voice. "It's unbecoming for a lady to cry."

I shook my head slowly, stilling her hands. "You're my mother," I uttered, wiping the tears she'd missed. "You're the most becoming person I know."

"You're only saying that."

"I'm not." I laughed lightly. "I'm pretty sure I cry more than you, so I know what I'm talking about."

Ma's eyes narrowed, and she cocked her head to the side, studying me. "You? Really?"

I nodded. The weight of her stare was disturbing. I was certain I could hear the cogs in her mind grinding and screeching, trying to make sense of something that was out of her reach too.

Eventually, Ma sighed, pulling my hands away from her face. "Well, as nice as it is to know that my son has a big, soft heart, you really ought to try to rein in those emotions. Really, what would Grayson think if he saw you weeping like a baby?"

My heart stuttered to a halt, a hot wave of grief settling into my bones. And there it was, the epiphany I had been struggling to reach, the one I didn't want anymore. She didn't recognize me. She thought I was—

"Warrick," Ma breathed sharply. "Promise me that you'll try. Grayson's such a gentle soul. He needs someone he can rely on and lean against."

Warrick. Of course. She thought I was Warrick. Why hadn't I seen it sooner? All the stupid, damning signs were there. I ducked my head, worried she would take one good look at my stormy blue eyes and realize they weren't Warrick's deep mahogany ones. At least we had the same unruly dark brown curls.

What was I supposed to do? Let Ma wallow in this delusion that her favorite son was still alive? Or break the illusion and risk the effect it would have on her fragile soul? My heart ached, more than I thought possible. It had only been broken twice in my life. The first was when Warrick died. The second was when Ma was sent away, scattering pieces of her as she went.

It was dangerously close to breaking again.

"I'll try," I choked out, nodding fiercely.

Whether it was the right thing to do or not, I couldn't bring myself to wreck the moment. Maybe it was selfish, but I wanted to keep hold of this finite pocket of happiness, to know what it felt like to be Warrick in my mother's eyes.

"He's such a good boy, you know," Ma went on. "That Grayson. How is he faring at the docks?"

Tears flooded my vision, and I blinked them away. "Well enough," I said roughly. "He's getting pretty good at mending nets."

Ma nodded, smiling, but then her face darkened, her mouth tipping downward. She bent her neck, pressing her forehead against my chest. Her shoulders began to shake, and for a moment, I feared she'd realized I wasn't her prized son, but the runner-up.

"Oh, Warrick," she moaned, her voice thick with emotion. "They're so cruel to me here! They treat me like an animal—less than one! My room is ghastly, the food's bland, and they won't even give me proper cutlery. I just . . ." She pulled away, her fingers digging into my sides. "I don't understand. What did I do to deserve this?"

My mind went blank. She thought I was Warrick. Therefore, in her mind, Warrick wasn't dead. Which meant she didn't have a reason to come completely undone and get sent to the asylum. I cringed as her fingers bit into my skin. *I wouldn't want to be in your head right now. Must be a very confusing place.*

"It can't be all that bad here," I forced, gently trying to pry her fingers free. "Who else can say they live in a castle?"

"I don't want to live in a castle. I want to be home with my boys!" Ma shook her head, her mouth a thin line. "Time and time again, I've repented for my sins, and still they won't let me leave. I'm not sure what else I can do to convince them that I don't belong in this wasteland." She crumpled into her seat, pinching the bridge of her dainty nose. "Oh, all this fretting is giving me a nasty headache."

The pocket of happiness was going to cinch shut soon. I crouched onto my heels and placed a hand on my ma's knee. "I'll talk to someone."

Ma's hand dropped from her face, and her crystal-blue eyes lit up like the summer sun. "Really? You will?"

I nodded, pasting a crooked smile onto my mouth, just like Warrick used to do. "I should be going anyway, but I'll be sure to talk to someone on my way out. In the meantime"—I winked at her, drawing inspiration from the charm my brother had once wielded like a weapon—"try to not get in any trouble. You'll hurt someone's feelings if you keep going on and on about the food."

Ma swatted at my arm playfully, a lilting giggle on her tongue. She sighed, cupping my face in her hands. "What would I do without you?"

You don't want to know. I smiled, but I was shaking as I took her hands and gave them each a quick kiss. "I'll be back again, hopefully in the next week or so. It'll all be sorted out by then."

Ma bit her lip and nodded, glowing with excitement. "You promise you won't wait so long to visit?"

"I promise that the next time I see you, we'll be leaving here together."

Cheeks burning with shame, I left Ma to tend to the flowers in the center of the garden. As I walked out, I caught sight of the nurse. He was lying in the soggy grass, a sizzling cigarette dangling from his lips as he stared up at the angry sky. His hands were clasped behind his head, his legs crossed at the ankles. He caught my gaze and saluted, a lazy smile pulling around his cigarette.

I opened my mouth.

Closed it.

And walked right by him.

I'd never been a good liar. But I guessed Warrick was.

I WASN'T SURE IF IT WAS THE WEATHER OR MY VISIT WITH MA, BUT Main Street was getting on my nerves. Too loud, too crowded, and the smell from the docks was worse than usual.

My foot slipped. At first, I thought I'd stepped in manure, but when I looked, it was a piece of paper. I moved my foot, and April Abbott's face stared up at me. Her unseeing eyes were fixed on something over my shoulder, her dimples barely showing through her knowing smile. The photo was black and white, but I wouldn't be surprised if the dress she wore had been purple—her favorite color, even though she couldn't see it. "I just like the way it sounds," she used to say. "Puuuuurple."

Thunder growled overhead as I glanced at the bulletin board next to Taylor's Trinkets. Her smiling face was plastered everywhere, a constant reminder she was still missing. A breeze stirred the papers, sending their edges fluttering. I stomped toward the board, lifting one of April's posters. And there was Harland Finch, the first boy to go missing. His photo, already faded by the sun, was speckled with grime. I let go of April's poster, and it flopped back into place, covering Harland's gap-toothed grin. Had people already forgotten him? Would it be only a matter of time before April's posters were buried too?

"Such a shame."

The voice came from behind me. I had been waiting for Jasper and Holly to finish up their shopping in Mott's Pharmacy, but the way my guts contorted told me it wasn't either of them. I clenched my hands into fists and looked over my shoulder.

Ambrose stood on the sidewalk, his hands in the pockets of his impeccably ironed trousers, his shoulders set rigidly in his gray double-breasted coat. He had said the words with a sort of blasé boredom, but the look on his face made me think he truly meant them. His normally pristine complexion had morphed into a weird mixture of mottled and waxy, and his jaw was set so hard it was making the skin around his mouth twitch.

But then Ambrose tsked, and he smiled, and the fraction of a human being I had glimpsed was gone. "So many poor souls going missing lately. God," he sighed dramatically, staring up at the darkening clouds, "who will be next?"

It sounded like a threat. Heat burst in my chest, embers dancing in my veins. "Why did you do it?"

Ambrose's jaw clenched again. Head still aimed at the sky, he flicked a heavy sidelong stare at me. "Do what?"

I turned to fully face him, squaring my shoulders and tilting my chin. "Take my shears. Why did you do it?"

Ambrose whistled, holding up his hands in mock surrender. "That's a pretty hefty accusation."

"You left me a note."

Ambrose barked out a laugh, the sound cruel and cutting. "A note? How dreadful!"

I took a step forward with a snarl. My nails bit into my palms, sharp and grounding, and for once, I didn't worry about seeing blood. I was already seeing red. "Stop being such an asshole and just admit you took them."

Ambrose sniffed, pulling out a pocket watch. "Look," he said nonchalantly, "calm down. The next challenge is only a couple days away. You can always try to beat me there."

As Ambrose frowned at the watch, I let out an incredulous laugh. "I *did* beat you before! I made top five, remember? And you didn't!"

Ambrose snorted, tucking the watch away. "You got lucky." He stepped off the sidewalk, waiting for an opportunity to sneak between traffic. "In all honesty, the challenges don't even matter; they're a waste of time, designed so cowards like you can pretend to be decent hunters without *actually* being put in harm's way. I'd like to see you beat me during the *real* ordeal. The Hunt." He looked over his shoulder and grinned. "Think you can stomach it, Shaw?"

I was sorely tempted to push him into traffic. His back was facing me. It would've been so easy to take two strong steps forward and just *push*. Watch as he collided with a buggy, maybe a car, if I was lucky. Laugh as his jacket ripped, his trousers became soiled, and his fancy pocket watch cracked. My palms itched, a flood of unfamiliar rage drowning me. It was awfully tempting, indeed.

I blinked, and Ambrose was already across the street. Sighing, I turned back to the bulletin board. Waiting for my heart to stop beating its war song, I unclenched my hands, started to look at my palms, and then decided against it.

"What's this about shears?"

Jasper and Holly had snuck up behind me, both carrying large brown paper bags that looked like they were going to split apart at any given second. Jasper was digging around at the top of his, fishing out a handful of small brown balls and popping them into his mouth.

I shook my head. "It's nothing." I held out my hands to Holly. "Am I bleeding?"

Holly peeked out from around her bag. "No?"

I gave a relieved breath, then collected the bag from her arms. Holly blushed, murmuring a quick thank-you before we resumed walking down the sidewalk.

Jasper took out another handful of the brown chunks. "Looked like that conversation was a little more than just *nothing*," he said around chewing. "Seriously, what happened?"

Holly, now with her hands free, tapped Jasper on the arm. "Don't pester him, Jasper." She hit him harder. "And stop eating the chocolate chips!"

"If I'm not supposed to eat them, then why are they so tasty?" Jasper asked, reaching into the bag to grab a couple more.

"They're for *baking*."

"Ah!" Jasper brightened. "So, that's why they are so. Dang. Delicious." He threw a couple into the air. The first one pelted his nose, the second dribbled down his chin, and the third got into his mouth.

Holly gasped in annoyance. "You're ridiculous. Those are from the mainland! Didn't you see how expensive they were?"

Chewing loudly, Jasper flashed Holly a cheeky chocolate-filled grin. "Mmm."

Holly folded her arms against her chest and burrowed her face into her tartan scarf. "When Ma gets mad at you, don't come crying to me."

Jasper rolled his eyes but stopped eating. "So, about those shears . . ."

I adjusted my hold on the bag. "He stole them. At the first challenge. Ambrose took my shears."

Jasper's eyes bulged, and thank God he wasn't still working on a wad of chocolate, because I was pretty sure he would've started choking. "Are you serious?"

I shrugged, but the movement felt stiff. "I mean, I can't prove it, but I'm, like, 99 percent sure it was him."

"And the other 1 percent?" Holly asked, her nose still buried in the green-and-blue-plaid fabric.

I shrugged again. "It was someone else. Peter, maybe."

"Oh," Jasper hissed next to me. "That slimy, cheating bastard. I ought to teach him a lesson. No one treats my best friend like that!"

Holly laughed, spinning on her toes and pinning Jasper with a coy look. "And just *how* would you do that? Are you going to fight him? Beat him to a pulp?"

Jasper faltered, ducking his head. "Or . . . give him a stern talking-to."

I couldn't help it; a chuckle ripped out of my throat. It felt like a release of some sort, like my internal pressure gauge had hit its maximum and was now deciding to level out. "Yes, Jasper," I said. "You do just that. Show him who's boss."

There were more stores closed than the last time I had walked along Main Street. Windows peppered with newspapers, doors boarded up, litter collecting on the forgotten welcome mats. Holly squeaked mournfully and rushed to one of the covered windows.

"Oh," she moaned, trying to peek through the slits of paper. "This was one of my *favorite* stores. The clothes they sold were always so fancy."

Jasper snorted. "Well, if you bought more than you window-shopped, maybe Dandy's would still be open."

Holly whirled around and stomped her foot. The tip of her nose was dark with dust. "You know Ma doesn't give me the same allowance as you. It's not fair!" She was about to stomp again when she stopped, her foot poised in midair. Eyes darting to mine, Holly gently put her foot back down, tipped her dirty nose in the air, and walked ahead of us.

"So," Jasper said, drawing out the word as he reached inside the bag again. "Ready for the next challenge?"

My stomach lurched. "Ready to die, you mean?"

"Please." Jasper snorted, spraying flecks of chocolate. "I hardly think Ambrose will be so bold as to try to drown you."

"I hardly think he'll have to; I'll be plenty capable of doing that myself."

Jasper hefted the bag onto his hip and mimicked a one-handed doggy paddle. "This. This is all you need to do."

I eyed his pathetic hand movement. "That's going to keep me alive?"

Jasper nodded firmly. "Absolutely. It's what I'll be doing."

"God. I was wrong. We're *both* going to die."

Jasper suddenly stopped, his mouth dipping into a frown as he stared inside the paper bag. "Well, damn."

Holly, a healthy distance in front of us, peered over her shoulder with a scowl. "What is it?"

Jasper winced, his cheeks going red. "We have to go back."

Holly let out an exasperated groan. "Why? What did you forget?"

"I, uh . . ." Jasper offered an apologetic smile that I wasn't entirely sure was genuine. "I sort of forgot to stop eating the chocolate chips."

Holly threw her hands into the air. "Oh, for the sake of Pete!" She stormed back to us, stopping only long enough to throw a glare Jasper's way. "You're useless, Jasper Warren. Useless!"

Jasper laughed gleefully as Holly marched back to the store. "I wish I could say that I'm sorry. But I'm not. I'm really, really not. They were so. Dang. Delicious!"

CHAPTER FORTY

EVANORA

APRIL 13 – MORNING

A PRIL 15 COULDN'T COME FAST ENOUGH.

My pod had been practicing relentlessly, stirring the water into such chaos it would make even the strongest swimmer sick with fear.

We couldn't waste time on training anymore. We were ready for blood. We were ready for war.

All I needed to do was find out when and where the challenge was being held. There was no room for error. Considering how quick Grayson had been to accuse me the second he saw those destroyed nets, I needed to be careful. I had practiced how I would ask. Concerned, and with simpering trepidation, like I was worried about his well-being and how he would fare in the water.

Because you are *worried*, my heart whispered to me.

Gritting my teeth, I buried the feelings deep down, snuffing out the ache in my chest. I didn't have time to waste on worrying about the boy. I didn't have time for anything except the plan. And the plan *would* work.

"Do you still like it?"

I blinked, remembering where I was and who I was with. Neptune spear me, I also didn't have time to fade into my thoughts like that.

Grayson was sitting next to me on the beach, eyeing me as I resurfaced from the confines of my mind. I had zoned out in the middle of staring at my bracelet. I nodded hurriedly. "Yes," I uttered, tilting my wrist back and forth. "We don't get a lot of light in the water. Watching the sun's rays dance along the silver band is quite addicting."

Grayson grinned. "I guess that means you'll have to come visit me more."

My heart clenched roughly. His smile would destroy me. And if I wasn't careful, I was certain I'd let it.

I could feel the boy's eyes on me, watching me with an intensity I was beginning to know all too well. It was the same intensity that riddled my own body, made each of my nerve endings feel alive, made my breath catch, my scales soft, my fins weak. Was it always going to be this way around him? Was the thread tethering our hearts together going to squeeze and squeeze until we finally acknowledged it? Would continuing to ignore the connection make it worse?

He was scanning my face, his ocean eyes darting from my lips, to the shimmering scales on my cheeks, to my eyes, to my lips, my lips, my lips. He was hungry. Ravenous.

I smirked, letting my gaze slide to him beneath my lashes. Grayson sucked in a sharp breath. I reveled in the sound. To have that effect on someone was intoxicating . . . But the problem was, he had the same effect on me.

"Have you noticed it yet?" I asked coyly, running my fingers over the silver band on my wrist.

"That you didn't bring a boat with you?" Grayson sighed, leaning back on his hands. "Not at all."

I nodded, shifting my fluke so it landed against the boy's crossed legs. "It's time for a real swimming lesson."

Grayson pondered my words, smiled, and said, "No thank you."

"Grayson."

"Evanora."

"*Grayson*." I giggled. "You'll be fine. I'm here, remember? I'll help you."

The boy's lips pulled to the side, his brows knitting ferociously. "I'd rather not."

I rolled my eyes. "Do you truly think I'd let you drown?"

"No." Grayson ran a hand through his messy curls, laughing helplessly. "I think I'll find a completely creative way to do it myself."

I slapped my fin against him gently. "I won't let that happen."

Shoulders drooping, Grayson opened his mouth hesitantly. It looked like he was relenting, but then his eyes skimmed the ocean. The expanse of it, the plunging waves, the deep grays and blues. His face grew pale, and his mouth snapped shut.

I sighed. "Look, you need to at least *try*. If you are swimming in the Balafor Ocean for the next challenge"—I gestured to the thrashing waters behind us—"you have to know what you are up against."

Grayson shook his head, his eyes not leaving the ocean. "We'll be back in Fariid, at Black Sands Beach. There are sandbars littering the area, so the water is gentler there. The waves don't act like they want to *eat* you."

I nodded, careful to keep my face neutral. Inside, I was overflowing with adrenaline. "Good," I said casually. "That's good."

Now just to find out *when*.

"Still," I said slowly, leaning back and letting my head roll to the side, "water can act differently depending on the time of day. I certainly hope the hunters are taking that into account." I frowned at him. "Please tell me they aren't sending you out during high tide."

Grayson looked at me, and for a dreadfully long second, I worried that he could see right through me. I waited for the accusations to start flying, the fear morphing into anger and hurt. I didn't know if I could handle seeing him like that again.

But then the boy chuckled grimly. "High tide, low tide . . ." He shrugged. "I don't think it's going to make much of a difference to me." He dug his fingers into the sand, watching as the grains squished between them. "But to balance the competition, the judges agreed that swimming during low tide would be best. Weather permitting, we will be starting the challenge just after sunrise, when the swell is lowest."

And just like that, I had both my answers.

So, why did the knowledge feel like poison in my mind?

I cleared my throat, dipping my head to my other shoulder. I flicked my gaze pointedly at the ocean. "So," I said, drawing out the word, "swimming lesson?"

Grayson let out a clipped laugh. "Yeah," he sighed quietly. "I don't think so. Not today."

I arched an eyebrow. "Might be fun?"

"Might be death. Not for you, obviously." He smirked. "Just me, the human. With my very human arms and very human legs." He inched his feet away as another wave crashed onto the beach and licked its way up the sand.

I waited a beat to see if the boy would change his mind. But I had a feeling it would be faster watching seagrass grow. I grunted, scooching myself into the water, wriggling my tail and pushing with my arms. "Fine," I said, tipping up my chin as the waves collided with me. "No swimming, then."

When the water was up to my chest, I unfurled my tail and turned back to the beach. I offered Grayson a soft smile as I stretched my arms out to him. "We'll just stand."

Grayson rose slowly, eyeing my hands like I held a poisonous jellyfish. His mouth was curled into a frown, but I could see the skin on his chin pulled taut, like he was using all his willpower to keep it from quivering. Any trace of hunger coursing through him before was replaced with fear.

I was about to lower my hands when the boy spoke, his voice barely above a whisper. "Just standing?"

I nodded, careful to keep my eyes on him. "Just standing," I repeated calmly.

Grayson reluctantly shucked off his jacket. The boots came off next, then the socks. As the boy rolled up his pants, a quiet whimper escaped his mouth. It sent a painful ache splintering up my spine.

I wanted to cave in, to tell Grayson that it was a foolish idea, a *stupid* idea, but when the boy stood tall, his mouth was set in a firm line, and there was a fire in his eyes that set my insides ablaze.

He needed to do this. And I needed to help him do it.

Head held high, Grayson planted his feet at the water's edge. He stood there for a time, breathing heavily, his entire body twitching with poorly contained nerves. Though the fire burned bright, another sickly moan escaped his throat.

"That's it," I urged quietly. I rolled my wrists in a slow circular motion, ushering him forward. "One foot, then the other."

The boy exhaled sharply, squeezed his eyes shut, and clenched his shaking hands into fists.

And he took a step into the water.

He gasped the second he connected with the rushing waves, but I knew it wasn't from the cold.

The water lapped at his ankles.

Then his calves.

Then his knees.

Grayson looked like he was convulsing, he was shaking so hard. He came to a shuddering halt, his breathing coming out in quick, frantic pants. "I do-don't think I-I can go any far-farther," he stammered out, his voice arching high with fear.

I shook my head, keeping my arms outstretched. "You can," I said simply. "You will."

Grayson closed his eyes again, his hands pressed tightly against his chest. "Please," he begged, "don't make me do this."

I resisted the urge to swim forward and collect the frightened boy in my arms, though everything within me screamed for it. "Grayson," I said firmly. "*Grayson*. Open your eyes."

The boy's eyes shot open. He swallowed hard as he looked at his submerged feet, at the waves collapsing in front of him, at the gaping body of water beyond.

"Don't look out there," I commanded. "That doesn't matter right now. Just look at me."

Grayson whimpered again, his eyes glazing over with the threat of tears. But he found me amidst the swirling waves and foam and held on as though his life depended on it. Biting his lip, he stretched out his arms, his fingers splayed as they hung in the air, reaching for mine.

"Just look at me," I said again softly. "Nothing else matters right now."

He took another step. Then another.

"Yes," I gasped quietly. "*Yes*, Grayson!"

The water was up to his thighs now, sinking into his trousers, drifting up his waist. The boy was crying unabashedly, but he was still moving, his steps inching him closer to my welcoming arms.

"A bit more," I breathed.

With a strained groan, Grayson surged forward, charging the last few steps until he collided with me. The air left my lungs the second he made impact—partly because of the way he slammed into my chest, but mostly because the boy was *here*, in my arms, pressing his entire body against me. He clung to any part of me he could get his hands on. I whipped my tail in strong, fluid strokes in an effort to keep us both upright; my fluke brushed the sandy floor, stirring up clouds of sediment and grit that swirled around us like mini whirlpools.

"You did it!" I cried softly, laughing with delight as I pressed my cheek against his hair. He smelled like the earth, and I had to fight the impulse to inhale deeply. "Gods, you're *incredible*."

Head buried into the crook of my neck, the boy fought to catch his fleeting breath. "Can I touch here?" he whispered, his grip tightening around my waist.

"Yes," I crooned. "But I won't let you go until you ask me."

Grayson gave a morbid chuckle. "That might never happen." Still holding on to me, he slowly straightened his legs, sighing with relief when his feet met sand.

Despite the angry pang in my heart, a chuckle escaped when I saw the horrified look on his face when I loosened my grip on him. I shook my head slowly, sliding my hands down his rigid arms until I found his trembling hands. "I told you," I purred, "I won't let go."

Grayson nodded reluctantly. The fire in his eyes was gone, replaced with a wary confidence that looked like a single rogue wave could sweep it away. He swallowed hard, his mouth pinched tightly as his eyes drifted from me to the ocean over my shoulder.

I needed to distract him. And gods be damned, I needed to distract *myself*. A Grayson on land was a sight to behold, but a drenched Grayson? Deadly. The wet fabric of his clothes clung to muscles I hadn't noticed before, and his wild brown curls caught the wind, tousled in ways that had my thoughts spiraling. Even the droplets of water dancing down his face, tracing his sharp cheekbones, pausing on his chin before falling to the ocean . . . I had an overwhelming, fire-hot urge to kiss every one of them, to taste the salt lingering on his skin.

I sucked in a breath, blinking rapidly. So much for distracting myself. I focused on our clasped hands, running my thumb gently along his goose-bumped skin. "I never doubted you for a second."

"Really?" Grayson made a face. "I doubted myself the entire time."

I squeezed the boy's hands, smiling warmly. "And yet you are here. With me. In the water."

Grayson's cheeks went red. "Yeah, well." He shrugged rigidly, his gaze darting away. "I'm currently trying to forget the *water* part."

As if in response, a particularly hefty wave rolled around us, slapping Grayson in the face as it went. The boy choked out a groan, his grip on my hands tightening. Panic filled his eyes as he wrenched his head to the side, looking at the shoreline behind him.

Distract him! For the love of the gods, distract him!

"I need to go back," Grayson mumbled, holding back an alarmed cry as another wave careened against his neck. He flinched away, tugging on my arms as he fought to get his footing. "Please! This was a mistake!"

"No." I shook my head quickly. "Listen to me. Grayson, you're okay. Everything's okay." I took our hands and plunged them into the water; the boy *did* cry out then. "The water is just being playful. It's saying *hello*." I moved our hands underneath the surface in a slow circle. "*Feel* it. *Move* with it."

"It wants me," he moaned. "It wants all of me."

I narrowed my eyes, a weird and twisted surge of jealousy rippling through my scales. Growling, I wrenched my hands free and brought them to Grayson's face. The boy yelped, his now-empty hands reaching blindly for a piece of me. They circled around my wrists, dangerously close to my flared fins.

"Please!" he wailed. "All of me. It wants *all* of me!"

Baring my teeth, I gave the boy a gentle shake, forcing his attention on me. "Well, it can't *have* all of you," I seethed. "Know why?"

Grayson sniffed, his feverish eyes seeking mine, worry creating deep lines along his forehead. "Why?" he croaked.

I could sense another onslaught of waves approaching. If I didn't act now, I'd lose him completely.

Distract him! Distract him! Distract—

I didn't think.

I pulled Grayson close, pressing my lips against his. The boy went utterly still in my grasp, his grip on my wrists going limp. I stayed there, breathing in his scent, memorizing the texture of his lips, the cold velvet of them, and, above all, pretending that I was simply there, kissing him out of necessity, out of the raging need to settle his rapidly manifesting panic.

I wasn't kissing him because I wanted to. Surely not.

I pulled away, breathing heavily. Grayson looked at me, mouth agape, eyes just as wide. I didn't think he was even breathing. We were so close that I could hear the pounding of his heart, the strain of it against his chest. It beat alongside mine, steady as it rippled through my veins.

I searched his eyes meaningfully before tentatively placing my forehead against his. "Because I want you too," I whispered, admitting both my fear and desire.

The connection tethering us together writhed, wishing to be set free.

Grayson remained frozen, a stone statue in my arms. Then, with a soft whine, he pulled me to him, his arms wrapping around me in a frantic, desperate way. He tugged me as close as possible, trying to erase every inch of empty space, to make the water between us disappear. His lips found mine again—slippery, wet, and heavy.

His hands moved up my neck, around my ears, through my hair, and the sensation was electric. Each touch, each spark, sent tremors through my skin, igniting every nerve. I ached for it, craved it, knowing that I'd never be able to get enough.

My Gift began to pulse, throbbing with the beat of my heart. My body hummed, and without warning, my magic surged forward, unraveling at an impossibly fast pace. Light poured out from my tingling scales, my twitching fins, my glistening skin. It bounced off the water's surface, echoed along the cliff's wall, shimmered within the mighty waterfall.

And for a brief, terrifying second, I absolutely didn't care if anyone saw.

I let out a tiny moan at the release of it all, and the boy hungrily ate up the sound, responding with desperate enthusiasm.

I reached for Grayson's hands, and when I pulled them into the water, he didn't flinch.

Waves swelled and crashed. Seagulls screamed overhead. And Grayson Shaw kept kissing me.

CHAPTER FORTY-ONE

GRAYSON

APRIL 14 – MORNING

ROUGH HANDS SHOOK ME AWAKE.

"What are you doing? Get up, you fool. Get up!"

I lurched from the bed, panting as I scanned the bright room wildly, trying to get my bearings. Pa had his hands on my shoulders, his face low and looming. His teeth were bared, and stray tendrils of hair hung over his eyes. I gave my head a hard shake and rubbed my eyes; they burned from the memory of tears. "What is it?"

Pa stood with a scowl. "You're late for work. Mr. Brightly expected you at the docks over an hour ago." He gave me a hard look. "Are you ill?"

My body suddenly burst with heat as I recalled my experience on the beach the day before.

Evanora gripping my face, her lips colliding with mine.

The look in her eyes when she told me that she wanted me.

The shock of her magic as it flooded from her scales, sending out wave after wave of beautiful blinding light.

I touched my burning cheeks and wondered briefly if I was. "I don't think so?"

Pa clucked his tongue, pressing a hand against my forehead. "You're sweating."

I chuckled tiredly, fighting the urge to flop back into bed. "Just a poor sleep, I think."

Pa placed his hands on his hips, eyeing my damp clothes, the wet imprint of my body on the bed. "Bad dream?" he asked reluctantly.

My stomach churned with butterflies.

Evanora's teeth grazing my bottom lip, giving it a tiny possessive bite.

The taste of her on my tongue.

A deep pressure began to build in my chest, sinking lower . . . lower. "Maybe. I can't remember it though."

Pa scoffed, but he looked relieved. "Well, if you aren't sick, then you best be on your way. I don't want to hear that blasted phone ringing again." He stared at me, still half asleep, still frozen in bed, and clapped his hands together briskly. "Go on, now. Get going!"

With a groan, I ripped off my covers and got out of bed with all the enthusiasm of a prisoner making his way to the noose.

I should've just said I was sick. Then I could've spent the entire day analyzing the way Evanora's fingers had haphazardly untucked my shirt so they could roam the expanse of my back.

Waiting to hear the bells again would be torture.

It didn't occur to me that Evanora might be regretting the kiss until I got back from work.

I was sitting at my desk, working on my sketch of her, when the link tethering our hearts together went eerily loose. I sat up straight, pressing a hand against my chest. I could still feel it—it hadn't completely disintegrated—but just barely. It had never felt so weak before, so fragile. I looked out my window, peering into the night sky. What was Evanora doing to make it go slack?

The one who was promised . . .

My breath got stuck in my throat. "No," I mumbled. "Not tonight, please."

Here. Come here, Promised One.

The night was quickly growing sour. First the sudden wasteland in my chest, and now the voices. I gritted my teeth together. "I don't have time for you."

I'd never tried talking *back* to the mysterious voices, but I figured that if I could hear them, they could hear me, no matter the distance.

Here. Here. Here, they whispered enticingly.

I squeezed my pencil so hard that I nearly snapped it in two. "*Where is here?*"

Come outside. We shall show you.

There was a knock at my door. I tore my eyes from the window and turned in my seat to see Pa in the doorway. For once, I was thankful for the intrusion; I needed a distraction.

"Hi," I said, closing my sketchbook with a casual flick of my wrist.

Pa leaned against the doorframe, his arms crossed against his broad chest. "How are you feeling?"

I shrugged, trying to block out the voices as they continued to slip through the open window. "All right. Mr. Brightly made me stay late to make up for my late start this morning."

Pa narrowed his eyes, suspicious. "With pay?"

I snorted, draping an arm across the back of the chair. "What do you think?"

Pa sighed, pushing off the frame and walking into the room. "That man pinches his pennies like a woman clutches her pearls."

I wilted slightly. "Sorry. I'll go in early tomorrow to make up for it."

Pa gave me a hard look. "The challenge is tomorrow."

A jolt of terror coursed through me, electrifying my nerves and causing the hair on my arms to stand up. "Oh. Right."

Pa continued to stare at me for a long moment before he strolled over to my bed and sat down with a huff. "Are you ready?"

Considering my only swimming lesson had really just been me wading through water and crying the whole time, no. Not in the slightest.

"I'm a little nervous," I admitted.

Pa rubbed his palms together slowly. "I wasn't sure what was best for you," he grunted, keeping his eyes trained on his hands. "You already knew how to build nets, and I knew I could teach you combat, but swimming . . ." He sighed. "I wasn't sure how to help you."

I bit my lip, shrugging. "Some things I need to do on my own, I think."

A crooked grin formed on my pa's face. "Spoken like a real hunter."

It was meant to be a compliment, but all it did was make me feel sick.

The one who was promised.

I felt an anxious spark in my veins. My gaze returned to the window.

Herrrrrre.

"Grayson?"

I whipped my head back in Pa's direction, startled. "What?"

Pa's eyebrows were drawn together. "I asked what you've been doing to prepare yourself for tomorrow." He looked briefly at the window. "Are you sure you're okay?"

My skin was crawling, a thousand ants burrowing deep. The cool night breeze was doing very little in the way of helping the fire in my chest. I could feel Pa's eyes on me as I slowly looked out the window. "It's just . . . I thought I heard . . ."

Pa's face hardened, concern etched into its cracks and crevices. "Heard what?"

I spared the window a final glance before turning in my chair again to face Pa. I had to word my question carefully. One misstep, and that concern would be quickly replaced with annoyance. "Are there worse things out there than mermaids?"

Pa stiffened, causing the bed to creak. "What do you mean?"

I had no clue what I meant. "It's just . . ." I sighed. "What's exactly *out there*, in the Barrens?"

Pa chuckled, but there was no warmth in it. Only exasperation. "Nothing, Grayson. There is nothing out there."

I chewed on my lip. "Are we sure? Like, do we know that for a fact?"

Pa stood abruptly. "Nothing is out there," he repeated harshly. "Anything you've heard is just made up fairy tales and urban myths."

I stood up too. "But where do those fairy tales come from? They have to have an origin. Why can't we swim at nighttime? Why does the ferry only set sail at sunrise? Why does no one fish near the Barrens?"

"What you should be asking yourself," Pa growled, "is why you insist on seeing your ma behind my back and letting her fill your head with this nonsense."

I rubbed my wrists, my fingers catching on the warped skin. "Does Ma know something about the Barrens?" The scars began to burn. "Is that why she—"

"It's time for bed," Pa said, cutting me off. "We both have a big day tomorrow, and I won't have you wasting the night away with these ridiculous thoughts."

"But—"

"Go to *bed*." Pa stormed toward the door, not bothering to grace me with a final scathing glare.

Pa was gone before I could tell him that it was barely past six o'clock. I sat back down at my desk with a grunt. That conversation hadn't gone nearly as smoothly as I had wanted it to.

Why was no one talking about the Barrens? Not even Evanora wanted to discuss it. But there was something out there, something sinister and evil. There *had* to be. Whatever it was, it had to be behind Warrick's death. And it had to be where the voices were coming from.

But . . . why?

Why now?

Why me?

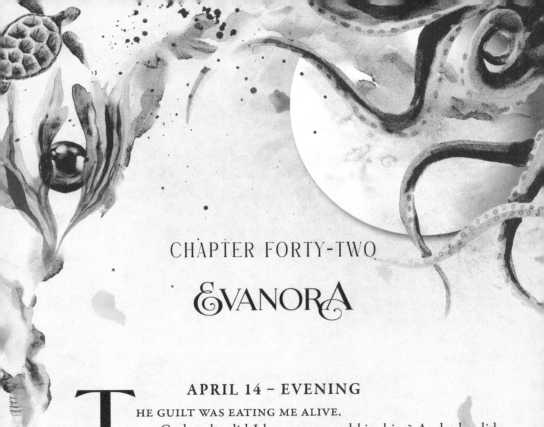

CHAPTER FORTY-TWO

EVANORA

APRIL 14 – EVENING

THE GUILT WAS EATING ME ALIVE.

Gods, why did I have to go and kiss him? And why did it have to feel so damn divine? My entire body burned with a mixture of shame and desire, but at least my magic wasn't threatening to burst out of my skin every single time I thought back to Grayson's lips on mine. It was there, though, bubbling at the surface, waiting for a break in my constant concentration to keep it locked away. One slip and I'd light up the entire ocean.

The kiss had not been part of the plan. It just felt like something I had to do. And the worst part about it was . . . I didn't even regret it. Not for a second. In fact, if I had the opportunity, I'd probably do it again. Though, after tomorrow, I highly doubted Grayson would feel the same.

In less than twenty-four hours, the world Grayson Shaw knew would be ruined, and he'd know it was all because of me, and nothing would be the same.

I avoided Mavi and Illeron for as long as I could. Part of me wanted to expel my knowledge like a violent sickness, purge myself of all the information I had. And a very large, very prominent, very *stupid* part of me wanted to keep it hidden, keep Grayson safe.

They finally cornered me in the garden, putting an effective end to my disappearing act.

"There you are!" Mavi cried, giving the sacred space a quick reverent glance before rushing into the center where I was resting. "We've been looking everywhere for you."

"Yes," Illeron mused, swimming around one of the boulders, his arms crossed. "It was almost as though you were hiding from us."

I propped myself onto my elbows, plastering on a smile. "Me? Hiding? Never."

Mavi frowned as she settled into the soft white sand next to me. "We haven't seen you since you left for the island yesterday."

"And time is of the essence," the warrior grumbled.

Mavi looked at Illeron, then back at me, her fingers worrying in her hair. "We were beginning to think you weren't able to procure any information on the next challenge."

I snorted delicately. "And I was keeping distant out of shame and embarrassment?"

Illeron's mouth flattened into a thin line. "Were you?"

I huffed, picking myself up off the floor. "I'll have you know that I've simply been busy." I waved a hand dismissively. "Lighting lanterns, healing fin rot, sneaking mermaids away to sunbathe. Boring things, but necessary things." *And most definitely hiding.*

The wielder gave me a wilted look. "Evanora, we haven't had to light the lanterns for a couple days now."

I froze. "Really?"

"Really. Our combined Gifts have been surprisingly quite effective."

"Well," I scoffed, shaking my head. "Then I've been doing other things. Poseidon drown me, I have a lot of things on my mind. Excuse me for forgetting."

Mavi looked at me expectantly. "So?"

"*So* what?"

Illeron rolled his eyes, shifting forward. "Did you find out the time and place of the next challenge or not?"

I swallowed hard, my stomach churning. The thread around my heart grew impossibly tight. *The plan*, I reminded myself. *Stick to the plan. Remember why you are doing it in the first place.*

I opened my eyes and stared hard at Mavi and Illeron. "They start at sunrise, on Black Sands Beach. We will take them by storm there."

Two things happened then.

The first: My heart went into a free fall, ripping itself from its confines in my chest and plummeting into the abyss that was my stomach.

The second: The link between me and Grayson went horrifically slack. It hadn't torn completely, but it was hanging on by literal tendrils, frayed and ready to snap at any given second.

My hand fluttered to my chest, and I stifled a gasp as I attempted to internally retrieve the loose threads. I wanted to wind them around my heart, cinch them tight, feel the connection between me and the boy throb back to life. But every time I tried to grip them, they slipped from my grasp. Without it taking space inside me, I suddenly felt empty, barren, a black void.

Luckily, Mavi was too busy being overjoyed with my news to notice. Illeron, on the other hand, was eyeing me heavily, his face tight, his ruby eyes flashing with concern.

"Are you all right?" His voice drifted into my subconscious, dark and suspicious.

Inhaling sharply, I forced my hand to drop from my chest. I cut a glance the warrior's way. *"I'm fine."*

"You don't look fine."

My upper lip curled into a snarl. "Then stop looking."

Mavi paused. "Looking at what?" she asked, her eyes darting from Illeron to me. Realization slowly set in, and Mavi tried—and failed—to mask her disappointment about the internal conversation she wasn't included in.

"It is nothing, Mavi," Illeron said briskly, his eyes not leaving mine.

"Illeron was just pestering me, as per usual," I added, severing the contact.

Mavi bit her lip, uncertainty clouding her features.

"It's about Grayson, isn't it?" Illeron pressed further. *"You're upset about the boy."*

A thin growl slipped through my clenched teeth. *"Stay out of my head, warrior,"* I snapped, a warning flicker of electricity scouring my scales. The agony in my chest festered.

"You are, aren't you?" Illeron sidled closer, his gaze drifting to the bracelet on my wrist. *"That human has completely clouded your senses."* He widened his eyes. *"Is that why you didn't come to us sooner with the information?"*

"Stay out of my head!" I demanded again, the warning flickers growing into bursts of crackling white light.

Illeron pulled away from my mind with a hiss, lightly touching his temples with rigid fingers.

Mavi groaned, lifting her hands up helplessly. "Can someone please tell me what's going on?"

"Nothing," I bit out, forcing my Gift back into its cage.

The black hole of pain was getting to be too much to bear. It was growing with each passing second, and I worried that it would continue eating at me from the inside out until it eventually swallowed me whole. I began to swim out of the garden.

"I must go," I said over my shoulder. "There is something I have to do."

Mavi's mouth dropped open. Illeron surged forward, one of his gnarled hands outstretched for me. "You can't! We have to prepare!"

I stopped long enough to cast a scathing glare Illeron's way. "We *are* prepared."

Illeron shook his head, flashing me his teeth. "Don't do this."

I raised an eyebrow, challenging him to say what was clearly crawling around in his mind. "Do what?"

"Leave us." He narrowed his eyes. "For *him*."

Mavi gasped, covering her mouth with her hand.

The pained expression on both their faces was almost enough to keep me in place.

Almost.

I forced out a laugh, but it came out cold and humorless. "Look at you, jumping to conclusions." Illeron opened his mouth, but I held up a hand, silencing him. "I'm going to Fariid. I want to assess the beach to figure out our best vantage point for the ambush." I tilted my head. "Did you honestly believe I'd go back to the boy? Don't be foolish. Why on earth would I go back to him?"

Illeron scoffed, though the pain remained on his face. He rubbed it off with a swipe from his hand. "I'll go with you, then," he said, lurching forward.

"No. I need you to rally up the team and tell them what I've learned. Let them know that we will be leaving tomorrow, before first light. We need to be there before the humans arrive, otherwise they'll see us." I lifted my chin. "Can you do that, warrior?"

A muscle feathered in Illeron's jaw. Mavi swam forward, nodding fiercely. "I can." She gave a little shrug. "I've hardly been able to do much in the way of help. I can at least do this."

My gaze flitted to hers, and I smiled sweetly. "Thank the gods I can at least rely on you, Mavi."

Illeron choked back a snarl.

For the briefest of moments, I felt a little bad for the warrior. I was being hard on him, torturing him for no reason other than the fact that he cared about me. It wasn't his fault that my heart was preoccupied; he was simply trying to protect it.

But then the agony in my chest became a yawning mouth, threatening to take another chunk out of me.

I swept for the island, trying not to think about how it was getting easier and easier to lie to my friends.

I RANG THE BELLS AS HARD AS I COULD. THE FIRST COUPLE TIMES, I followed the rhythm Grayson had shown me, but by the third attempt, I was rattling them in a sheer panic. Every single beat of my heart sent searing pain down my limbs.

The threads linking me to Grayson had finally quit being a frayed mess in my chest, but that almost felt worse now. I knew what it felt like to not have it there, and I had a feeling what I was about to say to the boy was going to send it unraveling again, this time for good. I didn't know if I could handle the emptiness, if my heart could take it.

By the time I saw Grayson loping down the stairs, my arms had gone numb from shaking the life out of the bells. His legs were moving so fast that they were a blur against the sand-colored cliff. With a grunt, he leapt off the last couple steps and tumbled toward the water's edge.

I took one look at the lopsided grin on his face, and any strength I possessed to remain strong left me. Ramming the bells between the rocks, I pulled myself onto the sand, fighting against the fear that clawed its way up my throat.

"I was beginning to think we weren't meeting up today." The boy was breathless, his entire face a beacon of happiness as he sat down next to me.

"I needed to see you," I whispered, reaching for one of his hands.

Grayson took it, his skin warm and rough against mine. He placed my fingers on his cheek. Closing his eyes, he leaned against my touch, inhaling deeply. "I couldn't stop thinking about yesterday," he uttered, his ocean eyes finding me in the dark.

I swallowed, my shoulders drooping. "Neither could I," I admitted.

Grayson's mouth quirked to the side, but his eyes filled with the faintest hint of worry. "You don't regret it?"

Holding his gaze, I slowly shook my head. "Not even a little."

The boy sighed with relief, the action causing his entire body to sag. "I'm glad. Part of me wondered . . ." Grayson's free hand went to his chest, his fingers tangling with the fabric of his shirt. "I was scared you did."

I bit my lip to keep it from wobbling. I was losing my nerve. If I didn't speak now, I'd never be able to; the words would get stuck in my mouth, and I'd choke on them. "Grayson, I—"

The boy pressed a finger to my lips, making a soft shushing sound as he leaned in.

My mind went deliciously empty, and for a second, there wasn't any fear of the Hunt, or the challenge tomorrow, or losing Grayson. There wasn't a plan to drive forward. There wasn't a swarm of heartache and loss. There was nothing but white noise.

I found myself falling forward to meet him halfway.

Grayson's fingers moved away from my lips, stroking my cheek. He let out a soft moan. "Beautiful," he breathed, his forehead pressing against mine. "You are so beautiful."

I wanted to crumble against him, completely dissolve underneath his fire touch. I wanted him to kiss me until I was breathless, until my fins drooped and my scales softened. I wanted to get drunk off his touch, his smell, his taste, and then keep going until it was embedded into my memory. I wanted to forget about my reason for rushing to the beach.

But I couldn't.

The white noise faded, and the wailing within my mind went back to being deafening.

I clenched my eyes shut, my sigh coming out in a hiss. "Grayson, I need to tell you something." I pulled away from him abruptly, staring willfully into his eyes. "Before another word is uttered. And I need you to listen."

The boy's brow furrowed, a frown drifting across the lips I was dangerously close to kissing again. "Sure." He placed a hand gently against my forehead before running his fingers through my hair. "Hey, are you all right? You're looking a little pale. Well . . ." He chuckled lightly. "Paler, I guess."

I was suddenly acutely aware of the sweat beading along my upper lip, the scorching heat in my cheeks. I placed my cool hands against my face. "To be truthful, I don't feel well. Not at all."

Grayson scootched closer, concern etched into his features. I hated how it made my insides quiver. "Do you need to go home? It's all right if you do." He forced a small smile. "I'll see you tomorrow, won't I?"

"No!" I blurted, surprising myself with the ferocity in my voice.

Grayson blinked slowly, trying to process my riddles but failing. "*No*, you don't need to go home, or *no*, I won't see you tomorrow?"

"Both . . . Neither . . . I—" I shook my head, groaning. Reaching forward, I gripped the boy by his arms. "Grayson, you can't participate in the challenge tomorrow."

The words came out so fast, tumbling off my tongue before I had a chance to even register them.

If kissing Grayson wasn't part of the plan, then gods be damned, this really wasn't either.

Grayson went still, the smile on his lips slowly slipping off.

I gripped the boy's arms tighter. "Did you hear me? You *cannot* be in the water tomorrow." I gave him a little shake. "Please, Grayson, promise me!"

Grayson felt limp in my hands. He drifted away from my probing gaze, staring out into the water and the day's fading light. "I don't understand," he said slowly. "The challenge . . ."

"It's tomorrow. Yes, I *know*. And you can't participate in it. Don't get in the water, not even a little bit." I sighed, dropping my head into my hands. "Please don't ask me why. I've already said too much as it is."

Grayson frowned. "No, I don't think you have. What's going on, Evanora?" He tried to pry my hands off my face. "What aren't you telling me?"

"Nothing," I said between clenched teeth.

The boy shook his head, a frustrated sigh on his tongue. "I deserve a bit more than that, don't you think?"

My head snapped up, eyes flashing as a burst of fiery anger replaced the guilt gnawing at my insides. It was a welcome change. "I'm risking everything by being here with you, Grayson Shaw, and yet you—a mere *boy*—think you deserve more than what I've already given?" I let out a bitter laugh. "Why is that?"

Grayson didn't flinch at my rage. He gave me a hard look and thumped his chest. "Because of this," he said, hitting his chest again. "Because of this *connection* between us."

"Connection?" I forced another laugh. "What connection?"

Grayson leaned forward, clasping my shoulder. "You feel it too. I *know* you do." As he spoke, he let his hand drift down, his fingers dancing along my shimmering scales, until he was resting just above my heart. "I can't explain it, but there's . . . I don't know . . . a *thread* that is linking our hearts together. I don't know what it is or why it's there. All I know is that it *exists*, Evanora."

I hadn't been prepared for that. Everything inside me turned to ice. Grayson took advantage of my silence, moving his fingers down my arm until he grasped my hand. He bent forward, pressing his lips against my palm. Shivers crept up my arm. Still kissing my skin, he lifted his stormy eyes to mine, pulling me under his calm. That quiet steadiness—so unnerving, so sure—was devastating to my worried heart.

"I know you're risking a lot." He laughed quietly, the sound sending vibrations through my nerve endings. "I am too. But something wants us to be together. I can feel it in my heart." He straightened, placing my hand on his chest. He held it there, his fingers trickling along my cool skin soothingly. Closing his eyes, Grayson inhaled slowly, then began to tap his fingers lightly against the back of my hand. It took me a second, but I realized he was following along to the rhythm of his heartbeat.

Ba-dum. Ba-dum. Ba-dum.

"Can you feel it?" he whispered, opening his eyes, his fingers not ceasing. "Can you feel how it's beating for you, Evanora?"

I could. And I could feel the deep, dull agony in my own as it matched his, beat for beat. A symphony of earth and ocean, of seconds and infinities, of a longing so terrible that I worried the connection would snap completely.

The key, my ancestors crooned. *The power of three!*

Grayson stroked my cheek, his thumb collecting the onslaught of tears trailing down my skin. "Tell me you feel it too."

His touch was so comforting. I ached for more of it.

And how cruel was that—to ache for something you were never meant to truly have?

The anger was gone in a violent *whoosh*. My breath caught in my throat, a wavering moan coming out instead. "I . . ."

Grayson was so close, and I couldn't tell if I was slipping into his orbit, or if he was getting pulled into mine. Time seemed to stand still. Even the crashing waves muffled their attempts at eating away the beach.

"Tell me why I can't go in the water tomorrow, and I won't," Grayson breathed, inching closer. He closed his eyes. "Tell me why, and I'll listen."

The boy's lips were on mine, and I was certain I could hear my heart breaking.

I twisted my head away, severing the kiss before it had a chance to fully form. I snarled at Grayson, ignoring the confusion and hurt riddling his features and trying to rekindle the rage that had fizzled into burning ash. "I need to protect my pod," I said firmly, and before anything else could be said, I dove into the receding waves.

I could hear Grayson calling out to me, begging me to stop. His hurried footsteps crashed into the water, unhinged and frantic. His cries continued, but it wasn't long before his steps came to a stuttering halt.

I didn't stop swimming until the island was long, long behind me.

CHAPTER FORTY-THREE

GRAYSON

APRIL 15 – MORNING

DON'T GET IN THE WATER.

Last night's visit with Evanora was a riddle. Or a puzzle. It didn't matter; I was awful at both.

The mermaid had been trying to tell me something—something big, something important—but all I'd been able to think about was trying to kiss her. The memory made me cringe. I'd have to apologize the next time I saw her.

If she even *wanted* to see me again. The thought was disturbingly bleak, and I quickly pushed it away. I couldn't stop the sudden presence of nausea burning up my throat though.

Everything felt off-balance now, and though the connection between us still thrummed with life, last night made me wonder if it was going to snap soon. Maybe it had reached its expiration date.

Maybe it wasn't even real. Maybe I was just imagining it because I wanted a love story like Pa and Ma, or Warrick and his mermaid.

Focus. I needed to focus.

The sun was just beginning to tease the looming clouds with its rays of light. The blue waters at Black Sands Beach were quiet and calm. In the distance, I could see three white-and-red-striped buoys bobbing lazily, their large yellow flags listless in the absent breeze. Even the seagulls seemed abnormally tranquil, content to rummage along the boardwalk instead of seeing which one of them could squawk the loudest.

By all accounts, today seemed like a good day for a swim.

You can't participate in the challenge.

Please, Grayson, promise me!

What had she meant by that? She knew how important the challenges were to the hunters. Was she just worried about my fear of water? Was she actually looking out for me and just having a hard time admitting it?

"Hey," Pa huffed, jostling me on the shoulder. "Pay attention."

I blinked hard, pushing my thoughts aside to focus on Mayor McCoy's voice as he paced along the water's edge with his hands clasped behind his back. His shriveled face was pointed at the sun, basking in its warmth as we watched him with rapt attention.

"Before you are three marked buoys, each one half a mile apart. Swimming to the farthest and back will total three miles." He raised a gnarled finger, grinning at us. "Three miles may not seem like much, but trust me—when you're out there, fighting the waves, braving the cold, it won't feel so easy."

His beady eyes fixed on us. "Your fingers and toes will go numb, your limbs will grow heavy, and your mind will go blank. You'll want to quit, to call for help, to wait for rescue. But I'm here to tell you that you're on your own today. No help will come. The boats are docked, life preservers are forbidden, and flotation devices are off-limits." He paused and faced us. "*Your* safety is *your* responsibility."

I swallowed audibly, earning a mildly concerned look from my pa.

Jasper, who was standing to my left, began to bounce on his toes, inhaling and exhaling sharply as he flicked his wrists. "Bring it on," he growled under his breath. His bad leg gave out, and he nearly tumbled to the ground.

I helped Jasper straighten, patting him on the back with a shaky hand. "Easy there, Poseidon," I uttered quietly.

Jasper offered me a confident grin and resumed his bouncing.

Peter, who was standing in front of us, twisted around with a snort. "We haven't even started swimming, and his legs are already failing him." He crossed his arms against his naked chest. "My money's on Jasper being the first to die."

Tommy, standing next to Peter, poked him in the stomach. "Calm down, Lyre. No one is dying today." He pointed at the open water. "Look how calm it is out there. Even the worst swimmer is going to make it back." He looked over his shoulder at us and frowned. "It just might take a while."

God bless Tommy. I was going to buy him a beer after this nightmare of a day was over.

"You'll notice," Mayor McCoy continued, sweeping a hand over to the desk just underneath the boardwalk, "that Mr. Grieves and Mr. Fowler won't be participating in the challenge today. That is because they were last year's best swimmers, and therefore, they will be this year's judges."

Mr. Grieves stood tall next to the desk, looking completely out of place in his crisp white suit and top hat. His usual silk cravat had been replaced by a black bolo tie, a large ruby brooch holding the strands in place. A white cloak clung to his broad shoulders, its deep crimson lining a striking contrast to his ensemble. I couldn't help but picture him spending hours choosing a brooch that matched the cloak. Hopefully the suit would be covered in black sand by the end of the challenge.

Mr. Fowler, on the other hand, fit right in. He was in the same uniform that all the hunters wore. The wide leather belt acted as a corset around his thick midsection. I didn't think he'd gotten the note that he could wear his own clothes. I also didn't think Mr. Grieves, in all his money-smothered splendor, enjoyed standing next to him.

Mayor McCoy pressed on. "They will be timing the hunters, taking note of who remains the most composed amidst the chaos, who has the best stride, and who returns to the beach first. When the challenge is over, they will deliberate and adjust the scoreboard as needed."

Mayor McCoy gestured to the large board above the judges' heads. Even from where I stood, I could see my name still written near the top. The pride of seeing my name amongst the top five hunters was going to be short-lived.

It wouldn't stay there—not after today.

Don't get in the water, not even a little bit.

"For all you gamblers and risk-takers, keep an eye on the board," Mayor McCoy said. "It'll help you decide who to vote for on the Night of the Betting."

"Or who *not* to vote for." Peter snickered, throwing another pointed glance over his shoulder.

Jasper forced a loud, exaggerated laugh. "Oh, that's *so* funny! Coming from the guy who is currently sitting in last place! Hilarious!" He abruptly stopped laughing. "Keep the jokes coming, you tub of lard; I've got all day."

Peter's mouth dropped open. He looked like a fish testing the air. Tommy calmly reached over and shut it for him.

"Fellas," Owen said sternly from next to Tommy. "Th-th-this is serious. T-try to focus here."

Owen's reprimand lost a bit of its edge with his stutter. Just the same, my cheeks burned with second-hand shame for Jasper.

There was a hand on my shoulder. At first, I thought it was Pa getting ready to scold me again, or goad me into another side bet. But then the grip went tight, and I could feel fingernails digging into my shirt. I flicked my gaze back to see Ambrose, a cool grin on his lips as his icy-blue eyes stared straight ahead.

I snapped my attention forward, a burst of red-hot adrenaline flooding my veins.

Ambrose's touch felt like poison. "Are you ready, Shaw?" he asked quietly, baiting me.

I clenched my jaw, exhaling slowly. "Ready for what?"

He laughed, low and sinister. "Let's face it—you're not setting a single foot into that water." His grip grew viselike. "I've seen you squirm the second you get too close to the water's edge. I've heard the sounds you make when the waves touch your skin. You're weak, and you're going to fail today."

I jerked my shoulder out of his grasp. "Don't touch me," I growled.

Ambrose whistled lightly, holding up his hands in mock surrender. "You'll be saying something different when you're drowning." He leaned in, his hot breath on my ear. "And I'll be looking the other way."

Another hand on my shoulder, but this time it was my pa. "No one is drowning today," he said gruffly, fixing Ambrose with a heavy glare. "Take a step back, if you know what's good for you, boy."

Still holding up his hands, Ambrose dutifully got back into his line. But his eyes were still on me, and his smug grin was more cutthroat than ever.

Sucking in a shaky breath, I turned my attention forward. And that was when I noticed that not only was I feeling the weight of Ambrose's attention on me, but someone else's.

I slowly craned my neck over the swarm of hunters to the desk, where Mr. Grieves was eyeing me up with such intensity it made my nausea come back with a vengeance.

Like I was something to eat, or something to squash.

Mayor McCoy strode over to the desk and retrieved the firearm. Holding it over his head, he pressed a hand over his ear. "Hunters ready?"

The crowd began to scream. I knew it was with excitement, but deep down, a part of me only heard the wailing of mourners.

Don't get in the water!

Mayor McCoy squeezed his eyes shut and pulled the trigger.

The hunters were off, tumbling over one another, eager to be the first into the water.

And I stood, unmoving from my place on the beach.

Ambrose pushed roughly against me, quickly surpassing Jasper's hobbling canter and Tommy's unhurried walk. He darted around Peter's flimsy excuse for a jog and caught up with Owen. Together, they crashed into the waves.

The water swallowed them whole.

There was a chorus of shocked cries as hunters burst into the water's icy grasp. A couple high-pitched shrieks and curse words reached my ringing ears. Still, they all continued forward, struggling to wade out until the sandy floor sloped and they could begin swimming with purpose.

My feet were anchors. My hands were lead. My mind was a swarm of bees, biting and stinging and humming with rage.

Pa had taken a couple steps forward, but he stopped to look back at me, his face contorted in confusion. "What are you doing? Come on!" he bellowed, waving a hand hurriedly at me.

My eyes darted to the water, its gaping mouth full of bodies.

Don't go into the water!

"Come on, Grayson!" Pa cried, desperation lacing his words.

"I—" I stopped, the words lodged in my throat.

Something was happening in the water.

The lazy blue waves that had been lapping the shoreline only moments before were speeding up, morphing into long icy fingers that lashed at the sand with an abnormal brute force. The water surrounding the hunters began to churn, dipping and coiling, angry at the sudden intrusion.

Like it was a beast. Like it was coming alive.

Like it was being controlled.

I looked back at Pa. The look of dueling disgust and disappointment dripping off his face was nearly enough to send me moving. He bared his teeth at me, spat on the ground, and thundered down the beach.

I took a panicked step forward. "Wait!" I cried.

But Pa was already in the water before my plea could reach his ears.

The waves were growing in size. The water had shifted from a soft aquamarine to an unsettling gray.

I forced my feet to move, but they only got me to the shoreline. The waves licked at my bare feet, and I scuttled back, a sickly moan escaping my mouth. "Please, come back!" I yelled, trying in vain to catch someone's attention.

Mr. Grieves observed from his place next to the boardwalk, his steely gaze burning into the back of my head. It took all my willpower not to run over to him, fall onto my knees, and beg him to call off the challenge. To do that would cost precious time. Time I certainly didn't have.

"Please!" I tried again. "It's not safe!"

The waves were like towers, rising and collapsing with a force that sent the hunters swaying in all directions.

I was frozen.

EVANORA

It's working!" Mavi cried from her place on the seabed. Her arms, outstretched and pointing at the surface, were already shaking from exertion, but the smile on her face was triumphant.

We were just beneath the second buoy, perched on a narrow seamount—close enough to see the hunters but hidden enough that they couldn't see us. The water wielders sat in a circle, arms raised, faces intense with concentration, their bodies glowing as their Gifts pulsed. Warriors stood watch, spears gripped tightly, fins stiff and ready.

I hovered just outside the group, eyes fixed on the surface, waiting to see a boy plunge into the water's grasp, praying that I wouldn't.

Mavi was right: Our plan *was* working. We had barely gotten started, and already the waters were in utter chaos. Waves tossed the hunters like they were mere playthings. Rip currents dragged them off course. Undertows threatened to pull them down. The water had shifted into a sickly gray, camouflaging us even more.

It was perfect. So, why did I feel so ill?

Illeron drifted away from his post and clucked his tongue beside me. "It would be so incredibly *easy* to just attack." He shrugged, glancing down at his spear. "We could pick them off, one by one, until there were no more hunters to even worry about."

I immediately shook my head. "No," I said firmly. "Grayson only told me the bare minimum about the challenge. Just because he didn't mention boats doesn't mean they won't be out there."

Illeron chewed on his lip. "If there were boats, we would be able to see them." His face lit up. "I'll bet our wielders are strong enough to take them down too."

"*No*, Illeron." I tore my gaze off the water to face him. "We are doing this my way. We stay down here, where it's safe."

The warrior's upper lip curled the slightest bit, but he dipped his head carefully. "As you wish, Your Majesty," he said out loud. *"Worried your boy will get caught in the cross fire?"* he asked in my mind.

I shot him a fiery look, my scales bristling. "Go back to your post, warrior. Before *you* are caught in the cross fire." To carry my point across, I let my Gift crackle to the surface for the briefest of moments, sparking at my fingers and shooting light through my fins.

Illeron's mouth quirked in the smallest of smiles, and he nodded curtly, returning to his post.

The wielders cheered, and I whipped my head back toward the surface in time to see a colossal wave smash into a swarm of hunters. Several submerged, fighting and clawing over one another to get back up. Just as they surfaced, another wave toppled over their heads.

I stifled a gasp, my heart aching with each frantic beat.

It was getting harder and harder to pinpoint each of the hunters. Spotting Grayson in the midst of them was like searching for a shell in the middle of a seaweed forest.

Please, Grayson, I inwardly begged, *stay out of the water.*

Out of the corner of my eye, I saw Illeron's head snap in my direction, a look of agony and betrayal coating his face.

I ignored it and continued searching for the boy.

GRAYSON

I WATCHED IN HORROR AS A SKYSCRAPING WAVE CRASHED ONTO THE heads of the hunters, followed by another, and another. The ocean was unrelenting, ruthless in its anger. It was hardly letting them come up for air.

Many of the hunters were persevering, fighting to make it to the final buoy. Others had stalled out, bobbing in place as they tried to figure out the water's erratic pattern.

If the waves weren't coming from every single direction, they might've been able to.

The crowd behind me had gone deathly silent, their encouraging cries getting stuck in their throats.

I cupped my hands around my mouth, praying my voice reached their ears. "Turn back!" I shouted. "It's not safe!"

As if to prove my point, a whirlpool erupted near the second buoy, yanking down a handful of hunters before spitting them back out.

"Please!" I wailed. "Come back to shore!"

I couldn't see Pa anymore. Fear gripped my insides as I dragged my gaze along every hunter I could see. With the crashing waves, it was nearly impossible to know if I was looking at the same person twice or a different person entirely.

Another whirlpool formed, nearly sucking the third buoy into its vortex. When it finally released its grip, the buoy sailed into the air, crashing into one of the hunters. The struck hunter didn't return to the surface for a painfully long time.

The crowd began to scream again, but gone were the sounds of joy and excitement. The only cries to be heard on the beach were those of bone-chilling dread.

I sucked in a gasping breath, clutching the sides of my head as I witnessed the frantic hysteria that enveloped the hunters. They cried out, fighting against the water as they rushed back for the beach. The sea was in no hurry to release them, however. It would let them gain distance, let them taste hope, but just when their feet were about to touch the sloping sand embankment, the waves would sink their foamy teeth into them and drag them back. It was the most gut-wrenching game, and I was starting to think that there would be no winners.

My eyes fell onto the second buoy, where a group of five hunters were struggling to climb on top of the metal device. They pushed and pulled at one another, fighting to get out of the water.

And there he was, clinging to the bottom rung, straining to get his legs out of the water's clutches. His hair had fallen out of its topknot and was plastered against his face. His mouth was in a tight grimace as his feet continued to lose purchase.

"P-Pa!" I shrieked.

Amidst the chaos, and the clamoring of hunters, and the raging of waves, Pa's eyes shot up, finding mine on the shore.

We stared at each other for an infinity. Then Pa's face relaxed, and he offered me the smallest of smiles.

And in that infinity, all I could see was Warrick.

The moment was wrenched from my fingers as the biggest wave I'd ever seen careened in the direction of the buoy.

It was moving fast, almost purposefully, aiming to take the buoy out.

I pointed a finger at it. "Pa! Behind you!"

Pa craned his neck in time to see the wave smash against the side of the buoy. The metal device groaned as it heaved onto its side, dunking several of the hunters back into the water. My pa clung to the metal bars as the buoy fought to straighten. But just as it started to correct, another rogue wave collapsed against the buoy's side, sending it sputtering in the opposite direction.

The world went quiet.

I watched, horrified, helpless, as Pa was flung from the buoy, his body like a rag doll as it collided with the roiling surface.

I didn't think.

I just moved.

EVANORA

No," I moaned, watching as a lone figure raced off the shoreline and into the water. "No, no, no!"

I didn't need my eyes to know. I didn't need my ears. I didn't even need my ancestors, who had begun screaming for my attention the second the figure's body collided into the water's open arms.

I could feel it in my heart. Every erratic beat spelled out his name with absolute crystalized clarity.

Gray-son. Gray-son. Gray-son.

The boy staggered as far as his feet would take him. The second they began to slip down the steep embankment, Grayson started to thrash, sloppily flinging out his arms and legs as he swam. He was aiming for the buoys, but against the pulsing waves, he wasn't getting very far.

I held my breath, my hands pressed against my mouth as I watched helplessly from my spot on the seamount. *Turn around*, I willed. *What are you doing? Turn around!*

"These fools just don't let up!" Mavi gasped, shaking out her arms before raising them again. "Look! Another one just jumped in!"

"I can take care of that one," one of the wielders growled, pointing her clawlike hands toward Grayson. "You just keep focusing on the waves."

Mavi bit her lip and nodded, her smooth forehead creasing with concentration as she sent another volley of waves upward.

Grayson was already starting to flounder, his head more under the water than above it. I was certain I could hear his choking gasps for air from my spot on the plain. Each one sent a spear of agony through my heart.

I didn't realize I was moving until a hand clamped down around my wrist. I came to a jarring halt, a burning pain in my shoulder as the ligaments stretched. I hissed as Illeron hauled me back. "What are you doing? Let go of me!"

Illeron didn't relinquish my wrist. His brows were low over his eyes, his mouth pulled into an ugly snarl. "Evanora, don't," he warned, his voice low and heavy.

I wrenched my arm free, turning back to see Grayson submerge completely, his legs kicking but getting him nowhere.

"He's not *worth it*," Illeron pushed.

The boy sank lower, and lower, his limbs quickly losing their momentum as the currents dragged him down.

I bared my teeth at the warrior, my magic flaring to the surface. "He is to me!" I seethed.

Tail writhing beneath me, I raced for the water's edge, fighting against time, praying that I had enough of it to reach Grayson.

GRAYSON

DROWNING WAS NOT NEARLY AS PEACEFUL AS PEOPLE WOULD HAVE you believe.

The pressure in my lungs was becoming too much to bear, and the ringing in my ears was nearly deafening. I had already swallowed several buckets of water, but still the water fought to get inside me. My mouth began to burn with the bitter taste of salt, and my stomach clenched viciously.

And, God, the water itself . . .

It slammed into me like a beast, tossing me back and forth, disorienting me until I couldn't tell which way was up. The cold was unbearable—a thousand needles sinking into my flesh, gnawing at my very bones. Mayor McCoy had been right: I couldn't feel my fingers or toes, but the searing agony that raked through me made that seem like a distant concern.

But the worst part wasn't the pain. It was watching the surface slip away, so damn close, but beyond my reach.

As I sank lower and lower, I wondered why I hadn't listened to Evanora.

The pressure was an unrelenting monster, squeezing my chest until I thought it would crack open. Blinding pain exploded behind my eyes, and I could feel the veins in my head straining, about to snap. My vision blurred, black dots crawling along the edges, and the world dissolved into a haze. I closed my eyes, choosing darkness over the fragments of reality. My mind slowed, heavy with fog. My limbs hung uselessly, limp in the water, as my strength bled away.

This was it. This was my ending. Unceremonious, lackluster, and goddamn poetic in how pathetic it was.

I wasn't going to become an ethnobotanist. I wasn't going to see Evanora again. Ma wouldn't care, but at least Pa would be proud that I'd died during a hunting challenge.

I allowed myself to sink and slowly began to let out my precious breath.

Strong hands were at my waist.

I shot up, my heart slamming in my chest, blood pulsing hot through my veins. I opened my eyes, and—

I wasn't sinking anymore. No, I was . . . soaring. The water fought against me, pulling at my face as I shot toward the surface, faster than anything humanly possible. My teeth clenched as I strained against the weight, tilting my head downward. Everything was a blur, but I caught sight of a glowing orb, surrounded by a halo of light.

It was weird how an oxygen-deprived brain could conjure up the things you desired most when you were about to die.

Because even though it wasn't remotely possible, I was almost certain that the orb had violet eyes, just like Evanora's.

I blinked hard, trying in vain to focus. As we drew closer to the surface and the blackness faded to a bleak gray, the orb began to take shape.

Long silky white hair flowing through the undercurrent.

Rigid iridescent fins.

A strong luminous tail.

A silver bracelet dangling off a dainty wrist.

If I had any more air to let go of, I would have gasped.

I broke through the water's edge, and it was like colliding with a brick wall. The second I was free, another wave collapsed on top of me, like it had been lying in wait. I had barely a second to cough out a lungful of water before I was back under, scrambling in the undercurrent.

Evanora's hands were on me again, soft and soothing as she collected me in her arms.

My mind stilled, but only for a moment.

I stared at her underneath the crashing waves. Her face was drawn tight with fear, her eyes darting to the hunters surrounding us. But whenever she looked at me, her gaze would soften. She hummed gently, one of her hands caressing my frozen cheek. It was almost enough to make me forget that I had nearly drowned a moment ago.

The pressure was beginning to build again. I glanced frantically at the surface looming just before us. I gripped my throat with shaking fingers, pulling my pleading stare back to Evanora.

The mermaid nodded, understanding. "I'm taking you back to shore," she said, her melodic voice crystal clear.

I remembered the very reason I had run into the water in the first place. "Pa . . . My pa!" I tried to croak out, though it came out in a warbled, bubbly mess.

Evanora's face fell, and she shook her head. "No," she whispered. "Just you."

Evanora's powerful tail undulated behind her, and suddenly, I was soaring again, racing toward the shoreline at a breakneck speed.

And then, with a final push, she let go, sending me tumbling into the sandy embankment.

For once, the waves worked with me, carrying my battered body the rest of the way. The second my head rose above water, I let out a ragged gasp, sucking in as much oxygen as my tender lungs would allow. Every breath resulted in a haggard coughing fit, but I didn't care.

I was on land, and I was alive.

And Evanora was gone.

When I collected myself, my eyes were back on the water, tracing the churning waves for any sign of her shimmering light.

All I could see was gray water slowly returning to pale blues and teals.

Most of the hunters had made it back, some crawling on hands and knees, others collapsed at the shoreline. The black sand was littered with bodies. Some were bleeding. Many were barely conscious. Peter was dry heaving into the sand, his large body convulsing violently. Rosemary Little was smothering Ambrose with frantic kisses, though he stared blankly ahead, oblivious to her love. Sebastian Brightly crouched next to Owen, steadying him as he hacked up water. Jasper lay on his back, hands clutching his chest, mumbling, "I'm alive . . . I'm alive . . . I'm alive!"

Panic seized my chest, but it didn't have time to claim purchase. There was a splash, and I ripped my gaze from the beach as my pa stumbled out of the water. His body swayed, but he managed to make it a couple steps on solid ground before he groaned and collapsed, sending up a spray of water as he connected with the waves.

And, once again, I was back in the water.

Thankfully, I only had to go up to my knees.

"Thank Christ you're all right," Pa bit out between heavy breaths as I placed his arm around my shoulders and guided him to the beach.

I could smell blood on him, sharp and metallic, and I wondered briefly if I was going to be joining Peter in the barfing department.

"The cut is on my arm," Pa wheezed, as if sensing my thoughts. "You can't see it."

I nodded, praying it wasn't the arm draped against my shoulders. "I hope you didn't like this shirt. I'm burning it the second we get home."

Pa started to laugh, but it quickly turned into a sputtering cough.

Even though it was futile, I peeked over my shoulder at the water, wishing to catch a glimpse of Evanora. She had to be long gone by now. It didn't even make sense for her to be near Black Sands Beach in the first place. She knew the challenge was today. To willingly be so close to so many humans? No, not just humans. *Hunters.*

My brain worked feverishly to make sense of it all, but it was still muddled, full of salt water and sea-foam.

As quickly as it had started, the waters were already settling. Any hint of the malevolent anger it had manifested earlier was gone, like the demon had been expelled and the sea was at peace again.

My knees nearly gave out, and I stumbled to a halt. Pa grunted, but he almost seemed relieved by the break.

It was an exorcism.

The hunters were the demons, which meant the exorcists were—

Sybil Morris pushed onto the beach, small whimpers escaping through her tightly sealed lips. She walked in quick steps, barreling roughly into the few hunters strong enough to stand. Her eyes, wide and full of terror, were trained on the sea.

We stood in stunned silence, watching as Mrs. Morris hurried to the water's edge. She stopped just as her pointed shoes met the reaching waves, and her whimpers turned into stifled sobs. She placed a trembling hand over her pale lips and sank onto the wet sand, her eyes not leaving the sea. If she noticed the water's frigid grip sinking into her dress, it didn't show. She just stared, and stared, and stared.

And that was when we all saw it.

A body, floating lifelessly next to the third buoy.

Tommy Morris.

CHAPTER FORTY-FOUR

EVANORA

APRIL 15 – MORNING

NO ONE WOULD LOOK AT ME. WHEN THEY DID, IT WAS with hurt and confused expressions. I had no idea how to acknowledge the looks, so I didn't.

I knew I probably deserved them, but I didn't want to acknowledge that either.

I pasted on a smile and swam next to one of the water wielders. "Excellent wielding today, Luvon. Your waves were impressive!" I said, placing a hand on his shoulder.

The mermaid recoiled at my touch. "Thank you, Your Majesty," he mumbled, swimming just out of my reach, his green scales bristling.

I gritted my teeth and forced the smile to grow. "And you, Daithi! Your whirlpools took my breath away," I said, gliding up next to the wielder with pink-tipped fins. "You played a great part in our triumph."

Daithi ignored me. She simply turned her petite nose into the air and pushed her long black hair out from behind her ears, creating a curtain between us.

My swimming nearly stuttered to a stop. Was no one in the mood to celebrate? My face was beginning to cramp when a purple tail swirling with faded spots passed in my peripherals. I reached out, gripping Mavi's arm. "Mavi!" I said, pulling her to a halt. "You were incredible today!"

For a split second, Mavi's fins went rigid, but then she turned to face me with a smile that looked as fake as my own. "Thank you," she said quietly.

I paused for a beat, then mustered a quick laugh. "Surely you can spare some joy in your heart. We were victorious, and the day belongs to us! Aren't you pleased?"

"Well, yes." Mavi's deep honey-gold eyes darted away briefly, catching the heavy looks of the other wielders. "Of course I'm pleased."

I gave Mavi's arm a playful shake. "Then what is it? What has you pretending to be happy in front of your dear friend?" I rolled my eyes, smirking. "At least the others are blatantly showing their disdain for me and not hiding behind false niceties."

Mavi's smile began to falter. "It's not disdain, Evanora." She dipped her head and lowered her voice. "They are just . . . confused, I think."

Ah, time to acknowledge it. "Confused? About what?"

Mavi bit her lip. "Well, it's . . . about that boy . . . the one you saved. We just . . ." Mavi let out a long breath, her brow furrowing. "Why, Evanora? Why would you do that?"

I opened my mouth, but a voice cut in from behind me. "Yes, I'd like to know the answer to that question as well."

I turned, and immediately felt the heat behind Illeron's scorching glare. I flinched back from the immense weight of it, guilt turning my guts into constricting reeds. Everyone had stopped swimming and was now crowding around us in a tight circle, and I realized that I had actually preferred them not staring at me; it hurt a lot less.

"I—" I bit out a laugh. "It was nothing! A minor error in judgement."

"That *minor* error," Illeron growled, "nearly upended our entire plan. Truly, Evanora, what were you thinking?"

"I wasn't!" I stammered out helplessly. "I saw him, and I reacted." I spun in a circle, desperately meeting the eyes of the wielders and warriors. "What would you have me do? Let him drown?"

"Yes," Mavi cut in, her voice carrying a level of ferocity I had never heard in her before. "Because of you, we had to cease all our attacks. There were still so many hunters in the water; we could have rained devastation down upon them." She covered her face with her hands and shook her head. "We could have done a lot more damage had you not gotten in the way."

I clenched my hands into fists, aware that my fins were growing rigid. "I didn't ask you to stop."

Illeron flashed his sharp teeth. "And risk you getting hurt in the midst of their wielding? Or worse, getting spotted by one of the hunters?"

I fought against the snarl that rose deep in my belly. "I think I can handle a couple waves and whirlpools."

Beside me, Daithi scowled. "Care to test that theory?" She raised her arms, and her Gift began to glow as the water pulsed around her fingers. It swirled and yawned, collecting more and more water as a churning vortex started to take shape.

It was strong. I beat my tail a bit harder in order to stay in place, but my fins lilted in the whirlpool's direction, my hair pulling at the roots as the water threatened to suck me in.

Illeron placed a hand on Daithi's arm, and she gave a disappointed sigh, reluctantly calling her magic back inward. The water immediately calmed.

The warrior looked at me. "The point of the matter, Evanora, is that your pod trusted you. They followed you into battle today, and you failed them." He winced, his mouth dipping into a frown. "Saving that boy from a plan *you* devised? We expected more from you." He turned. "*I* expected more from you."

The wielders and warriors slowly shrank away, shaking their heads, their tails drooping in defeat. I raised my arms and scoffed loudly. "Oh, what does it matter, really?" I let my hands fall back to my sides with a heavy slap. "Look, I said I was sorry. We shouldn't let my lapse in sanity put such a damper on things." I laughed brightly. "We . . . We won! We should be celebrating!"

Mavi, the last mermaid to leave, turned slowly to look at me. Her face was pinched tightly, barely holding her pain at bay. When she spoke, her bottom lip began to wobble. "Actually, Evanora, you didn't."

I faltered, the rest of my laughter getting stuck in my throat. "Didn't what?"

"Say you were sorry." With a final mournful look, Mavi swam away, joining the rest of the exhausted soldiers as they returned home.

I was alone.

I wanted anger. I wanted rage. I wanted to unleash my magic until the entire ocean was a crackling hive of light.

All I felt was self-loathing.

All I felt was misery.

CHAPTER FORTY-FIVE

GRAYSON

APRIL 16 – MORNING

TOMMY MORRIS WAS BURIED NEXT TO HIS FATHER.

Underneath the large cluster of birch trees behind their house, next to the small creek that ran through the backyard. Twenty-one stones created his cairn. Compared to his father's, which stood tall with forty-five, Tommy's twenty-one carefully stacked stones seemed almost comically small.

Dead at twenty-one.

The Hunt had claimed another life.

Pastor Kline had politely offered to hold a service at the church on the hill. Mrs. Morris had politely refused. God hadn't saved her youngest, nor had He saved her husband five years prior. If He didn't have time to fish her loved ones from the ocean's hungry grip, she didn't have time for Him either.

So, most of Lethe had gathered in Mrs. Morris's backyard instead. Chairs were brought out, benches pulled from the garden, picnic blankets tossed over the grass. Milk crates and soap boxes were flipped upside down, serving as makeshift chairs. Those without seats stood, straddling dead flower beds, huddling by the creek. People stamped their feet against the cold earth, rubbing handkerchiefs against reddened noses. No one complained. No one dared to think about the warmth of the church, the comfort of its pews.

The sun filtered through the birch leaves, casting its light down the pale trunks. The creek babbled beside us. Birds sang from the treetops. It was far too beautiful a morning for a funeral.

Pastor Kline still managed a prayer. Mrs. Morris had the decency to let him finish before she had Owen kick him out.

Now all eyes were on Owen, the eldest and last son. He stood before the cairns, head bowed low, shoulders slumped—like a flower desperate for water. He sniffled, wiped his nose against his sleeve, and then looked up at us, his dark eyes heavy with unshed tears. He reached into his coat pocket, pulling out a book—the same one Tommy had read on the beach while the others drank. It was well-worn: edges frayed, dog-eared pages, and book-marks sticking out in all directions.

Owen cleared his throat, opened the book, and began to speak. "*Death is-is-is extraordinary. You n-never t-truly know what it feels like until you are experiencing it yourself. N-n-no one has found a way to-to-to come back to tell us-us . . . us about it. Therefore, who can s-s-say whether or not it is the-the most beautiful feeling in . . . the world?*" Owen took a steadying breath. "*Death just might be our biggest adventure.*"

He closed the book and looked up with a small smile. "A quote from one of T-T-Tommy's favorite authors. If you kn-kn-knew . . . Tommy, you knew he always had a book in the crook of his arm. He was always reading, always quoting the-the-the—" Owen winced. "Sorry. The works of Gingham, Bing, and Pryce." He choked out a laugh. "Honestly, I could n-n-never understand half of what he was t-t-talking about when it came to books. But T-Tommy was . . . the smart one, not me."

The crowd rippled with gentle laughter, which was followed by a handful of sniffles and muffled sobs.

Owen glanced down at the book like it was a prized possession. "Tommy . . . He was s-such a quiet, brilliant s-s-soul, you know? He wasn't one for grand gestures or loud banter. He s-sp-spoke volumes with his s-s . . . silence, and when he did . . . speak, his every word was weighted . . . profound. And his love for books and th-thirst for knowledge enriched us all. He wanted to s-see the world . . . n-not just th-thr-through his own eyes, but . . . through the eyes of others. I think that-that-that's why he read s-so much."

Owen paused to duck his head, wiping his nose against his sleeve again. "It's going t-to be weird, n-n-not hearing him bicker with Mom about where sh-sh-she put his pipe, or him yelling quotes at me in the-the . . . the middle of a fight just s-s-s . . . so he could confuse me into losing." His smile began to wobble, his stutter making it nearly impossible for him to get the words out. "I'm going t-to miss his dry humor, the s-smell of his pipe on cold, crisp mornings. But most of all, I'm going to miss th-th-those quotes he would yell at me." Owen's face crumpled, his shoulders drooping. "I would give anything t-t-to have just one more fight with him."

It took him a long moment to collect himself. The sounds of his sobs filled the cramped space, mingling with the breeze singing softly in the trees. When Owen finally looked at us, there was a fierce determination in his tearstained eyes. "The-the-the Hunt," he bit out. "I'm doing it for T-Tommy."

Crouching next to the cairn, Owen set the book against the small monument's base. He then dug into his pockets, removing Tommy's glasses and pipe. He placed the objects around the book, his fingers lingering over each item. Owen let out a shaky breath, pressed his fingers to his lips, and touched the last stone on the stack. A final kiss goodbye.

As he stood back up, Mrs. Morris came forward, whimpering as she repeated the gesture. "Goodbye, my Tommy," she whispered, and though her words simply bounced off the cairn, the stones gladly collected her tears.

A line began to form as the people of Lethe trudged forward to pay their respects. One by one, they placed a hand on top of the cairn, uttered a condolence here, an apology there, and then gave the surviving Morrises each a hug that was more likely for their own comfort. My mind was buzzing with all the things I could say to make them feel better, but really, the one thing they truly needed was something I couldn't provide. No one could.

As I drew closer to the front of the line, I narrowed down what I could say to two things.

The first: I could offer the same surface-level sympathies that everyone was dishing out.

The second: I could unleash the confines of my chaotic mind onto Owen and tell him what I truly thought had happened to Tommy. There was nothing normal about that storm, nothing organic about it. Something had happened intentionally to throw off the second challenge . . . I just didn't know what. It felt more like a conspiracy theory than anything else. Deep down, I knew I had to talk to Evanora about it first. Until I confronted her about it, that was all it would be: a theory I was breathing an unhealthy amount of life into.

All I knew was that the more I thought about it, the crazier I felt and the more tangled my thoughts became. If I didn't do something about it, my mind would become a rat's nest, and any hope of unraveling it would be extinct.

Owen was in the middle of a long hug with Sebastian when I stepped up. His eyes met mine from over Sebastian's shoulder, and he pulled away, slapping Sebastian lightly on the back.

Sebastian reluctantly withdrew. "Feel better, friend," he said, lightly bumping Owen's jaw with his fist good-naturedly.

"*Feel better*?" Ambrose said from behind me, chuckling humorlessly. "He lost his brother. He's not suffering from a cold."

"Yes," Sebastian said, his amber eyes flashing as he gave Ambrose a hard look. "And I want him to feel *better*, all things considered."

"Uh, yeah." Ambrose coughed. "I'm pretty sure *feeling better* isn't on the menu for Owen at the moment."

Owen held up his hands. "I s-s-swear to God, if the t-two of you st-st . . . start fighting on my brother's grave, I'm going to-to-to kill both of you. *That* might make me feel better."

Sebastian's nostrils flared. But he stepped out of the line, and it was my turn. Owen offered me a sad smile. "Grayson," he said, holding out his arms, "th-thank you for coming."

I gave Owen a hug, quickly shifting from option two to option one. "I'm so sorry," I said quietly as I pulled away. "It's all so unfair."

Owen nodded, shrugging his shoulders. "You'd know that better than-than-than . . . anyone." The smile swiftly morphed into a quivering frown, and his red-rimmed eyes shone with unshed tears. "Sometimes the pain is s-s-so fierce, I can barely breathe." His hands flew to his chest. "It's like an anvil on my body; the-the-the pressure just won't ease up. I'll sometimes forget—" He gave an abrupt laugh. "If you can believe th-that. And when I remember he's gone, the-the . . . the grief comes back like a t-tidal wave, fast and ferocious and s-s-soul shattering." He sighed, dropping his hands. "I wish I were in . . . that grave instead of him."

I knew exactly what he was talking about. What he was saying was what I went through every single day without Warrick. I was a walking example, and now, so was Owen. Still, I shook my head fervently. "Don't say that. You don't mean it."

"Well, I certainly th-think it would hurt a hell of a lot less than-than . . . than how I'm feeling n-n-now." Owen heaved a long breath, running a hand through his hair. "How did you do it? With Warrick?"

I shrugged lightly, giving Owen a small smile. "One day at a time. One foot in front of the other. One night of rest, and then another."

A glimmer of hope caught light in Owen's eyes. "Does th . . . the pain go away?"

I didn't want to lie. "No," I said. "But you learn to carry it all the same. Some days it feels like it's going to crush you, and some days you almost feel guilty at how light it's gotten." I placed my hand on his shoulder and gave it a squeeze. "There will always be pain. It means you're human. It means you're still alive."

The tears finally broke free from Owen's lashes, and he whimpered, pulling me in for another hug.

"Hey," Ambrose huffed from behind me, "some of us are still waiting. God . . ." He snickered. "It's like the Symbolic Sign-In all over again."

Owen promptly let go of me, stepped around the cairn, and punched Ambrose in the nose.

Ambrose squawked and stumbled back, clutching his face as blood spurted between his fingers.

I was instantly queasy. The ground shifted violently, and it took all my effort not to sink to my knees and wait for things to level out.

Owen was clearly not as deterred by the sight of blood, and he went in again, fists raised, teeth bared. He landed two more punches before Ambrose had the wherewithal to actually try to avoid them. He managed to block one aimed for his chin, but he wasn't so lucky when it came to the knee in his gut.

The look on Ambrose's face made me think that he could count on one hand the number of times he'd been beaten up. The look on Owen's face made me think that he was right: Killing Ambrose *would* make him feel better.

Mrs. Morris swept forward, hands outstretched and nasty words on her tongue as she wrenched the boys apart. "Christ on a cracker!" she bellowed. "This is a funeral! Have some decency, you fat-headed bastards! You disgust me, the lot of you! Oh, Jesus H. Roosevelt Christ!"

"That's my cue to leave," I mumbled, swerving around the flurry of flailing fists and stomping feet, though I knew I'd mourn not seeing Ambrose get the snot beaten out of him—not to mention hearing Mrs. Morris talk like a sailor.

Pa was waiting for me at the end of the driveway, his arms crossed against his chest and the smallest smirk on his tightly sealed lips. "It's just not a funeral without a proper fistfight," he muttered, his eyes trained on the scuffle at my back.

"I'd hardly call that proper," I said, stifling a burp as bile shot up my throat. "Ambrose was *not* a willing participant."

Pa winked at me. "Even better."

We made it a measly five steps before there was a jarring honk behind us. I startled, bumping into Pa as a car slowed to a stop next to us. The car's back window rolled down, revealing Mr. Grieves's smiling face.

"Ah, just the person I wanted to see!" he said jubilantly, tilting his head out the window.

Pa instantly stiffened next to me. "If this is about the short-loin cuts you ordered, Mr. Grieves," he said hurriedly, "I promise it'll be ready by tomorrow morning. The delivery truck had a flat tire and—"

Mr. Grieves waved a hand dismissively. "No, no," he chortled lightheartedly. "I'm actually keen to speak to Grayson if you don't mind."

I started again. "Me?"

Mr. Grieves smiled invitingly, but all I could see was a rabid dog ready to bite. "Yes, you!" He pulled out his pocket watch and assessed the time. "I must be off, run errands and the like, but what say you drop by my house at three o'clock this afternoon?"

I caught myself frowning and smothered it with my hand. "Actually, sir, my pa and I were planning on practicing combat later today."

"Oh, ta!" Mr. Grieves shook his head. "You still have plenty of time to practice before the next challenge. I only need a small piece of your time."

Pa, who was not bothering to hide his frown, cleared his throat. "You clearly haven't seen my son with a spear," he said with a biting laugh. "He needs all the time he can get to practice."

Mr. Grieves put his pocket watch away. "I won't take *no* for an answer," he said with an air of finality. "I'll have my chauffeur pick you up this afternoon." He began to roll up the window. "Until then, young Shaw!"

I stepped forward abruptly. "Aren't you going to get Ambrose?" I glanced over my shoulder, where the fight was still going strong. "He's causing quite a scene."

Mr. Grieves paused briefly, the window opened just a crack. He shook his head. "Ambrose knows that whatever situation he gets himself in, he must be able to get himself out of. I'm not his keeper!" he said, rolling up the window the rest of the way.

"No," Pa uttered as the car drove away, leaving us in a cloud of dust, "just his father."

I gulped, my mind scrambling. What did Mr. Grieves want to talk to me about? What was so important that he couldn't simply discuss it with me here?

I could feel Pa at my back, huffing with pent-up nerves. I could hear the fight dwindle, then roar back to life. And it came to me:

Mr. Grieves didn't want witnesses.

T RUE TO MR. GRIEVES'S WORD, HIS CHAUFFEUR PICKED ME UP
in a sleek black car that felt completely out of place next to our decaying
barn and knee-high weeds. The chauffeur, a sharp-featured man with slicked-
back black hair and a thin mustache, introduced himself as Mr. Beaton. He
said I was to ask for anything I needed on the drive to Fariid, but his voice
lacked any real warmth. He opened the door for me with reluctant care, as
though being in Tully was beneath him—and by extension, so was I.

We set off down dirt roads that gradually became flagstone, past broken
fences that turned into winding stone walls. Even the weather seemed to
improve as we left Tully behind; the heavy clouds parted, replaced by soft
cotton-like wisps drifting across the high mountains and fading into clear
blue skies.

I'd heard rumors about Grieves Manor—how it loomed atop the highest
cliff in Fariid, overlooking the eastern Floria Sea. Nothing could've prepared
me for what I saw.

We stopped at the black wrought iron gates that enclosed the estate. Mr.
Beaton stepped out and, with deliberate steps, unlocked the ivy-clad doors,
pressing his gloved hands against the large gold *G* and *M* monograms until
they groaned open. As we passed through, he left them ajar, showing just
how long he expected me to stay.

Rows of neatly trimmed flowers lined the cobblestone path leading to
the house, with a gargantuan fountain angel crying over goldfish and water
lilies in the middle of the roundabout.

And the house. *God*, the house!

I could see why the Grieveses had passed on the castle in Maude. This
was a far better fit. Black brick walls shot up from the ground, interrupted
only by long, oval-topped windows. Sturdy turrets rose at each corner, their
pointed spires clawing at the sky. Gargoyle statues perched on the sleek black
shingles, their claws digging into the roof as they grinned hungrily at me. I
quickly looked away, squeamish.

It was a bright and sunny day, yet you wouldn't know it, standing in front
of Grieves Manor. The house—if you could even call it that; *house* was too
basic a word—seemed to suck the light out of everything around it, drawing
it in and snuffing it out.

Mr. Beaton cleared his throat, and I hurried up the steps, mumbling an apology as I walked past the door he had been holding open and into the gaping mouth of the house.

And just like that, I was in the belly of the beast.

I hadn't known such extravagance could exist in a place like Lethe. The island was known for tarnishing even the brightest splendors. Beautiful things weren't allowed on Lethe; the Hunt made sure of it. Perhaps the Grieveses were holding all of the beautiful things here in their mansion. They certainly had the space for it. The entranceway alone could fit my entire house inside it and still have enough room to host a party. A large chandelier dripping with crystals and candlelight hung from the domed ceiling, right between two staircases that snaked parallel along each opposing wall, leading up to the second floor. Thick red carpet ran along the stairs, but the rest of the floor was a crisp white linoleum. If I stared hard enough, I could see my reflection.

Along the crimson walls, towering family portraits hung in gilded frames—Mr. Grieves, Ambrose, grandparents, great-grandparents—each scowling, eyes narrow, jaws tight. Their anger was almost comical. I started to smile, remembered where I was, and quickly stopped.

Sitting just below the chandelier was a large circular table that was most definitely bigger than my bed. It housed a single vase smothered in flowers. It was the biggest pop of color the house—*mansion*—had to offer. Purples, pinks, yellows, greens. They bulged out of the vase's mouth, fighting for freedom.

A single table with the sole purpose of holding flowers. Seriously.

Mr. Beaton cleared his throat again. "When you are done sightseeing," he said wearily, "would you be so kind as to follow me?"

He was standing to the right of the entranceway, next to a hallway I hadn't even known was there. I looked at my boots, horrendously muddy and scuffed, and eyed the shining linoleum floor. "I—" I bent down, trying to rub some of the grime away. I only succeeded in smearing it. I straightened, my cheeks burning. "Should I take them off?"

Mr. Beaton looked at me like I had grown a second head. If it was possible for him to think any less of me, it was happening. "Mr. Grieves *really* doesn't like waiting," he said in answer.

I stepped off the entranceway rug, fighting the urge to look back to see the obvious trail I was leaving behind.

I didn't want to go down the hallway. It was lit, but the lights almost seemed to be for ambience more than anything else. Brass sconces glimmered on the walls, flickering with a weak light that the darkness devoured. I could barely make out my hand in front of my face. Mr. Beaton was a shadowy outline just ahead, his strict steps merging with my squeaky hurried ones. It felt like the hallway went on a lot longer than a hallway should, but it was hard to know in the ever-looming dark.

Mr. Beaton stopped abruptly, and I bumped into his back, a gentle "oof!" escaping my mouth. Mr. Beaton only sighed in response.

We stood before a heavy oak door. It was closed, and I could barely make out the sound of voices coming from behind it. They were heated, staccato with their rising and falling volume, punctuated by silence, and then a flurry of more words. I couldn't make out what was being said, but it sounded violent.

"Mr. Grieves will just be a moment," Mr. Beaton said, giving me a curt nod before stepping around me and marching back down the hall.

I shifted from foot to foot, debating whether to knock on the door or race down the hall back to Tully. I didn't have long to decide. As soon as I turned away, the door flew open, and there was Ambrose. My heart lurched at his sudden appearance. He was practically vibrating with energy—shoulders hunched, hands clenched into fists. Dried blood crusted his nose, and dark bruises shadowed his eyes.

I instinctively cringed, bracing for his usual belittling remarks. But instead of his typical scorn, Ambrose froze when he saw me, his hand snapping to his eyes. At first, I thought he was trying to hide the bruises. But when he wiped hard at them, I saw the light catch on the moisture clinging to his eyelashes.

My mouth almost dropped. Ambrose, crying? It felt like an impossible concept. But before I could process it, he growled and shoved past me, stomping down the hall and muttering to himself.

I swallowed, feeling unsettled. What had made him so upset? What had shaken him up so badly that he couldn't even be bothered to bully me? Was he being a sore loser about the fight? Was he being a real human for once and expressing *real* human emotions about the death of his friend?

I didn't have long to ponder that either.

"Young Shaw!" Mr. Grieves called from within the office. "Do come in."

That seemed like a terrible idea. Reluctantly, I moved toward the door. As I stepped inside, my feet shifted from hard linoleum to plush carpet, and the flood of light from the windows on the far wall made me squint. The room was large and circular, clearly in one of the mansion's turrets. I hated the realization; it meant there was no secret exit, no escape route. I was trapped.

Mr. Grieves sat behind his large desk, which was in the middle of the room and facing the door. To his left was a stone fireplace surrounded by fat velvety chairs and a table with an unfinished game of chess sitting atop it. On the right of the room were bookshelves that reached the ceiling, littered with so many books that they'd put the Tully library to shame.

Mr. Grieves was wiping his hands on a crisp white napkin, but he paused when he saw me, offering me what was probably meant to be an embarrassed smile. "I hope Ambrose didn't give you any trouble on his way out?"

I shook my head. "He seemed too upset to bother."

Mr. Grieves chuckled politely, folding up the napkin and sticking it into one of the desk drawers. "Please excuse him. I'm afraid the family business is putting a strain on his neck. His moods have been all over the place as of late. Now then." Setting his elbows on top of the wooden desk, he clasped his hands together and rested his chin on them, eyeing me. "I'll get right to the chase: You are a surprising one, Mr. Shaw."

I fumbled for a response that didn't include a full-body shudder. "A surprise? Me, sir?"

Mr. Grieves nodded, a slow smirk spreading along his lips. "Tell me, at the last challenge, how did you know?"

Cut to the chase, indeed. My shoulders ached from how tight they had grown. I knew where this was going. "Know what?"

My playing dumb did little to deter Mr. Grieves. "That it was too dangerous to get in the water *before* the water truly got to be as violent as it did." He leaned back in his seat, lightly gripping the chair's armrests. "Surely it wasn't a stroke of luck."

When I shrugged, a sharp pain cinched around my neck. I was already sweating. "Instinct, if I had to guess." I tried to smile and failed spectacularly. "I'm also tremendously afraid of water, which probably influenced matters."

Mr. Grieves's eyebrows shot up. "Ah," he said lightly, "that leads me to my next question. For someone who is so deathly fearful of getting wet, I noticed that while you struggled to get into the water, you had no trouble getting out of it." He mustered a laugh. "Why, you shot out of it faster than most!"

I faltered. "That's . . . not a question."

Mr. Grieves began tapping his fingers against the armrests, the only sign of his thinning patience. "How did you move through the water so effortlessly?" he asked, smiling around his gritted teeth.

"Adrenaline, I think." I stuffed my hands into my pockets. "Honestly, I couldn't get out of the water fast enough, it felt like."

He was digging, prying for information. I wouldn't give him any. Even if Evanora was behind this mess, I wouldn't say anything—not to anyone, and certainly not to this man.

"Oh, but you *did*," Mr. Grieves countered. "Exceedingly fast. It was almost as though you'd sprouted fins." He steepled his fingers together, bouncing them lightly against his chin. "Or you had help."

My vision was starting to swim. Had it always been so hot in here? As if in answer, the fire roared beside me, the wood crackling as it crumbled, sending up a spray of embers. I shrugged again. "I'm not sure what you are looking for," I said helplessly. "It was just me in the water." I set my jaw and willed my back to straighten from its wilted state. "I'm sorry if my answers aren't to your satisfaction."

Mr. Grieves said nothing, only continued to tap, tap, tap his fingers against his face. He stared at me like I was some sort of specimen that needed to be analyzed. He was waiting. Waiting for me to cave, to give in to his hypnotic icy-blue gaze and spew all my secrets so he could gobble them up. I glanced at the door. "Will that be all, Mr. Grieves?"

Mr. Grieves blinked, setting his hands back down on the armrests. The spell was immediately broken, and I found myself letting out the breath I hadn't known I was holding.

"You really are a peculiar sort, Grayson Shaw." He offered a smile, though there wasn't a single ounce of mirth in it. "Yes. Run along home now. Mr. Beaton will see to it that you get to your combat lessons in one piece."

A thirty-minute drive for a five-minute talk. I almost wanted to tell Mr. Grieves that I had a landline, that this could have easily been a conversation held over the phone. But I knew Mr. Grieves wanted to see me. He wanted to look at me as I lied, to see the cracks form in my morality, to watch me squirm under his interrogation. He wanted the grandeur of his mansion to unnerve me, to intimidate me, to fill me with so much jealousy that there was no more room for my secrets.

But it didn't work. My secrets were still my own, and while his home did intimidate me, it didn't fill me with lust for wealth, for power. Only disgust.

As I turned for the door, freedom at my fingertips, Mr. Grieves spoke up again, his words expanding in the office, swallowing up all the air. "I do hope you continue to . . . surprise me."

It was meant to seem lighthearted, casual, but I knew the truth behind Mr. Grieves's words. I could feel the carefully placed venom within them.

Mr. Grieves was going to be watching me, waiting for me to slip, waiting for me to let my guard down and give everything away.

I had to be careful. Almost everyone's eyes on Lethe belonged to Mr. Grieves.

Almost everyone couldn't be trusted.

CHAPTER FORTY-SIX

EVANORA

APRIL 16 - EVENING

THE BELLS WERE GONE.

I looked everywhere for them—between the rocks, swirling within the rock pools, nestled in the wads of seaweed dotting the beach. They were nowhere to be found. I was sure I had wedged them back between the rocks the last time I'd been at the beach. Had I not secured them enough? I glanced around, wondering if maybe Grayson had absentmindedly placed them somewhere after I had left. In the growing dusk, it was hard to tell. Everything was taking on a grayish hue.

I squelched my rising panic, my desperation to see the boy with burning blue eyes growing. I needed to see him, to feel the calluses of his hands, to hear the warmth in his voice as he promised me that things were okay, that my world wasn't crumbling around me. My heart—our connection—ached for it.

I looked up at the stone steps leaning against the cliffside. Should I cry out, call his name, scream? If he could hear the bells, surely he'd be able to hear my voice. But . . . so could others, probably. Bells were a lot more covert than a mermaid's wails for attention, after all. Biting my lip, I flicked my frantic gaze back to the base of the waterfall. When Grayson had first come up with the idea to use the bells, he had pulled an abandoned net from the rock pools. He had only taken a portion of the bells, then dropped the net back in. Perhaps there were more I could use.

I was just about to climb over the slimy boulders with their jagged teeth when the sound of footsteps met my ears. Immediately, my heart began to sing.

I wiggled onto the beach, stretching along the sand as much as my long body would allow, my tail flopping uselessly against the tired waves. As Grayson descended the last handful of stairs, I held out my hand to him, a relieved smile on my face.

"Thank the gods you are all right," I breathed. "I was so worried. The last time I saw you, I—"

Grayson didn't take my hand. He didn't even look at me. He sat down on a boulder bordering the sand and outcropping of wildflowers. Clasping his hands between his legs, the boy bent his head, letting out a long breath. "We had to bury Tommy today."

My heart heaved. "Tommy? Who is that?"

"A boy." Grayson's head rose, his eyes meeting mine. "A friend."

I didn't want to ask, but I knew I had to. "What happened to him?"

Grayson's gaze was careful, measured. "He died at the last challenge."

There was a tilting sensation in my stomach, like it was trying to leap up my esophagus. I placed a hand over my mouth, like that would stop its escape. "How awful."

The boy paused for a beat before nodding slowly. "You could say that."

There was a sharp pain in my shoulders, and I realized that, somewhere during the conversation, I had raised them nearly up to my ears. Forcing my muscles to relax, I glanced over to the rock pools. "I couldn't find the bells," I said quietly. "Did you move them?"

"They weren't sure if his death was from drowning, or from being crushed by the buoy that landed on top of him when it slipped out of a whirlpool," Grayson continued, either having not heard me, or just ignoring me outright. "We weren't allowed to see his body before it was buried. He was too damaged, hardly recognizable."

I swallowed hard. I didn't know how to navigate this. Grayson appeared to be grieving, but there was something else, a dark and burning anger brimming just underneath the surface. It would've been foolish to think that it wasn't targeted at me. I scooted forward, trying to erase the distance between us, which seemed cavernous and was growing by the second. If I could just get closer, if I could just *touch* him, I'd be able to break the ice that had formed around the boy, soften him up to me once more.

"Do you know what happened to the bells?"

Grayson looked at the rock pools with a frown. "I took them."

I stared at him, shock sending my fins bristling. "Took them? Why?"

Grayson sighed, shaking his head. "I don't think it's a good idea for us to see each other anymore."

Snap.

One of the threads tethering our hearts together ripped loose, sending our connection swaying on frayed ends. My hand fluttered to my chest, like I could reach inside and cinch the threads tight. Grayson winced, but that was the only sign that he had felt anything at all.

"Why?" I whispered, my voice tight. "Why would you say that?"

Grayson shrugged stiffly. "It's just too dangerous."

My fingers dug into my chest, scratching at the scales. "That never stopped us before."

Grayson's eyes found mine, and it was all hurricanes and hurling waves. "You were nearly spotted at the challenge. I was pulled into questioning because of it."

All the air left my lungs. I could feel my gills attempting to pull more in to replace what my body had lost. "What did you say?" I asked quietly.

Grayson looked at me for a long, agonizing moment before turning away. "I didn't say anything."

The relief I felt was short-lived. I pried my hand from my chest and reached out for the boy once more. "Then we should be fine. Please," I uttered soothingly, "come sit next to me."

Grayson turned to me sharply, his face contorted, lines running deep along his forehead. "Fine?" He forced out a cruel laugh, running a hand through his hair. "We aren't fine, Evanora! None of this is fine!"

I refused to drop my arm. I had to believe that if I continued to hold it out, Grayson would eventually take it. "Talk to me, Grayson," I urged, my fingers straining for a part of him. "Tell me what's wrong. Perhaps we can fix it together."

Grayson looked at my outstretched hand. "Fix it," he repeated. He mumbled the words, like he was processing them, testing how they tasted in his mouth. He stood, took a slow step over to me, and crouched so we were at eye level. I had wanted him closer, but this felt wrong. This didn't feel like he was wanting to try to fix *anything*. This felt like he was getting ready to attack. "Why were you at the challenge yesterday?"

I forced myself not to lean away, to retrieve some of the distance I had loathed only moments ago. "What?"

Grayson was an immovable force. He continued to penetrate me with his unblinking stare. "You want to help me? You can start by telling me why you were there."

Snap.

Making a helpless sound, I slowly lowered my hand. "I was worried about you," I stammered. "You know how you are with water. I didn't want anything bad to happen to you." I blinked slowly, trying to soften my features, though every part of me felt made of stone.

Quick as a lightning strike, the boy lashed out, grabbing my arm before it had a chance to fully drop. "Don't lie!" he bellowed. The outburst seemed to surprise him. He blinked, and when he spoke again, his voice was quieter. The urgency, however, remained. "You told me not to enter the water. You *knew* something was going to happen at the challenge, didn't you?"

Snap. Snap!

A whimper began to escape my mouth, and I bit down on the tail end of it. I tried to pull myself out of his grip, but it was too tight, too desperate. "Grayson, you're hurting me."

"You're hurting *me.*" Still, the boy let go of my arm, his fingers shaking as he withdrew them. "There was nothing normal about what happened in the water. The ocean . . . It's violent, it's unpredictable. But that?" He let out a long breath and shook his head. "There was nothing natural about those waves. Nothing."

The boy reached for me again, and like a fool, I willingly accepted his touch. It was gentler than before, deliciously tender. Our connection, threadbare and hanging by only a few strands, throbbed in my chest. Grayson rubbed his thumb against the back of my hand, watching as it glided along my scales. "You were there," he said quietly, finally bringing his eyes to meet mine. "You *helped* me. So tell me, *please*, did you have something to do with what happened in the water?"

I had no intention of telling him the truth.

Keep Grayson Shaw in the dark. Seduce him with broken words and empty promises. Manipulate him, lure him into a false comfort riddled with holes. Squeeze every detail about the Hunt that I could from him, until he was nothing more than a withered husk blowing in the ocean breeze. And, when it was time, release his barren soul into the night and not think twice about its departure.

That was the plan.

But then the connection binding our spirits together pulsed with the faintest glimmer of life, and my mouth was moving. "I told you to not go into the water. I told you to stay away!" I moaned, dipping my head until it landed against our clasped hands. "Why didn't you listen?"

There was silence. Too much of it. It was filling the entire beach, dulling the roar of the waterfall, muffling the lapping of waves. When I slowly picked up my head and looked at Grayson, I wished I hadn't.

Grayson Shaw looked crushed. Worse than crushed. Devastated. Shattered. Tears immediately pooled in his eyes, shifting the swirling blues to nearly black. He began to tremble, his hand going limp in mine. Letting out a wavering breath, Grayson pulled away. "No," he groaned, the first rush of tears dripping down his cheeks. "No, no, no."

I craned my neck, trying to find his eyes in the growing dark. "I need to look out for my pod, Grayson. Please understand that." I reached for him, but it was like touching a ghost. "I was just thinking about my family."

Grayson shook his head, my words falling on deaf ears. "The destroyed nets . . . That was you too, wasn't it?"

There was no point in lying. "My pod needed to find an upper hand in the Hunt. Surely you can see that," I pleaded. "Every year, more and more of us fall by your blood-hungry spears, your razor-sharp cunning. I truly think this would have been the year that finally ended us and our way of life. We needed to make a stand. And now we have." I gave his limp hand a squeeze. "You helped with that!"

"You *used* me!" Grayson wrenched his hand free. "All this time, you manipulated my emotions, toyed with my heart, said all the things you knew I wanted to hear." He glared at me, his eyes swimming with tears. "You . . . You *seduced* me, charmed me so that I'd share all my secrets, and like a fool, I fell for all of it. God." He rubbed his face harshly. "I'm such a fool."

I was losing him, and that hurt most of all. I shook my head vehemently. "You may be many things, Grayson Shaw, but a fool is not one of them."

Grayson looked away, his chin quivering. "I just wanted to believe that our connection was real, that this"—he gestured to the space between us—"was real."

"It *is* real," I urged. "It wasn't supposed to be like this, Grayson. You weren't supposed to find out—"

"What, that I was simply a pawn in your scheme?" Grayson cut in. He gave a sharp laugh, though his tears were like rivers on his face. "How can I trust anything you say now?"

Gods, I couldn't let it end like this. With a growl, I grabbed Grayson's hand and yanked him forward. I forced his fingers out of their clenched state and splayed them against my cheek.

"You can trust me," I whispered, turning my face into his feverish palm. "You *know* you can trust me." I offered a quiet, lilting laugh. "In truth, how I feel . . ." I opened my eyes and pinned Grayson with a desperate stare. "What we have is the realest thing I've ever felt."

Grayson began to shake. He was on the brink of realizing the truth coursing through my blood. I bit back my hope and pressed on. A final push—that was all that was needed. A final push, and the boy would be mine again. "No one has ever made me feel the way you do," I uttered into his skin. "When I'm with you, I'm not a healer, or a leader. I'm just . . ." I inhaled deeply, my burdens feeling the slightest bit lighter. "Evanora. Your Evanora."

There was nothing.

And then Grayson crumpled underneath the weight of my words, a hitching breath on his tongue. He sat there, his head bent low, his tears dripping onto my tail. I gave a lulling hum, stroking his back as he cried. I knew, at that moment, that I had him. We could move past this. We could mend the rift between us, pick up the loose threads and tie our connection back together. He was my Grayson, and I was his Evanora. Nothing else mattered.

But then the boy spoke. "Your words are honey, but all I hear is the humming of bees."

I faltered. "What?"

Grayson sat up, and though his stormy blue eyes were still shining with unshed tears, the resolve swimming deep within them was enough to cleave me in two. "You're nothing but a mermaid I found in a net."

My chest went tight. "Grayson," I gasped, "you don't mean that."

The boy nodded calmly. "I do." He stood, slipping out of my grasp in so many ways. He looked down at me, his wobbling lips shifting into a snarl. "I wish I had never saved you."

And just like that, the final thread snapped, and the connection between me and Grayson Shaw disintegrated.

I choked out a sob, reaching up for him. "Please," I moaned, "you don't mean it. Say that you don't mean it." I was blubbering, fumbling in my free fall. All my mouth could say were those four senseless words. All my mind could think was, *Don't leave me. Don't leave me!*

Grayson exhaled slowly, closed his eyes, and turned away.

"Grayson!" I wailed, tears smothering my vision. "Grayson, wait!"

The boy was already at the steps, and it was clear that he had no intention of stopping.

"Until next time," I cried out, my words collapsing in my throat. "Say *until next time*!"

But I knew he wouldn't. And I knew there wouldn't be.

I was moving before my brain could catch up, digging my hands into the wet sand, clawing up the beach, my tail battering against the receding waves as I fought to reach land. The ocean at my back, the unforgiving earth ahead, and Grayson walking up the stairs with my heart in his hands. A rock jabbed into my belly, but I kept going. The stairs seemed an eternity away, and Grayson had already climbed several with no sign of turning back. Another rock bit into my scales, tearing at my fins. I shook, but I couldn't tell if it was from exertion or the agony inside me.

"Grayson!" I called, desperate. "Grayson, stop! Please!"

I didn't know when it happened, but eventually, my frantic movements slowed to a crawl, then stopped entirely.

And I watched as Grayson Shaw walked out of my life without looking back.

E VERYTHING WAS FALLING APART.
Grayson wanted nothing to do with me. My pod's trust in me was failing. The plan was slowly slipping through my fingers, and I no longer had the strength to grab it. Even if I could, I hardly felt I had anyone's support to proceed with it.

I was on my own. And it was all my fault.

As I swam into the kingdom, I was met with the whispers of a melody. Quiet, warbling in the undercurrent, barely anything at all. Soft, but familiar. My fins flared automatically. Was it the Cursed Beings with their intoxicating lullaby? A siren practicing? Illeron playing a trick? Loosening my fins with a flick of my wrist, I pressed on.

The melody took me to the palace entrance, the dissonant notes bouncing off the sweeping steps and the thick stone arches leading to the throne room. I picked up my pace, my stomach in knots. As I drew closer, I was able to make out some of the words being sung.

"With cold dead hands they'll grab you. Your fears of death will come true. You can't scream, cry, or hide."

I'd heard that song before. It was a lullaby dedicated to the Barrens. The humans had come up with it as a way of scaring the children away from swimming at night, warning them of the ill fortune that awaited them if they did. My ammah sometimes sang it to me, usually when I was acting poorly and needed a reminder that the ocean didn't belong to us.

"They'll pull you down, until you drown, your corpse shall be their bride."

The voice was familiar. Old and soft, cracked along the edges. The haunting words hung in the empty spaces before the water whisked them away.

I approached the entrance, slinking up next to the lone guard standing watch. He was facing the throne room, his mouth in a grim line, his eyes narrowed and suspicious. His right hand was wrapped tightly against his spear, his left hanging at his side. His green tail flicked slowly against the stairs. The rest of him was a statue, stone still, unmoving.

"Matthias?" I whispered, unease tightening around me. "What are you doing? You're supposed to be watching over Jorah."

The guard nodded curtly, his dark eyes not leaving the throne room. "I am, Your Majesty," he said, gesturing to the center of the room.

I didn't want to look. Something in Matthias's voice set off a wave of alarms in my mind, screaming and wailing, fighting to be heard. Every single scale on my body was urging me to turn, flee down the steps, and never look back.

Still, I found myself shifting, inch by inch, the muscles in my neck bulging, tendons pulled taut as I slowly craned my head to look into the throne room.

There, in the center of the room, sat Jorah. His hunched back was to us, his spine jutting out like tiny mountains. His molting tail twisted unnaturally beneath him, and his head bobbed and jerked, as if he were sleeping.

But then he started to sing.

"They come out at night, they'll give you a fright, if you choose to swim in the dark."

His small voice echoed in the throne room, colliding with the walls, the pillars, causing the words to become distorted and fractured. I could hear the hollowness swelling inside Jorah, the impending insanity threatening to fill in the empty spaces until it swallowed him whole.

"He's been here for hours," Matthias explained, his eyes flicking to mine. "Just sitting there and singing to himself."

I bit my lip, trying to control the steadily rising dread. "Have you tried returning him to his room?"

The guard nodded, his armored shoulders slouching. "It is as though I'm not even there."

"So swim if you dare, but you better take care, for you shall become their mark." Jorah gave a small chirping laugh that sent my stomach flipping. "Oh, yes, swim, swim, swim!" he said in a high-pitched voice.

"I'll do it." Even as I said the words, I was turning away from the room, shutting out the image of a broken Jorah, sunken to the floor.

Matthias's face hardened. "Be careful." He handed me his spear.

I looked down at the weapon, trying not to laugh. "Gods, you sound like Illeron. What am I supposed to do with that?"

Matthias's cheeks reddened. "Protect yourself?"

I batted the spear away. "Poseidon drown me. Matthias, it's *Jorah*."

Matthias grunted as he lowered his spear. "That's not Jorah, Your Majesty," he said quietly, gesturing to my advisor huddled in the throne room. "I don't think that mermaid's been Jorah for a long time now."

Holding my breath, I swept to the side of the room. I wanted to give Jorah a wide berth so my sudden appearance wouldn't startle him. Because deep down, part of me knew that Matthias was right. That wasn't Jorah, not completely. Whatever was left of him was fragile, volatile, and unpredictable. One wrong move and the pieces of him would scatter.

Jorah's head was jutting forward, like he was inspecting something. He giggled again, his pincerlike fingers dipping into his lap. "*With cold dead hands . . . they'll* grab *you!*" His shoulders began to shake as laughter bubbled from his lips. "Dead and cold! Cold and dead!"

I wanted to get his attention, to make him stop singing, to have him look at me and *see* me. I opened my mouth to call out to him, then quickly slammed it shut, everything within me turning to ice as I drifted in front of him.

Jorah slowly withdrew his hand. He was clasping something between his fingers. It was long and slimy, blood mingling with the weblike scales.

His forearm fin. He had torn it right off.

Eyeing it with a grin, he flicked his hand, sending the fin sailing into the water. He got to work on his other arm, his long, crooked nails plucking at the bleeding sores, the blisters, sinking into his flesh like it was nothing but algae. Blood bloomed in the water, thick and black.

Black like the Barrens.

CHAPTER FORTY-SEVEN

GRAYSON

APRIL 17 – MORNING

I CLOSED THE WINDOW. IT SEEMED LIKE SUCH A FEAT, SUCH A morbidly symbolic gesture, yet it only took a handful of seconds to click the latch into place, blocking out the sounds of the outside world.

I could hear bells. I didn't know where Evanora had found them, but she'd been ringing them frantically for the past thirty minutes. With the window closed, I couldn't tell if I could still hear them or simply the memory of them, destined to forever haunt my mind with their music. They tangled with the only words my subconscious seemed capable of forming that morning:

She used you. She lied to you. She never cared for you.

On and on it went. The bells, the words, the ache in my chest.

With a growl, I walked out of my room and shut the door.

"Whoa there," Pa said as I strode through the kitchen, aiming for the front door. "Where are you going in such a hurry?"

I stopped, my hand hovering over the doorknob. I wanted to leave the house, leave Tully, get as far away from those bells as possible. "Trying to keep tabs on me?" I asked lightheartedly, forcing myself to turn away from my chance at freedom.

Pa was sitting in the kitchen, leaning back in one of the rickety chairs, his feet propped up on the table. He was holding a knife in one hand, a block of wood in the other, and it looked like he was whittling, or at least trying to. I couldn't make out what the wood was supposed to be—a dog, maybe, or a hunched-over man?

"Just trying to make sure you don't skip out on another training day." He flipped the wood around and began to work the other side. "We're already behind schedule because of yesterday."

"We were at a funeral."

Pa eyed me for a long, heavy moment before returning his attention to the block of wood. "No matter. We can practice this morning."

The wood shavings began to pile up. The clock ticked in the corner of the room. The wood fire crackled and spat. This was the part where I was supposed to nod, pick up the wooden sword stacked next to the front door, and offer Pa some banal comment about how I'd finally beat him in combat.

It was a test, and I was about to fail miserably.

"Actually, Pa . . ." I sighed, reaching past the wooden sword for the doorknob. "I really just need to get some fresh air first. Go for a walk. Clear my head." *Get those damn bells away from that damn mermaid.*

My pa remained silent, his knife carving thick chunks out of the wood.

"We can practice later," I added, a weak peace offering. "I just don't think I can focus until—"

"I don't think you've been able to focus on *anything* for a while, son." Pa set down the wood but held on to the knife. He twisted the blade between his fingers, his hard gaze flicking to me. "I'm not sure what's been going on in that head of yours, but it has you all sorts of scattered."

I could feel my cheeks beginning to burn with the telltale signs of guilt. I fought against the urge to cover them with my hands. "I don't understand."

Pa continued to spin the blade. "Well, you clearly didn't practice swimming, and now it sounds like you are trying to skip out of combat. Honestly, Grayson, it's almost like you want to fail."

I could have laughed. The heat in my face sank deeper, and I clenched my jaw. Whatever guilt I'd felt quickly shifted to anger. "Fail? This entire Hunting Season is a failure! I'm the only one who sees that!"

Pa's hands stilled. "What are you getting at?"

"Where do I even start?" I scoffed, running a hand through my hair. "People are going missing. The nets were destroyed not even twenty-four hours after we created them. The last challenge became so dangerous that someone died." I thrust my hands into my pockets. "And we are all expected to continue as though nothing is wrong? Everything is wrong!"

Pa shook his head. "The Hunt comes with its risks and dangers. Everyone knows that."

"I'm not talking about the occupational hazards of being a hunter, Pa. I'm talking about human lives." I let out a heavy breath, my rigid shoulders slumping. "We've lost sight of why we are doing any of this."

Pa slammed the tip of the knife into the kitchen table. The blade sank deep into the wood with a loud *thunk*. He stood, sending the chair skittering back. Pa was all heavy breaths and bared teeth when he stormed up to me. "Lost sight?" he growled, tendrils of hair slipping onto his forehead. "Lost *sight*?"

I took an involuntary step back, the doorknob digging into my spine. The wooden swords clattered to the floor, but the sound was muffled by my raging heartbeat and Pa's shouting.

"How on God's good earth can you even say that?" he bellowed, looming over me, daring me to find more distance to put between us. "Or have you forgotten about your brother, Warrick—dead because of mermaids?" Pa punched his fist against the door, sending the frame rattling. "Lost sight of why we are doing this?" He spat at my feet, then finally, blessedly, leaned away. "We are doing this for *him*."

Pa wasn't out of ammo, but I didn't let him reload.

"Did you even know your own son?" I snapped. "Warrick would've hated all of this. He wasn't the martyred hero you've made him out to be." I inhaled, taking in the shocked look on Pa's face, before pressing on. "Warrick was kind, gentle, and charming. He loved laughing, and getting his hands dirty with work. He hated sitting still for too long. He stole raw pastry dough and berries when Ma wasn't looking, and blamed it on me when she was." I met Pa's eyes, furious. "Warrick was also a liar. He hated the Hunt. He hated you for making him prepare for it."

Pa was shaking his head, fumbling with his ammunition. "No. No," he stammered, stepping away. "Stop talking nonsense. Stop it!"

I took a strong step forward. "Warrick dreaded turning eighteen. He wanted to run away, escape the island, pretend that he didn't come from a place soaked in bloodshed." I cocked my head to the side and raised an eyebrow. "Want to know why he never left?"

Pa's head couldn't seem to stop its hurried back-and-forth motion. "Because he *died*!"

"No!" I shouted, a hysterical laughter bubbling up my throat. "Because he fell in love! With a mermaid!"

It happened fast. If it weren't happening to me, I probably would have missed it.

Pa's fist shot out, landing hard against my cheek. I yelped, tumbling against the door. My head whipped back, the world growing black as it hit the wood. When color returned, it exploded in reds, oranges, yellows. Blinding flashes of pain surged down my neck, shoulders, and back. My skin tingled with it, hundreds of tiny daggers stabbing at my nerves.

Pa stood over me, his face dark, eyes full of rage, panting. Slowly, I brought my hand up to my cheek, and his rage seemed to clear, the storm in his eyes fading.

"Listen," he muttered, grabbing a cloth from the sink and running cold water over it. "I didn't mean for that to happen." He handed it to me, not meeting my gaze. "But I won't have you spouting lies about your brother under my roof."

Numbly, I pressed the cool cloth against my face. It quickly ate up the warmth, rivulets of water dribbling down my neck, soaking into the collar of my shirt.

"I'm not lying," I said quietly. "You know I'm not good at it."

Pa rubbed his hand, puffy and chipped at the knuckles. "I refuse to believe that Warrick would commit such a heinous act willingly. He must have been bewitched."

I started to bite my lip, then immediately stopped when a sliver of pain sliced through my face. "I saw it."

Pa went still. "When?"

I fidgeted, unable to meet his stare. "The night he died." Out of the corner of my eye, I could see Pa shift with a groan. "It wasn't a mermaid that killed him, Pa. It was something else. Something dangerous."

"For Pete's sake." Pa rolled his eyes. "Grayson, you were just a boy, and it was nighttime. You don't know what you saw."

I lowered the cloth. "I saw Warrick's boat split right down the center. I saw him slip beneath the ocean with a single tug. His mermaid was long gone before any of that happened. How do you explain that?"

"It—" Pa loosed a breath, slapping his hands at his sides. "I don't know, Grayson. It was an entire pod of mermaids, maybe."

I shook my head, my resolve growing. "No. Whatever was coming for Warrick had scared her. That's why she left." I peered up at my pa, narrowing my eyes. "So, *how* do you explain that? It wasn't a mermaid. It wasn't a pod. It was *something else.*"

Pa was shutting down. He had been since the second his fist met my face. He held up a hand, and I hated myself for flinching the way I did.

"Enough," he huffed. "I'm not talking about this anymore."

I pressed my lips into a tight line. We stared at each other, breathing hard, refusing to back down. I was shaking from pent-up nerves, hateful words ricocheting through my mind but never landing on my tongue.

"Fine," I bit out, lifting my chin. "Then I'll find someone who will."

Pa scoffed. "Don't be daft. We need to practice." He gestured to the scattered swords. "Pick your weapon and meet me outside."

He was already moving on, pretending the fight had never happened, that the swelling of my cheek was from something else entirely. I stared down at the wooden swords, the puddle of water next to them. Face burning with a mixture of tight pain and loose rage, I stepped over them, opened the door, and walked out.

Pa didn't even try to stop me.

MA WAS IN HER ROOM.
The weather had turned on my walk to Rose Hill. The wind, playful at first, had whipped into something fierce, tearing at my coat and hair. Clouds had rolled in, swollen and dark, snuffing out the sun. By the time I reached the facility, rain was falling. By the time I reached Ma's room, thunder rattled the walls.

She sat by the window, her dull blue eyes tracking raindrops racing down the glass.

I was given no warning of her mood. I didn't know whether I'd find a ticking time bomb, a ghost, or a delusional dreamer. On any other day, that would've made me hesitate. Not today.

Today, I walked in, shut the door behind me, and approached her with a steadiness that didn't feel like my own. Ever since Pa struck me, I'd felt hollow. I had told him the truth, and he'd spat it back in my face. My pa, like the rest of Lethe, was too scared to face reality. They all buried their heads in the sand, surfacing only when it fit their warped narrative. The missing people. The Barrens. The Hunt. I was done going along with it.

I needed answers.

Lightning lit the room in a furious flash. Thunder followed, booming off the cliffs. Ma's pupils dilated slightly, the only sign she'd noticed. She didn't flinch or smile or gasp like she once would have. My throat tightened as I neared her chair, tears threatening.

A lifetime ago, Ma had loved thunderstorms. As a family, we'd huddle on my parents' bed, tucked under quilts, counting seconds between lightning and thunder. We'd spin tales of gods bowling or giants warring on Lethe's peaks—anything to distract me from the chaos outside. I hated the storms back then, but Ma always held me close, humming softly until I stopped shaking.

Warrick had teased me, but Ma never did. Even when I learned to appreciate the storms, I never told her. I liked the world we'd built in that blanket fort.

I stopped beside her chair. She didn't acknowledge me; her eyes remained glued to the rain streaking down the glass. Slowly, I placed my hand on the armrest.

"Ma," I said, my voice tight.

Ma finally blinked. She slowly licked her chapped lips, her tongue dry and cracked. "Grayson," she croaked, still not looking at me.

My heart fluttered at the sound of my name on her lips. I wanted her to look at me, to see me. Not with burning hatred. Not as Warrick. As me, Grayson, the son she had, on one dark night, tried to kill.

Swallowing, I lowered myself to the floor, hanging on to the armrest like it was my anchor. "What's out there, in the Barrens?"

Ma made a low wheezing noise, and it took me a second to realize it was a laugh. "Didn't you pay attention in school?" she whispered, her hands twitching in her lap. "There is nothing out there."

I shook my head, keeping my eyes trained on her. "I don't believe that."

The tendons in Ma's neck went taut. "And why not?"

I took a breath, my heart spiking its rhythm to a bird's wingbeat, taking flight, soaring out of my chest. "Because when you dragged me into the ocean that night, it wasn't a mermaid's attention you were trying to get, was it? You were wanting someone . . . *something* else."

Ma made that wheezing laugh again. Slowly, she raised her hand and rested it over mine. Her fingernails dug into my wrist, tripping over the scarred ridges.

And the memories came rushing back to me, quick and vicious as a flash flood.

The memory of Ma standing over me, of the knife dragging over my wrists, of my hot blood splashing into the icy ocean.

Of her submerging me, forcing my body down, down, down into the water's open mouth. And no matter how hard I fought, no matter how loudly I cried out, she didn't let me up for a gasp of precious air.

I closed my eyes, a groan on my lips, and the memories slipped away like smoke. "Why did you do it?" I asked quietly, slowly cracking my eyes open to look at her again. "Why did you try to kill me?"

My ma turned. Her neck creaked with the effort of it. Then came her eyes, dripping downward, the whites of them bloodshot, the pupils nearly pinpoints. She cracked a sluggish smile, tipping her head to the side. "Warrick was always my favorite."

The words stung, tearing through the crumbled ruins of my guard and slamming into my chest. "I know."

Ma glanced down at my wrists, her thumb rubbing against the scars tenderly. "You needed to die. It was the only way I could get Warrick back. That was what I had found out. That was what they had promised me."

I fought not to wrench my hand away from her clammy touch. "Who?"

Ma didn't hear me. Lightning burst beyond the window, and thunder clapped. Her face grew dark, and her grip tightened. "It almost worked. I had done everything right. I could hear them coming."

My stomach curdled. "*Hear* them? Wait—" I sucked in a breath, scooting closer to the chair. "What did they say?"

The one who was promised.

Here.

Ma shook her head, her greasy hair toppling into her face. "They were nearly upon you." She let out a growl, her mouth curling into a thin-lipped snarl. "But then *she* appeared," she hissed. "With her snow-white hair and her amethyst eyes, she came and ruined *everything.*"

"Ma, wait. Slow down—"

Ma's eyes landed on her fingers wrapped around my wrist, and she gasped, pulling herself away from me. The movement, shocking in its suddenness, nearly had me crashing onto the floor. She blinked, breathing heavily. "It should have been you," she whispered, her sunken-in eyes flitting to mine. "It should have been you."

She was withdrawing, retreating deep into herself once more. I couldn't let that happen—not when I was so close to getting the answers I had been seeking for so long. Even if it sliced me in two, I didn't care.

I had to know. "Ma, please," I begged, reaching for her. "Just slow down. Start from the beginning."

Ma was back to looking out the window, her eyes tracing the raindrop paths, her lips moving around the words, "It should have been you," over and over again. There was no getting through to her, no getting her back.

When I left, the rain instantly soaked through my clothes, a deep chill curling around my bones. My heart ached, and my scars burned, and for the first time in my life, I wished that Ma had thought to put the knife to my throat instead of my wrists.

Surely death was far less painful than what I was experiencing now.

CHAPTER FORTY-EIGHT

EVANORA

APRIL 17 – MORNING

GRAYSON DIDN'T COME. NO MATTER HOW HARD I RANG the strand of bells I'd taken from the old net in the rock pool, there was no sign of him. No hurried footsteps, no crooked grin, no bouncing curls flopping over those ocean eyes. I cursed myself for taking those moments for granted, for not committing every detail to memory. I feared I'd never see those perfect pieces of Grayson Shaw again.

It was almost too much to bear. My heart sank into my stomach as tears clung stubbornly to my lashes. Turning away from the island, I slowly made my way back home.

Illeron's voice was in my mind the second I slipped through the kingdom's borders. *"Look, this isn't funny anymore. Are you giving me the silent treatment?"* It went quiet for a beat. *"At the very least, let me know that you're still alive."*

I stuttered to a stop. Silent treatment? Alive? How long had he been trying to reach out to me? *"Illeron?"* I probed tentatively.

I could feel the warrior's relief swarm my mind. *"Thank the gods! Where have you been?"*

I bit my lip, stifling the guilt circulating through my system. If I said anything now, he'd sense everything I was feeling. *"I thought you were giving me the silent treatment."*

"If you were within reach, you would have known I've been trying to contact you all morning. I'd hardly call that silent."

Blowfish. I spewed out a handful of bubbles.

There was a sigh. *"Just . . . come to the weaponry. Please."*

That was the last thing I wanted to do. I wanted to go to the garden, lose myself in prayer, or maybe swim the kingdom's border and check on the lanterns. Above all, I wanted to be alone, to mourn my failings, to reassemble the broken pieces of the plan and see where the fractures started. I wasn't in any shape to be around anyone.

Illeron was pacing when I arrived. His arms were clasped tightly behind his back, his tail flicking back and forth in a frenzy. I had barely swooped through the entranceway when he rushed forth, grabbing my arms. I gave a startled yelp. Illeron had sounded mildly annoyed in my mind, but he'd been composed. *This* Illeron was nearly undone. He bared his teeth at me, his eyes wild. "Where have you *been*?" he demanded. He was shaking so hard that his long hair was splayed out in the ocean's fingers, framing his face like a silver halo. "Do you know how worried I was?"

I pinched my lips together, aware of the emotion precariously held at bay in my throat, starved for attention. "I'm really not in the mood for dramatics right now, Illeron."

The warrior shook his head viciously. "No. This is not the time for joking."

I attempted to growl, but all that came out was a whimper. "Please, Illeron." The tears came back. I blinked them away, but I could feel the emotion lodged in my throat inching higher. My bottom lip began to wobble.

Illeron *actually* looked at me then. His grip loosened. "What's wrong?" he asked, his anger quickly morphing into concern.

And then I crumpled.

A sob ripped from my throat, and then another, and another. "It's over!" I managed between jagged breaths with sharp edges. "Everything is ruined!"

Illeron folded me into his arms. I hadn't realized how desperate I was for contact until I felt his strong chest pressed against my cheek, his fingers running gently through my hair. "Shh," he breathed, his words vibrating against the tip of my head. "Shh."

I cried. Cried for my pod, for my parents, for Jorah. I cried for the plan, ruined beyond repair.

But mostly, I cried for Grayson. How I had broken him, destroyed the magic between us, forced our delicate connection to completely unravel. If I was hurting this much, I couldn't imagine what he was going through.

Years' worth of pent-up emotion poured out of me, and Illeron was gracious enough to let it collect all over him. He said nothing save for the soft shushing sounds as I slowly exhausted myself. Eventually, the wailing turned into stifled gasps, then sniffling hiccups, then long, quiet breaths. But even after the tears, the warrior still embraced me, holding me protectively against his chest. I was acutely aware of the strength in his arms, the way his hands cradled me like I was something that could break. Maybe I was a little broken, but still, I couldn't help but think back to Grayson and how he'd held me.

Like I was a treasure, a miracle.

I tried to pull away, but Illeron's grip only tightened.

I placed my hands against his rigid chest. "I'm fine now, Illeron. Thank you."

The warrior surrendered his hold, but only enough so that he could look down at me. He stroked my face, his thumb sidling over my cheek, down my jaw. When it brushed against my lower lip, Illeron sucked in a short breath. "You're so beautiful."

Despite the sudden roiling in my stomach, I couldn't help but laugh. "Even now?" I was certain I looked a mess: all bloodshot eyes, red nose, and mottled skin.

Illeron cocked his head to the side, leaning in the slightest bit closer. "Especially now."

I turned my head to the side. "Why did you want to see me?"

The warrior pulled away slowly. His mouth opened slightly, but all that came out was an incredulous chuckle. He swam away from me, running his hands through his hair. When he turned to face me again, he was back to snarling. "I don't understand you. You come to me for comfort, but only when it suits you."

I lifted my hands helplessly before clasping them in front of me. "You asked *me* to come here, Illeron, not the other way around."

"Yes." Illeron nodded stiffly. "Because a lot has happened in the past couple days. You've been distant lately, choosing to spend more time with that *boy* than with your own blood. Forgive me for being concerned."

My lips formed a thin line. "Well," I said, my voice strained, "you won't need to worry about that anymore."

Illeron narrowed his eyes. "Why?"

"Because he is refusing to see me." I sighed, taking a lock of my hair and roughly combing my fingers through it. If I didn't focus on something, didn't put my hands to work, I was going to start crying again.

The warrior tensed. He closed his eyes, letting out a long breath. "Is that . . . why you are so upset?"

He asked the question in an eerily quiet tone that instantly had my fins rigid. "Seriously, Illeron? *That* is what you are choosing to focus on?"

A muscle in Illeron's neck twitched, and when he opened his eyes, all I could see was a crimson tide of rage. "Evanora, you knew that the boy would eventually expire in his usefulness. You knew that he would eventually have to be eliminated. So, either you are upset because he cut ties before you could and you are worried that he is now a threat, or because you let your feelings get in the way and therefore are suffering the consequences."

The hiss came out before I could stop it. My magic hummed just below the surface, begging to be released in a crackle of light. "Grayson would never—"

"Do you truly know that, Your Majesty?" Illeron bit out, cutting me off. "Do you, deep within your scales, down to your bone marrow, believe that he wouldn't just turn around and tell all of Lethe that we were the ones behind the tragedy at the swimming challenge? The reason behind the destroyed nets?" He peered at me, his gaze cruel. "How well do you really know him?"

I raised a single eyebrow, a cool wrath fluttering down my fins. "A lot more than you know me."

We hovered in silence, our breaths the only thing taking up space. Illeron looked like I had slapped him in the face. His eyes carried an ocean of pain within them as he slowly looked away.

I immediately wanted to apologize, to rush forward and take it back. I swallowed, forcing my resolve to harden. "You're jealous. That is why you insist on insulting me, my integrity, and my decisions."

Illeron ran a hand through his hair. "Of course I'm jealous," he muttered. His eyes still wouldn't meet mine. "Every day you've been abandoning me—" He cleared his throat; I could practically hear his mind scrambling to redirect his sentence. "The *pod*, only returning when you absolutely must."

"I'm leaving *for* the pod!"

"Do you know how your subjects are faring, Evanora?" Illeron scoffed, rolling his eyes. "Did you know that Jorah is hardly functioning anymore? That his eyesight is officially gone and the Dark Madness is likely just around the corner?" He leaned in close enough for me to see his sharp teeth. "Did you know that a flare-up of fin rot and bloat has affected many of the merlings?"

I faltered, scooting back. "The merlings? Why didn't anyone tell me?"

The warrior grinned, but there was no warmth to be found. "That's my point, Evanora; you are *never here*."

I fumbled for a response, but none came to my defense. "Well," I said haughtily, "not that you care, but I *did* know about Jorah." I crossed my arms against my chest. "I caught him pulling off his own fins. He's all right for now. He actually let me heal him for once. But that might've been due to the confusion. And lack of eyesight."

Illeron shook his head roughly. "We are running out of time. We need a new plan."

"Illeron—"

"The pod will *revolt* if anything happens to Jorah." Illeron looked out the window. "He is beyond saving at this point, but we can't let his end occur without having another plan to rally the pod with."

My chest felt too tight, and I could feel my Gift pushing against my skin, yearning to burst through it. I fought to catch my breath. "No," I said, darting for the door, "I refuse to accept it. I can still fix this."

Illeron shot in front of me, halting my movements. "How?"

I bit my lip. The ache in my chest was growing steadily larger. "I don't know. I'll try to see Grayson again. Our old plan can still work as long as our relationship with the boy remains strong."

The warrior tried to mask his disappointment, but he was too slow. "When will you realize," he said through clenched teeth, "that Grayson Shaw isn't the answer?"

My mind exploded with the voices of my ancestors, filling up all the spaces until the rest of my frantic thoughts settled into white noise.

He is the key.

The power of three.

I placed a hand over my heart, barren without our connection stirring within it. But I could still feel the threads dangling haphazardly, desperately wanting to be retethered. "I know it doesn't make sense to you, but he still has a part to play. I can feel it."

Illeron's face hardened, and he loosed a breathy chuckle as he shook his head. "Nothing good has come from you going to the island."

I wanted to shake my head and argue this blatant untruth, but the warrior pushed on.

"I'm tired of seeing you come home in tears. I'm tired of being the one having to pick up the pieces of your broken heart." His shoulders sagged, and he dropped his head, sending his fine silver-white hair into his eyes. "I've been patient. I've let you cry on my shoulder. I've comforted you. But no more." With a sigh, Illeron shifted out of the doorway. "I don't know what sort of hold this boy has on you, but if you insist on returning to him like a domesticated pet, then I won't stop you."

I waited for the anger, for the bloodred fury to soak into my scales and set my razor fins firm. But all I felt was guilt-laden sadness. "Thank you," was all I could think of saying.

Illeron shook his head. "Don't thank me." He turned his back to me, inspecting the weapons stacked on the shelves. "I'm done."

I blinked at the warrior. I didn't want to ask, but knew I had to. "Done with what?"

The warrior picked up a spear, touching his fingers against the pointed end. "Pursuing the tide." He put down the weapon and picked up another. "The water yearns for the sand, but in the end, it will always return to the ocean, where it knows, deep down, that *that* is where it truly belongs."

CHAPTER FORTY-NINE

GRAYSON

APRIL 17 - EVENING

I WASN'T SURE WHAT CAME FIRST—THE NIGHT, OR THE REALIZATION that I was drunk.

I had found an abandoned bottle of alcohol on my trek home. I didn't think twice about taking it. I needed something—anything—to numb myself. Evanora's betrayal, the voices from the Barrens, Ma trying to sacrifice me to bring Warrick back—it was too much. My head was already swimming, but the liquor softened the edges, turning thoughts into fragments I couldn't hold on to. Betrayal. Voices. Sacrifice. White hair. Amethyst eyes.

The liquor burned going down, stinging my throat and making my eyes water. Despite the warmth pooling in my stomach, I was shivering, cold and stiff from the storm. My soaked clothes clung to me, and my boots squished with every step. I knew I'd catch a nasty flu if I didn't get home soon, but I kept walking.

When I tripped, I cursed the ground. When I swayed, I cursed the wind. By the time I reached the Tully docks, the world felt surreal. Night transformed the place. The piers looked like tightropes, Mr. Brightly's office loomed like a witch's hut, and mist danced over the water. Ships rocked lazily, their bells clinking with each swell. Flickering lanterns created ghostly shadows on the road. For a moment, I felt like the only person awake—or alive—on all of Lethe. The quiet was absolute.

Save for the whispering.

I wandered to the end of a dock, leaving wet footprints behind me. I took a swig from the bottle, the movement sending me off-balance. My feet tangled, and I grabbed a support beam to steady myself. The bottle wasn't so lucky, slipping from my fingers and splashing into the water.

"Well, shit," I muttered, leaning against the beam.

The bright green bottle floated for a moment before sinking, water filling it inch by inch. I had the absurd thought that it might be a peace offering to whatever was whispering at me—maybe it liked alcohol or glass. The idea made me laugh.

White hair. Amethyst eyes.

I stopped laughing.

I pushed myself upright, swaying lightly on my feet. Those were the descriptions my ma had given for who—or what—had foiled her plans of killing me. I had seen my fair share of mermaids before. They were usually all dead, and while they were drenched in a vast array of colors, I had never seen one possess white hair and purple eyes.

Until I met Evanora.

My heartbeat pounded painfully, filling the empty space she'd left. I sifted through my hazy thoughts, trying to make sense of it. Could there be another mermaid who looked like her? Or had Evanora been the one to stop Ma's madness? It seemed unlikely, but mermaids lived ridiculously long lives. She had never told me her age; it was entirely possible she was old enough to have saved me as a child.

The thought made me queasy—but only for a second. Then I was laughing again, my stomach cramping, tears streaming down my face. "Oh, God!" I wheezed between hysterical gasps. "I like older girls! Lock up your grandmas and mothers, folks!"

"What's so funny?"

The voice came out of nowhere. I spun around to see Jasper shuffling toward me from the dock's entrance.

I wiped my eyes, looking back at the water. "Oh, you know, just questioning my life choices and whatnot."

Jasper had his hands tucked into his jacket. His mouth was puckered, his eyebrows raised high into his frizzy hairline. It looked like he was attempting an air of nonchalance. He was failing miserably. "And you're laughing because you realized that your life is one big joke?"

I snorted. "I never took you for a buzzkill."

Jasper came to a stop beside me. "Yeah, well, I never took you for a runaway. So I guess we're both full of surprises."

I turned back to him, my eyes wide. "Who told you that nonsense?"

Jasper kicked at a pebble, watching as it skittered over the dock's edge. "Your pa came by our house. Said he'd been looking for you for hours." He winced. "He said that you'd gotten into a fight and you weren't in any shape to be alone."

My mood shifted sourly. I was acutely aware of the burning in my cheek. "I can take care of myself," I mumbled.

Jasper eyed me apprehensively before scoffing. "Yes. I can see that. Wait." He stepped forward, sniffing loudly near my face. "Are you *drunk*?"

"No." I burped, and Jasper groaned, waving a hand in front of his face as he leaned away. "A little."

"Jeez, Grays. Did you drink the entire distillery?"

"Nope." I grinned, then promptly wiped at the drool that began to spill over my bottom lip. "Just an open bottle I found on my way back from Maude." I pointed uselessly at the water below. "It's down there now."

Jasper looked horrified. "That's really gross."

"It tasted really gross too. There was still some in the bottle when it fell. Can fish get drunk?" I gasped, raising a hand to my mouth. "Did I just murder a bunch of fish?"

Jasper rolled his eyes, sighing heavily. "All right," he grunted, stepping forward. "It's time to get you home."

He took my arm, but I slithered out of his hold. "I don't need a babysitter. I know where home is."

Another sigh. Jasper pinched the bridge of his nose. "You're certainly acting like a child right now."

He reached for me again, but I jumped out of the way with a laugh. "Takes one to know one."

Jasper lifted his arms helplessly. "I wish I could say that you are acting this way because you're wasted, but no." He shook his head. "You've been acting really weird for a while now. What is going on with you?"

I cringed away, pulling my shoulders up to my ears. "It's nothing."

Jasper hurried in front of me. "It's not nothing! You can tell me!" He planted his hands on my shoulders, and I was far too tired to fight him off. "You can tell me anything."

For a second, I thought about it. Just unleashing the confines of my mind onto Jasper, telling him about Evanora, about what she had done to the first two challenges, about how she had completely pulverized my heart. And while I was at it, I could tell him about Ma and how she'd tried to kill me in hopes of getting Warrick back. I wasn't sure how he was going to take the sudden influx of information, but whatever his reaction was, I was willing to bet it'd be better than Pa's. It was awfully tempting; I was certain I'd feel better getting it all off my chest.

But before I could get a single word out, I heard it again. The whispers.

The one.

The one who was promised.

I turned my head to the side, watching the water suspiciously. "Did you hear that?"

Jasper's frown deepened. "Yeah, it's called *the waves*."

"No." I shook myself out of Jasper's grip. "The voices."

Jasper folded his arms together. "I'm pretty sure it's just us out here, Grayson."

Here. Here. Here.

I gestured wildly to the water. "There it is again!"

"Okay," Jasper said, resigned. "You are drunk, and my leg hurts, and I'm sure Mr. Shaw is tearing Tully down searching for you. Let's get you home."

I looked at Jasper, uncertainty filling my bloodstream. "You really can't hear that?"

The one. The Promised One!

I pointed again. "There! Right there!"

Jasper stretched for my arm. "Grayson, *please*."

I swatted him away, transfixed by the waves and mist. "No," I growled, stomping toward the edge of the dock. "I'm getting to the bottom of this. Right now."

Jasper let out a choked laugh, hurrying to catch up to me. "What are you going to do? Go for a midnight swim?"

I shucked off my jacket and rolled up my sleeves. My fear was silent; I was sure I had the alcohol to thank for that. "If that'll get me answers."

Jasper gawked. "Wait, you're serious?"

I crouched, lost my balance, collected it, and began untying my boots.

Jasper stared down at me. "You're serious."

The one who was promised . . .

I stood, sucked in a breath—

HERE!

—and jumped off the dock.

"Grayson!" Jasper cried out as the water swarmed me.

The water hit my body like a sack of bricks. The air immediately wanted to squeeze out of my lungs, but I pinched my lips together, holding it hostage. And the *cold*. Seeping into my pores, sinking its teeth into my bones. I was definitely destined for a flu now.

I looked up at the surface. I could see Jasper's faint outline. It looked like he was on his knees, one hand outstretched, straining for the water. He was yelling, but I couldn't make out the words. And then he was gone, rushing down the dock, yelling more things I couldn't quite make out.

I was quick to sink.

My world went black.

For a second, it was painfully silent. There was nothing but the muffled rush of waves and the blood pumping in my ears. I wanted to hear the voices again. I needed to. If I heard them, that meant they were real, that I wasn't crazy.

The current fought to turn me around, to push me back to the surface. I struggled against it, willing my body to go deeper into the bleak nothingness.

It paid off.

The one who was promised. Here.

They were closer. Much, much closer.

I looked around wildly, but all I could see was darkness.

Here. Here. Here.

They were getting louder, a chorus of voices stacked on top of one another, calling out to me in different pitches and volumes.

I shifted clumsily, ignoring the burning in my chest, the ache in my head. I just needed to *see* them, then I would resurface.

Here!

Out of the corner of my eye, I saw movement.

It was like smoke, blooming and dissipating in the water, faster than I could track. There one instant, gone the next. I tried to follow it, but everything was so damned dark.

Then I figured it out.

The ocean wasn't black—the *thing* dwelling within it was.

And it was huge.

Dread pooled inside me, freezing my limbs into stillness.

It took up my entire vision. Everywhere I looked, the bitter blackness was there, shadows swirling and writhing. The very presence of it was impossible. There were no eyes, no mouths full of hungry teeth, no legs or flippers or fins keeping it in place.

Impossible. Yet there it was.

The movement I had caught wasn't the dark beast swimming—it was it *reaching*. With long, spindly arms and hands the size of dinner plates, dozens of fingers with claws like knives, they would thrust upward from the shadows, aching to get me. And then they would dart back into the folds of blackness, only for several more to spike up again. Over and over, relentlessly, recklessly, *impossibly*.

They had begun wailing, their cries pouring from the black void, spilling into the ocean.

I was frozen.

They reached for me, their twisted dead fingers spread apart, eager to touch me.

No.

To grab me.

To *kill* me.

My fear returned in full force.

The darkness didn't move. It simply rested on the ocean floor, a throbbing mass of tangled arms and screaming voices. I was stuck in their vortex, like their sheer desire for me was enough to hold me in place. One kick forward only sent me farther back. The surface pulled out of reach at a devastatingly slow pace, almost as if to taunt me. I gritted my teeth, making my body thrash and wiggle as hard as it could.

I kept sinking.

There was a different sound, louder than the keening, and much more violent.

It was laughter. They were *laughing* at me.

I'm going to die, I thought, forcing my legs to pump faster. *I'm going to die!*

When I saw the light, I thought I *had* died.

My eyes burned with the forcefulness of it, the unnaturalness of it. What had once been pitch-black was suddenly drenched in blinding light. I shielded my eyes briefly, flinching. It was another one of their tricks, to startle me into a disoriented state. It had to be.

I waited for the many hands to grab me, for their jagged claws to sink into my flesh. They were going to rip me apart, piece by piece, until there was nothing left of me. And they were going to scream and laugh while doing it.

When I lowered my arm, there was Evanora. And she was the most beautiful creature I'd ever seen.

She swam up to me, bathed in starlight, her entire body glowing like a thousand diamonds caught in the sun. Her teeth were bared, a growl on her

tongue as she wrapped an arm around me, her glittering tail kicking ferociously to hold me in place. She threw her free hand toward the shadows, her
magic sparking at her fingertips. The darkness halted.

The voices had gone silent. The laughter had ceased. They waited at the
edges of the mermaid's light, biding their time for when the black abyss crept
forth again.

A hiss rose from deep within Evanora's belly. She eyed the void, her
grip on me growing tighter. A single word slithered out between her
clenched teeth. A single word that sliced through the water, pierced the
darkness, and sent the shadows shrinking back. A single word that made
my broken heart sing.

"Mine."

A tsunami of crackling light burst from Evanora.

CHAPTER FIFTY

EVANORA

APRIL 17 – EVENING

I DIDN'T KNOW WHAT TO EXPECT.

My Gift was there, begging to be used. But after the emotionally tumultuous days I'd been having, I wasn't sure how much I had stored away; it might've been a lot, or embarrassingly little.

It was dangerous, foolish. I was either going to save us, or make a spectacle of myself, then die a slow, horrible death at the hands of the Cursed Beings.

But the second I laid eyes on Grayson, I knew none of that mattered.

I didn't think. I just acted.

I had merely held out my hand.

And all hell broke loose.

Wave after wave of burning light crashed out of me, electrifying the waters, erasing the shadows. It went unabashedly on, eclipsing everything around us until it was as though it were daylight. There was nowhere for the darkness to hide. The Cursed Beings hissed and shrank away, their tentacle-like arms quickly withdrawing back into the black mass. My light hurt them, but the act of retreat bothered them more. They groaned and wailed as they slinked away, trying to avoid my Gift's flaring beams.

With a growl, I pulled Grayson closer, clutching him tightly against my chest. Slowly, we inched upward, unwilling to turn our backs on the mass of shadows below. Every kick of my tail widened the gap, but I could feel my magic waning, sputtering toward exhaustion. Gritting my teeth, I channeled the last of my strength into the Gift. Just a little longer. Just until we reached the surface.

I glanced above. The water's edge seemed impossibly far.

Grayson made a choked sound that claimed my attention. His eyes were wide as he clutched his neck, his lips pressed tightly together. He pointed frantically at his chest, then upward toward the surface.

Oh, gods, I realized, *he's going to drown.*

My magic sputtered once, twice, then fizzled out completely, several lazy sparks streaking from my fingers before the black abyss ate them away.

We were out of time.

The Cursed Beings roared as we swam with everything we had. My tail thrashed, Grayson's legs kicked weakly, and we surged upward. I didn't dare look back. Grayson—always so strong—felt light and fragile in my arms, like a child. I held him closer, ignoring the burn in my chest, the ache in my body as it screamed at me to stop.

"We're almost there," I gasped, my voice raw. "Almost there!"

I could feel them closing in—their jagged claws slicing through the water with terrible precision. The surface was just ahead, but I knew they wouldn't stop, not even there. Twisting sharply, I bolted toward the shore, my fins skimming the water's edge. The night air kissed my scales as I zigzagged through the dock's wooden legs, narrowly dodging nets that hung like curtains.

The Cursed Beings shrieked, the sound clawing at my ears. They slowed, hesitating as the shoreline loomed closer.

Grayson strained against me, his entire body trembling with fatigue. I could see his eyes fluttering shut, his neck muscles spasming.

"Grayson!" I shouted, my voice stretching to the ends of the earth, fear enveloping my entire being.

The rocky shoreline was in sight.

The Cursed Beings lunged, snagging the tip of my tail in their jagged claws.

With all the strength left in me, I burst out of the water's mouth, thrusting us onto the hard earth. We smashed against the firm, unyielding rocks. They were cold and prickly, and the pain was glorious. It meant we were alive. *Alive.*

Hoisting my tail over the rocky ledge, I sat up on my arms and peered into the water. I could see the shadows lurking just underneath the surface, their fingers snapping and clawing at the rocks. As the waves swept in, the Cursed Beings surged forward, but they made no attempt to leave the water. And when the waves receded, so did they, pulling farther and farther into the ocean until I couldn't see them anymore. Their voices lingered on the sea-foam, in the night breeze.

The one who was promised. He is ours.

I bared my teeth at the ocean. "You cannot have him."

The Cursed Beings giggled at my defiance. *You do not own him.*

"Neither do you."

Oh? the shadows crooned, their words growing fainter. *Are you so sure?*

I wasn't. And, gods, I was exhausted. "Go back to the abyss where you belong," I growled.

The darkness didn't reply. They were gone, and I was left in a beautiful silence.

Silence. Grayson.

I spun to the boy, who lay crumpled on the rocky ledge. He wasn't moving.

"Grayson!" I cried, scuttling forward, ignoring the rocks as they bit into my scales and snagged my fins. "Grayson!"

I placed a shaking hand on his chest, where it remained still. No jagged gasps for breath, no hurried rising and falling. "No," I moaned, leaning forward, replacing my hand with my head. "No, no, no!"

His heart was beating, but it was terrifyingly weak. I shot back up, looking at Grayson's face. He was always pale, but he had gone practically white, his lips a mottled blue. I tapped his cheek, lightly at first, then with vigor. The boy's head lulled to the side unceremoniously. "Grayson, *please*," I begged. "Open your eyes! Wake up!"

I looked at my hands. Clenching and unclenching my fingers, I tentatively pressed them against the boy's chest. I loosed a low breath, closing my eyes. "If there is magic left within me, let him have it."

My Gift hummed inside me, an unsteady flicker. I could feel it sluggishly pool in my fingertips, the warmth spreading up my arms. I pressed harder against Grayson's chest. The warmth dripped off me and onto the boy, coating his chest in a dull light. It collected on his skin before seeping beneath, and I imagined it intertwining with his bloodstream, tangling with his heart, his lungs, returning life to them.

The light went out at my fingers, and the humming ceased. All I could do was wait. I pulled my hands away from Grayson and watched him closely, praying to every god I knew that the dredges of my magic would be enough.

Nothing.

Nothing.

Movement.

Grayson's chest spasmed. He lurched forward, coughing, his eyes shooting open, wild and frantic as he fought to collect his bearings. Water dripped out of his mouth in stringy, foamy gobs. He sucked in a ragged breath, coughed roughly again, and then looked at me, his eyes thick with tears. He swallowed, wiping his mouth. "Are you okay?" he croaked, his voice a thin, bedraggled thing.

I could have cried. Instead, I forced out a harsh laugh. "Am *I* okay? You nearly died! Honestly, Grayson, what were you thinking? Why were you swimming at nighttime?" I shook my head. "Why were you swimming *at all*? You know you can't!" I groaned, running a hand over my face. "Why do you insist on continuously scaring me?"

The color that had been slowly returning to the boy's face quickly drained away. He tried to smile. "Because I have a knack for it?"

My gaze drifted to my tail, where the fins were cleaved in two. I could still smell the Cursed Beings' rotten flesh on my scales. "We shouldn't have survived that."

Grayson turned to me. "Why did we?"

I looked down at my hands, searching for an answer. They looked so normal that it was hard to believe they had warded off an entire army of Cursed Beings only moments ago.

"I don't know," I answered truthfully. "In all honesty, I didn't know they'd react to my light like that."

The boy furrowed his brow. "Evanora," he whispered, glancing around. "Who—what—*are* they?"

I closed my eyes, letting out a low breath. I'd been dreading this. For the second time, I was going to ruin Grayson's life and shift everything he thought he knew. "What do you know about the curse?"

"Curse?" Grayson gave me a quizzical look before holding up a finger. "You mean . . . *the* curse?" he asked, adding emphasis on the words that seemed to mean a lot more to him than they did to me.

I shrugged. "Probably? How many curses can a single island have?"

Grayson tried to roll his eyes but only got about halfway before he stopped, closing them with a wince. "I was taught about it in school, about how we once had a great relationship with your kind. We worked together; the mermaids kept the waters safe, and we kept the island safe." He opened his eyes with a frown. "We were told that one day, without any explanation, the mermaids turned on us and began killing the islanders whenever they could. So . . ." He blew out a breath and shrugged. "We fought back. That was how the Hunt began."

"And the Barrens?" I prompted.

The boy scratched his head. "We were never taught about it. It's always been there."

I shook my head slowly. "But it hasn't."

Grayson chewed on his lip, his forehead cluttered with worry lines. Eventually, he let out a soft sigh. "I know," he whispered. "We have myths and stories about what lives in there, about the hateful evil that even death tries to flee." He snorted half-heartedly. "We even have a damn lullaby about it. But it's all just fairy tales and bedtime stories to keep children from making mischief in the middle of the night."

I raised an eyebrow and stared pointedly at the water. "Do you still think it's a myth?"

"No." Grayson shivered again and rubbed his hands together. He blew against his fingers for a couple breaths before looking at me. "I also think there was a lot that the school left out."

I nodded. "The curse is real, Grayson, and it should be feared. What you witnessed"—I gestured to the water—"was the spawn of it."

Grayson's skin took on a greenish hue, and he burped, swallowing whatever had entered his mouth with a grimace. "I don't want to hear any more."

I shook my head. "You need to. It's time you heard the truth."

"No, I—"

"A long time ago," I interjected, cutting off Grayson's protests, "there was a boy, and there was a mermaid. Just like Warrick and his mermaid." I held the boy's gaze. "Just like you and me."

Grayson bit his lip, scared but curious. "What happened?"

I offered a sad smile. "They were in love—a love so pure, it was etched into the earth, woven through the stars, and reflected in every crashing wave and whispering breeze. It was dangerous, that love, raw and new, an uncharted territory. No one knew what to make of it. Love between two species was unheard of, and even the wisest scholars couldn't decide if it was right or wrong." I chuckled softly. "The couple didn't care. Time meant nothing to them—every stolen minute became an eternity. Those moments held lifetimes, worlds within worlds. Their love was boundless, their desire to be together teetering on madness.

"Back then," I paused, lifting a finger, "peace reigned between your kind and mine. Humans and mermaids thrived together. War hadn't divided us yet."

Grayson frowned. "So, what changed?"

The smile slipped from my lips. "Death." I rubbed my face tiredly. "Death, I'm afraid, ceases for no one, not even those blessed with the truest of love."

The boy inhaled slowly. I could tell he wanted me to stop, but a larger part of him was hungry for answers.

"No one knows for certain what happened," I continued. "Some say their love wasn't lawful and they were ambushed by their own. Others claim there was a misunderstanding, a fight in the water that ended in bloodshed. No one knows who struck first—the mermaid or the boy. All that's certain is that their lives ended under the new moon, the night at its darkest. Their blood mingled with the ocean, and from that pain and hate, something new was born—an entity that only knew death, that thrived on fear and suffering."

"The Barrens," Grayson whispered.

I nodded. "They go by many names, but my pod knows them by only one: the Cursed Beings." A chill settled into my scales, and I knew that even the brightest sun and the warmest waves wouldn't alleviate it. "The Cursed Beings only leave the Barrens at night. Their hunger for bloodlust and pain is never satiated; they are always looking, always yearning for more. They claim any living thing they can get their hands on. Whales, mermaids, humans—it makes no difference to them. In their eyes, death is death, and it is never enough."

Grayson was shaking hard. He wrapped his arms around his drawn-up legs. It took everything within me not to scoot forward and pull him into a hug. He swallowed, dipping his chin into his knees. "I can hear them."

I went deathly still. "You're certain?"

The boy nodded. "It started on my birthday. It used to be only at night, and when I was near the water." He rubbed at his red-tipped nose. "Lately, it's all the time. Nonstop."

My heart was pounding. "Grayson," I said slowly, "what do they say to you?"

Grayson's body jerked, something between a shake of his head and a shrug. "I don't know. It's only whispers."

He was lying. Keeping secrets. But I didn't push him.

"The truth is, we know little about the Cursed Beings. Humans see them as myths; we know them as abominations. They hunt at night, avoid light, and dwell in the Barrens. They search by smell and sound, and their ability to speak is new." I sighed, running a hand through my hair. "Maybe that's why you hear them now. Perhaps they've only just learned how. I heard them for the first time a few days ago." I eyed him carefully. "But why you, I wonder?"

Grayson shrugged again, looking away as he rubbed at his wrists. "Your guess is as good as mine."

I really wished he would open up to me. Here I was, pouring my heart and soul out for him to see, and the boy remained tight-lipped as ever. I tried not to hold it against him. I had hurt him one too many times, and I had a feeling I wouldn't be seeing that adorable smile and unabashed honesty for a while.

"You are a special one, Grayson Shaw. Maybe that is why they speak to you."

The boy chuckled, but it was forced. "Well, that's comforting." He chewed on his lip, thinking. "The Barrens circle the entire island." He looked at me with sorrowful eyes. "That's why you can't leave." He let out a breath that sounded dangerously close to a sob. "That's what killed Warrick."

I nodded. "Yes, Grayson." I placed a hand on his shivering knee. "I'm so sorry."

The boy stared at my hand, at the touch he craved and loathed. "What happened?" he asked quietly. "After the couple died?"

I offered a sad smile. "The bodies were recovered, and chaos followed. Humans blamed the mermaids, and mermaids blamed the humans. Grief ignited war. The humans turned their nets and spears—tools we'd shared with them—against us." I shrugged tiredly, letting my head droop to the side. "And with the Barrens cutting off any escape, we were trapped."

"The Initial War." Grayson sniffed, swiping at his nose with his soggy sleeve. "Did you fight back?"

I shook my head. "Some wanted to. Some *did*. But my parents . . ." I inhaled sharply, a familiar ache stabbing through my chest. "They loved the humans. They believed in them, believed that someday the pain and confusion would fade, that we could find an understanding." I shook my head, a bitter laugh escaping. "They were wrong, of course. While they waited for that pain to subside, the Hunt began—and with it, a new kind of agony.

"The Hunt has claimed more lives than the Initial War ever did. Only recently," I whispered, my gaze dropping to avoid Grayson's, "did my pod decide to resist. It was our first, and only, act of defiance—to prove we weren't docile creatures destined to meet the tip of a spear."

Grayson's expression shifted, realization dawning, quickly followed by the shadow of pain. Silence fell between us, heavy and suffocating. "I would have helped," he mumbled, his tear-streaked face catching the dim light. "If you'd just asked me, I would have helped you end the Hunt."

I struggled to catch my breath. I squeezed his leg, painfully tight. "Grayson—"

The boy staggered to his feet. "But you went behind my back, treated me as a pawn in your twisted game." His lower lip was trembling. He pressed his hand against it, a moan slipping between his fingers. "I just don't think I can forgive you for that." He took a step away from me, shuddering softly. "And I want nothing to do with you."

Tears sprang to my eyes, hot and uninvited. I opened my mouth to protest, to plead, to scream until the tightness in my chest subsided, but another voice cut me off. It was thick, booming in the night, frantic echoes bouncing off the rocky ledge before slipping beneath the waves.

"Well, where is he?" it called out gruffly.

"He was *right* here! I swear it!" a meeker voice responded.

I jerked my attention up the rocky wall, a hiss in my throat, my fins razor-sharp and ready.

"I don't see him anywhere. You're certain you saw him here?" the first voice demanded.

"Yes," the second voice replied hurriedly. "At the end of the docks. I told him not to jump in, but he didn't listen. He was . . . He was in rough shape when I found him." There was a pause, then a heartfelt shout. "Grayson! Graaaaaysoooon!"

Grayson didn't seem alarmed to hear his name on the wind. He squinted up at the wall of rocks, his shoulders sagging as he sighed. "It's just Jasper and Pa." He glanced down at me. The tears had already dried in his eyes, and his mouth was set in a firm line. "You should go. I might've spared your life, but they will not hesitate to take it." He snickered weakly, kicking at loose rocks, watching them tumble over the ledge. "I'm almost tempted to let them."

A gasp quickly replaced the hiss. I faltered, inching closer to the water. "You don't mean that."

Grayson gazed at me for a long second before letting out a heavy breath. "No," he muttered. "I don't."

The relief was short-lived as another volley of anxious words tumbled over the rock wall.

"I don't get it. Why would he go in the water?"

"I *told* you; he was in rough shape! He wasn't making any sense, acting like a regular crackpot." There was silence, then a quiet, "Sorry."

Grayson peered up the wall again. "Trust Jasper to say something he shouldn't," he grumbled. "Seriously," he bit out, glowering at me, "you need to go."

I shook my head wildly. There were things I still needed to do, things I still needed to say. I couldn't leave when things between us were so broken. "Grayson I—"

"I'm right here," Grayson called out, raising his voice to be heard over the rumbling waves. His eyes never left mine. "Pa? Jasper? I'm here."

I swallowed a whine, torn between looking at the boy and the top of the rocky ledge. The water called out to me, begging me to return to it. But all I wanted to do was remain on the cold, hard rocks with Grayson. I bit my lip, fumbling back. "Is this what you truly want, Grayson Shaw?"

The voices were getting closer. I could see lights bouncing along the stone wall that hugged the island's side. Thick, heavy footsteps fluttered over the ledge, and my heart pounded in time with them. I looked back at the boy, growing frantic, waiting for an answer I would loathe.

Grayson's eyes softened, but his words hit me like a carefully aimed blow. "I've never had a say in what I want, Evanora. Not when it comes to you and me. You made certain of that."

CHAPTER FIFTY-ONE

GRAYSON

APRIL 18 – MORNING

GOD WAS PUNISHING ME.

It was the only explanation I could conjure as I huddled beneath my blankets, shivering so hard my teeth rattled despite the inferno raging beneath my skin. Every muscle ached, my nose was performing the cruel magic trick of being both blocked and leaking, and my chest was a tangle of misery. Getting sick after narrowly avoiding death—and having Evanora rip the remains of my heart out and scatter the pieces—was a cruelty so precise it had to be divine. Surely I was being tested, and I was failing spectacularly.

I was holding a book, seeing the swirling words but not reading them, wondering if I had broken a mirror recently, when there was a knock at the door. I looked up, glaring down the hall and the empty kitchen yawning after it. "Go. Away." I burrowed myself deeper underneath the blankets, like hiding myself from the outside world would deter it from bugging me.

The knocking persisted.

God was testing me, for sure.

With a groan, I slammed the book shut and peeled the mountain of blankets off, yanking one to drape over my shoulders like a makeshift cape. A few unsteady steps tested my strength. Satisfied I wouldn't collapse, I shuffled down the hall. I didn't need a mirror to know I looked awful, and I hoped whoever was at the door felt appropriately guilty for disturbing me.

Holly stood on the porch, her freckled nose and cheeks pink from the climb up the hill. A basket crammed with jars, herbs, and tea bags rested in her arms. Her smile faltered the moment she saw me.

"Good *God*, Grayson Shaw," she said in place of a greeting. "I *am* speaking to Grayson Shaw, right? Not a plague-riddled zombie?"

I let out a snort that quickly became a gravelly cough. "Well, hello to you too."

Her gaze traveled all over me—from my chapped lips, to my red nose, to the bags under my eyes, to the sweat seeping from my greasy hair. I tightened the blanket around myself self-consciously. "Did you come to ogle me like a specimen, or"—I stared down at the basket in Holly's hands—"are you here to nurse me back to health?"

Holly lifted the basket like it was a trophy. "I brought all the essentials. Ma's chicken soup, peppermint tea, garlic, ginger, echinacea root. You name it, it's in here."

I forced a smile. "That's very kind of you, Holly."

When I tried to take the basket, Holly stepped away, clutching it against her chest. "What do you think you're doing?"

I frowned, my hands outstretched and empty. "Trying to take the essentials?"

"Don't be ridiculous. You are in no shape to take care of yourself." Holly stepped around me, still holding on to the basket with a tight grip as she walked into the mudroom. "Go sit by the fire while I warm the soup up."

Mood sinking, I ambled into the kitchen. I didn't know what I hated more—having to remain in an upright, sitting position, or visiting when I'd rather be sleeping, or staring at the wall, or reading a book even though I'd been on the same page, same line, all morning. "I don't want to get you sick," I argued weakly as I did as I was told.

"Oh, hush." Holly had already tied an apron around her waist and was searching for a pot.

"Cupboard to your left," I offered, trying to ignore the ache in my chest at the sight of Ma's frilly apron on Holly. It still had flour on it from the last time she had baked bread. "No. Other left."

"Aha!" Holly said victoriously, brandishing the pot with a grin. "And your ladles?"

I rubbed my snotty nose with one hand, using the other to point to the jar of kitchen utensils on the end of the counter. "Really, Holly. You don't have to do this."

Holly waved me off, already pouring soup into the pot. A bit splattered onto the apron, and she absentmindedly wiped it with her hand, smearing it into the floral fabric. The stove hissed to life as she lit the burner. Settling the pot over the flames, she propped one hand on her hip and began to stir. She looked so at home it was both comforting and jarring.

Sensing my stare, Holly glanced over her shoulder, her cheeks flushing. "I hope you don't mind me taking over your kitchen."

I shook my head, watching the flames flicker beneath the pot. "Even at my best, you could run circles around me in here."

She bit her lip to suppress a smile. "With Ma busy with the twins and Jasper only good for taste testing, I had to learn fast."

I nodded. "My ma was the brains behind all our meals. Without her, well . . ." I laughed awkwardly. "It's a wonder Pa and I haven't burned the house down yet."

The stirring slowed. "Is that why Mr. Shaw isn't here taking care of you? Because he doesn't know his way around a chicken-soup recipe?"

The laughter died in my throat. "He's . . . He's down at the butcher shop," I said reluctantly.

It was true—Pa *was* at work. But telling Holly that he had gone to work before I was even awake, not to mention the silent treatment he had been giving me since he'd collected me off the rocky embankment of Bristling Bay, seemed like oversharing. "To be honest," I added quickly, "he was in such a state of shock last night, I don't think me getting sick even crossed his mind."

I knew without a doubt that it hadn't. The news about Warrick occupied every nook and cranny of Pa's brain and was likely not vacating the premises anytime soon. The fact that he had been out searching for me was a miracle. Or obligation. Or guilt.

The stirring resumed, but Holly's movements were stiff. "Jasper said you were hearing voices last night."

The conversation shift was about as subtle as a hammer to the head, and it was a shift I didn't appreciate. "I thought I could, yeah."

Holly pursed her lips. It looked like she was wondering how fast it would take the nurses at Rose Hill to get to my house for an emergency psychiatric test. "What did they say?"

"I don't know exactly," I lied. "It just felt like they wanted me to go for a swim."

Holly jerked her head in my direction. "You? Swim?"

"Maybe the voices didn't know that I'm not very good at it," I said jokingly.

Holly didn't laugh. As she slowly turned back to the soup, I wrestled to get the words rattling in my fuzzy brain to drop onto my tongue. "I think the voices came from the Barrens."

Holly snorted, not even sparing a glance my way. "The Barrens," she repeated. "You mean the place where monsters live? The ones our parents warn us about so we don't go swimming at night?" She gave me a pointed look. "Remember that lesson, Grayson? About *not* swimming at night?"

I gave a hearty sneeze in response.

Holly rolled her eyes and resumed stirring. "They are just fairy tales, Grayson. They aren't real."

"You're right." I rubbed my tingling nose. "I think I was just really, *really* drunk." There was no point in me trying to explain everything Evanora had told me. The Cursed Beings, the tragic love between mermaid and human, the real reason behind the Initial War. Anything I said would be damning and would get me a lot more than just a psychiatric test.

"Jasper told me about that too. He said you found an abandoned liquor bottle on the side of the road." She made a face over her shoulder at me. "Gross."

I couldn't help but laugh. "That guy really needs to learn to keep things to himself."

Holly spooned a large helping of soup into a bowl and set it in front of me. "Hell will freeze over before that happens." She rested her elbows on the table, threading her fingers together and tucking her chin into them. "You might want to talk to Pastor Kline." She waved my scowl away. "There might be explanations for the voices that we just don't know about. And if anything, he's got two large ears that are excellent for listening."

Yeah, and the loosest lips Lethe's ever seen. My ramblings would surge through the island like the plague. And then it would be Tully's lone practicing physician, Dr. Peele, knocking at my door, itching to poke and prod me with his dirty instruments and pick apart my brain like he had with Ma before she'd been sent to Maude. No, thank you.

The rich scent of broth, soft veggies, fresh noodles, and tender chicken attempted to assault my stuffed-up senses. I had absolutely no appetite, but Holly wouldn't stop looking at me, so I dug a spoon into the soup and slurped it down. I hissed sharply and dropped the spoon, sending it clattering onto the table.

Holly surged forward, worry tightening her porcelain features. "What's wrong?"

Lips pinched together in a grimace, I swallowed loudly and pointed to my neck.

Holly clucked her tongue soothingly, placing a hand on mine. "Is your throat sore?"

I shook my head, blowing out a lungful of scalding air. "No. The soup is *really* hot."

"Oh!" Holly chirped out a laugh, smacking me lightly on the shoulder. "Well, slow down, you silly goose! The soup isn't going anywhere."

"Seriously, am I breathing fire? I think I can see smoke."

"Grayson Shaw, your jokes are terrible."

I groaned, pushing the bowl away from me. "I'm sick. You're supposed to feel sorry for me."

Holly scoffed, pushing the bowl back. "You don't need to be sick for me to feel sorry for you."

I picked up my spoon, making sure to blow on the soup. "Well, that's mean," I said between breaths. "The Holly I know is kind and gentle and helps me find books in the library. *Hot!*" I screeched, nearly spitting the soup out.

Holly laughed, leaning away as I fanned my face. "Slow *down*! Are you trying to melt your mouth?"

"I can't feel my tongue," I said between loud pants, resisting the urge to stick my fingers inside my mouth to touch it.

Holly bit her lip, stifling her giggles. "You're hopeless." She plucked up one of her braids, running her fingers over the ginger ridges. "Do you really think I'm mean?"

I stopped panting. "A mean person wouldn't hike up the hill to give me soup." I hesitantly reached for my spoon again.

A blush crept up Holly's cheeks, blooming to the very tips of her ears. As my fingers curled around the spoon, two things happened.

The first: Holly placed her hand on mine. It wasn't the light, fleeting touch of concern she'd given me before. Her hand settled deliberately, her fingers lacing between mine. Her skin, pale and smooth, was a stark contrast to my flushed, fevered tone. Her fingernails tapped softly against the wooden tabletop, each sound reverberating through the silence like a distant quake.

The second: A spark jolted through me—not the fluttery chaos of butterflies in my stomach, or the tingling warmth where her thumb brushed my overly sensitive skin. It struck deeper, at the heart, where the frayed remains of Evanora's connection still simmered. Weak and sputtering, it flared to life, reminding me it wasn't gone. Not yet.

The connection rained down embers into the pit of my broken heart, sending spurts of pain that bit into me like shards of glass. The heart, impossibly, continued to pump around the pain. And with every beat, a word began to take shape in my sluggish brain.

Trai—tor. Trai—tor. Trai—tor.

Guilt seeped through my system, blazing a trail through my body. It forked in my bloodstream, splitting into two agonizing paths. I knew one of the guilt-charged streams belonged to Holly—I'd have to be on death's door to not catch on to that—but my sick-muddled mind couldn't figure out the remaining trail. Pa, maybe? For constantly letting him down? Jasper, for nearly dying in front of him?

Trai—tor. Trai—tor.

I refused to believe the guilt belonged to Evanora. She'd wronged *me*. She'd used *me*. There was nothing to feel besides hurt and betrayal when it came to the mermaid. No. Definitely not Evanora.

I looked into Holly's eyes, wide with nerves and hope. A smile played at the corner of her lips, twitching the gentle edges, trying to pull them upward.

Trai—tor.

Holly was showing an interest in me. I should have been ecstatic, not burrowing into myself, wondering why I was thinking about Evanora. The mermaid didn't deserve to take up all my thoughts—not when the prettiest girl in Tully was holding my hand. It was cruel and unfair and—

Trai—tor. Trai—tor.

And despite it all, I wished it were Evanora holding my hand, her icy grip cooling the fire on my skin.

Damn. Traitor, indeed.

"Holly . . ." I sighed, closing my eyes in a slow wince.

Holly froze, a statue in my kitchen. Her touch went rigid.

"If I have ever led you to believe that there was something between us . . ." The sentence tapered off. I didn't know how to end it. God, I wished a coughing fit would occur so I didn't have to continue. Or a fainting spell. Hell, I'd even take my house actually burning down to get out of this conversation.

Holly ripped her hand away from mine, placing it on her quivering lips. The deep red scorch mark of embarrassment burned her cheeks, and her eyes instantly welled up with unshed tears. When I hesitantly reached for her, she stuttered back, sending the chair careening into the sink. She took a staggering step away from the table, her flooded eyes not leaving mine. "Oh, God," she whispered, shaking her head rapidly. "Oh, *God*!"

"I'm so sorry," I tried, pulling myself to my feet, only to collapse back into the chair, weightless as a rush of flashing lights clouded my vision.

"Stop," she said, breathing hard around her fingers as she began to pace. "Just *stop*."

The poor girl was mortified, and I was too lightheaded to even comfort her. "It has nothing to do with you," I promised. "Trust me, you don't want to like me like that."

Holly gasped out a mixture of a cry and a laugh. She moved her hand upward, shielding her eyes. "I'm such an idiot!"

"No!" I exclaimed, trying again to stand. "I'm the idiot!" My legs were toothpicks, the ground soggy bread. I struggled not to tip over. "Any guy would be over the moon if you were interested in them." I took a shaky step forward. "You are amazing. And pretty. And bright."

Holly stopped her frantic pacing in the cramped kitchen and slowly lowered her hand. She leveled me with a cold stare, the tears finally dripping from her hazel eyes. "And that's not enough? That's not good enough for you?"

I didn't think my heart had the ability to hurt even more. I shrugged helplessly, the blanket falling to the floor. "I'm a mess. I can't ask you to be the one to help fix me."

Holly dropped her head, letting her tears fall onto the floor. Her hands balled up into fists at her sides. "You wouldn't have to ask."

I wanted to die. I suspected Holly did too. I forced a smile instead. "I know. That's why you're going to make someone *so* happy someday."

Her expression hardened, fury igniting like a spark to kindling. She stormed forward, her breath hot and her glare sharp enough to cut. I leaned back instinctively, toppling into the chair. For a terrifying moment, I wasn't sure if she was going to kiss me or kill me. "I don't *want* to be with *someone someday*," she growled. "*I* deserve to be happy too!"

Her fury was as quick as a viper, sharp as a blade.

So was mine.

I arched an eyebrow and smiled thinly. "So do I."

Holly's mouth snapped shut, but a small whimper escaped, fragile and raw. Her tears fell freely now, a cascade of unspoken pain. Straightening abruptly, she tore off Ma's apron and hurled it toward the counter. It slid into the sink, disappearing into the murky water. She froze, staring at it for a moment, as though debating whether to retrieve it. But instead, she turned on her heel and marched out of the room, leaving the house with a slam of the door.

The silence, the treasured solitude I had wanted that morning, was suddenly suffocating.

The shock of the situation numbed my burning skin like a salve. The whole thing had happened in a matter of seconds. If it weren't for the soup steaming on the table, I would have been tempted to think the ordeal had been a wicked fever dream. There was a gentle throb at the base of my spine—not enough to hurt, but enough to say, "I'm here." I had a feeling it was the same for Holly. The real pain wouldn't come to us until later, when we were alone, buried in an uncomfortable isolation—something that neither of us truly wanted—and left to lick our wounds. That was when the pain would come.

I sat back in the chair, felt my spine have its own heartbeat, and let the cursed, cherished silence wash over me.

SOMEONE WAS AT THE DAMN DOOR AGAIN.
I had barely made it back into bed—the soup left to go cold, Ma's apron still in the sink—when there was an eager knocking at my front door. Tossing the blankets over my head, I buried myself and my pitiful sorrows under the mountain of fabric. "No one's home," I growled, thrusting my face into the pillows.

"I swear, Grayson"—*thump*—"if you don't answer this door"—*thump!*—"for your best friend"—*thump THUMP!*—"then I'm going to seriously consider throwing your ass back in the ocean."

Jasper. It was just Jasper.

It was just Jasper about to cave my face in because Holly went home crying and told him all the nitty-gritty details about how I broke her heart.

I burrowed deeper into the blankets.

"Come on, Grays." Jasper knocked on the door a final time, but it was lackluster. "I know you're in there."

"No, I'm not!" I shouted from my room.

"Well, then the ghost haunting your humble abode sounds an awful lot like you!" Jasper drawled from outside. "Except a lot sicker and . . . phlegmy."

Sighing, I heaved the blankets off and staggered to the front door. I opened it a crack, peeking at Jasper from the small sliver. "Look, beating up someone at death's door is a low blow, even for you."

Jasper rubbed his bright red knuckles; how hard had he been knocking? "Huh?"

I opened the door the slightest bit more. "I'll let you get one punch in, but that's it."

Jasper's entire splotchy face pinched downward in an all-encompassing frown. "One punch?"

I squeezed my eyes shut and grimaced, readying my face for an explosion of pain. "Is one not enough?"

"Grays—"

"Fine! Two. I'll let you have two."

Jasper let out a guffawing laugh. "Why do you think I want to punch you? Don't you think you've suffered enough for the past twenty-four hours?"

I opened my eyes hesitantly. Jasper was staring at me like I had sprouted horns. The way my head was pounding, I wondered if I had. "You aren't here to beat me to a pulp?"

"Do I have a reason to?" Jasper snorted, pushing his hair off his sweaty forehead. "Also, do you really think I could?"

I considered, then relaxed, opening the door all the way. "No." *Not yet anyway.* "And no."

Jasper swatted my arm. "There's the Grayson I know and love." He leaned in conspiratorially, dropping his voice to a whisper. "You heard the news, right? Isn't it crazy?"

I blinked at Jasper, my mind trying hard to piece his words together, only to be left with a pile of nonsense. "News? What news?"

Jasper gawked at me. "You haven't heard? The entire island is in an uproar about it!"

"Jasper, I've been clinging to life in my bed since last night. What are you talking about?"

Jasper's entire face lit up, complete with a twinkle in his eye. "Oh, *cripes.* You really *haven't* heard!"

"Heard *what*?" I exclaimed, my illness and abundant self-pity making my patience dangerously short-fused.

Jasper grinned at me, his skin shining with freckles and sweat. "The unthinkable has happened."

My mind swam with ideas: The mermaids had attacked. The Hunt was being called off. The Cursed Beings had found a way to move in broad daylight.

I took a step forward, willing my hands to stay at my sides and not wrap around Jasper's scrawny neck to throttle the information out of him. "What?"

When Jasper spoke, there was a twinge of disbelief clinging to his words. And I realized that his grin, still larger than life, was the product of shock, not glee. As the words tumbled out of him, it grew, completely out of place, absolutely unhinged. "Rosemary Little—girlfriend of the untouchable, invincible, undisputed Lethe champion Ambrose Grieves—has gone missing."

CHAPTER FIFTY-TWO

EVANORA

APRIL 18 – AFTERNOON

"Ouch!"

"It wouldn't hurt as much if you held still."

Nienna's fin rot was the worst I had seen on a merling. It had eaten through most of the blue fins on her fluke and was creeping up her tail, mingling with her spots. It tangled with the scales on her arms and twisted around her forearm fins like a vine, leaving blistering welts and craters of pus.

Illeron was right—many of the merlings were struggling with the disease. I'd been so caught up in my own life that I had failed to notice.

Nienna hissed and tried to wrench her arm free from my grip. I held on to her tightly, my Gift flickering with the sudden shift in concentration.

Andoras huffed, peering at the merling from over my shoulder. "Such a guppy."

Not letting go of Nienna, I shot him down with a stern look. "Think you can do any better?"

Andoras uncrossed his arms and touched the gills at his neck, where the scales were inflamed and swollen. He gulped audibly. "I don't know. Probably."

"Well, we'll find out soon enough." I turned back to Nienna. "We're almost done. Just sit tight for a moment longer." Smirking, I glanced over my shoulder at Andoras again. "Then it's your turn . . . guppy."

The merling clenched his jaw in a scowl, but a flood of crimson swept across his sharp cheekbones. Nienna giggled, a soft chiming sound that briefly lightened the weight in my chest. I managed a smile for her—warm, reassuring—but it felt brittle, stretched. I was spent. Exhaustion ran through me like a current, and my magic, strained and sputtering, had begun its silent protest after the third merling I'd healed. Twenty more awaited me, and I prayed my strength would hold until the last little one was tended to. After that, my magic could burn itself out and die for all I cared.

I got to eight—eight of the precious merlings—before the light completely faded from my fingertips. I had burned through so much of it when I'd rescued Grayson Shaw, a boy who hadn't really wanted to be saved—not by me, anyway. And because of my error in judgement, the merlings suffered.

I had to announce a recess and send the sick ones home, promising to fix their ailments the next morning. I made sure to smile, to make a game of it, to chase and tickle the merlings until they were gasping with laughter and not thinking about the pain they were in, about how their queen was a failure.

I could not break, not in front of the merlings. The breaking could happen later.

I followed the path skirting our kingdom, weaving through the soft glow of the lanterns. Thank the gods for Mavi's Gift; they hadn't needed tending in a while. With my reserves utterly spent, the last thing I could manage tonight was to rekindle them. Still, a thread of dread crept in as I imagined their glow fading. If the lanterns snuffed out tonight, it would mean chaos— utter destruction of the pod. Pain. Darkness. Death.

At least then we wouldn't have to worry about the Hunt.

The bitter thought bubbled up unexpectedly, and a sharp, near-hysterical laugh burst from my throat. The release felt both cathartic and unhinged, the kind of laugh that edged too close to breaking. My gut churned, and another wave of giggles surged, as though my body reveled in unraveling. *The leader has finally lost her mind!* I imagined the whispers. *Insanity suits you, Your Majesty.*

Blinking away tears of mirth—and exhaustion—I swam onward. If Ammah were with me, she'd scold me for laughing so ungracefully. She'd insist I swim tall, lift my chin, arch my back just so.

She'd also probably tell me to put on that damned crown.

I swallowed the emotion pooling in my throat. "If Ammah were with me, I wouldn't be in this mess."

My parents had always managed to find a way to survive. The Hunt, the Cursed Beings—there was no danger they couldn't evade. Fighting back was never considered because it simply wasn't an option for them.

But they were dead, and things were different.

The darkness surrounding the pod felt endless, the Cursed Beings infinite. Their unseen hands clawed at our fragile borders, testing them, challenging us with reckless abandon. They were growing stronger, bolder—powerful in ways we'd never seen before. Even Grayson could hear them. The thought sent a shiver through me. Something was stirring, something vast and unknowable, and it terrified me. What had changed? What had unleashed them?

With the Cursed Beings breathing down our necks, the Hunt pinning us in place, and Grayson Shaw no longer wanting anything to do with me, fighting back was no longer an option—it was a necessity, an obligation. Fight, or die.

There was movement out of the corner of my eye, snagging my attention and sending my thoughts scattering.

I wasn't alone.

In the distance, past the safety of the lanterns, a lone mermaid drifted. They were dangerously close to the Barrens, their movements stiff, the flutter of their tail barely moving them. A spike of fear drilled into my heart.

It was a merling on a dare. Illeron had warned me about this. Sometimes the merlings goaded one another into swimming as close as they could to the Barrens. Whoever lasted the longest was the bravest. And most foolish.

Blood shuddering in my veins, I inched closer, a sick curiosity blooming within me. Whoever was dancing that close to the shadows had a death wish. "Excuse me!" I called out, putting as much authority in my voice as possible. "Just what do you think you are doing out here all alone?"

The figure twitched, veering closer to the cliff's edge. They managed to right themselves before slipping completely into the darkness. A heartbeat later, they popped back out.

I ground my teeth together, an exasperated hum locked behind them. "Where are your friends? Who do I have to thank for this particular exercise in courage?"

Again, I was ignored.

The hum shifted into a growl. I swept forward, forearm fins bristling with impatience. "Listen here, merling. Where are your manners—"

I stopped short, my annoyance settling.

It wasn't a merling. It was Jorah. He swayed, his tail a rigid mass of loose scales and decayed fins behind him. The smell of rot snaked through my gills, instantly sending them curling. A trail of dark blood followed behind him like smoke, a wake of ill omens.

An all-too-familiar fear sent my stomach shriveling.

I forced a smile, cocking my head to the side. "Out for an afternoon swim?"

Jorah said nothing. He merely danced in and out of light and darkness.

I swallowed hard. *"Jorah,"* I tried inwardly.

Still, nothing.

I looked around. The warrior watching over him was nowhere in sight. Which meant I had to have a stern talk with Illeron, whether either of us wanted it or not. I surged toward my advisor, trying to keep the fear from swelling into a full-blown panic. What was that insufferable fish doing? Any closer and he would slip right into the Barrens.

"Jorah," I sang playfully. "Where are you going?"

He is coming home.

The wave of voices pummeled into me so suddenly that I nearly scrambled back from the force of them. The Cursed Beings were talking in broad daylight. I didn't have time to be surprised by the horrific discovery. Jorah let out a keening noise, sweeping deeper into the shadows.

Home. Home. Home, the Cursed Beings whispered.

"He *is* home!" I bit out, stirring out of my shocked stillness and rushing forward.

I grabbed Jorah's dorsal fin just before he became completely submerged in the abyss's clutches. It felt slimy and frail in my hand, a second away from disintegrating between my fingers. With a grunt, I reeled him back, amazed at the half-dead fish's strength as he continued to press onward.

It is his time.

"No!" I yelled, shaking my head vigorously as I buried my nails into his fin and yanked.

Jorah didn't even flinch. He stared into the void, unaware of being stopped, unaware of me.

He suffers because of you, the Cursed Beings crooned wickedly. *Just let him go. He wants you to—*

"Enough!" I pulled Jorah back into the fading daylight.

He had stopped fighting me, his tail flopping uselessly underneath his hunched frame. Breathing hard, I squeezed my eyes shut and tried to tune out the calamity in my mind. Voices that shouldn't be talking—not in daylight—swarmed like a bloom of jellyfish, nestling warmly into the panic I had tried in vain not to create. Jorah bobbed beside me listlessly.

"Jorah," I panted, "what are you doing?"

My advisor said nothing. He wouldn't even look at me.

"*Jorah*," I pleaded. "Please answer me."

The silence lingered, thick and stained with the black eyes of a hungry audience.

I pulled him closer, careful to keep a grip on his molting dorsal fin.

I didn't mean to gasp, but I couldn't help it.

The mermaid I held on to wasn't Jorah—not anymore. It was a shell of the mermaid I had once known, one who had raised me, educated me, loved me. It wasn't Jorah at all. It was a husk, the brain already dead with the body not knowing.

Dark Madness.

It had crept in, slowly at first, then all at once—like a tidal wave crashing upon an unsuspecting shore. Jorah's eyes no longer gleamed silver in the light; they were completely milky white, thick veins snaking through them like twisted ropes. The few scales that clung to his skeletal body were dull, slick with a thin layer of slime. Every inch of him was ravaged by fin rot, but the black blood didn't come from there. With every wheezing breath, dark crimson seeped from his gills—a steady stream, carrying with it the promise of death.

I stifled a sob, my body trembling. I reached out to touch his face. "Oh, Jorah," I whispered, my voice breaking.

Yes, the Cursed Beings sang with glee. *You see. You know.*

I shook my head, my eyes not leaving Jorah's vacant ones. "No," I cried softly. "No, no, no."

Jorah's cracked mouth bobbed open and closed, a fish gasping for oxygen. He slowly turned to gaze into the Barrens, his unseeing eyes piercing the dark. His tongue, shriveled and black, darted out. When it dragged over his lips, it took an entire layer of skin with it.

Everything hurt. How could everything hurt this bad? All of me was breaking, shattering into a million pieces. It would be impossible to find them all again. "I can't do this without you," I whispered. "Please don't leave me to do this on my own."

He is ours, the darkness moaned.

"No!" I wailed, pinning Jorah in place as he began to wiggle for the shadows. "No! Not yet!" I slipped onto the sandy floor, shaking and crying as I held on to Jorah's tail.

My advisor stilled. I looked up, hoping to see a flicker of recognition, a glimpse of the strong mermaid I'd once known.

There was only Dark Madness.

I swallowed a sob. "Let me say goodbye," I begged. "I need to say goodbye."

The Cursed Beings slipped into silence, contemplating. *Time is not on your side. He is fading.*

"I know that!" I snapped, wiping my face as I forced myself to rise. I took Jorah by the shoulders and hugged him. It was all protruding bones and oozing flesh. The smell of pus and rot encapsulated us, but I didn't care. "My path has led me to you," I breathed, running my hand over his thin hair. I pulled back, blinking away the tears. I offered him a wobbly smile that he could not see. "May our ancestors' light guide you home."

The darkness laughed, deep and malicious. *There is no light down here.*

"Silence!" I shouted, my voice cracking.

The Cursed Beings relented.

I looked at Jorah. "My path has led me to you," I repeated. "May our ancestors' light guide you home. May your journey be swift and peaceful, your soul reborn, your body renewed. Go, and swim free." I closed my eyes, letting out a shaky breath. "Goodbye, my dear friend. Thank you for everything. And . . . I'm sorry." I bit back a sob. "I'm sorry I wasn't strong enough to save you."

Jorah blinked sluggishly. But as I loosened my grip, he turned his head to look at me. *Really* look at me. I knew, in that moment, that part of him was still in there. And it was time for both of us to let go. I sucked in a sharp breath and smiled, nodding. "Swim free, Jorah."

He turned for the shadows.

Here, here, here! they cried ravenously. *Yes, yes, yes!*

Jorah's movements were slow, rigid, almost mechanical. It was torturous, watching him slowly slip into the Barrens' black embrace.

I made myself watch.

The Cursed Beings' cries rose to a mournful shrieking, the multitude of hungry voices crashing into one another in a vicious dance. They climbed, higher and higher, approaching a frenzied hysteria, and I had to fight not to cover my ears.

Jorah's body disappeared. There was a great and violent wailing, and then silence.

With a choked groan, I leapt for the cliff's edge, pulling myself over the lip and peering into the abyss below.

Long, sinewy arms erupted from the darkness, grabbing Jorah's body, their razor-sharp claws sinking into his fragile skin. They moved as one—swift, precise, and relentless. Jorah didn't cry out. He didn't make a sound when his fins were ripped off, his hair was torn from his scalp, and his bloated stomach split open, spilling its contents. He didn't flinch or moan as his tail was shredded and his scales were plucked off one by one. He blinked, and let it happen.

I made myself watch.

I couldn't be sure if their desire for blood and destruction had been temporarily satiated, or if perhaps they'd grown bored of having an audience, but without warning, the arms began to drag Jorah's body down into the damning dark, into nothingness.

I looked away.

CHAPTER FIFTY-THREE

GRAYSON

APRIL 19 – MORNING

IS THIS PUNISHMENT OR PRACTICE?"

Pa stared at me through the small square window separating us. He sipped his coffee, looking perfectly warm on the other side of the freezer door. "Bit of both."

I rubbed the goose bumps coating my arms. "I'm still sick, you know."

Pa scoffed. "You were hardly sick to begin with."

You never bothered to check on me, so how would you know? "Well," I said, resigned, "aren't you going to feel bad if I die of hypothermia or"—I sneezed—"pneumonia?"

Pa said nothing, only took another agonizingly long drink. He wiped the coffee droplets off his mustache with his hand, smacking his lips. "Mmm, that's good," he uttered, swishing the steaming liquid around in the mug. "A bit hot though."

I kept my eyes carefully trained on the door. I could feel the slabs of meat at my back, hanging off their hooks, pools of icy blood on the floor. If I didn't look at them, I could pretend they weren't there. I hopped up and down, attempting to jump-start my circulatory system, which had grown dangerously sluggish in the cold. "Seriously, Pa, how much longer?"

Pa sighed, taking out his pocket watch and glancing at it. "If you think this is bad, you are going to have a hard time on May 1. What if your boat capsizes, or you lose an oar and need to jump into the water to get it?" He shoved the watch back into his vest pocket. "You need to be ready for the cold."

"I handled the cold just fine at the swimming challenge."

Pa leveled me with an eyebrow-raised glare. "Did you?"

I let out a strained laugh. "It wasn't the *cold* that nearly killed me. The *water* nearly killed me."

"No. Your fear nearly killed you."

Getting locked in the butcher shop's cellar wasn't how I thought my morning was going to go. I had woken up with the intent of setting things right with my pa. I figured the apology was going to be awkward but amicable and there would be laughter and back slapping involved. Phineas would purr in the corner of the room, and we would drink coffee, have a somber conversation about my near-death experience, and then vow to never speak of it again.

A surprise training exercise in the cellar did not fit into the agenda, and Pa didn't care.

I stared at the mug in my pa's hands, coveting the warmth he received from it. "Right now, *you're* nearly killing me. When are you going to let me out?"

Pa took another sip. "When you stop complaining."

I fell silent immediately. Five minutes of stillness passed before the lock creaked and the door swung open. I hurried out, rubbing feeling back into my arms. "Thank you."

Pa grunted in response, locking the door behind me. Phineas drifted down the stairs, winding around my legs lazily. He chirped when I scooped him up, his warmth like sunshine against my chest. He probably smelled the cellar on me, but I pretended it was just my company he appreciated, not the fact that I smelled like blood. "Did you ever do that with Warrick?" I asked as we reached the top of the stairs.

The question seemed to startle Pa. He lifted the counter flap, holding it longer than needed as Phineas and I slipped underneath. After a moment, he smiled, a sad curve of his lips that lit up his brown eyes. "Yes. A couple times. He didn't like it either." Pa looked at me ruefully as he eased the flap down. "But he knew better than to complain."

I smirked. Phineas squirmed, so I let him down, watching as he made his way to the windowsill, spun a few times, then tucked into a loaf-like ball. "I'll bet Ma wasn't a fan of your training methods, especially since he wasn't even eighteen."

Pa made a sound, and I realized it was a laugh. "She complained enough for the both of them, I think."

I chuckled, unable to help myself. It felt good to laugh. "I absolutely believe that."

But the laughter died quickly, leaving only a heavy silence as we both reflected on the one who had left us, and the one who'd simply left. Talking about Ma and Warrick felt strange, like we were crossing a line into unfamiliar territory. We'd avoided their names for so long that saying them now felt like an awkward act—like breathing air after forgetting how to.

Leaning on the counter, I tapped my numb knuckles on the wood. "Ma told me that Warrick was her favorite," I said quietly. "The last time I saw her, she said she wished it had been me. That I should've died instead of him." I gave a faint smile, glancing at Pa. "Guess I should've listened when you told me not to see her."

Pa slowly ran a hand over his face. I expected anger from him, a red-hot burst of fireworks and flares. But he reached forward and clasped my arm. I was acutely aware of his fingers avoiding the scars wrapping around my wrist. "Your ma loved you fiercely, Grayson."

I looked pointedly at my scars, chuckling. "She had a weird way of showing it."

Pa's grip tightened on me. "She was sick. She *is* sick. You can't take what she says as gospel."

His words felt stiff and not even remotely true, but I appreciated them just the same. Giving me a final squeeze, Pa let go and grabbed for a rag. "Now, off you get," he said gruffly. "I have work to do, and I won't have you late for your own shift. If Mr. Brightly attempts to dock your pay again . . ." He slapped the rag onto the counter and began to rub enthusiastically, drowning out the rest of his sentence.

I hadn't apologized like I had wanted to, but I had a feeling it didn't matter anymore; the moment was over before I had the chance to realize it had even begun, and Pa, allergic to emotions, proud owner of stony glares and protective barricades, wouldn't appreciate me attempting another heart-to-heart. He was already pretending that I was gone, so I took the hint, gave Phineas a scratch under the chin, and left.

There were sounds coming from the alley beside the shop: the crashing of boxes, splintering of crates, shattering of glass. Mixed in between the cacophony of noises were the unmistakable sounds of sniffling, followed by deep, guttural sobs. Uninvited fear spiked my bloodstream. Holding my breath, I peeked around the corner, squinting into the shadows.

Slumped over a pile of broken wood, a dark green bottle dangling from his fingers, was Ambrose Grieves. His head hung low, a trail of drool dripping from his lips as he stared at his foot, stuck inside a ruined crate. He kicked at it, lost his balance, and tumbled backward, spraying alcohol as he flailed before slamming into the brick wall of the store. He let out a sharp "oof!" followed by a laugh, then a groan.

I looked at the bottles scattered around him, then the barely visible sun peeking over the horizon. Hesitant, I stepped into the alley. "Ambrose?"

Ambrose was speaking, but I didn't think the words were meant for me. He remained pressed against the wall, as though an unseen force were pinning him there. He shook his head back and forth sloppily, his eyes shut, his moving mouth set in a grimace. "She's gone," he was mumbling. "She's gone, she's gone, she's gone and dead."

I took another step, the shadows leeching any collection of warmth I had on my skin. "Ambrose?" I tried again.

"Why her? Anyone else. Not *her*." Ambrose wiped the snot away from his nose, groaning with the effort of such a simple action.

My heart hammered in my chest. I'd never seen Ambrose like this—undone, broken. Any other day, I might've taken some twisted pleasure in seeing him so thoroughly drunk, on the brink of tumbling off his pedestal. Not today. Today, Ambrose wasn't just unraveling. He was feral, a wild animal cornered in the dark, with only one way out—the way I was standing in front of.

I took my hands out of my pockets, holding them loosely at my sides. I had to be ready for anything. "What are you doing in the dark?"

Ambrose finally looked at me, and I wished he hadn't. There were scratch marks etched along his sharp cheekbones, dried blood mixed in with his stubble. He swiped at his glistening eyes and gave me a hateful smile. "Why, I'm mourning the death of my girlfriend. Can't you tell?" He raised the bottle in a mock toast before bringing it to his lips and taking a large mouthful.

I fought against taking a step back. He reeked. Like old body odor, dried blood, and liquor all mixed together into a noxious concoction. I shook my head. "She's missing. Not dead."

"Oh, no." Ambrose laughed loudly. "She's dead. I know she is. They all are."

A shiver raced up my spine. "What do you mean?"

"I mean ..." Ambrose paused to burp. "That they are *dead*, Shaw. Are you stupid? Are you deaf?" He pierced me with a cold look, and for a splinter of a second, his icy-blue eyes were vacant, damned, Godless. He laughed again. "The name is uttered, and that's that. It's game over for those poor, stupid, sorry names."

Ambrose's face crumpled, and without warning, he threw the bottle to the ground, creating a storm of glass shards and alcohol. He picked up a half-broken crate and slammed it into the brick wall, watching as the wood fractured and spat chunks everywhere. "I'm sick of it!" he shouted, picking up another bottle and aiming it at the wall. "I'm sick of it!" An explosion of glass. "*I'm sick of it!*"

Ambrose punched the wall, kicked it, rammed his forehead into it. He spun and began tearing the boxes apart, stomping on the remaining crates, booting the discarded bottles. All the while, he screamed at the top of his lungs. Screamed, and screamed, and screamed.

I ran, leaving the broken man to his broken things in the dark alley.

CHAPTER FIFTY-FOUR

GRAYSON

APRIL 20 – MORNING

THE THEME FOR THE DAY WAS PAIN.

Out of all of them, the combat challenge was, by far, the most violent. The worst injury you could get from net building was a rope burn, maybe a sliver, and besides Tommy's death, the swimming challenge's biggest hurdle was the amount of salt water you swallowed.

The combat challenge was on a whole other level.

Bones were broken. Ankles and wrists were sprained. Bruises were created that lasted for days.

And blood. So much blood.

It was everyone's favorite challenge. I did not share the sentiment.

The crowd was especially hungry, pressed up against the ropes, straining to get closer to the beach, arms outstretched, fingers splayed. They roared in anticipation, chanting the names of their favorite hunters—Halston, Grieves, Morris, Simmons, Brightly. I heard my last name thrown in there once or twice, which was nice, if confusing. They hadn't scored us for the swimming challenge, so technically, I was still high on the betting board—a strong contender for the Night of the Betting.

Pa and a man from Fariid were by the judge's table. Pa stood tall with his arms crossed, while the other man—a towering Nordic Adonis with long blond hair and a braided beard—lounged in a chair that seemed on the verge of breaking beneath him. He leaned back, ignoring the chair's groaning protests as he pulled out a compact mirror to inspect his teeth. He tilted his face this way and that, smoothing his slicked-back hair, prodding the skin under his eyes.

"Finally," Jasper sighed beside me, "the island has someone more narcissistic than Ambrose Grieves."

I started to laugh, felt Pa's eyes blazing a trail in my direction, and quickly stopped.

Mayor McCoy clapped his hands, stealing everyone's attention. "Ladies, gentlemen, hunters! We have arrived at our final challenge!"

The crowd roared. The hunters cheered. I fought down the bile rising in my throat.

Mayor McCoy laughed, nodding at the audience. "Yes, yes. I know you've all been waiting for this!" He wagged a finger at them. "But first things first. Hunters!" He turned to us. "Welcome to combat—the challenge that will test you mentally, physically, and emotionally. It will make you question why you chose to become a hunter. It will ignite a hunger to find the answer." Pausing, he clasped his arms behind his back and paced before us, his expression grim. "You will sweat. You will bleed. Some of you will cry."

Peter Lyre snickered behind me. "Only the weak little piggies will."

Jasper rolled his eyes. "That's rich, coming from you."

Peter frowned. "What's that supposed to mean?"

"What do you think it means?" Jasper pushed his thumb against his nose and oinked loudly, earning a few questioning stares from surrounding hunters. I elbowed him in the ribs, causing his last squeal to come out like, "*Wheeeeee-uh!*"

Peter jutted out his bottom lip and covered his pushed-up nose.

Mayor McCoy waved an arm at the black sand, where multiple rings made of white rope lay. "Behold, your battle stadium, hunters!"

The crowd gasped and cheered. The hunters stood proud. I tried not to laugh.

Mayor McCoy closed his eyes and smiled, soaking in the sounds like a flower in the sun. His outstretched arm swept to the boardwalk, where a rack of equipment stood next to the judge's table. "And your weapons for battle! Choose wisely, hunters, for if your weapon should break, you will not be receiving another."

I tuned the mayor out when he started going over the rules. Pa had already drilled them into me mercilessly. It was a tournament set in a one-versus-one format. Competitors were matched based on age. This felt fair, but I wondered how many eighteen-year-olds ended up making it to the final round, only to get the shit kicked out of them by some forty-five-year-old. Competitors were to use wooden swords, blunted spears, fists, and wits. You needed five points to go ahead to the next round. A hit, along with exiting the ring, counted as a point. If you struck the opponent to the ground, that counted as two. The more blood and the flashier the move, the better. If no one was able to achieve five points at the end of the five-minute mark, both were eliminated.

Sounded straightforward enough—and completely barbaric.

I leaned forward, scanning the hunters for Ambrose. He was off to the side, next to his father, standing tall with his arms clasped behind his back, his face set in a steely expression. The stubble was gone, the blood washed away, but the red welts from the scratches on his cheeks remained. His right hand was bandaged, a souvenir from his fight with the brick wall, I guessed. I'd half expected him to be absent. But he looked nothing like the feral animal I'd found in the alley the day before.

Ambrose turned his head, leveling me with a cool look. The air left my lungs, but I forced myself to look back. Ambrose's mouth twitched, and he turned away, staring ahead at the beach.

I wanted to talk to him. *The name is uttered* . . . What had he meant by that? What did he know about the missing people?

Mayor McCoy's voice severed my thoughts. "Because Mr. Shaw and Mr. Erlandson are Lethe's best fighters, they will be today's judges." He opened his mouth to speak but was cut off by the sudden shrill cries of the crowd.

Many of the audience members began to jump up and down, waving handkerchiefs at the judge's table with a palpable desire. Pa pinched the bridge of his nose and bowed his head, but Mr. Erlandson, the Nordic god, smiled and stood, eating up the attention. He flicked his long billowing vest back, placed a black-trousered leg on the chair, and raised a thickly muscled arm, blowing kisses at the crowd. God, I could hear a woman crying.

"And your job, dear audience," Mayor McCoy pressed on loudly, "is to keep an eye on the hunter you are cheering for!" He nodded at the betting board next to the judge's table. "The hunters will receive points based on where they end up in the tournament. The higher they make it, the higher the points. This will help you decide—"

"Christ Almighty," a hunter cried out from behind me. "We know about the betting board. Let's get on with it already!"

The crowd cheered. The hunters shifted on their feet, itching to inflict pain. The wind shifted, and I could smell the primal tension in the air, thick and electrifying. Mayor McCoy's smile faltered. The show was over, and his fleeting seconds of fame were ripped from his fingers. "Very well," he grumbled, stalking over to the judge's table and snatching up a pile of papers from the desk. "I shall now read out your names. When you hear your name, pick your weapon and head to your designated ring."

He went in alphabetical order. Slowly, the pack of hunters began to thin. Waiting to hear my name was like standing with a noose around my neck and waiting for the floor to drop. My body was a prison, and my nerves ached to be freed. It seemed almost comical that the waiting felt just as painful as the challenge itself.

"Taylor Feeney. Owen Morris. Ring number six. Brook Garven. Travis Cranston. Ring number seven."

Who would I be paired with? Some thug with more brawn than brain? Someone who could dance circles around me? Someone who would beat me to a pulp and laugh while doing it?

"Harry Ian. Murray Thompson. Ring number ten. Cory Kroft. Jasper Warren. Ring number eleven."

The suspense was killing me. The people in my age group were lessening. I looked around wildly, trying to find potential opponents, trying to imagine how they would destroy me. *Calm down*, I warned myself. *You're not a dead man standing. You still have a chance. Remember what Pa taught you.*

"Peter Lyre. Grayson Shaw. Ring number thirteen."

Shit.

Peter looked at me and grinned. "Oh," he growled, "this is gonna be fun!"

I walked on feet that didn't belong to me and numbly picked up a sword. I could feel Pa's eyes on me as I trudged to the ring. The nerves had hunkered down in my stomach, twisting in my guts, oozing down my legs. I glanced quickly to make sure I hadn't pissed myself.

The rings looked a lot larger from afar. Standing inside one, it felt like even a single misstep could send you out of it. Peter stood on one end, bouncing from foot to foot, taking a couple practice swipes with his spear. His shirt was already off.

Pa and Mr. Erlandson were the challenge's main judges, but with so many hunters fighting at the same time, work had to be delegated. Each ring had its own separate judge to oversee the match. Mrs. Morris stood at the edge of ours, holding a clipboard in her frail hands. She pulled a pencil out of her frizzy hair, placing it delicately on the board. "Now," she said sternly, "I'll have no nonsense. You fight, and you fight well. You only have five minutes, so make each hit count. No wasting energy trying to be fancy."

She looked tired. Tommy's death had aged her, like years—not days—had passed since his funeral.

Peter lowered his spear. "The crowd loves a flashy move!"

Mrs. Morris shook her head. "The day is young. And in all honesty, Mr. Lyre, they aren't watching you."

Peter looked offended. But Mrs. Morris was right—our ring was pushed far back, nearly at the water's edge. The audience could hardly see us. They were going to be watching the first couple rows of rings, where the veteran hunters were.

Mrs. Morris cocked her head, pursing her thin lips. "You'll get your moment. Win the first couple rounds, and you'll find yourself in a ring close enough that the crowd can see each and every grain of sand stuck to your body. Go hog wild with the moves then." She looked at the watch dangling from the silver chain on her waist. "Ready, hunters?"

I nodded warily. Peter stomped his feet and huffed like a bull.

The word *fight* barely exited her mouth, and Peter was charging for me.

Time slowed down. Peter's steps seemed sluggish, the ground pulling at his feet, the sand he kicked up like dust in the breeze. The snarl on his face was frozen, the battle cry on his lips long and drawn out.

And then he was in front of me. One second, nothing. The next, blinding pain in my shoulder. I gasped, crumpling in half as I gripped the white-hot ache piercing my skin.

"Ah," Mrs. Morris sighed. "One point to Mr. Lyre." She jotted my failure down on the paper.

"It helps if you *move*, Shaw," Peter crowed.

I straightened with effort, biting back a groan as I slowly removed my hand. No blood. Thank God.

When Peter came at me again, I did as he suggested; I moved. Right out of the circle.

Mrs. Morris clucked her tongue. "That's another point for Mr. Lyre."

Peter barked with laughter. "I'm going to be in those big rings in no time!"

I gritted my teeth. I wanted nothing to do with the challenge, but losing to Peter felt downright dishonorable. I held up my sword. Peter whistled approvingly. "Are you going to participate now?"

There was no way I could match him in strength. Peter was large, built for something like this. I had to use my cunning and get creative.

I gave a hard smile. "Come at me and find out."

Peter scoffed, bent low, and raced for me again.

I was ready for him. When Peter jutted his spear forward, I swept to the side in a crouch, sticking out my leg. Momentum carrying him forward, Peter ran straight into my outstretched limb. He stumbled several steps out of the ring before catching his fleeting balance.

Mrs. Morris raised her eyebrows. "One point for Mr. Shaw," she said, a hint of approval in her voice.

Peter stamped his foot on the ground. "That's not fair!"

I stood. "Just because we have weapons doesn't mean we have to use them."

"But . . . But . . ."

"You're at three minutes, gentlemen," Mrs. Morris announced. "I suggest you hurry."

Scowling, Peter stomped back into the circle. "Try that again, Shaw. I dare you."

I smirked. The pain in my shoulder was lessening, a flutter instead of a throb. I went low, squatting on my heels, waiting for Peter to charge. He stared at me, spitting venom, and took the bait. Just as he came up to me, I grabbed a fistful of sand and threw it at his face. Peter sputtered, his eyes snapping shut, his mouth pinched tightly. His hands went loose in the air, the spear, the desire to strike, momentarily forgotten. I leapt to my feet and spun, striking him on the back with my sword.

Peter let out a roar as he crashed to the ground.

"Two points to Shaw."

Music to my ears. I was in the lead. Just two points left.

"That's cheating!" Peter cried. "That's cheating!"

"That's using your wit, Mr. Lyre. Now stop making a fool out of yourself and get up."

Peter lurched to his feet with a whimper. He wiped the sand from his eyes and squinted at me. I didn't pause to see if he was ready. It was my turn to attack. I surged forward, sword raised.

"Wait," Peter screeched, blinking rapidly. "Wait!"

I didn't wait. I darted left, then right. Peter blindly held up his weapon, but it was useless. I was a ghost, a breath of wind. He was stronger, but I was faster. Peter brought down his spear, but I was already at his side. I sank to my knees, arched my sword, and smacked it against the backs of Peter's knees.

The giant fell. Goliath was conquered.

Mrs. Morris gave a squeak of laughter that seemed to surprise her. "And that's another two points to Mr. Shaw." She made a note on the clipboard before pressing it to her chest. "Congratulations, you've made it to the next round." She looked around. "Some of the fights are still going. I suggest you use this time to drink some water, ice your shoulder, and strategize." She focused on me. "The judges will announce your next opponent shortly."

I couldn't catch my breath.

I won. I won!

Which meant I had to keep fighting.

Shit!

There was a muffled sound coming from the ground where Peter was.

Mrs. Morris rolled her eyes. "Oh, get up, Mr. Lyre. And quit your crying."

"I'm *not* crying!" Peter wailed, his face still turned into the ground. "There's sand in my eyes." His entire body was rippling with vibrations. He turned his head, pointing his tearstained face at me. "You got lucky this time, Shaw."

I tried to shrug, but a flood of pain returned to my shoulder. "Probably."

"Your next opponent won't go so easy on you. I can promise you that!"

I wiped the sweat off my forehead and smiled. "I sure hope not."

Peter looked like he wanted to yell, but all he did was bury his face back in the sand.

I walked to the judge's table, where cups of water rested, along with bags of ice. My pa was careful not to say anything, and his face hardly gave anything away, but I could see it in his eyes. Pride. He was practically glowing with it. He was proud of me for beating Peter. As I grabbed a bag of ice, I wondered how long that feeling would last for him.

The ice helped, but my shoulder was stiffening fast. If I didn't get back to fighting, it would seize up completely. I took inventory of the rest of my body. My hands ached from gripping the sword too tightly, and my knees burned from when I'd crashed onto the sand to finish Peter off. Apart from that, I was okay. For now.

The last fight ended, and Mayor McCoy was back to reading names.

I was paired with Owen Morris in ring number eight. As we sized each other up, I knew Pa's pride was about to be short-lived. There was no way I could beat Owen. He'd been through too much. His brother was dead, and the last fight had wrecked him—his left eye was nearly swollen shut, he was favoring his right leg, and his sword grip hinted at sprained or broken fingers.

I bit my lip, scanning him. Even *with* his injuries, I was at a ridiculous disadvantage. Owen was at least a foot taller, his long arms giving him a reach I could never match. I was going to lose, and he was going to make it look easy. I'd be lucky to land a single hit.

Mr. Craigsby, Tully's farrier and blacksmith, leaned against his walking stick and stared at his watch with boredom. "Are you ready, gentlemen?" he asked flatly.

Owen chuckled, adjusting his grip on his weapon. "Come on, Mr. Craigsby. Sh-sh-show a little excitement! It's the-the-the combat challenge, after all."

Mr. Craigsby glowered at us from underneath his bushy eyebrows. "Once you've seen one fight, you've seen them all, Mr. Morris." He glanced down at his watch again. "Your five minutes starts now. Fight."

Neither of us moved. We were statues, pausing with bated breath, waiting for the other to strike.

Mr. Craigsby scoffed. "Anytime, gentlemen."

Owen crept toward me, his moves slow, methodical. I countered, my feet crossing one over the other, matching his pace. We went in circles, staring at each other, swords raised, time dwindling, no points.

"It's not a dance, for heaven's sake!" Mr. Craigsby bellowed. "Fight!"

Owen swung, but it was far too high. The sword swept right over my head. I ducked, feeling the wind tousle my curls, and jabbed forward, pelting Owen right in the gut. Owen let out an "oof!" and staggered back, cradling his stomach.

"One point for Mr. Shaw," Mr. Craigsby announced dryly.

Owen's eyes darted to Mr. Craigsby, and then he crumpled to the ground with a loud groan. "Ohhhh my *God*!" he wheezed.

Mr. Craigsby glowered at him, scratched out his note on the paper, and wrote something else. "Make that two points."

I hurried over to Owen, helping him stand. "Are you okay?"

Owen let out an embellished moan as he fought to get his feet underneath him.

Guilt swept through me. "I'm sorry. I didn't mean to hit you so hard."

Owen lifted his head, cracked a smile, and blinked at me. I thought it was meant to be a wink, but with one eye swollen shut, it was hard to tell. "Don't worry, you didn't."

My heart lurched. "What?"

Owen leaned in, dropping his voice to a whisper. "You n-need t-t-t . . . to win." He stood, wincing as he took the pressure off his right leg. "And fast."

My mouth dropped open. "What do you mean?"

Owen spared a glance at Mr. Craigsby, then shoved me away with a grunt, his facial features shifting into something harsh and annoyed. He began to circle me, a predator stalking prey, until his back was to our bored judge.

"I mean," he whispered, his face returning to its regular soft expression, "th-that you n-need . . . to *win*." His shoulders sagged, and the movement seemed to cause him grief. "If I beat you, th-th-then it's only a matter of t-t-time before I'm up against Ambrose." He shuddered. "Th-th-there's no way I can go against him and come out alive."

I started to speak, but Owen was charging me, a howl on his tongue. I could read his moves from a mile away. Owen swept his sword low. I jumped over it with a gasp, stumbling away as Owen reared back and whacked his weapon against mine. "Hit me!" he barked, his voice low and gravelly.

I strained underneath the weight of Owen's sword on mine. "What?"

"Hit. Me!" He pushed me off and swiped again.

I blocked his sword just before it hit my face. With a cry, I thrust his sword away and pushed Owen. He tumbled back several steps before falling on his ass. Breathing hard, I looked at Mr. Craigsby.

Mr. Craigsby didn't look impressed. "I'm not counting that."

"What?" I shouted. "Why?"

"Because you didn't *hit* him. You pushed him. It's his own damn fault he fell."

I scowled. "I got a point in my last match for tripping my opponent."

Mr. Craigsby shrugged. "Well, consider it a judge preference, then."

Owen stood up slowly. "How much t-t-time do we have left?"

"Two minutes. Get a move on."

Owen glared at me. "We're both going to-to-to lose at . . . this rate."

I groaned helplessly and began to pace. "Why don't you just forfeit?"

Owen rolled his one good eye. "Th-they don't allow that. You either lose, or you run out of t-time. There's no in between." Owen slipped forward, slapping his blade against mine. "I don't want t-to run out of . . . time. We'd look like cowards." He looked into the crowd, where Sebastian Brightly stood in a flamboyant yellow suit, waving a sign that read, *GO OWEN MORRIS, GO!!!* Owen smiled shyly, then turned back to me. "I'd rather leave with my dignity intact."

I nodded, my heart thundering. I pushed Owen away and raised my weapon. "If that's what you truly want."

Owen grinned. "Just . . . make it look real, okay?"

The next two minutes went by in a blur. I did as Owen asked. A smack of my blade to his rib cage gave me one point. Headbutting him when our arms were tied up with swords gave me two, but only because he dropped to the ground with a theatrical flourish. Mr. Craigsby tiredly declared me the victor as I helped Owen back to his feet. Hugging his ribs carefully, Owen gave me a small smile. "*Thank you*," he mouthed before limping away.

Another fight down. I was so over it.

For a brief terrifying second, I wondered if, because I'd beaten Owen, *I* was going to have to go up against Ambrose. But when Mayor McCoy read out the names, I realized it was *so* much worse.

"Grayson Shaw. Jasper Warren. Ring number three."

As I made my way to the ring, a flurry of thoughts raced through my mind. If fighting Owen had been hard, going up against Jasper would be impossible. I couldn't fight against my best friend—not when this moment meant so much more to him than me. And the fact that Jasper had made it through two rounds was a miracle. I wondered if he'd talked the five points out of his opponents. But Jasper . . . *God*, Jasper! I couldn't fight him! Anyone but him!

I gripped my sword and stared hard at Jasper. Jasper stared right back, giving me a shaky smile. He tilted his head to our judge. "That's how you can tell we're in the big leagues."

I looked to see Pa standing at the ring's edge, clipboard in one hand, watch in the other. Great. My pa had a front row seat to watch me completely unravel. Pa frowned at us, his hard eyes lingering on me. "You boys ready?" he asked as he shifted the equipment and rolled up his sleeves, revealing faded tattoos and old scars.

I said, "No," at the same time Jasper yelped, "Totally!" with an enthusiastic nod.

Pa looked back down at the watch. "Five minutes on the clock. Fight!"

I glanced from Pa, to Jasper, and back to Pa. "Wait, this isn't really happening, is it?" I looked hurriedly to Jasper. "We aren't actually going to fight, are we?"

In answer, Jasper hobbled over and punched me in the face.

A flash of pain erupted on my nose. I stumbled back with a choked groan, clutching my face. Jasper leaned over me, his gaze pleading. "I'm so sorry. Please don't hate me!"

"What the hell, Jasper!" I croaked, afraid to move my hand, afraid of what I might see.

Pa let out a breath dripping with disappointment. "That's one point for Mr. Warren."

I looked up to see Jasper swinging for my head. I ducked in time to miss it. "Seriously? Another headshot?" I finally lowered my wet hand and wiped it on my pants, hoping in vain that it was just sweat and nothing else.

"I'm sorry!" Jasper squeaked, aiming for me again.

The punch was a decoy. When I bent to avoid it, Jasper's sword came down, striking me in the back. I squawked as pain flared along my spine.

"One point for Mr. Warren," Pa bit out.

"Oh, God," Jasper whimpered. "Please don't hate me!"

I scuttled away, rubbing my back. "I'll hate you less if you stop hitting me."

Pa growled, and I could hear the clipboard creak underneath his grip. "That's . . ." He sighed, restraining his annoyance. "Another point for Mr. Warren."

Jasper lit up. "Wait, really?" Confusion snaked through his features, and he scratched his head. "What did I do?"

Pa stared at my feet, where I had one inside the ring and one out.

"Oh, come on!" I shouted as Jasper whooped and danced.

Pa glowered at me. "Are you going to join in on the fight anytime soon?"

I slapped my sword-free hand against my side, isolated in my frustration. "This is ridiculous. Everyone is being ridiculous."

"No," Pa ground out, nearly snapping the clipboard in half, "*you're* being ridiculous. This is a *challenge*." He flicked his head in Jasper's direction. "Hit him."

Jasper squawked and raised his sword with trembling hands. "I'm pretty sure a judge can't coach the hunters. There has to be a rule about it somewhere."

Pa's features darkened, but he pressed his lips together.

I glanced from my pa to Jasper. "Can't we just talk about this for a second?"

Pa shook his head. "You're at two minutes. Stop talking, and start fighting."

Jasper raced for me. I held up a hand, halting him in his tracks. "Just hold on, Jasper!" I said hoarsely, fighting the urge to hop back out of the ring.

Jasper groaned, butting his head up against his weapon in irritation. "If we don't hit each other, we *both* lose."

I lowered my arm, anger coursing through me. "Maybe we should."

Jasper faltered, lowering his sword. "What?"

Pa narrowed his eyes. "What?"

I shook my head, sending a shock of pain through my face. "What is the point of all this? What are we doing this for?" I pointed at Jasper. "I'm *fighting* my best friend!"

Jasper's mouth dropped open. He pointed at the betting board. "Uh, hello? To get higher up on the board?" He cocked his head to the side. "Don't you *want* people to bet on you?"

I laughed, sharp and brittle. "I don't want *anything* to do with this!"

And there it was, the truth in all its ugly glory. Pa went eerily still. Jasper nearly dropped his sword. I hung my head, shame burning my cheeks. "I don't want anything to do with this," I said again, more to myself than to them. It felt oddly liberating to say. I had been holding those words in since the Symbolic Sign-In, and the weight of them had been slowly crushing me. "I'm done."

The cheers of the crowd, which I had drowned out since my first fight with Peter, came roaring back. The force of it nearly took me off my feet. I blinked at them, trying to find a friendly face but finding none. They were all ravenous beasts. They were all vultures.

Pa slowly looked down at the watch. "You're at one minute," was all he said, and when he looked back up, he wouldn't meet my eyes.

Jasper looked at me pleadingly. "Grayson," he whispered. "Please!" He jabbed. My reflexes kicked in, and I stepped out of the way. He tried again, and I dove, narrowly missing a chop to the side.

"Thirty seconds."

Jasper limped after me, desperation clinging to his features. "If you're not going to fight, at least let *me* go to the next round!"

I came to a halt. Jasper had the decency of letting me turn to face him. We stared at each other, breathing hard, everything hurting, everything shaking.

"Twenty seconds. You still need two points if you wish to make it to the next round, Mr. Warren," Pa uttered, still not looking at me.

Jasper gritted his teeth and raised his sword.

I dropped mine. "I'm done fighting," I said. "I'm just . . . done."

For a brief, beautiful second, I saw Jasper's fingers loosen on the hilt, his vibrating arms lowering. I started to smile.

And then his blade came crashing down on my head, and everything went black.

THE SMELL OF BLOOD WAS EVERYWHERE.

I woke with a start, surging upward, swinging an invisible sword in my noodle arms.

"Easy there, tiger," a voice said from in front of me. Hands touched my chest, pressing me back down onto the sand. "You have quite the goose egg on your noggin'. No sudden movements for you!"

"Holly?" I croaked.

The voice chuckled. "No, silly."

My eyes snapped open. "Evanora?"

Staring down at me wasn't the mermaid, but Mr. Erlandson. I hadn't realized his voice was so . . . high-pitched. Mr. Erlandson frowned at me. "Evanora? Who's that?"

I let out a low groan, squeezing my eyes back shut. We were underneath the boardwalk, where the shadows hung like curtains and the sand was blessedly cool. "Just . . . a girl."

"Well," he chuckled. "She sounds like a peach. Ah ah ah!" he admonished, pulling my hand away from its journey up to my head. "No touching."

"It feels like a walrus jumped on my head."

Mr. Erlandson clucked his tongue soothingly. "I'll bet it does. I really don't think Jasper had to hit you as hard as he did. What a brute."

When I tried to rise again, Mr. Erlandson helped me up. "Thank you, Mr. Erlandson," I mumbled.

Mr. Erlandson waved a hand. "Please, call me Petrie."

I nodded, knowing I never would. Squinting at the beach, I saw a few lingering fights, but most hunters had joined the spectators, cheering them on. Some stood, heads bandaged, arms in slings. Most sat, nursing bruises or fussing over swollen joints. One man, coated in blood, boasted it wasn't his. I quickly looked away.

I was grateful the sand was black. I didn't want to see the carnage.

My eyes latched on to a group standing off to the side. Through the crowd, I could just make out Peter, shirt still off, dancing and deking, retelling the valiant moment when he'd decided to let me win. Owen leaned against a cane, rolling his good eye. Ambrose, looking relatively untouched, wasn't paying attention. He stared ahead, past the battling hunters, out into the ocean. Searching for something, coming up empty-handed.

I had to talk to him. Now, before anything else happened.

I rose to my feet. The ground immediately shifted, my vision swimming. Mr. Erlandson jumped up with a hearty yelp, stabilizing me with his tree-trunk arms. "Whoa there!" he chirped.

I steadied myself, breathing in deeply, letting it out slowly. "I'm all right," I promised. "I just need to talk to someone."

Mr. Erlandson let go reluctantly. "Be careful," he warned. "No—"

"Sudden movements. I got it. Thanks."

I ambled into the sunlight, shielding my eyes and hissing as a blade of pain wedged itself into my brain. Resisting the urge to touch the throbbing lump, I pressed on, threading through hunters and spectators alike. Ambrose shifted into focus. As if sensing my purposeful approach, he turned slowly, locking eyes with me. He watched as I drifted in and out of the crowd. Closer, closer—

I was back in the shade. Ambrose dissolved from view. I glanced up to see Pa blocking my path. I sighed, blinking slowly. "Not now, Pa."

"What did you mean, *I'm done*?" he seethed, reeking of quiet fury. "What did you mean, *I don't want anything to do with this*?"

I tried to step around him, but Pa matched me, lurching to the side and blocking me again. "I don't have time for this," I grumbled. "Please let me pass. Just for a second! Then I'll come back, and you can yell at me and tell me how much of a disappointment I am."

"A disappointment? A *disappointment*?" Pa caught his voice rising and stopped. He ran a hand through his hair, pulling several strands out of the topknot. "God. All our training. All those hours of preparation. And for what? For you to make a fool out of yourself? For you to embarrass me?"

I scoffed, rolling my eyes. The world spun. I squeezed them shut. "This isn't about *you*, Pa!" I paused, and when I was certain everything was motionless, I opened my eyes again. "And this isn't about Warrick anymore, is it?" I laughed, crossing my arms stiffly. "Was it ever really about him?"

Pa's shoulders heaved with rage. "What are you talking about? Of course it's about Warrick. We bled into his bowl. We made an oath for him."

"Playing along with the Hunt isn't going to bring him back!" I spat. "Nothing is!"

Pa surged forward, teeth bared, hands mangled claws. I stumbled back. Right into Mr. Grieves.

"My word!" He chuckled, forcing me upright. "Looks like someone has a bit of fight left in them! It's nice to see it wasn't completely beaten out of you." He frowned sympathetically. "I was sorry to hear that you lost against that Warren boy."

Pa stepped back, making a clear effort to smooth out his features and relax his hands. "Mr. Grieves," he mumbled pleasantly. "I was just having a conversation with my son."

Mr. Grieves smiled politely. "How nice!"

"A *private* one."

Mr. Grieves nodded. "You know, I was just coming over here to do the exact same thing." He placed a hand on my back, guiding me away from my pa. "It'll only take a second!" he called out over his shoulder.

Pa's face had turned completely red, and I didn't envy the conversation future me was going to have with him later.

I let Mr. Grieves take me even farther from Ambrose. "How can I help you, Mr. Grieves?" I asked, unease settling into my veins.

"No help required," he said jovially. "I just wanted to mention how disappointed I was in your performance today."

Annoyance flared in my gut, red spots dotting my eyes. "Well, get in line," I said curtly. "I'm disappointing a lot of people today."

Mr. Grieves laughed, taking my hand and patting the top of it. "Yes. Shameful, truly. After your strength in the net building and your strong intuition with the swimming challenge, I had rather hoped to see your grit on full display today. I wanted you to surprise me, but alas"—he winked at me—"you didn't."

Only Mr. Grieves could insult in such a casual manner, like he was discussing the weather, or what to have for lunch.

"I'm not really sure what you want me to say," I answered dumbly. "It just wasn't in the cards for me, I guess."

"It certainly wasn't," Mr. Grieves agreed somberly. "In fact, it almost looked like you gave up."

"I'm surprised you were able to keep such a close eye on me," I said before I could stop myself. "Considering you were participating in today's challenge as well."

"Oh, I see a great many things, young Shaw. A great many things, indeed." Mr. Grieves ruffled my hair; I jerked out of his reach as his fingers skimmed the throbbing goose egg. "Hopefully you can renew my faith in you during the Hunt." Mr. Grieves's smile was venomous. "I'll let you get back to your pa."

Mr. Grieves strolled away, whistling a merry tune amidst the bloody sand and yelps of pain. I glanced down the beach, hoping to see Ambrose where I had last spotted him. The section was empty. I cursed under my breath and went with my second-best option. "What happened to Rosemary?" I called out after Mr. Grieves.

Mr. Grieves's whistling stopped. He slowed, peering at me from over his shoulder with a concerned frown. "Why, she's missing, of course. Terribly dreadful, that."

I raised an eyebrow, challenging him. "Your son says otherwise."

Mr. Grieves gave a surprised laugh that didn't match the darkness collecting on his face. "Does he now? Very interesting." He rubbed his chin, pondering. "I'll have to chat with the boy, see if he knows something I don't. You know those mainland girls, always unpredictable." He laughed again and shrugged elegantly. "She probably whisked herself back to her home across the water."

I cocked my head to the side, paused for a heavy second, and spoke. "But the ferry isn't running." I said the words slowly, letting them sink into Mr. Grieves one by one, letting him know that something was amiss, and I was aware. "The ferry only begins to run after the Hunt, doesn't it? Or . . ." I crossed my arms. "Is there another way off the island?" *Like in a casket?*

Mr. Grieves's smile stiffened, and for an instant, a snag of frozen time, I saw the burning rage underneath his carefully placed features. "Well," he said quietly, "it appears that you, too, see a great many things." He tilted his face up, appraising me. "Be careful, Mr. Shaw; seeing too much can get you into trouble."

CHAPTER FIFTY-FIVE

EVANORA

APRIL 20 – MORNING

EVERYTHING WAS NUMB, WHICH WAS PROBABLY A GOOD thing. I didn't want to feel anything.

Word of Jorah's death spread with the current, a dark whisper carried along the grains of sand. The kingdom crumbled quickly. First came the frantic questions, drowning with fear. Then the shouting—desperate, demanding answers, grasping for a different truth. When no other answer came, the wailing began.

Grief tore through the city, dragging uncontrolled magic in its wake. The water quivered as water wielders thrashed through the undertow. High-pitched shrieks echoed within our minds, threatening to unravel what remained of our sanity. Sirens sang their lamentations, their voices summoning whirlpools that tore through the depths.

And I was numb.

I sat alone in the garden. The pod needed their queen, their leader, but I was in no shape to address them. How could I? Without Jorah there, I was just as lost as they were.

The octopus was with me. Sensing my distress, it sprawled on my lap, clinging to my scales. The tips of its limbs fluttered up and down gently, attempting to console me. It looked at me with its large, infinite eyes, as if to say, *There, there. I'm here.*

I stared ahead blankly, absentmindedly rubbing its bulbous head. First my parents. Now Jorah. I was officially alone. I had never felt so isolated, trapped on the throne I never wanted, ruling over a pod I was not fit to rule. Hiding in my garden, I was a coward.

Jorah had not slipped peacefully into death. He had been torn from life, and I had done nothing but watch. I was a failure.

The sounds of hysteria increased. I closed my eyes, hugged the octopus against my chest, and cried.

Illeron shot into the garden. I hadn't even heard him coming. His entrance was vicious and unexpected. The octopus spooked out of my arms, shooting away in a burst of ink. I waved the cloud away, hurriedly wiped my eyes, and looked at the warrior.

I was expecting a stern mermaid, hell-bent on verbally beating some sense of duty into me. With Jorah gone, maybe Illeron felt an obligation to step up as my grouchy guide. I expected to see feral anger etched into his stony features, the words *duty* and *honor* and *leader* pouring out of his lips before he even came to a complete stop.

What I saw was horror. Pure, unfiltered horror.

The warrior hovered in front of me, breathing hard. The grip on his spear was iron, but the entire weapon shook with his poorly concealed fear. Illeron's face was stripped of all color, his eyes wide and wild, his mouth pinched so tightly that lines creased at the corners.

I was immediately at attention. "What is it?"

Illeron glanced over his shoulder, his hair whipping with the jerky movement. "You need to come quickly. The pod . . . They are . . ." He looked back at me, sorrowful, terrified, a merling back at the Barrens, frozen in place on a dare. *"Leaving!"* he finished in my mind.

I was up and swimming before the word had time to settle through the fog of grief swirling around me.

The pod had gathered in the kingdom's central square, squished next to the fountain, trailing up the stairs to the palace. They were talking quickly, clinging to one another. Some carried a few precious belongings. Others held swords and spears. All were crazed, possessed by an otherworldly terror.

I swept up the stairs, stopping at the palace pillars. "What is going on?" I demanded as I reached the top.

Mavi hurried up the steps to me. "I tried to convince them, Evanora. But . . . But they just won't listen!"

I pulled Mavi close. Her entire body was shaking, and broken whimpers slipped off her tongue. Illeron came to a halt at my other side. We hovered, staring down at the kingdom square. The three of us against the entire pod. It was beyond pathetic.

The crowd drifted into silence. No one would meet my eyes. I growled impatiently. "Well?" I called out. "Have you no nerve to speak to your queen?"

One of the pod members swam forward. They were wringing their hands together, their gaze downcast. "We are leaving, Your Majesty."

I looked at the mermaid, at the stiff curl of his deep red tail, the twitch of his hands. "To where?"

The mermaid looked at the others, and with a forlorn sigh, he drifted back into the crowd, all strength sapped from underneath my pensive stare. Another rose to the challenge and spoke up from the back, her voice high and shrill. "The Barrens, Your Majesty."

It was an effort to keep my forearm fins from flaring. "Do you wish for death?" I asked simply.

A ripple of whispers shuddered through the pod. "We are dead if we stay here!" the mermaid cried out in response. "Jorah is gone, and our hope of surviving has died with him." Her words seemed to surprise her, but they were out in the open, hanging over our heads in the water, and there was no way she could retrieve them.

I shook my head slowly. "Jorah's passing is devastating, but it was inevitable. He was a dead fish swimming long before the Dark Madness claimed him."

There was a cluster of audible gasps in the crowd. "Have you no shame? No respect for the dead?" one pod member yelled. "His body is not yet cold, and you offend his name!"

"Right now"—I raised my voice to be heard above the clamor—"my focus is on *you*. My pod, alive in front of me. To go into the Barrens is suicide, and I will not allow it."

"We are lost without Jorah!" a mermaid said near the front.

"I am your queen!" I roared. My magic rippled, and the pod quaked underneath my authority. "Jorah wasn't your leader. *I* am. Jorah didn't have a final say in caring for the pod. *I* do."

"Jorah was here far more than you ever were!" a voice rang out in the pod, and the crowd uttered their agreement. "Jorah actually cared for us! He didn't sneak off to the island to mingle with *humans*."

Beside me, Illeron cringed. What sort of tales had he been telling in anger? I offered him a scathing side-eye before turning back to the pod.

"Regardless," I said, holding my head high, "it is far too dangerous to swim into the Barrens—too unpredictable." I tried to pin each and every one of them with a heavy stare; there were so few left, I almost could. "Whether you consider me to be your rightful ruler or not, trust me when I say the Barrens are not to be trifled with."

The pod stilled, torn between fear and desperation.

Then a young voice piped up, tentative and trembling. "It is daylight," he said hopefully. "We have time to make it through." He looked at his ammah, his mouth quivering. "Don't we?"

Andoras clutched his ammah's hand, looking timid and so severely small. My heart ached at the sight of him.

"Don't you think we would have made the journey already if we deemed it possible?" Illeron interjected at my side.

"It doesn't matter that it is daylight." I sighed, straining to keep my voice a quiet, gentle thing for the merling. "I have reason to believe that the Cursed Beings are still awake during the day. Daylight will not aid you. In the realm of darkness, you will still be in danger."

"How can you possibly know that?" Andoras's ammah called out.

"Because . . ." I took a breath, stilling the sudden rise of nausea. "I have seen them. I have heard them."

The cursed memories came in a tidal wave.

Their touch on my tail as I rescued Solandis—cold and venomous, leaving trails of black death.

Their whispers, slipping out from the black abyss and into the daylight.

Their gnarled, sinewy hands grabbing Jorah, dragging him down, down, down.

The way those same hands had reached for Grayson, begging for a piece of him. Their chorus of voices singing to the boy, a lullaby of demise.

Andoras's ammah shook her head. "It is too late for you to try to guide us now, Evanora. We are your pod no longer."

I blinked, ripped out of my thoughts, and watched with growing dread as the pod began to pull away, swimming around the palace, aiming for the edge of our kingdom.

I saw faces contorted in anxiety, in bravery. I saw backs rigid and straight, others bent, resigned to the unknown that awaited them.

I saw death.

"What should we do?" Illeron gasped, his eyes snapping from the dwindling pod to me.

My mouth hung open, but no words slipped out. No ideas, no demands to stay, no pleas to avoid certain death. I watched in a frozen horror as Andoras was pulled away by his ammah, his face crumpled in misery. His mouth moved, and though his words never reached my ears, I knew, in my heart, what he was saying: *I'm sorry. I'm . . . sorry!*

"Evanora!" Illeron barked at my side. "What should we do?"

But I was a merling again, begging my parents to stay when they wanted to talk peace with the humans, crying tears they couldn't see.

Some of the pod had remained, my words holding anchor in their souls, but the number was dreadfully small in comparison to the amount that had left. We all watched in a stupor as the last of the mermaids slid over the cliff and into the Barrens without even a backward glance.

There was silence, and I held my breath, allowing a thimble of hope to bloom within me.

Maybe I was wrong. Maybe everything I knew about the Barrens and the Cursed Beings was wrong. Maybe the pod would make it out alive.

And then the screaming started.

CHAPTER FIFTY-SIX

EVANORA

APRIL 20 – MORNING

I DIDN'T THINK—I JUST MOVED.

I was following the screams, racing for the bitter dark.

"Evanora, no!" Illeron yelled, but his voice hardly registered. He was far behind me, an infinite distance away. He'd never be able to catch up.

And even if he could, he'd never be able to stop me.

The Barrens were upon me. I didn't give myself a second to reconsider my actions, didn't let the fear sink in. The pod was all that mattered. I knew the Cursed Beings loathed my light. If I used my powers, I could swim in, find the mermaids, and hurry them back to safety. I only prayed that I'd reach them in time, that the magic would last long enough. I couldn't handle any more death; I refused to let any of them go the way Jorah had.

I rushed into the darkness, pushing every ounce of my Gift to the surface. My light came forth like a cannon blast, piercing the depths of unspeakable black. It was stronger since the last time I had entered the Barrens, and the shadows instantly hissed and shrank away, long inky arms darting out of sight.

I blinked into the abyss, forcing my eyes to adjust. My ears filled with the sounds of terror, pain, and regret.

I looked around, my head swiveling, trying to find the mermaids that the horrified sounds belonged to.

They were everywhere. *Pieces* of them were everywhere.

I was too late.

A guttural sob ripped from my throat. *No*, I moaned inwardly, trying to catch movement that didn't belong to the Cursed Beings. *No, no, no!*

A mermaid streaked by me, wailing at the top of her lungs as blood-drenched claws raced after her. Another spun in frantic circles, his shredded fluke trailing crimson threads into the abyss. He turned and turned, as if the motion could somehow undo his doom. A third surged toward me, arms outstretched, desperation etched into every movement. She reached for my light, but her scream was ripped from her throat as shadowy hands shot up from the depths. They coiled around her waist like eels, dragging her into the blackness before she could even register the pain.

The arms were like tentacles, the hands like hungry mouths. They arced from the black void, sailing with a fluidity that made my skin crawl, my insides retch, my heart roar. One by one, they grabbed the defenseless mermaids, batting them around like playthings before sinking back into the dark. There were fewer cries of distress. Soon it would be silent again.

Dead. We were all dead. We just didn't know it yet.

No! I swallowed the terror rising in my throat, forcing my nerves into submission. *Not yet!*

Flashing my Gift like a beacon, I called out, "To me! To me!"

A garbled gasp came from my right. A strangled howl erupted to my left. A figure with pink-tipped fins slammed into my light, trembling and blood-ied. Daithi, the water wielder who had threatened me during the swimming challenge, now clutched the side of her face, where a vicious gash oozed dark ribbons of red. Her right eye was sunken, her eyelid a mangled mess. Her usual look of disdain was gone, replaced by sheer agony.

She stumbled into my arms, her breath ragged. "There are more," she croaked, black hair streaking my shoulder with blood. "Help them, please!"

I nodded tightly, swallowing hard against the lump in my throat. To-gether, we swam through the chaos, calling out for survivors, pulling them into my light.

More mermaids rushed into my beacon: Nienna, though her parents were nowhere to be seen; Andoras's ammah, but not Andoras himself; a handful of warriors; two water wielders; three sirens; one mind bender. My light became a sanctuary for the broken and battered. We drifted upward, the cliff's edge painfully close yet impossibly far.

Behind us, the screams of the lost rang out, begging me to turn back. Each cry tore at me, but I forced myself to swim onward, praying I could save more before it was too late.

At last, we breached the ledge. The pod members who had remained behind stared at us in stunned silence, their expressions a blend of relief and horror. Illeron was the first to move, lurching forward to take Daithi's limp body from my arms. His glare turned on the frozen crowd.

"Well, don't just float there," he barked. "Move! Do something!"

The others shifted into action, swarming us, collecting the mermaids too broken to swim on their own, guiding the ones who still could. Soon, the entire cliffside was littered with bodies. The second the last mermaid exited my bubble of light, I turned back to the Barrens.

There was a hand on my elbow. "Evanora," Illeron pleaded, sensing my desire to willingly throw myself back into the dark, "don't. It's too dangerous."

I looked at the warrior, at his strong, handsome, worried face. I felt eerily calm. "I'm going back."

Illeron's grip tightened. He shook his head viciously. "Please, Evanora, no! It's no use!" He leaned in, stroking my face with his free hand. I could feel his fingertips slide over the blood that didn't belong to me. It was like he was trying to memorize me, like he'd never get the opportunity to touch me again. "We can't lose you too," he finished in a desperate whisper.

I wrenched myself free, pulling out of Illeron's grasp. "I'm going back!"

And I did. Again, and again, and again. The Cursed Beings figured out my rescue mission and howled in misery as I took away their toys. I tuned them out, listening only for the screams. The Cursed Beings began to work faster, and so did I.

I was lightning in the dark, a ghost, a white-hot rage. "Just one more time," I kept telling myself when everything began to hurt, when each trip became more and more of a struggle. "Just one more time, then I can rest."

In and out. Up and down. Searching, saving, and returning to the light. That was all I knew, all I could focus on. I found a group of five mind benders huddled near the ledge that Solandis had fallen on top of forever ago, then a mix of three water wielders and three sirens scurrying deeper into the abyss, disoriented in their confusion. There was a small army of ten warriors trying their best to fight the Cursed Beings. By the time I got to them and surrounded them in my shroud of light, there were only five.

In and out. Up and down. Over and over. Until my light began to flicker. Until my tail went numb with exhaustion. Until the screaming stopped.

And it stopped much too soon.

The howling, however, went on until it was burned into my memory, until it was all I could hear.

By the time I had collected the last living mermaid and returned them to the cliffside, my Gift had completely extinguished, and I had only saved a third of my entire pod.

I knew I should have thanked the gods for letting me go on for as long as I did. But it was hard to make room for gratefulness in the midst of all my agony.

A third of my pod. The rest were dead with their limbs ripped off, their throats slashed, their blood dripping into a greedy dark that could never be fully satiated.

And I couldn't bear it.

I couldn't possibly bear it anymore.

CHAPTER FIFTY-SEVEN

GRAYSON

APRIL 21 – MORNING

THE DOCK WAS UNUSUALLY QUIET, LIKELY BECAUSE MOST of the workers were at home nursing injuries from the combat challenge. Even Mr. Brightly only emerged from his office when absolutely necessary. He'd taken a nasty hit to the back of the neck, and even though Dr. Peele had warned him that he was a sneeze away from paralysis, he still showed up to work, neck brace and all.

It was a strange contrast. Yesterday, we were at each other's throats, desperate to draw blood, to earn that winning point. Today? Business as usual.

My head throbbed. The sun mocked me with its unfiltered brilliance, each ray a piercing taunt. Even the thought of moving sent sharp, biting aches through my limbs. Staying home had been tempting, but the idea of disappointing Pa further had dragged me out of bed—albeit slower than usual.

It was too much work to concentrate on anything else other than the throbbing that vibrated down my rigid spine. I stared at the net in my hands, fighting the urge to touch the swollen lump on my head for the umpteenth time. Jasper was down the dock, sweeping at nothing, torn between pretending I didn't exist, and casting sorrowful glances my way when he thought I wouldn't notice.

I noticed.

But I was better at playing pretend. The silence felt good, a balm for my pounding head. I didn't want to relive yesterday—hit by hit, move by move, every gory, humiliating detail Jasper was clearly itching to recount. If he tried, I couldn't promise I wouldn't hurl myself off the dock.

Jasper broke first. He swept closer, pretending to study the dusty planks, whistling a made-up tune. When he finally reached me, he sucked in a breath, squared his crooked shoulders, and glared at me with all the courage his wiry frame could muster. "Are you mad at me?"

I slowly looked up from the untouched net and stared carefully at Jasper. I waited for a beat, watching the bravado drain from his face, the fidgeting shift of his feet, before speaking. "Mad? Why would I be mad?"

Jasper scratched his head awkwardly, cringing underneath the weight of my steady glare. "Because . . ." He blew out a sputtering breath, his lips flapping. "I beat your ass senseless yesterday?"

I held up a finger. "First of all, you beat me *after* I had set down my weapon. Hitting a defenseless fighter is supremely distasteful."

"You said you were *done*!"

"Secondly"—I held up a second finger, then groaned, rubbing the back of my neck as another stabbing pain raked down my spinal column—"did you *really* have to hit me so hard?"

The last of Jasper's flimsy courage left, and he crumpled to my feet, clasping his hands together, blubbering like an absolute idiot. "I'm so sorry! I just wanted those last points so *bad*! I didn't think I hit you that hard, but then you let out this weird groaning noise and dropped like a bag of potatoes and—oh, God! It was awful! You fell so hard! I thought I killed you for a second, I really did! And your pa awarded me the points but I didn't even *want* the points after that." He looked at me, blinking away tears. "I just wanted my best friend back."

I wanted to stay mad at him, but Jasper—sweet, stupid Jasper—was making it really hard. So, instead, I started to laugh. It almost felt as good as the silence, save for the sudden burning ache in my shoulder. "God, you're a goof."

The relief that washed over Jasper was like a tsunami. He let out a heartfelt sigh and clambered to his feet. "So . . . you forgive me?"

I rubbed at the ache in my shoulder and nodded. "How far did you make it?"

Jasper got bashful. He picked up the broom and spun it in his hands. "Only until the next round. I was up against Ambrose. How unfair is that?"

"Well," I said, picking up the net, "you *are* in the same age category."

Jasper shuddered. "It was terrifying. I saw my life flash before my eyes. I kept hopping out of the ring just to avoid getting clobbered. I didn't even realize I was doing it."

"I'll bet that did wonders for your score on the betting board."

Jasper began to sweep with conviction, sending dust everywhere. "Mark my words: If I could do it all over again—"

"You'd do the exact same thing," I interjected with a chuckle.

Jasper pondered my words, then made a jerky motion with his head and shoulders, a nod and shrug all crammed into one. "Probably, yeah." He started to sweep again, only to stop after two brushstrokes. "Ambrose ended up making top three. Can you believe that?"

I raised my eyebrows, remembering the haunted look in his pale blue eyes. "I can. Who made first and second?"

Jasper rolled his eyes. "Mr. Grieves got first." He waved his arms mockingly. "Shocker. And some girl from Fariid got second. Elena Doyle, or Delaney, or something."

I whistled appreciatively. "Wow. Don't mess with her."

"You're telling me! She could squish my head to a pulp with her thighs."

"Considering it's *your* head in between her thighs, I wouldn't blame her."

"Hardy har har." Jasper resumed sweeping. "She's not my type."

I laughed. "Why? Because she's real?"

Jasper pointed a finger aggressively at me. "I'll get a girl one of these days, Shaw. Just you wait!" He shrugged nonchalantly, twirling the broom around like a dancing partner. "Maybe at the Night of the Betting. Or the Final Festival." He winked at me. "Girls love being with guys before they go off to war. I read that in a book."

I scoffed, focusing on the net. "Sounds really romantic."

"Doesn't it?" Jasper sighed dreamily.

I felt eyes on me. Not Jasper—he was busy waltzing with his broom. And Mr. Brightly was still holed up in his office. My gaze swept the docks, the stone steps, the walkway curving into town.

Then I looked into the water, and I saw her.

Evanora.

She barely broke the surface, the gentle waves licking her jaw and tugging at her hair, pulling the strands toward the depths. Her eyes locked on mine, filled with a desperation so raw, so consuming, I could feel it across the distance. It wasn't just longing—it was something primal, a need that transcended words.

Evanora bobbed in place, holding my gaze for a dangerously long moment before she let the water overtake her and she slipped underneath the waves. When she resurfaced, she was farther out, near the curve of the island where jagged rocks thrust out toward the entrance of Bristling Bay. She rose as if conjured by the ocean itself, her skin glistening under the sunlight. Her head turned slightly, her chin resting delicately on her shoulder, and time seemed to shatter. No, not shatter—it ceased to exist. Until I spoke to her, nothing else would matter again.

She dipped under an approaching wave, and time jolted back to life, cruel and disjointed.

I stood up. The net dropped from my lap with a clatter. Jasper stopped his dancing to frown at me. "Where are you going?"

"I'll be right back," I said, my eyes not leaving the spot where Evanora had just been.

"Wait—" Jasper scoffed, looking around. "What if Mr. Brightly comes out to check on us? What am I supposed to tell him?"

"I don't know. Lie."

I quickened my pace, every ache in my body muffled to a distant echo. All I could hear was my rabid heart. All I could see were the droplets of water on Evanora's skin, the sun's rays kissing her. And nothing else mattered.

I followed the walkway toward Bristling Bay, clambering over rocks as I neared the water's edge. My thoughts ambushed me, hateful and unwelcome.

What are you doing? my mind demanded. *You're mad at her, remember? Did that blow to your head make you forget that small detail?*

My heart quickly stepped up to the challenge. *She seemed upset. And for her to visit us at the docks during the day . . . We should at least see what's wrong. It might be important.*

Almost as important as her using you? my mind interjected. *The last time you saw her, you said you wanted nothing to do with her.* If my mind could cackle, it would have. *Way to stick to your boundaries.*

I felt like I was having a full-on Jekyll-and-Hyde experience. I hadn't realized two parts of me could disagree on a single topic so ferociously. Still, I kept moving, inching closer to the water. Because I knew, whether all of me wanted to or not, I had to see her.

I stepped onto one of the lowest rocks and hunkered down on my heels. I glanced around, and when I was certain no hungry eyes were watching, I uttered, "It's okay. You can come out now."

Evanora emerged silently, her sudden proximity earning a sharp intake of breath from me—not because she was too close, but because of the jolt she sent through me. The sight of her was electric, a zap deep in my chest that ignited my blood.

The connection between us stirred—damaged, fragile, but alive.

Evanora rose from the water, her shoulders and chest gleaming. Droplets trailed down her pale cheeks, pooling in her collarbones and tangling in the delicate gills along her neck. She was close—an arm's reach away—but remained purposefully distant. Her face was unreadable, wiped clean of emotion by the waves, but her eyes betrayed her. They spoke volumes, worlds, eternities.

I wanted her to speak. God, I wanted it so badly. I wanted to hear the lyrical tones of her voice, the gentle lullaby wrapped around each word. I wanted to hear the chimes of her laughter, the soft sighs of her breath.

Evanora bit her lip, the first sign of her meticulously blank facade crumbling. "You said you would've helped me end the Hunt if I had only asked." She blinked, tears spilling down her pale cheeks. "Well, I'm asking now, Grayson Shaw."

I RETURNED TO THE DOCKS IN A FOG, EVANORA'S WORDS SWARMING my throbbing brain.

Her advisor's death.

Her pod abandoning the kingdom.

The Cursed Beings attacking during the day.

So much loss. So much bloodshed.

Evanora didn't have to explain herself—I'd decided the moment I saw her drifting by the docks that I would help her. No matter what it cost. My job, Pa's dwindling respect, my own safety—it didn't matter. Nothing mattered except ending the Hunt.

I only hoped we had enough time.

I'd wanted to stay with her, but it wasn't safe. We agreed to meet at our beach under the cover of night. There, in the shadows, we could share everything—our truths, our fears—away from prying eyes and judgmental tongues.

As she vanished beneath the waves, I had a feeling that the hours until nightfall would stretch endlessly.

I returned to work, my hands clumsy as I tried to mend the nets. I listened to Jasper ramble about foolproof ways to make a girl fall in love with him, but my thoughts never left Evanora.

The stars would come, and under their watchful gaze, it would be like before. Before the lies. Before the betrayal. Before the heartbreak.

None of it mattered anymore.

All that mattered was Evanora.

In a sea of chaos, confusion, and fear, there was only her.

CHAPTER FIFTY-EIGHT

EVANORA

APRIL 21 – EVENING

GRAYSON WAS WAITING FOR ME AT THE BEACH.

The sight of him standing there, kicking at loose stones with his hands in his pockets, his eyes furtively glancing at the open ocean, nearly brought me to tears. A large part of me hadn't expected to find him there; on my swim over, I had already begun to build up a reserve of disappointment to wallow in.

But there he was. His trousers were rolled up over his boots, a navy jacket to ward off the night's chill, and a cap trapping those unruly brown curls. He paced near the wildflowers, crushing them beneath his boots, his gaze lingering on the water but his feet avoiding it. I could see the hesitation in every stiff movement, and I couldn't blame him.

I swam closer, and Grayson stopped. He watched me warily as I pulled myself onto the wet sand, the waves nudging me along. I smoothed my scales, fiddled with the bracelet on my wrist, and tugged my damp hair over one shoulder. I knew I was supposed to speak first, but the words wouldn't come. *Hello* seemed far too casual, and rehashing the unspeakable events of the past few days felt even worse.

Start with the truth, my heart tried.

So, I did. Still playing with my hair, I trailed my eyes up Grayson's body, peeking at him from beneath my snowy eyelashes. "I didn't think you'd come," I confessed quietly.

The boy seemed to relax at the sound of my voice; the rigidness of his shoulders wilted, and he bowed his head, letting out a gentle chuckle. "I'm a little surprised to see you myself." He looked up, tapping on his chest, his heart buried underneath. "My heart told me to stay, that you'd show up." His smile grew uncertain. "That must sound stupid."

"No." I shook my head vehemently. "No, not at all." I wiggled up the beach, leaving a deep groove in the sand. Grayson didn't step toward me, but he didn't step away either. I counted that as a win. "You were right," I admitted. "There is something between us. I don't know what it is, or why it's there, or why it's with you . . ." I sighed, shifting my shoulders up to my ears. "All I know is that it was agonizing when the connection was severed. Every part of me ached with the broken threads. It felt like . . . like part of me was missing suddenly. Like I wasn't . . ."

"Whole," Grayson finished for me.

Holding his burning gaze, I nodded slowly. "Yes. Exactly that."

A light blush coated the boy's cheeks. "It still hurts a little," he whispered.

Pain bloomed in my chest. I wanted to reach for him, to hold him, to be held. "I suspect it does," I said. I slumped forward, rubbing my forehead. "I didn't mean to hurt you the way I did. I wish you could see that I was doing it for my pod." My skin prickled, but I didn't stop. I deserved the sting. "I didn't realize I'd come to care for you as much as I did." My laugh was a brittle thing. "But I did. I couldn't fight it or ignore it. It was always there, pushing and pulling, threatening to break free. Every time I looked at you, it was like my whole being wanted to shatter."

There was movement, and then Grayson's hand was on mine, pulling it away from my face. He held it carefully, though not because he thought I was fragile, or because I was some wild, untamable creature. He was afraid of me; I could feel it coursing through him. Still, he remained crouched, lacing our fingers together, intent on not letting the nerves win. Such a small act of courage, yet my heart swelled from it.

"You weren't supposed to be this wonderful," I said, the words escaping with a sob. "You were part of a plan, a job, and I wasn't supposed to feel this way about you."

Grayson tucked his free hand underneath my chin and tilted my face upward. He stared at me, his features carved from stone. His silence was ridiculously hard to read. Gods, I wanted him to speak, to yell, to demand an apology. The silence would drive me mad. The way I was blubbering like a fool, I suspected it already had. But I had started, and now that the words were pouring out, it would be impossible to stop them.

"I want you to understand, but I don't expect you to. I want you to forgive me, but I don't expect that either." I gave him a small smile, turning my face into his trembling fingers. "All I ask is this one kindness: Help me end the Hunt. We can work together, and when we are done, we can sever the connection." My smile began to wobble. "We will never have to see each other again."

Grayson's face remained fixed in darkness for a long moment before he closed his eyes, letting out a low breath. "Is that what you truly want?" he asked, his thumb sliding against my jawline.

The connection hummed with life. "It doesn't matter what I want."

Grayson leaned in, his lips dangerously close to mine. His blue eyes flicked up and down my face. "I want to know," he said softly. "Do you really never want to see me again?"

His words were kindling, his touch was a spark, and all of me was on fire. "No," I answered truthfully. "No, I don't want that. Not in a million years, a million lifetimes, do I want that."

Grayson's mouth quirked to the side. "Me neither."

My eyebrows shot up, a light gasp on my tongue. "Really?"

Grayson sighed, pressing his forehead to mine. "Evanora, there's nothing you could say or do that could push me away forever. We're linked, you and I. Whether I want to be or not, my heart will always lead me back to you." He pulled away just enough to meet my gaze, his eyes glinting with unshed tears. "These past few days were torture. I felt like I was dying. Like there was no reason to go on. But now . . ." He pressed our joined hands against his chest, his heartbeat thundering beneath my palm. "Now I can breathe again. I have a reason to breathe again."

He lifted my hand to his lips, kissing each finger slowly, reverently. "I'm yours, Evanora. My heart. My soul." His voice dropped, thick and warm. "Even my body, if you have a use for it."

The boy's eyes flicked upward, and my breath caught in my throat.

I was wrong.

It wasn't fear he was feeling.

It was hunger.

I wanted more than anything to be the one to satiate him. I wanted him to touch me, to feel each and every one of my scales, to run his fingers along my fins. I wanted to feel his lips on more than just my fingers. I wanted him. Gods, I wanted him, and I would never be content until I had him.

It felt like everything in our lives had been leading up to this one moment, a prelude to the line that, once crossed, we would not be able to backtrack over.

"We shouldn't," I whispered, allowing the boy to slowly pull me closer.

"We should," Grayson replied, tilting his head ever so slightly to the side.

"Could be dangerous," I said softly, trailing my hands up Grayson's back, relishing the shudder that followed my wake.

"I'm counting on it," Grayson said, cupping my face with his hands.

Closer, closer, closer. Until there was no space left, until we shared the same breath, until time stood still. We were on a precipice, staring over the edge. Grayson was asking me to leap off into the unknown with him.

Gods, if only he knew that I was already in a free fall.

"Grayson—"

His mouth was on mine, hot and slippery and pure heaven.

My heart was a weapon, threatening to carve through my chest in order to be with his. The pain was euphoric. The pain was liberating. The pain screamed, *I'm alive, I'm alive, I'm alive.*

Grayson groaned, a low, primal sound that sent shivers through me. His hands slipped from my cheeks into my hair, his fingers tugging, tangling, caressing. A soft croon escaped my lips, my skin prickling with ice as fire roared beneath. My mouth opened—a silent invitation he accepted eagerly. His tongue brushed mine, tentative but electric. I answered with a purr, a melody of silk, and he devoured the sound greedily.

His hands left my hair and began trailing down my spine, tracing the subtle ridges of bone. I arched, aching for more, more, *more*, knowing it would never be enough.

The boy tasted like the earth. Rich grass and wildflowers and sunlight. Like all things forbidden yet coveted. I could get drunk off his taste alone, yet I knew it wouldn't stop there. It couldn't. I wouldn't allow it. I slipped my hands up his chest, feeling the tight skin, the taut muscles coiling underneath. When I shuffled them roughly over his shoulders, Grayson obeyed, ripping off his jacket without breaking the kiss. When I returned to his chest and began clawing at the thin fabric that separated my skin from his, Grayson listened, tearing through the buttons on his shirt like it didn't matter. I could hear the plastic pieces plinking off nearby rocks, getting swallowed by the waves, never to be seen again.

"The plan," I whispered weakly against the boy's lips. "We need to go over the plan."

"Not yet," Grayson managed to say between fervent kisses. "Not yet."

His skin gleamed like milk under the moonlight, faint blue veins pulsing with the rhythm of his heartbeat. He was trembling—not from cold, but from the weight of us. I pressed myself to him, water meeting land, two souls fusing into one. He moaned at the contact, and the sound sent a jolt through me.

My body sparked, tensing as Grayson's teeth drew my bottom lip into his mouth. I could feel it—my Gift, bursting at the seams, threatening to spill over. I started to squirm, an anxious whimper ripping out of my throat as the boy released my lip and buried his face into the crook of my neck. His breath was quick and warm against my gills. He ran his tongue beside the delicate skin. I heaved viciously, digging my claws into his pale flesh.

"Grayson," I moaned. "I can't . . . My Gift . . . It's going to . . ." Gods, when had speaking become so hard? Not a single coherent thought could settle on my tingling tongue. My mind was full of Grayson, Grayson, Grayson.

"It's okay," Grayson breathed into my neck. "Let go. I want you to let go."

And I did. Light erupted from within me, a shock of pure energy that lit the night like dawn. Grayson gasped, his hands tightening on me as wave after wave of magic poured from my body. I convulsed with the sheer force of it, a cry of ecstasy breaking free. When the light finally ebbed, leaving only a faint crackle in its wake, Grayson found me again—hungry, desperate, unrelenting. I chuckled softly, wrapping my arms around him, ready to give him eternity.

A rogue wave surged onto the beach, splashing us. Grayson pulled back with a startled cry, water dripping from his curls and chest. I should have felt guilty, but all I felt was desire. Leaning in, I licked the salty trails left behind, tasting the ocean on his skin. His tension melted as he laughed quietly, his anxiety fading under my touch.

"I think the world is telling us to slow down," he whispered hoarsely as I pulled off his hat and squeezed the remaining drops out of his hair.

"Or," I countered, dropping my voice low, "it's telling us to keep going. I like my interpretation better."

Grayson laughed again as I sucked the water off my fingers. "No. You're right—we need to go over the plan." His laughter drifted into a sultry sigh as I flicked my tongue against his bottom lip, capturing a stray droplet. "You are going to be the death of me if you keep doing that."

I grinned, nipping his lip playfully before pulling away. "Then it'll be a most pleasant death."

The boy leaned back on his hands and reluctantly turned his gaze away from me to stare out into the black mouth of water. "It's already so dark out," he said with a whistle. He eyed the unblinking moon. "It won't be safe for you to return home."

I hummed coyly, sidling closer to the boy and running a finger down his chest. "I had no intention of returning home, Grayson Shaw," I admitted quietly, my eyes saying all the things my mouth wouldn't.

Grayson sucked in a hitching breath, and I could tell it took everything within him not to pull me close, search for the not-so-hidden meaning behind my words. He shook his head. "Truly, the death of me."

"It should at least please you to know that I would mourn forever."

The boy's mouth quirked to the side, and he reached forward, pushing a strand of hair behind my ear. "Forever is an awfully long time, you know."

I smiled, but it was a fleeting thing. "I know more than most, I suppose."

Grayson's face dipped into shadow. The meaning was on full display now, and neither of us cared for it. He cleared his throat. "Is your pod safe without you?"

I nodded, relieved for the conversation shift. I didn't want to be reminded of Grayson's horrifically short lifespan compared to my practically immortal one. "Yes," I said quickly. "I made sure all the lanterns were lit. But, as a safety precaution, I had one of the warriors make sure the path to the cave was clear in case everyone needed to evacuate at a moment's notice." I bit back a giggle at the boy's blank face. "None of that makes sense to you."

"Not even a little bit." He scratched his head, grinning sheepishly. "But it sounds like they are in good hands."

I softened, thinking back to how tender Illeron had been since Jorah's passing. He was constantly undertail, doing everything he could think of to make my life easier. He hadn't been particularly agreeable when I told him about my plan to see Grayson again, but after the nightmare in the Barrens, he knew better than to speak up. We were out of options, and we were running out of time.

"Yes," I agreed quietly. "Yes, they are."

Grayson placed a hand on my tail. Such a simple act, yet it sent my scales wilting, my skin vibrating, my heart bursting. He rose to his feet, severing the contact, and it honestly felt like a wound splitting open. I tried to hide my disappointment as I traced the outline of where his hand had been. "Off home, then?" I forced a smile. "You must be tired. It's been a long day for you."

The boy made a quizzical face. "What? No. We still have a great many things to discuss." He gave me a devilish grin, his eyes dripping over my body. "Amongst other things."

I giggled, settling back onto my hands. I was the picture of nonchalance, though every part of me was throbbing with want. "I'll be here in the morning. We can sort things out then."

Grayson shook his head. "Don't be silly. Time is of the essence. Besides," he said, smiling shyly, "I want to be with you. For as long as I can."

I pursed my lips, trying to hide my grin. "All right, Grayson Shaw."

The boy began to walk toward the steps before quickly turning back. He leaned down and kissed me hard on the lips. I sputtered out a laugh but accepted it merrily. One long embrace, followed by two quick pecks, and then the boy was walking backward, unable to tear his eyes away from me. "I'll be right back," he whispered, nearly stumbling on the first step.

I tilted my head back with a laugh. "*Go.*"

It felt like only a handful of minutes that I was alone on the beach, the moonlight and ocean my only companions. I could hear the Cursed Beings whispering at my back, longing, craving, but their voices were swept away by the tsunami of peace in my soul. I was whole. I was complete. Nothing could change that. Not even the epitome of evil could dampen my spirits.

The boy returned, his arms full of firewood, thick wads of fabric, and a basket. I watched with growing curiosity, but Grayson would simply return my questioning looks with knowing ones of his own as he worked. He set the fabric—a blanket, he called it—on the beach and gestured for me to settle on top of it. I'd never felt such softness before. I sighed with contentment and lay down, my tail swishing against the plush fabric. He opened the basket and wordlessly handed me a sticky lump the size of my palm. It was soft and gooey, thick tendrils of not-quite-liquid coating my webbing. It smelled rich, almost sickly sweet. As I stared at it in confusion, I could feel my body react bizarrely; my mouth began to water inexplicably, and my stomach roiled.

"Take a bite," Grayson instructed.

Tentatively, I did. The second the lump entered my mouth, it dissolved into a puddle of texture, taste, and sensation. A punch of flavor—sweet warmth and tangy aftertaste on my tongue. I closed my eyes and moaned my pleasure, taking another bite.

The boy laughed at my reaction. "It's a lemon honey cake. I picked some up from the bakery on my way home from work."

"It's absolutely delightful!" I inhaled the cake and licked the remnants off my fingers. I hadn't realized how hungry I was. I'd never tasted anything so utterly divine. Nothing in the ocean carried such mouthwatering flavors; everything was cold and bland with the sole purpose of sustaining. I eyed the basket greedily, earning another laugh from Grayson.

"There's more in there," he said, mirth coating his voice. "Go ahead."

"I really shouldn't," I said, reaching into the basket and pulling out another.

As the boy worked on building a fire, we began to strategize. The challenges were over, leaving little for Grayson to sabotage directly. He looked uneasy, his worry evident in the furrow of his brow. I assured him there was still much he could do. He would be my eyes and ears on land. He could map Lethe, uncover the designated beaches where the hunters docked their boats and hid their nets. He could learn where they waited, how they laid their traps, what weapons they wielded. Even the smallest ripple could make waves, I reminded him.

Grayson sat beside me on the blanket, pulling its edge over our shoulders. He rubbed his hands briskly and extended them toward the fire. I marveled at the flames—how something so small could radiate such heat and power. The flickering tongues of orange and yellow beckoned to me, but when I reached toward them, the boy stopped me with a gentle warning. Instead, I nestled closer, resting my head in the crook of his shoulder. He sighed, content, and leaned his head against mine.

"Tell me about your family," I murmured, taking one of his outstretched hands and curling my fingers around his.

Grayson chuckled, but the sound was sad. "There isn't much that you don't already know. My brother died when I was young. My ma went mad with grief and tried to take me down with her when she spiraled out of control." He slowly flipped his hands, showing me the multitude of scars on his wrists. I held back a gasp, lightly rubbing my fingers along the warped skin. "All I remember is her slicing me open and pushing me into pitch-black water."

A shudder ripped through me. "How are you alive?"

The boy shrugged. "I don't know," he answered honestly. "I don't know why it didn't work. I was in the water, bleeding out, dying, and then, suddenly, I wasn't." He cocked his head down and smiled at me. "But I'm awfully glad I am."

I brought his wrists up to my lips, placing soft kisses along the scars. "So am I."

Grayson nuzzled the top of my head. "So, it's just me and Pa. Pa is over-protective. I can't blame him for that. Ma is at Rose Hill now. I visit her from time to time, but—"

"That witch?" I interjected bitterly. "After what she did to you? Why?"

Grayson went quiet for a long moment. "Because she is my mother. I love her."

I didn't know how to reply. We sat in silence for a heartbeat before the boy let out a heavy breath. "What about you? What was your family like?"

I bit my lip, focusing all my attention on Grayson's scars. "They were mighty," I breathed. "Rulers of the ocean. Ferociously just, effortlessly kind. For the longest time, I thought they were untouchable; nothing could kill them."

Grayson sighed quietly. "And yet . . ."

I nodded, stifling the surge of emotion barreling its way up my throat. "My appah, Rainos, was claimed by last year's Hunt. He traveled to the island just prior to Hunting Month in order to talk peace with the humans." I gave a wobbly smile. "It didn't go very well. He followed Ammah into the afterlife. At least, I *think* my ammah is in the afterlife." I shivered; Grayson wrapped the blanket around us tighter. "I don't know what happened to her. It kills me, not knowing."

"What was she like?"

"Oh," I sighed dreamily. "Nereida was lovely. The very essence of beauty, with a personality that shone like the brightest jewels. Her siren song could calm even the most chaotic riots. Her love for her pod was unending and passionate; there was not a single thing she wouldn't do for them." I chuckled dolefully. "After she left one day and failed to return, I was often mistaken for her. On more than one occasion, I had to witness the disappointment in my pod's eyes when they realized that they weren't addressing their great queen, but her less-than-adequate daughter."

Grayson went rigid beside me, his breath hitching. "You look similar to her?"

"A mirror image," I replied. "From our violet eyes, to our long white hair, to our shimmering, iridescent scales." I frowned, gazing at my glowing tail. "I used to hate it, sharing such a likeness to her. I wanted to be my own mermaid. I wanted to be unique." I looked up and smiled at the boy. "But now, I realize that it's a gift, and I treasure it deeply. I wouldn't change any-thing." I laughed lightly. "When I finally decide to wear her crown, then I'll truly be just like her. That'll certainly send a few members of my pod into a confused frenzy."

Grayson opened his mouth, which had grown tight with nerves, but before he could speak, I gripped his arm tightly, my eyes growing wide. "What's that?"

Grayson blinked at me. "What?"

I pointed to the stars. "*That.*"

The boy followed my outstretched arm to the tip of my finger, and then farther still, to where the night sky was suddenly bathed in bright splashes of color. Reeds of greens and pinks and reds whipped against the stars, undulating and frolicking in the night air. He relaxed, chuckling under his breath. "It's an aurora borealis."

"A what?" I asked, not daring to take my eyes off the dancing colors.

"The northern lights," Grayson said. "They happen from time to time. You can't always see them; the village lights often dampen their appearances." He whistled lightly. "I haven't seen them this powerful in a while."

I watched the lights zigzag through the sky, effortless and free. "They are beautiful."

"Yes," the boy agreed, though I could tell he was looking at me and not at the night sky.

I snuggled deeper into Grayson's chest, watching as the lights raced alongside the beat of his heart. "I'm going to take this as a good omen."

The boy smiled. "Me too."

We sat in silence, watching time slip by in the form of dancing lights. We should have been talking, coming up with more plans to gain the upper hand. We should have been strategizing and discussing the fall of the Hunt. I should have been questioning Grayson on why the topic of my ammah sent him stiff and on edge. I should have delved deeper into the scars on his body, about *why* his witch of a mother would ever try to kill him.

But I didn't, and we didn't. To talk, to strategize, to question, would mean ruining such a devastatingly perfect moment.

Nothing else mattered. Only this moment, this stolen piece of time, this small, impossible instant I could hold in the palm of my hand.

CHAPTER FIFTY-NINE

GRAYSON

APRIL 22 – MORNING

I DIDN'T KNOW WHEN I FELL ASLEEP, ONLY THAT IT WAS THE best sleep I'd had in ages. No nightmares. No voices needling into my ears. No thoughts of the Hunt wrenching me awake, gasping for air, drenched in sweat.

When I opened my eyes, Evanora was leaning over me, her delicate lips curved into a smile as she twirled a stray curl of my hair around her finger. Blinking against the haze of sleep, I took in the golden halo of sunlight framing her snow-white locks. Drops of seawater clung to her shoulders from a quick dip, shimmering like tiny salt kisses.

"Am I dreaming?" I asked.

The mermaid hummed softly, her fingers twirling. "Do you want to be?"

I smiled and closed my eyes, relishing her touch. "No."

Evanora's fingers went from tangling with the rogue strands to pushing them off my forehead. "I love your hair," she whispered, as if sharing a secret.

"Thank you. I can't do a thing with it."

Evanora leaned down and kissed me. My hands moved on their own, sliding to her neck, tangling in her thick, silken hair. Her skin was warm from the sun as she lowered herself onto me, her hands pressing against my chest, claws digging in just enough to send a shiver down my spine. I sucked in a breath, and Evanora deepened the kiss, her lips coaxing mine into surrender.

Her mouth moved to the space just below my ear, pressing a kiss there, then a bite, then a flick of her tongue. I squirmed, every nerve alight as her touch sent shock waves coursing through me. My hands roamed, tracing the smooth, glasslike scales along her sides. They quivered beneath my fingertips, her body trembling with anticipation.

Evanora pulled away, breathing hard, her eyes unfocused and heavy lidded. She gazed down at me, a smile pulling at the corner of her lips. "You can touch me," she whispered. "I won't break."

She took my hand and guided it, painfully slow, over the curve of her hip, then up her side, until it rested on her bare breast. Her rabid heart thrashed just underneath my fingertips, her magic pooling in her scales in a heavenly glow. She threw her head back and whimpered as my fingers splayed over her exposed skin, sidling against the cool scales collecting there.

God, I would never tire of seeing her in such a state of elation. My fingers danced along her goose-bumped flesh, and she burned brighter, and brighter, a star about to burst. I pulled away, my pulse quickening. "Neither will I," I said.

Chest heaving, Evanora tilted her head forward and watched with unabashed desire as I took her hand and guided it down my chest. I held my breath, steadied my nerves, and then finished the journey, placing Evanora's shaking fingers over the waistband of my pants.

Warmth. Hard. Desperate.

The mermaid gasped with delight, her eyes growing hypnotically wide. I throbbed underneath her touch, aching for more. I was about to beg for it when Evanora began to move, shifting her hand in firm, slow circles. I squeezed my eyes shut and flopped onto the blanket, completely surrendering to her. Evanora purred encouragingly and dipped her head back into the crook of my neck. Her mouth found that irresistibly tender area again, and she bit. Hard.

I let out a squawk, but the sound quickly morphed into a groan as the mermaid planted her mouth on my neck and sucked, a low, feral moan escaping through the cracks of her lips. I began to shake as she moved faster and harder, multitasking between stroking me through my pants and working absolute magic on my neck. My legs went numb, all my bones jelly, the blood zapping and racing through my veins. I was close. Just a couple more seconds, and—

I opened my eyes, and I was back in the water. Ma was standing over me, her hands clasped around my neck, holding me down. The Cursed Beings were close, too close, screaming for me, calling me by name. A bright burst of light, white and pure and all-encompassing. A rush of movement—

But then she *appeared. With her snow-white hair and her amethyst eyes, she came and ruined* everything.

Ma's voice rang in my mind, clear and deadly. I sat up, shocking Evanora into stillness. I couldn't catch my breath; the guilt was a vise on my chest, the pressure building so quickly that I was certain I would split in half. Why was I thinking of that damning moment? I should have been rapidly approaching bliss, not on the verge of throwing up. My scars burned so ferociously that I had to look to make sure the skin was still intact.

The mermaid looked at me with a frown, then at her hand still on me, now embarrassingly soft. "Was I doing it wrong?" she asked quietly, her words drenched in confusion.

Evanora's voice seemed distant, thousands of years away, and I struggled to bring myself back to the present with her. I shook my head quickly. "No. It was perfect. *You* were perfect."

"Then . . ." Evanora slowly removed her hand and placed it on her lap. "What happened?"

My stupid thoughts. My stupid ma. That's what happened.

The mermaid cocked her head to the side, chewing on her lip thoughtfully. She brightened suddenly. "*Was* that supposed to happen?" she asked, hopeful.

God, kill me now. How could I possibly explain to Evanora, the most beautiful creature I'd ever seen, the one I wanted, body and soul, over and over until we were both numb from exhaustion, that my conscience had literally made me flaccid? How could I explain something that even I didn't understand?

"Well," I tried, "in a sense."

Not the truth, but not a lie. Evanora seemed content with my answer. She leaned in for a kiss. Our lips met—

Snow-white hair. Amethyst eyes. She ruined everything.

I cringed, pulling away. "I'm sorry." I sighed, resting my forehead against hers. "I just don't know what my problem is right now."

I could tell Evanora was disappointed, but she smiled. "It's been an eventful couple of days. It's all right to be tired."

I sighed with frustration and shook my head, my skin skimming along hers. "Trust me, I want this so badly. Ridiculously badly. You-have-no-idea badly."

Evanora gave a soothing chuckle, clasping my face in between her hands and planting a soft kiss on my hairline. "Don't worry. We'll have more time."

I smiled, but a tremor of dread fluttered through me. *Will we?* I wondered inwardly.

As if sensing my thoughts anyway, Evanora tilted my head up and pegged me with a determined look. "After the Hunt, we'll have all the time in the world. I'll be yours, and you'll be mine, and no one can say otherwise."

I wanted to believe her. But I couldn't help but feel that Evanora was wrong. Something deep and dark was telling me that there wouldn't be an *after* anything.

Time was slipping through my fingers. I picked up my belongings scattered throughout the beach and made a half-hearted excuse about needing to start my day before it got too far ahead for me to catch up. Evanora was reluctant to leave but agreed; her pod would be thinking the worst about her absence. We ended our time together with an embrace, a flurry of kisses, and a round of, "Until next time," and then I was wandering back up the hill, casting looks over my shoulder, watching the mermaid and her glow slip away from the island.

I missed her immediately.

The house was mercifully quiet. Pa was already down at the butcher shop. I was late for work. Mr. Brightly would certainly have words with me about it. Still, I took my time. I made sure the animals were fed. I replaced Penny's bandages and mucked out her stall. I took a bird bath in the sink and changed my clothes. And I waited for my thoughts to make sense.

Nothing made sense anymore.

I felt like I had a pile of puzzle pieces, but none of them fit together perfectly. God, some of them belonged to a completely different puzzle. Evanora's and Ma's words rippled through my mind, sloshing around like a ship in the middle of a turbulent storm. I attempted to sort through them, save the capsizing ship.

Ma had thought she could exchange my life for Warrick's. She'd tried to kill me because of it. She'd failed. She'd mentioned someone with snow-white hair and amethyst eyes coming and ruining everything. I could only assume she meant the exchange from being completed, but I wasn't certain.

Evanora had snow-white hair and amethyst eyes. So did her mother.

Had Nereida been there the night I was nearly murdered? Did she have something to do with my life having been spared?

Was I the reason she was no longer here?

And the bright burst of light that I suddenly remembered . . . What was that? Why was I remembering it now, during a most inconvenient time?

Why did it remind me of Evanora?

My head was beginning to hurt, and I was no longer just a *little* late for work. Unraveling mysteries would have to wait.

I hurried down the hall, thrusting my arms into my jacket and hopping into one of my boots. I passed my parents' bedroom and came to a stuttering halt.

Voices. I could hear voices.

I turned slowly, staring at the closed door. The remaining boot slipped out of my hand, clattering to the floor, temporarily forgotten. Holding my breath, I leaned forward, hesitantly pressing my ear against the door.

Yes. Definitely voices.

But . . . not anyone familiar.

They were hushed, hurried, almost violent in their urgency.

A spark of anxious trepidation burned through me. Had someone broken into the house in the slice of time between when Pa had left and I'd returned? My heart thundered at the thought of strangers invading our home, our little space of safety, and tearing that safety to shreds. It seemed unlikely, but just to be safe, I carefully retrieved my boot and gripped the laces. Gritting my teeth, I reached for the doorknob.

Grayson.

I stopped, my heart in my throat. The voices crept underneath the door again.

Grayson Shawwwwww.

Whatever was in the room wasn't just whispering. They were talking, trying to get my attention.

In herrrrrre, the voices drawled.

I knew I should ignore them, shove them away, rebuke them. But I found myself opening the door a crack, peeking my head inside the room.

It was empty, and the voices went quiet.

I stepped over the threshold, the creaking floor announcing my reluctant arrival, and the voices burst back to life.

Here, here, here! they cried, a multitude of bodiless voices, belonging to no one, and everyone.

Swallowing hard, I looked around the room. "Hello?" I called out hesitantly.

Closer, the voices breathed.

I followed, feeling almost possessed as I listened for their faint trail. *Madness. This is absolute madness*, I thought as I lowered myself to the floor and looked underneath the bed.

Dust bunnies, some books, a single sock.

No, no, no, Promised One. Here.

Feeling slightly emboldened, I rose to my feet and glanced around the room. I hadn't been in there in a while, but nothing appeared to be out of place. Pa's dirty laundry sat on the chest at the end of the bed. The bookshelves underneath the window had a hearty layer of dust on them. Family portraits hung crookedly on the wall, save for the one of Pa and Ma on their wedding day—that one had been removed a long time ago, leaving a dark patch of wallpaper behind. The dresser with a broken leg sagged against the far wall, one of the drawers half open.

The closet door was closed. I stared at it with growing dread.

Yes, the voices crooned. *Yes.*

The closet. The voices were coming from the closet.

I forced my feet to move, step by measly step. As I drew closer to the door, the voices grew louder, stronger, until they were part of me, *in* me, until they were all I could hear, feel, and sense.

Yes! they cried out. *Here!*

I opened the door and peered into the dusty shadows.

Rows of clothes lined the walls on steel rods. Stacks of papers, books, and porcelain dolls littered the floor.

And in the center of the small space was a box.

Yes, yes, yes!

I crouched, grunting as I pulled the box into the room. It was small, weighing almost nothing. The voices turned to vicious shrieks as I carefully pulled off the lid and looked inside. But simply looking wouldn't satisfy the voices, and what started out as a low throb in the back of my head had turned into roaring agony. I needed them to stop. I would go crazy if they didn't.

The box held Ma's things. I pushed aside a paisley dress, several dried flowers, and a hairbrush with long blond strands still tangled in the teeth. There were a couple family photos, the edges soft and curling from constant touching. A pile of newspaper clippings. And then I saw it. A book.

HERE!

I placed my hands on the leather-bound book, and the voices abruptly ended. The silence that I had wished for was nearly deafening. I pulled out the book and leaned against the wooden bed frame. The book was old, the leather cracked from oily fingers, the pages torn and faded. I ran my twitching fingers over the cover, brought it up to my nose, and inhaled deeply.

It smelled just like her. Hints of floral, traces of ink, the perfume she hated but used because Warrick and I had given it to her for Mother's Day.

Settling it back onto my lap, I cracked open the cover and looked inside.

What I saw didn't make sense at first. The pages were filled with hurried handwriting that sometimes curved up the margins and looped back into the lines. The entire book was full of it. Some of the words were in English, and some weren't. Some were circled, and some were scratched out so deeply that the page had torn, an angry blue mouth. Sketches played along the warped corners, of black beasts with long hands reaching upward, of mermaids with beady eyes and long fangs, of knives covered in blood. I fingered through the pages again, and again, and again, my stomach sinking.

It was a journal. Ma's journal. And it was full of the Barrens, the Cursed Beings, and the Hunt. It was everything Lethe didn't want us to see, everything the island didn't want us to know. All wrapped up in a single book.

But . . . why was it hidden?

And why was I supposed to find it?

CHAPTER SIXTY

EVANORA

APRIL 22 – MORNING

THE POD—WHAT WAS LEFT OF IT—WANTED TO FIGHT.
My return to the kingdom was hailed as a victory, though partnering with a human left some mermaids with rigid scales and razor-sharp glares. Desperation outweighed disdain; we needed all the help we could get, even if it came from someone who couldn't breathe underwater.

At my command, groups formed and dispersed. Sirens, water wielders, and mind benders clustered together, forging alliances and honing their skills. We couldn't afford division. We had to be strong, united, prepared for when the battle reached our waters. No more retreating. No more hiding.

The pod focused on Illeron as he demonstrated a jab, a strike, and a parry with his spear. The warrior was the epitome of power, his face of chiseled stone and grit. It was hard to remember the blush on his cheeks as he gently guided my movements during our private lesson. Watching him now, there was nothing gentle, nothing soft. Only fire. Only determination.

"Watch it!" Daithi growled at the mind bender next to her. "You almost got me with your spear."

The bender sniffed, tilting his pointed nose into the air. "You were clearly crowding me." He glanced at the bandage swaddling her face. "If I didn't know any better, I'd say the Cursed Beings tarnished your left eye as well as your right."

"Hey," Illeron barked, baring his teeth at the pair. "Daithi, Forthis. That's enough. Work together. *Move* together."

The bender sighed, lowering his head. He stared pointedly at Daithi, who relaxed her shoulders and nodded. "Apology accepted."

The next attack they did, the mermaids were in sync, smiling at each other as their weapons sliced through the water.

I watched my small army, heart swelling with hope. *This could work*, I thought. *We have a chance.*

Contentment swirled through me like a gentle current as I left the training grounds. Back in my room, I drifted along the walls, past the wide-open window, until I reached my bed tucked into the corner. The seaweed spread lay untouched and inviting, its softness promising the reprieve my aching body desperately needed.

But my gaze didn't linger on the bed. It climbed instead to the crown resting on the smooth slab of rock beside it.

The intricate piece gleamed with gemstones, their light refracting in shimmering hues as my fingers brushed its surface. The weight of it, even unadorned, was staggering. How had Ammah borne it with such grace all those years? I hesitated, dread tightening my chest. How could I wear something so laden with responsibility when I was nowhere near Nereida's caliber?

"That would look far better on you," a voice uttered in my mind.

Illeron was hovering in the doorway. I dropped my hand from the crown, feeling like a merling caught sneaking food from the kitchen before dinner. "What are you doing here? Shouldn't you be with the pod?"

Illeron swam into the room, shrugging. "The other warriors can handle them for a moment. I wanted to check in on you." He moved with nonchalance, but I could practically see the waves of unease crashing over him, thick and toxic.

A defensive vine riddled with thorns cinched around my heart. "You mean," I scoffed, "you came to talk me out of the plan to use Grayson Shaw as an ally."

Illeron's jaw clenched, but he made no effort to deny my words. He ran his fingers along the windowsill as if he were checking for sand deposits. "I think," he said, inspecting his fingers, "that we can do it without him."

I immediately began to shake my head. "No," I said, resolute. "We need him. *I* need him."

The warrior laughed, forced and brittle. "You sound like an addict."

I clasped my hands together, sinking onto the edge of the bed. "I'm not going to fight you on this," I said, keeping my voice calm despite the warning flicks of my forearm fins. "Grayson is a part of this just as much as we are. I refuse to cast him aside again." I leveled him with a hard stare. "I will not do it, Illeron."

The warrior tapped his knuckles against the windowsill. Eventually, he sighed, dipping away from the window and sitting on the bed next to me. His silver-and-crimson tail brushed against mine as he collected my hands into his. "Can you help me understand?" he asked, keeping his focus on our hands, on the way his thumb grazed mine. "Tell me why we need this boy so badly."

I wanted to rip my hands away. Instead, I closed my eyes, pretending it was Grayson's cool fingers playing along my skin. "The ancestors have been talking to me. I didn't understand it at first." I chuckled lightly. "I *still* don't think I do."

"What have they been saying?"

I opened my eyes. "That he is the key to all of this."

Illeron exhaled slowly. "No pressure, Grayson Shaw."

I laughed, the stiffness in my back ebbing away. "They also mentioned something about the *power of three*, about unlocking my Gift." I shook my head, frowning. "Which makes no sense. I have my Gifts already—healer and light bringer. What else is there to unlock?"

Illeron shrugged, his shoulder rubbing against mine. "The ancestors do enjoy speaking in riddles." He huffed out a quick breath. "So, Grayson is the key to . . . *something*. And that's why you need him." He finally turned his attention to me, clucking his tongue. "Even though you don't know what the key actually is or what it unlocks."

I nodded. "All I know is that I've been looking at it wrong this whole time. I wasn't meant to use him. I was meant to work with him." My heart hummed, the connection throbbing with so much life that it ached. I smiled. "I don't expect you to like it, Illeron." I gave his hands a squeeze. "But I expect you to help. So, please say you will."

The warrior looked at me, *through* me, before offering a faint smile. "I'll help," he agreed quietly. "But you're right: I don't like it."

"Do you *like* anything, oh great warrior?"

Illeron gave me a heavy look, and though he said nothing, I could feel the words resting on his tongue: *You know the answer to that.*

Instead, Illeron's eyes darted to the crown resting beside the bed. "You should wear it."

His attention had been all captivating, enough to sink a battalion of ships. Without it pinned on me, I could finally breathe. I shook my head. "Not yet."

"Why?"

I gave a crooked smile, staring at the mighty piece of jewelry. "Because I don't deserve it."

Illeron opened his mouth, then quickly shut it when Mavi burst into the room.

"There you are!" she cried, triumphant. Her victorious grin shifted into a devious one when her large eyes landed on our clasped hands. "Am I interrupting something?" she asked coyly.

The warrior glared daggers at the water wielder before slowly withdrawing his hands from mine and rising off the bed. He cast one last longing look my way. "I better get back to the pod, make sure they aren't starting a war of their own." He pressed a hand to his chest, dipped his head, and then let his hand fall back to his side in a graceful sweep. *"Wear the crown,"* he commanded in my mind.

I laughed, folding my arms over my chest. "Not yet," I repeated. "And I'm not doing it back."

Illeron's mouth twitched to the side before he turned and brushed past Mavi. "Excuse me," he said gruffly.

Mavi swept to the side, giving him a wide berth. "You're excused," she said, arching an eyebrow at the sullen warrior as he swam by. The second he was gone, she placed her hands on her cheeks, grinning from ear to ear. "What was *that* all about?"

I waved a hand dismissively before flopping back onto the bed with a sigh. "Trust me, it's never clear with that fish."

Mavi laughed, twirling around the room in playful circles. "Oh, that looked *very* clear to me."

I lifted my head with a scowl. "Did you come in here for something? Or to simply insult my intelligence?"

Mavi stopped spinning and dropped onto the bed beside me. Her tight ringlets swept in front of her face with the movement, and she brushed them aside haphazardly, revealing a look of blazing determination. "I want to help."

I softened, reaching forward and cupping her full cheek. "You will," I promised. "Once the plan is more solidified—"

"No," the wielder pressed. "Now. I want to help now." She pushed herself up onto her elbows. "What can I do? I can't just keep sitting still, watching you from the shadows."

"You *are* helping," I argued. "You've helped make the lanterns last *much* longer. Not even my parents found a way to make that happen. And you've already proven yourself to be a better healer than I am with your salves and ointments."

Mavi looked helpless as she let her head drop onto the bed. "I want to do *more*," she said, her words coming out in a long, drawn-out groan. "Our reserves are officially depleted. I've foraged every last inch of our kingdom." She turned to me, frowning. "There's nothing left, nothing but scraps and sand. When the last jar runs out . . ." She sputtered out a heavy breath and shrugged. "That's it."

"Mavi," I gasped, "why didn't you tell me?"

The wielder bit her lip, blushing. "You've been so busy. I didn't want to burden your already-hectic schedule."

I shook my head viciously. "No. This is important." I took her face in my hands again. "*You* are important."

Mavi wouldn't meet my gaze. "There's more."

I narrowed my eyes. "Neptune spear me—more?"

"We have also run out of food."

"Mavi!"

"I'm sorry!" Mavi shook her head. "Illeron told me not to tell you."

"Why?" I asked carefully, gritting my teeth.

"He didn't want you to worry. He directed us to set aside what was left of our usual meals for you so you didn't grow suspicious."

An incredulous laugh bubbled through my tightly sealed lips. "I'm the leader of this pod. It's my job to worry." I forced myself to relax. "What has everyone been eating?"

Mavi made a face. "Seaweed."

My stomach twisted; I was already imagining the bellyache that often came with the bitter greens. "Hardly sustaining."

"It's been getting the job done." Mavi sat up, shaking her head. "I want to be brave, *need* to be brave. I want to prove to you and the pod that I'm not just some merling who can't seem to get rid of her spots." She offered me a determined smile. "How would you feel about finally expanding our borders? Just a little," she added quickly when I widened my eyes. "Just enough so that I can find more food and medicinal plants."

I chewed on my bottom lip. "Jorah wouldn't be impressed with your devilish desires, Mavi."

"Well," Mavi said with a grimace, "Jorah is no longer here. Please?" she pleaded, clasping her hands together. "Expand them just a little?"

My heart began to race. It was true. Jorah wasn't here to forbid me from doing what should have been done a long time ago. But I wasn't thinking about my kingdom's borders anymore. I was thinking of a much larger scale. "I can do you one better, I think." I took the wielder's hands in mine. "Mavi," I said with a slow grin, "how would you like to go on a little field trip?"

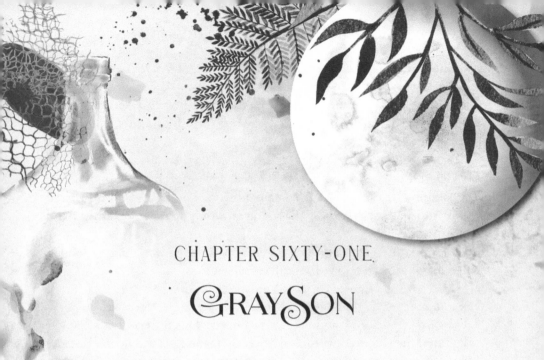

CHAPTER SIXTY-ONE.

GRAYSON

APRIL 23 – MORNING

AND . . . YOU'RE DEAD."

I flinched when Pa's sword rested against my shoulder. Uncurling from my hunched position, I craned my neck back to see Pa towering over me and the hay bale I had chosen to hide behind. "I really thought this was a good spot," I said with a resigned sigh.

"It was," Pa agreed. "The first time you chose it."

I scrambled to my feet, flicking off the straw that clung to my shoulders. "I didn't think you'd check there again."

Pa huffed out a breath. "Honestly, Grayson—are you even trying? You need to focus! The Hunt is days away, and you're acting like your head is in the clouds."

"I *am* trying."

That was partially true. I was trying, but focusing? That was a different beast entirely. Every time I attempted to concentrate on the stealth drill Pa had forced on me, my mind wandered back to Ma's journal, hidden beneath my bed. Or to last night, when Evanora had visited with a mermaid named Mavi, whose expression wavered between terror and exhilaration. And the voices—the whispers that used to hover gently outside my window—had grown into a monsoon of banshee wails, demanding, *Go to the water. Come to the water. Get in the water.*

Pa's scolding broke through my haze. "Any false move, any second you let your guard down, you're a dead man, Grayson. Those bloodthirsty mermaids won't hesitate to slit your throat."

"Yeah," I scoffed. "That's why we need to get to them first, right?"

Pa glared at me, weighing my words, trying to figure out if I was being genuine or not. "Right," he said slowly. "And that's why you need to be in top shape." His eyes, analyzing and judgmental, shifted up and down my body.

I lifted my arms and spun in a slow circle. If my pa was going to look at me like that, I wanted to give him full viewing access.

"Don't joke at a time like this," Pa growled, but there was a twinkle in his eye, a softening in the roughness of his jaw. "Come on, let's get back to it."

I saw my opportunity and pounced. "I need a longer break than that."

Pa lifted his wooden sword and rested it against his shoulder. "Because hiding from me is grueling work?" He jerked his head toward the house. "You know the drill; I'll close my eyes and count to sixty. In the meantime, you hide and evade me like your life depends on it. Because mark my words— come May 1, it will. Now, hop to it."

I shifted on my feet, desperate to avoid another drill that would end in disappointment. "About May 1 . . ."

"No," Pa said, cutting me off. "Quit stalling. Go."

"I'm not stalling," I lied. "Seriously, Pa, I know what's going to happen on the day of the Hunt. But I know next to nothing about the days leading up to it. Like . . . what are the rules? Where is our boat going to be? When can we cast nets? How does it all start?" I shrugged, my arms slapping against my sides. "I'll be useless if I don't understand even the basics."

Pa's eyes narrowed, his annoyance palpable, but the corners of his mouth betrayed a flicker of approval. That part of him won out. With a grunt, he sank onto the hay bale and began carving into the dirt with the tip of his sword.

"So," he said, drawing a rough outline of the island. "This is Lethe." He marked four *X*'s around its perimeter. "These are Fenharrow, Fariid, Maude, and Tully. Each village starts at its designated beach." He pointed to the eastern *X*. "Fariid starts at Black Sands Beach. Tully"—he tapped the western *X*—"starts at Hannigan's Cove, and so on. Got it?"

When I nodded, Pa continued. "The Hunt lasts a week. The hunters must start at their designated beaches on May 1, but after that, they can travel to whichever beach they think will best suit them." He nodded, pride puffing out his chest. "You'll find a lot of the islanders will travel to Tully. Our beach has proven most profitable when it comes to hunting mermaids."

I suddenly hated Tully. Fighting against a shiver, I asked, "And when can we dock the boats?"

"April 26," Pa said. "After the Night of the Betting."

I nodded, wishing I had my sketchbook so I could take notes.

Pa continued, circling the entire island with the tip of his sword. "Nets can be dropped anywhere, but only certain ones are allowed to remain in the water at night. Each hunter is given a color on the morning of the Hunt. You use your color to mark which nets belong to you." He gave a wry chuckle. "There were many fistfights before that problem was ironed out. A lot of scoundrels tried to claim nets that didn't belong to them."

"Has there been much success catching mermaids at night?" I asked, knowing the answer.

Pa shook his head. "Strangely enough, no."

I wanted to be glad, but all I could think of was the reason *why* the mermaids weren't caught.

They were hiding.

Grayson Shaw. Here. The one who was promised. Here!

"Hey!" Pa snapped, tapping me on the knee. "Are you paying attention?"

I had turned my head in the direction of the ocean without realizing it. The pull was strong today. It took everything in my power not to heed the call. The fact that I ached to go into the ocean despite my all-encompassing fear was unnerving. I nodded hurriedly. "Yes."

Pa clucked his tongue, annoyance rearing its ugly head again. "You were the one who wanted this lesson."

"I do!" I crouched, inspecting the crudely drawn map with embellished interest. "What else can you tell me?"

Pa stood. "Nothing. That's enough for one day. Back to training."

"Oh, come on!" I protested. "There has to be more." I gestured to the map. "Can we hunt all hours of the day? Are there limits to how far we can venture out?" I bounced on the balls of my feet. "Come *on*, Pa. Don't be mad." I had gotten some good information out of him. I was testing my luck by pressing for more.

Pa loomed over me, an unmovable force of strength and stubbornness. "I'm not mad. I just didn't realize you have the attention span of a toddler."

I could feel an itch in my neck, a pull in my tendons and muscles as my body began to turn toward the ocean again. I kept still. My body grew hot with the effort. "It's not that! It's just—" I gave in, shifting to where I knew a body of water waited for me.

Here. Here. Here.

Pa took a step forward, his face all lines and creases. "Just *what*, son?" There was a sudden gentleness to his voice, a tenderness I had forgotten was there. It made everything within me ache.

I bit my lip. I could feel my body sway with the phantom waves crashing inside my soul. I came to a shuddering halt, clenching my hands at my sides. "It's just . . ." I sighed, hanging my head. "I think something's wrong, Pa. Wrong with *me*." The confession came out in a whisper, and part of me hoped that the wind would sweep it away, keeping it a secret. "I think something terrible is going to happen. I don't know what, or when. But I can feel it." I lifted my head slowly, praying the waves hadn't reached my eyes, which had grown warm and dangerously moist. "A promise."

Pa tilted his head to the side, his lips pulled in so tightly that all I could see was beard and mustache merged together. The concern was there, the desire to comfort despite not knowing how. Pa was broken too, and how could two broken people possibly hope to fix each other without cracking even more? He smiled, patted me on the shoulder, and handed me the wooden sword. "If you don't become a better hunter, you could be right."

I couldn't help but laugh, the sound thick and wet. "I thought you said not to joke."

Pa's smile faltered. "I'm not."

THE LIBRARY WAS TOO WARM, TOO QUIET, AND HOLLY WOULDN'T stop glaring at me from behind the counter.

The last time we'd crossed paths, things had ended badly—hurt feelings, harsh words, slammed doors, and Ma's apron ruined. Given the venom Holly was throwing my way, I doubted she'd welcome a casual chat about the weather.

I tried to avoid her. God, I hadn't even wanted to go to the library. Pa had given me good information—Evanora would be pleased—but Mavi's sudden appearance on the beach had complicated things. She was asking about Lethe's plants. More specifically, the ones Evanora had picked long ago—the prayer reeds. Mavi wanted to know which beaches had the best batches of them, which herbs made effective healing salves, and which flowers were both edible and medicinal. I knew a fair amount about the island's flora, but I wasn't an expert. I couldn't even map out Lethe from memory, let alone list every single plant that grew here.

I needed books.

Hence the warm, quiet, angry-stares library.

After what felt like an eternity scouring the shelves, I considered asking Mrs. Humphries for help, but she looked as thrilled to see me as Holly did. Every time I got close, she'd skitter away, bury her nose in a book, or shush me before I could speak. With my heart pounding, I sighed, resigned, and walked up to the desk. "Hi, Holly."

The positive: Holly had stopped glaring at me.

The negative: She was now blatantly ignoring me, writing fervently on a piece of paper.

I shifted, leaning my elbows on the counter. Ma's journal dug into my ribs. I wasn't sure why I'd brought it along. It had felt necessary when I left my house. Now it felt awkward in my pocket and disturbingly heavy. "I need some help," I said quietly.

"Find someone else," Holly said without looking up.

I glanced at Mrs. Humphries from over my shoulder. The librarian, who had been staring at us with intense interest, dove her face back into a book so quickly that her glasses slipped off her nose. I turned back to the desk, smiling ruefully. "I'm getting the impression that Mrs. Humphries still hasn't forgiven me for the last time I was in here."

Holly scoffed as she flipped the pencil around and began erasing furiously. Rubber shavings darted everywhere. "Well, the last time you were in here, you destroyed the flooring. I can't say I blame her."

I held up a finger. "To be fair, I was trying to stop Jasper from playing around with the knife. The floor was an unfortunate casualty."

Holly slapped her palm against the paper, whipping her head up. Loose ginger curls framed her reddened face, her freckles standing out like pale beacons. "What can I do for you, Mr. Shaw?" she asked with thinning patience.

I sighed, scratching the back of my neck. "I need some books."

Holly tilted her head to the side. "Obviously."

I could feel my own cheeks burn. "An updated map of the island. And a complete list of all plant life, on land and in water, if you have it."

Holly shifted her attention back to her paper. "Aisle seven, rows E, F, and G."

I shook my head. "I looked there already."

Holly's shoulders hunched in defeat. Letting out a long breath, she stood, flipping her braids behind her shoulders. "You can never find anything, can you?"

I shrugged, offering a pleasant smile. "The sooner I get those books, the sooner I leave."

Holly took the bait. Wordlessly, she walked around the desk and disappeared into the shelving. I waited at the front, tapping my fingers against the wood top and avoiding Mrs. Humphries's disapproving looks. Holly returned moments later with her arms full of books. She dropped them onto the counter with a solid *thunk!* I let out an appreciative whistle. "Wow. Those were all hiding in there?"

"Yes," Holly said curtly, smoothing out her deep green skirt before sitting back down. "Pick the ones you need and be on your way please."

I sorted through the pile, pulling out three books claiming to know all there was about Lethe's vegetation and one that had been published recently, called *Lethe—Hidden Gem of the Balafor Ocean*. I showed Holly the books. She wrote them down dutifully. Holly returned to her crumpled piece of paper. I waited.

And I waited some more.

Eventually, Holly set the pencil down forcefully and glowered up at me. "Will that be all, Mr. Shaw?" she asked coolly.

Heart in my stomach, I glanced around the room. Thankfully, Mrs. Humphries had found something else to turn her attention to: a boy not-so-stealthily eating crackers in the corner of the room. I pulled the journal out of my jacket. "Actually," I whispered, "I was hoping you had something that could help me with this."

Curiosity piqued, Holly leaned forward, inspecting the book. "What is it?"

I handed it to her carefully, like I was holding a bomb and not a clump of papers wrapped in leather. "I don't know. I found it in my parents' closet." I watched as Holly opened it and began riffling through the pages. "It has to do with the Barrens, but the writing is jumbled and all over the place; it's hard to make any sense of it."

Holly immediately slammed the cover shut, her face pale. "Grayson," she hissed, thrusting the book back into my hands. "Things like this are *banned*."

I fumbled with the journal. It was hot against my skin. "I know, but—" I bit my lip, straining to grasp my scrambling thoughts. "Do you have something that could . . . I don't know . . . help me decipher it? Seriously, anything will help."

"We don't have anything like that in here."

"Holly, *please*," I begged. "If anyone can help me figure out the damned riddles inside this thing, it's you!"

Teeth bared, Holly shook her head rapidly. "My life doesn't revolve around you, Grayson Shaw! Stop trying to get me in trouble. Quick!" Holly scanned the room with wide eyes. "Put it away before someone sees it!"

"Sees what?"

Holly and I froze as Jasper sauntered up to the counter. He nodded at us. "Sister. Friend." His gaze zeroed in on the journal, which was wedged half in, half out of my jacket. "Ooh!" he squeaked with delight. "What's that?"

"Nothing," Holly and I said in unison.

Jasper snorted. "Doesn't look like nothing." He reached for the journal. "Let me see!"

I frantically tried stuffing the rest of the journal into my pocket as Jasper lunged forward, fingers like daggers as he ripped it out of my hands. We struggled for a heartbeat, both clutching the journal, a mini game of tug-of-war. I had the sudden fear that we would tear the thing in two, and Ma's riddles would be buried in shredded confetti, never to be solved. My grip gave out, sending Jasper scuttling back with the journal in his hands. He let out a victorious "aha!" before turning his back to me, warding off my attacks with one hand as he cracked the book open with the other.

"Well, well, well!" he chirped, undeterred by my anxious hands snaking over his shoulders and around his waist. "What have we here? A *banned* book?"

"Keep your voice down!" Holly pleaded, wringing her braids together. "Do you want to get kicked out again?"

"That was Grayson's fault, not mine," Jasper said casually, flipping through the journal. "Look at all this chicken scratch! How can you make any sense of it?" He turned the book upside down, then began turning the pages right to left. "Is there a special way to read it or something?"

"Give it back, Jasper," I growled, fighting to get around his lanky frame.

"In a sec." Jasper peered at one of the pictures Ma had sketched, a woman and her baby standing in the water, surrounded by a mass of black tentacles that seemed to reach beyond the page. She held her baby out to the outstretched inky arms, an offering, a sacrifice. A murder. "I've never seen a banned book before."

"There's a reason for that!" Holly cried, ducking behind the counter.

I could feel Mrs. Humphries's eyes burning into the back of my head. Sure enough, the librarian was watching our pathetic spectacle, her face shifting into a devastating shade of red. Sweat crept onto my forehead, desperation flooding my system. My fingers snagged a corner of leather, and I tugged as hard as I could. "Jasper, I swear, if you damage even a page in my ma's journal—"

Jasper's eyes twinkled with delight. "Oh, this is your *ma's*! Well, now it all makes sense. This thing has *crazy* written all over it."

Holly gasped. I went deathly still. Jasper's left eye twitched, the glimmer rapidly retreating. He'd gone too far, and he knew it. But just to make it crystal clear, I clenched my fist, cocked it back, and slammed it into his face.

Jasper let out an "oof!" as his head snapped back. His grip on the book immediately went slack, and I quickly snagged it before it toppled to the floor. Jasper's bad leg gave out; he collapsed against the front desk with another grunt, sending piles of papers scattering.

Holly covered her face with her hands. "Oh, Grayson," she moaned.

Jasper righted himself, clutching the side of his face. He opened and closed his mouth, testing out his jaw, and gave his head a quick shake like he was trying to recenter his brain. "Jeez, Shaw. I was just kidding around."

I was breathing hard. The sweat was in my eyes, burning them with every blink. I shoved the book into my jacket pocket, fighting the urge to punch him again. "Talk about my ma like that," I seethed, "and I'll break your other leg."

Jasper laughed, but his face went ghastly pale. He rubbed his bad leg, the damaged bones tucked beneath scarred skin. "That's a little harsh. It was just a joke."

God, the anger. Never had I felt so much of it. It filled every single part of me—every crack, every pore, every seam. I was overflowing with it, a geyser of power and rage and hate. Jasper might've been joking, but I certainly wasn't.

I didn't know where it was all coming from, didn't understand it. But in that moment, as I stared at Jasper and his swollen cheek, at the hand prodding at his leg, I didn't care.

Mrs. Humphries was stomping toward us, steam practically coming out of her ears. As she opened her mouth to give us the scolding of a lifetime, I held up my shaking hand in placation, tucking my collection of books underneath my arm. "You don't have to say anything, Mrs. Humphries," I said, turning away from the two people I'd thought were my friends. "I'm leaving."

I didn't make it very far.

Two steps out of the library, I found myself walking right into Sybil Morris.

"Oh!" she cried out in alarm, stumbling back from the impact. The box she had been holding tightly against her chest went crashing to the ground, its contents toppling out like popcorn. "Oh, damn it all."

It took me a moment to collect myself. I was still seeing red from the library, and for a split second, I wondered if Jasper had followed me out, wanting to restart what I had ultimately finished. But then I blinked, and the haze was gone, and Mrs. Morris was on the ground, struggling to collect the long rods and tubes that had fallen out of the box. "Shoot," I groaned, hurrying to grab the pieces that had tumbled into the street. "I'm so sorry, Mrs. Morris."

Mrs. Morris lifted her head, blowing away the frizzy strands of hair that had fluttered into her face. "Nothing to be sorry for, Mr. Shaw," she said brightly. "I can't see a thing over this confounded box."

I grabbed another tube, inspecting the thin stem protruding from one end. "What is all this?" I asked, tapping lightly on the other side, which was cone shaped and pointy.

Mrs. Morris rolled her eyes as she picked up the box. "Toys." She chuckled. "That's what I'd call them, anyway. The men would prefer to call them fireworks and flares, but really"—she leaned in, dropping her voice to a whisper—"they just want any old excuse to light something on fire and watch it explode."

I laughed politely, dropping the tubes into the box. "What are they for?"

Mrs. Morris adjusted her hold so she could see me over the bouquet of explosives. "The fireworks are for the Final Festival. The flares are for signaling the start of the Hunt." She beamed at me. "All from the mainland. Can you believe that?"

Considering that Lethe's idea of a good time was a somewhat cold beer after work with a side of bloodshed and murder of innocent mermaids, I could. "Not teaching today?"

Mrs. Morris clucked her tongue in annoyance. "The school board figured it would be best for my mental health to let me have the rest of the month off for grieving purposes."

I eyed the box. "I'm sorry that the people running the Hunt don't feel the same way."

Mrs. Morris tried to shrug, but the box nearly slipped out of her hands again, and she stopped. "Honestly, it's nice. It gives me something to think about. Keeps my hands busy. Owen's been burying himself in work, so the house is . . ." She sighed, giving me a sad smile. "It just feels too empty, too large, too quiet."

I knew the feeling well. "How are you doing, Mrs. Morris?"

Mrs. Morris nodded sharply, her bun of graying curls bouncing. "Oh, you know. Good days and bad days."

I smiled softly, taking a small step forward. "I know I'm just a boy who annoyed you way too much when you taught me, but you don't have to pretend if you don't want to."

Mrs. Morris paused, her stiff shoulders softening. In an instant, she seemed to age years. Her cheeks hollowed, deep bags pulling under her eyes. Wrinkles creased around her lips, pale and thin. "There are no good days, only bad. Owen's a ghost—barely eats or sleeps. It's like I lost both my sons. I know he's grieving, but I wish he wouldn't shut me out." She laughed bitterly. "Some days I wonder what I did in a past life for God to hate my family like this—so many trials, so much pain." She inhaled sharply. "If there's a lesson, I don't know what it is. All I feel is sorrow and a hole in my heart."

I shrugged gently. "Sometimes I don't think there *is* a lesson. It's just life, and it's cruel and unjust and unfair. It's not always meant to make sense."

Mrs. Morris blinked rapidly. "Well, amen to that. And for the record, you never annoyed me. Jasper, on the other hand . . ." She barked out a laugh. "That clown knew just about every single one of my buttons and pushed them ceaselessly." Mrs. Morris looked at me, pinching her thin lips to the side. "Thank you."

"For what?"

"For not tiptoeing around my broken heart." She chuckled softly. "It can't get any more broken, so no need for treading lightly. Everyone else is so careful. Half the village crosses the street when they see me, and when they don't, they treat me like I'm this fragile thing. They avoid talking about family or the Hunt. The safe topic is weather. Just weather. If I weren't angry enough to spit lava, it'd be comical."

I wanted to tell her that there was always a way for the heart to break more, for its remaining pieces to crack and crumble into a fine powder. Instead, I said, "I think it's more damaging to pretend the pain doesn't exist."

Mrs. Morris sighed softly. "You'd know better than most. You're no stranger when it comes to pain." She hefted the box onto her hip and placed a hand on my shoulder. "You've been through the wringer with the best of them."

I smiled, but my entire body was a single mournful heartbeat. "I'm well-versed in it, unfortunately."

Mrs. Morris nodded. "Amen to that too." She gave my arm a squeeze before going back to balancing the box. "Well, I best be off. I want to get these to Fariid before the children are released from school. I don't want any of them seeing these *toys* and demanding an ear-shattering sample."

I laughed. "Heaven forbid."

Mrs. Morris cocked her head to the side, blowing away those stray strands again. "It was good seeing you, Grayson. Thank you for being a real human being."

I smiled, nodding. "It was really nice seeing you too, Mrs. Morris."

In the distance, the school bell chimed. Mrs. Morris groaned, rolling her eyes. "Cheese and crackers, the Lord is testing me today. Goodbye, Mr. Shaw!"

I waved goodbye as she hurried past me. She crossed the street just before a swarm of kids surrounded her. Over the noise of Main Street, I heard her squawk in protest as the kids demanded to see the contents of the box. Then I heard her laugh—loud, amused, and full of love for children who weren't even hers.

And I wondered if it was possible for bad days to carry pieces of good in them—a glimmer of light that kept Mrs. Morris going.

I wondered what would happen if that light was snuffed out.

CHAPTER SIXTY-TWO

EVANORA

APRIL 23 – EVENING

GRAYSON WAS WAITING FOR US.

My Gift thrummed with excitement at the sight of him. It took everything not to rush over, drag him into the sand, and kiss him senseless. Was this how it would always be—the wanting, the *needing*? The desire to have our souls become one?

Mavi sighed beside me, and I suddenly remembered I wasn't alone. "For a human boy, he *is* pretty cute," she muttered begrudgingly.

I bit my lip, fighting a smile, but the glow of my scales gave me away. "He's alright," I said carefully.

Grayson glanced over his shoulder to the steps, then tiptoed to the water's edge. "I can't stay long," he said quietly, looking up at the cliffside again. "Pa thinks I'm out feeding the animals." He smiled shyly at us. "Hi."

Mavi dipped her chin and brought her hand to her chest. She peeked at us, and when she realized we weren't formally greeting each other, she blushed, lowering her hand. "Sorry, I forgot."

Grayson shook his head. "I think your way of greeting each other is a lot neater than ours." He lifted his hand and waved it back and forth. "Pretty lackluster, isn't it?"

Mavi watched with wide eyes as the boy's hand drifted back and forth in front of her. "I like it!" She mimicked his movements, giggling at the sight of her webbed fingers tangling with the air.

I grinned at Mavi's childlike wonder. "Trust me, our greeting ... it gets tedious."

Still waving, Mavi looked at me, giddy. "We should bring this back home with us!"

I scoffed. "The pod is barely on board with us working alongside Grayson. I doubt they will welcome more changes anytime soon, especially ones that feel a little on the *assimilation* side."

"Right," Grayson said with an exhale. "About that." He reached behind him and pulled an over-stuffed bag onto the beach. "I did some research, and I think I have information that'll make you both happy."

Mavi stopped waving only to clap her hands together instead. I scooted further up the beach eagerly. "What did you find out?" I asked, flicking my tail into his legs.

Grayson's cheeks flushed at the contact, and his eyes darted to Mavi. When she wasn't looking, his fingers brushed against my scales, sending a spark through me. Satisfied, he quickly went back to focusing on the bag, fumbling with the clasp, his fingers twitching. "For you, Mavi," he said, pulling out a thin block with soft fluttering insides.

"Oh." Mavi accepted the block with a forced smile. She turned it back and forth in her hand, watching as the fragile insides shivered in the breeze. Colorful ribbons dotted the edges. "Thank you," she said with strained enthusiasm.

Grayson laughed. "It's a book. Open it."

Mavi bit her lip and hesitantly cracked the hard cover open, revealing lines of unfamiliar words and pictures of plant life in all shapes and sizes. "*Oh!*" she cried with more genuine excitement. "A book! How exciting!"

I looked over Mavi's shoulder at the scribbles. "What does it tell us?" I asked, running a finger over the delicate insides. It felt fragile, like dried leaves.

Grayson took the book back and flipped to the middle. "It shows all types of plants that live both on Lethe and the surrounding waters. I've made bookmarks for the ones that will be most beneficial for you." He tapped one of the ribbons. "Each color corresponds with a plant and its properties. Purple means anti-inflammatory. Red means hemostasis. Yellow means infection and fever. Green means food. And blue means—"

"Prayer reeds!" Mavi squealed, jostling up and down.

Grayson nodded. "Humans don't really have any use for them, so we usually leave them be." He flipped to another page, revealing a large map of the island. "This map shows where most of them can be found." He winced apologetically. "Unfortunately, the prayer reeds seem to like shallower water, which puts you in a great deal more danger."

Mavi shook her head passionately, her dark brown curls flying. "It doesn't matter. I'll get them all!" She looked at the sun slowly sinking and whined. "I wish I could start now."

Grayson smiled. "You can." He rummaged through his bag and pulled out jars of flowers, herbs, and ointments. "They're not prayer reeds, but they might help." He handed Mavi the jars, and she held them up to the fading light, inspecting each one. "Since you can't come on land, I grabbed these. I also made a couple salves. I color-coded them like the book, so you'll know what each jar does." He added more to her pile. "You can keep the jars too. For anything else you find."

Mavi's grin lit up the whole beach. "This is amazing!" She shot me a scowl. "Why didn't you let me see him sooner? Look at all the supplies I could've gotten!"

I laughed. "You didn't ask!"

As Mavi fussed over the jars, cooing at the salves and herbs, I looked at Grayson, my heart swelling. "This must've taken a lot of time. Thank you." I placed my hand on his.

Grayson looked at our hands, smiling at our fingers dancing alongside one another. "It was nothing."

Feeling bold—and a little stupid—I leaned forward, planting a quick kiss on his unsuspecting cheek. I was back in my spot before the boy could even register it.

Grayson's hand went idly to his cheek, where the skin was moist with salt water, the presence of my phantom kiss still lingering. His entire face had gone red, a goofy grin slowly staking claim to his lips. "Is that my payment?" he asked in a low voice.

I laughed, lilting and soft. "Oh, just a portion." I leaned forward, my smile a devilish thing as I licked my bottom lip. "Your full payment will come later."

"Wait," Mavi said, alarmed. "We have to pay him?" She looked at the jars cluttering her arms with so much concern that Grayson and I erupted into laughter. Mavi slowly joined in, though it was obvious she didn't know what we were giddy about.

"Grayson can't possibly accept payment when he hasn't assisted me in *my* endeavors," I said, wiping my eyes. "You've made Mavi happy, as you promised earlier." I shrugged, pouting playfully as I crossed my arms. "What about me?"

The boy looked at me, tilting his head coyly and arching an eyebrow, and I could tell that he wanted to make me happy in ways that didn't just include providing information. Dangerously divine ways. Tantalizing ways. For the umpteenth time, I wondered what we would be doing if Mavi weren't with us. Probably nothing productive, but certainly fun. I laughed again and mouthed the words, "*Settle down.*"

Grayson bit back a groan and stood, grabbing a stick from a pile of driftwood near the rock pools. He traced a rough outline of Lethe in the wet sand, then marked four *X*'s along the farthest points up and down, side and side. He explained that, after April 26, the boats would be left where the *X*'s were. He looked at me, determination blazing in his blue eyes. "They will be left unattended."

I sucked in a breath, my insides contracting. "What sort of boats can we expect to see?"

"Nothing with motors," Grayson said. "Typical rowboats. Wooden." He smirked. "Susceptible to damage."

I nodded, mind racing. It was valuable information. A little overwhelming, but valuable. "What do you have in mind?"

"Anything and everything." Grayson smoothed out the sand, then drew a boat. "If the boats are near the water by April 26, that gives us four days to tamper with them. I think we should go out at nightfall when we're less likely to get spotted. One night for each location." He pointed to the bottom of the boat. "We can weaken the keel and the flooring, though nothing too obvious—just enough damage to avoid suspicion. Then, during the Hunt, one nicely aimed spear jab would be all that's needed to splinter the bottom and send the people spilling out."

I shook my head. "Even if we did do that to the boats, how would we know when to attack?" My shoulders slumped, and I looked at Mavi with a frown. "In all my years of being alive, I've never known the exact moment when the Hunt begins. They always seem to catch us off guard." I sighed, running my hands through my hair. "It's beyond frustrating."

Grayson chewed on his lower lip. "As far as I know, it starts at the same time, every time." He shook his head. "Always on May 1, always at the crack of dawn. They fire flares on the four beaches to signal the hunters to begin."

I squinted at the boy. "They fire *what*?"

Grayson chuckled at my confusion. "Flares. They are like . . . I don't know . . . explosions of fire that shoot up into the sky. They pop and hiss and send down showers of sparks. You can see them from miles away."

"How about miles *underwater*?" Mavi asked, unconvinced.

"It'll be dark," Grayson said. "If you have someone on the lookout, staring in the direction of the island, they should be able to spot them." He glanced from Mavi to me. "When you see the flares, that's your sign to arm yourselves and spread out amongst all four beaches, catch them all by surprise."

I nodded slowly, loosening my grip on my hair. "Four days. Four beaches. Many, many boats."

"It'll be a lot of work," Grayson admitted softly.

"Not to mention dangerous," I added, my forearm fins bristling at the thought of it all. "What if I'm seen?"

Grayson shook his head. "I won't let that happen. I'll travel with you to each beach and stand guard while you wreak havoc. And who knows? Maybe I'll break a couple oars while I'm there, mess with a rudder or two."

Unable to help it, I leaned forward, cupping Grayson's cheek. "My brave heart," I crooned.

Mavi stifled a weird sound, something stuck between a giggle and a gasp. Grayson's eyes went wide with shock. I didn't move my hand. The boy's skin was much too nice and warm and soft for me to do that.

Slowly, Grayson melted into my touch, his breath coming out in a long contented sigh. "Well," he mumbled into my fingers. "Does it sound like a plan?"

Guilt rippled through me. It *did* sound like a plan, save for one small detail.

"I'm not very good with a spear," I admitted, already regretting what I was about to say next. "But I know someone who is."

CHAPTER SIXTY-THREE

GRAYSON

APRIL 24 – MORNING

ANOTHER DREAM.

More screaming. More waves crashing on top of me. More hands holding me down, and more hands reaching for me.

When I awoke, I was standing at my bedroom door, my hand on the doorknob. I stumbled back, a gasp stuck in my throat. I had been gripping the doorknob so tightly that it had left a red imprint on my palm, hot and stinging. There was a vicious tugging in my heart, a need to be in the water. Lost in sleep and utterly defenseless, my body had moved of its own accord, following that need like a mouse smelling cheese in a trap.

What would have happened if I hadn't woken up?

I shuddered, my body tense and aching. I was covered in sweat, my pajamas sticking to me like a second layer of skin.

What would have happened? Would I have made it out of the house? Would I have made it down to the ocean's edge?

Would I have walked right in?

Grayson Shaw. The one who was promised. Here.

I turned to my desk, where Ma's journal sat. It was open, its pages rustling, beckoning me closer. As I walked to the desk, a gust of wind fluttered through the window, and the pages began to whip back and forth, turning so quickly that the words became a blur. As the horrific sound of paper tearing met my ears, I surged forward, slapping my hand onto the tumbling pages.

The wind stopped abruptly, the sudden silence heavy and ominous. I peeked down at the pages trapped beneath my splayed fingers.

The woman and her baby stared up at me. The baby's eyes were scratched out, and the mother was grinning, her mouth full of blood.

I ripped my hand away with a gasp, heart pounding in my ears. But when I looked again, the woman was back to standing in the water swarming with black tentacles, gifting her baby to them. Chest heaving, I scanned the page. Barely legible lines now made sense, chicken scratch became gentle words with swooping letters. Several trembled and jumped in place, bolder than the others.

> Bargain
> Blood oath
> Linked

My scars burned. I bit my lip, letting out a choked laugh. "Shit." It felt good to swear, so I did it again.

The one who was promised, the voices sang through my open window. *Here.*

I slammed the window shut.

The journal was screwing with me, making me see things that weren't there, hear things that weren't there. It was leaking into my dreams, feeding into my paranoia, making me insane.

Unable to help it, I turned the page, hoping it would return to scribbles.

> They come out at night
> They'll give you a fright
> If you choose to swim in the dark
> So swim if you dare
> But you better take care
> For you shall become their mark
> With cold dead hands they'll grab you

Your fears of death will come true
You can't scream cry or hide.
They'll pull you down
Until you drown
Your corpse shall be their bride.
So do not swim in the dark.

The Barrens' Lullaby littered the lines. Over and over. Words stacked on top of each other, letters tumbling over one another. Some words were circled until the page had torn through. Some were underlined. Others were repeated, like Ma was stuck in a cycle, obsessive, intent on getting the point across.

Night. Night. Night.
Cold Dead Cold Dead Hands. Hands. Hands.

My lungs began to scream, and I realized I'd been holding my breath. I let it out in a quick *whoosh*. I could feel it, the beginning of a great culmination. It was all connected somehow . . . connected to *me*.

But how? And, God, *why*?

The clock in the kitchen chimed, time passing, uncaring of my troubles. I was late for work again. Mr. Brightly would have my head, my payroll, or both.

I closed the book with shaking fingers, peeled off my wet pajamas, and quickly filtered through the rumpled clothes discarded on the desk chair. Sand still clung to my pants from the night before, a faint dampness to the shirt sleeves, a whiff of salt air. I shut my eyes, inhaling deeply, allowing the memories of Evanora to wash over me, sending the feelings of dread back into the crevices of my mind. Her lips on my cheek, her hand cupping my jaw, her teasing smile as she whispered, "My brave heart."

The clock chimed again, and the dread returned.

I left the room.

I circled back.

I grabbed the journal.

YER FIRED."

I stared at Mr. Brightly, waiting for him to crack a smile, slap me on the back, and bark at me to get to work.

It didn't come.

Mr. Brightly planted his hands on his hips, sighing loudly through his fat nose. "Are ya deaf, boy? I said yer *fired*." He tapped his boot heavily on the ground, jerking his head in the direction of town. "Go on," he snapped, like I was some stray dog that had wandered in looking for scraps, "git!"

I took off my cap and began wringing it with my hands. "But . . . But . . ." I stammered out. "But I'm the best net mender you have!"

"Aye," Mr. Brightly agreed somberly. "Ya *were*."

"Please," I begged, seconds away from dropping to my knees in a full-on grovel, "Mr. Brightly, I *need* this job. Pa and I barely get by with both our payrolls combined."

Mr. Brightly was brutally stubborn, his one good eye slicing right through me. "Ya should've thought about that when ya decided to keep droppin' in whenever it pleased ya."

I looked around desperately, grasping at straws. "I'll do a week's worth of labor for free."

Mr. Brightly began to shake his head. "Now, Grayson—"

"Two weeks. Three!"

He held up a hand when I opened my mouth to sell my soul. "That's enough, boy." He looked at me with a moderate amount of disgust. "Don't ya have any dignity? Pleadin' the way ya are . . . Have ya not a single ounce of shame?"

I didn't. I glanced down at my rumpled cap, feeling hot tears of frustration sting my eyes. "Please, Mr. Brightly. Don't fire me," I said quietly. "Net mending is all I know. It's the one thing I'm actually good at." I looked at him, mouth clamped tightly to keep it from wobbling. "It's the one thing that helps me stay connected to Warrick."

Mr. Brightly softened, the cruelty slipping off his face like water on a duck's back. "Perhaps ya should've thought about that too." He crossed his arms against his wide chest. "Collect yer things and begone from 'ere.

The next time I leave my office, I don't wanna see ya 'ere, loiterin' and wastin' time."

Red-hot anger flared in my veins. "Are you serious?"

"As serious as a sinner in church." Mr. Brightly turned his back to me. "Ya can expect to see yer last payroll in the mail. Now, git."

Rage. I was practically convulsing with it. As Mr. Brightly stormed back to his office, I stared at the scattered chum buckets, the discarded brooms, and the nets I'd never fix again. I wanted to smash everything—kick over the buckets, snap the brooms, slice through the ropes. A mess so big even Jasper would be impressed.

Pa would be furious. Worse, he'd be disappointed. I needed to fix this— before word got out that I'd lost my job. Easier said than done. In Tully, gossip spread faster than fire. I had to get another job. Maybe Dick's Home Goods needed someone to stock shelves. I could perhaps be a bagger for Mott's Pharmacy. Maybe the Welcome Home Tea Room could use a dish-washer. I needed something lined up before Pa found out.

But instead, I wandered aimlessly, my hands itching at my sides, Ma's journal heavy in my pocket. Without realizing it, I found myself in Han-nigan's Cove.

The air was thick with voices, laughter, jeering taunts. A man leaned against the cave wall, knife in one hand, wood in the other. Two others tossed rocks into the waves, while two more circled each other in a crude ring drawn in the sand, shouting obscenities behind wooden spears.

Peter stopped circling Jasper and raised his spear at me. "Shaw!" he called out. "Come down here! Let's have a rematch!"

I just wanted to be alone. Shoving my hands into my pockets, I glanced at the sandy steps I had just crept down. "I don't really feel like kicking your ass again, Lyre."

Jasper, who was very clearly avoiding eye contact with me, snorted out a laugh. "Oh, *burn*!"

Peter smacked the blunt end of his spear into Jasper's gut. "Shut up! He didn't kick my ass. He got lucky."

Jasper, hunched over and rubbing the tender spot on his stomach, shook his head. "Didn't look that way from where I was standing," he wheezed.

My heart lurched at Jasper's loyalty. Even in the middle of a fight, he came to my defense. I felt a little bad about threatening to break his leg the last time I'd seen him.

Peter scoffed, turning to Ambrose, who hadn't looked up from the block of wood he was whittling. "You believe me, right?"

Ambrose's knife slid across the wood in slow, methodical movements. He paused, blowing off the loose shavings before twisting the block back and forth, inspecting it. "You lost, Peter," he said, almost sounding bored. "What else is there to believe?"

Peter's face twisted into a pout. He threw his spear into the sand and stormed off, glaring at me. Owen and Sebastian stopped tossing stones, watching him with mild amusement. Owen raised a hand in a small wave. His face was still bruised, but his left eye was open again. "Hey th-th-there, Grayson."

I nodded in greeting. "Owen. Sebastian."

Sebastian waved at me to come closer. "Come on down, chap! The water's warm."

I trudged down, avoiding Sebastian's gaze, still bitter about his bastard uncle firing me. Jasper returned to slashing at imaginary foes. Ambrose kept carving his block, but his eyes stayed on me. I met his piercing blue gaze and held it, refusing to look away first. "Ambrose," I said carefully.

Ambrose's upper lip curled into a sneer, but all I saw was the cornered animal in the alleyway, drunk and destructive. Ambrose glanced back down at his carving. "What do you want, Shaw?"

To be alone. To have my job back. For the voices to stop whispering. "World peace," I said, keeping my steps light, my pace even.

Sebastian slapped his knee. "Too late for that, I'm afraid."

"Yeah," Owen said, tossing a handful of pebbles into the water, watching as they rained down in little droplets, "world peace means no Hunt."

Sounds amazing. I wondered if Evanora and I would have met if the Hunt didn't exist. Would we still have this unexplainable connection? Would I still crave her like Pastor Kline craved his alcohol, or like how Ambrose craved violence?

Sebastian bent to pick up a shell. "That doesn't sound so bad, in all honesty." He tapped Owen on the shoulder, leaning in to show him his findings. Owen touched the shell's rigid edges, whispering something that caused Sebastian to throw his head back and laugh.

Peter snorted from his spot underneath the tree. "Uh, hello? Lethe needs the Hunt to survive." He rolled his shoulders and looked away. "Dipshit."

Jasper fumbled with his spear, accidentally dropping it into the sand. He jutted out his bad leg to pick it up. "Well," he grunted, straightening, "if there was world peace, then that would mean the mermaids and humans are still in harmony, right?" He shrugged, passing the spear from one hand to the other. "From what I can remember in school, Lethe was thriving when peace reigned between our species, and we wouldn't need the Hunt to survive."

I raised my eyebrows, impressed. "I didn't think you paid attention in school," I said before I could stop myself. "You were too busy trying to make everyone laugh."

Jasper grinned at me. Then he remembered that we were in the middle of a fight; his cheeks went red, and he turned the smile into a scowl. "I pay attention to a lot of things," he said quietly, looking away.

Ambrose sighed loudly. "Why are we even talking about this?" He tilted his head, his knife slipping through the wood like butter. "World peace doesn't exist. The Hunt does. So, stop talking about stupid things that aren't real."

Everyone went silent. Peter kicked at the sand. Jasper blocked an invisible attack. Owen and Sebastian remained huddled together underneath the lip of the cave's mouth, moving on from throwing rocks to collecting shells. Ambrose's knife kept moving.

The wind whistled through the caves, tearing across the beach like a phantom. It ripped at my jacket, pulling on the ends, revealing the inside lining. Ambrose's hands stilled. "What'cha got there, Shaw?" he asked, nodding to Ma's journal peeking out from the top of the inside pocket.

I smoothed my jacket back into place. "Nothing."

Ambrose chuckled, low and dark, as he pushed off the rock wall. "Come on, now," he said, tucking the knife and wood away. "Share with the class."

Peter, sensing approaching shenanigans, stumbled to his feet. Wiping the sand from his pants, he trotted toward us, a cynical grin on his face. "Sharing is caring!" he called in a singsong voice.

I began to hurriedly button up my jacket, my feet moving on their own as they took me backward, step by step. "It's nothing," I tried again.

Ambrose and Peter were in front of me. "Doesn't look like nothing," Ambrose said, his fingers inching toward the edge of my jacket. "Looks like something you're trying to hide."

I wrapped my arms around my waist and jerked away, my body twisting out of Ambrose's prying reach. But there was Peter, behind me and ready for the escape attempt. I slammed into him, feeling small against his Goliath stature. He grabbed my arms and spun me back toward Ambrose, pinning me against his stomach, crowing with joy.

"I got him!" He laughed. "I got him!"

Ambrose's lips curved into a half grin. Wordlessly, he popped my buttons back open. He worked slowly, knowing I was defenseless to stop him.

"Please," I tried, squirming. "Please don't—"

The last button was released, and Ambrose's hands were inside my jacket, feeling for the hidden pocket.

"Please!" I cried out, sounding weak and hating myself for it.

Ambrose's fingers latched on to the book, and he wrenched it out of my jacket. "Well, now," he said softly, eyeing the cracked leather cover. "What have we here?"

Peter's grip on me remained strong, but he groaned loudly, his breath hot and vile on my neck. "A book? Are you serious? We're bugging him about a book?"

Ambrose clucked his tongue. "Not just any book, Peter." He cracked the journal open, his fingers slipping over the pages almost reverently. "A *banned* book."

Owen stopped inspecting shells. "A banned book? Really?" He started to hobble over. "I've n-never s-s-seen one of . . . those before."

Sebastian pressed a hand against Owen's chest, halting him in his teetering tracks. "Maybe don't go over there just yet," he whispered.

Jasper lowered his spear, his face sweaty and pale. He swallowed hard, the sound nearly audible over the crashing waves. "Lay off him, you guys," he called from the circle.

"Shut up, cripple," Ambrose said idly, turning the pages, his eyes glued to the scribbles and pictures. "A banned book," he said again, shaking his head in mock amazement. "I have to hand it to you, Shaw—you're a lot more of a rebel than I took you for."

Sebastian's hand was still on Owen's chest. "Dare I ask what a banned book is?"

Owen glanced at him, looking positively miserable that he was standing in the cave's mouth and not in the sunlight, looking at the journal. "Lethe used to-to-to have a t-ton of books that t-t . . . talked about mermaids—th-their origins, culture, and how . . . they helped the island grow. When the-the-the—" He stopped, wincing a silent apology. "The Initial War happened, all books pertaining . . . to . . . them were banned." He shrugged. "Most were burned in order t-t-t . . . to n-not encourage open minds to get any ideas. We are t-t-taught only what . . . the elders of Lethe want us to kn-know. Everything else is-is-is ancient history and"—he shrugged again—"eventually forgotten."

"Boring!" Peter drawled, his grip on me growing loose.

"Seriously, guys," Jasper said, inching out of the circle. "Let's just give it back to Grayson."

"Let's just mind our own business, village idiot!" Peter snapped, the tension holding me still going completely loose.

I leapt forward, a coiled spring finally released. Peter let out a guffawing gasp, his frantic hands reaching for me. But I was already far out of reach, racing for Ambrose.

Ambrose looked up from the book in time to see the last bit of my charge. I tucked my body, tight as a bullet, before pummeling right into his chest. The momentum carried us onto the ground, a tangled mass of limbs, mouths full of sand and swear words.

"Oh, *God!*" Sebastian cried.

"Oh, *sh-sh-shit,*" Owen groaned.

Jasper gasped. Peter laughed.

When the dust finally settled, I was on top, hands gripping Ambrose's shirt, lifting his head off the ground. "Give me back my book!" I shouted, fire and fury spitting from my mouth.

Ambrose coughed, hacked, and wheezed, the air knocked clean out of his lungs. But even as he struggled, he managed to grin up at me, a devilish gleam to his eyes. "I don't *have* your book." He jerked his head in the direction of the crashing waves, his eyes not leaving mine.

Horror sent my veins withering, the blood pumping inside them ice-cold. I looked up, and there was Ma's journal, soaring through the air, a bird made of paper. It landed unceremoniously in the ocean and floated precariously on top of the churning gray water, a high stakes balancing act. Foam licked at the cover. The waves batted playfully at the pages, pulling the book farther and farther from the shoreline.

Ambrose's coughing turned into a laugh. "Go for a swim, Shaw."

Rage exploded in me. I slammed Ambrose back down. I had to get that book. I needed it—desperately. I needed it like air. My entire body screamed for it.

Ambrose's hands shot up, grabbing my jacket. I stumbled, nearly falling on top of him. He bared his teeth, breathing heavily, eyes wild. "On second thought, maybe I'll keep you right here," he snarled.

Then he yanked me down. His forehead crashed into my nose with a sickening crack.

Pain exploded in my skull. I gasped, but it came out as a strangled wheeze. Blood gushed from my nose, flooding my mouth. My vision blurred, the world spinning. But Ambrose wasn't done.

His forehead hit me again—harder. Agony ripped through my face like fire, and I struggled for breath, fighting against the crushing pain. Something was broken. My cheek? My nose? I couldn't tell. Everything burned, burned, burned.

My fingers dug into the sand as I tried to push back, but Ambrose was relentless, yanking me down again. The pain flared with each brutal thud of his skull against mine. I couldn't breathe. I couldn't think. I had to fight back.

I grabbed for anything—his jacket, his shirt, his chest.

His neck, warm, exposed, vulnerable.

I wrapped my fingers around it and squeezed as hard as I could.

Ambrose's grip on my jacket immediately went soft. His breathing grew high-pitched and strained, his mouth opening and closing like a beached fish. His hands became claws as they ripped at my clothes, fighting for a piece of me, returning empty.

I squeezed. Harder and harder, my teeth gritted, blood pouring from my nose like a faucet. Flecks of crimson began to dot Ambrose, but even that didn't stop me. I wanted to squeeze until the smile was off his smug face, until the feral glimmer was gone from his eyes.

I wanted to squeeze until he was dead.

Ambrose squeaked out a whimper, his legs flailing behind us, gaining no purchase in the sand. His face was shifting from a speckled red to a mottled purple, his eyes, wide and frantic, growing bloodshot.

I howled, loud and primal, and squeezed harder. Power that felt foreign surged through me. I was strong, an immovable force.

Hands were on my back, then my shoulders, then under my arms, wrenching me backward. I shrieked and fought against Owen as he pulled me farther and farther from Ambrose. "Let go of me!" I cried. "Let go!"

"For Pete's s-s-sake, Grayson! Enough!" Owen yelled, hauling me back despite my efforts to break free. "You're killing him!"

Peter was already at Ambrose's side, rubbing his back as Ambrose curled into himself, gasping for air, his neck swollen. Dark bruises from my hands already bloomed across his pale skin. The sight made my stomach lurch.

Nausea finally made an appearance, and I doubled over, moaning as my stomach heaved and clenched. My face barked with pain, but even the promise of exacerbating it didn't stop the dry heaving. When my stomach was empty and my mouth tasted of blood and bile, I slowly straightened, light-headed and feeling more like myself—embarrassed, ashamed, and scared.

Owen's face was contorted with concern. "What's wrong with you?"

I tried to shake my head, but a dizzy spell sent the ground teetering. God, I had wanted to kill Ambrose so badly only moments before. Now I could barely look at him without remorse flooding my system. "My . . . My book," I mumbled. "I need my book."

The sound of sloshing footsteps pulled me from my spiral. Jasper emerged from the waves, soaked to his waist, the journal clutched in his hand. He peeled seaweed from it with disgust, flinging the strands back into the water.

Relief hit me like a wave. But as I reached for the journal, I stopped. Blood—my blood—covered my hands.

I froze.

Sebastian stepped forward, his expression distant, and handed me a blue handkerchief. He didn't look at me, keeping a safe distance as he stretched his arm out. "There you go," he said quietly.

I uttered my thanks and quickly wiped off my hands. When they were clean and the blood was just a memory, I worked on my face, tenderly dabbing around my throbbing nose and burning cheeks. I tried to give the handkerchief back, but Sebastian quickly shook his head and held up his hands. "Oh, no," he stammered. "It's all yours."

Jasper offered me Ma's journal. I took it with shaking hands. There was the smallest smile playing on Jasper's lips. His eyes carried admiration with a hint of fear. "Good job," he said jovially. "I'd say more, but I'm pretty sure we're still in a fight." He started to walk away, then wheeled back, frowning. "Shouldn't you be at work?"

I swallowed, the taste as vile as my mood. "I was fired."

Jasper whistled. "Yikes. Well"—he clapped me on the back—"good luck explaining that to Rowan. I'll sing a song at your funeral." And with that, Jasper collected his socks and shoes, blew Peter and Ambrose a raspberry, and marched off the beach.

"You sh-sh-should go," Owen said quietly. "You don't want t-to be here when Ambrose gets his s-st-strength back."

"Honestly, I don't think any of us do," Sebastian admitted. "The death glare Peter's giving us right now is a sight to behold."

I left the beach, my head bent low, my heart hanging even lower.

I had a feeling that not even confessing my sins to Pastor Kline would save my soul this time.

CHAPTER SIXTY-FOUR

EVANORA

APRIL 24 – EVENING

ILLERON AND I LEFT FOR THE ISLAND AS SOON AS THE WATER temperature dropped and the sun began casting its long shadows. Despite my nearly delirious desire to see the boy, I couldn't shake the nerves gnawing at me.

This would be the warrior's first time meeting Grayson. He'd seen him from afar—always distant, never close enough to speak. His perception of Grayson was like a warped reflection in rippling water. I didn't expect Illeron to like him as much as I did, but I hoped he could develop feelings beyond hate and mistrust.

Tonight wasn't just about discussing how best to turn boats into splinters. It was about their first meeting, and I wanted it to be more than a clash of egos. Illeron would wage a battle of pride, Grayson a battle of wits. Both would fight to win my favor—whether they realized it or not. Feelings would get hurt, and I wanted it over as quickly as possible.

I scooted onto the beach, the sand biting into my scales. I hoped Grayson would bring his soft blanket with him. The warrior remained in the water, poking out just enough to expose his armored chest. I patted the sand beside me. "You can come up here, you know."

Illeron stayed put, his gaze flitting to every little thing that made noise.

I could see the tension in his neck, the tightness running along his jaw. "We should both be in the water in case we need to leave quickly."

I giggled, flopping onto the sand. "Nothing is going to get us, Illeron. Do try to soften your fins."

I could feel the warrior's eyes settle on me. I lifted my head with a frown. "What is it?"

Illeron shook his head, a smirk on his thin lips. "It's nothing."

I slapped the wet sand in mock fury. "You will tell me this instant."

Illeron cocked his head, scrutinizing me. "It's just that . . ." He sighed out a quiet laugh, running a hand over his head. "There are moments when I look at you and think, 'There's no way this is the same mermaid from a month ago, sneaking off to avoid her royal duties. She really has become a great leader.' " He gave me a sardonic smile. "Then I watch you beach yourself on the sand without a care in the world and think, 'Ah, there she is. Dashing headfirst into danger, as usual.' "

I squawked and threw a clump of sand at the warrior. He swooped to the side without even flinching. "You are so *rude*!" I laughed.

Illeron shook his head somberly as he narrowly missed another shower of sand. "Telling the truth is a fatal character flaw of mine, I'm afraid."

I stopped, arm poised in midair, a wad of wet sand in my grasp. I gaped at Illeron. "Did you just make a joke?"

"Me? Never." The warrior tilted his body so that he was almost lying on top of the water's surface. There was a flash of crimson in the fading sunlight, the quick flick of his tail, and then a wall of water was careening toward me.

I squealed and covered my head with my hands, but it was no use. I was instantly drenched, my hair dotted with sand, the strands sticking to my shoulders and chest. I sputtered, swiping the water droplets off my face. "Rude *and* mean!" I shrieked, grabbing fistfuls of sand and aiming them at Illeron.

The warrior held up his hands. "Truce! I do not want to be caught attempting to drown my queen when Grayson Shaw arrives."

Sniffing delicately, I pointed my nose into the air and let the sand fall between my fingers. "Very well," I said, slapping my hands together. "But only because you know I'd win."

Illeron chuckled, shaking his head. "I think it's a rule; always let the royals win."

I settled back onto my hands, watching as the sun dipped lower in the sky. "I think my appah created it."

"I think so too."

A heavy silence drifted between us, full of memories that brought as much pain as they did joy.

"You know," Illeron said, "I used to patrol with Rainos."

Shock electrified my nerves. "Really?"

The warrior nodded with a smile. "Yes. He taught me almost everything I know. How to hunt, how to fight." He shrugged gently. "I owe him everything. I wish I could tell him that."

I bit my lip, stifling a sudden uninvited flood of emotion. "I never saw that side of him." I made a face. "In all honesty, I didn't even know we were at war with the humans until it was nearly too late."

Illeron's smile went sad. "I think he did that on purpose. He wanted you to maintain your innocence for as long as possible."

I snorted, flicking away the rogue tear that raced down my cheek. "And look at where that got us—an unfit leader who can't even bear the weight of her crown."

The warrior shook his head. "I maintain what I said earlier." He moved closer to the beach. "You really have become a great leader."

I scoffed, wiping a couple more damned tears away. "Through trial and error."

"As it should be," Illeron offered. "You understand heartache and loss because you were forged in it. You've witnessed death and decay, and yet you refuse to let it break you. Gods, Evanora, you traveled into the Barrens for your pod. You've raced through the darkness and surfaced victorious."

I tried to smile, but I felt hollow, pain and regret sifting through my veins like sludge. "I would hardly call rescuing a third of the pod victorious."

"If you hadn't gone in there at all, that number would be severely different," Illeron countered. "Those trials and tribulations aren't to be taken lightly; they are what's made you stronger."

I looked at the warrior, my war-torn heart beating anew. "Thank you," I said softly.

Illeron shook his head. "No need to thank me. I'm simply stating facts."

Still, I could see the rosy tint in his cheeks, his eyes flitting from mine, the fidgeting of his tail beneath the lulling waves.

"What do you think life will be like?" I asked. "After the Hunt?"

Illeron laughed dryly. "You mean if we survive?"

I shot him a wilting glare.

The warrior cleared his throat. "I haven't really thought about it, to be honest." He rubbed his lower lip in thought. "The Hunt is all I've known—all *we've* known. Cowering in fear at every shadow that passed over us, barely getting by on the limited resources we have." He shrugged stiffly. "Not even visiting the surface to feel the sun on our scales, the fresh air. I think . . ." He shook his head. "I think we've forgotten what it's like to be free."

He looked at me, smiling. "That's what I think life will be like after the Hunt. It'll be free. Free to do whatever we want, go wherever we want. No more fear, no more starving, no more gods-forsaken Dark Madness and fin rot. Just . . . complete and utter freedom."

I closed my eyes and inhaled deeply, trying to imagine it all. "Sounds nice."

Illeron shifted closer, almost fully out of the water now. "Sounds like a fantasy?"

"No," I said, opening my eyes and gazing down at the bracelet encircling my wrist. I touched it lovingly, my fingers drifting to the octopus charm. "It sounds like a promise."

There was a beat of silence, then movement; Illeron's hand rested on top of mine, uncertain and careful. "That will eventually rust and break," he said in a low voice.

My heart stuttered. "The sentiment will remain," I said softly.

Illeron kept his hand on mine, his grip tightening ever so slightly. There was a sound deep in his chest, a rumbling that crept up his throat and into his mouth. "How old are you, Evanora?" he asked suddenly.

I whipped my head up to look at him. "What?"

"How old are you?" He laughed sharply. "And how old is Grayson?"

I faltered. "I don't understand how—"

"Humans are *built differently*. They aren't designed to last long. It might be fun, being with him now; by life's sordid standards, you two are probably about the same age. But mermaids have different timelines compared to humans, and eventually, you'll see it: the aging. It'll be impossible to ignore. You'll see gray hairs speckling his head, large creases around his eyes and mouth. You'll see his body, strong and tall, become frail and weak, twisted and gnarled like a root."

I shook my head, my scales crawling. "No," I bit out. "No. That's enough, Illeron."

The warrior persisted. "You will stay young forever, and he will grow old right before your eyes. Your visits on this decrepit beach will become shorter and fewer, until eventually they won't happen at all because he will be too fragile to even make it down the stairs."

My magic coursed within me, crackling against my rigid fins in warning. "That's enough!"

"It's going to happen, and you won't be able to stop it. You'll only be able to sit back and watch as he slowly forgets all about you." Illeron clutched my hand and pulled it against his chest. "But *I* wouldn't, Evanora. I would *always* be there for you." He dipped his chin, brushing my fingers against his cold lips. "Don't you see that?"

My Gift flared, a burst of wild light mimicking the rage igniting my blood. I ripped my hand away from the warrior, my teeth bared, a hiss on my tongue. Summoning all the power I possessed, I leaned forward, intent on planting my hands on Illeron's chest and giving him a shock that would have him regretting every foul lie he had said.

But what came wasn't an endless stream of magic. It was words, spiked with fury as they tumbled off my lips, filling the heated space between us, never to be taken back. "It's never going to be you, Illeron!"

The warrior went utterly still. The waterfall roared, and the waves carried on with their shushing lullaby. The cliffs howled above, and the hungry seagulls cried. Time continued to pass by, and the silence between me and Illeron was deafening.

Illeron placed a hand over his heart, trying in vain to keep his stoic expression from crumbling. "I see," he said, his voice catching, his words thick and scratchy.

I moaned, dropping my head into my hands. "Illeron—"

The warrior held up his free hand. "No. Don't. You don't need to make excuses or shower me in all the reasons why it's not me."

Keeping my face hidden, I shook my head. "But you don't understand."

Illeron laughed coldly. "You're right—I don't." He sighed, the sound coming out in a low groan. "I'll never understand why you are choosing him over me."

I lifted my head, my bottom lip wobbling, pain etched so deeply into my face that I was certain my skin would crack. "I don't have a *choice*."

The warrior clenched his jaw so tightly that I could see the arteries in his neck bulge. "See, that's where you're wrong, Evanora. You do have a choice. You'll always have a choice. And you made it loud and clear that it'll never, ever be me."

I so desperately wanted—no, *needed*—to tell him about the connection Grayson and I shared. He would understand that I truly didn't have a choice in the direction my heart was taking me. The cursed thing was in charge, and I was merely a hostage to it. My heart belonged to Grayson. It had since the moment he'd found me on the beach. And it was completely out of my control. "Illeron . . ."

"Forget it," the warrior said curtly, turning away. "Let's just wait for Grayson."

Illeron returned to the water. He didn't look at me, didn't talk to me. He was a black void, back to being the warrior with icy ocean water in his veins. The one who didn't know how to smile, or make jokes, or comfort. The one I'd fondly call an uptight sea urchin. The one who loved me and kept it hidden, afraid to stir the waters.

It was suddenly painfully obvious that I wasn't the only one who had changed. Now, staring at the warrior, at the shell he had reverted back to, I feared that I had just ruined any chance of seeing his smile ever again.

We waited in silence for the boy to arrive.

We waited for a long time.

CHAPTER SIXTY-FIVE

GRAYSON

APRIL 24 – EVENING

WHERE DO YOU THINK YOU'RE GOING?"

I froze, elbows deep in my bag. I craned my head over my shoulder to see Pa standing next to the door. "Nowhere."

Pa remained in my doorway, leaning stiffly against the frame, his arms crossed against his chest. He stared pointedly at my bag, bulging with blankets, cinnamon buns, and a few jars of salves I had found in the back of my closet. "I find that really hard to believe."

My heart pounded in my chest, the unease suffocating. I should've left for the beach sooner—no, I should've left *hours* ago. Pa had been late coming home from work, and my mind raced through a hundred possible reasons why. But even as my thoughts spun, I knew I should've taken the chance to slip away, to avoid this moment. Yet, like a fool, I'd wasted that precious window of time with cleaning my face, slathering ointment under my eyes to hide the bruising, and drying Ma's journal by the fire. Thank God I'd at least had the sense to bring it back to my room instead of leaving it on the kitchen table where Pa could find it.

If I had been gone, I would have avoided the awkward talk that was clearly about to happen, the one I had been dreading ever since speaking to Mr. Brightly that morning.

"You know," Pa said, pushing off the doorframe and leisurely strolling into the room, "I had the strangest conversation today." He chuckled wryly. "All sorts of tall tales that had me scratching my head."

I gulped, slowly pulling my hands out of the bag. "What did Mr. Brightly tell you?"

Pa's gaze fixed on me, his smile curdling into something sour. "Mr. Brightly didn't tell me anything. But I can tell you what I heard from Jasper. That clown walked into the shop this morning, dripping wet, raving about how you lost your job and nearly beat the life out of Ambrose Grieves." He shook his head, half in disbelief. "And you know what I thought? I thought, 'No way. Not *my* son. This ginger-haired fool must be talking about someone else. Because there's no way my son could ever do such things. Not when he knows how badly we need the money and how dangerous the Grieves are.' "

I winced, wishing the floor would turn into a mouth and swallow me whole. "Pa . . ."

Pa unfolded his arms and slammed a hand against the desk, causing me to flinch. "Christ above. So, it is true! It is, isn't it?" He turned away, running his hands through his hair before resting them on the back of his neck. "What on God's green earth is wrong with you, Grayson?"

"I don't know!" I pleaded, watching Pa pace. "I don't know what's wrong with me!"

And it was true—I didn't. I could understand the Brightly thing, but the anger? The need to hurt Ambrose over a book? That was a different story.

Pa shot me a scorching look. "Well, you better figure it out, and soon." He stopped in front of me. "I will not be the laughingstock of Tully. Not again." He shook a finger at me. "I will not resort to walking in the shadows because everywhere I go, people are whispering about our mess of a family. First Warrick, then Persephone, and now you?" He sucked in a breath, staring up at the ceiling. "God, am I the only sane person in this family? What did I do to deserve this?"

"None of it was my fault, Pa!"

"Oh, of course not!" Pa fired back. "Nothing ever is! You're just this saint, aren't you? This perfect little child who can do no wrong. I tell you not to see your ma, and you go anyway, getting hurt in the process. I try to train you for the Hunt, and you practically get kicked out of the last challenge. Warrick got you a decent-paying job—not at the butcher shop like I wanted, because heaven forbid you see even a drop of blood—and you throw that away too! But, of course, *none* of it is *your* fault." He pointed a finger at me. "It's time to wake up, boy. Own your mistakes for once in your life!"

I stepped away from Pa and sat on the edge of my bed. "Do you think I *wanted* to get fired? Or that I *wanted* to get in a fight today?" I laughed humorlessly, shaking my head. "Do you think I woke up and decided to be a violent degenerate? Look at me!" I gestured to my swollen nose, the splashes of color underneath my eyes. "This *isn't* me!"

Pa pursed his lips, then let out a long breath through his nose, shrugging as he did. "Honestly, Grayson, I don't know what to think. All I know is that you're right about one thing: The boy I'm staring at right now isn't my son."

His words were a blade slicing into my heart. I lowered my head so Pa couldn't see the tears of frustration welling up in my eyes. "You're not listening to me," I whispered. "You are so focused on how angry and disappointed you are that you aren't hearing a single word I'm saying."

Pa went quiet, and I could feel the energy in the room shift, thick and electrifying. The tension could be cut into a million pieces and still demand to be felt. He tapped his foot on the ground, thinking, deciding which way he wanted to parent me. The options were slim: scold and discipline, or comfort and nurture.

Talk to me, I begged inwardly. *Ask me what's wrong. Sit down on the bed and just* listen.

"You're grounded," Pa snapped. "No more racing away to God knows where. No more visiting your ma. No more pretending that nothing is your fault. You hear me? No more." He shook his finger at me. "You're stuck in this house until I say otherwise. I expect you to use that time to work on yourself; this isn't a vacation, all right?"

Head still bent low, I laughed, quiet and helpless. There was no use arguing. Pa had spoken, and as far as he was concerned, his word was a step below God's. "Fine."

My pa nodded sharply. "Good." He walked to my desk and grabbed my sketchbook and pencil. "You can start now," he said as he thrust the book into my arms.

"What do you want me to do?" My voice was small, the tears I had been holding back spilling over.

Pa cleared his throat, his face tightening with discomfort as my tears hit the paper. He pointed to the blank page, his voice almost mechanical. "I want you to make a list of all the places in town that might be hiring. Think of things to say that make you sound like a desirable employee." He glared at the droplets staining the page. "And don't you dare mention the fact that you were fired. If they ask about any of that, be polite. I won't have you dragging Mr. Brightly or anyone else through the mud just because you messed up."

"I didn't—" I swallowed the rest of my sentence at the dark look in Pa's eyes. "Fine," I said instead, the sudden weight of exhaustion pressing down on me.

Pa closed the window on his way out, the act feeling like the final nail in my coffin. Even long after he'd left the room, I didn't open it. I just sat there, perched on the edge of my bed, feeling like I was on the outside of my life looking in, watching helplessly from the sidelines as other people tampered with the timeline, orchestrating events completely out of my hands. I wanted to scream, to shatter the glass separating us, to seize control. But all I could do was sit and watch the nightmare unfold on repeat.

The next morning, after Pa had left for work, I raced to the beach, holding on to the hope that Evanora was still there. *Maybe she spent the night*, I thought as I stumbled down the stairs, my hand barely grazing the steel railing. *Maybe she stayed.*

The beach was empty.

APRIL 25 – EVENING

It was the Night of the Betting, and not even being grounded could prevent me from not going.

"Grayson!" Pa called out from the kitchen. "Pastor Kline is here. Quit your dawdling."

I peeked my head around the door, staring down the long hallway. "I thought I was grounded."

Pa paused from working on his tie long enough to heave an exasperated sigh. "Tonight is an exception. I've said that about ten times now."

I thudded my head against the door, scrambling to find another reason to stay home. "It's going to look pretty ridiculous when I show up wearing the best suit I own and my face looks the way it does."

Pa snorted, which I assumed was his version of a laugh. "Well, you have no one to blame but yourself for that one." He turned to the hallway, trying to catch a glimpse of me hiding behind the door. "Ambrose Grieves will certainly be there despite the walloping you gave him." Pa flicked his hand impatiently in my direction. "Come on, now. We don't want to be late."

I want to be late. I want to miss the entire thing.

What was so exciting about parading around the audience like I was on display? The whole idea of people betting on hunters to encourage them to kill more mermaids made my skin crawl. It wasn't about the money that was shared amongst the gamblers and the hunting victor—it was about the need to destroy something beautiful, the desire to provoke as much bloodshed as possible.

"Grayson," Pa barked, slipping into his dinner jacket. "I'm not going to ask you again."

Admitting my defeat, I slowly emerged from behind my bedroom door. I held my hands away from my body and did a slow spin. "How do I look?"

Pa assessed me, raising his eyebrows appreciatively. "Not bad."

I scoffed. "I can't believe I still don't fit into Warrick's old clothes." I lifted my arms. "The sleeves are too long. And the pants are too big."

Pa approached me, running his hands across my shoulders in sharp, staccato movements in an effort to flatten the creases. He then went to my tie, straightening it out. "Well, it's not like we can afford a tailor."

I shook my head. "I wouldn't want to change it anyway." I smirked despite the flare of pain that shot up my nose. "Maybe I'll grow into it."

"Unlikely." Pa frowned at my unruly curls, eyeballing the one spiraling down the center of my forehead. "All that time getting ready, and you couldn't do anything with your hair?"

My cheeks burned with shame. Most of the time spent *getting ready* wasn't me getting ready at *all*. It was spent sneaking out my window, picking purple wildflowers, running to the beach, and tossing them onto the sand. We weren't meeting tonight, but after missing our last rendezvous, I hoped Evanora would come anyway, see the flowers, and wait for me. I needed to see her—my heart ached for it. I'd sneak out after the Night of the Betting, even if it meant adding more time to my grounding.

By the time I'd returned home, I had five minutes to pull myself together. My hair was hopeless, a casualty of the rush. "Untamable, I think."

There was a hint of pain in Pa's dark eyes. "You get that from your ma, I suspect." He scanned my face, the creases on his forehead deepening. "Amongst other things."

Like being crazy? Having bizarre moods? An intense fascination with the Barrens and the evil that lives there? I forced a crooked smile. "I'll take that as a compliment."

Pa huffed out a breath. "Pastor Kline is never going to give us a ride anywhere ever again if we keep him waiting like this."

"Don't worry," I joked. "I'm sure he has friends in his pocket to keep him occupied."

I was right. By the time we reached Fariid, Pastor Kline was a stumbling drunk. The ride was awkward—the wagon would veer off course, the horse would whinny with concern, and the pastor would overcorrect, almost throwing us into a ditch. Thirty minutes felt like hours, and I wasn't sure if my nausea was from the ride over or from the unknowns the night held.

The courthouse was packed, hot and thick with sweat and anticipation. The dimmed lights, the ominous piano, and the cloaked figures on the stage put my stomach instantly in knots. Flashbacks to the Symbolic Sign-In nearly had me coming to a shuddering halt, but Pa's glare kept me moving.

The bowls that we'd bled into rested on the platform's edge. The rusty blade was nowhere in sight, and I wasn't sure if that was better or worse.

Behind the figures, the betting board displayed the hunters' names. After my last challenge, mine had dropped down the rankings. I couldn't help but smile.

I was about to file into one of the pews when Pa grabbed me again. "No, no," he said, shaking his head. "Up front with the others."

They really *were* going to parade us around. "Please tell me I don't have to cut myself again," I whispered loudly.

Pa rolled his eyes. "I'll cut you now if it'll get you moving faster."

I trotted up to the front.

When the last of the hunters had assembled on the stage, the figures clad in robes wordlessly lifted their wrists and began to ring their bells in unison. A hush swept over the crowd, enraptured by the delicate jingling, all eyes on the front. It grew louder, and louder, until nothing but the bells could be heard, a chaotic carol that filled the entire courtroom.

I closed my eyes and pretended that Evanora was calling me to the beach. *Grayson Shawwwwww.*

I snapped my eyes open, dread turning my blood to ice.

The one who was promised. Hereeeeee.

The bells didn't drown out everything. They didn't silence the one thing I wished they would.

The man in the golden cloak raised his arms, and when he lowered them, the bells came to a crashing halt. Clasping his hands together, he strode to the center of the stage, staring down at the audience through his long, drooping hood. "People of Lethe," he announced, gesturing to us with the sweep of his arm, "your hunters!"

The crowd erupted into applause, cheers, and . . . God, was that a moan? They were ravenous, hungry for violence, for blood. The air crackled with a carnal energy.

Mayor McCoy, sitting near the front, shuffled toward the stage. The golden man's gaze snapped to him. They stared at each other. The mayor hesitated. "You don't want me to . . . I don't know . . . give a speech?"

The man in gold said nothing. The silence was thick. Mayor McCoy fidgeted, laughing awkwardly. "I could announce the hunters, say a prayer . . . recite a poem? A poem might be nice." He gave up when he was met with more silence. "Or I can sit back down," he muttered, trudging back to his seat and slumping like a scolded child.

The gold cloak turned back to the crowd. "People of Lethe," he said, his voice laced with power. "You've been with them from the beginning. You cheered for them during the First Festival. You watched as they pledged their loyalty during the Symbolic Sign-In. You've witnessed their struggles—against the nets, the ocean, one another." He paused, letting the words hang in the air. "It's all been for you. Every tear. Every drop of blood." He walked across the stage, stopping before each bowl. "Every blister, every callus, every ounce of sweat. All. For. You." He chuckled, a slimy sound that made my skin crawl. "And they would gladly do it again. They fight for change. For justice."

"Hell yeah!" Peter said from behind me, already sounding well lubricated with alcohol.

The gold-robed man stopped at the last bowl. "Now has come the time for you, dear audience, to return the favor. To give back to the hunters what they are owed." He looked up at the crowd, his hood swooping back and forth. "Can you do that, people of Lethe? Can you spare a few coins for your great and fearless hunters?"

The crowd screamed—actually screamed. At first, I thought something was wrong; we were being attacked, the building was caving in, someone was getting stabbed. But then, just barely, I could make out the sounds of purses snapping open, the clinking of coins spilling into sweaty palms, the flapping of paper bills against gloved hands.

Pa scoffed beside me. "It burns holes in their pockets if they don't spend it quick enough."

The hooded man placed a hand over his heart and bowed his head. "I thank you. The hunters thank you. Now"—he clapped his hands together—"you know how all this works. Everyone received their designated bidding card upon arrival, correct?"

A few audience members nodded. One man playfully waved his card at a young woman, earning a giggle from her, and a slap from his wife.

The man in the gold cloak nodded. "Good. When a hunter is brought forward, raise your card high and keep it there until we tally the bets. The more desirable the hunter, the fewer winnings for you, of course." He glanced at us. "And take heart, young hunters. If the odds are against you, use it to fuel your fire. Show Lethe you're not to be underestimated."

A couple hunters grunted in agreement. One literally punched himself in the face and screamed, "It's our time!"

The gold cloak turned back to the crowd. "You can bet on as many hunters as you'd like—well . . ." He chuckled darkly. "As long as your wallet allows for it."

The audience rumbled with laughter.

"Just get on with it!" a man shouted from the back pew. "I have money to spend and drinks to drink and women to fu—"

"As you wish." The golden man held up his hands in supplication. "When the last of the hunters has been betted on, please stick around for drinks, music, and joy. Our board members will approach you to discuss the details of your bets—to clarify who you bet on, the amount you are placing on which hunter, and so on and so forth. Now"—he waved a hand to several of the members in cloaks—"let us begin!"

One of the black-robed figures took a seat behind a desk, poised, pen in hand. Three others prowled the stage, eyes hidden beneath their hoods. The final one began lining us up. Feet shuffled, shoulders jostled. A fight almost broke out, which a red-robed figure quickly quelled. The black cloak herding us forward started with Ambrose.

The bastard looked immaculate, making me wonder if I'd even hurt him. His gray suit fit perfectly, and his navy-blue pocket square highlighted his eyes. His light blond hair was slicked back, not a strand out of place. The only thing out of character was the large blue plaid scarf around his neck.

The figure in the black cloak stood beside Ambrose and hovered their hand above his head—or tried to; he was so tall that their hand was only able to dance in the air beside his ear. "Ambrose Grieves," the black-robed figure called out in a voice that I instantly recognized to be Mrs. Morris.

The entire crowd erupted, hands shooting up, cards waving wildly. The black cloaks began counting, hands moving like orchestra conductors. When the tally was done, the numbers were whispered to the one at the desk, who scribbled it all down. For Ambrose, there was a lot to write.

Ambrose smirked arrogantly, dipped his head to the crowd, and took a step back.

And so, the Night of the Betting commenced.

Some received many bets. Some received none. Peter Lyre gained one bet from his mother, who waved her card wildly in the air like she was on fire. Pa received an impressive number of bets. Owen's number was nothing to laugh at. Even Jasper's name sent the crowd into a frenzy. Everyone loved an underdog.

Then it was my turn.

Mrs. Morris placed a hand on my back, lightly pushing me toward the edge of the stage. "This way, dear," she said softly.

I tried to steal a glimpse of her from behind the black hood's shadows, but her face was swallowed by darkness. It was a shame; the way my heart was pounding, I could've really used her comforting smile and gentle eyes.

Mrs. Morris placed me in the center of the stage and hovered her hand above my head. "Grayson Shaw," she announced loudly.

Almost everyone's hand shot upward. A sea of bidding cards flapped around frantically. People shrieked and panted, dogs in heat, thirsty for blood. There were so many cards in the air that, for a second, I thought it was a joke. I could feel Pa's pride simmering on the back of my head. Even Mrs. Morris, who was meant to be an unbiased member, gave my shoulder a squeeze when she returned me to my spot in the line. "Well *done*, Mr. Shaw! Well done!"

When the bets were tallied, the board was adjusted. Names moved up and down. Pa, Ambrose, and Mr. Grieves topped the board. I was expecting my name to nearly tumble off the bottom, but to my surprise, I slipped into fifteenth place. It wasn't the highest, but it was respectable.

Not everyone thought so.

"What the hell!" a voice cried out in frustration.

Jasper was stalking toward me. His bright blue suit still showcased the stain he had gotten before the First Festival. He looked anything but happy, and I had a feeling that it didn't have to do with our current fight, but a new one entirely.

"What the hell!" he said again, this time when he was standing in front of me.

"What's wrong?" I asked, keeping my voice neutral.

Jasper sputtered, spittle flying everywhere. "You know damn well what's wrong." He pointed a finger at the board. "I've done everything right, and you still got more bets than me?" He grabbed at his hair, pulling on the strands until they stood up in a wild, frizzy mess. "This is bullshit!"

I held up my hands. "Jasper, calm down." I lowered my voice and leaned in, hoping the die-hard fanatics couldn't hear me. "It's just a game."

I forgot that the die-hard fanatics included Jasper Warren. He gaped at me, his pale complexion shifting to a disturbing splotchy red. "A game?" he seethed. "A *game*?"

I winced, rubbing my forehead in exasperation. "Jasper, you know what I mean."

"This *game* is *everything* to me!" he shouted, pushing me in the chest.

I flinched away when he tried to shove me again. I could feel a thousand eyes on us, the feral desire pumping through the room like a toxin. "Jasper, lower your voice."

"Or what? Or everyone is going to find out what a fraud you are? That you hate the Hunt?"

There was a collective gasp in the room. Even the piano stuttered to a jarring halt.

I clenched my jaw. "That's enough, Jasper."

Jasper laughed incredulously, spreading his arms wide. "You aren't even trying! You don't even want to be a part of the Hunt!" He stomped forward until we were nose to nose. "Well, for your sake, I hope you lose. That way, all those dumb bets beside your name will mean nothing, and the money that you don't care about will go to someone else, someone who deserves it, someone who *wants* to be in this *game*."

Ouch. Harsh but true. Still, *ouch*. I frowned. "Well, that's not fair."

"What did you say?" Jasper demanded, breathing heavily in my face, still itching for a fight.

"I said I need some air," I lied. "Excuse me."

The music resumed. But the toxic carnal rage remained.

I pushed my way out of the main courtroom, avoiding the waiters dancing around with their trays of appetizers and champagne, ducking between fat men wielding cigars like weapons. By the time I made it to the grand entranceway, I was sweating inside my too-large dinner jacket and choking on cigar smoke.

I'd never seen Jasper act like that. Sure, we weren't exactly seeing eye to eye lately, but what had happened to the whole defend-the-best-friend-at-all-costs mission statement he constantly carried around like his very own cross?

The game—*the Hunt*—was getting to his head. No. It was already *in* his head. It had been since the day he was born.

The front doors were completely blocked with stuffy women in stuffy dresses, loud men in loud suits. Mr. Brightly was amongst them, laughing hard at a joke told by Petrie Erlandson. He slapped the Nordic Adonis merrily on the shoulder. Mr. Erlandson went stumbling back. This caused another wave of laughter. The sound was grating on my already-frazzled nerves.

I turned away from the front doors and began creeping up one of the double staircases on either side of the room, my mouth full of *excuse me*'s and *oh, pardon me*'s as I inched around more people. God, where did they all come from? I was out of breath when I reached the top, feeling like I had conquered a great mountain instead of a handful of steps.

The air was still stifling on the second floor, but the cantankerous volume was blessedly muffled. Peace and quiet was nearly in my grasp. I'd wait in one of the offices until Pa had had his fun—or rather, until Pastor Kline was blacklisted from the open bar—and then I would be home free. I could do it. I could survive until then. Unless I died from heatstroke or smoke inhalation.

I rounded into the right hallway, lined with large oak doors and heavy paintings of Fariid's previous judges, only to press myself against the first door as a wall of people streamed by. Women cackled and fluttered their lace fans, batting their eyelashes at me as they waltzed by. Men sank their teeth into too-small sandwiches, ravenous after a night of betting. Wave after wave of people. Skirts brushed against my shoes, thick tweed jackets snagged on my loose buttons, threatening to yank them right off.

God! Where did they all come from?

The doorknob dug into my spine. Fighting back a pathetic whimper, I spun around, gripped the warm metal, and thrust the door open. As I clicked the door shut behind me, I marveled at the fact that even the rooms felt hot and stuffy, carrying hints of body odor and carnage.

And then I realized why.

I slowly turned, and there, in the dim office light, was Sebastian, perched atop the desk in the center of the room. Owen was wedged between his legs, his hands roaming all over Sebastian's body, trying to get a piece of him. Sebastian's hands were nowhere to be found, tucked somewhere between his and Owen's legs.

Owen growled, ripping his head away from the crook of Sebastian's neck and thrusting his face right into Sebastian's. But instead of squirming away, Sebastian let out a cooing sound and wrapped his legs around Owen, locking his ankles together.

They looked like they were wrestling. And judging by the sounds they were making, they were both winning.

My mouth dropped open when Owen gazed into Sebastian's eyes, tilted his head, and kissed him with enough force that it made my own face hurt.

Sebastian's missing hands were clearly *not* missing, because Owen's legs began to shake. "Yes," I heard him moan against Sebastian's lips. "*Yes!*"

More sounds. More roaming hands. More winning.

Sebastian's eyes opened, latching on to me. The horror that immediately encompassed his sweaty face was nearly comical. He unsuctioned himself from Owen and began to furiously wipe his mouth dry. "Oh, God!" he cried between swipes. "Oh, *God*!"

Owen turned to look at me, his eyes glazed with remnants of passion, his tie undone, the first buttons of his dress shirt open. We realized at the same time that the zipper to the front of his pants was splayed open, revealing a long and hard—

"I didn't see anything!" I yelped, smacking my hands over my eyes. "I didn't see anything!"

As Owen tucked himself back into his pants and hurriedly pulled up the zipper, Sebastian gave a mewling wail and launched off the desk. "That's not true," he cried, huddling into Owen's busy arms. "He saw *everything*!"

Owen began working on his shirt buttons next. "Calm down," he soothed, looking at me from over Sebastian's head. "It's just Grayson. If he s-s-says he didn't . . . see anything, th-the-then he didn't s-see anything." He raised his eyebrow. "Right?"

I nodded rapidly. "Absolutely." I peeked through my fingers, a nervous laugh bubbling up my throat. "Is . . . everyone decent after the thing I *definitely* didn't see?"

Sebastian stifled a sob, but Owen laughed—a full-on throw-your-head-back-and-howl sort of laugh. The sound caused me to jump, but Sebastian relaxed, letting out a giggle of his own before slapping Owen on the shoulder.

"Maybe next time, lock the damn door," I added helpfully.

That sent Owen off again, his shoulders shaking as he doubled over, clutching his stomach. "Seriously, *s-st-stop*!" he cried. "I'm gonna piss my pants!"

I lowered my hands, laughing as well. "That would make two of us."

Sebastian rolled his eyes and waited for us to finish cackling like hyenas. He fluffed his purple handkerchief, fixed his ascot, and smoothed out the front of his suit, and we were still in hysterics. "I think some drinks of the alcoholic variety are required," he finally announced loudly.

Owen wiped his eyes and straightened. "Th-that's a great idea," he said in between spurts of tapering giggles. "You go down first. I'll catch up."

Pulling out a pocket mirror from his pants, Sebastian gave himself a quick once-over before tucking it away and slinking out of the room. Owen leaned against the desk, watching Sebastian leave, a goofy love-drunk smile on his face.

I stuffed my hands into my pockets and whistled. "So . . . *that* happened," I said, making my way over to the desk.

Owen ducked his head, suddenly bashful. "Yeah." He peeked up at me. "Are you s-s-surprised?"

I pursed my lips together, then shook my head. "Not really. The signs were all there. I was just too caught up in my own life to really notice them." I leaned on the desk next to him. "It's kind of sweet, actually; the small-island hick falling for the mainland rich boy."

Owen snorted, but his face grew tense. "So . . . you don't th-think it's . . ." He made a weird shrugging motion. "I don't know . . . wrong?"

I smiled. "Love is love, and at least one of us is experiencing it."

Owen shrugged again, warmth spreading to his cheeks. "After T-Tommy I . . . I was just so s-s-s . . . *sad*, you know? St-still am. And S-S-Sebastian . . ." He stared longingly at the door. "He helps. He makes me happy."

I placed a hand on Owen's arm. "You deserve to be happy."

Owen grinned ruefully. "I wish everyone else felt that-that-that way. S-sp-speaking of which . . ." He straightened, looking me dead in the eyes. "Don't t-tell anyone, okay?"

I cocked my head to the side, my face riddled with confusion. "Don't tell anyone what? I didn't see anything, remember?" I gestured to his pants. "Your fly's still down, by the way."

Owen did a double take on his zipper, groaning when he realized I'd tricked him. He grabbed his jacket from off the chair in the corner of the room. "You might not want to s-s-stay in here," he said as he slipped it on. "I'm pretty s-su-sure . . . Sebastian and I are coming back up here to-to-to finish what we st-st-started."

I cringed, lifting my hands in surrender. "Duly noted."

Owen laughed as he limped to the door. "S-s-see you around—but not t-too . . . soon!"

"Make sure you lock the door next time!" I yelled as he closed it.

The room became a sanctuary of stillness and quiet, and I was sour that I had to give it up. I opened the door.

And walked straight into Ambrose Grieves.

Before I could react, he shoved me against the wall hard enough to rattle the paintings. The air whooshed from my lungs, and Ambrose was in my face, snarling. His bloodshot eyes were wild, his body trembling. With a primal growl, he punched the wall, narrowly missing my head. "Watch where you're going!" he bellowed, voice hoarse from the damage I'd caused.

I opened my mouth, ready to apologize, but stopped short. His scarf had loosened, revealing the bruises I'd given him, and the crescent-shaped cuts from my nails along his neck. But the long scratch running from his collarbone to his chin wasn't my doing. It was fresh; blood dotted his shirt. The salt of the ocean hung in the air, the dampness of his jacket unmistakable.

"Ambrose," I croaked. "What *happened*?"

Ambrose's lower lip began to quiver, his tightly cinched brow unfurling.

"Ambrose," a deep voice barked from down the hall, tucked behind an open door. "Get in here."

Ambrose took a step back, his eyes like daggers, his teeth still bared.

"Ambrose!" the voice demanded. "Enough!"

Ambrose looked me up and down, his red-tinged eyes wild. He spat at my feet before stomping down the hall.

I clutched my chest, feeling my raging heart underneath, and loosed a shaky breath. "Ambrose," I called out. "Ambrose, wait!"

He was already at the end of the hall, marching through the last office door. I hurried after him in time to see him collapse into Mr. Grieves's arms, muffled sobs escaping him. Mr. Grieves, still drenched in his golden cloak, stiffly patted his son's back, murmuring, "There, there," in a soothing tone that felt fake.

Mr. Grieves and I locked eyes, and all the air was out of my lungs again.

Mr. Grieves settled his son into the desk chair, still uttering those snake-oil words. Then he marched to the door. He gripped the heavy wood, his face tight at the edges, his smile sharp. "Mr. Shaw," he grumbled politely.

"Mr. Grieves," I replied slowly, my eyes flitting to Ambrose's slumped form and the box next to him. The fireworks and flares. Mrs. Morris had managed to get them to the courthouse after all.

Ambrose whimpered. Mr. Grieves hummed delicately, his smile slipping. "Do excuse us," he crooned, and before I could get another word in, he was shutting the door with alarming power.

I stumbled away from the door's rapidly closing mouth.

Right into Holly.

Why was everybody I knew in this godforsaken hallway?

We crashed together like a magnet to metal, complete with smacking foreheads, bumping chests, and stubbing toes. The drink in Holly's hand went all over her, soaking her crimson dress and tangling in her long ginger curls. Her glass toppled to the carpeted ground and rolled beneath a table, leaving a trail of deep red as it went.

"Grayson Shaw!" She said my name like a curse word.

I backed away a step, mortified. "Oh, jeez! Holly, I'm so sorry!" I hurriedly yanked the handkerchief from my pocket. "Here, let me help."

Holly, who had been in the process of squeezing her hair dry, froze. She glanced down at her soiled chest, where the majority of the spilled drink had collected, before eyeing me warily. "I'll pass on that, thanks," she said flatly.

My mind, full of images of Owen and Sebastian, and now Ambrose and Mr. Grieves, had me spinning. And it took me far too long to realize I was staring at Holly's chest. Again. I slapped a hand over my eyes. "Oh, God, I'm sorry! I don't know how that keeps happening."

Holly laughed. The sound surprised me. I couldn't remember the last time I'd heard her laugh. It felt like her anger toward me had lasted a lifetime with no end in sight. "You're a hopeless thing, Grayson Shaw."

I lowered my hand hesitantly. "Is your dress going to be all right?"

Holly went back to wringing out her hair. "I'm not sure. At least I'm already wearing red. Maybe it'll blend in."

Despite the choking smoke, the aromas of food, and the scents of carnal desire, I was able to smell it wafting off Holly's dress: hints of fermented grapes. "Wait," I stammered. "Holly, are you drinking wine?"

Holly grinned mischievously. "Jasper snagged me some. It was gross at first, but the taste is growing on me." She suddenly went pale, and her hands drifted from her hair to her chest. She clasped them together in a pleading motion. "You won't tell on me, will you?" Her eyes darted around the hall anxiously. "Ma and Pa will kill me if they find out!"

I mimed sealing my lips, locking them tight, and throwing the key over my shoulder. "I'm a locked vault. But"—I winced, catching another whiff of wine—"maybe you should make yourself scarce until it dries."

Holly's shoulders sagged with relief. "Thank you!" Relaxing, she finally accepted the handkerchief I was waving like a white flag and began blotting the front of her dress. "What are you doing up here anyway?"

"Trying to find the judge's liquor cabinet. I heard he has a fantastic brandy locked up." I laughed sheepishly, pointedly looking at anything that wasn't Holly's breasts. "Trying to find an exit, actually. I've been attempting to leave for the last twenty minutes."

Holly's hands stilled mid-blot. "Really?"

"Hey," I said, holding up my hands defensively, "this place is a maze."

Holly shook her head dubiously. "Truly hopeless." She cocked her head to the side, smiling. "I know a back exit. Follow me."

The fresh air hit me like a cool wave, the salty smell of the sea replacing the heavy smoky air of the hall. I pulled at my tie, unbuttoned my jacket, and breathed deeply, savoring the crispness. Holly poked me in the stomach, forcing me to exhale like a deflating balloon. "Rude," I gasped, rubbing the tender spot.

Holly tilted her nose into the air. "Consider us even."

"For what?"

"For making me spill my drink all over my dress. Do I need to show you the state it's in again?" she asked, beginning to unwrap the shawl she had draped around herself.

I quickly averted my eyes. "Nope."

Holly grinned up at me. "Good."

We walked away from the courthouse, neither of us leading the way, both of us content to keep it that way. Our wandering led us to Black Sands Beach, the lights and sounds of the pier bright and loud with life. Vendors hollered at us to try their cotton candy and hot dogs, their freshly made popcorn. Merchants shoved handmade jewelry in our faces. Carnies crowed at us to throw darts in the hopes of winning a rare prize.

"It seems that not everyone drops everything for the Hunt," I mused, handing a red-faced vendor with an eye patch the precious spare change in my pocket. I pointed at the pale pink wad of cotton candy hanging in a bag above our heads.

Holly shrugged, eyeing the cotton candy eagerly as the vendor placed the bag in my hands, bobbing his head repeatedly in thanks. "This is Fariid. They probably don't have to."

I ripped the bag open and tilted it in Holly's direction. Holly immediately shook her head despite the longing in her eyes and the way she licked her lips. "Oh, no," she said hurriedly. "I couldn't possibly."

"Holly." I laughed. "It's me. You don't need to be so polite."

Holly bit her lip. Unable to resist, she dove into the bag, ripping off a sticky chunk the size of her fist. She nibbled along the edges and closed her eyes, savoring each bite. "I've always wanted to try cotton candy!" she moaned between mouthfuls.

I popped a chunk into my mouth, letting the too-sweet candy melt on my tongue. "I never really cared for it," I admitted. "But Ma always brought it home after the Night of the Betting." I smiled, thinking back to the moments of me and Warrick racing around the house, crazed with sugar highs, our fingers coated in sticky splotches of blue and pink. "It brings back happy memories."

Holly peered up at me for a second longer before returning to the wilting candy in her hand. "How's your face? It looks painful."

I snorted, then immediately regretted it. "You should see the other guy."

"I did. The scoundrel was wearing a blasted scarf!"

"Right?" I laughed. "What a coward. I thought the people of Lethe proudly showed off their war wounds. I would have worn a scarf too if I'd known he was going to."

"I don't know if a scarf would have helped you."

I gasped jokingly. "Well, no more cotton candy for you!" When I eyed the leftovers in Holly's hand, she quickly pushed them into her mouth, grinning impishly around the thick wad. "If you choke, I'm not helping you."

Holly swallowed and opened wide, revealing an empty mouth and an artificially pink tongue. "Ta-da!"

"It's like a magic trick."

"Speaking of magic tricks . . ." Holly went for another handful of cotton candy. "Did you see Jasper at all tonight? He made himself scarce right after getting me my drink."

Heat flooded my entire body. "I did," I said carefully. "He was a little sour that I'd received more bets than him."

Holly sucked on the tips of her fingers and pondered. "He's just jealous, is all. He's been waiting his whole life for this. It's hard for him to see someone not care as much and still do better."

The words stung, even if she hadn't meant them to. "I know."

Holly frowned, still in thought. "He's also probably still upset about the altercation in the library. Threatening to break his one good leg was a bit of a low blow."

My heart squeezed painfully at the memory. "About that . . ."

Holly held up a hand and immediately began to shake her head. "You don't need to say anything, Grayson."

"No," I pushed. "I do. I want to apologize. Not just for what happened in the library, but for . . . you know . . . everything else."

We had reached the end of the pier. The sounds of life had faded, the glowing string lights casting long and daunting shadows on the wood. The entire Floria Sea loomed before us, the moonlight dancing on the aqua waves and white-foamed caps. Holly leaned against the wooden rail and crossed her arms, her gaze searching the distant waters. "The thing is, Grayson, part of me always knew." She tucked her chin against her shoulder and looked at me with a small smile. "I could wish and hope and pray all I want, but I always knew." She laughed quietly. "How could you ever like your best friend's sister?"

"I *do* like you, Holly," I said hurriedly.

Holly sighed, her eyes returning to the sea. "Not in the way that counts though."

I shrugged, feeling a surplus of emotions, none of them mattering. "Life is just . . . It's so complicated right now. I feel like it's racing by without my knowing. Half the time, I'm simply trying to catch up. I'm constantly making mistakes, messing up, and hurting feelings. It's like . . ." I clucked my tongue, fighting to find the right words. "It's like I'm stuck in a loop of doing damage control and stomping out fires before they have a chance to ignite anything and everything around me. Even if I wanted to be with you, I'd worry the entire time that, eventually, you'd get hurt too."

Holly blew out a long breath, leaning deeper into the railing, peering at the waves below. "So, where does that leave us?"

I hesitantly held out my hand, a meek peace offering. "Friends?"

"Barf." Holly stared at my outstretched hand, and her lips slowly cracked into a grin. She accepted it, shaking it firmly. She tilted her head, analyzing me. "I'm too young to place bets," she said begrudgingly. "But if I could, I would have bet on you, Grayson Shaw."

I smiled, feeling warm despite the cool night surrounding us. "That counts in my book, Holly Warren."

Holly released my hand and turned back to the water. We stood in silence, contented, at peace.

As all good things go, it didn't last.

Holly froze, her entire body growing rigid beside me. "What's that?" she asked, pointing at the approaching waves.

I squinted, leaning hard against the wooden railing. "A piece of driftwood?"

Holly frowned, curling a strand of hair around her fingers, an act of self-soothing. "It's a weird shape, don't you think?"

I blinked, rubbed my eyes carefully, and looked again. The mass bobbed against the waves, edging closer and closer to the boardwalk. As it slipped and skidded atop the water, I realized that the branches and roots were too loose, too disjointed. Too *wrong*. The bark hadn't been stripped clean either;

the shape was still covered in it, dark and wet, flashes of blue, brown, and red gleaming in the moonlight. And there were leaves still cluttering the tip of it, clumping together, the water running its cold, foamy fingers through them.

Warning bells sounded in my mind, but Holly heard them first.

Holly gasped, wrenching me from my spot on the railing and pulling me into a hug. She swung me away until my back faced the sea and all I could see were the flashing lights of the shacks we had passed. My heartbeat was in my ears, making the vendors' shouts and the carnies' cries sound like wailing sirens.

"Grayson," she breathed, holding me tight, "don't look."

I looked.

It was nestled atop the water, the waves gently pulling it toward the shore like a gift.

A body. Large, still, and covered in blood.

CHAPTER SIXTY-SIX

EVANORA

APRIL 25 – EVENING

I EYED THE WILTING FLOWERS, STONES IN MY STOMACH.

They were obviously from Grayson. He wanted me to wait, but the sun was already sinking dangerously close to the horizon, the warm air shifting with crisp undertones.

Something didn't feel right. It was too quiet, too still. My body was on edge, every single one of my scales stiff. My nerves told me to leave, to return to the island another day. But my heart, my cursed heart, begged me to stay. Something inside the connection holding us together told me that he desperately needed me tonight, that the boy was unraveling, that seeing me would anchor him again.

I decided to stay.

Illeron didn't come with me. Grayson's absence had done little to stimulate his faith in humans. The fact that I returned the following night did little to stimulate his faith in me.

It didn't matter. I sat on the beach, watched the sun set, and waited.

The moon was a narrow slice in the sky when I finally heard the stumbling of footsteps. Grayson walked at a slow pace, swaying against the metal railing, tripping on his feet and the wooden stairs. His head drooped nearly to his chest, his shoulders hunching forward as if to ward off the cold. He came to a stuttering halt on one of the stairs, his hands gripping the rail fiercely. I could hear him take several long, slow breaths before he resumed the trek downward.

A flush of anger ripped through me. Was the boy . . . intoxicated?

"Grayson Shaw!" I barked, snapping my tail impatiently against the wet sand. "It is one thing to miss our scheduled visit and embarrass me in front of Illeron, but to leave me flowers and then arrive in the state you're in?" I sniffed, folding my arms tightly against my chest. "It's very rude, indeed."

"I know," Grayson moaned, stumbling again. "I know."

"You know *what*? That you're late? That you're in no shape to be useful? That—"

And then I stopped.

Something was wrong. Very, very wrong.

For starters, Grayson was covered in blood.

All hints of rage exited my body with enough force to leave me breathless. I gasped, hands fluttering to my mouth. "Grayson!" I cried out, trying to pull myself farther up the beach. "Grayson, what happened?"

The boy tumbled over the last step and collapsed into the sand, a heap of skin and bones and blood. He sat there in a daze, barely noticing me as I scrambled beside him, my hands frantically searching his body, looking for a source of all the blood.

"It's not mine," he mumbled, his eyes hazy and unfocused as they stared ahead at nothing.

I needed to be sure. The amount of blood on him suggested a wound of catastrophic size. He was coated in it. His hair, his face, his hands, the front of his suit. Nothing was left untouched. I forced my panicked mind to focus. *If the blood was his, he would be dead.*

And the boy was alive. Broken in so many ways, but alive. There was a bump on the bridge of his nose, a flurry of bruising coating the skin underneath his dull eyes. It looked painful, but the wound wasn't fresh. I couldn't find anything else. I breathed a quiet sigh of relief, allowing the tension in my shoulders to loosen. I took his hand in mine, squeezing it gently. Grayson gave no indication that he even felt my soothing touch.

"What happened?" I whispered.

The tremor that began at the corner of Grayson's lips was the only way I knew he had heard me.

"Please," I pressed, growing desperate. "Don't shut me out. Talk to me." I lifted my free hand and cupped Grayson's cheek; it skidded against the blood, still disturbingly wet. "Let me help."

Grayson took in a stuttering breath, the sound getting stuck in his throat. When he exhaled, it came out as a whimper. "It was the Night of the Betting tonight," he started, his voice thick, syrupy, stunned. "I didn't want to go, but Pa made me." A shiver raced through the boy's back. "The air felt charged when we got there, violent. People were excited." He grimaced, shaking his head. "I can't explain it, but the entire night felt . . . cursed . . . in some way. The audience was almost ravenous, feeding off this weird energy that poured into the room. And the hunters were no better. Everyone was acting unhinged and wild." He shrugged, his shoulders looking so frail in the bloody jacket that was too big for him. "It's like, the closer we get to the Hunt, the more insane people become. They are desperate for carnage."

I gave his hand a squeeze. "Did something happen during the betting?"

Grayson shook his head slowly. "No. After." He made a sudden jerking motion, his hand slapping against his mouth. He took a heavy breath, swallowed, and continued. "I needed fresh air. Everyone was acting so crazy in the courthouse, and I didn't want to be a part of it. So, my friend and I went for a walk. We ended up at the Fariid boardwalk, next to Black Sands Beach. Everything was *fine*." Grayson's lip began to wobble with conviction.

I hummed softly, scooting closer. "What did you see, Grayson?"

A moan escaped the boy's mouth. He squeezed his eyes shut, a flood of tears slipping down his crimson cheeks. "A body. Floating in the water." The jerking motion happened again. "It was fresh," he whispered from behind his hand. "He had died recently. The blood—" Grayson began to shake violently, making his words skip and stutter. "Th-th-the blood wa-was still leav-ing his bo-body."

Grayson shuddered, leaned over, and vomited on the sand.

Helplessness drifted over me like a fog. I wished, not for the first time, that my Gift could heal more than physical wounds. Grayson's pain was trapped deep in his heart, and there was nothing I could do about it.

The boy slowly straightened, wiping the remnants of bile off his lips with the back of his hand. "I'm sorry," he whispered, looking pale and disgusted with himself.

"No," I said softly. "It's okay." I swiped my tail, covering the vomit in sand. "You don't have to keep going. If it's too painful . . ."

Grayson shook his head. "I'm all right." He wasn't. But he continued. "My friend ran for help, but I couldn't just leave him in the water, waiting for help to arrive. I didn't think—I just raced to the beach and charged in." He dropped his head into his hands. "The voices, Evanora," he moaned. "They were *so loud*. I could feel their desire. Their desire for me." He peeked at me through his fingers. "It's almost unbearable; I feel like I'm going crazy."

A surge of defiance raced through me, sending my fins rigid all over again. I couldn't heal the boy's shattered heart, but gods help me, I could protect what was left of it. "You're not going crazy," I promised, pulling Grayson into a hug. "I don't know why the Cursed Beings want you so badly, but they can't have you. I won't let them."

Grayson sucked in a sharp breath, his body tense in my arms. Then a choked cry escaped him as he buried his face into the crook of my neck, sinking into me like quicksand. He stayed there for a long while, unleashing the agony of his heart—days of festering doubt, wondering if he was going mad, if he was following his mother's path.

When he finally pulled away, his face was flushed with embarrassment, and he quickly rubbed his eyes, sniffling into his jacket sleeve. His cheeks were a raw red, matching the blood still staining his skin. He cleared his throat, voice thick and wet. "I tried to help. I did chest compressions until others arrived and took over." He looked nauseated. "It didn't matter. The man was dead. Someone hit him in the head and dumped him in the water."

Grayson retched again, emptying his stomach violently. I rubbed his back, keeping my hand steady until the heaving stopped.

"Grayson," I whispered, my voice a soft anchor in the storm, "it isn't us."

"I know," Grayson croaked, wiping his mouth again. "I think it's someone far more dangerous." He looked at me, his eyes losing their dull haze. "People have been going missing since the start of the month. This was the first time a body was actually recovered; whoever is behind all this is getting sloppy. Maybe they *want* to get caught."

I bit my lip. "Do you think it's connected to the Hunt somehow? Some strange, nefarious plan to inspire . . . I don't know . . . more violence?"

Grayson shrugged, his brows pulling together. "I don't know," he answered honestly. "All I know is that we are running out of time."

Unease welled up inside me. "You're right," I said carefully. "Which is why we need to meet at the times we previously agreed upon." I leaned forward, trying to find Grayson's eyes in the moonlight. "I can't afford to come here and spend the entire night waiting for you."

The boy nodded, but he was staring at his hands, curling and uncurling his fingers, watching as the blood stretched and tightened.

I sighed. I wasn't Jorah; scolding in the hopes of stirring motivation wasn't the answer.

Grayson flinched when I took one of his hands, but he allowed me to guide him to the beach's edge. "What are you doing?" he asked.

The water kissed my scales, cool and refreshing. "Giving you a bath."

The boy sucked in a breath. "I don't think that's a good idea," he said, his eyes wide as they darted anxiously along the waves. "The voices . . ."

"They won't get you. Not while I'm here." I smiled warmly, coaxing him farther. "You're safe with me, Grayson Shaw."

A whimper on his tongue, Grayson let me gently tug him into the ocean's embrace. The water unfurled around us, happy to have our company. I pulled the boy into my chest, cradling him against me as I pushed away from the beach.

Grayson's fingers dug into my skin. "Not too deep!" he yelped.

I laughed, a quiet, crooning thing. "Do you trust me?"

The boy bit his lip, squeezed his eyes shut, and nodded. "Yes," he bit out. "But I don't trust the water."

"That's healthy," I admitted. "She can't be trusted at the best of times."

"She sounds delightful. A real treat."

I laughed again, folding my tail beneath me and setting Grayson down on the sand. He lashed out when my grip loosened, then stilled when he realized the water barely reached his chest. I found his shaking hands and gave them a comforting squeeze. "You're safe," I whispered, pressing his fingers to my lips, kissing each one gently. "You're safe."

Grayson swallowed and nodded.

I dipped my hand beneath the water, scooping up a clump of sand. I began rubbing it over his skin, massaging it into every crevice of his fragile human body. Slowly, the caked blood flaked away, leaving behind only haunting memories that I washed into the water. As I hummed a lullaby my ammah used to sing, I could feel Grayson relax just a little. He wasn't whole yet, but I saw pieces of him emerging from the cracks of his ravaged heart.

Every spot the sand touched, my lips followed. I kissed his cold hands, now bright pink from the scrubbing. I kissed his nose, red from the chill. His cheeks, his eyelids, his lashes. I was thorough, making sure he was clean, inside and out.

"I don't think we have time for this," Grayson mumbled.

"Yes, we do." I hummed the soft melody, and the boy closed his eyes.

It wasn't until I got to his hair that Grayson began to shake again. He allowed me to pour the water over him twice before the panic set in and

I had to carry him back to shore. He trembled furiously upon the sand. I huddled up next to him, knowing my cool scales were likely doing more harm than good.

Grayson placed his head against my shoulder. "Tomorrow," he managed between chattering teeth, "the boats will be on the beaches."

I nodded somberly. "We must make our move then. I was hoping you could have met Illeron beforehand." I winced, guilt stirring in my stomach. "That mermaid is a pretty hard clam to crack open."

Grayson snorted. The sound seemed to cause him pain. "What a nice way to call someone an asshole."

I was tempted to ask Grayson what *asshole* meant, but I had a feeling I already knew. Not to mention, it was *my* fault that Illeron was back to being an uptight clam in the first place. "Just . . . don't be alarmed if he isn't all that friendly at the start."

The boy chuckled. "Don't worry. I'm sure I'll have him cracked open and laughing in no time."

Good luck with that.

Grayson's fingers danced along my scales, outlining each one. His shivering had shifted into convulsions. "Pa is being a tyrant at home right now. It's almost impossible for me to leave the house without him knowing."

Everything within me went utterly still. I was certain the boy could feel my heart pounding against my rib cage. "You won't be able to help?"

Grayson sighed with frustration and shook his head, his curls tickling my chin. "Oh, no. I'm definitely helping. I'm just letting you know now that if I suddenly go missing, search the house first."

A shocked laugh bubbled up my throat. I looked purposely at my tail shifting through the sand. "I shall lead the hunt."

"Oh," Grayson groaned. "Poor choice of words."

A silence settled between us, soft as the breeze, lulling as the waves. Grayson's head began to bob.

"You should go," I whispered, nuzzling the boy's curls.

Grayson groaned sleepily, sinking deeper against my body. "Not yet."

"Tomorrow's a big day."

"Not yet."

I craned my neck to look at him. "Why not, my brave heart?"

The boy pinched his lips together, his tired eyes following the ever-moving ocean. "Because I can still see him. I can still hear them. I just . . . I don't want to be alone."

So, we stayed together. Huddled on the beach, trapped in our private paradise, pretending the world and all its horrors didn't exist.

And with hope flowing in my veins, I allowed myself to believe that, one day, we wouldn't have to pretend, that such a dream *could* become a reality.

I just hoped the cost of such a reality wouldn't be too great.

CHAPTER SIXTY-SEVEN

GRAYSON

APRIL 26 – MORNING

THE BODY BELONGED TO MARKUS BRIDGE.

He was a mechanic from Fariid, one who couldn't partic-ipate in the Hunt because of his bad heart. Pa knew him, but I didn't. When Pa invited me to join him and Pastor Kline—who didn't know Markus either but liked to be involved—I politely declined. I could see Pa was disappointed—not because he wanted me to share his grief, but because he didn't want to be alone with Pastor Kline. Honestly, I couldn't blame him.

"Might be good for you, you know," Pa offered, taking the steps leading away from our front door one by one. He was squeezing the life out of his hat, pouring all of his ill-concealed emotions into the poor piece of fabric. "Might give you some closure."

I gave a half smile, fighting the shudder that crawled up my spine, one vertebra at a time. "I don't know if closure is what I need," I said, shrugging. I needed distance, to not be able to close my eyes and see Markus Bridge's dead ones staring at me through the void. I could still feel his blood coating my face, still hear his ribs crack underneath my hands as I tried to save him.

Pa pursed his lips together, nodding reluctantly. "All right."

He made it down two more steps before he paused again and turned. "You're sure?"

I laughed, but all I could hear were the waves as they carried Markus to shore. "I'm sure."

Pa nodded again. "All right," he repeated.

When Pa looked pleadingly at me from atop the wagon, all my resolve to stay behind crumbled. I'd never seen the man look so pathetically desperate; it felt good to be the reason for his relief and not the more negative emotions I was growing used to.

So, I found myself attending another funeral.

Two funerals in one month. God.

The church was practically empty. Markus hadn't left behind many friends and family. Still, that didn't stop me from getting wedged between Pa and Pastor Kline despite there being ample space on the pew. I sat with my hands in my lap, my shoulders pressed between the two, my knees knocking into theirs, feeling claustrophobic in the middle of the largest church on all of Lethe. Safety in numbers.

It was a magnificent building. Stained glass windows towered beside solid-oak pews—not like the cheap ones at the Tully church that felt ready to collapse. Plush red carpet lined the aisles, leading to the podium covered in hundreds of candles.

And, of course, there was a plain wooden casket sitting on the stage, its lid askew, limp flowers scattered across its edges. Pastor Kline had wanted to sit closer, but as soon as we entered, Pa had steered me to the farthest row. Just because I was here didn't mean I wanted to see the body, and I appreciated the distance.

Pastor Kline tsked when the Fariid reverend finished his short-and-sweet prayer and began the somber sermon. "Look at him, getting right to it," he muttered. "What is he saving his breath for? The second coming of Christ?"

I adjusted the tie strangling my neck. "Maybe he's saving time for the eulogies."

Pastor Kline grumbled. "Look around, young Shaw. There's hardly anyone here. The eulogies will be over and done before I've finished tying my shoelaces." He shrugged, his shoulder shimmying tightly against mine. "I'm just saying, if he wants to hold the congregation's attention, he needs a bit more pizzazz."

Pa snorted. "Is that what you think you do? Pizzazz the crowd?"

"I certainly do a better job than this heretic. Why," Pastor Kline scoffed, "he's already closing his bible!"

Pa rolled his eyes. "For Pete's sake. Not everyone is blessed with being long-winded like you, Pastor Kline."

If he were sober, Pastor Kline might've caught Pa's snarky remark. But he wasn't, and he beamed, his beady eyes brimming with admiration for himself. "Thank you." He leaned back into the pew, nearly squishing me. "I *do* have a way with words, don't I?"

"That's not what I—"

I elbowed Pa in the ribs before he could finish.

The sermon wrapped up swiftly. It *did* feel rather quick, but then again, I was used to Pastor Kline's droning services; being able to leave before my backside became completely numb felt like a treat.

When I stood, wiggling life back into my limbs, the reverend gestured to the measly congregation. "If you wish to observe the body and pay your respects, come forth."

Pastor Kline immediately began to amble to the front, but I had a feeling the spring in his step had less to do with paying respects and more with providing the poor, unsuspecting reverend with unsolicited advice.

I couldn't move.

I was back on the beach, pulling Markus Bridge onto dry land, listening for a heartbeat in his hollow, silent chest.

Pa squeezed around me.

I was screaming for help, wiping the man's blood from my eyes before I began pressing my hands against his chest.

The congregation continued to plod to the front.

I was swallowing down vomit as I felt his chest give, his ribs crumbling away to dust. Each frantic compression sent a spurt of blood oozing out of Markus's mouth.

The room began to shift in my blurred vision, the floor tilting and sighing, ready to cave in. My hand shot out, clamping around Pa's wrist.

Pa jolted to a halt. He frowned at me from over his shoulder, but his quizzical expression immediately softened when he took in my shaking body, my hyperventilating breaths, my eyes glued to the floor.

"Hey," he said, shifting to face me. "Grayson."

I shook my head, a quick jerky motion. "I can't," I uttered, unable to tear my eyes from the ground, where the plush carpet began to morph into pools of crimson. "I can't."

Pa's gaze flitted to the front of the church, where the casket waited like a gaping mouth. He placed his hand on top of mine, slowly prying my death grip off. "Nothing can hurt you up there."

He was right. The damage had already been done. "Please, Pa," I whispered. "I can't."

Pa's hand stilled against mine. He sighed slowly. "Of course you can't."

I forced myself to look at him, ready for the wall of displeasure to be back in place.

All I got was kindness, and it nearly ripped me in two.

"Honestly, I'm just happy you came with me. But it was foolish of me to ask in the first place." Pa's mouth quirked to the side as he gestured to the door. "Go get some fresh air. Pastor Kline and I will be right behind you."

Adrenaline shot through me like a bullet, and I let Pa finish unfurling my clammy fingers from his wrist. "Really?"

Pa nodded. "It's too stuffy in here anyway. I never liked this church; I don't want to stay in here longer than I have to either."

I could have wept. The ground ceased its roiling, and the room settled back into its stoic structure. "You'll be right behind me?"

"Even if it means I have to pull Pastor Kline out by his crooked white collar."

I choked out a laugh, earning a handful of glares from the podium. Even Pastor Kline paused from his impromptu lecture to stare in my direction. Ducking my head and giving my sweaty face a quick wipe, I skirted around Pa and dashed for the door.

The waves of bloody memories began to wash away the second I was in sunlight. I tripped down the front stairs, gulping in as much fresh air as my lungs would allow. And with every step I took, I reminded myself that I was on firm ground; I wasn't at the beach, stumbling through sand, colliding with the freezing waves to save a man who no longer needed saving.

My knees gave out on the last step, and I fell onto the stone stairs in a heap. That was okay; it wasn't like I could outwalk the memory of Markus Bridge anyway.

As I hung my head between my bent knees and fought to slow my breathing, a car honked down the barren street, shattering the blessed stillness. I slowly raised my head and pushed the curls out of my eyes.

The car honked again, drawing closer. There was the squeaking of brakes, the crackling of gravel. As the creak of the window joined the chorus of sounds, my adrenaline made a valiant return.

"Young Shaw!" Mr. Grieves cried with delight. "How nice to see you. Are you enjoying Fariid?"

Everything within me collapsed. I gulped around a wobbly smile. "Hello, sir."

Mr. Grieves stared at me for an uncomfortable moment, taking in my pale face, my sweaty skin, and the trembling in my fingers. "What brings you to Fariid on this fine morning?" he asked.

I glanced at the church behind me, hoping Pa would barge through the doors, saving me from Mr. Grieves and his false niceties. No such luck. "It was Markus Bridge's funeral."

"Oh, dear." Mr. Grieves clucked his tongue. "That was today? How dreadful that I missed it."

Yeah. Dreadful. "It's still going if you want to pay your respects," I offered.

Mr. Grieves immediately began waving his hand dismissively. "No, no. I couldn't possibly. However . . ." He chuckled. "I'm a little surprised to see you here, considering you were one of the poor souls unfortunate enough to find him. Must have given you quite a fright."

I nodded carefully. "I came to support my pa. He—"

"You know," Mr. Grieves said, cutting me off, "when Ambrose found Mr. Bridge, he had a very similar reaction to yours. Why, I think you even witnessed the tail end of his panicked spiral."

My blood went cold. "I did?"

Mr. Grieves nodded solemnly. "Of course! On the Night of the Betting, when he stormed into the office, he was in quite a state of shock. Covered in blood, shaking like a mouse." Shadows spread across his face, flickers of disgust. "It was most unbecoming," he added quietly, more for himself than me.

"That doesn't make sense." The words tumbled out before I had a chance to stop them.

Mr. Grieves frowned at me, his eyes sparking. "How so?"

I should have just kept my mouth shut. I should have gone back inside the church. "Well," I started slowly, "Mr. Bridge was still in the water when I found him. And when Ambrose passed me in the hallway, he *did* have blood on him. From a cut on his face." I dared to look Mr. Grieves right in the eyes. "But he wasn't wet. Damp, sure, but not wet. So . . ." I cocked my head to the side, raising an eyebrow. "How did Ambrose manage to find Mr. Bridge and remain dry?"

The shadows swallowed Mr. Grieves whole. He tilted his face up, appraising me. "You are rather keen, aren't you?" he asked, the corner of his mouth twitching upward. "If a little nosy." He pointed a finger at me lightheartedly. "I'd hate for you to put your nose somewhere it doesn't belong—that's how even the most well-intentioned people get hurt."

He didn't answer my question. He had chosen to threaten me instead. I forced a smile despite my bladder loosening to a dangerous degree. "Duly noted."

I wanted to push it. I wanted to make Mr. Grieves uncomfortable. I wanted to make him snap. *What are you hiding?*

But then Mr. Grieves cracked a large smile and began rolling up his window. "Always a pleasure, Mr. Shaw!"

"Pleasure," I mumbled as the car sailed down the street, "is not what I'd call it."

My entire body was itchy. I wanted to jump into a bath of scalding water and scrub my skin raw, until I could no longer feel Mr. Grieves's serpentine gaze on me, until his sinister words washed down the drain.

I would not let Mr. Grieves's threats stake claim within the confines of my mind. They were just words. They were nothing more than a child's temper tantrum when they didn't get their way. I'd dealt with worse, and I had bigger things to worry about.

I slowly stood and turned back for the church.

I made it up three steps before I sank to my knees.

CHAPTER SIXTY-EIGHT

EVANORA

APRIL 26 – EVENING

I DON'T LIKE HIM."

"All he said was 'hi'!"

"And then he tried to make a mockery of me."

"By attempting to be respectful and using our hand gestures?"

I could practically hear Illeron sighing in my mind. *"It was physically painful to watch. If he ever tries to do something like that again, I'm going to rip off his arm and show him how to actually do it."*

Biting back a snort, I swam up to the beach, where Grayson was crouched next to one of the boats lining Hannigan's Cove. "How was that?" he asked in a quiet, breathless voice. "I think I messed up at the end, but the rest of it was good, right?"

I slithered onto the wet sand on my belly, pulling my fluke into the air so that the tips of my fins grazed my hair. "That was great!" I said, taking his feverish hand. "But you don't need to try so hard. He'll know what you're doing and harden right up."

Grayson sighed. "How much harder can a clam get?"

"What did he call me?" Illeron's voice demanded in my mind.

I scowled over my shoulder at the warrior as he bobbed in the water a healthy distance from shore. "You know, you *can* talk to him."

"I'm fine over here."

"Yes," I said, "you'll be *so helpful* way over there." I waved my hand over, slapping my fluke against the water, scattering droplets like rain. "Get over here, before I lose my patience."

Illeron rolled his eyes, but he unfolded his arms and swept to the shoreline. His gaze was cold and calculating as it roved over the boy.

To his credit, Grayson didn't shy away. He leaned forward, extending his hand to the warrior. "It's nice to finally meet you, Illeron," he said with a polite smile.

"I cannot say that I share the sentiment," Illeron grumbled.

I growled thinly, flashing the warrior my teeth. "We will speak English when we are with Grayson. I refuse to be your translator, Illeron."

Illeron clucked his tongue. "Neptune spear me," he groaned in our language. His eyes flitted from Grayson's to the hand hovering in front of him. "Get that thing out of my face. You smell awful," he said in careful, crisp English as he tilted his head back, his upper lip curling with disgust.

"Illeron!" I scolded. "That's rude!"

Grayson shook his head. "No, it's all right." He slowly withdrew his hand. Gods bless him, his beautiful smile remained. "I imagine I *do* smell weird to you."

The warrior's eye twitched. He remained quiet, baiting the boy to speak more, to offend him so greatly that he could throw his arms into the air, declare that I'd made the world's biggest mistake, and swim home without looking back.

Illeron stared at the boy. Grayson stared right back. To my surprise, it was Illeron who backed down first. "All right," he sighed. "So, what's the plan?"

Grayson rose to his feet and clapped his hands together gently. "Well, I was thinking that—"

"I wasn't *talking* to you." Illeron hissed the words so violently that the boy flinched against the boat and nearly toppled into it.

I slapped my fluke against the ground again. But this time, instead of water shooting everywhere, sparks went flying, my Gift making a surprise appearance. "That's *enough*, Illeron." I bared my teeth at the warrior. "This is *my* plan. *I* decide what we are going to do." I exhaled, pausing to compose myself and give my scales a chance to loosen. "And right now," I continued, my voice calmer, "I want us to listen to Grayson."

Illeron chewed his bottom lip, his deep crimson eyes flashing. He reluctantly placed a hand on his chest and bowed his head. "Of course, Your Majesty," he mumbled around gritted teeth.

I gave Grayson a reassuring smile. "You have our attention, Grayson Shaw."

"So choose your words wisely," Illeron said quietly, eyes remaining firmly on the sand.

I shot the warrior a final warning look before turning to the boy expectantly.

Grayson glanced between Illeron and me, swallowing. "You brought your spears?"

Illeron nodded curtly.

"Good. I think it will be awkward to work on the boats while they're still on the beach; you won't get the leverage or strength you'll need to damage the bottoms. I figured I'd push them into the water for you."

The warrior scoffed.

I smacked him on the arm, forcefully ending his snide mirth. I nodded encouragingly to the boy. "Keep going, Grayson."

There was a rigidness to Grayson's shoulders. "I brought some rope. I can tie it to the bow eye, toss you the rope, and then you can pull the boat into the water while I push on the back." He winced apologetically. "It'll be a slow process, but thankfully, Tully doesn't have a lot of boats." He looked over his shoulder at the rows of wooden beasts. "I counted fifty-seven when I was waiting for you."

"Tully doesn't," Illeron said, "but what about Fariid? Or Fenharrow?" He finally looked at the boy, his entire face coated in ice. "What are we going to do when the boats double or triple in numbers, and there is still just the three of us?"

The boy tilted his head to the side. "I don't have to push the boats in at all."

I let out a spurt of laughter. Illeron looked like he had been punched in the face. He pursed his lips together, then shook his head the slightest bit. "I don't feel like getting sand on my tail today. Pushing them into the water will work fine," he relented quietly.

Grayson smiled stiffly, the only sign of his thinning patience. "Once the boats are in the water," he continued, "it'll be up to you and Evanora to damage them. Not too much—just a light bruising. Focus on the keel and skeg. Those are the most vulnerable parts. And if a boat has a rudder, don't hesitate to knock it around." He pointed at the bottom of the boat. "Inside the boat's riskier though. Aim for just under the seats, especially the center one. That's where you'll want to strike during the Hunt."

An excited shudder rippled through me. I grinned devilishly. "I cannot wait to see all those poor, foolish humans floundering around in the water, having no clue what hit them."

"Hey, now," the boy said with a soft laugh. "Don't forget that I'm also a poor, foolish human."

I blinked innocently, placing a dainty hand against my chest. "Me? Never."

Illeron rolled his eyes. "Oh my *gods*." He pushed himself back into the water, growling under his breath. "When you two are done being merlings, we have work to do."

Blushing, Grayson grabbed his bag and began heaving long wads of rope out. Unable to help it, I reached forward, placing my hand on his. "If it means anything, I don't think you smell awful," I whispered.

The boy coughed out another laugh. "Really?"

"Yes." I nodded. "You smell like fresh air and pure sunshine. Like all the beautiful wild things grown from the richest soil, with the deepest roots." I stole a look over my shoulder at Illeron before leaning closer to the boy. "Do *I* smell weird to you?"

I thought Grayson might laugh again, but instead, the crimson on his cheeks deepened, creeping down his neck. "No," he said quietly. He curled a strand of my hair around his fingers, watching it slip through like glass. "When I first met you, I thought you smelled like . . ." He shook his head abruptly. "Never mind."

"What? Now you *have* to tell me."

The boy's eyes wouldn't meet mine. "It's embarrassing."

I crossed my arms tightly against my chest and leaned away; the strand of hair fell out of his fingers. "If you don't tell me, I'm going to think that I'm the worst-smelling thing your poor nose has ever encountered."

Grayson bit his lip, his hands fidgeting at his sides, begging to touch me again. He groaned quietly and drifted closer. His breath was warm on my ear, tickling my sensitive skin. "When I first met you, I thought you smelled like home," he uttered softly.

My heart stammered to an unhealthy halt. "Really?" I asked, looking at him out of the corner of my eye.

Grayson leaned in, pressing a whisper of a kiss against my neck. "Really," he breathed, sending electric shivers through my skin. "I can't explain it, but when I saw you in the net, caught your scent on the wind—I thought of home. Like I was meant to find you. Like I was supposed to be with you."

He pulled away, but I wasn't ready to let him go. I tugged him back, drawing him close enough to be eye to eye, nose to nose, heart to heart. "Your answer is a lot better than mine," I said with a pout, brushing my forehead against his, my fingers creeping into his hair.

Grayson gave a crooning chuckle. "Comparing me to dirt sounds about right."

"I'm going to be old as dirt if we don't get started soon," Illeron called out from the water.

"You already are!" I shot back.

The warrior raised his eyebrows at me. "Clever."

Grayson shook his head, a sardonic smile on his lips as he stood. "He's right. We'd better get started." He eyed the drifting moon, the army of boats behind him. "While time is on our side."

The words were ominous, the weight of our situation suddenly crushing.

We devised a plan. Grayson would tie the rope to a boat's bow eye, and Illeron would pull it into the water. While Illeron worked on the first boat, Grayson and I would haul out the second. Grayson would stand guard while we worked, ready to alert us if danger was near. We'd chip away at the boats closest to the shoreline, moving down the line until they were all tarnished.

The hardest part was watching Grayson struggle to haul the boats back onto the sand. Illeron seemed to take pleasure in it, grinning each time Grayson stumbled on the shifting ground. I snapped my teeth at him. "I'd like to see you do any better."

That wiped the grin clean off his face.

When we got to the third row of boats, Grayson heaved a sigh from the beach. "It's so late," he said loudly. "I should go home."

I froze, the spear in my hands turning to lead.

"That was the signal," Illeron said in my mind. *"Where are you?"*

I swallowed a shaky breath, squeezing my eyes shut. The wood around me suddenly felt suffocating, a casket carrying my body to sea. I wanted to scratch at it until I was back in the water, collect splinters underneath my nails until I was free. But I was paralyzed, struck still by my fear. I was stuck. No, I was *trapped*. *"I'm inside the boat."*

"Poseidon below," Illeron cursed. I could feel his presence drifting until he was underneath my coffin. *"Stay put, Evanora. Don't breathe, don't move."*

Clamping my lips tightly together, I gently laid the spear at the bottom of the boat, flinching when it bumped into the siding. It sounded like a cannon roaring through the silent night air, an alarm blaring my location: *She's here, she's here, she's here!*

"Careful, now," the warrior warned. *"Careful."*

I sank to the floor, pressing myself hard into the wood and curling into the tightest ball I could manage with my long tail. The stars winked overhead, playful and not at all concerned by my being trapped. The ocean swelled, the waves caressing the boat, as if to remind me that it was still there. I pressed my hand against the siding, imagining the water's soothing touch on my skin. Without it, I felt naked, vulnerable, a beacon in the cold and ruthless night.

"*What's happening?*" I dared to ask. "*Can you see anything?*"

There was silence, and then: "*There is a figure on the beach with Grayson Shaw. It looks like they are talking.*"

"*Is Grayson safe?*"

"*He looks . . . on guard. Stiff.*"

I shifted, the chips of wood biting into my scales. "*What if he's in trouble?*"

Illeron's sigh entered my mind. "*He knew the risks in coming here. He can take care of himself.*" He sucked in a sharp breath. "*Neptune spear me.*"

I was instantly alert. "*What is it?*"

"*The other man just shoved Grayson. Hard. Grayson's on the ground.*"

A growl escaped my throat, and before I knew what was happening, I was moving.

"*Evanora, you're jostling the boat,*" the warrior warned.

"*Grayson needs me.*" I unfurled my tail and flipped over, moving with the waves as I clawed my way over to the bow.

"*Evanora, no. He's back on his feet. He's—*"

My magic crackled, sparking against the dull sun-washed wood like embers. I flicked my wrists, my forearm fins deadly. "*He needs me, Illeron!*"

I gripped the boat's edge and slowly pulled myself up. My tail lashed out behind me, banging against the wooden insides like they were nothing more than kindling.

I could see him, standing next to a figure drenched in shadow. The stranger swayed on his feet, his fists raised. Grayson, covered in sand, raised a hand in a quiet plea. His other hand was at his side, reaching for something. He was talking, but his voice was muffled by my own raging heartbeat. The shadow took a strong step forward, then another. The boy held his ground.

The stranger's fists slowly turned into wagging fingers. He patted Grayson on the head roughly, took a stumbling step back, and then wandered back up the hill, tripping in the sand and weeds. Grayson watched him go, his shoulders drooping with exhaustion, before he turned back to the boats and let out a long whistle.

The coast was clear.

Heart in my throat, I launched myself out of the boat and sailed for the shore. "Grayson," I whispered harshly, worry withering my fins. "Are you okay? Did he hurt you?"

Grayson shook his head dolefully, but he was pale, a haunted look dancing in his tired eyes. "Just my pride. I'm pretty sure I have sand in my pants."

Illeron appeared next to me, his mouth set in a thin line. "It was probably wise that you didn't fight back."

Grayson roughly rubbed the sand out of his hair. "What," he said, his voice carrying an edge, "because you don't think I'd be able to defend myself?"

Illeron's eyes widened in shock. "No. Because we wouldn't want any added attention." He proceeded to surprise us all with a small smile. "I have no doubt in my mind that you would've been able to put him in his place."

The boy opened his mouth, only to quickly shut it. "Right," he eventually agreed, the fire doused on his tongue.

"Grayson," I said, pushing myself farther up the beach, "who was he? What did he say?"

Grayson looked at the hill with a shrug. "Just some drunkard. He was rambling. I couldn't understand half of what he said." He turned to me with a wilted smile. "It's all right. I'm all right."

When I refused to budge, the boy laughed lightly and took me by the shoulders. "Really, Evanora, everything's fine!" He nodded to the two boats floating in the water, the remaining rows still waiting for our handiwork. "We need to keep going. We still have several hours' worth of rope burns, sweat, and destruction to get through."

Both the boy and I pretended that I couldn't feel the way his hands were shaking.

We returned to work—reluctantly on my end, and with renewed vigor for Illeron. Grayson put on a brave front, making sure to smile at me whenever he caught me looking.

It was when he didn't, though, that had me worried.

When Grayson wasn't smiling at me, or hauling boats back to shore, or busying himself with expertly tied knots, he was watching the hill. Not for nosy villagers passing by, but for someone to come back.

Because he was scared of whoever he was waiting for.

CHAPTER SIXTY-NINE

GRAYSON

APRIL 26 – EVENING

WATCH YOUR BACK, SHAW. THAT WAS WHAT AMBROSE had said to me. *Or you're next.*

Next? Next for what?

Ambrose had reeked of alcohol and had a wiry, wild-animal look about him. The same sort of look he had when I had found him in the alley—violent, self-destructive, unpredictable. When I'd asked what he was doing in Tully, his response was a smile, a shrug, and shoving me to the ground. If he hadn't backed off, I wasn't sure what Ambrose would have done next.

But what scared me more was that I knew what *I* would have done.

I hadn't even realized I was unclasping my hunting blade out of its sheath until the cool hilt was biting into my sweaty palm, the pale moonlight dancing on the hungry blade. When I saw it in my hand, I was afraid. Afraid that my body had moved on its own accord without my knowing it. Afraid that, once the blade was in my hand, I wanted nothing more than to plunge it into Ambrose's chest.

Ambrose wasn't afraid. When he saw the knife in my hands, he actually smiled. He took a step forward, taunting me, daring me to do it.

And, God, I'd wanted to.

I shuddered violently at the residual feelings floating inside me. They'd felt so *damn good* in the moment. Now they were poison, clogging up my bloodstream, choking the air out of my lungs with their barbed fingers. I sighed, rubbing my eyes, trying to wipe away the memory of Ambrose's smile.

I shifted to my side, staring out my window. The voices were too loud. I couldn't bear to tell Evanora how difficult it had been to be on that beach with her and Illeron. It had been torture. All I'd wanted to do was crawl into the water, sink my teeth into the unblinking darkness.

Even now, when I was in bed, as far from the ocean as I could get, I could hear their whispers, feel their promise of death wrapped in a lullaby swaddle. They wanted me. The Cursed Beings wanted me. And what scared me the most, more than pulling a knife on Ambrose, more than wanting to tear into his flesh, was that I was beginning to want them.

I didn't know how much longer I could resist their call.

I closed my eyes and waited for sleep to take me. And if it didn't, maybe insanity would.

APRIL 27 – MORNING

I OPENED MY EYES. SUNLIGHT DRENCHED THE ROOM. BIRDS OUTSIDE my window chirped their morning hellos.

And there was Evanora.

I lurched forward with a gasp. "Evanora!" I cried out hoarsely. "What are you doing here? How did you get into my house?"

The mermaid giggled. She was perched on the edge of the bed, leaning over me, her flowing tail sweeping along my bedroom floor in long snakelike movements. She brushed a curl off my forehead. "It wasn't all that hard," she said, her voice deliciously soft. "I just climbed and climbed and climbed."

It didn't make sense. Even in my half-asleep, muddle-minded state, I knew that. A million questions formed in my head, but Evanora's fingers were combing through my hair, gentle as the breeze, and not a single one of them landed on my tongue. I closed my eyes and relaxed beneath her touch. "If Pa finds you here . . ." I mumbled lazily.

Evanora made a gentle shushing sound, her finger drifting from my hair to my lips. "He won't find out. He's gone off to work. It's just you and me."

My body was instantly alert, nerves awakening from their slumber and giving me their full, prickly attention. A slow smile crept onto my face as warmth traveled from my heart and collected in my groin. "We're alone?"

Evanora moaned softly. "We're alone." She sank on top of me, her normally ice-cool body feeling like an inferno.

I wrapped my arms around her, unable to pull the stupid smile off my face. "I know I saw you last night, but . . ." I cracked my eyes open, heat pouring into my cheeks. "I missed you."

Evanora licked her lips, slowly, enticingly. "Just how much?"

I chuckled, bringing her closer. "I'll show you."

The mermaid resisted. It was like trying to move a brick wall. She laughed at my pouting frown. "Trust me," she breathed, nuzzling her nose against mine, "I want you just as badly. But I need your help with something first."

I cocked an eyebrow. "Now?" The word came out in a whine, causing Evanora to laugh again.

"Yes, now." Her tail slapped against my bookshelf, sending its innards scattering. Had her tail always been that long? "You see, the climb up to your house wasn't hard, but I scraped my stomach a little on the way." She winced. "I think some rocks got stuck between my scales."

I sucked in a breath. "Are you okay?"

Evanora nodded reassuringly. "Oh, yes. It's a bother more than anything." She grinned at me. "Can you take a look?"

It was an open invitation to not only ogle the body belonging to the most beautiful creature I'd ever seen, but to also touch it. *All* of it. "God, yes."

The mermaid laughed. "You're too kind." She began to pull away from me. It felt like trying to pry two pieces of Velcro off each other. "I don't think I can focus on anything else until we get them out. It's just so . . . *itchy*."

She rose higher, but the warmth of her body remained pressed against my skin, slippery and wet.

"It's almost like . . ."

A sharp metallic scent hit my nose. A deep, gurgling sucking sound met my ears. Evanora's impossibly long tail collided with my desk chair, splintering it into kindling. The hair on the back of my neck stood up, a wave of goose bumps scattering along my arms.

"I could rip . . ."

Evanora reared in front of me, a hissing cackle on her tongue. The tongue that hung loosely in her mouth. Her bottom jaw was gone, replaced with a bloody stump of bone shards and shredded lips.

"My own skin off!"

Evanora spread her arms wide, and I realized with growing horror that it wasn't just her jaw that was missing. The front of her entire body was cut in half, from her missing jaw to the scales rising up her belly. Blood poured from the gaping wound, beading off her exposed rib cage, leaking out of her furiously beating heart. Skin and sinew hung loosely along the newly made borders of her naked chest, warped and stretched. Boils began to emerge amidst the blood and erupt, volcanoes of hot oozing pus that dripped onto my bedsheets.

Evanora smiled a crimson-drenched smile, running her hands over the broken edges of her body, moaning with delight as her fingers slipped into her wound, squelching, coming back soaked.

The mermaid I'd fallen for had become the death that searched for me in my nightmares.

I yelped and pushed away from her, thudding into my headboard with enough force to send the entire frame shaking. I covered my eyes with my hands, swallowing down the bolus of nausea that shot up my throat. "This isn't happening," I cried, peeking through my fingers at the monster before me. "This isn't happening!"

Evanora's fingers slid up and down her open chest, snagging on the broken bones, tugging on the torn skin. "Help me, Grayson," she whined. "I'm just *so itchy*!"

"It's a dream!" I yelled. "Just a dream gone bad. Wake up, wake up, wake up!"

The mermaid's hands traveled up to her face, and with a hysterical laugh, she sank her daggerlike claws in and raked her fingers down, slicing through the skin like it was nothing but paper. Blood splattered across me, so hot it sizzled against my skin. I choked out a gasp, frantically wiping off the crimson. Deep red burns remained, dotting my sweaty arms.

"Wake *up*!" I screamed.

Over and over, Evanora's fingers ripped through her face until nothing but shreds remained. "Can you see the rocks, Grayson?" she asked breathlessly. "Can you see them?"

I shook my head wildly, grabbing at my hair and pulling until the pain had me seeing stars. "No," I groaned, my heart in my throat. "No. No no no!"

Evanora cocked her head to the side, the tips of her silken hair clumping together in blood and pus. "You can't?"

I shook my head again. "Please," I begged. "Just stop. You're not Evanora. You're not my Evanora!"

The mermaid's fingers fluttered away from her face. "If you can't see the rocks," she said, grabbing the edges of her broken rib cage, "then look *harder!*"

Not-My-Evanora pulled. The fractured bones snapped and collapsed, nothing more than brittle fragments. Her entire chest caved in, exposing more of her blistering insides. Her sagging lungs, her withered windpipe. Her angry beating heart. The smell was like rotting meat.

"Stop!" I shrieked, fighting to be heard above the crunching of bone.

"Make me!" she howled back, her voice drenched in a euphoria that sent my stomach squeezing. "Find the rocks. Dig them out! Help me, Grayson! Help me!"

I sobbed, dropping my hands into my lap. "How?"

Not-My-Evanora grinned wickedly; a handful of her teeth toppled out of her mouth. "Why, with your knife, of course. The one you wanted to use on Ambrose Grieves."

"I don't have it," I whispered weakly. "I don't . . ."

The mermaid's smile grew. "Sure you do."

I looked down at my lap. There, in my sweaty palms, was the hunting knife. I screamed hoarsely, flinging it away from me as hard as I could. It clattered into the floorboards and bounced off Not-My-Evanora's tail.

When I looked back at my hands, it was still there, glinting in the blood-drenched sunlight. I threw it again, and again, watching it fall, watching it reappear in my hands. It was laughing at me—I *knew* the damned knife was laughing at me. Desperation welled up within me. "Please just make it stop."

The mermaid clucked her tongue, waving a gnarled finger in my face. "Only you can stop it." She bared her chest at me again. "Find the rocks. Dig them out! Cut me the way you wanted to cut Ambrose Grieves!" Her voice was a wheezing hiss, a cancer in my mind. She watched as I weighed the blade in my shaking hands. "You can try to throw it again, but we both know what will happen."

I bit my lip, a whimper mixing with the bile in my throat. *I could stab her. Then I'll wake up. None of this is real.*

"Yes, Grayson Shaw." She moaned, tilting her head back, her entire body expanding and contracting with every haggard breath. "None of this is real."

I raised the knife, aimed it at her heart.

And then I froze. It was wrong. This *was* real. It had to be. If I stabbed her . . . I shuddered violently. Something bad would happen if I did.

Not-My-Evanora's head craned forward at an awkward angle, the bones in her neck like jagged pieces of glass. "What's the matter, Grayson? Don't you want to wake up?"

"I can't do it," I cried. "Please don't make me do it!" I dropped the knife and covered my face with my hands. Of course, the knife came with me, still in my clutches, still yearning for the blood I was denying it.

The mermaid growled, thick and wet. "Fine," she seethed. "If you won't do it, then I will."

Not-My-Evanora grabbed my hand holding the knife. She wrapped her mangled fingers around my wrist, squeezing so tightly that I could hear my bones pop.

"No!" I screamed. "No, no, no no *no*!"

She thrust the blade into her chest.

My eyes shot open.

I was in the bathroom, standing in front of the sink, staring at my reflection in the cracked mirror hanging above it.

The hunting knife was in my hand, pressed neatly against my scarred wrist.

I gasped, dropping the knife into the sink. It tumbled against the porcelain before coming to a halt next to the drain. I sank to my knees, leaned over the toilet, and vomited everything I had inside me.

It took a while to stop dry heaving. It took even longer to stop shaking. I leaned against the bathtub, sucking in stale breaths and rubbing my wrists. As I rested my head against the cool lip of the tub, something teetered into the porcelain belly. It sounded heavy and ominous. I peeked over the edge, my stomach shifting at the movement.

It was Ma's journal. I wanted to be surprised to see it, but I wasn't.

The book was splayed open to pages I was growing uncomfortably familiar with. A woman, knee-deep in water, handing her baby to tentacle-like arms. The ocean swept around her, yanking at her dress, as if to say, *We want you too.*

Next to the sketch, two words were circled in thick, bold lines. They were made into an island, cut off from the other words, isolated, important.

Blood
Rage.

I shut the book, forced my legs to work, and returned it TO my room. The thing was cursed, and I was becoming cursed because of it. In that moment, as I gently placed it back onto the desk, my desire to burn it, to rip it into shreds, was so strong that I almost acted on it. To show that damned journal that I was in control, that it had no power over me.

But I was tired, and I was so close to finding answers. I could feel it.

Find the answers, then destroy it. That was the plan.

It wasn't until I was entering the kitchen that I realized I had retrieved the knife. I would've laughed if I didn't think I was going to be sick again.

I was fulfilling my pa's wish. The knife was becoming a part of me.

Pa was sitting at the table, a cup of coffee in one hand, a scrap of newspaper in the other. "You're awake early," he commented without looking up.

Even in my dazed state, I could tell when the scent of my sweat and vomit assaulted his senses. Pa glanced at me, his face scrunched in distaste. "God," he said, "you smell awful. Are you all right?"

No, I thought. *I'm not. I haven't been all right for a while.* I glanced warily over my shoulder, numb all over. "The . . . The bathroom," I whispered. "I saw . . . I saw . . ." My sentences fractured, only letting me spit out pieces of them at a time. Fractured, like Not-My-Evanora's ribs.

Pa carefully set down his coffee and leaned forward. "A spider?" he guessed. "A mouse?"

My mind was a blur of bloody smiles and ripped skin. "No." A vicious shiver raced through me. "I saw . . . her. *Her.* The kn . . . The knife." I turned back to Pa. "I tried . . ."

Pa's eyes dropped to the hunting blade dangling between my thumb and finger. "Whoa now," he said, standing and striding over to me in quick, strong steps. "Drop that thing and you'll be missing some toes, son." He slowly pried my fingers away from the hilt and gently placed the knife on the table. I had never felt so barren. Pa gently took me by the shoulders, looking me up and down. He frowned when he removed his hands and found them slick with my sweat. "You don't look well, Grayson."

"I'm sick." Finally, a sentence that didn't slip out in stuttering fragments.

Pa nodded. "Right. That much is obvious. Let's get you back to bed. I can put the kettle on for you, make you some of your magical tea."

When he tried to put his hands on me again, I jerked away. "No," I said, shaking my head vehemently. "I'm *sick.*" I began wringing my hands together, the skin cracking underneath the pressure. "I tried . . . God . . . I almost . . ." A wave of nausea vaulted up my throat. Unable to finish my sentence, I looked down at my wrist, the skin between my scars still red from the knife's teeth.

Pa sucked in a breath, his eyes instantly moving away. He didn't like looking at my scars. "Did you hurt yourself?"

I shuddered, my entire body tensing and contracting, trying to become smaller, invisible. Trying to become nothing. "No."

Pa nodded sharply. "Good. That's good." He turned and swiftly picked up the knife with an expertise that made my insides itch. Itch, like Not-My-Evanora's skin before she began to peel it off. "Maybe I should hold on to this for a bit. Until you get more comfortable around it."

Until you're sure I'm not going to hurt myself? My knees began to quake again. I walked gingerly to the table and sank into one of the chairs. "I need . . ." I sighed, frustration blooming. Taking the knife away wouldn't work, but trying to explain that in an eloquent manner didn't seem possible. "Help. I need help."

Pa softened. He placed the knife back on the table and patted my bowed head, his fingers getting stuck in my tangled curls. "That much is obvious too, son."

The clock chimed. Pa cursed, pulled out his pocket watch, and cursed again. "I'm going to be late for work."

My head shot up, my heart spasming painfully in my too-tight rib cage. "Please," I bit out. "Don't go. Don't. I need—"

"Help," Pa said with a sigh. "Yes, I heard you."

"So . . ." I glanced at the knife worriedly. "*Stay.*"

Pa bit his lip, tapping his foot. We both knew he couldn't afford to. We both knew he wouldn't. He crouched in front of me, planting his hands on my bouncing knees. "Later," he promised. "We will talk about all of this later."

I was the only one who knew, deep in my bones, that there wouldn't be a *later*. Not because Pa didn't have time, or because he didn't care, but because life wouldn't allow it. Life would get in the way, as it always did, and then it would be too late.

"We can pay Pastor Kline a visit. Maybe even Dr. Peele. Right now," Pa continued, "you are home. You are safe. Nothing bad can happen to you here."

I am alone. The words began to tumble in my mind. Around and around, growing larger, taking up too much space, until it was all I could think, all I could focus on. *I am alone.*

Pa was walking toward the front door, throwing on his jacket, kicking on his boots. "I'll be home before you know it."

I am alone.

Pa stood in the doorway, one foot inside the house, one foot out. "I'll . . . I'll see you later, son."

I am alone.

The door closed, trapping me inside the house, a captive in the safe haven that suddenly felt cold, unfamiliar, and foreign.

I. Am. Alone.

No, you aren't, the voices whispered lovingly. *We are here, Promised One. We will always be here.*

The worst part was, I believed them.

The voices would always be there, and there wasn't a damn thing I could do about it.

CHAPTER SEVENTY

EVANORA

APRIL 27 – EVENING

GRAYSON WAS STRUGGLING.

He was too proud to admit as much, but I could see it. His eyes were haunted, pained, as if the ocean itself kept sneaking up on him. Sometimes I could hear the faintest whimper carried by the waves as he fought against his fear of the water, and the pull to be in it.

There were more boats in Fariid—too many. My heart sank. The number had doubled, maybe tripled, since Tully. Illeron kept quiet, but I could feel his worry. There was no way Grayson could get all the boats into the water alone. But when he jogged over, grinning despite the stiffness in his body, he said breathlessly, "The tide's coming in."

Illeron and I looked at each other. "So, you won't be able to help us," the warrior guessed, slightly sour.

Grayson shook his head. "You won't need my help. By the time the tide is fully in, you'll be able to reach the boats at the farthest point of the shore." He chuckled under his breath. "I don't know who's looking out for us right now, but they must like us a lot."

Hope soared within me. "That's brilliant!" I gasped.

Illeron nodded begrudgingly. "That's acceptable."

Grayson was already tying his rope to a boat. "I'll help for as long as I can," he said, tightening the knot in the bow eye. "But I'd like to remain dry tonight, if I can help it."

The warrior cocked his head to the side. "Afraid of a little water, human?"

Grayson returned Illeron's look with a dark one of his own. "Afraid that I'll do a better job than you, fish?"

I sucked in a breath, my fins reflexively growing tough.

Grayson stared at Illeron. Illeron stared right back. Then the warrior snorted, shook his head, and turned away. "So feisty for a human."

Grayson's shoulders relaxed. "So uptight for a fish."

We got to work, the routine smoother than in Tully. Less arguing, more competitive banter. Grayson goaded Illeron to hurry when he waited to push a boat in, while Illeron slapped his tail impatiently whenever Grayson fumbled with the knots or slipped on the sand. It was strange, seeing them get along—but nice. I'd expected them to hate each other until the Hunt was over, if not a bit longer.

Grayson worked on the boats lining the water's edge, and when the waves began to lick at their bellies, he would push them in as much as he dared, then set out to tie up the next row.

On and on we worked. We didn't stop. We didn't take breaks. If there was no rest for the wicked, there certainly wasn't any for the righteous. We were a well-oiled machine with only one thing in mind: to destroy the Hunt or, at the very least, make it a very uncomfortable and inconvenient experience for the hunters.

And Grayson was struggling.

The look on his face broke my heart—the way he both avoided looking at the water, and couldn't keep it out of his sight. The faint whimpers that escaped him tore at me. It was like watching an animal trapped in a cage, keening for freedom, knowing that death waited on the other side with knives for teeth and razor-sharp talons for fingers.

I tried to comfort him with soft smiles and fleeting touches, but my words slipped off him like waves retreating from the shore. All he saw was the sea; all he felt was the water kissing my skin.

When we were working on the third row, the tide eating up half of the black sand of the beach, Illeron went still, his spear poised underneath the boat. He craned his neck, his ear pointed toward the shore. "I thought he said he didn't want to get wet," he muttered.

I kept working beside him, digging the spear's tip into the boat's wooden underbelly. "He doesn't," I said, gritting my teeth as the wood finally gave way.

Illeron heaved a sigh and began poking at the skeg. "Well, I hate to break it to you, but your lover boy is up to his knees now." He stopped again. "Make that his waist."

I paused, listening.

And that was when I heard it.

The sloshing of footsteps. Hurried, panicked, erupting in the water like sonic blasts.

Fear squeezed my insides. "No!" I whispered, dropping my spear and lurching around the bobbing boat.

The warrior looked at my abandoned spear with confusion, then at me. "Wait, what's wrong?" he asked.

But I was already gone.

Grayson was at the far side of the beach, a faint shadow in the midst of the pier's long, spindly legs. He had been right next to me only moments ago. How had he made it down there so quickly?

I cursed myself for not focusing on the boy enough. In my goal of destroying the boats, I had ignored the connection throbbing in my heart, pretending that the incessant tugging was simply nerves, both Grayson's and mine.

But I realized now that it was a cry for help.

I broke through the surface, searching the open ocean wildly for a glimpse of him. The boy was nearly up to his shoulders. I could just make out the strained look on his face as the waves splashed against his chin and cheeks, the way his mouth was peeled back in a silent shout. He didn't want to be in the water, but he needed to be.

"Illeron!" I screamed, submerging underneath the swelling waves and whipping my tail as fast as I could. "Illeron, help!"

The warrior was behind me in an instant. "What do you need me to do?" he asked firmly.

"We can't let him get any deeper. We can't lose him!"

Illeron nodded and abruptly swam right, his silver-and-crimson tail disappearing in the moonlit waters. I aimed myself for Grayson. When I reached him, I barely slowed; my body pummeled into his, knocking him off course. "Grayson!" I shouted. "Grayson, enough!"

The boy shook his head wildly, trying to step around me, though the tips of his toes bounced off the sloping sand. "No!" he screeched, pushing me away. "I need to go! They need me! They're calling for me!"

Illeron popped up in front of us, a barrier to deeper waters. His face was a mask of fury, dripping with salt water and concern. "If you don't turn around and head back to the shore, I'll drag you there myself," he barked.

The boy didn't hear him. He continued to fight to get around me. "They're calling for me!" he cried out again. "If I don't go, I'll go mad! I just know I will!" He squeezed his eyes shut and began hitting the sides of his head with his fists. "Make them stop! Please make them stop!"

A shudder ripped through me, cold and ferocious. I grabbed his hands and pulled them away from his head. "If you go any farther, you'll *die*. And I'll be damned if I let that happen." I bared my teeth and hissed, tugging the boy into a tight embrace. "I promised I'd protect you. I won't let them have you! You'll just have to live and be a little mad."

Grayson wailed and tried to claw his way out of my grip. But I was firm, my arms locked around his frail body like a cage.

"You can hate me all you want," I whispered viciously. "You can scream and scratch me until you're numbed by exhaustion. But they cannot have you."

The boy swung his head back, but before he could smash it into my face, Illeron was there, his hand pressed against Grayson's forehead, keeping it craned back at an awkward angle. It looked painful; the boy squawked in alarm, the bones in his neck creaking underneath the warrior's pressure. Illeron gritted his teeth and pressed harder, pushing Grayson's head back, and back, and back, until the boy was staring at the shining stars, the naked moon, the blanket of night.

"Illeron, stop!" I begged. "You're hurting him!"

"He wanted to hurt *you*!"

I shook my head rapidly. "He's not in his right mind. Please let go of him."

Illeron snarled and leaned forward, his mouth hovering next to the boy's ear. "Listen here, human. You try a stunt like that on my queen again, and I'll end your life so quickly, you won't even have time to send a prayer to your god." He dug his nails into Grayson's forehead. "I'll gladly give you to the Cursed Beings myself."

Grayson's eyes flicked to the warrior's, full of self-loathing and hate. "Do it," he growled, sounding completely vile and inhuman.

Illeron shook his head. "Lucky for you, Evanora deems you too precious to kill." He leaned away slowly. "Now, I'm going to remove my hand, and you are going to quit your childish antics; we've already lost a lot of time because of you. I doubt we will be able to break all the boats now."

The warrior's words seemed to hold weight in the boy's soul. He blinked, the fog in his eyes lifting, the stiffness of his body replaced with trembling. "I'm sorry," he moaned quietly. "I'm so sorry."

When Illeron took his hand away, Grayson crumpled into me, cold and frozen with fear. He buried his face into my neck, sobbing. "I'm sorry," he said over and over. "I'm so *sorry*, Evanora."

"It's okay," I promised, knowing that nothing was.

I took him back to the beach, swimming slowly and with great care. I was carrying fragile goods; one wrong move and they'd surely shatter. The boy was limp when I pushed him into the wet sand, a pile of bones trapped in soggy skin. I was hesitant to let go of him, but Grayson was too tired to move, let alone leap up and march back into the water. I wiggled up beside him, pushing the sopping-wet curls out of his face. "I think you should go home, Grayson," I said softly, taking his hands and blowing on them.

The boy shook his head weakly. "No," he bit out. "I can still work. I can still help!"

I smiled against his shivering hands. "But I won't be able to. I'd be too worried about you."

Grayson's mouth dipped into a low frown. "I lost control just for a *second*."

"And who's to say it won't happen again?"

"It won't!" the boy proclaimed. "I won't let it."

I nuzzled my nose into his cheek, hoping Grayson couldn't feel the emotions brimming against the surface of my skin, the fluttering beneath my scales. "Please go home. Warm up, get some rest. Illeron and I can finish up here. We'll meet at the beach in Maude tomorrow night."

Grayson looked at me, uncertain. "You promise you'll be all right?"

I chuckled, planting a soft kiss on the corner of his frown. "Only if you can promise me the exact same thing."

"I can," he lied.

"Then I can too," I lied back.

I sank beneath the crooning waves and watched the boy leave the beach. When he got to the stairs, he looked back at me, uncertainty clouding his features as he whispered, "Until next time?"

I buried my sob with a grin and nodded reassuringly. "Until next time, Grayson Shaw."

The warrior slipped in beside me, a statue of resilience, the edges cracking. His mouth was set in a thin line. "He can hear them," he guessed when the boy was out of sight. "The Cursed Beings."

I nodded carefully, my eyes flitting to his. "Their grip on him is getting stronger every day." I rubbed at my forearm fins, softening their hard edges. "I fear that one day he will completely succumb to their call, and I won't be there to save him."

The warrior massaged his temples wearily. "You know what this means, don't you?"

I looked at him, my arms still wrapped around myself like a hug. I didn't want to know. All I wanted was to keep Grayson safe. And my ability to do even that was slipping through my fingers.

Illeron sighed, long and worn out. "It means he's been touched by them. They nearly had him once." He slowly raised his head, his eyes narrowed as they pierced into me. "And they will stop at nothing until they have him again. It is not a question of if they get him, but when." His gaze drifted to the beach, heavy with worry. "And I have a feeling they are growing impatient. Your boy is running out of time."

CHAPTER SEVENTY-ONE

GRAYSON

APRIL 28 - MORNING

KNOWING I WAS DREAMING MADE EVERYTHING WORSE.

I knew I was dreaming, and I knew there was no way I could wake up.

The only way to end the dreams was with death.

I was back in the water, cold hands tightening around my neck, pulling me under. Blood from my wrists swirled around me like smoke. I tried to blink it away, but the crimson curtain kept coming, sweeping across my eyes, filling my nose, pouring into my mouth. My lungs spasmed, and I gasped for air. Water flooded in, drowning me inside and out, until I was nothing but blood, water, and the screams locked in my throat. The waves ebbed, the wind and rain howled. I looked up and saw—

It should have been you!

—Ma.

But it wasn't my ma. It was my face staring down at me, my hands around my neck, my vicious grin spattered with my blood.

The Cursed Beings screamed, long and delirious. No, not the Cursed Beings. *Me. I* was screaming. Every time I opened my mouth, the creature wearing my face opened its mouth too. We screamed in unison, dreadful and loud, in perfect sync, in perfect madness.

"Wake up!"

I wanted to. God, I wanted to wake up so badly. I clenched my eyes shut, fear coating me like a second layer of skin.

"Wake *up*!"

I opened my eyes. I wasn't in the water anymore. I was above it, holding Evanora beneath the waves by the throat. Her tail thrashed in panic as I squeezed the life out of her. Her violet eyes bulged in silent terror. She clawed at my hands, but I didn't feel the pain. Only power.

"Grayson, wake up!"

It was Evanora's voice, chapped and tight from my hands around her neck. Wind and rain ripped at my clothes, my hair clinging to my face. I gasped and tried to pry my hands off the mermaid. My grip only grew more steadfast. I tried to say, "Swim! As fast as you can. *Swim!*"

All that came out of my mouth was, "It should have been *you*!"

The knife was back in my hands, aimed at Evanora's chest, where our connection beat hard against her ribs. She squirmed, but my strength was inhuman, godlike.

My strength was death.

I knew how the dream was going to end.

With a hoarse cry, I plunged the blade into her.

Evanora let out a bloodcurdling scream.

The world fell silent, Evanora's cries echoing in the deadly quiet.

I released her neck slowly, a dark laugh bubbling in my throat as I stared down at the knife in my own chest. My heart tried to beat around it, blood pouring out, blood promised to someone else.

"Wake up, damn it!"

I clasped the hilt with my shaking hands. It was buried deep, growing slick with my blood. I gritted my teeth, growled darkly, and wrenched the blade free.

"*Grayson!*"

I opened my eyes in time to watch my left foot slip off the edge of Howler's Hill, sending a torrent of pebbles cascading down into the yawning ocean below. I yelped and tried to scurry back, but the momentum of my steps carried me forward, over the ledge, into the promise of a free fall. The wind roared, the rain spitting fury, and I was falling down, down, down—

There was a hand on my arm, yanking me back.

I gasped at the force behind it, the desperation buried within the grip, as I was dragged back over the cliff face. The cliffs continued their screaming, mourning the death they hadn't been given as Pa hauled me back to the tree line. My bare feet slipped and skidded in the mud, but Pa didn't stop. He tugged on my arm so viciously that I was certain it was going to dislocate. We were both in our pajamas, so drenched that our clothes clung to us.

Pa's face was bone white, clenched tight with fear. I stared at his wide eyes, his heavy breaths, his rapidly moving mouth. "Are you awake?" he was asking, though the wind stole most of his words. "Please, God, be awake!"

My heart was a pistol, my blood the ammunition. I looked at the beckoning cliff, then back to Pa. There was no sign of the knife, no sign of Evanora, no sign of blood. Still, I had to ask, "Is this a dream? Are you real?"

Pa's expression morphed into a look muddled with both relief and pain. He nodded hurriedly. "Yes, son, this is real. *I'm* real."

The rain suddenly felt too heavy on my back, and I sank to the ground, the mud suctioning me in place. Waves of nausea rolled through me, sending me into convulsive shudders. "What is wrong with me?" I sobbed into my dirty hands. "Why is this happening?"

Pa knelt next to me, shielding me from the rain's cold touch with his upper body. "I don't know," he uttered, his voice tightly cinched. "I just don't know, Grayson."

"I'm scared," I wept. "I'm so scared!"

Pa's hands were on my back, making large soothing circles. "I am too."

I swallowed a lungful of air, feeling suddenly starved. "How did I get here?"

Pa pulled away slowly. "You don't remember?" He pushed his long unkempt hair out of his eyes and inspected me carefully. "You really don't remember anything?"

I shook my head. I remembered leaving the beach, taking Penny home, and putting myself to bed as quietly as possible so I didn't wake Pa up. Everything else was blank.

Pa frowned. "I was in the kitchen, finishing my coffee, reading the morning paper. I heard you get up. I figured that, despite the bad weather, you were wanting to train or something." Long creases appeared on his forehead as he grimaced. "But the second you walked into the kitchen, I knew something was wrong." He looked at me, the memory—the terror behind it—fluttering over his face. "You weren't . . . responsive. It was like you weren't even there. You were . . ."

A dead man walking. "Asleep," I whispered, another violent shiver racing through me, the threat of tears returning.

Pa nodded. "But I couldn't wake you up no matter how hard I tried. I talked to you, poked and prodded you. I even stepped right in front of you in hopes of getting you to stop walking." He groaned, running a hand over his face. "But you kept moving, like I wasn't even there. Eyes open, mouth shut, barely even breathing. Like you were possessed. You just kept walking into me until I finally got out of your way. You walked outside, and I followed you. You just . . . kept walking."

Pa looked like he didn't want to keep talking. I didn't want to hear the rest. I knew how it ended.

"Listen, Grayson," Pa bit out. "I'm sorry if it felt like I wasn't taking you seriously before." He clamped his hands on my shoulders and helped me to my feet. "I am now. I promise I am." He patted me on the back. "Let's get you inside and dry you off. I'll stay home. I'm sure Tully can survive without its butcher for one day. We'll get this sorted out. We'll put an end to it."

I wanted to believe him. But it wasn't that simple. There wouldn't be any sort of *end* to anything. Not until the Cursed Beings had me. "We need to go see Ma."

Pa's hand became a fist on my back. "Absolutely not."

"She is going to know better than anyone else what is happening to me," I pushed, tripping out of Pa's grip. "She's the reason behind it all, I'm sure of it."

And I was. The voices, the obsessive pull of the water, the journal—they all circled back to Ma. She would have the answers. She would know what was going on and how to fix it.

Doubt flickered on Pa's face, but only for a second. "She's only going to fill your head with more nonsense. That's the last thing you need."

What I needed was answers. "What happened that night?" I asked, squinting at Pa in the gray morning light.

Pa suddenly wouldn't meet my eyes. "What night?"

I growled, shaking my head. "You *know* what night! When Ma dragged me down to the beach and tried to kill me. What happened?"

"Grayson." Pa sighed exasperatedly. "That has *nothing* to do with this!"

I choked out a laugh. "It has everything to do with this!" I pushed around him, jogging through the trees, following the muddy trail that led back to the house. "I'll show you."

"Grayson—wait!" Pa let out a chirp of disapproval, but he chased after me, stumbling to keep up with my sudden burst of frantic energy.

I was in my room and grabbing the journal before Pa made it to the front steps. By the time he closed the door, I was already sitting at the table, riffling through the book with nervous enthusiasm. "It's in here," I muttered under my breath. "It's all in here. I'll show him, and he'll understand."

Pa was panting. It was hard to tell what was sweat or rain on his slick skin. "What is going on?" he demanded when he finally caught his breath, only to grow still when he saw what I was looking at. "What is that?"

"Ma's journal," I said absentmindedly, my fingers working furiously to find the cursed page that plagued my every thought. "I found it in your room." I held up a hand in Pa's direction when I caught his furious shade of red in my peripherals. "You can scold me about things like privacy later. This is important." I shoved the book across the table in his direction. "This! This is it!"

Pa chewed on his lip, still clearly torn between scolding me now or saving it for later. Curiosity won, and he leaned over and peered at the journal. It didn't take long for him to sigh and straighten. "Grayson," he said, folding his arms, "this is just gibberish. Nothing but scratches and scribbles."

"It's *not*," I pleaded. "It's a message! For me! It's about me!" I pointed vigorously at the picture. "Ma literally sketched me!"

Pa stared at the picture of the woman, knee-deep in the ocean, showing her baby to the tentacle arms. "That's a mother and her child."

"Yes," I agreed heartily. "Ma and *me*. She is giving *me* to the water." I pointed again. "To the Cursed Beings."

Pa's face scrunched together. "Cursed Beings? What—" He shook his head abruptly. "This is ridiculous. Grayson, this book is nothing but garbage. Your ma clearly didn't know what she was doing when she wrote it."

"She knew *exactly* what she was doing!" I argued. "She knew that the Cursed Beings lived in the Barrens. She knew that if she struck a bargain with them and sacrificed me, she could get Warrick back."

Pa scoffed, turning away from me. "Do you hear the words coming out of your mouth right now?"

I jabbed the words that only I could seem to read. "Bargain. Ritual. Link." I pointed at my wrists. "*Blood oath*. Tell me this doesn't make sense!"

"This doesn't make sense." Pa took a step forward and clasped my arms in a viselike grip. "Now, you listen to me, and you listen good and well, boy. Persephone has filled your head with fantasies. This book has only exacerbated them. You are fixating on them, *obsessing* over them, intent on finding truth when there isn't any to be found. No wonder you're sick and having nightmares!" He gave me a rough shake. "Grayson, they are nothing but fairy tales—"

I shoved Pa away. "If someone tries to talk to me about fairy tales one more goddamn *time*!" Spittle flew from my mouth as I yelled the words at the top of my lungs.

Thunder boomed outside, causing the windowpanes to shake and the glass in the cabinets to rattle. And then there was silence, a tension-filled quiet that ached to be full of loud voices and hateful words and brutal force. All of my fear was replaced with red-hot rage. I was gnarled and twisted with it, all gnashing teeth and claws. Breathing hard, I looked down at my shaking hands, wanting so badly to weaponize them.

Pa stepped away, shaking his head slowly. "I can't talk to you—not when you're like this. There will be no getting through to you in the state you're in."

I chuckled low, almost a growl. "Fine." I picked up the journal and tucked it underneath my arm. "If you won't talk to me, then Ma will."

Pa was immediately in front of me, a barricade before the door. "No, Grayson—" He held his hands out in front of him, warding me away. "She'll only make it worse!"

I ducked underneath his arms, grabbed my coat and boots, and sprinted out the door.

I didn't know if Pa was chasing after me. I didn't know if he was calling up Pastor Kline, or Dr. Peele, or spitting rage on the wind as he changed the locks on the front door, effectively banishing me from the house. I didn't care.

I didn't care about anything except for getting to Maude and getting answers.

THE RAIN HAD STOPPED BY THE TIME I REACHED MAUDE, BUT THE clouds still hung low, swollen and black, promising more. Ma sat outside, not in the gardens like before, but beside them, her rickety wheelchair facing the horizon beyond the cliff edge. The wind tousled her hair and played with the blanket in her lap, but Ma didn't notice. If the sky broke open and wept, I doubted she'd even blink.

A nurse sprawled across a bench, long legs dangling off the armrest, neck bent awkwardly against the other. His book rested atop his face, a shield from the sunlight peeking through the clouds. As I passed, he lifted the book and squinted at me. "Haven't seen you in a while," he mumbled, voice thick with sleep.

"Perhaps it's because you've been sleeping," I snapped, my steps not slowing.

The nurse raised the book higher, showcasing his surprise. "Wow, the kitten comes bearing claws." He glanced in my ma's direction. "I'd be careful today. She woke up in a foul mood, insisting nonstop that I was to take her outside. In the rain!" His face puckered, and he took on a falsetto voice. " 'Oh, I need to be outside,' " he moaned loudly. " 'I need to be near the water.' " The nurse snorted, his voice dropping back down to its snively egotistical tone. "When I told her we had to wait until it eased up, she threw a raging fit. Launched her breakfast tray at me." He self-consciously swiped at the green splotch on the front of his white shirt. "Spinach stains, you know."

I frowned at him. "Shouldn't you be closer to her?"

The nurse gawked at me. "What, so she can assault me again?" He sighed, lowering the book back onto his face. "No, thank you."

My eyes wandered to the cliff's edge, exposed and tempting to vulnerable, lost souls. "What if she . . . I don't know . . . tries something?"

The nurse laughed, causing the book to nearly slide off his large nose. "That woman hasn't left her chair in *years*. I highly doubt she is going to try *anything*."

Gritting my teeth, I resumed walking down the pebbled path, hoping that the next time Ma found fault in the nurse, she'd hit him with a lot more than just spinach.

Ma had one hand tucked under the blanket, the other idly picking at dead flowers on the hedges. Her fingers dragged across the thorns, her skin scratched and red, but she didn't seem to notice. Her eyes were fixed on the churning waves below, her head tilted slightly, listening to them. She closed her eyes, inhaled the salty air, and spoke. "I know why you're here."

Her words crippled my heart, sending it out of rhythm.

Ma held her tilted pose, but her eyes flicked to me as she opened them. "They are calling to you, aren't they?"

The blood drained from my face.

Ma chuckled morbidly, shifting her gaze back to the open ocean. "I knew they would."

I swallowed hard. "What do they want to do with me?"

Ma's head jerked to the side, the movement stiff, irregular. "They don't want to do *anything* with you. They simply *want* you."

"But . . ." I ran a hand through my hair, wishing my heart would stop its hellish rhythm. "But why?"

"I told you already." Ma slowly folded her arms; I could hear her bones crackle and snap. "I made a deal with them. The deal was not met. They are angry." She was talking so casually, like we were discussing the weather, not the root of all evil that circled the island and hungered for me.

I shook my head, impatience causing my skin to itch. "That's not good enough." I marched in front of the chair and stood before Ma, blocking her view. "I'm going to need more than that. You at least owe me that much."

Ma leaned to the side, finding the ocean again. "It should have been you. I don't owe you anything."

A burst of fire in my gut propelled me forward. I snarled, slamming my hands onto the wheelchair's armrests, bending low until we were face-to-face. Ma didn't even flinch. "You've *cursed* me!" I roared.

The journal slipped out of my jacket pocket. It bounced off Ma's knees before tumbling to the ground. Ma's eyes darted to the book, watching as the wind ruffled the pages.

"Oh," she crooned, a coy smile on her lips, "you've found my journal."

"Yes," I ground out. "And you're going to tell me everything."

Ma clucked her tongue. "Am I?"

I grabbed the book and shoved it into Ma's lap. "You can start with the night you decided to try to kill me."

Ma stroked the book's cover like she'd been reunited with a long-lost friend. "It wasn't easy, you know. Getting information that was considered toxic for Lethe's close-minded people. All books pertaining to the old ways of the island were banned, most of them burned or torn to shreds. Almost everyone had forgotten what really happened centuries ago." She shrugged. "Fact became fiction, then fairy tales, then silly lullabies to scare wild children tame. Everyone knew not to swim at night but couldn't remember why. They couldn't remember the real evil that lurked underneath the waves, always starving, never satisfied. It wasn't the mermaids." She laughed dryly. "It was never the mermaids. It was always them."

I bit my lip, a shiver crawling up my spine. "The Cursed Beings."

Ma nodded. "People chose to focus on the mermaids because it was easier than accepting the creature with godlike power hidden in the Barrens, the one that longed for death, that fed off the darkness and still wanted more. They chose to hate the mermaids instead, pretending that Lethe's downfall was all their fault when really"—she rolled her eyes—"humans were to blame too. We are a pathetic species. We can never accept when we are wrong. Too proud."

The irony sent a rush of hysteria through me. I gave a hurt laugh. "Well, I guess you're an expert on that."

Ma held up a finger. "I did what I had to. A mother's love is not something to be trifled with."

Uninvited tears filled my eyes. "You were my mother too," I whispered.

A flurry of emotions passed over Ma's gaunt face, but none of them showed a hint of compassion. "I found out about the Cursed Beings during my comfort calls with Pastor Kline at the asylum," she said, her voice flat. "Honestly, I probably shouldn't have been leaving the house. After Warrick, I was broken. Broken people shouldn't be trying to help other broken people. But the crackpots in here? They'll talk about anything. And with those visits . . ." She raised her hands with a grin. "An epiphany. I consumed every morsel of information the patients gave me. What they were, how they were created, what they wanted. I devoured as gospel the things everyone else called lunacy."

Ma clapped her hands together. "My eyes were opened to a whole new world. After the calls, I'd race home and write down everything, no detail spared. I had to know what Lethe wanted to keep secret." She looked up from the book, cocking her head. "Which brings us to you."

Blood rushed into my ears. I could feel the dread building.

Ma blinked, analyzing me. "I knew I had to act when the moon was new, a sliver in the sky. That's when they're strongest. So I drugged you, playing it off as an illness. I tucked you in, kissed your forehead. And then, in the dead of night, I stole you from your bed and took you to the ocean." Her eyes dropped to my wrists, hidden beneath my jacket. "I cut your wrists. Slipped you into the water." She laughed, low and bitter. "Guess I didn't drug you enough. You woke up the second the water soaked into your pajamas. Kicking, screaming—like a little drunkard."

I stared at her, sickened.

"Easy to subdue," she went on, unconcerned. "I held you in the water, called to the Cursed Beings, begging for a bargain. To give me back my Warrick and have you instead." She leaned forward, tilting her face to catch a ray of sunlight. "They spoke to me, Grayson. I heard them, clear as day. Their voice, like a thousand gods in one. They heard my pain, my plea. The deal was struck."

I exhaled a sharp breath. "I don't understand. How could you make a deal with them?"

Ma's grin widened, her bottom lip splitting. Blood dotted the cut. She licked the droplets away with a lazy flick of her tongue. "Even deals with the devil can be made." She scowled suddenly. "But then—just as the darkness was ready to claim you—a bright light. Daylight in the middle of the night. Hateful. Burning. So pure, it made me sick. The Cursed Beings fled before the ritual could finish. Left us both empty-handed."

She sniffed, almost indifferent. "With all their strength, they erased that light from existence. Killed it dead. And as they left, they warned me: An unfinished bargain carries consequences."

My pulse raced. "What does that mean?"

Ma smiled, dark and knowing. "They've tasted your blood. And they want you. More than anything. More than death, more than fear." She leaned forward, eyes glinting. "Now they're restless. Hungry. They're done waiting for you. You feel it, don't you? That pull? The irrational rage eating at you?" She snickered. "You're a dead man. You just don't know it yet."

The one who was promised. Here.

The voices drifted up the cliff, carried by the wind, needling into my mind. My ears began to ring, my vision spotting with bright, white-hot light.

I had been promised. And the promise hadn't been fulfilled.

I gave my head a quick shake, trying to knock the voices out. I could hear their laughter, gentle and lulling. *Here*, they crooned. *Herrrrre.*

Ma smirked, watching my unraveling with amusement. "How long can you refuse their call, I wonder?"

I squeezed my hands against my head. "I've lasted this long."

"Barely." She tsked, settling into her seat. "It won't be long now. Whether it's willingly, or by force. They will have you." She beamed at me. "And I'll have my Warrick back."

I ripped my hands away from my head and pointed at the cliff and the thrashing waves beyond it. "Ma, they tricked you! They were never going to give you Warrick! He's gone! He's dead! He's never coming back!" I began to pace, desperation clawing at me. "You're lucky that light—whatever it was—came when it did, because if it hadn't, you would have been left with no sons and a shattered heart, and they would have laughed, Ma. They would have rejoiced in your agony. Because that's what the devil *does*."

Ma's eyes followed me, the amusement still riddled across her wilted features. "It was a mermaid's light that saved you."

She said the words so quietly, so offhandedly, that I had to stop pacing in order to register them. "What?" I asked stiffly, suddenly terrified to know the answer.

"A mermaid saved you," she said casually. "I met her once. My boat capsized off the coast when I was searching for Warrick. She saved me. Her light . . . It was pure. Joyful. Even when I screamed hateful things at her, she still helped me." Ma's voice dropped. "I despised her. With her long white hair, amethyst eyes, iridescent fins. The kind of beauty that hurts to look at. And her crown!" She snorted. "So wretchedly hideous."

She trembled, the wheelchair creaking beneath her. "I'm glad she's dead. Her glow still haunts me, but I find peace knowing it's gone. Some lights don't deserve to shine."

The world went eerily quiet. I couldn't breathe.

Evanora didn't know what had happened to her mother. It ruined her, not knowing. And it ruined me, seeing her in so much pain, seeing her hide it with a carefully placed smile.

If only she knew the truth was just as painful.

Evanora's mother, Nereida, was dead because of me. Evanora suffered every single day because of *me*. Guilt swept through me, slicing through my own heartache, tearing it asunder. With a broken gasp, I sank to my knees. There was no way I'd ever be able to look at Evanora without feeling the shame of her mother's sacrifice. Her blood was on my hands, staining, condemning. Nereida was the thread that connected us—she had to be. She was the reason behind our linked hearts beating as one.

And she was dead because of me.

Ma was talking, but her words were miles away, tucked underwater, sinking deep, deep down. "If Warrick won't come to me like you claim, then I will go to him."

I was staring at my hands, at the blood I couldn't see but knew was there. "What?" I croaked, numbly looking up in time to see Ma launch out of her chair and take off in a sprint.

Straight for the cliff.

Time slowed down.

The wheelchair teetered on its back wheels before toppling over with a crash. I screamed, the wind ripping the sound out of my mouth as I scrambled to my feet. The nurse shouted in alarm as he leapt off the bench, tripping over his gangly legs as he fought against the syrupy seconds to turn meters of distance into inches.

But Ma didn't look back. She didn't slow. She was determined to find her favorite son at the bottom of the cliff.

I dove forward, snagging the hem of her dress between my fingers. I tugged back as hard as I could. I was suddenly a child again, yanking on Ma's dress, begging for her to look at me, to love me, to choose *me*. Not her dead son. Me.

The sound of fabric ripping met my ears, loud as gunfire. It mingled with the howling wind, with my screams, with the nurse's frantic shouts.

It wasn't enough.

Ma's body spun from the force of my desperate pull, giving me one last fleeting look at her face before she stumbled over the ledge.

And she had the biggest smile on her face.

CHAPTER SEVENTY-TWO

EVANORA

APRIL 28 – EVENING

"SOMETHING IS WRONG."

The sun was setting with the promise of approaching night. Illeron and I had been hiding on the edge of a sandbar, staring at the ten desolate boats strewn along Maude's rocky bay. Even from our spot in the water, it was obvious they were in rough shape: heaps of rotten wood covered in algae and bug-bitten holes. Little effort would be needed to render them completely useless. But without the boy, the ten pathetic boats resting atop the shale-covered beach were untouchable, out of reach and immune to our desire for destruction.

My body was stiff from not moving, my tail cramping against the sandy slope. I looked at Illeron, worried. "Grayson should have been here by now."

The warrior adjusted his grip on his spear, flexing his fingers. "Perhaps he isn't coming."

I immediately shook my head. "No," I forced out. "He knows this is important. He knows he needs to be here."

"Evanora," Illeron sighed. "He had a close call last night. He was really shaken up about it. You can't blame him for getting cold feet."

It was possible. But I couldn't shake the feeling that something terrible was unfolding, something bigger than mere nerves. Biting my lip, I tugged on the thread holding my and Grayson's hearts together, focusing all my energy on it.

The thread, normally thrumming with life and love, was dangerously slack. The sudden emptiness was terrifying.

Illeron's hand was on my shoulder. *"I'm sure he's fine, Evanora,"* he whispered in my mind.

The warrior's words did little to calm me, but they did give me an idea.

"Try reaching out to him," I said, pushing myself off the sandbar and into the ocean's embrace. The cool water was a salve on my aching body, coaxing the tight knots out of my muscles with its massaging waves. "See if you can listen in on his thoughts. Maybe we can find his location through them."

Illeron gave me a look. "That won't work."

"Why not?"

"Because he's human." He shook his head. "Even if I wanted to, I doubt I'd be able to access his mind. I'm sure I'd be locked out."

I rolled my eyes, exasperated. "You haven't even tried. Besides, don't you constantly claim that mermaids are superior to humans? With that logic, you should be able to reach out to him easily."

"Humans are dumb and dangerous. It's an awful combination." Illeron pinched the bridge of his nose. "All we would find out is that Grayson is safely tucked away in his home on the hill, out of harm's way, with no intention of helping us tonight."

"Well," I said, shrugging, "then at least I wouldn't have to worry about him."

The warrior glanced at the beach, at the taunting boats resting on their bed of shale and rock shards. "I'm sure we can find a way to do this on our own."

"Illeron, don't fight with me on this." I turned to him, my tail swishing pensively. "I am asking you to do me this one kindness. I will never ask you for anything else as long as I live."

"I find that very hard to believe."

"Illeron, *please.*"

The warrior groaned under his breath. He closed his eyes, exhaled slowly, and went completely still.

I waited for a heartbeat. Then two. Then three. When the silence got to be too much, I let out a quiet whine. "Anything?"

Eyes still closed, Illeron quirked his mouth. "It helps if I'm not rushed."

"Sorry."

After another weighted silence, the warrior opened his eyes with a frown. "There are a lot of voices to sift through. It's hard to tell which one belongs to him."

I swam away from the sandbar. "Perhaps we should try moving."

He sighed again. "Evanora . . ."

But I was already leaving, and Illeron had no choice but to follow.

The sun dragged its rays across the sky, painting the clouds with pinks and oranges. The warrior's eyes were watchful. "It's going to be dark soon."

I remained resolute despite the tendrils of fear slithering along my spine. "Then we'd better hurry up and find him."

We circled back to Tully, scouring Hannigan's Cove, the docks, and Bristling Bay. I looked at Illeron hopefully. The warrior went quiet, then shook his head. "He's not here."

My hand went subconsciously to the bracelet on my wrist, my fingers on the octopus charm. "Should we head to the waterfall?"

Illeron chewed on his lip thoughtfully before shaking his head again. "No. If he were close by, I'd be able to sense him." He frowned. "At least, I *think* I'd be able to. It's a guess, at best."

He wanted to give up. I could see it in his eyes.

"Well, don't stop," I hissed. "Keep listening!"

Illeron gave an incredulous gasp. He spun in a circle, his arms outstretched. "Evanora, this is impossible. There are too many variables. He could be anywhere. Gods, he could be *sleeping*. There are too many reasons why I'm not able to find him. I don't know his mind. I don't know what it sounds like. How can I—" He suddenly stopped, craning his head to the side, listening.

I surged forward, clasping my hands to my chest. "What, do you hear something?"

Illeron's face cinched tightly, his body all stiff angles. "It's faint, hardly anything at all." He turned to me with a frown. "It's around Maude, where we just were." He shrugged slowly. "I can't even be sure if it's him. Whoever it is sounds . . . weak, barely hanging on."

I was already swimming, heart in my throat, nerves on fire. The connection within me stirred to life, a flicker of light in a cavern. It was a tired, limp thing, but it was there. "It's better than nothing."

We followed the edge of the island, ducking low when we heard voices, veering away when we saw moving shapes. Illeron continued to reach out in his mind, dictating our direction. We hurled ourselves over coral beds, under rock arches, around seawalls and moored ships. We raced against time, but time still continued. The sun slipped below the horizon.

And the darkness crawled forth.

"This is dangerous, Evanora," Illeron warned, glancing at the moonlight creeping along the blanket of stars. "The Cursed Beings feel especially close tonight."

I kicked my tail faster, fear spurring me forward. "Which means Grayson is in danger."

We reached Maude's rocky bay with its ten broken boats. I looked at Illeron without slowing. The warrior clenched his jaw.

"No," he said inwardly. *"Keep going. We are close."*

So, we continued.

I could feel the Cursed Beings whispering at my back, their darkness playing within the water's shadows. I growled, diving deep into the reserves of my magic, sending out a scatter of light from my scales. The darkness bristled, retreating.

We sailed around the southern point of the island, where the border suddenly vaulted upward in a dramatic cliff wall. It raced straight up, nothing but sheer slabs of basalt columns. The base of the cliff was littered with mounds of broken lava rocks. They erupted from the ocean's depths like gnarled fingers reaching for the sky. Waves crashed upon them mightily, splashing into the boulders, spraying them with sea-foam.

And there, sprawled against the rocks, with the waves pulling at his legs, was a boy with oceans in his eyes.

He wasn't moving.

I sucked in a breath, my heart stuttering to a halt. "Grayson!"

Illeron's gaze darted up the cliff wall. "Evanora, wait!" he shouted, reaching for me. "There are lights up there. Someone will see you!"

I ripped myself free from the warrior's panicked grip. "Let them!"

The lights from above darted their weak beams against the water, moving back and forth along the waves. I zigzagged between them, one with the ocean, the current, the tide. The distant sound of yelling rippled along the surface. I ignored it, letting the water wash it away.

I swam forward, breaking the Balafor's edge, sailing through the air. The lights blurred by, searching, but I was faster. I collapsed onto the rock formation, slamming against the slippery stones with enough force to knock the air out of my chest. I gasped, tears flooding my eyes as my tail scraped over the rocks' sharp teeth.

Grayson was on his stomach, his limbs sprawled around him in awkward angles. Blood trickled from his hairline, pooling around his head in a crimson halo. He moaned, his face contorted in pain.

The beams of light danced, drawing closer and closer to the rocks. I collected my breath and pulled myself forward, grimacing as scales tore off my belly. "Grayson," I wheezed. "Grayson, open your eyes!"

The boy turned his head slowly in my direction. He opened his mouth, revealing blood-soaked teeth, a chunk of flesh missing from his tongue. "Ma . . ." he whimpered, the word slurred. Crimson and saliva seeped between his lips, and he went quiet again.

I clenched my jaw tightly and hauled my long body over the gnarled rock. The lights were upon the boulder's base. They began to crawl upward, stalking, hunting. Groaning, I stretched my hand up, my fingers brushing against Grayson's cheek, his freckled constellations. He flinched, but his eyes remained shut.

"Grayson," I sobbed. "*Please.*"

The lights climbed higher.

I shoved myself upward, dropping my hand from the boy's face to his jacket. I tugged as hard as I could. Grayson's limp body skidded along the slick rocks, bumping over lips and ledges. He tumbled into my arms, wet and cold. I let the momentum carry us back, and together, we splashed into the water as the beams of light trailed up the remainder of the boulder.

I could hear them the second we were in the water.

The one who was promised, the Cursed Beings cried joyously. *Here, here, here.*

They were close. Too close.

I pressed against the boulder and buried my face into the boy's bloody hair. "It's okay," I whispered. "You're okay." I didn't know if I was talking to Grayson or to myself.

We want him. We need him. He is ours. Ours!

My Gift crackled to the surface. I wanted to blast the darkness away, unleash my earth-shattering light on them, watch them experience the fear I was feeling. But I would expose us to the watchful eyes up above if I did. Clutching Grayson against me, I leaned against the rock's side, my heartbeat filling my ears.

The lights slowly began to retreat, pulling back up the cliffside.

"Are you all right?" Illeron asked from afar.

Grayson coughed up a wad of blood. It splattered against my chest, hot against my icy skin. *"Grayson is hurt badly, and the Cursed Beings are here."*

I could feel Illeron's terror as his words sank into my mind. *"The lights are leaving. Now is your chance! Swim!"*

I moved. Pushing off the rocks, I bolted for Illeron, holding back my frightened tears and the scream in my throat.

The lights snapped off the cliffside and landed right on us.

Holding Grayson close, I froze, squinting at the blinding light.

"A-a mermaid!" a voice rang out from the top of the cliff. "A mer-mermaid has him!"

"Grayson!" another voice yelled. "Don't you hurt him, you white-devil bitch!"

I hissed at the light, my magic flaring out of my scales like fire, and dove beneath the waves, the disembodied voices echoing behind me.

Spots filled my vision. I couldn't see where I was going, and Grayson was beginning to stir. Eventually I'd have to resurface so he could breathe. I weaved left, then right, uncertainty mixing with my dread. Was I heading back to the boulders or away from them? Was I still aimed for Illeron or the Cursed Beings?

The one who was promised! He is ours! the Cursed Beings shrieked, closing in.

I snapped my teeth at them, squelching the whimper on my tongue. "You cannot claim him!" I yelled, my voice cracking like thunder.

The Cursed Beings laughed, high-pitched and hysterical. *Foolish mermaid. We already have.*

My magic flooded the ocean. It burst forth, as simple as breathing, a torrent of pure light as bright as the sun. The darkness scattered, moaning with disappointment. *No, no, no!* they cried.

The Gift unfurled again, emitting another wave of power that ate away at the shadows. "He is *mine*!" I roared.

The Cursed Beings wailed, their long black arms shrinking back into the depths.

I panted, reeling my magic back in, feeling dizzy from the sudden exertion. The Cursed Beings were gone, spitting curses as they fled, and Grayson and I were safe. For now.

Except, we weren't.

Because the boy was writhing in my arms, clawing at his neck, his eyes wide and wild. He gave a spurting cough, sending wisps of blood into the water. His throat clicked, squeezing shut. Heart racing, I thrust us toward the surface, pumping my tail as quickly as I could. "Hold on, Grayson!" I pleaded.

The boy sucked in a ragged breath the second we broke over the waves, only to start hacking up blood and salt water. His entire body thrashed with the effort. "Ma," he choked out between gasps for air. "Ma is back there!"

I shook my head. "Grayson, we need to get you to shore."

"No!" he cried, trying to pull away, nearly delirious in his panic. "We need to go back! We need to!"

Illeron surfaced next to us, his eyes flashing with alarm. "What's going on?"

I tried to hold the boy still, but it only caused him to kick and struggle more. "I don't know," I snapped. "He isn't making sense."

"My ma!" Grayson sobbed, searching the cliff face and surrounding waters frantically. "She fell. She fell, and I . . . I couldn't . . ." He looked at me, mournful. "Please, we have to go back. We have to save her!"

Illeron clucked his tongue, glowering at the boy. "We don't have time for this. The humans spotted you. We aren't safe here. We have to leave, *now*."

I nodded. "Grayson, we have to go," I said as softly as I could.

The boy shook his head wildly. "But she's still out there!"

I could see the flashing lights bouncing along the cliff, following the edge until it began to slope downward, closer to the ocean. The voices were growing louder, the sound of heavy footfalls reaching my ears. I adjusted Grayson in my arms, trying to meet his darting gaze. "Grayson, look at me."

The boy didn't listen. He was biting his lip so hard that a thread of blood seeped out of the corner. His eyes were on the darkening waters. I jostled him. "Grayson! Look at me!"

Grayson whipped his head in my direction, and for a moment, he looked like a little lost child, alone and afraid.

"I didn't see your mother. Only you."

The boy's face crumpled. "No." He sniffed, shaking his head. "No . . . She's out there!"

I blinked away my own tears. The pain Grayson felt was all too familiar. "No, my brave heart. She's not."

Grayson held my gaze for a long moment, trying to sort through my truth and find the lie. He let out a sob, burying his face into my neck as waves of grief washed over him.

The footsteps were louder, the lights brighter, the voices full of hate and death.

"Evanora," Illeron growled. "We have to leave!"

I curled the boy into me. "I couldn't save your mother," I whispered. "But I can save you. Will you let me do that?"

Grayson whimpered, the epitome of sorrow, and nodded against my neck.

I took off, lightning in the night sky, Illeron racing behind me.

The Tully docks were empty save for the seagulls and dead fish. When I tried to keep going, Illeron pulled me to a stop. "We can't go to the waterfall."

I glanced down at the boy in my arms, shivering and crying quietly. "I want him to be as close to home as possible."

The warrior shook his head, eyeing Grayson with a surprising amount of concern. "Grayson is not in any shape to wander up all those stairs. You need to leave him somewhere where he will be found. Besides, you were spotted with him. If you go to that beach, the humans will know that *you* know that beach. It will be compromised."

Horror fluttered through me. I looked up at the docks, biting my lip. "I just want him to be safe."

Illeron hummed softly and placed a hand on my shoulder. "He is."

The warrior was trying to be kind, but I couldn't shake the feeling that there was no such thing as safety anymore.

I swam up to the dock and hoisted Grayson on top of it. He curled into a ball, his face a mask of agony. His moans had long faded, but the tears still streaked down his cheeks, mixing with the blood. I pulled myself onto the wooden planks, my fluke trailing in the water, and ran my hand over Grayson's face, caressing his cold skin. He opened his bloodshot eyes and met my gaze, his mouth tight and trembling. There was so much I wanted to say, so much I wanted to do. I wanted to tell him I was sorry, that I understood his pain. I wanted to kiss away his tears, wrap myself around him until he felt how scared I was.

But I simply stroked his face and smiled. Because none of it mattered. None of it would make a difference. I would leave, as I always had to do, and Grayson would be alone with his broken heart.

The boy silently uncurled one of his hands away from his body and held it out to me.

I took it in mine, squeezing it gently. "I can't heal your shattered soul," I whispered, "but if you'll let me, I can fix the other things that are bringing you pain."

Grayson nodded, a whimper escaping with the movement.

I closed my eyes, summoning my magic. Instantly, warmth spread across my skin, touching my scales with its soft light. I directed it down my arm, sending it into him. The glow swept over Grayson's body, focusing on his injuries. The bruises beneath his eyes faded, the bump on his nose smoothed away. The cut on his hairline sealed without a trace. His tongue became whole again.

The boy's wounds healed.

But the heartache remained.

The light faded, and Grayson shuddered. "Thank you," he whispered.

I leaned forward, pressing his hand to my lips. "I wish I could do more."

Grayson closed his eyes, turning his face into the wood. "Just . . . don't leave me. Not yet."

I wiggled farther onto the dock and laid my head next to his. "I'll never leave you, Grayson Shaw."

I stayed with him as long as I dared.

Even when hurried footsteps bounded down the boardwalk, and Illeron shouted at me to flee. Even when flashing lights lit up my skin, and a pistol roared its warning through the air. Even when Grayson began to push me away, his tears like floods on the wooden floor.

I waited until the last second to let go of Grayson's hand and push myself off the dock.

My body left, but my heart stayed behind.

CHAPTER SEVENTY-THREE

GRAYSON

APRIL 29 – EVENING

I WOKE UP IN MY BED. THE ROOM WAS DARK WITH APPROACH-
ing dusk, shadows dripping off the bookshelf and desk. I was trapped
beneath a pile of blankets I couldn't recall climbing under, in a new
set of pajamas I didn't remember putting on.

I wasn't sure how I had gotten home. The last thing I remembered was Evanora splashing back into the ocean, leaving me and my misery
alone on the dock. I contemplated being stuck in another nightmare, but it
was unlikely. I had already experienced the worst nightmare imaginable.

I was the reason behind the death of Evanora's mother. And now, my
own ma was dead. Also because of me.

We have her, the voices hissed through the cracks beneath my window.
Come see her. Come see herrrrrr, Promised One.

The persistent whispers aside, it was quiet—the kind of silence that
made you wonder if you'd gone deaf. The birds were still, the waves muted.
Even Howler's Hill was silent, a blessing and a curse. I craned my neck to the
window and saw the cause of the eerie stillness: The window was shut, a large
lock dangling off the latch like morbid jewelry.

I shifted, trying to pull myself into a sitting position. The blankets were
so damn *heavy*. I flopped back onto the bed, admitting defeat. All those times
training with Pa, and I couldn't even get out of my own bed.

A rustling from the corner of the room made my heart skip. Maybe I *was* still trapped in a nightmare. I glanced at the source of the sound, half expecting to see Persephone, her body broken and bloated, seaweed tangled in her hair, blood and water dripping onto the floor.

Instead, I found Pa, standing with his hands clenched into fists at his sides. He was breathing hard, and even in the darkness, I could see his eyes glimmer with unshed tears. "You're awake," he uttered, his voice thick. "Thank Christ you're awake."

I blinked at him as he rushed to the bed, a sob catching in his throat. He pulled me into a tight hug, and in that instant, Pa became undone. He cried out, gasping, years of suppressed emotions spilling over—tears for me, for Ma, for Warrick, for everything he had been holding in. The collar of my shirt was instantly soaked.

I didn't think I had any more tears left to shed.

I was wrong.

My entire body ached with the release. My eyes stung, my lungs pulsed, my heart clenched. Even my arms and legs felt heavy, which I couldn't blame on the blankets. Everything hurt when I just wanted to be numb.

"I'm so sorry," Pa moaned. "I should have listened to you."

"You tried," I offered meekly.

"I should have tried harder." He pulled back, sniffing. "You were begging for help, and I turned my back on you when you needed me most. No son should have to fight so hard for his father's attention. I should've seen how much you were hurting. I should've believed you." His face twisted, fighting more tears. "How can you ever forgive me?"

I didn't know how. Because, deep down, I knew Pa was only partially telling the truth. I knew he believed I needed help—not because the Cursed Beings existed and hungered for me. Not even because of my nightmares that carried the promise of harm.

He believed I needed help because I was following in Ma's footsteps, growing more insane with every passing day.

He didn't want to help me figure out a way to survive the Cursed Beings' hold on me. He wanted to help me not completely break apart like Ma.

Both felt like very real threats, and I didn't know which was worse.

"Pa . . ." A whimper crawled up my throat. "Ma's dead."

Pa closed his eyes, his breath leaving in a long moan. "I know, son," he said, tugging me back into a hug. "I know. The nurse called me after . . ."

After she told me all about the bargain. After she smiled while talking about Nereida's demise. After she threw herself off the cliff.

She is herrrrrre. The Cursed Beings laughed. *Don't you want to see her? She is waiting for you. Both she and Warrick are.*

"I tried to stop her," I groaned, pulling away.

Pa glowered at me, his face as dark as the shadows in my room. "The nurse told me about that too." He took me by the shoulders. "What were you thinking, Grayson? You could have been killed!"

"Part of me thought . . . I don't know." I shrugged helplessly. "I could still save her."

"Yes, and you nearly ended up busting open your own head." He said the words sternly, but I could have sworn I saw a hint of admiration drift across his eyes. "They said you scaled the wall almost to the very bottom. It wasn't until the basalt got slippery that you lost your footing." He grew pale. "Pastor Kline and I got there as fast as we could, but I . . ." He shuddered, his entire body jerking. "I thought the worst. And when I saw that mermaid drag you into the ocean, I . . ." He bit back a sob, his deep brown eyes filling with tears. "I lost it, Grayson. I absolutely lost it."

His grip on me grew deadly tight. I patted his arm reassuringly. "I'm all right, Pa. She didn't hurt me."

"But she could have!" he growled. "She could have ripped you to shreds so there was nothing left for me to find."

I shook my head. "But she didn't. Pa, she *saved* me. You saw it yourself."

Pa chewed on his bottom lip. "No," he said eventually. "I don't know what I saw."

Stubborn until the bitter end. I almost laughed. "You saw me on the Tully docks, safe, *alive*, with not a scratch on me. *She* put me there. And she waited with me until help arrived." I smiled. "There was nothing vicious about her. She was peace and light and—"

"Evil, Grayson. She is evil. All mermaids are." But he sounded uncertain, troubled by the mantra he spouted every day of his life.

"No!" I shrugged out of his arms. "Pa, I have no doubt in my mind that if the mermaid had wanted to kill me, she would have. But she didn't. She isn't evil. She is *good*." I tilted my head softly, peering into Pa's unsure gaze. "Maybe some mermaids are."

Pa narrowed his eyes, fighting to grasp a concept that had never once crossed his mind. He sighed, wiping his tear-streaked face. "Maybe so," he agreed begrudgingly.

That was the best I could hope to get from Pa. Too much, too quickly, and the man would begin to question everything, a midlife crisis in the making. But it was a start. "Maybe so," I repeated, smiling.

I began to shove the blankets off me. The combination of body heat, flooding emotions, and a closed window was making the room stifling, and I had a sudden desperate desire to escape it all. Pa clamped his hands back onto my shoulders with a barking laugh.

"Whoa, there." He whistled. "Nope. No, sir. It's bed rest for you."

I struggled to get out of his grip. "But I feel fine."

Pa forced me down and piled the blankets back on top of me. "You suffered a great ordeal last night."

My heart lurched in my chest. "Wait . . . Last *night*?"

"You went unconscious the second we collected you from the docks. When you didn't wake up this morning, I grew worried." Finished tucking me in, Pa straightened, inspecting his handiwork. "Dr. Peele said it was just from the shock of it all and that I should keep an eye on you. I was just thinking about calling him again when you finally woke up."

I'd lost an entire day. We were running out of time preparing for the Hunt, and I was in bed, watching as that precious time drifted by. I had ruined our chances of messing with the boats in Maude, and now Evanora and Illeron were expecting me to go with them to Fenharrow Bay. If they weren't already there, waiting for me.

I tried to get up again, the blankets suddenly suffocating. "No . . . really, Pa, I'm fine—"

Pa chuckled, placing a hand on my chest, pinning me in place. "Well," he said, "that makes one of us. Just humor me for a bit and stay in bed, son. You don't have a scratch on you, but you probably have a concussion. After a fall like that, you're lucky it's not worse."

I didn't have a concussion. With Evanora's help, I felt better than I had in ages. Not that I could tell Pa that. He could barely grasp the concept of mermaids being good. A good mermaid that could also heal would send him right over the edge.

Pa was still talking. "I also received a pardon from Mayor McCoy."

I stopped trying to shimmy out of the blankets. "A pardon? For what?"

"To pull you out of the Hunt."

I whipped my head in Pa's direction with a gasp. "*What?*"

Pa strode to the desk and leaned against it, crossing his arms and ankles. "Come on now, Grayson. We both know you never wanted to participate. You were only doing it for my sake."

I shook my head hurriedly. "No . . . No . . . I-I-I need to participate. I *want* to participate!" I stuttered out.

Pa held up a hand reassuringly. "No, you don't. And that's okay." To his credit, he sounded completely at peace. "I pushed you to join; that's my fault. I wanted so badly for you to crave the Hunt like I did. I thought I could drill that craving into you, make you see things the way I did. And you tried!" He chuckled, shaking his head. "God bless you, you tried. The pressure of it all grew to be too much for you. I see that now." He stared at me from across the room, eyes burning into my soul. "And thanks to you, I see other things."

I swallowed hard. "Like what?"

"That I lost sight of what I was truly fighting for, *who* I was fighting for. I got so caught up in the beast of it all that I forgot what the Hunt is truly about." Pa cocked his head to the side, smiling warmly. "It's about coming together, *fighting* together, fighting for *family*. I'm no longer fighting for just Warrick. I'm fighting for your ma. I'm fighting for *you*, Grayson. So that, one day, we can live in a peace they never got to experience, a world that they left too quickly."

"No, you don't understand. I need to—"

"You need to be in bed," Pa said firmly. "I appreciate your enthusiasm, I really do. But what's done is done, Grayson. Mayor McCoy is already bent out of shape about me asking for him to pardon you, one of his top betting participants. He would lose his head if I crawled back and asked him to revoke it."

"But—"

"*No*, Grayson." Pa pushed off the desk and walked to the door. "Getting worked up isn't good for your health. I think it's time for you to get some more rest."

I groaned, thudding my head against the pillow. "But I've slept all day!"

Pa looked over his shoulder at me with a sour expression. "And yet you're acting like a sleep-deprived child." He smiled thinly at me and began to close the door. "Good night!"

I scowled at the door, listening as the latch *clunked* into its home, as the lock *clicked*—

Wait . . . lock? *Clicked?*

With an annoyed grunt, I hoisted the blankets off and vaulted out of bed. I stumbled to the door and tried the handle. It rattled in my hand, but the door didn't open. Patience thinning, I pulled harder. The door didn't budge. I growled, slapping my palm against the wood. "Since when does my door have a lock on it?" I demanded.

"Since you decided to become an escape artist in your sleep," Pa called from down the hall. "It's for your own safety."

"My own safety," I muttered, resting my head against the wood. "Gee, thanks."

The room felt too small, the air too hot, too tight. I paced the narrow space, anxiety building.

There was still so much to do. Fenharrow and Maude still had their boats, imperviously intact. Evanora and I still needed to finalize the plan; we had most of the pieces in place, but not all of them. I didn't have time to be stuck in my room. I had to break out somehow, flee my cage. I couldn't let Evanora down after all she'd done for me.

After what I'd done to her mother.

I shook the lock on the window. It squeaked in protest but held firm. I let out an exasperated groan and punched the wall. Sparks flew underneath my skin, lighting my nerves on fire.

And then the worst thing happened.

I could hear bells.

CHAPTER SEVENTY-FOUR

EVANORA

APRIL 29 – EVENING

H E'S NOT COMING."

I scowled at Illeron, but I knew he was right. I had been ringing the bells for so long that I heard them even when I stopped. "Are you absolutely certain?"

The warrior nodded. "I can sense him. He's close by, but he seems . . . stuck." He laughed morbidly. "He's not happy about it either."

I lowered the bells with a sigh. "I was really hoping to see him, make sure he was okay."

"*I* was really hoping he'd be able to help us with the boats," Illeron retorted. "I have a feeling neither of us will be getting what we want tonight."

I scoffed, placing a hand on my chest. I could feel the connection brimming with life. Grayson was alive, and he was safe. Angry, but safe.

"So?" I asked, shoving the bells next to the rock pool. "What now? What do we do?"

Illeron tossed his spear from one hand to the other. "I think it's rather obvious. We go back home."

The idea hung in the air between us, smelling foul. I scrunched my nose and stuck out my tongue. "The great warrior admitting defeat? Unheard-of."

Illeron snorted, shaking his head. "I know an unbeatable battle when I see one. We can't do anything without the boy."

"Not a battle," I argued. "Just a hurdle." I rubbed my forehead, trying to stimulate some semblance of strategy. "What if one of us was on the beach, and one of us waited in the water with the spear?"

"Then one of us would be caught if a human were to appear, and the other would get to watch."

"Illeron, be serious."

The warrior raised his eyebrows. "I am. Are you?"

I rolled my eyes. "Well, then what do you suggest?"

"I suggest we go *home*." He shrugged. "We've affected half of the island's boats. I'd count that as a victory."

"We can do *more*." I chewed on my lip, searching the water for answers. "What if we were both on the beach?"

Illeron frowned at me. "*Are* you being serious? Because I'm really starting to question it."

I held my hands out in front of me, miming clasping a ledge. "The boats are just sitting there, right? We should be able to slide into them, cripple the insides without difficulty. Then, when we are done"—I gripped the imaginary ledge and pulled downward—"we should be able to tilt the boat onto its side so that we can access the bottom." I shrugged. "Being on land, it will take longer, but it *can* be done."

Illeron rubbed his jaw. "It's just too dangerous, Evanora."

"Leaving them is dangerous too," I countered.

The warrior raised his arms helplessly. "Why can't we just wait until tomorrow? Perhaps Grayson will be able to help us then."

I shook my head. "Tomorrow is the Final Festival. The island will be swarming with humans. They will be high-spirited, drunk, and nearly insane with excitement about the Hunt the next day. If we want to act, it has to be tonight."

Illeron grew pale. "I wish we had more time."

"But we don't. This is all we get, and we've wasted too much of it squabbling here."

Stubbornness fading, Illeron gestured toward the island. "We don't even know where Fenharrow is. Should we just go back to Maude?"

I met his gaze with grim determination. "I know where it is." I dug the tip of my spear into the sand, retracing the map Grayson had drawn for me. I marked X's on the four corners of the island. "These X's are the beaches with boats. We've already checked Hannigan's Cove and Black Sands Beach." As I spoke, I scratched out the western and eastern X's. "Maude's boats are already falling apart. With enough force, we can splinter through them." I shuddered. "Besides, just looking at that shale-covered beach gave me cuts and slivers." I circled Fenharrow's *X* at the northern tip. "That leaves one option."

Illeron squinted at the map. "Evanora, that's too far. The Balafor is too dangerous up there." He traced the island's edges. "Trying to go around would take too long, and we'd risk running into the Cursed Beings."

His fingers stopped at the map's center, where a large crack cleaved the island in two. "We'd have to . . ."

"Cut through the island," I finished for him in a quiet voice.

A muscle feathered along the warrior's jaw. "No," he huffed, dragging a hand through the sand, erasing the map with a single swipe. "That is absolutely ridiculous."

I scoffed, my spine stiffening. "Do you have a better suggestion?"

"We would be completely exposed!" Illeron shook his head. "We don't know anything about that section of the island."

I resisted rolling my eyes and redrew the map. "Grayson told me there are three bridges." I traced my finger along the land's crevice: bottom, middle, top. "The first and last are wooden suspension bridges. The middle one is made of stone, with only a narrow gap to get through. That one will be a problem." I laid my hand on his. "It's hard, but it's possible." At least, I hoped so.

Illeron still shook his head. "What about people? Houses near the channel, nets, traps? There's too much we don't know."

I grabbed my spear. "Grayson's counting on us. We have to try." Illeron opened his mouth, flashing his canines. I raised a hand, silencing him. "I'm going with or without you. We're in a battle, Illeron, and right now, we have the upper hand. We need to act before it's too late." I offered him the spear. "Time to be brave."

He eyed the spear before sighing and taking it. "Lead the way, Your Majesty."

THE CHANNEL'S OPENING NEAR MAUDE, WHERE WE'D FOUND Grayson, was framed by towering basalt columns. Gargantuan waves crashed through, slamming against the rocks before spilling into the ocean. It looked like a mouth, forever open, its jagged teeth waiting. The sky above groaned, black clouds rolling with thunder, as though warning us to turn back.

I tried to ignore the pounding of my heart, the beats strangely resembling the drums of a death march. I glanced at Illeron, my scales prickling. The warrior's eyes were fixed on the large opening. He let out a heavy breath, nodding gravely.

Together, we dove into the churning water, pushing through the current. Rocks and silt swirled around us as fish fled, anemones recoiling. The stone walls around us rose, towering and intimidating, their algae-covered edges carved by years of water. Sometimes the channel constricted, forcing us to leap over narrow gaps; other times the walls leaned away, mountains so high the tops were hidden in clouds.

I relaxed when we reached the first bridge. Grayson had been right. The old wooden beast hung above us tiredly, creaking in the wind. The posts, bent and loose from neglect, held the sagging structure, and several planks were missing, the rope ties frayed.

"When I was a merling, Jorah told me that giants once lived upon these lands," I whispered as we passed underneath the bridge. "Long before it became Lethe. They were as tall as the mountains and as ferocious and unforgiving as the ocean. They could make it from one side of the island to the other in a couple steps, and they could walk into the water and never be completely submerged."

Illeron gave me a long withered stare but said nothing.

I skirted around a mound of red sea whip, its long tentacles tickling my tail. "They were a territorial species; they didn't want to share the island with anyone. And they didn't, for a time." I smiled coyly. "But then the mountains began to move."

The warrior sighed wearily. "Trolls? Really?"

I nodded. "The trolls were getting tired of constantly getting trampled on, of hearing how great and terrible these giants were. So, they rose from their peaceful slumbers. The ground shook, the water trembled, and the valleys quaked as the mountains fell away, revealing an army of very disgruntled trolls."

Illeron ducked underneath an abandoned dock, the wood rotted and brittle. "So, what did these disgruntled trolls do?" he asked reluctantly.

"They waged war on the giants, claiming the winner could stay on the island. Blinded by greed, the giants accepted. They howled, slammed their clubs, stomped their feet, and gnashed their teeth. But the trolls weren't scared. They were one with the earth. With a single breath, they cracked the ground open, swallowing the giants whole. The earth ripped itself apart, creating this very channel as the giants' graveyard." I glanced at the smooth pale debris scattered below, wondering if they were stones—or forgotten bones. "They say when it storms, you can still hear the giants' battle cries echoing."

"Forgive me, but I have a really hard time believing any of that."

I shrugged. "It was Jorah's story, not mine."

The current died down, the sudden absence of it sending me and the warrior skyrocketing forward. The water level dipped, the surface pressing on our backs. The evening air was cool on my exposed skin, leaving deadly kisses on my neck and dorsal fin.

Illeron sucked in a sharp breath. I couldn't blame him. The second bridge loomed ahead—a wall of stone and cement. The sweeping arch between the two landmasses was the only thing delicate about it. Smooth stones stacked high above the bridge acted as a barrier, held together by a rusted steel grate. It was built to withstand any weight, weather, or rogue wave. Algae clung to the fence, the only color on the colossal structure.

And it was crawling with people. They trudged along the stones, heads bent against the wind, clinging to their jackets. Wagons passed by, horses plodding along, their hooves stumbling on the flagstone path.

The warrior growled, low and annoyed. "How did I let you talk me into this?"

But I wasn't staring at the people passing overhead, oblivious to us.

I was staring at the pinhole opening in the center of the bridge, the one we were expected to crawl through.

I fought the urge to glance at my tail, at the thick muscles beneath the scales, the curve of my backside, the flowing dorsal fin. My confidence plummeted. Parts of me were slender. Those parts would fit. The rest . . . not so much.

A hand was on my shoulder. "You'll be fine," Illeron breathed, his gaze darting from the villagers and their carts to the gap ahead of us. "Just think narrow thoughts."

I snorted, but I was already envisioning myself getting stuck, feeling human hands on my tail as they yanked me out, their breath hot, their eyes delirious, their knives hungry.

Illeron loosed a breath. "I'll go first."

The warrior crept to the gap in the bridge, where the water trickled out in slow, lazy drips. He dared a final look at the humans passing by, then slowly, carefully, rose above the surface. He moved so smoothly, the water barely stirred around him as he tossed the spears through the opening, gripped the slimy rocks, and hoisted himself into the man-made structure.

The darkness swallowed him. I could hear his quiet breaths and pinched grunts as he worked through the hole, wriggling his tail and pushing himself forward on his arms. An eternity passed, then two.

I swallowed a whimper. "Illeron?"

His response was a faint splash on the other side, then a rueful chuckle. "It's cold, tight, and slimy, but manageable."

I peeked over the lip of the hole and found the warrior's silhouette looking back at me. He nodded reassuringly, holding out a hand in my direction. "You can do it, Evanora."

Silencing the voices screaming at me to turn away, to abandon the battlefield, to *flee*, I crawled into the pinhole gap.

I was instantly met with the scent of death and decay. Fish bones cracked underneath my arms, algae clung to my body in thick gobs. The rocks closed in around me, forcing the air out of my lungs as they pressed against my shoulders and back. I ducked my head, tucked myself as small as I could, and pulled myself forward, bit by bit.

Illeron hummed encouragingly. "Yes. Just like that. You're doing great."

My hands scrambled for purchase, my fingers digging into patches of cold slime that squelched deep underneath my nails. My tail slapped against the wall, and pain flared straight into my spine. Illeron's shadowy figure wasn't getting any closer. I was going to be stuck in the belly of the bridge forever.

Illeron reached farther into the tunnel, his hand outstretched, warm and inviting. "Don't look at anything but me."

I groaned and scooted closer. Illeron's hand was almost within reach, a beacon of hope in the dark. Relief flooding through me, I unfurled my arm and stretched it forward. My fingertips grazed his, a whispering touch. I gasped, desperate.

"You're almost there," Illeron urged. "One more push and I'll be able to pull you out."

I jerked my head in a shaky nod and went to move.

My hips wouldn't budge.

I hissed, craning my head back to see my hips pinned between the narrowest part of the tunnel. I shifted back, then tried again. No luck. My relief quickly curdled into dread. "Illeron," I croaked. "I think I'm stuck."

The warrior bared his teeth at me, shaking his hand in front of my face. Tantalizingly close, yet so far. "Keep trying."

Panic crept through me, vicious and uninvited. "The gap is too small.

I can't get through." My tail coiled painfully, thrashing against the stone walls encasing me, finding no purchase. I was suddenly back in the net, stranded on the beach, locked away from freedom and waiting for my approaching death.

Illeron tilted his shoulders back into the hole. His hand found mine. His touch nearly made me weep. "Yes, you can," he growled. "Eyes on me, Evanora."

I sucked in a moan, my frantic gaze finding his.

Illeron's mouth quirked to the side in a half smile. "Good. Now, deep breath."

I took in a long, shuddering breath, the bridge's belly pinching against my sides.

The warrior nodded gently. "Perfect. Now, again."

I did. Until my heart rate slowed, and my nerves calmed. I could feel my muscles relax, the tension lacing itself between my scales loosen. Illeron tightened his grip on me. "All right. Clear your mind and close your eyes. Everything is fine. I need you to believe that."

I nodded, tears clinging to my lashes. "Everything is fine."

"Good. Say it again." There was a burning pressure in my shoulder, a throbbing tightness in my forearm.

"Everything is fine."

"One more time, Evanora."

My arm was ripping out of the socket. Scales were tearing off my body. Everything was *not*—

"Everything is fine!"

My hips shifted, the rocks gave way, and I flew out the other side of the hole, landing on top of Illeron with a splash. The second I was out of the gap, Illeron was pulling me along, away from confused murmurs and puzzled stares from atop the bridge. We flew underneath the surface, fighting against the current. We were breathless, our nerves in frazzled tangles, our bodies slimy and dirty, but we didn't stop moving. Even as the pain threatened to collapse me from the inside out, as the memory of being confined in the stone walls clung to my bruised and broken skin. We didn't stop moving.

We finally slowed when we got to the third bridge, blessedly far over our heads.

"I don't know about you," Illeron huffed, "but I'm pretty sure I'm going to have the stench of algae on me for the rest of my life."

I laughed shakily, the sound chipped and brittle. "That was hell."

The warrior rolled out his shoulders, poking at the tender muscles. "Finally, we agree on something," he said around a crooked smile.

I looked at Illeron, my heart swelling. "Thank you for helping me get out." I shook my head, a shiver tracing its icy fingers along my scales. "I couldn't stop panicking. I kept thinking—"

"I know what you were thinking," Illeron interjected, his mirth rapidly retreating. "I'm never going to let that happen, Evanora." He placed a hand on my shoulder. "My job is to keep you safe. As long as I'm around, I will do just that. Which, as it turns out"—he chuckled sardonically—"is a full-time profession."

I let out something between a laugh and a sob, batting him away. "Sounds unbearable."

"Just the worst."

Something in my chest relaxed, and I realized that I'd missed this. Bantering with Illeron, laughing with him, *caring* for him. Things I'd taken for granted, things I'd worried I would never experience again.

Illeron raised his spear. "Now, onto the battlefield."

The channel opened into a vast inlet, where towering trees with sweeping vines crowded the water on one side and a beach of bleached white sand curved along the other. The bay stretched in a wide half circle, narrowing toward the farthest point, where the ocean poured through a craggy gap in the rocks—strikingly similar to the one I had just crawled through. A chill of fear prickled my skin. It was narrow. I could hear the waves fighting to get through from my position in the channel.

I immediately noticed two things.

The first: The tide was coming in, and many boats were in the water.

The second: We weren't alone.

Humans huddled by a fire at the inlet's tip, two of them laughing and chirping, their youth written all over them.

Which made them more dangerous.

"Neptune's spear," Illeron growled with disgust. "*Teenagers.*"

The flames reached for the night sky, embers dancing in the breeze. The air was rich with the scent of nectar and burning wood, but all I could smell was the blood dripping down my chin from the cut I'd given myself from biting my lip too hard.

The weight of defeat was almost painful. We had worked so hard to get to Fenharrow Bay. We'd risked going through the channel. We'd almost gotten *caught*. We were scraped and raw and reeked of silt and algae.

All for nothing.

I stared numbly at the spear in my hands. Exhaustion creeping up on me, I turned for the channel. "What a waste of time."

The warrior blinked at me. "Where are you going?"

"Home," I said without stopping. "You were right. We never should have come here."

Illeron's hand was around my arm. "No."

Resisting the urge to shake him off, I peered up at him, raising an eyebrow. "No?"

Illeron's mouth was set in a thin line. "No. I did not sit through your ridiculous story about giants and trolls and nearly get the life squeezed out of me by a bridge to just give up. We've come too far."

I cocked my head at him in amazement. "Who *are* you?"

Illeron groaned. "A fool." He wiped the blood off my chin, clucking his tongue at the state of my broken lip. "You're so dramatic sometimes."

"I wouldn't have it any other way."

The warrior smiled, his fingers lingering. "Neither would I." He scanned the bay, analyzing. "There are thirty boats, and over half of them are in the water. That works in our favor."

He was forgetting a very large, key detail. "Yes," I said, drawing out the word in a hiss, "and we likely won't get a chance to damage any of them. Those boys will be on us the second we start tapping on the wood."

Illeron grinned wickedly at me, and my stomach clenched. "When *you* start tapping on the wood." He straightened, clutching his spear to his chest. "I'll distract them, draw them away from the beach."

I was shaking my head before he even finished talking. "No. Illeron, that's absurd! Do you have a death wish?" I bit my lip again, ignoring the throb of pain that split across my face. "What if they catch you?"

Illeron shrugged. "If a handful of boys catch me, then I really need to reconsider my role as a warrior."

"Illeron, I'm serious!"

"So am I." He planted his hands on my shoulders. "Attack as many boats as you can. Leave the ones on the beach. I can't guarantee I'll hold their attention for long, and I won't be able to help if they find you on land. Once you've done all you can, head back to the last bridge we passed. You should be safe there. If I don't return in an hour, assume I'm not coming back at all." His grip tightened, his ruby eyes gleaming in the moonlight. "Do not come after me."

Helplessness plundered through me. "But—"

"Do as I say, Evanora!" The warrior bent down and pressed his lips against mine.

Firm, urgent, and desperate. He was pulling away before I even had a second to process it.

It felt an awful lot like a kiss goodbye.

And then he was gone, hurling himself toward the inlet's tiny opening, slipping beneath the thrashing waves, one with the water, a drop in the ocean. The last thing I saw was the tips of his silver-and-crimson tail slicing through the foam.

I knew better than to call out or chase after him. But it took everything within me not to do either of those things. I held my breath and waited.

There was nothing but silence.

And then a thunderous crash. A tail slapping against the water.

The boys immediately sat up, their eyes wide as they craned their necks in the direction of the noise. Muffled voices met my ears.

"What was that?" one asked in a low voice.

"The wind, you dummy," the other retorted, waving a hand dismissively.

More silence. Another slapping sound as Illeron's fluke connected with the water.

The first boy rose to his feet, scratching his too-small head with stubby fingers. "Definitely not the wind."

The second unfolded his long limbs and stood, grabbing a metal rod that lit up with the flick of a button. "Let's go check it out!"

The lumpy boy nodded eagerly, grabbing a bundle next to the fire and waddling to catch up.

I strained my eyes to see what he was carrying. A bag? A blanket?

A net.

My blood ran cold. *"Please come back,"* I called out to Illeron.

I was met with an unearthly quiet, and I knew the warrior was choosing to ignore me. I thought to try again but decided against it; to distract him could potentially prove fatal.

I waited a heartbeat, then two, then three.

And then I moved.

Eighteen boats bobbed in the water, held fast by their metal anchors. I went to work, slicing through the bottoms with reckless speed. I knew I should be more careful, take my time, make sure they'd pass inspection without raising suspicion. But desperation drove me. The faster I worked, the sooner I could leave. The sooner I left, the sooner Illeron could escape—and I could give him the verbal thrashing he deserved.

Between my spear thrusts, panting breaths, raging heart, and strained groans, I could make out a third tail slap, followed by excited yelps and howls.

"A mermaid! It's a bloody mermaid!" one boy cried.

"Quick! The net! Throw the net!" the second crowed.

I forced my hands to move faster, until they were nothing but a blur of bleeding skin and calluses. Desperation clawed at my insides, threatening to tear me apart. I hopped from boat to boat, holding back tears as I wedged my spear into the floorboards, prying them loose. The wood groaned under my force but always yielded.

By the time I slipped out of the eighteenth boat, three more had drifted into the water, bobbing with the rising tide. I made quick work of them, barely noticing the pain in my body. Sweat stung my eyes, my palms, the raw patches on my tail where the scales had been torn away.

When I was done with the three, two more were on the edge of the water. And when I was done with those, another two began to settle into the ocean.

I didn't know what was worse—the fact that I could no longer hear Illeron's tail slap taunts, or the fact that I also couldn't hear the humans hunting for him. I didn't know how much time had passed; maybe the warrior was in hiding, catching his breath and making the boys squirm a little.

I forced my mind to quiet. My thoughts were making me sick with worry. I attacked the two boats with vigor. The faster I worked, the sooner I could leave. The sooner I left, the sooner—

"There it is! I see it!"

"Don't let it get away!"

My hands slipped. The wood bit into my skin, leaving a path of splinters in my raw palms. I yelped, dropping the spear and pressing my unsteady hands against my chest. The weapon clattered against the boat's insides. The sound was like an explosion.

The boys went eerily quiet.

Illeron slashed his tail into the water emphatically.

"Wait . . ." one said slowly. "Are there *two* of them? Do they hunt in pairs?"

I didn't hear a verbal response. But I did hear footsteps. They were hurried, clumsy with excitement. And they were getting closer.

Twenty-five boats. Twenty-five out of thirty. I could make peace with that number. I tumbled over the boat's gunwale and splashed into the water just as the lanky boy clambered over the sandy hill.

Heart heaving, I raced for the channel's entrance, not daring to look back. I didn't stop until I reached the bridge.

Panting, I sank to the ocean floor, trembling with pent-up nerves. Every muscle in my body screamed for rest, but my mind wouldn't allow it. My fingers tingled, the phantom weight of the spear still there. My head throbbed like a beast, pounding relentlessly. I longed to shut my eyes and sleep through the rest of the night.

But even then, I refused to relax. I kept my eyes on the channel's opening in the distance, desperate to catch a flash of crimson, a glimpse of silver-white hair in the moonlight.

Illeron would come. He had to. He wouldn't leave me like this. He would find a way to make it back.

I waited.

And waited.

I reached out in my mind, knowing it was futile but trying anyway. Illeron didn't respond. My heart contracted with unease. I tried to convince myself that he was fine, that he was just out of reach, but that was futile too.

Time dripped by. The moon carried on its merry way, settling on the water in a soft glow.

Something was wrong, I was sure of it. I could feel it in the current, taste it in the salty waves, smell it on the wind. Everything felt charged, dangerously close to snapping.

I swam back. I couldn't help it. I had to know if Illeron was all right. I didn't care if he chastised me the entire way home. I had to know.

The inlet was deathly still. I wanted to scream just to hear something. I feared I would grow mad in the stillness.

And then I *did* hear something.

Not the flutter of a tail or the hoarse gasps of tired lungs. Not the crashing of waves or the rustling of seaweed.

Something far, far worse. A sound that made my heart shatter.

A victorious laugh. It was high-pitched, a hysterical cackle that cracked along the edges. And it didn't belong to Illeron.

"We caught it! We caught the mermaid!"

CHAPTER SEVENTY-FIVE

EVANORA

APRIL 29 – EVENING

O NOT COME AFTER ME.
Do as I say, Evanora!
A kiss that felt like goodbye.

Those were the things racing in my mind as I swam as hard as I could through the inlet. Over and over, a plague of pain, terror, and a heartache so deep that I couldn't breathe.

I couldn't lose Illeron. The loss in my life was already so great, there was no more room in my soul to mourn another.

Ammah. Appah. Solandis. Jorah. Most of my pod. All gone. Lives cut too short, leaving behind gaping holes in my heart that grew larger with each day. Days that only grew darker.

No more. I couldn't possibly bear any more.

I wouldn't lose Illeron. I refused to grieve for him.

The sky split open, fat raindrops pummeling the water. The sand turned bloodred. A heavy fog rolled in, coating the ground, dancing on the ocean's surface.

The fire hissed in protest as I swam by, the flames dying under the relentless rain. Lightning cracked the sky, thunder right behind it. Through the sheets of rain and fog, I spotted the faint bounce of light along the drenched sand. The humans were still on the other side of the embankment. I'd have to take the inlet's entrance to reach them.

I ducked under the thrashing water, catching my breath. The opening to the ocean seemed impossibly small, waves crashing through with brutal force. I had to time it perfectly. The waves slammed into the trees, pulling roots and earth back into the sea. The trees groaned, the sand eroded. Then the waves retreated.

I shot forward, kicking hard as the water surged. The waves tore at my back like a thousand knives. My flesh burned, but I pushed on. Through the small opening of rocks, out the other side as the water began to coil again.

Faint voices drifted on the fog.

"Come on! Pull him in!"

"He's . . . so . . . *heavy*."

The humans. I was close.

I turned around and hovered in place, blinking through the turbulent silt and sand pummeling my face. The light was just ahead of me, whipping back and forth frantically like a beacon. My magic crackled with life, but I eased it back down gently. Not yet. It was too soon. I had to get closer.

There was a low snarl that reverberated through the water, primal and animalistic. The boys immediately skittered, giggling nervously.

Illeron.

Illeron was still alive.

I crept closer, keeping my Gift brimming along the surface of my skin.

The small-headed boy was knee-deep in the water, struggling to pull Illeron to shore. The net was too small, more for minnows than a full-grown mermaid. Illeron was twisted inside, his tail bent at awkward angles, blood trailing from a deep gash on his face. His teeth were bared as he clawed at the net, hissing whenever the boy adjusted his hold.

"Oy! Stop making that disgusting sound!" the gangly boy barked, stomping into the water and smacking the warrior with the lit-up metal rod.

Illeron jerked away, a feral groan deep in his throat. Another bloom of red on his shoulder, bright against his pale skin.

My stomach contorted, an insane fury building within me. My Gift pulsated within my fingertips, itching to be unleashed. *Not yet.* I slipped even closer to the shore.

"What sort of money do you think we'll get for him?" the boy holding the metal rod asked.

"I dunno," the boy reefing on the net replied. "Honestly, I'd settle for enough to keep Dad's printing shop open. We've been seeing a lot of red lately. It's not looking good."

"Yeah," the second one chirped, smacking the light source against his palm. "Same with my parents' grocery mart." He ducked his head, blushing. "I mean, I'd love a new bike too."

The lumpy boy scowled at Illeron. "The whole island's struggling. It's all because of them." He shrugged. "We have to lower our expectations though. The Hunt's in a couple days. There's gonna be a lot of mermaid carcasses for the hunters to make money off of. I say we keep this one alive. When the tourists come, we'll showcase a *live* mermaid. They'll pay anything for a look."

Now.

I held my breath and rose from the water, my head and shoulders glowing in the damp night air. "Hi there."

The boys spun to look at me, their eyes wide, mouths hanging open. I cocked my head to the side and bared my teeth in a malicious grin.

The light holder hurriedly wiped his sopping-wet face and pointed a shaking finger at me. "S-s-see! I t-told you there were two—"

I didn't let him finish his sentence. Exhaling sharply, I lifted my hands above the surface, cracked my fingers, and forced all the magic inside of me out.

A burst of brilliance, blinding as the sun, fierce as fire. It leapt from me, showering the boys with electrifying sparks. They screamed, stumbling over one another as they tried to flee, but there was nowhere to run. My magic was everywhere—on the beach, in the water, curling through the grass. It was endless, a force of nature they couldn't escape.

When the magic finally ebbed, the beach was empty save for one boy. The small-headed one, clutching the net in a death grip, shaking uncontrollably. The scent of urine hit my nose as I lowered my hands. I slithered forward, locking eyes with him. "Your friend is gone," I said, my voice low.

The boy whimpered, high-pitched and pathetic, but remained frozen in place.

"Which means no one will hear you scream." I grinned, tracing a nail along the boy's jawline. He quaked and quivered, squeezing his eyes shut, trying to lean out of my touch. "But you know, I think I just might take you home with me. Not a lot of my pod has seen a *live* human before." I gripped his chubby chin and dug my nails in, not enough to break the skin, but enough to make him squeak. "I hope you're good at holding your breath."

The boy sprang to life, ripping out of my grasp and dropping the net. He spun on his toes, wailing as he high-stepped out of the water and scrambled up the embankment.

The second he was over the sandy hill, my hands were on the net, ripping and tugging to find the opening they had crammed Illeron into. The warrior grunted, his scratched hands working feebly from the inside, trying to help.

"You shouldn't be here," he barked hoarsely.

"I'm a terrible listener," I retorted, sinking my teeth into a knot and whipping my head back in forth, more animal than mermaid.

"They might come back," Illeron said before letting out a shuddering cough and clutching his ribs.

"Then we'd better get you out of here, and fast."

The net began to loosen, the snapping of threads tumbling in my ears. With a strained yell, I grabbed the ropes and pulled as hard as I could. The opening tore. I reached inside and grabbed the warrior's hand, yanking him out of the rope's chokehold.

Together, we dove into the deep water and tumbled back into the inlet, letting the current carry us to the channel. Illeron dragged behind me, his grip on my hand weak. The gasping breaths he took rattled in his lungs before exiting his gills with a wheeze. The blood was still flowing freely from his face and shoulder, and when I looked back at him, I realized his other hand hung limply at his side, his elbow swollen, the muscles above it warped and misshapen. I sucked in a breath, fighting off a shiver. *Broken.*

We finally slowed as we approached the bridge. A cloud of sand puffed up as we pressed our backs against the basalt wall and sank to the floor. My hands were immediately on Illeron, sorting through his wounds. The warrior was clearly annoyed, but was also too tired to fight off my pokes and prods.

"You shouldn't have come back for me. I told you not to come back for me!" he whispered roughly.

I clucked my tongue, my fingers pinching the cut on his eyebrow. "And leave you to have all the fun? Absolutely not."

"Fun is a weird way to put it." Illeron's chuckle turned into a grimace as he touched his side. "I should be saving you, not the other way around."

I leaned away, raking my eyes over the warrior's huddled body. He was scrunched into a tight ball, his tail wrapped around him, like he was still stuck in the net. "I used up a lot of my Gift back there. I can't guarantee that I'll be able to heal all your wounds, so you're going to need to tell me which ones are a priority."

Illeron tried to scoff, but it came out as a groan. "I'm *fine*. Don't waste your magic on me."

I raised my eyebrows delicately, then tapped his side. The warrior let out a scathing hiss, jerking away. "Yes, you're totally fine," I quipped sarcastically.

Illeron chewed on his lip, then wheezed out an exhale. "I can't feel my arm, and I think my ribs are cracked," he offered reluctantly.

I smirked. "Was that so hard, proud warrior?"

I tapped into the depths of my magic, willing it back to the surface. It hummed to life, crackling at my fingertips. I pressed my hands to Illeron's body, wincing as he moaned at the contact. The magic flared, coating his pale skin, sinking into his scales, then into his torn muscles. I felt bones realign, tendons tighten, nerves spark. Illeron opened and closed his hand tentatively.

"Not bad," he said appreciatively when I pulled away.

I looked at my hands, still crackling with the last remnants of my power before it faded. Exhaustion tugged at my scales. I let my hands drop to my lap. "That's the last of it." My gaze lingered on the cut on his face. "Mavi can stitch that when we get home, but you'll likely have a scar."

The warrior lightly touched the broken skin slicing through his eyebrow, cleaving the space in two. He gave me a half smile. "I can handle a scar. It's Mavi's way with a needle that scares me."

I laughed, feeling the weight of the night slowly ebbing away. "I got twenty-five boats."

Illeron's eyes widened. "Twenty-five?"

I nodded, bobbing up and down excitedly.

The warrior laughed dubiously, pulling me into a hug. "Twenty-five out of thirty!" he exclaimed quietly, squeezing me tightly. "That's incredible!" He pulled away breathlessly, his eyes like glimmering rubies. He ran a hand along my cheek, gently pushing a strand of white hair away. "How on earth did you manage that?"

I shrugged, heat warming my insides. "Insanity, I think."

Illeron shook his head, his eyes not leaving mine. "Insane, yes. But also strong, brave, and . . . gods, so *powerful*. To single-handedly take down twenty-five boats, and the way you brandished your magic on those boys . . ." He gave a gasping laugh. "Just breathtaking. I've never seen anything like it."

My breath caught, my heart shifting violently in my chest. "Really?"

Illeron nodded. "You became starlight, Evanora. Not even the heavens could compete with you." He smiled gently, his eyes bright with wonder. "You were dazzling. Utterly and irrevocably dazzling."

Fear flickered in me, memories of a fleeting kiss crashing through my mind. Was he going to bring it up? Try again? It had been a grim farewell, nothing more. But what if it meant something else to him? Did he remember what I said that night we were waiting for Grayson? Did he remember, but not care?

The Illeron I'd grown to enjoy—even care for—was slipping in and out of focus. I didn't want to hurt him again, but I didn't want him retreating back into his shell either. I didn't want us to end up back at that painful stalemate.

Please don't, I prayed inwardly. *Don't do anything we will both regret.*

The warrior sighed with contentment and slowly released me. He rested his back against the stone wall and stared up at the rain as it plunged from the skies above. A smile staked claim on the corner of his lips, wistful and dreamy. He didn't look pained, like I was worried he would. Not upset, or angry, or withdrawn. He looked . . . happy. It suited him.

"We just might have a shot of winning this thing yet," he said quietly, stretching out his tail, letting it flop playfully against mine.

Soul feeling so ridiculously full, I settled in beside him, my mind's roar quickly dying down to a gentle hum. For the first time in a long time, I felt like my heart could beat freely without anyone—not even me—wondering who it was beating for. "We just might."

CHAPTER SEVENTY-SIX

GRAYSON

APRIL 30 – AFTERNOON

I
T WAS THE DAY OF THE FINAL FESTIVAL, AND I WAS STUCK IN
the goddamn house.

Pa didn't believe that I was feeling better. I'd been fine the whole
time, but the way he hovered made me wonder if I was missing something. Maybe I *was* unwell. The voices slithering in from underneath
my windowsill suggested I was. The way I kept waking up by slamming into a
door that refused to budge definitely indicated it.

I needed to see Evanora. No—*had* to see her. It felt like withdrawal, like
at any moment, I'd crumble. My brain would dissolve into mush. My body
would collapse into a pile of bones and blood. The connection between us
felt dangerously thin, but that could've been the guilt gnawing at me. Every
time I thought about Evanora, I thought about her mother. Her death. Her
blood on my hands.

And, God, the plan.

I had no idea where she was with it. Had she and Illeron gotten more
boats? Had they given up? Were they still trying to stop the Hunt? Not
knowing was driving me just as mad as the voices.

The next time Pa opened my door, I'd be ready. I'd shove my way
through and run. Where? I didn't know. I'd told Evanora not to come to
the island; the festival made it too dangerous. But I had to do something.

There had to be a way to get to her. To let her know I was still here. That I still wanted to help.

Footsteps thundered outside my door. I spun and tiptoed to the wall, pressing myself into the corner. My heart raced as I grabbed the first thing I could find—my sketchbook. The soft cover flopped in my hand. Hardly intimidating, but it was all I had. Before I could look for something better, the lock clicked.

The doorknob jostled, twisting to the side. I gripped the sketchbook tighter.

The door flew open.

"How's my favorite little weirdo—ow!"

Jasper stumbled back as my sketchbook collided with the top of his head. It took another swing and a satisfying *thwack* before I even realized I was attacking the wrong person. I pulled the sketchbook to my chest, my mouth dropping open in shock. "Jasper?"

Jasper was cradling his head, wincing as he rubbed at his frizzy ginger curls. "Who did you *think* it was, dummy?"

I quickly put my weapon back onto my desk, hiding the evidence. "No one."

Jasper squinted at me suspiciously, still touching his head. "Right."

The door was still open. I was tempted to bolt. Seeing Jasper only reminded me of the last time I had interacted with him. My stomach twisted sourly at the bad-tasting memories. "What are you doing here?"

Jasper's hand went still. He straightened, his pale cheeks suddenly bright with color. "I wanted to check in on you." He shoved his hands into his pockets, his eyes not meeting mine. "I feel awful about how things have been between us. And"—he nodded at the open door—"I ran into your pa in town. He told me everything."

My shoulders hunched as I sagged onto my bed. "Everything?"

Jasper nodded solemnly. "I'm . . ." He groaned, dropping his head to his chest. "I'm not good at this."

"At what?" I snorted, feeling prickly. "Apologies?"

Jasper nodded again, slinking over to the desk. He fingered the sketchbook, catching the edge, pulling the pages apart. "I shouldn't have been such a bastard at the Night of the Betting," he mumbled, staring blankly at my drawings of plants and flowers, not really seeing them. "And I shouldn't have joked around with your ma's journal like that." He pinched his lips together and finally looked at me, his large hazelnut eyes filled with sorrow. "I'm really sorry, Grayson. I've . . . I've been a shit friend lately." His breath hitched as he inhaled. "And, oh my God, your poor ma! That must have been a nightmare for you, witnessing what happened."

Nightmare was an appropriate way to put it. Since that night, every time I slipped into sleep, Ma was there, tumbling off the cliff. Sometimes she did it freely, other times I pushed her. But no matter how she fell, she was always grinning, screaming into the wind, "It should have been you!"

I didn't know if I preferred those dreams to the standard ones I had grown used to. Both were exhausting. Both left me gasping for breath and soaked in sweat, with my heart pounding so hard in my ears that I thought my skull would splinter.

Jasper was looking at me, biting his lip. "I heard a mermaid saved you." He said the words carefully, but his curiosity was poorly concealed. It was all over his face like a damned beacon. He was practically glowing.

I sighed wearily, falling back onto my hands. "Go on, ask."

For courtesy's sake, Jasper feigned shock. But it didn't last long. "What was it like?" he blurted, leaning forward. "Was she cold and slimy? Did she try to lure you to sleep with her siren song? Did she try to drink your blood? I heard they like doing that."

Funny how Pa had told Jasper everything except the part that truly needed to be shared. "No," I ground out. "She was gentle, and kind, and even healed me."

Jasper blinked. "Really?"

"Really."

Jasper blinked again, not convinced. "Seriously, Grayson. What did she do?"

"Nothing," I snapped, failing to keep the growl out of my voice. "She wanted nothing more than to keep me safe and put me in a spot where Pa and the others would find me. She made sure nothing bad happened to me."

Jasper almost looked dissatisfied, like he wanted me to share some awful horror about the mermaids, show him some grotesque wound, give him another reason to hate them. My ma had committed suicide. I had watched her do it. And all he really cared about was whether or not he had grounds to loathe mermaids more than he already did. My desire to leave the room swelled within me—leave, or kick Jasper out so I could be alone again. "I'm sorry to disappoint you," I said with a humorless chuckle, "but that's the whole story."

"Hmm," Jasper grunted, shaking his head. "That is pretty boring, if I'm being honest."

"But at least I'm alive, right?" I asked sarcastically.

Jasper waved a hand dismissively. "Yeah, yeah." He heaved a sigh, the action sending his entire skinny body rising and falling, before flipping through the sketchbook again. "Did you hear about the two mermaids spotted in Fenharrow?"

I froze, my spine seizing. "What?"

"Oh." Jasper rolled his eyes. "Of course you didn't. You've been stuck in here. Sorry." He shook his head. "Last night, some boys were hanging out at the bay when they heard splashing. When they went to investigate, they found a mermaid swimming along the beach." He sputtered out a breath. "They sure are getting gutsy, hey?"

I swallowed, acutely aware of the clicking in my throat, the heartbeat in my ears. "So . . . what happened?"

Jasper frowned. "Well, they almost caught one."

Could Jasper hear the way my heart was racing? It sounded like it was echoing throughout the room. "*Almost?*"

Jasper's scowl deepened. "They got away. While they were trying to haul the first one back to shore in their net, the second one snuck up on them. One of the boys claimed the mermaid cast a spell on them, while the other said she rained down lightning from the sky, trying to strike them." He shrugged. "But mermaids so close to the island a day before the Hunt. Spells and lightning aside, it must be a good omen."

I exhaled, allowing the tension to leave me in a rush. So, Illeron and Evanora *had* managed to get to Fenharrow Bay. Had they been able to sabotage some boats? Or had they gotten caught right away? Maybe that was how Illeron had wound up in the net; he was distracting the boys so Evanora could wreak havoc. It must have been terrifying for him, being trapped in that net. No mermaid, not even that uptight clam, deserved that.

But I wasn't able to dwell on it.

Because Jasper was at the last page of the sketchbook, where my portrait of Evanora stared up at him.

Jasper sucked on his teeth, tapping his foot against the floor. "What is this?" he asked quietly, lifting the book to show me, as if I didn't know what he was looking at.

I jerked my shoulders, the movement stiff. "Nothing. Just a drawing."

His foot wouldn't stop tap-tap-tapping. "I can see that. A drawing of what?"

"Just . . . a woman." It took everything in my power not to leap from the bed and rip the sketchbook out of his hands.

Jasper tore his scathing gaze from the picture to me. "Not a woman. A *mermaid*." He pointed viciously at the drawing. "What on earth would prompt you to sketch such an ugly, ungodly creature?"

The skin on my hands barked in pain. I looked down to see I had wrapped them together so tightly that I was pinching the skin, creating bright red marks that streaked between my fingers. "It's just . . ." I winced, fidgeting helplessly. "I just wanted to remember the mermaid who helped me."

Jasper's upper lip curled in a disgusted snarl. "That mermaid didn't help you. She *spared* you! She was going to kill you, but she ran out of time." He scoffed, shaking his head at me. "How can you possibly think otherwise?"

I clenched my jaw, my body growing hot with anger. "How can *you* possibly think that every single mermaid out there is evil?" I spread my arms wide. "News flash, Jasper: Not all mermaids are out to get you!" I thrust my fingers into my chest. "I'm living proof of that! Is it really so hard to believe?"

Jasper's head shook slowly, disappointment settling across his face. "Look"—he raised a hand to silence me—"you've clearly been brainwashed. I don't know what happened with that mermaid, but she obviously filled your head with lies." He gestured wildly around his own head. "She fed you all these ideas! She saw you were vulnerable and manipulated you into thinking nonsense. Not evil?" Jasper laughed cruelly. "Give me a break, Grayson!"

He turned back to the picture, his eyes narrowing as he scrutinized it. "Does your pa know about this? About your obsession with the very creatures we're supposed to be hunting?"

The blood in my veins froze. I wanted to grab the sketchbook, hurl it into the ocean, create confetti with its innards—anything. But I was stuck. Stuck in this nightmare that wouldn't end. I swallowed, the dry feeling in my throat choking me. "Jasper," I breathed, "don't."

Jasper whistled. "So, he doesn't. Well . . ." He loosed a breath, folding his arms; the book crinkled in his grip. "Isn't he going to be disappointed when he finds out."

My body still wouldn't budge. *Wake up*, I moaned inwardly. *Wake up, wake up, wake up!* I kept my gaze on Jasper, my voice even. "He does know," I forced out. "He already knows all about it."

Jasper barked out a laugh that was devoid of mirth. "Look at you, trying to lie to your best friend. Come on, Grays. We both know you aren't good at it."

"If you were my best friend," I spat, rage bursting above the calm facade, "you wouldn't be doing this to me."

"To you?" Jasper shook his head. "No, Grayson. I'm doing this *for* you. The sooner you stop thinking mermaids are your friends, the sooner you start thinking straight, the sooner I get my best friend back." He shrugged, casual, but there was a hard edge to his words. "It'll hurt, sure," he added, as if to soothe me. "But it's necessary. You need to feel this pain so you can move on from this . . . this *sick* fascination."

"Jasper," I begged, blinking away the sudden blurriness that crept along my eyes. "Please, just . . . wait a second!"

Jasper looked out the window, at the sun-kissed clouds beyond the trees. "The sun's nearly down. The festival is going to be starting soon." He pursed his lips. "I wish you could come. But we both know what would happen if you did. Trust me, Grayson." He sighed, closing the door. "This is for your own good."

The second the doorknob slid into place, the trance was over, and I sprang free from my numb state. I charged to the door on flimsy legs, pulling as hard as I could on the handle as the lock condemned me with its damning *click*. I pounded on the door. "Jasper!" I screeched. "Jasper, open this door!"

I was met with silence.

Jasper was gone, on his way to Fariid, to find my pa and blow up my life more than it already was.

I couldn't let that happen.

I barreled my shoulder into the door, a strained yell ripping from my throat as I heaved my entire body into the unmoving wood. Again, and again, and again. Until my shoulder ached, my skin was on fire, and my bones rattled. "Why . . . won't . . . you . . . open?" I bellowed with each slam.

The door wouldn't budge, ignoring my frantic attempts to escape. Panting, I slumped against it, clutching the useless doorknob like a lifeline. Defeat coiled in my chest, but I forced it down. I couldn't give up yet. My eyes darted to the window. Heart hammering, I stumbled to my feet and lurched toward the desk. Books and jars crashed to the floor, but I didn't care. Hunched on top of the slanted tabletop, I grabbed the lock, twisting it in my sweaty hand. It was old, the bolts thin and rusted, digging into the frame. If I had something strong enough to break them, I could take the whole lock out—no key needed.

My eyes landed on Ma's jewelry box.

Gripping the desk, I leaned toward the bookshelf, careful to avoid the glass. I could just barely reach it. I inhaled sharply, flicking it closer. When it skidded into my hands, I yanked it back, a triumphant shout on my tongue. The box was cool under my fingers.

I spared a precious second to hug the box against my throbbing chest. I bowed my head, pressing my lips to the lid. "Thank you, Ma," I whispered, "for finally being here for me when I need you."

And then I rammed the box into the lock as hard as I could.

The window shook, the lock groaned, the entire room vibrated.

If you come out, the Cursed Beings crooned, *then we come in.*

I gritted my teeth and brought the box down again.

It took three solid hits before the bolts popped out of their holes and ricocheted onto the ground.

I was throwing open the window and bursting out of my prison before the lock even had a chance to fall onto the desk.

CHAPTER SEVENTY-SEVEN

GRAYSON

APRIL 30 – EVENING

PENNY WASN'T THRILLED TO SEE ME WHEN I STORMED into the barn with a bucket of grain and her bridle. "Time to test out your new shoes," I said as I hastily tacked her up. Her mood sank even lower when I immediately tapped her into a gallop. She tried to settle into a trot. We compromised on a canter.

The festival was in full swing when we arrived, and Fariid was alive and hungry.

The sights, sounds, and lights of the Final Festival were overwhelming. Fireworks popped beside the broken fountain, their crackling bursts met with gleeful howls. Vendors hollered in cracked voices, trying to sell their beer, pastries, and hot dogs. Music blared from the stage, and the crowd danced around a roaring fire that reached for the stars. Women shimmied their bare chests and teasingly lifted their skirts. Men salivated, pawing at their pants.

It was similar to the First Festival, but the air felt different—hot, sticky, and primal, thrumming with a thirst that left my nerves taut and my cheeks burning.

I tucked Penny into a nearby alley and ducked under a string of lights, eyes scouring the crowd, searching for a single person amongst the sea of people. It hadn't taken me all that long to break out of the house. I had to remind myself of that every time the fear needled its way into my lungs, making my breath tight, my head spin. There was no way Jasper had already found Pa. I still had time.

I weaved my way through the crowd, head swiveling, trying in vain to find a gangly boy with ginger hair, a limp, and fiery determination in his eyes.

"Whoa there, Shaw!" There was a hand clamping around my shoulder.

I jerked away, spinning on my toes to find Mr. Brightly. He swayed on his feet, the beer in his pewter mug sloshing everywhere. The buttons of his collar were undone, revealing a chest full of coarse dark hair that glimmered in the twinkling lights. Mr. Brightly blinked slowly, focusing on me with his one good eye. "Where ya off to in such a hurry?"

I tried not to grimace. Mr. Brightly smelled like he had taken a bath in a vat of beer. "I'm trying to find Jasper," I said, taking a step back. "Have you seen him?"

"Nah." Mr. Brightly shook his head sloppily. "But I've seen many fine ladies. Take yer pick. I'll help ya woo 'er."

I held up my hands, smiling politely. "I'll pass on that, thanks."

Mr. Brightly scowled. "Yer no fun, Mr. Shaw. Never have been."

I wished I could blame the insult on the alcohol, but I knew better. "Can you let me know if you see him?"

But Mr. Brightly was already gone, staggering away, jeering at a group of women who were taking turns feeding one another cookies dipped in melting chocolate. The chocolate coated their fingers, their chests, their teeth as they laughed.

I turned around.

And ran into Peter Lyre.

"Grayson!" he crowed, slinging an arm around me. "Fancy seeing you here!"

I clenched my jaw. "Why wouldn't I be here?"

Peter snorted. "Because you're a scaredy-cat pansy who dropped out of the Hunt. This"—he gestured to the festival with a sweeping arm—"isn't *for* you. It's for us." He thumped a fist against his chest. "The *real* heroes."

I shrugged out from underneath his arm. "The festival is for anyone who wants to celebrate."

"Yeah." Peter laughed heartily. "And considering you look like you constantly have a stick shoved up your ass, I'd say you don't fit into that category."

I balled my hands into fists. I couldn't get distracted by Peter. I couldn't let my temper get the better of me. "I don't have time for this," I grumbled, shaking my head and turning away.

Peter pouted mockingly. "Aww," he moaned, "are you going to go cry now? Run off to your daddy so he can fix your hurt feelings?"

I looked over my shoulder at Peter, and the venom in my eyes was enough to wipe the snide grin off his face. I could see the memories of what I had done to Ambrose flutter through his rapidly paling chubby cheeks. "Burn in hell, Peter," I growled before letting the crowd envelop me, putting me deeper into the city square.

Still no sign of Jasper. My feelings of helplessness were beginning to grow. A flash of ginger curls.

My heart staggered in my chest. I picked up my pace, narrowly avoiding a dancing couple careening to the side. I sidestepped around a child holding a chocolate in the shape of a mermaid, wincing as she bit into the tail and let out a dreamy, "Mmm."

Jasper was by the stage, watching the band. Had he not found Pa yet? Or had he and, after sharing every bit of my secrets, was now enjoying the festivities?

I ducked underneath a man swinging his arms wildly, miming a conductor. I reached forward, hands gnarled into claws, and grabbed Jasper's shoulder.

But it was Holly who whirled around to face me. Her mouth was open in a surprised O shape, and her rosy cheeks were dusted in powder sugar and glitter. Her large hazel eyes danced with fire and twinkling lights.

At the sight of me, Holly's lips morphed into a huge grin, and she squealed with delight, pulling me into a hug. "Grayson Shaw, as I live and breathe!"

It must've been like hugging a plank of wood. I tried to loosen my stiff muscles, adrenaline racing through me. "Hi, Holly," I said absentmindedly, still hunting the crowd for another head with ginger hair.

Holly pulled away. "Have you come to make a wish?"

I furrowed my brow. "A what?"

Holly rolled her eyes. "You know, a *wish*." She gestured to the stage behind her.

That was when I noticed the large brass bowls lining the sides and the coins Holly was clutching to her chest. I made a face. "You know that money lines Mayor McCoy's pockets, right?"

Holly's face darkened. "Well, you're a buzzkill," she huffed, tilting her delicate nose into the air. "The money might, but my wish doesn't."

Placing coins into one of the bowls and making a wish seemed almost as violating as cutting our fingers open and bleeding into them. First our bodies belonged to the Hunt. Now our money. What was next? Our souls? I tried to soften; I didn't want to be the reason why Holly lost that sparkle in her eyes—not when I had snuffed it out so many times before.

"What are you wishing for, then?"

Holly smirked. "Well, if I told you, then it wouldn't come true, now would it?" But the rouge in her cheeks deepened, and she wouldn't meet my eyes. She swished her hips back and forth, sending the lavender layers of her dress ruffling. "If you were making a wish, what would it be?"

To end the Hunt. To leave this island and never look back. To not have these god-awful voices plaguing my thoughts.

"To find your brother, actually." I craned my neck to look at the crowd. "Have you seen Jasper?"

Holly seemed disappointed at my not playing along. But she turned, pointing at the hot dog cart in the corner of the square. "I saw him there about five minutes ago."

Five minutes might as well have been an eternity. Still, I nodded my thanks. "I have to go, Holly. But, please, do me a favor." I took her hand in mine and carefully folded her fingers around the few precious coins. "Don't spend your money on a wish." I offered a half smile, but it was tinged in sadness. "They hardly ever come true. Lethe won't allow it."

I left her at the stage, pushing my way through the swelling crowd to the hot dog cart. The smell of soggy buns and old meat assaulted my senses, but I waved away the clouds of steam, intent on ending this sordid cat-and-mouse chase.

"Buy!" the vendor screamed at me, thrusting a wilted hot dog into my face. "Buy!"

I leaned back with a scowl. "Jasper Warren," I yelled above him. "Tall, ginger hair, has a limp. Have you seen him?"

The vendor shook his head fervently. "Buy! You buy!"

I pushed the hot dog away. "Please," I tried again. "I really need to find him!"

"You touch, you buy!"

Growling, I grabbed the hot dog from the vendor's hand and threw it onto the ground. Everything was red and loud, pounding in my ears, eating away at any of the lingering sane thoughts I still possessed. "I'm not buying a goddamn thing from you!"

The vendor balked, his almond eyes trailing down to the pieces of hot dog, which were immediately trampled by people passing by. "You pay!" he roared, pointing at the ground. "You pay for that!"

But I was already walking away, my hope of finding Jasper rapidly dwindling. It was hopeless. The square was too large, too full of people nearly hysterical with excitement, hunger, and passion. I would have been better off not leaving the house at all.

"Rowan Shaw! Have you seen him?"

My breath caught. I jerked my head up, following the scratchy voice.

"No, I don't want your cotton candy! Rowan Shaw! Where is he? Where's his cart?"

Close. Jasper was close. I spun in a circle, my chest tight, my gaze swimming with blurred faces and jack-o'-lantern grins.

And there he was.

A handful of feet away, Jasper was leaning over a stand selling cotton candy and lollipops, yelling to be heard above the vendor's demands for money. He kept shaking his head and ducking around the fluffy pink-and-blue candy being shoved in his direction, his demands falling on deaf ears. As if sensing me, Jasper pushed off the stand and straightened, his entire body turning slowly in my direction, the sketchbook dangling from his fingers.

We locked eyes, and everything went still.

I exhaled quietly through clenched teeth and shook my head, careful to keep my gaze on him. "*Please*," I mouthed.

Jasper's lips pinched to the side, his eyes flaring with stubborn determination. He held up the sketchbook for me to see, cocking his head to the side in challenge.

And then he bolted.

Letting out a hiss of frustration, I chased after him, dodging dancers and leaping over carts of trinkets and food. Jasper veered left, then right, moving with surprising agility despite his bad leg. I slipped, slamming into a table full of mugs. Beer splashed everywhere, drenching bystanders; they erupted into sarcastic applause and jeers. I regained my footing, wiped foam from my face, and looked up.

He was gone.

I had chased Jasper to the edge of the square, where the festivities were quiet, the streets were dark, and the only people to be seen were a few drunkards wandering aimlessly, merrily singing out of tune.

Forcing my breath to slow, I crept along the dark buildings, peeking into alleys. One had a man moaning as he pissed against a wall. Another housed a couple relieving themselves in a very different way, and I quickly moved on. My heart pounded as I neared the last alley before the road split into four directions. Jasper *had* to be in there. If he wasn't, my chances of finding him would drop sharply.

I held my breath and tiptoed into the shadows.

At the far end of the alley, with his hands on his knees, gasping for air, was Jasper.

Keeping my eyes trained on him, I inched closer, careful to remain as quiet as possible. *Don't breathe. Don't blink. Just one foot in front of the other.*

I stepped over a collapsed crate, wincing as broken glass cracked underneath my boot. I didn't know what I was going to do when I finally made it to the end of the alley and cornered him.

You'll have to knock him out.

The thought momentarily stunned me into stillness. Nausea burst through the pit in my stomach and burned up my throat.

I didn't know if the thought belonged to me or the Cursed Beings. And that realization terrified me.

Just hit him over the head. Lights out. Do it while his back is turned, and he'll never know it was you.

My thoughts. Definitely my thoughts. Which made it so much worse.

Jasper had collected his breath and was beginning to straighten. He grunted, rolling out his neck and shoulders, kicking life back into his feet.

I was running out of time. It was now or never.

I crouched, fumbling blindly for anything to get the job done. I was sweating all over, my hands itchy and hot. My fingers circled around a piece of broken crate. I lifted it carefully. The piece of wood felt too light, too fragile. I pulled my eyes away from Jasper and looked for something sturdier.

Jasper sighed and began to twist.

Time's up.

I raised the wood into the air.

Jasper turned in time to see me slam the plank onto his head.

To my surprise, the piece of wood didn't immediately shatter in my hands, and Jasper dropped to the ground. His bad leg was the first thing to give out, and with wide eyes and a wheezing groan, Jasper toppled backward, collapsing into a pile of garbage bags.

He didn't get back up.

I let out an unsteady breath, followed by a violent retch as my insides threatened to contort themselves out. The broken wood slipped from my shaking fingers, the sound of it clattering to the dirt floor echoing in the alley. Swallowing down the bile pooling in my mouth, I took a timid step toward Jasper. "Oh, God," I whispered hoarsely. "Jasper?"

No response.

I knelt, pressing my ear to his mouth. A breath—faint, shallow, barely there. Thank Christ he was alive. I scanned his head—a nasty bump already forming, but no blood. Closing my eyes, I took a deep breath. "Get ahold of yourself, Shaw."

When the nausea subsided, I stood, quickly considering my options. The sketchbook. I had to destroy it. And when Jasper woke up, he'd have no evidence to show my pa—just a bump on his head and a crazy story Pa likely wouldn't believe.

I grabbed the sketchbook from where it had fallen next to Jasper and started to leave.

But then guilt hit. I glanced over my shoulder at his unconscious body, discarded like trash.

I sighed, conscience weighing me down, and checked if any of the back doors tucked within the alley were unlocked. One was. I dragged Jasper inside and closed the door quietly. The cramped room smelled better than the alley—warm, dry, free of piss and garbage.

I stepped out of the alley like a bullet, heart pounding in my ears.

The square had descended into chaos. Two vendors were fistfighting, wares scattered across the ground as they kicked and punched. The crowd cheered and laughed. The dancers—more like animals than people—pressed against one another, tearing clothes off in feverish hunger. I turned away, shielding my eyes, moving faster.

Were the days leading up to the Hunt always like this? Always so . . . feral?

I hurried around a man as he pressed a giggling woman down onto a table and began pulling up her skirts with a mad look in his eyes. I nearly backed into Mr. Brightly, who was drinking beer as it waterfalled onto a woman's naked breasts. Cheeks burning, I quickened my pace.

Someone was shoving me. "Where are you running off to, Shaw?" Ambrose howled. "Where's your pretty knife now? Do you still want to cut me with it?"

I took off in a run.

God, I needed to get home. I needed to escape this nightmare. I needed to—

Come here, Promised One.

A throbbing in my chest. My head lurched upward. I was nowhere near Penny, where I had pointed my feet and told my body to go. I was at Black Sands Beach, my feet buried deep in the dark sand.

Yes, the Cursed Beings moaned. *Here.*

The water was a violent coil, pulling back before springing onto the shoreline. The waves were loud as they towered in the sky before crashing back to earth.

I gasped, my hands flying subconsciously to my throat. No. No, not the beach. Home, I needed to go *home.*

This is home.

No.

Home. Here.

No!

The ache in my chest grew with every rabid heartbeat. I groaned, fighting against the pull with all my might.

It was too strong.

My feet moved of their own accord, dragging me closer and closer to the mouth ready to swallow me whole.

Grayson Shaw.

Please.

Grayson Shaw!

Please!

Flashes of a bloodied Markus Bridge tumbled into my mind, pictures of an unmoving Tommy Morris floating atop the waves. Still, my feet moved. My boots lined the water's edge. The waves showered me in mist. The salt air stifled my gasping whimpers. One more step and I'd be in the water. I'd be theirs.

"Grayson Shaw!"

A voice rang out in the night, clear as a bell, soft as wind chimes, as beautiful as the mermaid it belonged to. I stopped. The grip on my chest loosened, giving way to a connection that pulsed with so much life that I worried it would snap from the sheer force of it.

Blinking through the mist, I looked along the shoreline, anxiously scanning the water, praying that she wasn't there, praying that she was. My gaze trailed to the pier, where a pair of large violet eyes stared back at me from underneath the wooden legs, enveloped by a soft, warm glow.

Evanora.

YOU SHOULDN'T BE HERE!" I SCOLDED AS I HURRIED OVER TO HER, slipping underneath the pier's shadow. "What if someone sees you?"

Evanora shook her head, her beautiful eyes shining like amethyst jewels. "I had to see you," she whispered, placing a hand against her chest. "And it's a good thing I came too." She cocked her head to the side, her face tight with worry. "What were you doing so close to the water?"

I crouched, offering her an unconvincing smile. "Going for a night swim."

Evanora clucked her tongue, reaching up with a wet hand and cupping my cheek. "They are getting worse," she breathed. "The voices. The Cursed Beings' hold on you." Not a question, but a dreadfully accurate observation.

I leaned into her touch, closing my eyes as I breathed in deeply for the first time that night. "It's okay," I promised quietly. "I'm okay." I took her hand in mine and clutched it against my chest. "I have you here to protect me."

Evanora's lips quirked, but I could see the concern rippling underneath. "I might not always be here, you know. I almost wasn't tonight."

I squeezed her hand tightly. "Why *are* you here, Evanora?" I glanced over my shoulder, at the festival that loomed dangerously close by. "Things are out of control right now. You should see what's going on at the festival. People are acting crazy, utterly possessed. I've known about the Hunt since the day I was born. I've been to Final Festivals. They've gotten wild, sure, but this . . ." I sucked in a sharp breath. "This feels different. A culmination of something. I feel like . . ." I sighed, dropping my head, my lips brushing against her pale knuckles. "I feel like everything is falling apart."

Evanora hummed gently, her tail swishing rhythmically behind her. "It *is* the culmination of something, Grayson Shaw. It is the beginning of the end . . . the end to all of it."

I looked up at her, enveloped in her moonbeam glow. Goose bumps erupted on my skin, but my heart settled into a soft rhythm, and my muscles loosened. "Let's go over the plan again," I said with grim determination.

Evanora grinned wickedly at me. "I thought you'd never ask."

I jerked my chin up. "When the Hunt begins, flares will be ignited all over the island, signaling the start. Showers of red fire in the sky."

Evanora's delicate brows wove together. "We will know it's time to move when we see them."

"Exactly." I stared hard at her. "What will you do next?"

Evanora counted the steps off her fingers. "My pod will break apart into groups and head to the four beaches. The wielders will create a storm within the ocean, making the waters unruly. They will have a harder time spotting us then. The sirens and benders will taunt and scare the hunters into oblivion. The warriors will then attack the boats, splitting them apart with spears." She winced, her cheeks growing red. "I wasn't able to get all the boats in Fenharrow."

I shrugged. "Attack them all anyway. If they don't give after several spear jabs, leave them and move on to the next."

Evanora nodded, the color slipping off her sharp cheekbones as her confidence bloomed. "The second the boat has collapsed, we will snag the floundering hunters and take them back to shore."

"If they try to hurt you, hurt them back," I added hurriedly. "Only kill when absolutely necessary."

Evanora nodded again, though without as much vigor. "I doubt the humans won't put up some semblance of a fight." She sighed wearily. "But we will keep the killing to a minimum."

A playful wave splashed the mermaid's face, droplets clinging to her lips like a cruel tease. My heart skipped at the sight—I wanted nothing more than to lick them off, to drown myself in her. *Focus, damn it.* My free hand quivered as I curled it through her hair, winding the wet strands around my fingers. "And at the end of the day?"

"We return home—not to the kingdom, but to the caves. Safer there," Evanora replied, her voice dark with determination. "We'll regroup, heal, eat, and prepare for the next battle." She brightened, her expression softening. "Mavi has been wildly successful. Our stores of medicinal plants and prayer reeds have grown—she even managed to steal a couple traps full of lobsters, crabs, and snails!"

I smiled grimly, but my shoulders sagged. "I'm really hoping you won't have to use much of her stolen goods; with any luck, there won't be a battle to return to the following day." I leaned forward, resting my forehead against Evanora's. "But it's a good plan. The hunters won't know what to make of any of it." I nuzzled my nose into hers. "I almost wish I could join in the fun."

The mermaid went stiff. She pelted me with a look so horrified that it almost made me flinch. "Promise me you won't get in the water during any of it!"

I choked out a laugh, startled by her intensity. "I hate the water."

"But that hasn't stopped you from trying to get in it lately. Your fear has been overridden by something far more deadly." She removed her hand from mine and clutched the sides of my face. "Please, Grayson, promise me you won't even go near the ocean during the Hunt. You *must* stay on the shore. Even if we are struggling, or losing by a tidal wave, you cannot try to help. The risk of someone mistaking you for a hunter will be too great, and while I vow to honor your request to not kill the humans, I doubt all of my pod will be so lenient. Please"—she gave me a little shake—"please just promise me?"

I wrapped my hands around hers, feeling the tremor in her touch. "I promise."

Evanora's face softened, but the cracks remained. She closed her eyes, exhaling slowly. I could see the tension in her body start to ease, but it didn't fade completely. It wouldn't. Not while the Hunt loomed over us.

She pulled away, her fingers slipping from mine before she ran them through her hair nervously. The strands twisted like frail threads as they fell over her bare shoulder. "I don't know what I would do if I lost you," she whispered, her voice cracking.

The words sliced through me. I shook my head quickly, fighting the lump in my throat. "You don't need to worry about that. Not now. Just . . ." I sighed, my voice low. "Focus on what's ahead. I won't go near the water. You have my word."

Her eyes opened, the lashes heavy with unshed tears. The sight of them—glittering with a fear I couldn't alleviate—shook me to my core. I wanted to kiss those tears away, make everything hurt less.

Focus, indeed.

Evanora took my hands and kissed my palms, her lips soft, tender, shaking. Her tears slid onto my callused skin, burning where they touched. The scars on my wrists felt like they were on fire.

And the memories flooded back—vicious, relentless, damning.

Evanora's mother.

Dead because of me.

Nausea lurched up my throat, so sudden and uninvited that I reared back, a groan on my lips as I hunched to the side, clutching my chest. The mermaid gave a startled hiss, then quickly recovered and lunged for me. "Grayson!" she cried. "Grayson, what's wrong? What is it?"

Evanora's mother.

Dead.

My scars burned with the memory of the blade. My shoulders ached with the pressure of Ma's fingers as she pushed me farther underneath the thrashing waves. Lungs tight, heart pounding, eyes full of fear.

And then light.

And then death.

Nereida. *Dead.*

Evanora's hands were on me, trying to pull me upright. "Grayson," she moaned. "I can't help you if you don't tell me what's wrong!"

How could I tell her? How could I possibly tell her that I was the one responsible for her mother's death? Wave after wave of agony ripped through me as the mermaid anxiously searched my face for answers.

"I can't," I gasped, squeezing my eyes shut and turning into the sand. I couldn't even look at her. Not when she looked at me the way she did. Not when she didn't know what I had done. "I can't!"

"Please," she begged, wrenching me toward her. Her embrace was tight and cold. "Grayson, you aren't alone. I swore I'd protect you. I meant that with every fiber of my being. Please. You must tell me what's wrong."

"I can't," I whispered again. "Because if I do, I fear . . ." I swallowed hard around the lump in my throat, a whimper squeaking through the cracks. "I fear it will change everything."

Her response was immediate, her face resolute as she shook her head fiercely. "It won't," she insisted, her voice steady. "Nothing you say will ever change what we are to each other. Our bond is too strong, Grayson Shaw. We can carry anything together." She placed her hand on my chest, her fingers vibrating. "Our hearts beat as one. They always will."

I met her eyes—those tear-streaked eyes—and I knew she was wrong. The truth would shatter us. "It's about your mother," I choked out, the words more painful than I could bear.

CHAPTER SEVENTY-EIGHT

EVANORA

APRIL 30 – EVENING

THE WORLD WENT DEATHLY QUIET. I TRIED TO KEEP MY face serene, but it was hard; I could already feel fractures racing along my cheekbones, my forehead, my lips. "My ammah?" I asked lightly.

Grayson wouldn't meet my searching gaze. "The night my ma tried to kill me . . . Do you remember what I told you about it?"

I nodded slowly, my chest growing tight. "Yes," I breathed. "She pulled you from your bed, carried you down to the beach while you were trapped inside a dreamless sleep." Unable to help it, my eyes flitted to the scars on his wrists. "You couldn't defend yourself as she sliced you open and plunged you underneath the waves."

The boy shook his head, tears breaking free from his thick lashes and tumbling down his cheeks. "I never knew why she had tried to kill me that night, why my life meant nothing to her." His ocean eyes finally met mine. "So I asked her."

My spine stiffened. "Grayson . . ."

He continued, his voice a thick, broken thing. "I should have given up on her like she had with me. The second she tried to end my life, I should have cut all ties with her, pretended she didn't exist, like Pa did." He grimaced.

"But I *had* to know, Evanora. I just had to know. Not knowing..." He shuddered viciously. "It was killing me."

"So," I whispered, "what did you find out?"

Grayson swallowed hard. "At the pinnacle of her brokenness, she discovered the Cursed Beings." He looked at me, those stormy blues full of pain. "But her view of them is ... *was* ..."—he swallowed again— "warped. She didn't think of them as these vile, evil creatures that dwell in darkness and thrive on suffering. She saw them as gods that could grant her any wish."

I let out a stark laugh. "The Cursed Beings? Granting wishes?"

Grayson nodded. "I know. The notion itself is crazy. But Ma had it in her head that she could bargain with them, that she could make an offer they couldn't refuse."

"Grayson," I uttered slowly, "what did she do?"

The boy's face went tight with disgust. "A life for a life."

I sucked in a sharp breath. "Your life ... in exchange for Warrick's." I shook my head. "But that doesn't make sense."

Grayson shrugged, but his jaw was clenched. "It did to her. And that was all that mattered."

The pieces were slowly lining up, mashing against one another before slotting into place. It was making my head spin. "The bargain ... *That's* why you can hear the Cursed Beings. They were promised you, and didn't get you."

The boy sighed, giving me a tired smile. "And they won't stop until they do."

The voices, the pull of the ocean—it all made sense now. Grayson was trapped in a promise his mother had made, forced to pay the price for surviving. But there was still one piece missing, one piece out of place. Nausea twisted my stomach, turning my skin hot. I didn't want to know how it all fit together.

"But I don't understand." I narrowed my eyes, frowning at Grayson. "What does any of this have to do with Ammah?"

Grayson went pale, staring out at the sea. Could he hear the voices now? Were they pulling him toward the death they thought he owed them? "When I was in the water, I could hear them ... the Cursed Beings. I didn't know what they were. I thought I was losing my mind, thought I'd slipped into some wretched fairy tale." He trembled, his face twisting in pain, as if speaking the words cut him deeper. "They were hungry, Evanora. Hungry for me. For my life. For my blood." A tremor racked his body. "I couldn't see them in the dark water, but I felt them, speaking to my soul. Their voices were many—male and female, old and young. They kept saying, 'The one who is promised . . . Come here.' "

Grayson bent forward, crying into his lap. The waves kissed his feet, fireworks danced in the sky, and time stopped for him. He was stuck in that moment, bleeding beneath the waves. I placed a shaking hand on his shoulder. "What happened?"

He shook his head violently. "I felt their tentacles reaching for me, long black arms from the depths. I tried to fight back, to scream, to escape. But Ma was strong, and their pull was stronger. I was at their mercy." He inhaled sharply, a whimper escaping. "Then it happened." He lifted his head, his eyes full of sorrow. "A light in the darkness."

All the warmth leeched from my skin, leaving me naked in my coldness. "A light?" I repeated, voice so low that the waves ate up my words.

Grayson licked his quivering lips. He closed his eyes and turned away, his face becoming a mask of shadow. "Your . . . Your mother's light."

A gasp slithered through my tightly clenched teeth. I brought my hands to my lips, my eyes wide and wild as I shook my head numbly. "No," I moaned from behind my fingers. "No."

The boy crumbled beneath the weight of my useless pleas. His shoulders bowed forward, and his head sagged into his hands. "My ma said that she came out of nowhere, blasting away the dark with every ounce of magic that flowed through her. In one breath, she was able to erase the night, send the Cursed Beings scattering. It was unlike anything Ma had ever seen before, such raw *power*. For me," he said, his voice catching. "She used her Gift to save me."

My hands moved from my mouth to my ears, desperately trying to block out the boy's words before they slipped into my mind, took festering root, and grew into poisonous weeds that would infect me. "Stop it! I don't want to hear any more."

Grayson gritted his teeth, his dark eyebrows knitting together with rage. For himself, or the Cursed Beings, or the unfairness of life, I couldn't tell. "Your mother stopped the bargain before it could be completed. And—"

"Stop!" I shrieked, squeezing my eyes shut.

"—in their anger, the Cursed Beings—"

"Enough!"

"—took her life when she had no more magic to defend herself."

And there it was. The awful truth to the questions that kept me up at night, the questions that had me staring at her crown for hours upon hours, begging the ancestors for answers, and finding none. Nereida, the great queen of the waters, beautiful and kind and pure, had died at the hands of the Cursed Beings.

For a human.

A boy.

Grayson Shaw.

The last piece slowly shifted, the sound of it settling into place echoing in my mind, my aching heart.

"It isn't true." I leaned forward with a hiss, grabbing Grayson's face and forcing him to look at me. "Tell me it isn't true!"

The boy winced as my nails bit into his skin, but his gaze remained firm. "I'm so sorry."

I bared my sharp teeth, a snarl on my lips. "You're *sorry*," I spat. "My ammah is dead because of you!"

Grayson flinched at my words, words he had likely said to himself over and over. "You can't hate me more than I hate myself," he whispered, his eyes a storm-drenched night. "Your mother is the reason I'm still alive. She is the reason we are connected, Evanora. She is the thread tying our hearts together."

My heart squeezed in response, the bond holding me and Grayson together suddenly feeling too tight, suffocating. I wanted to claw through my own skin and pull the damn thing out, just to alleviate the pressure. I wanted to rip the connection to shreds, tear apart the frayed strands, watch the boy's own heart break as I did it.

But it wouldn't bring her back. It wouldn't fix what he had done.

"I wish I could take it all back," Grayson pushed hurriedly. "I wish I could have just died that night."

My blood was fire within me. When I didn't say anything, Grayson slowly lifted a hand to his chest, feeling the strain of our connection as I willed the life to bleed out of it. "I didn't ask Nereida to save me—"

I gave a thorny growl. "Do *not* say her name so casually! You have no right to hold her name in your mouth!" My Gift sparked out of my skin, a crackling spit of light dancing on the waves.

Grayson held up his hands in quiet surrender. "I understand your anger."

My anger? I was rage and venom. I was crashing waves and rockslides. I was thunder in the sky and coursing lava far below, and still there was room inside me for more. Anger? The word didn't even scratch the surface. My magic hummed and buzzed, fighting to be freed. "How could you possibly understand?" I seethed.

Still holding up his hands, the boy scooted closer. "Because I've experienced that sort of anger too."

I laughed, but it carried no warmth. Ammah was dead because of him, because she'd seen a helpless child and couldn't bear watching him suffer.

He is the key, my ancestors pleaded. *The power of three.*

I shut out the voices, mentally slamming the door I had always taken great care to keep open for my ancestors. Their words of wisdom were of no use to me right now. I didn't need a key. I needed my ammah back.

"Just . . ." Grayson bit his lip, lowering his arms until his open palms hovered between us. "Just tell me what I can do, Evanora. Tell me how I can make things right."

I needed him to not say my name like that, like it was a rare jewel in his hands, a decadent dessert on the tip of his tongue. Like it was a gift that I had the power to wrench from his fingertips.

"Please, Evanora." The boy slowly turned his hands and placed them delicately on my lap. His fingers stroked my scales, his touch hot but steady. "Tell me what you need."

"I need . . ." I stared at his hands, torn between wanting to rip his arms off, and bury myself into them. "I need . . ."

I needed the gaping hole in my chest to close. To have something else besides pain in every fiber of my being. To not feel like my connection to Grayson Shaw was a curse. "I need—"

"Grayson?"

The meek voice had come from above us. The boy whipped his head upward, but I was faster. I glimpsed a girl, bright coppery hair with a tangle of white flowers woven into it, a shawl wrapped around her narrow shoulders, a deep purple gown flowing in the sea breeze. And eyes, large hazelnut eyes, awash in horror.

Grayson staggered to his feet, face pale, his mouth twisted in shock as his gaze stretched up, up, up the pier. "Ho-Holly!" he gasped, his hands clutched against his stomach.

The girl took a step back from the railing. She gripped the shawl tightly, her wobbling mouth pressing into a thin line. Grayson was staring at her with a desperate urgency, but the girl was looking at me, unblinking, unmoving, a mixture of disgust filtering into that wall of horror.

I didn't want to be gawked at. The way her stare dragged over my body made my scales crawl, my fins taut. I bared my teeth at her and snarled.

She took another step back, a squeak escaping her tightly cinched throat, along with the word, "M-mermaid!"

I grinned, flashing my sharp canines at her. "Very perceptive."

The girl pressed a hand to her mouth, her pale skin taking on a sea-weed-green hue. Yet she couldn't stop staring.

I thumped my tail against the wet sand, the sound sending her flinching back another step.

"Holly," Grayson said again. "Please wait." He took a step to the side, shielding me from that unwavering stare. "I can explain—"

The second our staring contest was severed, the girl was running, her footsteps echoing down the pier at a rapid pace that was immediately swallowed up by the festivities around her. Grayson choked out a groan and stumbled forward, only for his steps to come to a jerking halt. He swiveled on his toes to look back at me, still nestled in the sand, a glowing ball of broken pieces and prickly fins.

He had to choose. Me, or the girl.

He surged forward and grabbed my hands, and for a moment, I thought he had picked me. And despite the pressing ache in my caved-in chest, I felt a flicker of warmth, a bud of hope that our fractured hearts and the wavering connection within them could be salvaged. But then I realized how hot and sweaty he had become despite the night chill, and everything inside me sank.

"I'll be right back," he bit out, glancing over his shoulder, searching for a girl with flowers in her ginger hair amidst the dancing festival lights. "Please, Evanora, stay right here. I . . ." He grunted, squatting in front of me. "I can still fix this."

Fix this? Which part? Everything was ruined.

"Just stay here," he pleaded quietly, running a hand over the curve of my cheek. "Believe in me. Believe in the plan. I just . . ." He stood, his knees cracking with the effort. "I have to go."

Grayson took another handful of steps away from me before stopping again. Shoulders hunched, he looked back at me, his eyes heavy. "Forgive me," he whispered, knowing I couldn't.

I said nothing as the boy bolted across the beach, kicking up sand as he flew. He yelled the girl's name, over and over, until his voice was raw, his words cracked along the edges. I watched until he vaulted up the stone steps leading away from Black Sands Beach, until the dancing festival lights swallowed him whole, until I could no longer hear his frantic voice drifting in the wind.

And in the sudden enveloping stillness, in the company of purring waves, twinkling stars, and a sliver of moon, I could have sworn I heard my heart shatter completely.

CHAPTER SEVENTY-NINE

GRAYSON

APRIL 30 – EVENING

DON'T LEAVE.

I could feel the words tumbling along the thread that connected our hearts together.

Don't leave me.

I didn't want to. God, I didn't want to leave Evanora. Leaving her by the pier felt too much like I was abandoning her, like I was throwing away everything we had built. Castles made of sand, plans made of sea breeze, a fire of passion and hope made of toothpicks.

I knew that even if I did return to the water's edge, the mermaid wouldn't be there.

Gritting my teeth, I pressed on. My lungs were already burning, my boots filled with sand, my legs on fire.

I had to get to Holly. I had to find her before more damage could be done, before she found someone and explained the horrors she had witnessed. Who would she find first? Her parents? Pa? Mayor McCoy? Who would bother to listen to her in her state of panic?

My boots slapped onto the stairs, the sudden transition from liquid sand to unmoving stone sending my heart slamming into my rib cage, my bones jarring, my teeth clattering. I took the steps two at a time, willing my aching body to remain intact and upright. After I found Holly, it could do whatever it wanted. It could collapse, break apart bit by bit. It could cease to exist for all I cared.

"Holly!" I cried out in a gasping breath as I cleared the last step and stumbled in the direction of the city square. "Holly, let me explain!"

The streets were empty, the city silent. I wasn't chasing her anymore; I was yelling after a ghost. If I weren't so consumed by desperation, I might've marveled at how well the Warren children could hide.

I turned down mazelike streets, panic twisting inside me, sharp and raw. It battered at my chest, roaring for release. I could feel its heat in my ears, its growls in my mind. *Find her. Catch her.* For a brief, terrifying moment, I didn't want to find her. I wasn't sure what I'd do if I did.

The city square loomed, lights flashing, sounds crashing over me. My heart raced, but my body froze. The music had stopped, but the bonfire still blazed, filling the air with heat that scorched my lungs. The crowd danced, wild, half naked, their bodies twisting with the flames. Stomping their feet as they howled at the crescent moon, they weren't human anymore.

The Hunt had begun.

Unable to shake the cold shiver crawling down my spine, I forced my eyes away from the thrashing crowd. I had to find Holly. I had to—

"Grayson?"

The muscles in my neck went taut as I slowly turned to the voice. It was deep, dark, drenched in anger.

A small group was huddled next to the wooden stairs at the farthest edge of the stage. Holly was sitting on the steps, doubled over and breathless, and even amidst the thundering bellows of the crowd, I could hear her sobs, see her tears as they dripped onto the ground. She was sitting next to Jasper, who was clutching his head and wincing, pulling his hand back every so often to inspect it for blood. The siblings were surrounded by Mayor McCoy, Mr. Grieves, and Pa.

Shit. *Pa.*

It was his voice I had heard, his fury I felt pummeling me from across the square. At the sound of my name on his lips, the small group, in the middle of whispering comforting words and handing out handkerchiefs to Holly and Jasper, froze.

They all stopped and stared at me.

Pᴀ's ɢʀɪᴘ ᴡᴀs ɪʀᴏɴ ᴀs ʜᴇ ʜᴀᴜʟᴇᴅ ᴍᴇ ᴜᴘ ᴛʜᴇ ᴡᴏᴏᴅᴇɴ sᴛᴇᴘs ᴀɴᴅ onto the stage. Breaking out of it was next to impossible, but it didn't stop me from trying.

"Let go of me!" I growled, ripping uselessly at his fingers clamped around my arm. "What are you doing?"

Pa's face was stone—silent, implacable. He didn't entertain me with a response. Mayor McCoy, struggling to silence the crowd, shouted, "Citizens! Your attention!"

The people didn't stop. They continued to cackle and shake their naked skin at the fire. Sighing, Mr. Grieves strode across the stage, casting a disdainful look at me as he passed. His voice cut through the night like thunder. "Brothers and sisters of Lethe! A moment of your time."

The crowd immediately fell silent.

Mayor McCoy stepped back, defeated. Mr. Grieves continued, his face grim. "The Final Festival: A night to unleash your wild nature, to become one with your kin, your people. To prepare your body, your mind, your *soul*, before the Hunt tomorrow." He paused, pinching the bridge of his nose. "But it seems there is someone here who doesn't share our mindset. There's a traitor in our midst."

He snapped his fingers. Pa jerked me forward with a grunt.

Mr. Grieves sighed, as if the act pained him. I almost believed him—until I saw the wicked grin creeping up his lips. "Grayson Shaw."

As one, the crowd began shrieking, a great wave of noise that sucked the air from my lungs. The sea of people gnashed their teeth at me, stomped their bare feet, mangled their hands into crude gestures that would've made me blush on any other given day. I ducked as a shoe was thrown at me, clenching my jaw as a pewter mug—still full of beer—collided with my shoulder. Pa's grip was steadfast. His expression didn't even change when a second mug pelted my left shin, causing me to yelp and hobble back a step.

Mr. Grieves held up his hands, stifling the mob's outcries. "Yes," he agreed somberly, "yes. I understand your outrage." He patted his chest. "I'm angry too." He swung out an arm, gesturing at my hunched form. "The makings of a great hunter. Young, strong, and brave, with a keen eye for detail and instincts that border on the supernatural." Mr. Grieves tucked his hands behind his back and turned to face me. "I'm very, *very* disappointed in you," he said in a low voice for only me to hear.

Words failed me, so I spat at him instead. A thick glob splattered across his cheek. Mr. Grieves recoiled with a grunt of disgust. Mayor McCoy rushed forward, snatching Holly's handkerchief and offering it to him. Mr. Grieves waved him away, wiping the spit off with a flick of his wrist and sending it to the floorboards.

"Do you care to know what Grayson was doing?" He scowled at me, still talking to the audience. "While you were all celebrating at the Final Festival, do you wish to know where he was?"

The audience boomed, the volume of their voices causing the stage to vibrate.

Mr. Grieves pointed a condemning finger at me, the tip of it shaking in my face. "He was at the beach, consorting with the enemy. A *mermaid.*"

Several members of the crowd dropped to their knees, wailing as they clutched their faces in horror. Others made the sign of the cross against their naked chests. Some raised more things in the air to throw at me. My eyes swept over a blur of pewter mugs, glass bottles, and half-eaten hot dogs. I growled as a bun sailed over my head. Crazy. This was *crazy.*

"History's repeating itself!" someone from the crowd yelled.

I wanted to shout that we weren't repeating history. Evanora and I were *creating* it. But another pewter mug whizzed by my ear, and I clamped my mouth shut.

"Oh, yes," Mr. Grieves sneered, his voice dripping with malice. "While we were here, pledging ourselves to the Hunt, cleansing our bodies, minds, and souls, this boy was with a mermaid. He sat there, fondling her scales while she exposed her *wretched,* unholy nakedness for him. And what do you think they were talking about?" His teeth flashed at the crowd. "They were planning which of you would go missing next! They discussed which soul would leave this world too soon."

I whipped my head at him, my bladder clenching. "What?" I choked out, my voice stolen by the audience's hateful gasps. "That's not true!" When Mr. Grieves ignored me, I turned to Holly, shaking so hard that Pa had to adjust his grip. "Holly," I uttered. "What did you do?"

Eyes filled with tears, Holly dropped her head, her bottom lip trembling.

"Harland Finch, April Abbott, Rosemary Little, Markus Bridge," Mr. Grieves continued, his voice cold and commanding. "A few names in the ever-growing list of the missing or dead. Because of people like *him.*" He shook his head as if the betrayal pained him. He clenched his fists and shook them at the crowd. "Enough! Enough with the bloodshed! Enough with the broken hearts mourning lives stolen too soon!"

The crowd erupted in deafening agreement, stomping and shouting.

"The mermaids didn't do it!" I cried out, fighting to be heard over the thundering affirmations of the crowd. "They had nothing to do with those missing people!"

Mr. Grieves tossed me a scornful look. "And let me guess—*she* told you that?"

I jutted out my chin, looking him in the eyes. "Yes."

The crowd boomed with laughter, but I didn't cower.

"And you know what else she told me?" I asked, turning my glare at the crowd.

Mr. Grieves raised an eyebrow but didn't respond.

"She told me that they don't want to fight," I bit out. "They never have. They have absolutely no desire to quarrel with us; they only retaliate because we constantly force them to." I swallowed hard, turning my pleading gaze to Pa. "They don't want the Hunt. They just want to be left alone."

The crowd went silent. Jasper scoffed. Holly kept crying. Mayor McCoy's mouth dropped open with shock. Mr. Grieves sniffed, shaking his head.

Pa's mouth pressed into a thin line, and though he didn't look at me, his grip loosened the slightest bit. I tried again, focusing solely on him. "Pa . . ." I whispered. "There doesn't have to be a Hunt."

Someone jolted to their feet in the crowd, pointing an accusing finger at me as he adjusted his stained collar. "He's been seduced!" Pastor Kline cried. "The mermaid has worked her witchcraft on him. He's been bewitched!"

"I haven't!" I argued. "I—"

Mr. Grieves was beside me in an instant, pulling me out of Pa's grip. "He's a danger to us all!"

"Justice!" a crowd member cried.

"He deserves to pay!" another screamed.

Pa tugged me back toward him with a confused scowl. "What are you doing? Let go of my son!"

Mr. Grieves's face darkened, his fingers pinching the skin beneath my jacket. "Hand Grayson over, Mr. Shaw." He smiled coolly. "Unless you wish for me to use force." His icy-blue eyes flicked over to the edge of the stage, where Mr. Brightly, Peter, and Ambrose were making their way to the front of the crowd, fists raised, hate bleeding from their tongues.

Pa's grip slackened again, but he didn't let go. "What are you going to do with him?"

Mr. Grieves sucked on his teeth. "Grayson Shaw has been caught fraternizing with the enemy. He will remain in the jail cells underneath the courthouse until a proper trial can run and his guilt can be exposed for all to witness." He nodded his head at the restless audience. "He's betrayed them all. They deserve to watch justice take place, don't you think?"

When Mr. Grieves yanked on my jacket, Pa resisted once more. "I'll take him home," he offered quickly. "I'll make sure to punish him properly."

Mr. Grieves was already shaking his head. He held out a soothing hand at the writhing crowd. "I think it's fairly obvious that that won't suffice. Now"—he cocked his head to the side, his eyes sparking with a quiet madness—"if you don't hand Grayson over, I'll have no choice but to assume that you are involved in this devilry."

Pa's breath hitched, and his hands slipped off my arm.

"Pa," I begged as Mr. Grieves heaved me toward him. "Pa, don't do this!" But he just stared at the ground where I had once been. "Pa!" I tried again as Mr. Grieves pulled me to the stage's edge.

Pa gritted his teeth, his eyes like daggers when he finally looked at me. "I will not let you drag me into your mess. Not again . . . not anymore."

My mouth went dry, and I stopped fighting Mr. Grieves. My pa thought, to some extent, that I deserved this. And maybe I did. But watching Pa hardly resist Mr. Grieves, hearing him say that he wouldn't help, was a knife to the guts. It was worse than watching Ma fling herself over the cliff, or seeing the hate in Evanora's eyes when I told her about Nereida.

It was so much worse.

Because, in that moment, I realized that I had lost my remaining parent, and Pa had lost his last living son.

We were alive, and we were both alone.

"Grayson Shaw's trial will be held after the Hunt," Mr. Grieves announced. He glanced at the quiet night sky, sucking in a breath as his gaze danced amongst the stars. "And the trial will be the only thing you have to wait for." He looked back at the puzzled crowd. "The Hunt starts now."

My blood turned to ice. A collective gasp raced through the audience. Even Mr. Brightly, Peter, and Ambrose seemed apprehensive, their fingers like wilted flower petals on the stage's ledge.

"Now?" Jasper croaked.

"We aren't ready!" Mayor McCoy moaned.

The voices began toppling into one another, clambering over each worried groan to be heard. Mr. Grieves held up his hands. "The Hunt starts now," he repeated firmly. "The mermaids are prepared. And with Grayson whispering in their ears, who knows what else they have schemed up. We need to strike now, when they least expect it, when their guards are lowered." He squared his shoulders and stared the crowd down. "It's now or never."

The audience began to nod slowly, and when they all cried out again, there was not even a single trace of conflict. There was no groaning, or complaining, or muffled disagreements. Only vicious shrieks of enthusiasm.

"Tonight!" the crowd bellowed. "Tonight!"

"You . . . You can't!" I stammered, fighting to catch someone's attention, someone who would listen. Someone. Anyone!

"And why is that?" Mr. Grieves asked with a dreary sigh, humoring me.

A sea of eyes were on me, hungry, waiting for my response.

I swallowed. "Because . . . Because of the Cursed Beings."

The crowd immediately erupted with laughter.

"I'm serious!" I yelled, fighting to be heard above the hysteria. "They're real! I've seen them. I can *hear* them. If you go into the water now, you're all dead! Every last one of you!"

"Dead?" Holly whispered from her spot on the stairs, her tearstained eyes slowly rising to meet mine.

Mr. Grieves snorted. "Don't concern yourself with this crackpot, Ms. Warren. He's as insane as they come." He grinned, the act completely serpentine. "Don't let this betrayer strike fear into your hearts over a bedtime tale. Hurry home. Tell everyone you pass on the streets. Knock on every door, shout through every open window. Everyone needs to know that the Hunt is happening now." He shooed the rumbling crowd. "Go! Grab your weapons. Fight hard! Show those vile creatures that they cannot, *will not*, mess with us!"

"The superior species!" Peter screamed.

"The hunters!" another yelled.

The others joined in, chanting, "The hunters!" so loud that even the bonfire withered with fear.

"We will flood the ocean with our nets. We will aim true with our spears! We will not rest until every single mermaid is vanquished! Everyone must make a stand and fight!" Spittle flew from Mr. Grieves's mouth as he slashed his hand in the air. "Go!"

The footsteps of the crowd sent the ground rumbling. They had been hungry for my blood only moments before. Now they were marching out of the city square, yearning for the blood of others.

Mermaid blood.

Evanora's blood.

I ripped out of Mr. Grieves's grip enough to snarl at him. "Maybe I am some criminal for trying to find out the truth. That doesn't make me a monster!"

Mr. Grieves's grin returned. He smoothed out the loose strands of hair framing his face. "No," he sighed. "But it does make you into something far worse. It makes you different. And being different makes you dangerous."

I tried to find Pa again, but he was already walking down the stairs. I looked at Jasper urgently, my eyes wide as they reached across the space between us. "Please!" I choked out. "Jasper, don't let them do this!"

Jasper's lips curled back with disgust. "You chose this path, Shaw." He gestured at Holly, who went back to staring at her feet. "We tried to stop you. We tried to help. But you made your bed," he scoffed. "Now go sleep in it."

Mr. Grieves yanked me by the arm toward the steps. I planted my feet on the wooden platform, resisting with all my might. "You can't do this!" I shouted, my body heaving against his grip. "The mermaids . . . They won't know!"

"Yes," Mr. Grieves agreed, a muscle in his jaw twitching. "That's the point."

I had no choice but to let Mr. Grieves drag me off the stage. He ignored my weak cries, my twisting and fighting. He only held me tighter, until pain from his fingers was all I could feel, and blood was all I could see, and the cries of mermaids were all I could hear.

The Hunt. Not tomorrow, not at dawn, with the ceremonious rise of the sun. *Now.*

The mermaids would be blindsided.

It was all my fault.

CHAPTER EIGHTY

EVANORA

APRIL 30 – EVENING

DEVASTATED.

Beyond devastated. Utterly destroyed. Totally, irrevocably broken.

My ammah was dead because of Grayson Shaw. Her light had been snuffed from the world because of him.

I didn't know how I made it back to the kingdom. The moon hung like a sliver in the sky, and the Cursed Beings were hungry. Their voices slithered through the water, their tentacles and inky hands brushing against my tail. They didn't grab me. Didn't drag me into that slow suffocating death. They knew I wouldn't fight. In that broken, empty moment, I wanted nothing more than to die. But they denied me that. Another cruel game. The fun was in the struggle—the chase. They wanted me to suffer more.

I wanted to tear at my own skin, rip out my hair—anything to feel something besides the hollow ache filling every part of me. How could I possibly suffer *more* than *this*?

And, gods, my heart. I wanted to rip it out. It had betrayed me. Every time I dared to open it, someone tore it apart. Grayson, Solandis, Jorah, Illeron—they'd all taken pieces that couldn't be replaced. They'd hurt me, even if they hadn't meant to.

Never again.

I wouldn't open myself up again. The bond I shared with Grayson? It was a lie. There was no greater purpose. No fate. No serendipity. It was nothing. None of it was real.

Grayson was wrong. The ancestors were wrong. I was wrong.

"You're back!" Mavi cried when I entered the throne room. She swam up and wrapped me into a tight hug. "Thank the gods!"

The gods. I had a bone to pick with them too.

Illeron shifted from his spot near the empty throne, a grim smile on his face. "Well, do you feel better now that you've seen the boy? Have you gotten the last bit of recklessness out of your system?"

"Yes, *Grayson*," Mavi breathed, pulling away. "How is Grayson?"

I opened my mouth, but the only thing that came forth was a sob.

The warrior was immediately by my side, guiding my shaking body up the coral dais. Mavi's hands were on my back, her nervousness sending ripples cascading into the large stone pillars. I crumpled onto the throne and folded my tail up to my chest, wrapping my arms around it and burying my face into my lap. And I wept.

Illeron knew better than to speak up as I cried. But Mavi was becoming almost as inconsolable as I was. "What is it?" she whispered, stroking my hunched back. "What's wrong, Evanora?"

The warrior gently pulled Mavi away. "Let her be," he uttered. I could feel his eyes, swimming with concern, all over me. "She will talk when she is ready."

It took some time, but eventually I was drained dry of tears, and all that was left was a gaping hole in my chest that pulsed with the beat of my broken heart. I lifted my head and laid my cheek against my tucked tail. "It's over," I mumbled numbly, staring out at the kingdom beyond the throne room's gaping mouth.

Illeron blinked at Mavi, then looked back at me.

"What does that mean?" Mavi asked hesitantly.

I chuckled bitterly. "What do you think it means? It's over. Finished." I flicked my gaze to them. "We've reached the end of our little game, and it was fun while it lasted, but it's all over."

The warrior shook his head, confusion darkening his sharp features. "Evanora, you aren't making sense." He reached for me, his icy fingers a salve on my burning skin. "You are obviously tired and need to rest. We have a big day tomorrow."

I ripped free from Illeron's grasp. "You aren't listening to me!" I growled, my Gift flaring to the surface in a warning flicker. "I said it's *over*! We aren't going to pretend that we stand a chance against the humans and their spears and nets. We aren't going to fill our heads with delusions that we can actually fight back." I sighed, unfurling my tail and slipping deeper into the throne. "It's all hopeless."

Mavi tugged at her hair, anxiety radiating from her. "But . . . we're ready."

Illeron nodded, jaw clenched. "We've worked too hard to throw it all away now. The boats we've tampered with. The training. Mavi's worked tirelessly to stock us with food and supplies for the week. Are you really going to say it was all for nothing?"

It was a challenge. But I couldn't summon the strength to argue. "Yes," I said, voice hollow. "It was."

Mavi slid forward, her hands clutching the throne's armrest. "Please, Evanora." Her fingers slid forward, taking my hand. "*Talk* to us! Whatever has happened, whatever has changed, I'm sure we can fix it."

A fresh flood of tears stung my burning eyes. I laughed coldly, shaking my head. "I very much doubt that."

Illeron clutched his spear tighter. "What happened?" he asked in a low voice. "Up there, with the boy." He cocked his head to the side. "What did Grayson do?"

I gasped out a whimper, leaning my head against the throne's backrest and blinking away the tears as they pooled on my lashes. Gods, what *hadn't* Grayson done? "I don't . . ." I bit my wobbling lip. "I don't know where to start."

Mavi squeezed my hand. "At the beginning. Start at the beginning."

So, I did. I told them everything. From the moment he'd found me tangled in the net, and the bond that pulled us together. I told them about the manipulations, the betrayals, about how we'd come together in our brokenness, briefly feeling whole again. I told them about the Cursed Beings and their grip on his doomed soul, how it had twisted his mind. And I told them about Queen Nereida—how she'd died because of a boy she'd never even met.

By the time I was finished, the words were being ripped from my tight throat, shredding the skin as I forced them out. The pain in my chest had doubled in size, squeezing against my organs, making it hard to breathe.

Mavi blinked back tears. "Oh, Evanora," she moaned, leaning forward and resting her head on our clasped hands. "How awful."

Illeron ran a hand over his face, letting out a long breath. "To think . . . this *entire* time . . ."

"Her death was the thing that connected us," I finished for him. I snorted softly, shaking my head. "What a cruel joke."

"The gods and ancestors have a strange sense of humor—that's for sure." Mavi tilted her face to look at me, her dark curls swaying in the water like anemones. "But, Evanora, this shouldn't have to change anything. Our plan—"

I hissed, pulling my hand out from underneath hers. "Don't you understand? This changes *everything*!" I sat forward. "I refuse to trust a human who allowed my ammah to die so that he could live."

"He was just a child, Evanora," Illeron pressed quietly. "He had no choice in what happened that night."

"It doesn't matter," I snapped. "Even as a child, he . . . he should have known better." I pointed at them, my finger trembling. "Not long ago, both of you said boys like him couldn't be trusted." I laughed, a harsh, cruel sound. "Well, congratulations. You were right. I'm the fool." I dug my palms into my eyes, squeezing the tears from my lashes until my vision blurred. "I'm such a fool."

Illeron's hand landed on my shoulder, but I shrugged it off, twisting away. "How can I ever look at him again and not see her blood on his hands?" I whispered.

"I'm sure he's asking himself the same thing, Your Majesty," Illeron said, staring down at his empty hands.

Mavi swam closer, her voice soft. "It sounds like he's deeply remorseful." She cupped my cheek, her touch gentle. "We just need to get through one week, working alongside him. Then you can forget about him forever. Never see him, never speak to him again." She offered a fragile smile. "You'd only have to visit the island to sunbathe."

I tried to smile, but it shifted into a grimace. Her words filled the cracks in my heart with fleeting hope, but the connection, that damned connection, throbbed inside me, bright and undeniable. It filled the hollow space, lighting up the darkness. I turned away from her touch, scowling.

"You can't sway me," I said firmly. "My mind is made up."

I raised my voice to cut through Illeron's growl and Mavi's quiet plea. "We'll hide in the caves for a week. No one leaves. We'll be safe there."

Illeron's gaze flicked to the ceiling, teeth bared. "The cave system is for emergencies. We'll be cramped."

"And it's too dark," Mavi added, cringing. "Being in the caves for that long will make everyone's fin rot worse. Dark Madness will creep up on half the pod. Not even your Gift or my salves will stop it."

"We'll make it work!" I snapped, my voice sharp. "I won't risk my pod for an unpredictable human. We can endure for a week." I crossed my arms, ignoring how they shook. "Not fighting worked for my parents. It'll work for us."

Illeron's upper lip curled. "Yes, it worked," he snarled. "But *barely*." He swam in front of me. "We have a plan, Evanora, and it's a good plan, a *solid* plan."

Mavi crept forward. "We've worked so hard. All of us have!"

My heart throbbed painfully within me. "I refuse to work with the boy who murdered Ammah. I refuse to have anything to do with him!" I bared my teeth at them, scorching them with a rageful stare. "I would rather die."

Illeron didn't flinch. His eyes locked on to mine, unyielding. Slowly, he leaned his spear against the throne. He stretched his arms out to me, palms up, inviting. "It wasn't a human who killed Nereida," he said softly. "It was the Cursed Beings. Your ammah died fighting. She died for something she believed in, with everything she had." His hands encircled mine, and I didn't pull away as he guided me off the throne. "She would want us to fight. Your appah too. They made you a fighter, Evanora. A brave, reckless fighter made of starlight."

Mavi pressed her clasped hands against her lips. "Please," she whispered, lowering her gaze. "We know you're hurting, but don't let it swallow you whole. Don't let the world steal your light."

Illeron tugged on my hands, guiding me to the back hallway. A half smile curled the edges of his lips. "Pick up your crown. Be the queen your pod needs you to be. *Fight*."

Over the warrior's shoulder, Mavi nodded hurriedly, daring to smile around her fingers.

I could feel the determination in both of them, the fierce need to make me see clearly.

But I *was* seeing clearly. For the first time that month, my eyes were finally open, and I was seeing everything.

I would bear the weight of my pain alone. I would pick myself up, force a smile, and lead my pod—not to victory, but to surviving, like we always did. Because that was all we were capable of doing. It was all the gods and the Cursed Beings would allow. Surviving. Anything else was just too unsafe.

And when the week was over, and yet another Hunt was put to rest, and the waters calmed and the blood was washed away, I would sever the connection with Grayson Shaw completely.

I slowly pulled out of Illeron's grip, careful to keep my face clean of any trace of emotion. "Tell the pod that we leave for the caves at first light," I said calmly, turning away.

"Wait," the warrior started. "Where are you going?"

"To pray, Illeron," I said, swimming out the palace's entrance. "I'm going to pray."

For mercy. For a miracle. For an explanation.

Poseidon drown me. We needed all three.

CHAPTER EIGHTY-ONE

GRAYSON

APRIL 30 – EVENING

I LOST TRACK OF TIME.

How long had I been locked in this cramped basement cell? The low rumble of people rushing by the barred window reached my ears, their excited chatter about a surprise attack. Despite the nausea churning in my stomach, the sounds gave me hope—they weren't in the water yet. I still had time to warn the mermaids. I just needed to escape first. But I knew it wouldn't be as simple as breaking a rusty window lock.

I scanned my surroundings once more. A small square room. A thin mattress in the corner, propped on pallets of wood. A cracked sink and toilet along the wall facing the street. Flaking blue paint, the only color in an otherwise dreary space. A single bulb swayed overhead, its dull light barely reaching the corners. Beyond the bars of my cell, a dozen more stood in a dim hall, and at the end, a door to the alley. Escape. So close.

But . . . how to get there?

The bars holding me in were solid. Not a single one shifted or creaked out a complaint when I heaved on them. I hopped onto the stained toilet and tried the window. The bars against the glass were the same, and even if I were able to snap one out of place, the window was far too thin to squeeze through.

So, I tried yelling. I screamed at the top of my lungs for someone to help me. I beat my fist against the glass whenever someone passed by, shouting for them to stop, to set me free, to end this madness.

No one stopped.

My hand throbbed, my throat was raw. But I kept going. I had to believe someone would hear. Someone would see my innocence. Because if I didn't, I'd unravel. And I didn't have time for that.

I watched helplessly as the outside traffic slowed, then stopped. Tears stung my eyes. Maybe being locked up was a mercy. I'd caused enough damage. Freed, I'd only do more harm. "Please," I croaked, my voice cracking. "Someone—"

The back door creaked open, and the sound echoed down the hall. A figure stood in the threshold, cloaked in shadow, moving slowly—purposefully. I hopped off the toilet and rushed to the bars, gripping them tightly.

"Pa?" My voice was weak, stretched thin from shouting. I swallowed, trying again. "Pa?"

The figure chuckled, a honeyed sound that made my skin crawl. "Do you really think someone will save you? That you're worth saving?" He clucked his tongue. "The writing's on the wall for you, Shaw: guilty, guilty, guilty."

Helplessness welled within me. "Please, Mr. Grieves, call off the Hunt. This isn't right, and you know it."

Mr. Grieves laughed, such a bright sound from a dark man. "Strong words coming from a boy who was caught with a mermaid."

"It's too dangerous! To go out at nighttime . . . You're putting everyone at risk—"

"Oh, that old nursery rhyme again?" Mr. Grieves waved a hand dismissively. "The hunters will be fine. If I were you, I'd worry a little more about your mermaid friends." He frowned mockingly. "Caught unawares, with you stuck in here, unable to warn them?" He placed a hand delicately to his cheek. "Whatever will become of them?"

Pain, dismemberment, death. I gritted my teeth, my grip on the bars tightening until my knuckles cracked. "Please, Mr. Grieves." I closed my eyes, exhaling slowly. "Yes, okay? *Yes*, I was with a mermaid. *Yes*, I went against everything Lethe stands for and formed a friendship with her. *Yes*, I care for her—deeply—despite all mermaids being our enemies." I opened my eyes and glared at him. "But we weren't doing anything wrong. I wasn't feeding her names of potential victims to snatch away. We weren't strategizing how to make the list of Lethe's missing persons larger than it already is."

Mr. Grieves raised his eyebrows as he blinked at me in surprise. "Oh, I know that."

Everything shifted within me, the silence of the room threatening to swallow me whole. "What?"

The grin that grew on Mr. Grieves's face was a dark, deadly thing. "I know the mermaids aren't behind the people going missing."

Blood pounded through my ears. "And . . ." I swallowed hard. "How would you know that?"

"I know," Mr. Grieves crooned, "because *I'm* the reason they are missing." He shrugged nonchalantly. "But *missing* isn't really the correct term. *Dead* is more appropriate."

My mind was a swarm of locusts, buzzing and itching, eating me alive. "What?" I asked again.

Mr. Grieves shook his head. "You know, young Shaw, for being such a bright boy, I'm rather disappointed that you didn't catch on sooner."

"It's . . . It's been you?" Mr. Grieves swam before my eyes. The ground tilted and swirled. I stumbled back until my feet hit the wooden pallets, and I slumped onto the bed. "All this time, it's been you?"

Mr. Grieves tilted his head to the side. "You sound rather upset."

Dizzy spells be damned, I jerked my gaze back up to snarl at him. "You killed innocent people! You . . . You killed children! You should be in here, not me!"

Mr. Grieves held up a finger. "To be fair, I targeted people who were considered useless to society, those who could never participate in the Hunt. Harland was deaf. April was blind. Markus had a bad heart." He sniffed drearily. "You get the picture."

A strangled laugh tore through my throat. "That doesn't make it any better!"

"Of course it does." Mr. Grieves began to pace outside my cell, hands tucked neatly behind his back. "The island is faltering. Businesses closing, more people fleeing to the mainland, fewer tourists arriving after the Hunt to buy our goods." His polished shoes tapped sharply on the stone floor, his midnight-black cloak snapping at his heels. "I needed to stir the hearts of the islanders. Give them a reason to fight. A reason to make this the best Hunt ever."

He stopped and spread his arms, as if presenting an award. "And it worked! I've never seen such passion in the hunters. The more hunger they have, the more effort they put into hauling mermaids in. And mermaids,

Shaw, are money. Those scales? Makeup. Their hair? Wigs, dresses, blankets. Mermaids are the answer to our dying island."

He grinned, leaning closer, wagging his finger. "And you getting caught with one of them? That was the icing on the cake. The islanders were in an uproar. I should be thanking you. You gave them the final push."

Mr. Grieves was looking at me like I was supposed to break out into applause. Instead, I sneered at him. "You're a monster."

"Ah." Mr. Grieves shook his head. "My hands may be dirty, but so are yours. People will eventually forget the poor souls snatched away in the middle of the night. They will grieve, and then they will move on. But you?" He grinned at me. "They will never forget the fact that you fell in love with a mermaid."

My breath caught in my raw throat. The connection hummed with so much energy that I wondered briefly if I was going to spontaneously combust. Love? I'd never been brave enough to say it, let alone think it. But the way Evanora's smile made every inch of me hurt, the way her touch made me want to explode into a thousand colors, the way I wanted to steal time just so I could spend it with her . . .

Yeah. Love.

It was suddenly ridiculously obvious. I was a blind fool for not noticing it earlier. As my heart continued to swell, my mind a kaleidoscope of everything Evanora, I allowed myself to wonder if she felt the same way.

After what I had confessed about her mother, probably not.

"I wasn't alone in my endeavors, you know," Mr. Grieves went on, oblivious to my internal turmoil. "Ambrose was the muscle behind the plan. And he was good at it too." Mr. Grieves puckered his lips, rubbing at his chiseled jaw. "Up until Rosemary, that is." He sighed with disappointment. "He didn't want her to be a target."

I had a desert in my mouth. I swallowed, trying to ease the painful dryness. "Why did you make her one, then?" I croaked. "There was nothing *wrong* with her."

Mr. Grieves rolled his eyes. "Maybe so, but she wasn't pure-blooded; she wasn't from the island."

"She was Ambrose's girlfriend!"

"She was the one no one expected to go missing," Mr. Grieves explained patiently. "If we had picked another health-challenged individual, it would have been too suspicious. We needed someone healthy to build panic. And she was close to our family; no one would dare to think we were behind the dastardly deeds if our sweet Rosemary Little were to disappear." Mr. Grieves pointed a finger at me. "But you did."

I slowly stood from the bed. The ground still shifted and bent at my feet, and my body felt like a thousand pounds. I wanted nothing more than to curl up in a ball on the bed. "What?"

Mr. Grieves's mouth quirked to the side. "You suspected something, didn't you? At the combat challenge." He whistled lightly. "You were really pushing my buttons about it, really asking the hard questions." He picked an invisible speck of dust off his pristine cloak. "I wanted you to be next, after that."

He said the words so lightly, so casually, like he wasn't talking about death . . . *my* death. I couldn't help but scoff, lifting my arms helplessly. "Well?" I asked haughtily. "Why didn't you kill me?"

"Oh, I tried. Trust me." Mr. Grieves grinned. "I tried. It was Ambrose who struggled. He said the first time he tried, you threatened him with your hunting knife." He shook his head, tsking. "Naughty, naughty. And the second time, at the Night of the Betting, you were causing a scene with that Warren boy, so he had to improvise."

My stomach heaved violently. "Markus Bridge."

"Markus Bridge," Mr. Grieves agreed. "A rather solid plan B, but still, I must say, I was rather disappointed when Ambrose stormed into my office later that night and I found you, alive and well, hot on his heels."

I ran a hand over my face. "What makes you think I won't tell Mayor McCoy any of this? Or the police?" I laughed, looking up at the ceiling. "God, I could tell literally anyone what a scumbag you are, anyone at all!"

Mr. Grieves cocked his head to the side. "And what makes you think they'll believe you?"

My blood turned to ice.

Mr. Grieves rubbed his thumb over his lip. "After all, you're the traitor who was found sharing information with the enemy, not me." Mr. Grieves shifted away from the bars, sighing heavily as he turned for the back door. "You know, I really had high hopes for you," he said somberly. "Too bad you had to go and ruin everything." He tipped his hat to me with a wink. "Well, I must be off. I don't want to miss any of the fun!"

And with a whirl of his cloak, Mr. Grieves descended into the shadowy hall, cackling under his breath, more beast than man. The door slammed behind him, and before the silence could sink in, the voices crept forth.

The one who was promised.

I groaned, squeezing my eyes shut. "Get out of my head!" I shouted, clamping my hands over my ears.

Promised One!

"Make it stop!" I shrieked, high-stepping onto the bed. The room was too small. The walls were closing in, the ceiling collapsing on top of me.

Here.

"Stop it!" I twisted into the corner, cowering in its shadows as the voices wailed, and wailed, and wailed.

Here!

Blood was pouring into the room, thick and hot and—

"Grayson."

I flinched into the wall so sharply that I smacked my elbows into it.

The screaming abruptly stopped, filling my body with their fading echoes.

"Grayson?"

Holly was standing behind the barred wall, clutching her shawl tightly, her long hair loose and unkempt. Her eyes darted between the room—perfectly in one piece and blood-free—and me. "Is . . . Is this a bad time?" she asked hesitantly.

I should have been furious with her. I should have felt scathing rage at the fact that she was standing in front of my cell when she was the reason I was in it in the first place. But all I felt was joy. I clambered off the bed, my legs nearly buckling with the impact. "It isn't safe for you to be here!" I said, grabbing the bars that separated us, daring a peek at the back door. "Mr. Grieves is—"

Holly shook her head. "Mr. Grieves is heading to Black Sands Beach with the rest of the hunters." Her brow furrowed with concern. "They really mean to set out tonight."

I groaned, leaning my head against the bars. "What a mess."

Holly bit her lip. "Are there really monsters out there?" she whispered. "Those . . . Cursed Beings?"

Mouth set in a grim line, I nodded.

Holly's chin quivered. "And if the hunters go out now . . ."

"They will experience something far worse than mermaids," I finished for her. "And the Cursed Beings won't stop until every single one of them is dead."

Holly placed a hand to her chest, sucking in a shuddering breath. "It's all my fault. If I hadn't run off after seeing you, they wouldn't be . . ." She choked back a whimper. "Oh, God, it's all my fault."

I wanted to agree with her. A sick, twisted part of me wanted to rub her dainty nose into the problem she had created until it was nothing but a stub. I sighed, wilting against the bars. "You should probably go," I said. "Before someone catches you in here." I shrugged stiffly. "Can't be seen with the traitor."

Holly blushed, smiling shyly. "About that . . ." She unfurled her shawl, revealing a string of keys around her neck.

I blinked at her. "Where did you get those?"

Holly took off the necklace of keys and immediately began sorting through them. She picked one and lined it up to the door's keyhole. "I searched each office until I found them." She tried another. "As it turns out, I'm fairly good at breaking into desk drawers."

I widened my eyes in surprise. "I never took you for a thief, Holly."

"Well . . ." Holly gritted her teeth as she stuck another into the keyhole. It went into the lock but didn't turn. "I never took you for a daredevil who associates with mermaids."

"Fair enough." I watched as Holly tried another key, then another. "If that's how you feel about me, why are you here?" I gestured to the thinning pile of keys in her hands. "Why are you helping me?"

Holly paused, blowing out a heavy breath to get a strand of hair out of her eyes. "I don't agree with you playing around with mermaids, especially the day before the Hunt. But you being locked in here seemed . . . wrong."

It seemed wrong. One of the first things Evanora had ever said to me. That day on the beach, when she was planning to kill me. But instead of ending my life, she'd asked for my name. My chest tightened at the memory. "Holly, you know that once you set me free, I'm going to fight back, right? I'm going to try to put a stop to it all?"

Holly grunted, thrusting another key into the hole. "I know," she growled, twisting the key with all her might. The lock clicked out of place, and with a groan, the door eased open. "Because I'm going to fight back too." She straightened with a relieved sigh, giving me a sardonic grin. "We aren't on the same side," she clarified, pointing her finger at me. "But I refuse to let my family rush into an ocean crawling with monsters."

My heart leapt into my throat. I held out my hand to her. "Care to stop a war with me?"

Holly snorted, rolling her eyes. But she took my hand, her grip warm and steady. "Absolutely."

We started for the door, but I stopped, forcing Holly to a halt. "Wait!"

Holly resisted as I began to lead her back down the hall. "What's wrong?"

"I need to grab something."

Holly tugged on my hand. "This isn't the time to raid the judge's liquor cabinet!"

"What? No." I coaxed her down the hall. "Though a boost of liquid courage sounds good right now. Did you see anyone else in the courthouse when you were snooping for the keys?"

Holly shook her head. "No," she said, letting me drag her forward a handful of steps. "No one's here."

I nodded, sucking in a breath. "Perfect. They still might be upstairs, then."

Holly dug her heels in. "Grayson, wait—stop!" She let out an exasperated sigh. "What is so important that you would risk losing time over?"

I turned to Holly with a grin, the shadows of the jail dripping over my face. "A signal."

T HE CITY SQUARE WAS ABANDONED, THE BONFIRE NOTHING BUT smoldering embers and a snowfall of ash. Holly stuttered to a stop, her hand tightening in mine. "Everyone's already gone!" she squeaked, looking around at the empty space frantically.

I tried not to let my panic show. It was happening too fast. Time was flying before my eyes; I'd never be able to catch up. "Where is your family?"

Holly wiped her freckled cheeks, which were shining with tears. "They must've gone home to prepare like Mr. Grieves asked."

I nodded quickly. "Then we might still have time." I pulled her forward. "We can ride Penny together."

Penny was less than impressed to carry two riders, and she was downright annoyed that we expected her to gallop.

She eventually did, but only after I promised to never ride her or put her to work ever again.

We rode in silence, our minds too full and our tongues too heavy. We raced as fast as we dared in the night, tears streaking from our eyes as we searched the darkness for signs of life—or signs of death. Holly jostled and twitched in front of me, a ball of nerves, afraid of what she might see, and what she couldn't.

I dropped Holly off at the Warren house. The home was wrapped in shadows; not even the porch lantern was lit. No one was home. "Run as fast as you can to Hannigan's Cove," I directed as she slid off Penny's back. "Try to stop anyone you come across from getting in the water."

Holly brushed the hair out of her face, looking up at me with eyes wide with fear. "Where are you going?"

I clenched my jaw and bundled up the reins. "To sound the alarm."

I didn't wait for Holly's reply. I kicked Penny into motion again, thankful the Clydesdale was still game to run.

I wasn't surprised to find my own house empty and dark. I leapt off Penny before she came to a complete stop and raced as fast as my legs could carry me.

Past the house, past the barn, and into the woods looming beyond.

I followed the trail I knew by heart. Under the sweeping trees. Across the chirping brook. Through the weeds, over the fallen trees with their mangled roots sticking up like daggers. I didn't flinch when branches clawed at me. I didn't yelp when brambles tried to slow me down with their thorns. I crashed through the tree line and into the clearing of Howler's Hill. Breathless, sweating, and bloody, I made my way over to the ledge.

I could just make out Hannigan's Cove from my spot on the cliff's edge. The beach was spotted with lights. They flickered back and forth excitedly, the movements looking almost like dancing ghosts. There were so many that I couldn't count them all. I couldn't hear anything above the wailings of the cliff, but I didn't need to. I knew who the lights belonged to.

Hunters.

A whole sea of hunters.

Heart in my throat, I scanned the water. No lights visible there yet. The boats weren't in the ocean. I still had time.

Swallowing hard, I pulled the flares from my pocket. They had remained tucked away in the office, just like I had hoped. Mr. Grieves hadn't thought to grab them yet, likely blinded by his self-righteous madness and need for blood. I could only carry three. I prayed it would be enough.

I strode over to the cliff, leaned as far over as I dared, and raised my hand in the air.

I pulled the trigger.

CHAPTER EIGHTY-TWO

EVANORA

APRIL 30 – EVENING

I DID NOT PRAY.

I did not sit in solitude, meditating on the words of my ancestors, daring to ask for enlightenment.

I did not pour my heart out to the gods, casting my cares and troubles into their plane of existence.

I did not silence my mind, hoping to hear more riddles that I would not be able to decipher.

I raged.

I stormed into the garden, my body a blur of glowing white. I screamed at the top of my lungs and created sandstorms with my tail. I shrieked and slammed my fists into the boulders. I cursed the world and ripped up the colorful plants. Schools of fish spooked and fluttered off. A seal sailed into the safety of the seaweed forests.

I raged, and raged, and raged.

And when I stopped, hovering in the middle of the shattered remains of the garden, my shoulders heaving with heavy breaths, my nerves like lightning in my veins, I felt nothing but emptiness. I was swollen with it, a hateful loneliness that bloomed within me, threatening to staunch my blood flow, suffocate my lungs, choke my heart.

I sank to the floor next to the scattered sand and plant debris, wanting so desperately to be numb, wanting to feel anything other than the agony that coursed through every inch of me.

Unfair. It was all so unfair. If only I had listened to Jorah and hadn't gone off on a scouting mission. If only I hadn't gotten caught in that net. If only I hadn't met Grayson Shaw. If only I were braver, and stronger, and better at being a leader.

If only Ammah and Appah were here.

So many if-onlys, I didn't know what to do with them all.

Blinking back my tears, I curled up my tail and slipped onto my side. "I wish . . ." I murmured into the empty garden. "I wish it were different. I wish I could take it all back."

A flicker of movement beside me. I lifted my head enough to see wide onyx eyes full of galaxies staring back at me. The octopus cocked its pale head, sliding one of its limbs along my quivering arm. Soft, soothing, its suction cups popping gently as they pressed and released. I hastily wiped my eyes, sniffling as I opened my arms for the creature. The octopus took my silent invitation and sidled into the space I'd created, nestling against my chest and sticking its long arms against me. Our heartbeats mingled, and my breathing slowed. I closed my eyes and tucked my face into the octopus's soft head.

Evanora.

I opened my eyes. I was still alone in the garden, nothing but the undercurrent stirring in the broken reeds and torn flowers. But the voice had sounded close.

Evanora.

I shifted, clutching the octopus against my chest as I looked around. I swallowed, my eyes darting from boulder, to coral, to the darkness beyond. There was no way of knowing who it was, but I could feel in my singing blood that it was friendly. It wasn't the Cursed Beings playing tricks. It was like . . . home.

"Hello?" I called out hesitantly, my voice shaking and unsure.

Evanora, here.

The octopus was looking right at me, its large endless eyes peering into my soul—beyond it, into the fiber of my being. I blinked at the creature. It narrowed its eyes at me, a shudder of blue rippling through its pale white skin. It's grip on me tightened—not painfully, but enough to get my attention. And, gods, it had my attention. I sucked in a breath.

"Who are you?" I breathed.

The octopus's arms slackened. *A friend. A messenger.*

I glanced around a final time, making sure no one was pulling a hoax on me. The octopus raised a limb and pressed it against my cheek. *Not there. Here.*

I gulped audibly. "How is this happening? How is this . . . possible?"

The octopus's syphon sputtered. *The ancestors are growing restless. They've been trying to reach you.* The octopus cocked its head to the side, fluid and graceful—much too graceful for an animal. *Have you shut them out?*

Guilt burned at my cheeks. I *had* shut them out. "They kept speaking in riddles. It didn't make sense." A startled laugh escaped my throat, and I covered my face with my hands. "None of this makes sense."

The octopus sighed—actually *sighed*—and relaxed into me. *I imagine it doesn't. You've been through a lot recently. My poor Evie.* The octopus's eyes grew heavy, sadness sweeping through them. And for a second, just a split second of frozen time, I saw a splash of violet mix in with those black orbs.

My breath caught in my throat. "Ammah?"

The octopus paused, as if in thought, then slowly shook its head. *A piece of her. Channeling.*

My heart leapt against my rib cage. Nereida . . . talking to me through an octopus. How absurd and impossible and perfect. Tears sprang to my eyes, and I straightened, taking one of the octopus's arms in my hands. "It's really you, Ammah? This isn't some . . . trick?"

The octopus's suctions tickled my fingers. *For now. I can't stay long.*

Stay long? I had too many questions, too many thoughts weighing on my heart. She had only just arrived, and for the second time in my life, she was threatening to vanish without a trace. Fear swept through me, brittle and biting, and I gripped the creature harder. "You can't leave me again!" I begged.

The octopus vibrated in my arms, and I realized it was laughing. *I'm always here, little Evie. You only need to open your heart and clear your mind.*

I steadied my breathing. We couldn't have any semblance of a normal conversation if I was a frazzled mess. I wiped my face and nodded shakily. "What is your message?"

The octopus stilled. *You need to fight, Evanora.*

I barked out a laugh. Of course that was the message. Why had I expected anything else?

Your story isn't done, Ammah continued through the octopus. *And neither is Grayson's. You both still have parts to play. Together.*

I bit back a snarl. Over my dead body. "Please," I said quietly. "Please don't make me go back to the boy who murdered you. I can't . . ." I swallowed around the lump in my throat. "I can't bear to see him again, knowing what he did."

The octopus vibrated again, shifting into a gentle red hue. *The boy didn't do anything to me, Evanora. I wanted to help him. His life wasn't meant to end that night, and mine was.*

Growling, I ran a hand through my hair as frustration blossomed within me. "Why?" I moaned. "Why didn't you tell me what happened sooner?"

It wasn't time.

Such a stupidly simple answer. I didn't care for it at all. "It wasn't time?" I laughed bitterly. "I've spent years, literal years, wondering what happened to you, and your answer is that *it wasn't time?*"

The octopus continued to stare at me, its limbs undulating delicately. *Yes.*

I placed a hand over my chest. I wasn't sure when my heart had begun roaring again. "I just . . ." I sighed. "I just don't think I can do it, Ammah."

Yes, you can. Because you are my daughter. Because you are queen. Because you have to.

Another simple answer. I shook my head. "It's not that easy."

It is. The octopus gripped my shoulders. *All you need to do is believe that it is.*

"You and Appah weren't fighters."

Ammah chuckled. *Oh, yes we were. We simply fought for different things. We fought for love, for peace, for understanding. So desperately we wanted to mend our broken ties with the humans.* The octopus's arms rose in a shrug. *Alas, we failed. Perhaps we were too quiet. It is time to be loud.*

The connection strained, signs of life tumbling along it. I hated how it still took my breath away, the very essence of it, of being tied to Grayson Shaw, of being part of him. I hated how much I wanted to sever it, knowing that I likely couldn't survive without it. "Will you tell me about the power of three? About Grayson being a key?"

The octopus melted against my chest. *All will be revealed.*

A spike of impatience in my bloodstream. "When?"

Soon. Tonight.

I opened my mouth, then quickly clamped it shut when the octopus stirred. *I must leave now. Don't shut the ancestors out again. They might appear to you in a shark next time.*

Despite the joke, the fear returned. Unable to help it, I held the octopus closer. "Please don't leave."

The octopus gazed up at me, and I saw those splashes of violet. *Go, Eva-nora*, Ammah commanded through the octopus. *Go, and finish your story.*

Panic gripped me. "Wait," I whispered. "Wait!"

The voice began to fade. *The power of three, Evanora. He is the key. The key. The key.*

I let out a shuddering sob. "Ammah, please!"

The octopus looked at me, and I knew.

Nereida, the great queen of the waters, was gone.

Silence fell upon the garden. The ruined flowers tossed and turned in the undercurrent. The seaweed danced. The sand drifted and settled.

I wanted to stay there forever, wrapped in the warmth of the memory of my ammah.

But I couldn't. Because there was a fight to be won.

I uncurled from the octopus, running my fingers gently over its bulbous head. "Guess I'd better go now," I whispered. "This riddle isn't going to solve itself."

The octopus sighed heavily, its syphon expanding and contracting. It lifted a limb and stuck it to my cheek.

I laughed, something between mirthful and mournful, and peeled it away. "Oh, you."

The octopus stared at me for a long moment before curling up its limbs and hovering in front of me. I smiled. I felt . . . lighter . . . liberated.

Free.

Something shifted inside of me, allowing space for hope to take seed. I couldn't remember the last time I had felt anything so pure. It was almost euphoric.

I couldn't forgive Grayson for what had happened. But I could work with him. For my ammah, for my pod, I could.

I SWAM AS FAST AS MY TAIL WOULD LET ME, YET IT STILL DIDN'T SEEM fast enough. The lava-rock path was a steady stream of white beneath me, illuminated by the faint glow of my nerves.

I had to get to Illeron and Mavi before they told the pod. I had to tell them that we were going to—that we *needed* to—fight.

The night surrounded me like an obsidian cloak, sapping all light and life from the surrounding waters. It felt especially ominous tonight. I glanced at the surface overhead, eyeing the small sliver of moon anxiously. Barely any light danced from the thin slice before the encroaching darkness swallowed it.

The darkest night. An ill omen.

I started to look away, focusing on the path blitzing ahead of me, when I saw it from the corner of my eye.

A flash of red. Bright as the stars scattering across the sky.

I stuttered to a halt, blinking hard, breathing harder. But as quickly as they had come, the lights were gone; the sky was clear, no trace of red. I rubbed my eyes and looked again.

And there it was, a cascading fire flurrying in the night.

The flares.

The hunters were setting off the flares.

I gasped, my hands fluttering to my mouth. *No*, I moaned inwardly. *No!*

Illeron burst into view, racing along the path like the Cursed Beings were at his back. "Something is wrong," he choked out, coming to a rigid stop in front of me. His hair was ruffled, like he had been dragging his hands through it, and he was clutching his spear so tightly that I feared the weapon would snap in his grip. Every single one of his silver-and-crimson scales was rigid and raised, the fins on his arms like razors.

I ripped my gaze from the warrior and dragged it along the surface, watching as the showers of red blinked and fizzled out and the world grew dark once more. I felt like I was dreaming, stuck in a warped vision my ancestors had created. "I thought we had more time."

Mavi came next, tumbling through the dark in a rush of purple scales and wild honey eyes. "The flares!" she squeaked. "The hunters are firing the flares!"

"I don't understand," I said slowly, my words feeling thick. "It is not yet dawn."

"It can only mean one thing." A muscle twitched in Illeron's sharp jawline. "The Hunt," he breathed. "It's begun."

My scales instantly tensed. We had run out of time.

Mavi clutched her hands at her stomach, a whimper on her tongue. "No," she moaned. "No, no, no, no!"

The warrior's grip grew impossibly tighter on his spear. "What do we do, Your Majesty?"

I stared at the surface. The dream was swallowing me whole. I was drowning in it, seeing nothing but an abyss of night and fire stars and hungry hunters with spears for teeth. I wondered when we would see the boats, feel the nets in the undercurrent, hear the ugly cackles of humans.

"Evanora!" Illeron barked, taking my arm. "What do you want us to do?"

The warrior's touch was grounding. I loosed a wavering breath and gave my head a quick shake. I couldn't unravel again, not when my pod needed me. I turned sharply to the warrior and Mavi. "Where is the pod?"

Mavi continued to wring her hands together. "They are in the throne room. We had begun telling them about"—she started to frown but quickly stopped—"about the change in plans. But then we saw the flares, and—" She gave a meek whine, tangling her fingers into her hair roughly. "Oh, gods. The flares. The flares!"

I exhaled sharply. The pod was together. The pod was safe. "Good," I said firmly. "That's good." I looked at the wielder. "Tell everyone to return to their homes."

Mavi's mouth dropped open, her hands slipping off her head.

Illeron growled. "Neptune spear me—now is not the time to gather precious belongings!"

I pursed my lips together, leveling the warrior with a cool glare. Illeron grunted, lowering his eyes. "Tell everyone to return to their homes," I repeated, slowly turning back to Mavi. "And tell them to grab their armor and weapons."

It was Illeron's turn to be shocked. He nearly dropped his spear and had to fumble to retrieve his grip.

Mavi lurched toward me, a hopeful smile on her lips. "We're going to fight?"

My heart, which I had thought was so hollow, so shattered, brimmed with love. I chuckled lightly, taking the wielder by the shoulders. "Yes, Mavi," I breathed, pulling her close. "We are going to fight."

Mavi sucked in a gasp, her eyes shining, her grin so large that it nearly lit up the ocean. Illeron threw his head back and howled, raising his spear into the air. I shied away, my light mirth turning into something deeper, something far more delicious than being numb.

Another flare darted across the sky, and the laughter was quick to fade; the weight of reality pressed against our shoulders with a sickening dread. I waved my hands at them, coaxing them into silence. "We must make haste. Grayson told us we would have time to travel to the beaches when we saw the flares." I frowned. "However, with the flares going off now and not tomorrow morning, it would be wise to assume that some of the Hunt's rules have been adjusted."

Illeron's face became stoic once more. He rubbed his bottom lip thoughtfully. "We will simply have to make changes of our own."

I looked at Mavi, determination swimming within me. "Tell the pod that we will meet back up in the throne room when we have gathered our supplies. We will devise a plan together."

Mavi nodded hurriedly and broke out in a swift stride, aiming for the palace.

I turned to the warrior. "Take the merlings and those who do not wish to fight to the cave system. They will be safe there." I glanced at the surface. "We don't know how many flares they will fire before the hunters are in the water." I looked back at Illeron with a sigh. "I wish we had more time."

Illeron dipped his head, but he didn't move. He continued to stare at me, his expression unreadable.

I faltered, frowning at him. "What?" I asked, self-consciously tugging on my hair.

Illeron finally swam forward, his brittle expression cracking to produce a coy smile. He passed his spear from one hand to the other. "What changed your mind?"

I pondered for a moment. "An octopus," I said with a laugh.

The warrior arched an eyebrow at me before shaking his head with a snort. "You will never cease to amaze me, Evanora."

My chest went tight. I nodded at the path. "Make sure everyone is ready," I said as I began to swim away. "We have to hurry."

Illeron blinked at me. "Wait . . . Where are you going?"

I turned, my tail flicking playfully as I swam on my back. I winked at the warrior. "Accessorizing."

Illeron's mouth dropped open, but he quickly recovered. Placing a hand on his chest, he bowed deeply. "My queen," he said with a low chuckle.

I swam to my room. In the distance, I could feel the wielders breathing life into the water, hear the excited shrieks of sirens. The benders stretched out their Gifts, practicing, preparing. I inhaled deeply, my heart swelling with hope. Only moments before, we'd been about to flee to the cave system to cower in the dark for a week. Now we were rising to meet the night with our spears.

The crown sat on the table in its eight-year slumber. My fingers fidgeted at my sides as I gazed upon its might. Fear wedged its way into my thoughts. *What if it doesn't fit?*

I bit my lip and slid closer.

What if it's too heavy?

I reached out my hand.

What if I look ridiculous?

I closed my eyes when my fingers touched the arch of jewels.

It wasn't made for me.

I opened my eyes. No more swimming away. No more hiding. "Yes," I seethed into the empty room, "it was."

Before the fear could punish me further with a reply, I picked up the crown and placed it gently atop my waterfall of hair. The wreath of woven metal and shells hugged my head, its center gem dangling against the middle of my forehead. I traced my fingers along the edges of shells and jewels as they swept like frozen waves, undulating together until they crested in the middle. The jewels glistened and shimmered as I turned my head left, then right. It didn't move. It was a perfect fit. It was heavy, but I could bear it. I *would* bear it.

I exhaled slowly, a giddy chuckle escaping with it.

A night of war lay before us, a night of pain, and bloodshed, and death. I bared my teeth, my Gift crackling beneath my scales, power surging through my skin. Let the hunters come. I was ready. We all were. Because our stories weren't yet finished.

Illeron was right: We had a solid plan. But we would have to make some adjustments. It was nighttime, after all.

And there were things out there far worse than the Hunt.

CHAPTER EIGHTY-THREE

GRAYSON

APRIL 30 – EVENING

I was out of flares. There was nothing left for me to do but wait. Wait to see if they saw my signal. Wait to see if they would act.

Holding my breath, I peered down the cliff at Hannigan's Cove. The boats were hovering at the water's edge, the lantern lights glinting like a thousand winking eyes.

They were getting into the water.

My feet moved on their own. I rushed back to the house, panting as I scanned the abandoned space. Penny was near the barn, sniffing the wooden siding. I scrambled onto her back, offering her a quick pat on the neck as she huffed in annoyance. "Just one more ride," I promised as I dug my heels into her sides. "Just one more, then you can rest."

No further persuasion needed, Penny shook her head, reared up a step, then bolted down the path. She moved so fast that I nearly toppled off her back. I gripped the reins and leaned down, ignoring the pain as tendrils of her mane whipped against my cheeks. We blazed a trail of dust down the road, a blur of movement as we sailed through Tully. We were like lightning, like the wind.

I couldn't let them get into the water.

Was Evanora still going to follow through with the plan? Did she still believe in it, in us?

I ground my teeth and coaxed Penny faster.

The boats were off the shore by the time Penny and I tumbled onto the beach. I leapt off her back and stumbled forward, breathless, my heartbeat throbbing in my ears. A ragged gasp lurched up my throat as I watched helplessly from the safety of the sand. The boats swayed amongst the waves, the hunters within them crowing and cackling as they raised their nets and spears.

I was too late.

A final boat was being pushed into the surf, its lone rider thrusting the wooden beast forward, steering it around the waves. I took a small step forward, holding out my hand. "It's . . . It's too dangerous!" I tried to call out, my voice cracking, getting lost in the wind.

The hunter stilled, his thick tattooed arms rippling as he gripped the stern. The waves thrashed against the boat, pulling it farther out into the ocean. They licked at the hunter's clothes, soaking him up to his waist. In the sliver of moonlight, I could see his hands shaking as he turned back to the beach, his dark eyes finding mine.

Pa and I looked at each other for a long, heavy moment.

I took another step. "Pa," I whispered, knowing he couldn't hear me. *Turn around. Come back to shore. I'm sorry I'm a failure. Come back to shore!*

All the things I wanted to say to him. All the things I couldn't.

Pa's gaze was scathing as he shook his head slowly, and even with the distance separating us, I could feel his disappointment. It clung to me like a second skin, made me want to break out of my frozen stupor and race onto the boat with him. Anything to make him proud, anything to make him know that I still loved him despite everything that had happened.

But all I could do was watch numbly as Pa clambered onto the boat and paddled away from shore.

It was like watching Ma fling herself off the cliff all over again.

"Grayson!"

I blinked through my tears to see Holly running toward me. I had been so focused on the boats that I hadn't seen her near the caves. Her deep purple skirts were covered in sand, her cheeks ruddy with exhaustion. She pushed her hair out of her face, the flowers wilted and missing petals. She gulped down breath after breath, her eyes wild with fear as she looked into the ocean.

"I tried to stop them," she wheezed, wiping her wet nose. "I tried everything! But . . . But they wouldn't listen!"

I bit my lip, my insides contracting. There was nothing I could say that would make the morbid situation any better. We were too late. We had failed. I placed a hand on her hot shoulder, giving her a gentle squeeze. "Thank you for trying," I mumbled, unable to take my eyes off the retreating boats.

Holly sniffled again, straightening from her hunched state. "What happens now?" she asked meekly.

My mouth went dry. "I . . . I don't know."

We stood in silence, the weight of it pressing down on us, our lungs too tight to breathe, hearts pounding too wildly to settle. We could only watch. Wait. And pray death wouldn't come.

What would it look like? Tentacles ripping through the water, hauling hunters from their boats, swatting away spears like twigs? Or would the Cursed Beings creep closer, their clawed hands raking the hulls, splintering through the wood with disturbing ease? Would the hunters panic, diving into the water, only to be swallowed whole? Or maybe they would hear the voices that had tormented me for so long—voices that would drive them mad enough to turn on themselves.

There was nothing.

Then, movement in the water. My breath caught.

Heads broke the surface, slow and deliberate. One by one, droplets glistening on their silken hair, water clinging to them like they were born from it. They weren't just rising—they were claiming the ocean as their own.

The hunters stared at the mermaids.

And the mermaids, they stared right back.

EVANORA

THE BOATS DREW CLOSER.

I held my breath, bobbing in place, Illeron at my side, the warriors and mind benders behind me. The hunters paused from their grunting and rowing to stare at us. A handful pointed, open-mouthed and breathing heavily. Some grabbed for their spears. Whispers fluttered along the water's edge, sidling up to me and draping me in poison.

"Mermaids! They're really here!"

"There are so many."

"That white-devil bitch will make us a pretty penny!"

"Is that . . . Is that a *crown*?" There was a laugh. "Pretty jewelry won't save you, princess! We'll still cut you to pieces!"

Illeron growled beside me, lifting his spear.

"Wait," I breathed.

The boats crept closer.

I loosened my grip on the spear, my fingers instinctively reaching for the lantern tied to my waist, the seaweed now slick with sweat. One of the last-minute adjustments. Every mermaid had one. A lantern buzzing with my light, reinforced by Mavi's water.

Below, Mavi, the sirens, and the water wielders huddled on the ocean floor, encircled by a ring of lanterns. The eerie glow stretched far, casting long shadows across the sand, wrapping around the beach and most of the boats. But not all.

Mavi blinked up at me, her face tense, waiting for the signal.

The Cursed Beings were closing in, moaning against the lantern barrier, testing for weaknesses. Predators above. Predators below. We were surrounded.

I smiled grimly. Perfect.

A flash of movement. I flinched, expecting to see a spear sailing toward me, to feel cool steel biting into my flesh. But the boats were still too far away, the eager hunters busy rowing. I jerked my head in the direction of the beach, where two figures stood on the shoreline. A girl with vibrant copper hair smothered in dying flowers, and a boy with oceans in his eyes.

Grayson Shaw.

His gaze found mine. Wordlessly, he pressed his hand to his chest, his eyes locked on me.

Despite the incessant tugging of my heart, I glowered and looked away, focusing on the boats.

Let him stand there and worry. If he still had a part to play, his window to play it was rapidly closing. It wasn't my problem. *My* problem was slowly lumbering toward us through unruly waves and crawling below us in the depths where light dared not tread.

We are hungry, the Cursed Beings lamented. *So very hungry.*

I looked down just in time to see one of the lanterns flicker, then go dark. Mavi gasped as an inky tentacle shot through the gap, thrashing as it searched for its prey.

The sirens and water wielders scrambled to the center of the circle, huddling together as the tendril pulsed and split, transforming into a gnarled hand with claws the size of my arm. Black blood swirled through the undercurrent as the hand began dragging itself forward with a shriek.

"Evanora," Mavi whispered, panic enveloping her cracking voice.

"Wait," I urged again.

The boats were closer now. Many of the hunters had given up paddling and were pressed against the bows, leaning over the wooden edges, their knuckles white as they held their spears above their heads. The butts of the weapons were wrapped in thick strands of rope—a vicious tool to stab, secure, and reel in. Other hunters gathered their nets into bunches, shaking the wads of rope so the bells jingled tauntingly.

"Come here, fishy," one of the closest hunters crooned, tapping his spear against the bow playfully. "I'm not gonna hurt ya . . . much."

Illeron looked at me expectantly, his eyes flashing with a loud fury. I gritted my teeth and shook my head.

"Evanora!" Mavi cried out again as another lantern extinguished and more tentacles surged through the new opening.

We are hungry! the Cursed Beings bellowed.

The boats were upon us. In the distance, thunder clapped in the sky, an earth-shattering roar carried on the backs of the blanket of clouds. A spark of lightning, and then the sky split open, showering us with icy rain. The wind picked up, howling in my ears, in my thoughts, as the heavens mercilessly poured onto us.

The closest hunter stood on steady legs as the boat tipped and jostled amidst the growing waves. He closed one eye and aimed his spear right at me, grinning like he was deranged. "Yer mine!" he growled.

Illeron choked out a gasp and made to move in front of me. "Wait!" I barked.

The warrior reluctantly froze, his tail twitching with barely contained aggression.

The hunter threw his arm back, grunted, and sent the spear hurtling toward me. It sliced through the air, strong, true, deadly. I jerked my head to the side just in time, feeling the rush of wind and the heat of the wood as it passed by my ear. The tip of the metal brushed my skin, a sharp sting of warmth trailing down my neck, the scent of blood and metal thick in the air.

The spear barely hit the water before the hunter yanked it back, cursing under his breath, rope sliding through his hands.

Another lantern went out.

"Evanora!" Mavi shrieked from below.

FEED US! the Cursed Beings screamed.

I grinned at the darkness. *As you wish.*

I found Mavi's desperate gaze and bared my teeth. "Now!" I screamed, my voice filling the entire ocean.

Mavi sucked in a breath, furrowed her brow, and unleashed her Gift onto the circle of lanterns. A wall of water spiraled forward, working its way outward from the center where Mavi hovered, until it connected with the remaining lights with so much force that I could feel the ripples of its power in my scales.

The lanterns toppled to the ground, empty, drained of magic.

And the darkness came.

GRAYSON

EVANORA SCREAMED SOMETHING, A SINGLE WORD, BUT I COULDN'T hear what it was above the sound of crashing thunder and the droning of rain.

But I watched in horror as the dim lights dancing underneath the water flickered out. I wiped my drenched face and squinted. I could still make out a couple faint orbs of light glowing underneath the ocean's swell, but they were scattered, shifting and undulating in the undercurrent.

Holly clung to me, whimpering as she buried her face into my shoulder. I held my breath. The icy rain pricked my skin, made all of me numb. But I didn't dare move. I didn't dare look away.

But . . . nothing happened.

The hunters sat in their boats, their spears and nets still poised above their heads, ready to send down a shower of their own upon the mermaids. But Evanora didn't move. Neither did Illeron, nor the other mermaids behind them. They just kept bobbing at the water's edge, watching the hunters.

Watching . . . and waiting.

There was a startled cry as a boat lurched—not with the waves, but to the side. The boat went still, then darted again. The movement was strong, fluid, calculated.

A mermaid couldn't move it like that.

The hunter gripped the gunwale, staring at the water with wide eyes, peering into the darkness.

There was a deep, malicious groan, the sound of wood splintering.

The boat disappeared.

Not split down the middle like Evanora and I had planned. Not broken just enough to pull the hunters into the ocean. Not even capsized.

The boat just . . . vanished.

Alarmed mumbles filtered through the air as the waves crested and crashed. Hunters hesitantly lowered their spears and looked at one another, confusion and panic gripping their weathered faces.

Another boat slipped out of sight.

Then another.

Another.

And all I could see was Warrick getting pulled to his watery grave. Over and over. Every time a boat was pulled beneath the waves, I saw his face. Every time a hunter cried out before getting swallowed by the darkness, I saw Warrick's scared smile.

The Cursed Beings were here. And they were famished.

The hunters started to scream, their voices hoarse and riddled with fear. They began blindly throwing their spears into the water, hurling their nets. Some still aimed for the mermaids. Most were aimed at nothing, clearly hoping to strike whatever silent, invisible terror preyed upon them. But their spears returned empty, their nets hollow.

"Don't be a bunch of sissies!" I heard someone cry. "They're just trying to scare us!"

"Well," another voice squeaked, "it's working!"

My breath caught. Holly clutched me tighter as she began to cry.

Jasper. That was Jasper's voice.

I searched the battlegrounds, flinching with every strangled wail that reached my ears, my heart leaping every time I heard the sound of wood being torn apart. "Where are you?" I moaned, my eyes darting from boat to boat. "Where are you?"

The ocean began to churn, its deep gray color shifting to almost black. It was phase two of the plan: The water wielders were using their Gift to make the water unruly.

And, God, it was working.

Waves the size of cars, the size of buildings, began spilling against the boats, knocking them around like they were nothing but pieces of driftwood. Fat gobs of foam splattered the hunters, blinding them and making their grip slippery. With the storm raging above and the storm swarming from below, it would be impossible to see, to swim, to steer.

The hunters were trapped, and they didn't even know it.

"There!" Holly cried, pointing a shaking finger at the carnage.

I followed her finger to the boat that was stuck in a whirlpool. It spun and spun, slow, lazy circles that grew faster with each turn. The boat creaked and groaned as it fought to remain upright.

And there was Jasper, caught in the middle, his arms wrapped in a net that he was desperately trying to fling over the edge. Like it would save him. Like it would stop his impending doom. The boat tilted and veered, nearly throwing him overboard. Jasper clung to the gunwale, his pale face tight with fear as he slowly righted himself with his limp arms. He swiped the hair plastered to his forehead and began to sort out the net again.

"Oh, *God*," Holly sobbed, covering her wobbling mouth with her hand, her eyes bright with tears.

"He's okay," I whispered, pulling Holly in close. "He's okay."

Holly, knowing I was lying, only cried harder.

Jasper finished untangling the net and lurched to the side of the boat. He began to slowly push it over the edge, a hopeful smile on his face.

The smile was wiped off when a webbed hand reached from the center of the whirlpool and clamped around his wrist.

The net slipped out of Jasper's hands. His eyes went wide with shock as the head of a mermaid slowly broke through the water's surface, a cruel grin on its face as it tightened its grip on him. It leaned in, nose to nose with Jasper, its eyes never shifting, its grin never leaving. Jasper was frozen, his face turning a deathly shade of white as he stared into the mermaid's eyes.

I blinked, and the mermaid was gone. And then, so was Jasper.

With a single yank, Jasper was ripped from the safety of the boat and into the wild water below.

"*No!*" Holly screamed.

I was already moving.

Blood pounded in my ears as I searched for something, *anything*, that could get me into the water.

Jasper couldn't die. I wouldn't let him. I refused to think anything otherwise.

My blurred vision fell onto a boat tucked against the caves. Huddled next to the lip of the craggy rocks, it almost blended right in.

I raced to it as fast as my legs could carry me.

EVANORA

WHAT ARE YOU DOING?" I MURMURED AS GRAYSON RAN DOWN the beach. "What are you *doing*?"

And that was when I saw it.

The abandoned boat next to the caves.

I cursed under my breath as the boy slowed to a stop before it, his shoulders stiff, his chest heaving. "Don't do it," I moaned. "Don't do it!"

Grayson's worried gaze trailed along the water a final time before he grabbed the bow and began hauling it toward the water with quick, vicious tugs.

I sighed quietly. The damned fool. I told him not to go into the water!

I gave my head a rough shake. I could not focus on that right now. I had bigger things to worry about, like not dying.

The key, my ancestors whispered in my ears. *The power of three!*

I growled, tempted to shut them out again. The heart had no place on the battlefield, and I refused to let it get the better of me. "Illeron!" I called out over my shoulder as I propelled myself underneath a boat and began stabbing at the wood. "How's it looking?"

The warrior grunted as he broke through the boat he'd been working on and thrust his hand into the opening. "Just *peachy*," he replied as he ripped the hunter through the space and carried him deeper into the water. When he returned, his hands were empty, and there was blood dripping from his lips. "Everything is going as planned," he said, dragging his forearm against the crimson stain.

Another change—kill any and all hunters. Illeron was especially pleased with that adjustment.

I paused from assaulting the boat to raise an eyebrow. "War looks good on you."

Illeron dipped his head sarcastically. "That is the highest compliment you've ever given me."

I glanced down, taking quick inventory.

The water wielders were pressed together, maintaining the unruly whirlpools, the crashing waves. The sirens shrieked and wailed, creating a hysteria that pulsated throughout the undercurrent. The mind benders worked at coaxing the remaining sane hunters to leap into the wild ocean. The warriors paired off, one attacking the boats, the other waiting to snag a hunter once the hole was made.

The Cursed Beings ate up our scraps—sometimes reaching the boats first, pulling them under in a single swipe.

As I searched the water, attempting a head count, I realized with growing dread that, sometimes, the scraps included us.

I couldn't see the high-spirited Daithi anywhere.

Reading my mind, Illeron shook his head slowly. "Daithi is gone," he uttered softly. "Matthias too."

I gasped, my fins flaring as a flood of grief drowned me. "How?"

Illeron winced. "Matthias took a spear to the chest. And the Cursed Beings got Daithi."

My hand subconsciously went to my lantern. Glowing, alive. "That's not possible," I seethed. "The lanterns—"

"They've been burning for a long time," the warrior reminded me gently. "It must be tiring, constantly having to spend your Gift on keeping them lit while simultaneously fighting for your life. And with there being so many lanterns, some might be weaker than others. Some of them were bound to go out, whether you want them to or not."

I growled, gripping my spear tighter. "Mavi!" I barked. "How are you?"

The wielder glanced up at me, and the look on her face was answer enough. She was exhausted, the color drained from her vibrant skin, the purple sapped from her scales. Her tail wilted as she forced a twitching smile. "Never better!"

Liar.

Illeron placed a hand on my shoulder. "Stick to the plan," he said forcefully. "We knew this would be dangerous. We knew there would be casualties." His grip softened. "You can't save everyone." He nodded at the boats above us. "The hunters are confused and scared right now. We have them right where we want them."

I exhaled sharply. "In the middle of chaos."

The warrior cocked his head to the side, a hard smile on his tight lips. "Exactly." He brushed the hair out of my eyes. "You know"—he chuckled—"war looks good on you too."

I scoffed, batting him away. "Get back to work."

Illeron rolled his eyes. "Your Majesty," he drawled before fixing his gaze on another boat and swimming for it.

I rammed my spear into the boat I was working on, the wood splintering with satisfying force. Grinning wickedly, I reached through the hole, snagging a confused hunter. He barely managed a yelp before I pulled him under.

His eyes were wide, mouth puffed with air. I smiled sweetly, batting my eyelashes. He squirmed, muffled whimpers rising in my ears.

I raised my fin to his neck, ready to strike.

Only kill when necessary.

Grayson's words sifted through my mind. I hissed at their intrusion. The hunter gaped at me, a rush of bubbles exiting his tightly sealed lips. I bared my teeth at him, my fins pressed tightly against his vulnerable neck. But they had grown frustratingly soft as Grayson's words played on repeat, until his voice was all I could hear.

If they try to hurt you, hurt them back.

The hunter before me didn't look like he wanted to hurt me. He looked like he was going to be sick. With a sigh, I pushed him away. "Swim to shore," I growled, glaring at him. "Now."

The hunter nodded hurriedly and began to paddle to the surface.

Ours! the Cursed Beings snarled from behind me.

Two slimy black hands surged forward, catching the hunter's legs and dragging him into the shadows. But not before tearing him in two first.

Nausea burned inside me, but I gritted my teeth against it, swallowing the bile down. Clouds of blood sifted into my vision, pooling around me.

Then long strips of skin, then twisted tubes of intestines. Then an eyeball, wide and unblinking as it floated by me.

I choked out a disgusted groan and swam upward, fighting to get away from the blood-soaked horror. When I surfaced, I took a long, cleansing breath, ridding my lungs of the scent of torn flesh. I wiped off my face and ran a hand through my hair, hissing with annoyance as it came back bloody and flecked with skin.

Ours!

I turned to see a dark hand surging toward me, claws dripping with blood.

I inhaled sharply, extending my arm. A weak flare of light shot from my fingers. The Cursed Beings recoiled, howling as they retreated.

Panting, I placed a shaky hand over my heart and tilted my head back, letting the rain wash the gore off me. *Breathe*, I commanded inwardly. *Just breathe.*

When I opened my eyes, I found myself face-to-face with a hunter. He was huddled in his boat, trembling, eyes wide with fear. He shivered so violently that he nearly slipped out of his seat. His hat drooped from the rain, his black robes dripping like liquid night.

I nodded at the spear he clutched against his chest. "I think that's meant to be pointed at me," I said smoothly.

The hunter gulped, fidgeting with the white collar tucked around his neck. Hesitantly, he lowered the shaft with gnarled hands, his narrow face taking on a waxy pallor. I nodded encouragingly as he leveled it with my chest. The hunter was shaking so hard that the tip kept losing its mark.

I cocked my head to the side. "Go ahead," I offered, rising higher out of the water and straightening my spine, exposing more of my vulnerable chest to him. "Give it a try."

The hunter's thick, wispy brows pinched in concentration, and he thrust the spear forward with a cry.

The weapon toppled out of his numb fingers before he had a chance to finish the attack, tumbling into the water with a pathetic splash. Mumbling rapidly under his breath, the hunter began reeling the spear back in.

But I was there, clutching the gunwale, pulling myself up so we were eye level and nearly nose to nose. I smiled at him politely as I leaned over the lip of the boat. The hunter whimpered, and the biting smell of urine filled the air. Fumbling in his pocket, he pulled out a small silver container. He brought the bottle to his lips, drinking long and hard. The next thing he pulled out was a glass vial. Without taking his eyes off me, the hunter popped off the lid and began splashing the fluid onto my face with vicious, poignant strokes. "The power of Christ is upon you!" he cried with every vehement pass of his hand. "With this holy water, I cleanse your spirit, demon!"

I paused, then daintily wiped my cheeks with a small sigh.

"Are . . ." The hunter swallowed hard. "Are you cleansed?"

I grinned at him, flashing my sharp canines. "Oh," I crooned, "absolutely."

I grabbed him by the crooked white collar and gave a hearty tug. The hunter's shriek was cut short as he tripped over the boat's side and fell face-first into the water.

Laughter bubbled up my throat as I slowly lowered myself back into the awaiting waves. *Humans*, I thought ruefully, rolling my eyes.

I was almost underneath the surface when a hand landed on the back of my neck.

I didn't even have a chance to scream.

CHAPTER EIGHTY-FOUR

GRAYSON

APRIL 30 – EVENING

I COULDN'T TELL IF THE BOAT HAD BEEN TAMPERED WITH.

I didn't care.

I grabbed the boat by the bow and began hauling it toward the ocean.

Promise me you won't get in the water.

I froze, Evanora's voice clashing through the sirens in my mind like a tidal wave, muffling their roars.

You must *stay on the shore.*

I clenched my jaw, my fingernails digging into the wood. I had promised her that I'd stay as far away from the beach as possible. But Evanora had also promised me that nothing I could ever say would affect our bond. She had said that our connection could hold the burdens weighing down my soul.

She had lied.

And so had I.

I pulled the boat against the sand, grunting as the bottom dug in, resisting my desperate tugs. The boat wouldn't budge; it was stuck in a deep groove of sand and rocks. Panic flared within me as I yanked with all my might. "No," I moaned. "No, no, no!"

I had to get into the water. I had to help Jasper. I had to do *something*! I let out a roar of frustration as my cramping hands slipped off the bow. "Move, damn it!"

Hands sidled up to mine as Holly gripped the boat. Her face, splotchy and sweaty, was grim with determination. Her eyes flitted to mine, and together, we began to pull, wordlessly working to wrench the boat free.

I could have wept when the boat began to move. Slowly at first, and then the sand gave way, and the boat sailed toward the shoreline. The waves rose to meet the boat, arching the bow into the sky.

"Get in!" Holly cried as she moved to the stern.

Yes, the Cursed Beings seethed. *Get in, Promised One. Get in.*

I scrambled into the boat's belly, not giving my fear a chance to fester. There was no time for it. I could still see Jasper's boat, circling in the whirlpool. Every once in a while, his head would burst above the waves beside it, thrashing wildly underneath a tangle of ropes before getting dragged back under.

It was only a matter of time before he stopped coming up at all.

Holly continued to push me in. Foam covered the hem of her skirts, the waterline inching its way up her legs. She squawked at the biting chill, but she didn't stop. I fumbled for the oars and seated them in place. The boat lurched forward, the ground disappearing beneath it.

Come to us, the entire ocean seemed to shout. *Come to us!*

"Go," Holly panted, backstepping onto dry ground. "*Fly.*"

I dipped the paddles into the water.

I took a breath, my heart beating its own death march.

And I rowed as hard as I could.

The waves tossed my boat like it was weightless. Every muscle in my body was clenched as I fought the ocean, steering blindly, praying I was heading toward Jasper. I passed boats—some abandoned, some still holding frightened hunters, battling the hands reaching for them.

I locked eyes with Mr. Brightly before his boat vanished beneath the churning depths. Owen Morris screamed as webbed hands tore through a hole in his boat, claws trying to drag him down.

Faster, I thought as red-hot pain burned down my arms. *Faster!*

Ahead, Jasper surfaced, gasping, writhing in his net. I was close—just a few more strokes and I'd be able to reach him.

But then the mermaid rose to the surface, yanked the net, and dragged him under.

Painful stillness, and then Jasper broke through the waves again, his eyes wide in panic. A heartbeat later, the mermaid pulled him back down.

They were playing with him.

Rage surged. I grabbed the spear nestled at the bottom of the boat. When Jasper resurfaced, I lunged, seizing the net. The rope burned in my hands as I held him above the water.

Jasper coughed out a lungful of ocean. "Help," he croaked. "Help!"

I clenched my jaw and began sawing my way through the rope. "Hold on, Jasper!"

The mermaid's hands were on the net again, playfully tugging at the loosening strands. I gasped as pale green eyes rose above the surface and stared up at me, a coy smile on the mermaid's lips. He gave the net a teasing pull. I jerked it back in my direction and kept hacking away. A loop snapped free. Then another.

"Help!" Jasper cried again.

The mermaid narrowed his eyes into slits, tightening his hold on the net. He pulled on the ropes again, and there wasn't anything teasing about it. He was growing tired of games. He was ready to kill.

I bit my lip and poured all my strength into the net. When a third loop frayed open, I buried my hand inside the tangled ropes, grasping frantically for any piece of Jasper I could find. My fingers grazed the collar of his shirt, and I dug in, gripping as much of it as I could before pulling up. "Kick, Jasper!" I bellowed.

Jasper's legs began flailing. Little by little, he began to rise. The net slipped over his shoulders, tumbled down to his waist, and wedged around his legs.

The mermaid hissed and reached for the net, his claws like daggers as they ripped at the ropes clinging to Jasper's knees. Jasper yelped frantically as the nails shredded through his pants and found skin.

"Come on!" I roared, hauling Jasper higher. "*Fight!*"

The mermaid stuttered to a halt, his grasp around Jasper's legs slackening. A strangled cry left his mouth as he glanced down at his waist, where the glowing lantern dangling there fizzled out.

The mermaid swallowed a whimper, his green eyes finding mine once more. He gave me a long beseeching look before three tentacles arced through the murky water, wrapped around his waist, and wrenched him into the dark.

A deep, inky-black laugh echoed in my mind. *You'll be next, Promised One. We see you.*

I swallowed my shock and finished pulling Jasper into the boat. Jasper tumbled over the ledge, falling into a heap on the floor. He coughed and gagged, salt water and spit dripping from his lips as he clutched his twitching leg where the mermaid had left his mark. Blood oozed through the ribbons of fabric, coating his fingers. Through the rain, the hot metallic smell wafted up my nostrils.

But he was alive. Hurt, dazed, scared shitless, and alive.

I stifled a gag and reached for the oars again, preparing to return to shore.

The Cursed Beings knew I was there; I had to get out of the water as soon as possible. It was too dangerous to linger. Like the mermaid with Jasper, the Cursed Beings were toying with me. They had been all month. It was only a matter of time before they grew bored of the game and wanted the prize.

Jasper sucked in a ragged breath, his head swaying as he looked up at me. "Why?" he whispered, voice so quiet that I had to lean forward to hear him.

I furrowed my brow and pushed the paddles into the water. "Why what?"

Jasper gulped, wiping his mouth with a limp hand. "Why did you save me?" He shook his head slowly. "After everything... After..."

I gave him a long, heavy look, daring to slow my rowing. "Because you're my best friend, Jasper."

Color returned to Jasper's cheeks, and his face crumpled as he dropped his head and began to cry.

"I'm sorry," he moaned. "God, I'm so *sorry*, Grayson!" He wobbled upward until he was sitting. "I promise I'll spend the rest of my life making this up to you. I'll become celibate. I'll let you break my other leg. I'll pick stupid flowers for you so you can practice botany! I'll do whatever it takes for you to know how sorry I am."

Jasper continued to prattle off ways he could fall back into my good graces as the boat connected with the shoreline and he toppled out of it.

But I wasn't listening.

Because through the crashing rain and the turbulent waves, I saw Mr. Grieves.

Mr. Grieves, who should have been in Fariid. Mr. Grieves, who should have been hunting far, far away from here.

Mr. Grieves was here, in Tully, hunting at Hannigan's Cove.

And he was holding Evanora by the neck.

EVANORA

THE HAND YANKED ME UP, ITS GRIP ON MY NECK SO VICIOUSLY tight that every tendon and muscle screamed in protest, my vertebrae cracking, the blood in my system grinding to a sickening halt. The pain was a blinding inferno as the hunter hauled me into the air.

With unnatural strength, he lifted me from the water with one hand, throwing me into the boat with a savage howl. My back collided with the hard wood. Pain lanced through me, my dorsal fin in agony as I slithered to the floor, my tail curling helplessly beneath me.

He was on me instantly, grabbing my flailing arms with one hand, reaching for my neck with the other. I gasped, my neck muscles already anticipating the brutal squeeze, twisting and spasming in reflex. My eyes darted to my forearm fins, limp and useless. The hunter straddled me, pinning me down, his weight crushing me into the boat. His grin was twisted, dark as the Cursed Beings, dripping with malicious satisfaction.

"Out of the water, away from your friends." He cocked his head to the side. "Not so tough now, are you?"

I wrenched one of my hands free, and with a growl, I dragged my nails across his cheek. The hunter jerked his head back with a bellow as blood immediately began to gush from the four deep gouges. I scuttled back, but there was nowhere for me to go in the small boat.

The hunter lurched forward and grabbed at me again. He snarled, bending low until his face was close to mine. He grabbed my hands again and threw them above my head. "You know, you're awfully pretty." The hunter dragged a finger lazily up my waist, between my breasts, until he was caressing my jawline. "For a vile creature."

I snapped my teeth at him, missing the tip of his finger by a breath. The hunter wrenched his hand back with a loose chuckle, shaking a finger at me. "So much *fight* in you!" He pushed a lock of white-blond hair out of his eyes and reached back, pulling out a knife sheathed at his leg. "I'd like to see you fight your way out of this." He touched the tip of the blade against my cheek, sliding it carefully up to my eye. The knife's teeth kissed my eyelashes.

I swallowed, leaning away from the blade. "If you start with my eyes, then at least I wouldn't have to gaze upon your wretched face."

The hunter pulled the knife away, tapping it lightly against his chin as he assessed me. "Perhaps I should start elsewhere, then." He grinned, cold and vicious, as he lowered the tip of the blade onto my abdomen. "So you're able to see the fun I have planned for you."

The blade dug in, the tip disappearing into my flesh.

I hissed, squirming as blood leaked around the wound. The hunter bared his teeth at me, looking more monster than man. "When I'm done with you," he seethed, "I'm going to make sure I carve up every last mermaid on this godforsaken island!"

The knife bit deeper, my fragile skin posing no obstacle. My hiss turned into a feral cry.

"But I'm going to take my time with you, beast," the hunter continued, twisting the blade, savoring my pained moans. "I'm going to make sure you feel every single thing I do to—"

Thwack!

The hunter's eyes went wide, his jaw dropping in disbelief. A trickle of blood appeared at his widow's peak, running down his forehead and dripping off his nose. He tried to follow the trail with his eyes for a dazed moment, the knife slipping from his hand. Then he lurched backward, crashing onto my tail with a shocked groan.

I surged upright with a growl, kicking his legs off me and pressing my hand against the wound, blood still leaking from the cut. It wasn't deep, but without magic, it wouldn't heal anytime soon.

I stopped, my breath a fleeting thing.

Grayson stood in a boat next to the one I was in. He held an oar with shaking hands, his shoulders heaving with heavy breaths.

I blinked, not trusting my eyes. "Grayson," I whispered.

Grayson dropped the oar and clambered into my boat, his movements jerky and lethargic. He pointedly kept his eyes off the downed hunter. "Are you okay?" he asked shakily as he crouched next to me.

I eyed his green complexion, the way his hands trembled. "Are you?"

The boy's body convulsed as he stifled a gag. Hand covering his mouth, he nodded.

With the threat gone, my anger flared to life. I smacked Grayson's arm with a growl. "What are you doing here? I told you to stay out of the water!"

Grayson rubbed at his arm where I had struck, his eyes narrowing. "That's a bizarre way of saying *thank you*."

I rolled my eyes. "*Thank you*. Now go back to shore."

The boy looked like he wanted to agree with me, but he still shook his head fervently. "Not until I know you're okay." He dared to peek at my hand on my stomach, letting out a shuddering exhale. "You're hurt."

I gritted my teeth. "I've experienced worse pain."

Grayson's head jerked up, droplets of water spraying everywhere. His eyes swam with sadness as his hand clutched his chest, pulling at his shirt, like he wanted to tear at the skin hiding underneath. "Because of me," he whispered.

Something inside me caved, my heart crumbling along with it, and I found myself shaking my head, though every part of me wanted to shout *yes.* "Grayson," I breathed, wincing as I shifted closer. "We are bound by something deeper than fate, something older than . . . gods . . . than life itself. I meant what I said before: Our hearts beat as one. They always have, and they always will, and nothing will ever change that." I exhaled slowly, tilting my head. "I've experienced worse pain, but not because of you. *Never* because of you."

Grayson shook his head. "But . . . But your mother. I—"

"My ammah chose her path." I lifted a hand, placing it gently against his tight cheek. "I've chosen mine too."

The boy bit his lip, turning his face into my palm. He steadied his breathing, and when he looked at me, his eyes were clearer. "Me too."

My mouth quirked to the side. "Does it involve returning to shore?"

Grayson smiled, placing his hand atop mine. "It involves you." He kissed my hand before curling his fingers around it and bringing it to his chest. "I'm yours." His grip on my hand tightened, and the connection between us sparked like a thousand suns, a million gems, hot with need and yearning and everything we didn't have time for, but everything I wanted. "I have been since the second I saw you in that net." He swallowed hard. "If you'll have me, of course."

The key, my ancestors hummed. *The key.*

Tears sprang to my eyes. Was this what the ancestors meant? Grayson was binding himself to me, for as long as he lived. Was this what the ancestors wanted?

And I realized that it didn't matter, because it was what *I* wanted.

Letting out a mixture of a sob and a laugh, I blinked through my tears and leaned forward. Grayson smiled, wiping at my cheeks. "Don't cry."

"Foolish boy. You're crying too."

The boy wrapped his arms around me, and when we kissed, it was like the world had fallen away, ceasing to exist.

It was desperation and urgency, shared breaths and hurried heartbeats. It was life ending, and creation blooming. It was the dawning of a new day after the longest, darkest night. It was the crashing of waves upon the dry shoreline. It was nothing, and everything—*so much* of everything that a single kiss couldn't contain it all.

Grayson bit my lip possessively. "Mine," he whispered into my mouth.

I clutched him tighter, my fingernails digging into his skin. "*Mine*," I murmured back.

We were both breathless when we pulled away from each other. I glimmered on top of Grayson, a star just for him. The connection between us thrummed violently; I thought it was going to burst from my skin, explode inside me, split me in two.

If we survived the night, I would gladly let it.

"You really do need to return to shore," I finally said, gazing mournfully at the boy. "There is too much death in these waters, too much danger."

Grayson went rigid, all hints of warmth fleeing his body. "The plan was not to kill anyone," he said stiffly.

I sighed, caressing the boy's face, taking in the beautiful naivety that rested upon his skin like armor. "Plans change, Grayson," I whispered. "When they stop killing us, we will stop killing them."

The boy bit his lip, nodding reluctantly. "I'll . . . I'll think of something. I'll try to make them stop." Courage blazed a trail across his face. "I can't go to shore. Not yet. I . . . I want to help."

Heart swelling, I clucked my tongue. "My brave heart," I crooned, running my hand through his soaked hair. "Battle does not suit you."

And before Grayson could fight me further, I leapt out of the boat, soaring through the water like I had wings.

GRAYSON

I WAS SO BUSY WATCHING EVANORA SURGE THROUGH THE DARK waters that I didn't notice Mr. Grieves slowly climbing to his feet. When I did, it was too late.

Mr. Grieves lunged forward, grabbing me by the shirt collar and dragging me into the air. His breath was hot on my face as he snarled at me. "Grayson Shaw," he growled. "You're becoming quite the headache."

I opened my mouth, but a strangled yelp escaped as he threw me toward the bow. My neck snapped back on impact, my head slamming into the unmoving wood. Blood pooled in my mouth, my tongue throbbing where I'd bitten it. I blinked rapidly, struggling to clear my vision, and raised a hand weakly as Mr. Grieves crept closer.

"Oh, yes," he breathed. "Just a little nuisance."

The knife was back in his hand, still covered in crimson. I swallowed down a mouthful of blood and bile and pressed my back against the bow. "You . . . You shouldn't be here!" I choked out.

Mr. Grieves smiled, his expression pure malice. "Neither should you. But you know"—he gestured with the blade—"right before we launched the boats, I saw flares going off in Tully's direction. Odd, don't you think? Flares are rare here, imported, expensive." He tilted his head, eyes narrowing. "Not just any old soul can get them. So, I figured that someone was up to no good." Mr. Grieves tapped his forehead. "And I figured that that someone was *you*. I docked my boat and marched right back to the courthouse. And you know what I found? Nothing." He laughed mockingly. "You weren't there."

I squeezed into a ball, terror crawling up my spine.

Mr. Grieves crouched low, grabbed my collar again, and pulled me toward the blade. Blood from his head splattered against my cheek, hot and slick. "I was a fool to think Ambrose could kill you, the useless bastard," he growled. "I'll do it myself!" His arm reared back, poised to plunge the knife deep into my chest.

I didn't have time to breathe, or blink, or think anything besides, *Oh God, oh God, oh God!*

And neither did Mr. Grieves.

Just as his blade began its deadly arc downward, an arm reached out from behind Mr. Grieves, slashing a blade against his exposed throat.

The arm withdrew, but Mr. Grieves remained frozen with his head tilted back. The thin line at his throat began to bubble with blood, pinpricks dotting the barely noticeable cut. But when Mr. Grieves gave a gurgling cough, his entire neck erupted, spraying me in boiling crimson. It poured from his neck, his mouth, a waterfall of bright red that stained everything it touched. He tried to take a breath, but all the air fizzled through the gaping gash on his neck. Mr. Grieves's head rolled forward, his eyes, already lifeless, fixing on me. He slowly straightened, staggering forward a step, then another, the walking dead. The blade slipped from his hands, and he reached out to me, a great wet groan on his frothing lips.

I cringed away, shutting my eyes from the nightmare. When Mr. Grieves heaved a final wheezing sigh and crumpled onto me, I couldn't help but scream.

Ambrose Grieves was standing in a boat next to mine, enveloped in a shimmering red hue, the tip of his knife drenched in his father's blood. I took a gasping breath and hurriedly wiped my eyes. "Ambrose," I managed to choke out. "What . . . ? Why . . . ?"

Ambrose's shoulders rippled with a mixture of exertion and poorly re-strained nerves. His eyes, normally sharp and cruel, were blank, seeing and not. He slowly tore his bleary gaze from me and pointed it to his shaking hand, sucking in a quick breath at the sight of the bloody knife in his grasp; his fingers loosened against the hilt, then tightened, his knuckles cracking and turning white. "I'm . . ." he breathed, the word coming out slow and warbled. "I'm not a useless bastard."

I wanted to crawl out of my skin. Every inch of me was smothered in blood. I was hot and sticky and smelled like a thousand rusty nails. Slowly holding up a hand in placation, I nodded. "You aren't," I agreed carefully.

Ambrose was still looking at the blade, watching as his father's blood drip, drip, dripped from the tip of its teeth.

"Ambrose," I said quietly. "The knife." My eyes darted from his face to the blade, which was pointing—whether Ambrose intended it or not—at me. My fingers twitched, the frozen rain biting into my inferno skin. Mr. Grieves spasmed violently, then finally went still, the last of his soul parting with his wretched body. I was acutely aware of his weight on my legs, of his blood seeping into my clothes, his smell of death clinging to my skin. "Give me the knife."

Ambrose let out a morbid chuckle. He jerked his head, sending the water droplets clinging to his blond strands scattering. "Scared I'm going to finish what my father started, Shaw?"

I shook my head slowly, my hand still hovering in the space between us. "No," I uttered. "You aren't like him."

Ambrose reared his head back, the vacant expression on his face smoth-ered by a snarl. It took everything within me not to flinch back. He raised the weapon in earnest. "I could be," he growled. "I could be just like him."

I swallowed hard, not daring to take my eyes off the man who had claimed so many lives, the man who looked so much like a little lost boy in that moment. I reached forward tentatively, my fingers inching toward the bloody blade. "You could be," I said, my hand drifting closer to his. "But you aren't. You won't."

Ambrose's shoulders heaved upward, a stifled sob cinching his throat shut when my hand slowly rested atop his. His grip was iron against the hilt. Gaze fluttering from the shaking knife to the pain swimming in Ambrose's eyes, I gently pried his fingers loose. Ambrose's jaw clenched, the muscles bulging in his neck as he fought to keep his lips from wobbling. The sob broke free, and his grip tightened. I stopped.

"Ambrose," I whispered, "you *won't*."

After a strained heartbeat, Ambrose slumped forward, surrendering his hold on the weapon. Letting out a small breath, I tucked the knife beside me, my entire body trembling as all remnants of adrenaline vanished. Ambrose rubbed his face, his tears mingling with the rain on his cheeks and the blood on his hands. When he straightened, the sharpness had returned to his icy-blue eyes, but the cruelty was gone.

"This doesn't mean I like you," Ambrose spat as he clambered into his seat. "This doesn't mean we're friends."

"No," I agreed quietly as he began to paddle away. "No, it doesn't."

But I knew with utmost certainty that it meant one thing to both of us.

Ambrose was done fighting. And, God, so was I.

As soon as Ambrose's boat was a healthy distance from mine, I let out a strangled groan and shoved Mr. Grieves's legs off of me.

And then I leaned over the lip of the boat and retched until I was as empty as Mr. Grieves's cold, dead heart.

EVANORA

I WAS BEGINNING TO DREAD FINDING OUT WHAT MY ANCESTORS meant. I thought that Grayson and I committing ourselves to each other, body and soul, would have been the answer, and while that kiss was . . . gods . . . it was incredible, I didn't feel any sort of shift inside me. I didn't suddenly understand what the key was, or how it included Grayson. I wasn't any closer to knowing what the *power of three* meant.

I wasn't certain I wanted to know anymore.

"Evanora!" Mavi cried, racing up from the depths and reaching for me.

Alarms shattered through the wall of peace I had built around myself. "What's wrong?"

Illeron swam up to us. He had a cut on his bicep and a nasty rope burn on his hands. He wiped the blood off his arm with a disgusted grunt. "Is everything okay?"

Mavi shook her head with a whimper. "The lanterns! The lanterns are burning out!"

I snapped my attention to the ocean floor. Sure enough, the lanterns glowing at multiple mermaids' hips began to sputter out. One by one, they vanished from existence, leaving the mermaids vulnerable to the Cursed Beings' infinite reach. They huddled with those who still had working lanterns; some, in a fit of panic, even tried to pry them free to steal for themselves.

It didn't work, and it didn't matter.

The Cursed Beings snatched them all the same.

I sucked in a breath, my heart clenching. "Neptune's spear . . ."

Mavi's bottom lip began to wobble. "I tried to reinforce my water orb. I tried everything!" Her shoulders drooped. "But . . . I'm just so *tired*, Evanora."

I ripped my eyes from the horrors below and focused all my fury on Mavi. "No!" I snapped, grabbing her by the shoulders. "You cannot give up! Not yet!"

"Evanora," Illeron uttered. "She's doing her best."

I bared my teeth at the water wielder, ignoring Illeron's placation. "Daylight is hours away. We still have a lot of war and carnage ahead of us. I need you strong, focused!"

Mavi stiffened underneath my grip, but she didn't flinch. She only nodded her head, the color draining from her face. "I'm *trying*."

"Evanora," the warrior said again. "Let go. You're hurting her."

I snarled but relented, releasing Mavi from my grasp. The wielder rubbed her arms where my hands had been. She didn't deserve my wrath, but it needed to go somewhere; I was too full of it to keep it all contained.

Illeron swam between us, holding his hands up in supplication. "Tensions are high," he said firmly. "Emotions even higher. We need to keep level heads and work together, otherwise we'll never win."

I opened my mouth, then immediately closed it. I hated how right he was.

The warrior looked at me and nodded to the ocean floor. "Go with Mavi," he said softly. "We'll be fine up here. Light the lanterns again. Help your pod. They need you, now more than ever."

Again, he was right. I shook my head with a scowl but let myself slowly sink. "I'll only be gone a moment," I promised.

Illeron gave me a lazy grin. "I'll save some of the fun for you."

I spun on my tail and raced for the depths.

GRAYSON

THE STORM ABOVE WAS GETTING WORSE, BUT THE WAVES AND whirlpools were lessening. I hated to think why.

Because we are feasting on them. The Cursed Beings laughed. *We are feasting on their flesh, like we will feast upon yours. See how their lovely lights twinkle out. Out, and eaten.*

I ground my teeth together. "Shut up," I growled, digging my paddles into the dwindling waves. The shore. I had to get to shore.

Promised One, they crooned in reply. *We see you, Promised One.*

My boat jostled viciously to the side. I yelped and gripped the gunwale as the boat veered in the opposite direction, sending my head spinning, my frayed nerves coiling. "Wait!" I cried out. "Stop!"

The boat dipped low, then sprang high, nearly tipping vertically as it arched into the sky. I shouted in alarm as the entire weight of it crashed back onto the waves, nearly sending me toppling out of my seat.

We see you, Promised One. We see you, and we want you. Here, here, here.

I wiped the spray of the ocean from my eyes, the salt and blood burning them.

And through the foam and the blood and the rain, I saw Pa.

He was leaning over the gunwale of his boat, hauling up a mermaid in his net.

I steered my boat for him.

There was a thump at the side of my boat, then another. The third one sent my entire boat vibrating, my teeth chattering. A long black tentacle sidled up the side and waved at me lazily.

Promised One, the Cursed Beings chimed playfully, their many voices lilting. *Where are you going, Promised One?*

"You can't have me," I barked, raising my oar and swinging. "Not yet!"

The Cursed Beings ducked away with a hiss, narrowly avoiding the wrath of my oar. The tentacle shrank back into the water.

I paddled as hard as my arms would let me. The blisters on my palms tore, exposing the raw flesh underneath. I never knew my shoulders could ache so badly, like a hundred knives were wedged deep into the contracting muscles.

The net was nearly over the boat's edge. Pa grinned at the mermaid trapped inside.

With a snarl, I shoved the paddles down one last time, letting the waves carry me the rest of the way. My boat slammed into his with a violent *thunk!* Wood groaned, then splintered, chips flying like teeth. Pa stumbled forward, the net jerking out of his hands. His eyes went wide as the mermaid tumbled back into the water, slipping free from the net with a fluid twist. He stared, dumbfounded, at the empty net. Then his gaze snapped to me.

His eyes bulged, his mouth dropping open. I didn't blame him. I must've looked like hell—blood that wasn't mine staining my skin, shivering, eyes blazing with a reckless bravery.

He was in rough shape too. His left eye was screwed shut, a long, jagged cut slicing through the eyelid. His clothes were torn, and from underneath his soggy rolled-up sleeve, I could see four long claw marks tucked away on his right arm.

"What are you doing?" he roared, pointing at the water angrily. "You made me drop her!"

I ran my hands through my hair. "I don't know," I said. "It's all wrong!"

Pa shook his head at me, cursing. "Who are you fighting for?"

I threw my hands up. "We shouldn't be fighting at all! Pa . . ." I laughed incredulously. "It doesn't have to be this way. Mermaids versus humans . . . It's messed up! We are *fighting* for the *same thing*!"

Pa rubbed his face, narrowing his good eye. "And what's that?" he asked, humoring me.

"Peace!" I laughed again. "All they want is peace, to be left alone, to be—"

Eaten, the Cursed Beings moaned. *Eaten, eaten, eaten!*

I swallowed hard as the boat shifted. *Not yet*, I begged inwardly. *Please, not yet!*

The boat stilled. I gave my head a rough shake and flicked out my wrists, trying to expel the fear that gnawed at me. "Free," I finished. "They want to be free."

Pa looked up at the sky exasperatedly. "No," he said, resolute. "I refuse to believe that." He shook his head and looked at me, almost pleadingly. "It's us or them, son. Choose."

"I—"

"Choose!" he bellowed.

But I couldn't. There was no way I could pick a side. My body was made of flesh and bones, and my heart belonged to a mermaid, and my mind . . . God, my mind was a mess.

It didn't matter.

The Cursed Beings chose for me.

If we can't have you, the Cursed Beings growled, *then he will do just fine.*

I sucked in a breath, panic cloaking me. *No, no, no!* I wanted to shout the words. I wanted to leap from my boat and onto Pa's, switch places, tell him to row as fast as he could back to shore.

But all I could do was watch as four long arms burst from the ocean and grabbed Pa, unceremoniously yanking him into the darkness below.

EVANORA

I KNEW SOMETHING WAS WRONG BEFORE I HEARD HIM SCREAM. I could feel it in my heart, running along the frayed edges of the bond.

An untethering.

My breath caught in my throat, the magic stuttering at my fingertips as I worked on the last lantern with Mavi. My eyes snapped to the surface, letting the connection guide me.

Through the crashing waves, I could make out Grayson's blurry form. He was leaning over the edge of the boat, peering into the water, screaming at someone, anyone to help.

And I saw the Cursed Beings, their tentacles full of a man struggling to get free. The tentacles ripped and tore at his clothes, cackling with delight as the man squirmed. The man squeezed his eyes shut and grunted in pain as one of the tentacles morphed into a grotesque hand and began clawing at his exposed belly. The man jerked his leg up, pulled a knife out of a hidden sheath, and stabbed the hand, his teeth bared, the fight not yet drowned out of him. Red and black blood mingled in the water, a morbid dance of smoke and crimson. The Cursed Beings hissed, their grip on him loosening.

I knew better than to hope as the man scrambled back toward the surface. The Cursed Beings lunged for him again, the tentacle tips peeling away to reveal more hands that grabbed at each of his flailing limbs.

I didn't know who this man was to Grayson, but I knew he was important.

And I knew I was too far away to help.

I was too far, and my Gift had been bled dry.

From above, Grayson wailed. The bond went taut again. He was calling out to me, begging me to help. I could feel it, and I couldn't do anything about it. I blinked through my tears. "I'm sorry," I whispered, unable to tear my eyes away from the man.

The Cursed Beings unfurled, pulling on the man's limbs. The man's panicked groan flitted through my ears as he was stretched. He gritted his teeth, trying to withstand the pain, but I could see the realization in his eyes; eventually his body wouldn't be able to handle the strain anymore, and the Cursed Beings would take delight in tearing him to shreds.

And I would have to watch Grayson fall apart because of it.

The man's eyes fluttered shut, and his head drooped onto his chest.

It happened so slowly, dragged out so I could watch every detail and be powerless to stop them from unfolding.

A flash of silver and crimson.

A ferocious battle cry that sent the sands shifting beneath me.

And a well-timed body slam that sent the man tumbling away from the Cursed Beings' grasp and Illeron into it.

His lantern snuffed out.

CHAPTER EIGHTY-FIVE

EVANORA

MAY 1 – EARLY MORNING

THE WORLD WENT DEADLY QUIET. I COULDN'T EVEN HEAR the screams coming out of my own mouth. But I could feel it, coiling in my belly, rumbling in my chest, ripping through my throat. I could feel it as everything inside me splintered into oblivion. "*No!*"

The tentacles, made of darkness and shadows and pure evil, wrapped around the warrior. Illeron managed to give me a final smile before they enveloped him completely from head to tail.

And then they squeezed.

Clouds of blood bloomed around the darkness.

"No!" I screamed again, the word broken apart by sobs.

Mavi keened beside me, her mouth stretched wide in horror, her hands bent into gnarled fists as they pressed against the sides of her head.

The Cursed Beings laughed, their grip on Illeron growing tighter. He didn't cry out, didn't beg to be released, didn't try to fight back with a futile effort.

He accepted his death like the warrior he was.

But I didn't accept it. I didn't accept it at all.

I leapt forward, the water posing no resistance to me as I sailed through it. I snarled at the Cursed Beings, stretched out my claws, made my forearm fins as rigid as I could. A scream on my tongue, I raced for the dying warrior, hell-bent on unleashing a wrath unlike anything the Cursed Beings had ever seen. I withdrew into myself, becoming a mindless predator, intent to kill or die trying. "Let go of him, you beast!" I shrieked.

A tentacle sprang loose and zeroed in on me. It instantly split apart, one tentacle becoming two, becoming four, becoming eight. Eight little writhing tentacles, each with a sharp claw on the end. The legion reared back, poised to strike.

Through the opening the tentacles had created, Illeron's arm slipped out. He held it up weakly to me, his palm tilted upward. His fingers were bent into claws as the Cursed Beings' grip grew tighter, and the pain grew to unfathomable heights. But his hand was steady, his message clear.

No, he was telling me. *Stop*.

I bit back a sob, shaking my head. How could I stop? How could I stop and just let them mangle his body?

I tried to swim forward again, but the eight-armed tentacle followed my every move. I hissed at it. It hissed back.

Stop. I could almost hear his voice, calm and soothing, in my mind. *Let go*.

"I can't," I whispered around a hitching sob. I dared to reach around the tentacle, my fingers grazing Illeron's. The tentacle watched my every move, held back only by the light dangling from my hip. I clutched the warrior's hand. I could feel his stuttering heartbeat in his fingertips, the warmth in his skin rapidly retreating. Illeron's hand spasmed, then gripped mine tightly. And for a moment, I was back under the docks, clutching Solandis's hand as she was wrenched out of my life, her light snuffed from our beautiful, unkind world.

Let go.

I was back at the Barrens, giving Jorah one last hug before he trudged to his death in the darkness.

Let go.

So, I did.

"My path has led me to you." I closed my eyes, forcing the words out. "May our ancestors' light guide you home. May your journey be swift and peaceful, your soul reborn, your body renewed. Go, and swim . . . swim . . ." I choked back a sob. "Swim free, brave warrior."

I let the warrior's limp hand fall away from mine.

And I watched as the Cursed Beings wrapped around him again and squeezed with all their might.

Tighter.

Bones crunched. Scales crumbled.

Tighter.

Organs squelched.

Tighter.

Then the most horrific *popping* sound I'd ever heard. Like the bursting of a giant bull kelp head. The cloud of blood turned into a geyser.

I closed my eyes as the Cursed Beings slowly retracted their long slimy arms.

I couldn't take it. Any more pain. I just *couldn't*. I was already too full of it. There was no space left within me.

The man floated listlessly, his body swaying in the undercurrent.

The man Illeron had given his life for.

The Cursed Beings, done with Illeron, swept for him.

With a seething growl, I surged forward, grappling for the unconscious man just as their tentacles circled around his legs again. I yanked him out of reach, screeching at the Cursed Beings as I held out my hand in warning. My Gift sputtered and crackled at my fingertips, nothing more than a faint glow. Still, the Cursed Beings hung back, their probing hands dancing in the water.

You are running out of magic, they guessed correctly. *You are running out of time.*

"Stay back!" I roared, not daring to lower my quavering arm.

The Cursed Beings laughed, plucking up Illeron's lifeless body. The warrior's broken arms hovered in the water, disjointed and loose. His tail was crimped and bent. Blood continued to seep from his mouth, his nose, his eyes. Eyes that would never roll at my expense again, that would never look at me as though I were made of sunlight. All of him was broken, and so was I.

Such a shame, the Cursed Beings moaned, *that you won't be able to give him a proper burial.* They tossed his limp body around from tentacle to tentacle. His torn fins flapped at the movement. *But you know, there is a way to end your suffering.*

Clutching the man tighter to me, I swallowed. "How?"

A single inky arm stretched toward me. *Why, just give us the boy. Give us the Promised One, and everything will be made right.*

I snapped my teeth at the gnarled hand; it darted away. "I don't believe you," I snarled. "Never!"

The Cursed Beings laughed again. *Suit yourself.* And without letting me glance upon the fallen warrior a final time, the darkness circled around him and dragged him out of my life forever.

A sob rattled through my shredded vocal cords.

It was all coming undone. I didn't know how much more I could take. I didn't know if I could take any more losses. My battle-weary heart simply couldn't bear it.

The man twitched in my arms. His right eye flew open, bubbles seeping from his tightly sealed lips. I growled as he continued to writhe, desperate for oxygen. The man's eye settled on me, and it went wide with fear.

I gripped him tighter, baring my teeth, letting my agony and anger pour out of me like the ocean itself. "You are alive because of Illeron. Do not let his death be in vain!" I whispered viciously.

The man blinked at me, his hands at his neck. He bobbed his head hurriedly.

I pushed him toward the surface, an anguished cry on my tongue.

GRAYSON

NOTHING. NOTHING BUT WRETCHED SILENCE AND PANICKED thoughts.

And then, in a mighty splash that sent my boat bucking to the side, Pa erupted from the ocean, coughing and choking as he reached blindly for the boat. Adrenaline coursed through me, and I let out a relieved sob as I helped him out of the water. Pa crashed to the bottom of the boat, gasping and convulsing, his hands pressed against his throat. Thick red marks marred the skin around his wrists, and there were deep angry grooves crisscrossing along his stomach.

But my pa was alive. *Alive!*

Still hunched over, Pa looked at me. His good eye was unfocused, still trapped in the horrors of the water. "They . . ." He coughed again. "They saved me. From those . . . those . . ." A shudder tore through his back as he lurched forward and vomited up buckets of water. Whether the nausea came from nearly swallowing the entire ocean or finally witnessing the Cursed Beings, I wasn't certain.

I placed my hand on his back. Pa shied away, fear still clinging to him. "You're safe," I uttered, moving closer. "You're safe, Pa!"

Pa shook his head, pressing the heels of his palms into his eyes. "*Why?*" he groaned. "Why would they do that for me? Why would they sacrifice their own kind for . . . me?"

Because of me, I realized with growing dread. *Because the Cursed Beings want me, and Evanora won't let them.*

A wave of panic swept through me, scattering my nerves. I crouched next to Pa and clutched his face. "Pa, what do you mean *sacrifice*?" I gulped hard. "Did someone die in your place?"

Pa's lip began to wobble, and he tried to pull out of my grip. But he was too weak, and my fear was too great. "Yes," he moaned.

I gave his face a rough shake. "Who?" I demanded. "What did they look like?"

Please don't say violet eyes. Please don't say scales made of sunlight. Please don't say it was Evanora!

Pa shook his head stiffly, his right eye meeting mine. "I . . . I lost consciousness. I don't know who did it. But the mermaid who brought me back up here . . . the one who told me not to waste this gift . . ." His shoulders heaved again. "She was the purest white I've ever seen."

I blew out the breath I hadn't realized I was holding. "She's still alive," I murmured, more for myself to hear the words than for Pa. "She's still safe."

Pa raised his eyebrows as realization dawned on him. "That was your mermaid, wasn't it? The one bathed in white."

I pinched my lips together. "Yes."

Pa nodded slowly, still dazed by his dance with death. "She . . . She's your mermaid," he mumbled softly before contracting as another coughing spell tore through him.

I moved my hands from Pa's face to his shoulders. "Come on," I said, tightening my grip. "We need to get you to shore."

Pa spat on the boat's floor and slowly sat up. "What . . ." He looked at me, horrified. "What *were* those things?"

There was no time, but I knew Pa's stubbornness; he wouldn't let us leave until he got an answer. "They live in the Barrens." I glared at him. "All those nursery rhymes, all those myths and fairy tales and folklore . . . They're all true, Pa." I pointed at the water. "Those evil creatures, the Cursed Beings, want nothing but death, and they aren't picky about who is their next meal." I hastily seated the oars. "Which could be us, if we don't hurry."

Pa looked at me, really *looked* at me. "I believe you," he whispered. "Everything you told me this month, I . . ." He shook his head in wonderment. "I believe you." He bit his lip, remorse washing across his face. "I'm so sorry I didn't listen."

I gritted my teeth. "No time for apologies. We need to get to shore."

Pa grabbed my hands, stopping them mid-row. "No," he bit out.

I stared hard at him. "No?"

"No."

"So"—I laughed mirthlessly—"you want to just die, then? Because that's what will happen if we don't move."

I could feel the Cursed Beings lurking underneath my boat, whispering, calling out to me, *begging* for me.

Pa shook his head again. "You said the mermaids didn't want to fight, that they would stop attacking us if we stopped attacking them." He squeezed my hands gently. "I *believe* you." Slowly standing, Pa clambered into the boat next to ours, slumping into the seat with a grunt. He slapped on his soaked hat and gave me a firm smile. "What's the plan?"

EVANORA

THE LANTERNS WERE ALREADY SPUTTERING OUT AGAIN. Helplessness tugged at my insides as I saw more and more of my pod getting pulled into the shadows surrounding us. The Cursed Beings were relentless, darting out from the darkness, snagging the mermaids the second their lanterns extinguished, their dying screams forever imprinted in my mind.

"Mermaids without lights!" I cried. "To me!"

A throng of mermaids hurried to the bottom of the ocean floor, fighting with one another to get to me first. As Mavi and I busied ourselves with their empty lanterns, exhaustion crept up on me. Gods, I was tired. Tired of fighting, of surviving, of this night that never seemed to end. I wanted to be back on the boat with Grayson. I wanted to be home. I wanted my ammah, my appah. I wanted to never feel this much emptiness again.

My arms began to shake as Mavi and I approached the last empty lantern. But when I lifted my fingers and urged my Gift out of its slumber, nothing happened. I gave Mavi an alarmed look and flicked out my wrists. I tried again. Still, nothing. The mermaid stifled a cry, his blue eyes piercing mine desperately. I bit my lip, guilt a tsunami in my soul. "I'm . . ." I swallowed a sob. "I don't have any more to give."

The mermaid sucked in a breath, his eyes flitting to the lantern still tied around my waist. "Give me yours!" he demanded.

Mavi swooped in front of us, hissing. "How dare you ask your queen for such a request, Forthis!"

Forthis pushed around Mavi, reaching hastily for my light. "I deserve to live too!"

I blinked, and he was gone, wrenched into the shadows.

Mavi let out a shaky whine and tucked close to me. I numbly wrapped my arms around her twitching shoulders. I kept searching the waters, looking for Grayson, praying he was safe. I looked for a sardonic grin and the flash of silver and crimson, only to feel the loss of Illeron all over again.

Tears sprang to my eyes, and I didn't have the strength to wipe them away. If Nereida were with us, she would know what to do. She would know a way to get out of this mess, to pull up the last dredges of my magic.

A warrior tumbled from the surface, a wild fear cloaking her eyes. Her hands shook against her spear as she beckoned me. "Your Majesty," she panted. "We're getting eaten alive up there! The hunters won't give up! I don't understand," she growled, running a hand through her short green hair. "How are there still so many boats? Why haven't the Cursed Beings grabbed them all?"

Because they are playing, I thought with a sickening sense of dread. *The thrill is not only in the kill. It is in the chase, the hunt. We are simply playthings for them, toys made of flesh and bone and fear.*

"There are still countless boats," the warrior went on. "At least ten of our fighters have been caught. We need your spear!"

Mavi pulled at my arms. "No!" she yelped, her voice cracking with panic. "We need her down here to manage the lanterns! You'll need to make do without her, Meddoh!"

I didn't have the heart to tell her that there was no point anymore. Once they were out, that was it. Without my Gift, the unlit lanterns were nothing more than a beacon for the dark.

The warrior pointed at the surface. "We need you up there!"

Mavi shook her head wildly, her amber eyes pleading. "We need to stay down here, where it's safe."

An insane laugh bubbled up my throat. "There is no such thing as safe!"

It's time! my ancestors suddenly roared. *It's time! It's time! The key! It's time!*

Heart in my throat, I gazed up at the surface, hoping and praying that whatever plan Grayson was implementing would start to work, and fast.

GRAYSON

My arms were on fire. I wondered briefly if tearing them off would be less painful. I gave in to the aches coursing through me and paused, leaning over the gunwale and peering into the water below.

I couldn't see Evanora.

I also couldn't see a lot of glowing lanterns left.

Motivation laced with desperation, I approached Pa's boat, ignoring the biting protest in my back. "How's it looking?" I called over.

Pa wiped the rain from his face, catching his breath. "I found Mr. Erlandson and Officer Crowley and told them to return to shore. They were more than happy to oblige." He scowled. "A lot of them don't want to stop. Mayor McCoy is still out there, along with Owen Morris, Peter Lyre, and Mr. Krieg. And that's just off the top of my head." Pa sighed heavily. "I don't understand—why are so many hunters *here*, at *this beach*?"

I ducked my head. "That's my fault. Mr. Grieves saw the flares I set off to warn the mermaids. He followed my scent back here, along with a horde of other hunters."

Pa straightened. "Where is that ray of sunshine, anyway? I haven't seen him."

I swallowed, nausea pressing against my stomach. "In a boat. Not breathing."

Pa scrunched his nose. "Do I want to know?"

"No. I wish I didn't."

Pa pursed his lips together, nodding firmly. "We need to keep going. The sooner we convince the hunters to get to shore, the sooner we can rest."

I blew out a heavy breath and forced a smile. "I'm barely winded. I could go for hours."

Pa snorted. "You just might have to."

I steered my boat back into the open ocean.

"Wait!"

I turned to see Pa fidgeting with his leg, wincing as he bent over to unclasp buckles and unravel leather strands. He straightened with a grunt, holding up a hunting knife. *My* hunting knife. The gold flecks in the white hilt glimmered in the night. Fat raindrops tangled with the knife's sharp teeth. "I think this belongs to you," he said, leaning over the edge of the boat, holding the blade out for me.

I took the hungry knife hesitantly, flicking my gaze to Pa. "You might need it."

Pa shrugged. "Maybe so." He peered into the midnight water. "But you might need it more."

I had a feeling that a mere blade wouldn't stop the Cursed Beings from sinking their claws into me. But as I clasped the knife onto my leg, I couldn't quite shake the sensation that I was meant to have it, just like

Pa had been meant to give it to me on my birthday, like I'd been meant to use it to free Evanora.

It felt good. It felt *right*.

I was meant to carry it tonight. I was scared to know why.

"Thank you," I whispered, meaning it.

Pa, ever allergic to affection of any kind, grunted again. "Get back to work."

I chuckled, shaking my head. "No rest for the wicked."

Promised One, the Cursed Beings breathed as I rowed away. *Where are you going, Promised One?*

For a Sunday paddle, I thought sarcastically.

My boat shuddered to a halt. I dug my oars into the waves and pushed. Nothing happened. Biting my lip, I peered over the edge.

Three long tentacles gripped the boat's wooden walls, holding me in place.

I gasped and reared back as one of the tentacles slinked up the side and over the gunwale, hovering in front of my face.

We grow tired of waiting for you. Their words echoed in my mind, drenching me in a poisonous fear that left me immobile. *We want you. Now.*

I held up my hands. "Wa-wait!" I stuttered.

The tentacle shifted, like it was a head cocking to the side. *Wait? You want us, the rulers of the dark, the lords of the night, to* wait?

The boat groaned as the tentacles began to apply force on the outer walls.

"I-I-I just mean . . ." I cleared my throat, my mind going dangerously blank. "I want to bargain with you."

The Cursed Beings laughed, the sound turning my blood to ice. But I had their attention. *What sort of bargain?*

I licked my lips, scrambling for an idea, *any* idea, that would get the Cursed Beings off my boat. "How about . . . you let me help all the hunters I can. You let me finish this."

The tentacle vibrated with impatience. *That sounds like a demand, not a bargain.*

I shook my head. "If you let me do those things, I'll . . ." I sighed, lowering my head. "I'll offer myself to you freely." My heart squeezed in my chest, the bond throbbing painfully, but I kept going. "I won't fight. I won't let Evanora get in the way. I'll walk into the water and let you take me."

The tentacle snapped back violently, a serpent ready to strike. *We could just take you now.*

I nodded hurriedly. "I know you can. But you won't." I straightened my shoulders. "I'm giving you my word. I'm yours the second this is all over."

The tentacle drooped with a hissing sigh. *A mere human's word is a fickle thing.*

"But what about the word of the Promised One? Surely that holds weight." When I got no reply, I raised an eyebrow in challenge. "I thought the Cursed Beings loved to bargain. Am I wrong?"

Slowly, the tentacles detached from the boat. *We're watching you,* they growled. *Any false move, any breach in your promise, and you—and the rest of the lives on this miserable beach—are ours.*

I nodded again. "Deal."

The tentacles retreated.

With shaking hands, I grabbed for the oars. They tumbled out of my wet fingers twice before I managed to get a proper grip on them.

I rowed away slowly, pretending I hadn't just made a deal with the devil, pretending this was all just another terrible nightmare, that all I had to do was wake up and open my eyes, and it would be over.

EVANORA

EVANORA, LOOK!"

I followed Mavi's shaking finger as she pointed at the surface. "The boats! They're . . . They're returning to shore!"

She was right: The boats were slowly drifting back to shore. I fought the relief swelling in my chest, forcing myself to stay grounded. Not yet. The Cursed Beings were still picking us off, one by one, as each lantern failed. Too many deaths had already proven that hope was a dangerous thing.

Above us, the warriors shook their spears and cheered as more boats veered toward the beach.

"Is this really happening?" Mavi dared to ask around a feeble smile. "Is it really almost over?"

The exhaustion was a weight on my shoulders. I slowly sank to the ocean floor, wincing as my stomach wound protested the movements. "I think so," I whispered, pressing a hand against the open flesh.

Mavi shifted closer, eyeing the blood leaking through my fingers. "Are you okay?"

I nodded, but my hand stayed firmly in place. "It's more of a bother than anything. If my Gift cared to return, I'd fix it." I held out my free hand, testing the magic. A spark flickered, then vanished. I sighed and lowered my hand.

"It doesn't matter. We just need to survive a little longer." I pointed upward, past the warriors and the retreating boats. "Look at the sky."

Mavi blinked. The storm was breaking, revealing orange and red beneath. She gasped. "It's almost dawn!"

I smiled grimly. "Almost. Not quite."

As if in answer, a nearby warrior's lantern blinked out. The Cursed Beings roared, diving for him. His screams were muffled as they dug their talons into him. I shut my eyes. Mavi's grip on my shoulder tightened.

"We're close," she moaned. "So close! We just need to hold on."

Easier said than done. I had nothing left. No magic, no strength. Keeping the lanterns lit was becoming a fight I was losing. I could feel the fatigue breaking me down, my edges fraying, bleeding away. Soon there wouldn't be enough of me to keep fighting. Would I flicker out, like my magic?

Mavi went rigid, distracting me from my spiraling thoughts. "Look at that boat."

I frowned, forcing myself to look beyond the remains of blood and fins.

Amidst discarded nets and broken spears and wooden splinters, there was a single boat. It wasn't moving toward the shore, only turning in slow circles, as though the hunter inside was still waiting for more mermaids to emerge.

An anxious whine seeped from Mavi's throat. "Why isn't it moving? It . . . It should be moving!"

I grunted, shrugging lightly. "Perhaps they lost their oars."

Mavi's fear-drenched eyes slowly turned to me. "What if they still wish to fight?" she whispered. She wrung her hands together, the webbing between her fingers twisting and stretching. "What if they still want our blood? What if . . ." She lurched her gaze back to the circling boat, the movement jerky and strained. "What if they won't stop until we're all dead?"

I placed a hand on Mavi's arm. Her muscles tensed underneath my touch, her nerves coiling and vibrating. "They won't get us all the way down here. We're safe."

A whimper slipped through Mavi's tightly pinched lips. "No." She shook her head quickly, sending her tight curls into a tangled frenzy. "No!"

"Mavi," I urged, giving her arm a squeeze. "We're *safe*."

The wielder flinched out of my touch with a strangled cry. "There's no such thing as safe!" Her hands flew up to her face, pulling frantically at her skin, sending the scales on her cheeks taut. Her wild eyes found my spear nestled in the sand beside me, and she sucked in a sharp breath, her hands growing deathly still. "No such thing..."

I swallowed, scared to make any sudden movements. Before me wasn't my dear friend, but a trapped animal, drowning in panic and hysteria. "Mavi," I said quietly. "Don't."

I blinked, and Mavi was moving. I reached for the weapon, but she was quicker. With an otherworldly screech, she surged forward, hastily snagging the spear from my fumbling fingers.

And before I could say anything more, Mavi took off, aiming the spear at the bottom of the unsuspecting boat.

GRAYSON

TAKE A BREAK, MY BODY SCREAMED. *CATCH YOUR BREATH.*
I reluctantly gave in, sitting back in the seat and rolling out my shoulders.

The plan was working. More boats were heading back to shore. Mayor McCoy had taken very little energy to convince; he'd eagerly rowed away, muttering, "I didn't sign up for this."

Peter Lyre, on the other hand, had needed to be tied up with a net by Pa and hauled back, kicking and screaming.

Owen Morris scooted by, giving me a wry smile. "I n-n-never really liked the-the-the Hunt, anyway."

I craned my neck, inspecting the sky. The rain was lessening, the plump clouds breaking apart, showing the pale dawn approaching. The blood-soaked night was nearly over.

The beach was filling with abandoned boats and weary hunters, huddled together near the rocks, watching as Pa and I retrieved more souls who didn't know they needed saving. The sight warmed my exhausted heart, fueling me with the strength to keep going.

Now? the Cursed Beings prodded.

I shook my head. "No, not yet."

Their grumbles shook my boat, but they went silent.

Pa approached me. "That's the last of them," he panted, wiping thick strands of hair off his sweaty forehead.

I frowned, my gaze darting to the boats farther out. "What about those?"

Pa shook his head, his expression grim. "Those are the diehards. Mr. Fowler, Mr. Craigsby, and Dr. Peele are amongst them. A little rain and un-ruly waters don't scare them."

I made a face, though I didn't hate the idea of Dr. Peele dying at the hands of the Cursed Beings. "Did you tell them that the unruly waters include beasts that could tear them apart, limb by limb?"

Pa leaned forward, resting his elbows on his knees. "I did," he said carefully. "They only laughed."

I reached for my oars, holding back a groan as the wood bit into my broken calluses. "I'll give it a try."

Pa shrugged. "Don't expect them to come in. Expect them to laugh. Hard."

I rolled my eyes. "Go back to shore. I'll be there shortly."

I watched as Pa aimed for the beach, slightly jealous that I wasn't joining him. I sighed, cracked my neck, and dug my oars into the water.

Bump!

I froze, my oars hovering just above the surface. I waited to hear the chirp of the Cursed Beings, their sizzling laughter as their tentacles crept up my boat.

Bump-bump!

I gritted my teeth and pulled out my oar, preparing to strike against the oncoming attack of inky black hands. "I said not *yet!*" I growled.

Bump! Craaaaack! The bottom of my boat split in two. Water immediately began to gush in through the splinters. I gasped at the ice-cold intrusion.

Oh, the Cursed Beings sighed. *That isn't us.*

Crack! The split grew wider, becoming an opening with sharp wooden teeth.

An opening large enough for a hand to fit through.

EVANORA

MAVI PUMMELED MERCILESSLY AT THE BOTTOM OF THE BOAT. I had to give her credit—she looked more like a warrior than I ever had. The way she handled the spear, how she held it firmly with every lunge. Like it was an extension of her. Like she'd been born to wield it. Uninvited tears latched on to my eyelashes. Illeron would've been proud of her.

The wood gave way, the tip of her spear smashing through the bottom of the boat. She let out a guttural growl and thrust her hand inside the opening, grappling blindly for an unsuspecting ankle. The spear slipped out of her grasp, sailing to the ocean floor beside me.

But Mavi, more monster than mermaid, no longer needed it. She hacked at the damaged wood with her claws, slashed it to splinters with her fins. She was wild with fear, drunk on panic.

The hole grew larger.

My heart pounded in my temples, unease rising in my gut. Something was wrong, but I was useless. Every movement sent agony through my wound. All I could do was sit in the sand, watching as Mavi's desperation edged toward destruction.

The wielder went eerily still.

She cast a final terror-filled look my way.

And then she yanked down as hard as she could.

The hunter tumbled through the small hole, scraping against the jagged edges before becoming weightless in the water's grasp.

The unease grew into a snarling beast as the hunter flailed, his long limbs tearing through the water, grappling for purchase, finding none.

The key! The key! my ancestors shrieked. *The power of three! It's time! It's time!*

My breath caught in my throat, my chest caving in.

The hunter jerked his head back, waves of unruly brown curls dancing. His eyes, full of the ocean, full of panic, searching, searching, searching.

His heart, connected to mine, beating with the ferocity of a thousand drums.

Grayson. The hunter was Grayson.

Mavi was about to kill Grayson.

I slowly rose from the ocean floor, feeling trapped in my sluggish body. "Wait," I croaked, my voice too small, too quiet, too fragile. "Wait!"

The boy was covered in blood. Mavi couldn't recognize him underneath all the layers of it. Gods, even my eyes had a hard time seeing Grayson—*my* Grayson—through the clouds of crimson and terror.

But my heart. My heart *knew*.

"Mavi!" I cried. The light began to drain from my vision. All I could see were flashes of blue and red. "Mavi!" I surged forward, but I was too slow, too weighed down by the night's events. I held out my hands, willing my magic to the surface. It only sputtered and sighed against my skin. "Please!"

The key! my ancestors screamed. *It's time!*

I kicked harder than I'd ever kicked in my life. But it wasn't fast enough. I was stuck in place, in time. The space between me and Mavi and Grayson yawned, growing impossibly larger, infinitely farther. "Please!"

If he died, I would surely die too. I was certain of it. I would crumble into a million pieces, shards of stardust scattered in the water. Never whole, never warm, never to shine again. Nothing but a shell. I couldn't live without him. I couldn't. I wouldn't! Desperation clawed at me as I reached out my hands for the boy. "*Mavi!*"

Grayson's squirming went still as his eyes latched on to the water wielder. He tried to smile.

Mavi tilted her head to the side.

She didn't smile back.

GRAYSON

Water. So much water. I couldn't see anything the moment I slipped through the boat and landed in the ocean's grasp.

Pain ricocheted through my body from where the broken shards of wood had bitten into me. I blinked through the burning salt and the clouds of blood, trying to decipher the darkness surrounding me.

The one who was promised! the Cursed Beings roared. *Here!*

I clawed through the water, unable to make sense of the shadows. I couldn't die—not like this. I had promised to give myself to them, but I thought I had more time. I needed more time!

The darkness growled. *He is ours! He is ours! The bargain must be completed!*

I needed to say goodbye to Pa. I needed to thank Holly for all her help. I needed to—

Feed us! Feed us! He is ours!

—tell Jasper to smarten up, to look into something other than working at the docks, because his net-mending skills were piss-poor.

Here! Here! Here!

I needed to see Evanora one last time. I needed to tell her that I would do it all again for her, that I would go through every ache, every heartbreak, every fear, if it meant I got to spend more time with her.

I whipped my head around, searching the waters for my inevitable death. But I didn't see misshapen claws hungry for my flesh.

I saw Mavi.

She was hovering in front of me, her head cocked to the side, her mouth stretched in a snarl, her golden eyes glazed. Her deep purple tail flicked pensively beneath her.

I relaxed, offering the young mermaid a small smile.

Mavi's eyes traveled down my body, coming to a stop on my leg. I followed her gaze hesitantly, my nerves tight and tingling.

The knife. She was looking at my hunting knife.

With a lilting purr that sounded much too sinister, she reached forward, deftly unclasping the sheath and pulling out the knife. She looked at the blade, at its sharp tip, at its hungry teeth. Another haunting hum rippled off her lips.

I made a face and held out my hands, confusion surging through my body. *Mavi*, I thought stupidly. *It's me. It's me!*

Mavi's eyes flicked to mine, and the realization sank in, heavy as death.

She couldn't recognize me.

My entire body began to burn with panic as Mavi pulled the weapon back, intent to strike. In the distance, I could hear someone screaming.

I opened my mouth, fighting against the water to speak, to scream, to do anything I could to show Mavi that it was me, not some hunter, me!

Mavi let out a ferocious battle cry as she sprang forward, quick as lightning, and drove the knife deep into my flesh.

CHAPTER EIGHTY-SIX

EVANORA

MAY 1 – MORNING

MY HEART DIDN'T STOP.
It shattered.

CHAPTER EIGHTY-SEVEN

GRAYSON

MAY 1 – MORNING

THERE WAS NOTHING.
And then there was pain.

CHAPTER EIGHTY-EIGHT

EVANORA

MAY 1 – MORNING

M Y SCREAM TORE THROUGH THE EARTH, DIVIDED the ocean, and sent the mountains crumbling. It gouged craters into the sand and shattered something deep inside me.

It splintered me in two.

I hadn't known pain before this. *This* was pain. A hand digging into my chest, wrapping icy fingers around my heart, and ripping it out while it was still beating. Like Mavi's hand, plunging into the boat. Like the way she'd yanked Grayson through the jagged hole.

All of me was caving in, folding inward over and over, collapsing into nothing.

When I reached them, Mavi was pulling the blade from Grayson's stomach. The sound of steel grinding through flesh, muscle, and bone rang in my ears. My sob, caught between a howl and a wail, erupted as I shoved her aside and threw myself over the boy. I buried my face in his neck and wept. Gods, I wept.

Pain. So much pain. I was drowning in it.

Mavi lowered the knife, her face a mask of confusion. She reached for me hesitantly. I flinched back with a feral hiss, blinking through the haze of tears. My glare froze her in place, her hand recoiling as her eyes filled with hurt. I leveled her with that dark, searing stare until my strength gave out and I collapsed back into Grayson's lifeless arms. Blood poured from him—too much, too fast. My trembling hand pressed against the wound, desperate to stop the flow, but it seeped through my fingers. Thick, warm, relentless.

"Why?" I rasped, crushing Mavi with another glare. "*Why?*"

Her mouth opened and closed, fumbling for words, finding none. She shook her head, wide-eyed and shivering.

And then it clicked.

The knife slipped from Mavi's fingertips, fluttering into the darkness below. She choked out a gasp, her hands moving of their own accord as they pressed against her naked stomach. Like *she* had the wound. "Gra-Grayson!" she stuttered out.

A whimper slipped through my tightly clenched lips, and I turned back to the boy, running a hand through his deliciously thick curls, across his full eyelashes, against his pale thin lips.

"I . . . I didn't know," Mavi stammered meekly. The fear that had been coursing ruthlessly through her was gone; dread had claimed its place. "I didn't recognize him. With all the blood . . . all the panic . . . I didn't know!" She dared to reach for me again. "Please, Evanora—believe me!"

I wrenched away with a snarl. "Get away from me!" My Gift crackled pathetically, but it was enough. Mavi's eyes filled with pain, and she lowered her hand.

A spurt of bubbles exited the boy's mouth, a groan clogged with water. I whipped my head to him hopefully. "Grayson?"

The boy's eyes darted underneath his closed lids, his limbs spasming. The blood gushed around my hand.

Then he went still.

Moaning, I carefully cradled him against me. He felt so small in my arms, so fragile. A flicker of light dangerously close to burning out. I searched the waters, desperate for a solution, for an explanation. Wrong. It was all *wrong*. This couldn't have been what the ancestors had intended. If I had known that finding the answers to their mundane riddles meant Grayson's demise, I never would have listened to them.

Which was probably why they'd never told me.

I closed my eyes, shutting out the thoughts.

Keys and powers and riddles be damned. I had to save Grayson. Nothing else mattered.

My eyes landed on the beach. It was swarming with hunters.

Mavi followed my line of vision. She squeaked worriedly and shook her head. "Evanora, *no*." She looked around frantically. "Maybe there's still a boat that's intact. We can put him on it and push it toward the shore. It's . . ." She swallowed, her throat bobbing. "It's just not safe!"

My upper lip curled, and I turned my head slowly, meeting Mavi's frightened eyes. "If you think," I seethed quietly, "that I am going to abandon Grayson right now, when he needs me the most, after what *you* did to him, then you can leave." I raised my chin defiantly. "Leave. Now. You are no friend of mine."

The wielder's bottom lip began to wobble. "Evanora . . ."

I growled. Time was running out. "Fine!" I barked. "If you're not going to leave, then I am."

"Evanora—"

I shot toward the beach. A wicked trail of blood followed our wake.

Promised One! the Cursed Beings shrieked at our backs. *He is ours, ours, ours!*

I didn't look back as I said, "He is *mine*!"

I broke through the surf like a shooting star, sending the hunters scurrying back in a flurry of sand and curse words. Some raised their spears, though their eyes held very little fight in them. It took one flash of my teeth and sharpened fins to get them dropping their weapons and scuttling back another step.

One hunter stepped forward. He was a mess; the cut over his eye bleeding into his beard, an artwork of deep scratches on his stomach, thick welts lining his swollen wrists.

The man Illeron had saved.

"My son," he uttered, staggering forward another step. "My son!"

I gritted my teeth and dragged Grayson farther along the shore. A moan dribbled off his lips with every sharp tug. The sound did terrible things to my heart.

"Grayson," the man breathed, approaching on stiff legs. I could feel his scorching glare on my shoulders as I continued to pull the boy's limp body away from the water. "What happened? What did you do?"

I didn't bother answering. I only shuffled forward on my belly, dragging myself across the sand with one arm, heaving on Grayson with the other. Sand bit into my skin, sinking deep into my own stomach wound. I grunted, pushing past the pain that threatened to cloud my vision. My pain didn't matter. Only Grayson mattered.

"What did you do?" the man roared, lunging forward a step.

Sucking in a breath, I lurched on top of Grayson's cold body, shielding it with my own. I lifted a clawed hand at the man and hissed, snapping my tail against the wet sand.

The man stumbled back a step, lifting his hands in quiet surrender. But there was nothing quiet about his eyes as they bored into mine. Pleading, hating, already mourning.

I waited until the man had retreated a handful of steps before I pulled away from the boy, inspecting him closely. "Grayson," I whispered, cupping his face. "Grayson!" I stifled a sob as I gently pushed the hair off his forehead, traced the constellation of freckles on his cheek. "You're safe now." My hand slowly crept down his neck to where his heart beat faintly against his chest— far, *far* too faintly. "Please wake up!"

The silence was nearly too much to bear. I wanted to scream just to fill it. Instead, I held my tongue and stared unblinkingly at the boy, feeling his pulse, watching his shallow breaths, hoping with every ounce of my being that I'd get to look into his ocean eyes a final time.

I wasn't sure how much time had passed. The hunters began to stir restlessly. The man shifted on his feet, hovering close by. But no one dared make a sound.

Grayson's eyes opened.

CHAPTER EIGHTY-NINE

GRAYSON

MAY 1 – MORNING

M Y SENSES DRIFTED AWAKE SLOWLY.

Everything was blurry, nothing but blobs of color wrapped in shifting shapes. I could barely make out the glowing being floating above me.

But I could taste blood in my mouth, thick and strong.

I could hear the gentle waves as they tumbled onto the shore, the shuddering gasps and shocked cries of faceless people hovering in my peripherals.

I could smell the salt of the ocean, the wildflowers that bloomed along the hill.

And I could feel the gaping wound in my stomach, large as a mouth, spitting out blood.

I wanted to scream.

The pain. God, the *pain*. Like someone had tried to tear me apart from the inside out. My head pounded, my heartbeat encasing my entire broken body as dizziness swept through me. Black spots flooded my blurry eyes, the threat of losing consciousness lurking along the soft, sandy edges. Tommy Morris's favorite author was wrong. There was nothing peaceful, nothing beautiful about this.

There was a whimper above me, a cool hand pressing against my sweaty forehead.

"It's okay," the glowing shape whispered tightly. "You're okay."

I wished I could believe that soothing voice. But the agony that raked its fingers through every single one of my nerve endings suggested otherwise. I clamped my mouth shut, biting so hard that I tasted fresh blood. I knew that if I opened my mouth—to breathe, to speak, to cry for help—the only thing that would come out was a wretched howl.

"He's not okay," a voice moaned. He sounded so far away, like he was in as much pain as I was. "He's dying!"

I knew that voice. All my life, I'd heard its hardened edges, its prickly tone. I'd memorized the spitting anger, the quiet rage, and the way stubbornness dripped off each word, so ingrained into the person the voice belonged to. I'd heard that voice scream my name, and whisper it like a prayer. I'd heard it sigh out rare apologies, and bark out even rarer laughs that sent the ground shaking.

But never had I heard Rowan Shaw speak with so much devastation. It nearly broke me apart.

I blinked to clear the fog from my eyes. Evanora blinked back at me, smiling through her tears as she continued to stroke my face. Pa stood to the side, his hands bunched in his pockets, his body rigid, his face washed of all color.

Evanora tilted her head at me, her snowy hair fluttering in front of her face. "Hi," she murmured gently.

I still didn't trust myself to speak. I pinched my lips together, a groan pressed tightly against them.

The second I could see, the whispers began.

The one who was promised! the Cursed Beings cried. *You lied, you lied, you lied!*

I wanted to squeeze my eyes shut, but I feared that if I did, I'd never be able to open them again. I turned my head in slow, jerky movements to look at the ocean. The waters were calm, but I knew the beast that raged underneath.

You promised us, Promised One, they screeched. *You gave us your word!*

I could feel them swarming my mind, tugging at my torn muscles, biting at my shredded skin. Doing everything in their otherworldly power to get me back into the water. My legs, bloodless and numb, twitched uselessly as their unfathomable reach infiltrated my nerves.

Here! Here! Here!

A groan slipped through my lips as I turned back to Evanora. The cacophony in my mind and the war waged in my body left me raw, but somehow, I found my voice. "Make it stop," I whispered roughly. "Please."

Evanora nodded, but her smile wavered. Her hands shook as she withdrew them from my face and rested them hesitantly on my stomach. She bit her lip, closing her eyes in concentration. A warmth spread from her fingertips, a burst of white light flickering over my pale skin—but it was gone too soon.

With a frustrated growl, she pressed harder, willing the magic to come. Again, the Gift surged forward, a crackling glow, only to fizzle out almost instantly. She tried once. Twice. Over and over. But the wound didn't close. The blood didn't stop. The whispers didn't cease. Each attempt left the light in her hands dimmer, weaker, until it vanished completely.

With a hoarse cry, Evanora collapsed beside me, her body quaking with grief. Tears streaked her cheeks as she shook her head. "I can't," she sobbed. "I'm sorry. I . . . I can't!"

The one who was promised! Here!

The pain began to ebb, lightning strikes shifting to soft, whispering thunder. I knew better than to think it was a good sign. Grunting, I shifted, placing my heavy hands on top of Evanora's where they still perched on my bleeding stomach. Everything was so cold, so numb. "Thank you for trying," I said weakly.

Evanora sat up slowly, her eyes fixed on me. Her mouth quivered, caught between a sob and a frown. She was trying so hard to stay strong for me, but her tears betrayed her. They landed on my face like salty kisses. I wanted to reach up and wipe them away, but my hands no longer obeyed me.

I turned my gaze to the ocean. The wreckage of war was everywhere—splintered wood bobbed on crimson-tinged waves. There were no bodies, human or mermaid, only the bottomless hunger of the Cursed Beings. They weren't picky about who they devoured.

Except for me.

The horizon glowed with streaks of deep red and burnt orange as the sun clawed through the clouds. The first rays climbed through the water, but all I could see were black tentacles reaching for me.

"Is it over?" I asked quietly.

Evanora nodded gently. She gave my hands a squeeze. "You did well, my brave heart. You fought so fiercely."

My eyelids grew heavy. The siren call of sleep tugged at me, but I fought to stay awake, knowing it was a battle I would eventually lose. Groaning, I tried to shift, but my body felt heavy, wooden—a casket for my damned soul.

Evanora caught me, guiding my head into her lap. From there, I could see the hunters on the beach, clustered together, watching my slow death with muted horror. Holly clung to Jasper, her whole body vibrating as she sobbed into his shoulder. Jasper stood rigid, his spear still in hand, his face taut as he fought against tears of his own.

I tried to remember the last thing we'd argued about, but my mind was clouded, a throbbing cotton ball. Was it even important? I hoped he knew how sorry I was, how much I loved him, even if he was a pain in my ass.

Then I saw Pa. He stood apart from the others, his broad shoulders sagging under the weight of an unspeakable grief. His hat was crushed between his trembling hands, tears carving paths through the blood and dirt on his face.

"Pa," I croaked. I tried to lift my hand to wave him over, but all I managed was a weak twitch of my fingers.

Pa's eyes darted nervously to Evanora before falling back on mine. He hesitantly stepped forward, wringing his hat tightly as he sank to his knees. "My boy," he murmured, the words thick and wet in his mouth.

My fingers twitched again, and Pa dropped his hat, slipping his hand beneath mine. Evanora bristled, a low, protective rumble in her chest. Despite my fading state, I found enough strength to chuckle. "You have . . . to share."

The mermaid clenched her jaw, a quiet hiss slithering between her teeth. But her fins relaxed, and the scales beneath my head softened.

Pa quickly rubbed at his one good eye and forced a smile. "Good to see you haven't lost your sense of humor."

I wanted to laugh again, but I couldn't catch my breath. My chest felt too tight, my lungs full of lead. I coughed, a string of spit and blood spurting onto my chin. Pa carefully wiped it off, and though his touch was kind, his eyes were full of worry as he shared a quick look with Evanora. "Hey now," he said wryly. "Don't you know the sight of blood makes you vomit? You *are* Grayson, aren't you?"

I tried to roll my eyes, only to realize with a burst of panic that I had closed them. I forced them open; it was like lifting a thousand pounds of sand. "You . . . You have to promise . . . me." I sucked in a rattling breath. "Both of you."

Evanora and Pa looked at each other again before nodding together.

"Anything," Evanora whispered, taking my other hand and clutching it close to her chest. It killed me that I couldn't feel her touch.

I swallowed hard. "No more . . . fighting. No more Hunts. It's over . . . okay? It's done."

Pa chewed on his lip, his eyes drifting to the sea of hunters. "That's a big promise, Grayson," he said softly.

"You . . . have to promise. You have to . . . try."

Pa inhaled sharply, then nodded. "All right, son. All right." He ran a hand through my sand-covered hair, his fingers curling around each strand, committing them to memory.

Evanora nodded gently. "We promise."

Relief filled me, flowing alongside my weak pulse. It was short-lived; the whispers crept back in, taunting my slipping mind, toying with my rapid heartbeat.

Promised One, they whispered. *You are close, Promised One.*

I winced as I flopped my head back toward the ocean. Red waves crashed upon the shore. "The waters . . . are still. But I can . . . I can feel them underneath. Wanting . . . me, calling me. I can . . . still hear them."

Pa blinked rapidly, his smile wobbling. "They'll quiet down soon enough."

I let out a shallow breath, gazing up at Evanora, searching her vibrant eyes. "Will you . . . Will you put me in the water? When it's . . . time?"

Evanora moaned, and she closed her eyes, an ambush of tears slipping down her porcelain cheeks. "Yes," she said, dipping her chin and running her lips along my cold knuckles. "Yes, I will."

The blurriness returned, and no matter how many times I blinked, it didn't flutter away. And despite the larger problem rapidly approaching, I was more devastated that I'd never see Evanora again. I'd never get to see her smile, never get to gaze into her large violet eyes, trying to capture every color, every shade, every flicker of emotion that rolled through them. I'd never get to see her hair made of snow-kissed silk, her iridescent scales that sparkled with every color in the sunlight.

Too quickly. It was happening all too quickly. I was so cold, so tired. My body begged me to give in to the dark void that crept across my eyes, to wrap myself in the black velvet that sidled along my bloodstream. I fought to keep my eyes open. It was an insurmountable effort.

Come to us, the Cursed Beings begged. *You gave us your word.*

I spasmed, arching my spine as a flare of pain shot through me.

Pa gripped my hand. "You can let go, son," he whispered, choking up. "You can let go."

But I didn't want to let go. I wanted to fight back. I wanted to find a way out of this. *Let me stay*, I begged inwardly. *God, please, let me stay.* I forced my eyes open again, searching the encroaching void for Evanora. Only darkness stretched before me, a road calling me home. I redirected my quiet pleas to the listening ears in the ocean. *Let me see her one last time.*

The Cursed Beings chuckled, their heartless mirth filling my broken, empty body. *Another request?*

I began to shake violently. *Please.*

I blinked, and there she was again. As beautiful as the day I'd met her—pure and vibrant, as though the sun, moon, and stars had conspired to shape her. A magnificent crown sat upon her head, and her winter-white hair spilled over slender shoulders. Delicate sun-kissed scales dotted her cheeks and neck, glittering like diamonds in the light. She smiled, and it illuminated her face with such warmth that I could have wept.

My hand slipped from hers, falling limply onto the sand. I pressed against the void, desperate. *Let me touch her.*

The Cursed Beings growled. *You are pushing us too far, Promised One.*

Just a touch, and then I'll go, I promised hurriedly.

Feeling rushed back into my hands. I felt them shudder and twitch as the frayed nerve endings pieced themselves together, a flood of warmth as blood returned to my fingers. I lifted my hand and held it in front of my face, flexing tentatively. Looking past my fingers at Evanora, I grinned. The mermaid widened her eyes, a choked sob in her throat as she gave me another smile that shook me to my dying core.

And with a strength that didn't belong to me, I reached up, sliding my hand behind Evanora's curtain of hair, and cupped the back of her head. Evanora raised an eyebrow, her eyes shimmering with tears and so much life. She laughed, and, *God*, the sound was like angels singing.

I pulled her into me.

Our lips met in a kiss that defied the void, the world, time itself. It coursed through every broken piece of me, igniting sparks beneath my numb skin and racing through my veins like wildfire. Her lips, wet with tears, slid against mine with urgency—a shared desperation. We were on borrowed time. We both knew it, but it didn't matter. A low, possessive growl rumbled in her chest, resonating through me like pure, unadulterated love.

The connection between us soared in my heart, weightless, a living, breathing entity, a miracle.

When we pulled away, breathless and smiling like fools, Evanora rested her forehead against mine. She didn't move, didn't look away. Even when the strength left me, and my hand fell back into the sand, she didn't waver. Even when the void slithered forward, and my vision blurred, I could still feel her there, feel her ferociously beautiful eyes on me.

The darkness drew closer, settling into my bones, wedging its way through the hole in my stomach. I could feel it—the need to rest, to sleep, to die. I pushed against the velvet blanket one last time, made my lungs take in a final breath, forced my tongue to form the words trapped in my fuzzy mind. "Until next time," I whispered.

Evanora's wavering breath rippled softly against my cheeks. Her fingers cupped the sides of my face, warm, calming. Home. "Until next time, Grayson Shaw."

I closed my eyes, and let the darkness take me.

I'm ready.

CHAPTER NINETY

EVANORA

MAY 1 – MORNING

HE WASN'T MOVING. HE WASN'T BREATHING. Stifling a sob, Grayson's father crumpled back into the sand, covering his face with his hand, his other still clutching the boy's. Even a couple of the hunters in the crowd began to sniffle and turn away.

I refused to accept it.

An anxious whine on my tongue, I scuttled to the side, gently resting Grayson onto the sand. I pressed my head against his chest, my own heart pounding as I listened for his.

There was nothing.

I gritted my teeth and pressed my head harder into him. There had to be a heartbeat. There *had* to be.

Nothing. Not even a flicker. Not even an echo.

A hand grazed my shoulder. "Enough," the man said, his voice guttural and heart-wrenching. "He's gone."

I shrugged him off with a hiss. "No!" I spat. "He isn't! He can't be!" I straightened abruptly and jostled Grayson's stiff shoulders. "Wake up, Grayson! Wake *up*!"

The man whimpered, sinking back into the sand.

The sun crept upward, its pale morning rays trickling along the beach.

The water, smooth as glass, began to ripple.

I bit my lip, my eyes brimming with tears. I gave him another useless shake. "*Please.*"

The ripples grew, swelling into violent waves.

He is ours! He is ours! the Cursed Beings cried.

Several hunters began to slowly back away as the ocean continued to surge and buck, a feral creature straining against its cage.

I didn't move. Even as the Cursed Beings screeched in my ears, even as the waves they were causing began to lick at my tail. For once in my life, I wasn't scared of the darkness that lay beneath.

I was angry.

Pressure began to build in my chest, sifting through the marrow of my bones, undulating in my core. It whispered down my tail, coating my scales in a warm humming glow. It tickled my fins and sent my hair fluttering. My heartbeat was everywhere, pulsing, beating, raging.

I was unraveling. The pain was swallowing me whole. I was on the brink of shattering completely, and I didn't care.

I wrapped my arms around Grayson with a broken sob, burying my face into his neck as my glow grew from pale embers into wildfire. It consumed my entire body, enveloping me in a light that sang in my blood.

Here! Here! Here! the Cursed Beings screamed.

The waves broke, revealing the flash of groping black hands underneath.

The hunters gasped and cowered back another step, sounds of fear slipping out of their slackened jaws.

It was impossible. Impossible to keep living with this much pain. Impossible to imagine my life without Grayson in it. "Come back to me," I whispered into his frozen skin. "Please . . . come back!"

The slippery hands hovered above the crashing waves for a long, pensive moment.

And then they lurched for the beach.

The hunters screamed, scrambling over top of one another to get away from the writhing mass of tentacles and hands. Even Grayson's father took a faltering step back. But his eyes were on me, not the Cursed Beings. On my glow, which was growing into a beacon of pure white light, shining out of my skin like I was the sun itself. He shielded his eyes with a grimace as my light grew, and grew, and grew.

He is ours! the Cursed Beings roared.

They surged onto the sun-drenched sand, defying all logic, all laws that bound them to the darkness of the ocean.

The pressure was consuming me, coursing through my body, my fractured soul, my destroyed heart.

The hands drew closer, clawing through the sand as they reached for Grayson. I could feel their hunger growing with every inch they gained, their insatiable thirst giving them an unholy speed. *GIVE HIM TO US!*

I opened my mouth.

And screamed.

The sound tore out of me in a bloodcurdling howl, and with it, a burst of light. It crashed onto the beach like a tidal wave, swallowing everything in its path, enveloping the darkness in a single splash of blinding white.

Another wave of light.

Another.

They poured out of me, unrelenting, powerful, an unshackled beast flooding the beach in devastating brightness. The Cursed Beings bellowed in fear, in agony.

Good. I wanted them to hurt as much as I was.

Their long, lithe limbs curled in on themselves, spasming and retracting. They withered away, shriveling as my light tore through them like paper. Chunks of rotten black flesh ripped off their bleached tentacles as they tried to pull themselves back into the water. Their screams slowly turned into defeated whimpers and wails.

The pressure did not cease, so I did not stop. I needed to purge it from my body. I needed to release all the pain inside me. My throat was raw, but I couldn't stop screaming. Not until I was numb.

The Cursed Beings shrank back, their power rapidly diminishing underneath the weight of mine. Their power was insignificant, nothing. Mine was almighty, endless. They snapped their claws. I shattered them. They reached for Grayson again. I shredded through their tentacles. Their black blood drenched the earth, hissing and steaming against the sand, and I did not stop.

Eventually, the pressure began to subside, though the ache in my chest remained. The waves of magic lessened from hurricanes to a gentle breeze. The outpouring became a slow trickle, then a drip, then nothing. My scales tingled with the presence of it; the Gift was still there, shifting eagerly beneath the surface. One whisper of a command and it would surge forth anew, an unfathomable force in the palm of my hand, a magic that could rip mountains in two and sink entire fleets of ships.

A magic that could snuff out the darkness.

When I opened my eyes, the Cursed Beings were gone.

And everyone was staring at me.

I LET THE HUNTERS SAY GOODBYE.

I expected a handful of them to step forward to pay their respects. To my surprise, almost everyone did. It made my hollow heart flutter with a foreign love for humanity. The hunters formed a line, each crouching in the sand to take Grayson's hand, offering some encouraging words that were more for themselves than for the boy. One hunter tried to make a joke, but he was stuttering so hard that he couldn't even finish his sentence. Another gave Grayson a light thump on the cheek, mentioning reluctantly that Grayson had definitely *kicked his ass* during the combat challenge.

Another hunter, with pale blue eyes and strong shoulders, merely stood over him. With his hands in his pockets and a sneer on his face, the hunter looked down at Grayson with an unreadable expression that made my scales tighten. I was poised, ready to unleash my wrath again, when the hunter shook his head. He whispered, "Not even you deserved this," before turning away and stalking off the beach, wiping his face quickly as he climbed the hill.

The girl with ginger hair crumpled into the sand next to Grayson. She gave him a hug and, after stealing a quick glance from me, a kiss on the cheek. She made room for the young hunter next to her, who was openly sobbing as he dropped his head full of frizzy copper curls onto Grayson's unmoving chest.

"You idiot," he moaned, snot and drool dripping off his face. "You weren't supposed to die! How could you die? How could you?"

My throat tightened, tears welling up in my burning eyes.

Gods, I needed to get off the beach.

When I began to pull Grayson's body back into the water, some of the hunters stepped forward, their spears raised. But the boy's father held them back. He'd heard Grayson's last wish.

"I never listened to him before," he uttered softly as he ran a hand through Grayson's hair. "I'd like to listen to him now."

With a final kiss on the forehead, the man stood, wrapping his arm around the girl with ginger hair, and then, hesitantly, around the lanky hunter with a bad leg. The hunter turned his face into the man's shoulder and cried. They all watched me as I dragged the boy into the awaiting surf and let the waves carry us out.

I didn't realize how long I'd been on the beach until I was back in the water. My scales soaked up the ocean's cool embrace, my dry, cracked skin instantly smoothing. I took a shuddering breath, my burning lungs quenched.

But I couldn't enjoy it.

I couldn't rest.

I carried Grayson farther from the shore, away from his home, his life, and the people who loved him. My arms clung to his still body, desperate to protect what was already gone. I avoided looking at him—the hands that had once caressed my scales with wonder, the lips that would never smile again, never speak my name. His eyes, those endless oceans, would never open again.

The remnants of the pod were gathered in the open water. So few of us remained, yet their cries of joy filled the ocean, a symphony of victory. They danced, embraced, and wept, their voices rising in gratitude and relief. Some turned their faces toward the bloodred sun, basking in its warmth for the first time in years. Others dared to breach the surface, letting sunlight kiss their battle-worn scales.

It was a celebration, a moment of triumph.

The Hunt was over. The war was done. And the Cursed Beings were nowhere to be found.

But I knew where they were. There was only one place they could have limped back to.

The sounds of life and laughter quickly faded as I approached, replaced with shocked whispers and awe-filled silence. I didn't look at the mermaids celebrating as I passed. I only swam forward, my head high, eyes staring straight ahead, the glow of my barely contained Gift crackling in my wake.

The mermaids watched in a fervent silence as I went by. One by one, they bowed their heads in reverence, their hands pressed to their chests before swooping gracefully to their sides. But they couldn't hide their smiles, couldn't resist running their hands through my trail of shimmering magic, watching as it collected on their fingertips and sent their skin glowing. "My queen," they uttered as I swam past. "My protector."

The one who had led them into a battle we had no business being in, somehow emerging on the other side victorious.

Unable to help it, I glanced down at the boy in my arms. I jerked my head upward, a whimper stuck in my throat. Gods, *how* was this victorious? How could winning be this painful?

The Barrens were a canyon of darkness when I approached the edge. And though my heart trembled, I held no fear in my soul. Cradling the boy tightly, I peered into the depths, at the shadows that had caused so much grief, so much pain, at the darkness that had taken so much from me.

It seemed so small now, so insignificant. My glow bled through the cracks of pitch black, seeping down the walls, burning through the shadows like they were nothing but wisps of smoke.

I could sense the Cursed Beings far below. They were still there, lurking and hiding, but they were lesser now, weaker—a fragile infant lost in the dark, calling out to a mother who would never return.

They were nothing to me, and I was everything to them. For once, *I* was the one to fear, to loathe, to revere.

I wished I could have been happy about it.

The Cursed Beings moaned from the depths. *The one who was promised,* they whispered feebly. *He is ours.*

My heart clenched tightly, and I bared my teeth at the darkness, a deep hiss slithering up my throat. The Cursed Beings shrank back with a whine. *Please,* they begged. A limp tentacle reached up from the shadows, its black palm stretched upward in supplication. It began to shake the closer it got to my light. *The bargain. It must be completed.*

I pulled back from the cliff's edge. Grayson's head thudded softly against my shoulder, the water tousling his curls. And I finally allowed myself to look. I gazed upon his eyelashes, his lips, his freckles. His callused hands, his pale skin hiding a machinery of muscles beneath. So many wondrous things about him that I couldn't count them all. I didn't want to say goodbye. I wanted to spend the rest of my life finding those wondrous things.

But I was out of time.

"The one who was promised," I uttered, running a hand along Grayson's cheek. "He is yours now."

The black hand crept closer, beckoning.

I pressed my lips to his, soft and quivering, a final goodbye. "Until next time, my brave heart," I murmured, smiling through the pain, through the hollow ache in my chest where our connection had once been.

With shaking arms, I released him.

The tentacle lashed out, coiling around his waist, pulling him toward the abyss. I watched as they took him, their cries of joy rising like a storm. The shadows swirled, writhing with their triumph, their eerie chorus shaking the water.

I dug my nails into my palms, forcing myself to stay still, to resist the screaming urge to dive after him, to steal him back from the darkness. The euphoric cries arched higher, whistling through my bloodstream, wailing between my ears, burning into my memory like a promise. It grew louder, and louder, until all the voices merged into one, a single shattering howl that sent the ground vibrating. My tail anchored me to the seabed as I watched Grayson Shaw disappear into the void.

The boy who had given me everything.

The boy I would never stop loving.

The abyss consumed him, leaving only silence.

CHAPTER NINETY-ONE

EVANORA

MAY 2 – AFTERNOON

I WOULD NEVER BE BLED DRY OF MAGIC AGAIN.

The ancestors were right—Grayson had been the key to unlocking my power . . . my *third* power, an impossible concept to comprehend.

Light binding. A power to bind and seal away the darkness, eradicate the shadows that plagued our every waking moment and every second that we slept.

I sighed, waving my hand in front of my face, watching as my Gift shimmered and coiled beneath my skin, sending flurries of glitter into the water whenever I moved.

If only unlocking this fearful magic hadn't come at such a price. I would have gladly lived my life without it.

"There you are."

The voice came from behind me. Soft and careful, like Mavi was talking to a scared, wounded animal and not her queen.

I dropped my hand and stared out into the Barrens, drooping my fluke over the edge of the cliff. They were so quiet now, so empty of life and death and darkness. It looked like a regular canyon instead of a black void ready to suck you in. Light binding, indeed.

Still, Mavi was cautious as she approached. She came to a stop a healthy distance away from the ledge, her tail flicking nervously. "You really shouldn't be that close to the edge."

I snorted dully, propping my head against my hand. "What's going to happen? Are the Cursed Beings going to gobble me up?" I shook my head, gazing at the deep dark as a ferocious spark of pain tore through my heart. "They got what they wanted. They won't bother us anymore."

"About that . . ." Mavi slowly lowered herself beside me. Her eyes were still on the Barrens, watching for any sign of the evil I had vanquished—a flash of slippery black tentacles or the scratching of thick nails on walls. She inhaled slowly, but her shoulders remained uptight and next to her ears. "I was thinking—" She shook her head quickly, wringing her hands in her lap. "Well, a lot of us were thinking, actually . . ." She dared to peek at me, her eyes traveling up my body, at the glow that permanently emanated off me now. "With the Cursed Beings now gone, we might . . . you know . . ."

I closed my eyes, letting out a steady breath. "Might what, Mavi?"

The wielder swallowed hard. "We were thinking of venturing out. Seeing what else the ocean has to offer." She stopped fidgeting and gave me a determined look. "Try to find a new home."

I wanted to laugh, but I had no energy to even try. "What's wrong with our kingdom?"

Mavi shrugged stiffly. "Nothing!" she said hurriedly. But then she paused, biting her lip. "Actually, that's not true."

I gave her a heavy sidelong stare. Mavi placed a hand tentatively on my tail; I could feel her trembling pulse beneath her fingertips. "Evanora," she breathed, "there is *nothing left* for us here." She gestured to the Barrens, *past* the Barrens. "And there is a whole world out there, now within reach. Imagine!" She exhaled sharply. "A world without Hunts or Cursed Beings. Without death and pain and sorrow. Where we aren't fighting just to stay alive every single day. Where we can bask in the sun and lie on the beach and never have to experience things like fin rot or Dark Madness or hunger again."

I wanted to feel something. Gods, I wanted to feel red-hot rage, a blistering inferno of hate and malice. I wanted to feel an ocean of sadness, to cry enough tears to flood the entire world.

I felt nothing. Nothing but emptiness, fathomless, unending. I had become the Barrens.

I looked back at my hand, at the glittering magic beneath my skin. "Did we not just go to war for those things?" I asked quietly.

Mavi nodded carefully. "Yes."

"Did we not lose countless members of the pod for those things?"

The wielder winced. "Yes," she replied again.

I paused, my hand hovering before me. Flicking my gaze to Mavi, I offered a sad smile. "And you still wish to leave?"

Mavi covered her face with her hands. "Too much has happened here," she groaned between her fingers. "We are all drowning in blood-soaked memories. We need to find a place to start fresh, begin life again." She slowly lifted her head, her gaze searching, pleading. "Will you lead us?"

I looked at her tight features, the hope brimming underneath. All I could see was the knife that had stabbed a hole in Grayson's stomach. All I could see was his blood on her hands. I turned away, biting my lip to keep it from wobbling. "If you want to leave," I said with a sigh, "then leave."

The wielder dropped her hands into her lap, growling softly. A bold sound, but useless. "Did you not hear me? We want you to come with us."

I slowly rose, my glow trailing behind me. My heart felt light—too light, with phantom throbs of a connection that no longer lingered there. "My place is here."

Mavi clambered upright. "But Evanora—"

"My place," I repeated calmly, "is here." My eyes drifted to the Barrens, to the bottomless abyss that mirrored my tormented soul. "You do not need my permission, Mavi. You can go if you wish to."

Mavi narrowed her eyes. "I don't understand why you're digging your fins in." She raised her hands helplessly before letting them slap against her sides. "Why do you insist on staying? There's nothing—"

"If you say *there's nothing here* one more time," I warned stiffly, my Gift sparking in my scales. The briefest moment of delicious anger sifted through me. But I blinked, and it was gone, and I was a void once more.

I wanted to tell her that *everything* was here.

Solandis. Jorah. My appah, my ammah. Illeron. So many fallen members of my pod. *Grayson.* I couldn't leave this place knowing I was leaving them all behind.

I was forever connected to this part of the ocean, forever connected to the island.

But sweet, innocent Mavi, with her spots still dotting her tail, her naivety like a blossoming flower, wouldn't understand. None of them would.

The wielder growled again, but she relented. "You really mean to stay, then?" she asked hesitantly.

I inhaled deeply, the ghostly pains in my chest warming my body. I touched the bracelet circling my wrist. And through the pain, through the heartache, I felt strangely at peace. "Yes."

Silence drifted between us, stretching as deep and far as the Barrens. Mavi opened her mouth, but I knew what she wanted to say, what she wanted to ask. I wasn't ready to talk about it yet.

"When do you plan to leave?" I asked.

Mavi's open mouth dipped into a frown. "I don't know," she said slowly. "Soon. Before nightfall. We want to make it to the other side of the Barrens before it gets dark." She laughed awkwardly, running a hand through her hair. "But since none of us have ever made that trek before, we don't really know how long it'll take."

I nodded, tilting my face to observe the surface and the sun's glimmering rays. "The days are getting longer, but not by much." I turned away from the Barrens, drifting along the lava-rock path. "If you wish to leave, I suggest you hurry."

Mavi raced to catch up, ducking around the shower of glitter trailing behind me. "Where are you going?"

"I'm returning to the island. I want to make sure the humans are keeping their word."

The wielder faltered. "You don't wish to see us off?"

I shook my head. I didn't feel pain in knowing the pod wanted to leave; a small hollowed-out part of me had expected it—dreaded it, but expected it nonetheless. But I knew that watching them abandon our home would be utter torture.

Mavi tripped to a halt, fumbling with her words. "Wait!"

I paused, hovering in the stillness, not turning to look at Mavi as she tried to find the bravery to say the words I didn't want to hear. "Will . . . Will you ever forgive me?" she asked quietly. I could hear the pain in her voice, the utter remorse behind each word. "For what happened? For . . . For what I did to Grayson?"

I clenched my jaw, tightening my hands into fists. I glanced at Mavi from over my shoulder. She was on the ground, bowing so deeply that her forehead pushed against the sand. I sighed, facing forward. "No," I said, feeling eerily calm. "I don't expect I will."

Mavi didn't move, but a gasping sob escaped her bent body.

I swallowed, blinking through the stinging tears. "Goodbye, Mavi."

I continued swimming, blocking out the sounds of Mavi's cries as I left her in the sand.

There was no going back. Only forward.

My pod was wrong. *Mavi* was wrong.

Despite the pain and the bloodstained memories, there was so much life left to live here. Even if the others couldn't see it, or feel it, or understand it, it didn't matter. I could.

I belonged here. Even if that meant in isolation.

Not alone, my ancestors whispered in the shadows of my mind. *Never alone.*

I saw a flash of movement. The shifting of pinks and blues and purples. Large, endlessly dark eyes.

I smiled softly as the octopus fluttered by me, its limbs flapping as it danced in the undercurrent. It gave me a long, unblinking stare. I touched my chest and dipped my head. "Hello, you."

The octopus darted closer. It rested a sticky arm on my cheek, sputtered out a breath, and surged away in a flurry of colors. *Never alone*, my ancestors repeated.

The phantom bond was a weak song in my chest. I let it carry me along the path I knew by heart.

THERE WAS A HUNTER ON THE BEACH. AND HE HAD A NET IN HIS hands.

My scales bristled, my magic like lightning in my veins as I picked up speed. *No*, I thought. *No, no, no!*

They'd promised. The hunters had promised to stop fighting. And, like a fool, I had believed them.

Retrieving the broken remnants of my fury, I surged for the beach in a wash of blinding light and crackling air. The sands at Hannigan's Cove were still stained with blood. The smell of it, of death, of heartbreak, hung low like clouds. I shoved the nausea aside as I skidded onto the beach, my teeth bared, claws raised, my fins flared and shining. "How dare you!" I snarled. "You swore!"

The hunter dropped the net with a hiss, backing away from me and my brilliant light. "Christ Almighty!" he gasped gruffly, covering his eyes. "What on God's good earth?"

I sucked in a breath at the sound of the familiar voice and quickly squeezed the magic beneath my scales. The light immediately snuffed out save for the glowing on my skin. Grayson's father waited a heartbeat more before lowering his hands and scowling at me. I opened my mouth, then quickly closed it.

I could see so much of the boy in his face, so much of him in his eyes. So much pain too, an agony that would never fully leave. I had to look away. "Forgive me," I said slowly. "I thought you were hunting."

The man stomped forward and collected the net. He glanced at me before focusing on the ropes in his hands. "I'm not," he grumbled, gripping the net tightly. He jerked his head to the side, gesturing down the beach. "This is one of Grayson's nets." His mouth pinched together tightly, his thick eyebrows knitting. "It's been collecting dust in the barn, and I . . ." He sighed sharply, his shoulders sagging. "I wanted to do something nice."

It was hard to pull my blurry gaze away from the net in his hands, knowing that Grayson had once touched it, had once spent countless hours mending and creating something from nothing but a pile of ropes. All for something he hated. I forced myself to look across the beach, past the wreckage of broken boats and blood, to the small wooden cross planted crookedly in the sand. There were letters crudely etched along the horizontal plank, and it was surrounded by white and purple wildflowers. My breath caught, the wildflowers swimming in my tearful eyes.

The man shifted on his feet. "I know it's not much to look at." He scoffed, rubbing the back of his neck. "Grayson was the creative sort, not me."

"No," I gasped, shaking my head. "It's beautiful. Grayson would have loved it." I crawled over to the cross, grazing my fingers against the soft, velvety flowers, feeling the sun's warmth on their petals. "One of the first times we met," I whispered, picking up a purple flower, "Grayson picked a whole bunch of these flowers for me."

The man walked over to the cross, standing close to me. Any fear of me was gone. He crouched, groaning as he clutched his stomach. "I didn't realize he was so romantic," he mused, cracking a small, sad smile.

"Well . . ." I forced a quiet laugh, plucking up another. "He certainly wooed me."

The man watched as I began to string the flowers against one another, creating a small circle of alternating colors. My fingers trembled as I worked, memories of Grayson crashing through my mind like the persistent tide. I missed that crown of flowers he had made me. I would have given anything to wear it again.

Heart in my throat, I placed the flowers on the top of the cross, draping them along the wooden arms. Grayson's father grunted approvingly. He swaddled the net around the base of the cross. I plucked up a couple more flowers and wedged them into the net's open spaces, blending everything in. We sat back, admiring our handiwork. The man wiped his face.

"God," he chuckled wetly, "I miss him."

I blinked away my tears and rested a hand on his back. "I miss him too."

The man sucked in a breath, his shoulders heaving. "He was lucky to have you in his life." He winced, peeking at me through his good eye. "I'm sorry I accused you of . . . of being the one who . . ."

I shook my head. "It's okay. I would have too." I rubbed his back reassuringly. "You are a good father. Grayson was lucky to have that as well."

The man scoffed, but thick tears dotted his eyelashes. "A good father would have tried *harder*—"

"You *did* try!" I interjected firmly. "His fate was written in blood, and nothing could have altered it." I sighed, sitting up straight. "Grayson would hate it if he saw how much you're torturing yourself over something that even he had no power over. Enough."

The man's good eye widened, and despite the pain coursing through his features, he threw his head back in a laugh. "God, you're feisty."

So much like Grayson. I looked away with a smile. "I don't think Grayson minded."

"No," the man sighed. "I suspect he didn't." He bit his lip, his gaze slowly getting pulled back to the blood-tinged waves. "The people of Lethe have seen enough death and bloodshed to last them all a lifetime. The decision to never have a Hunt again was . . ." He chuckled darkly. "Enthusiastically unanimous." He smirked at me. "You and your pod never have to worry about us again."

I didn't have the heart to tell him that it was just me now. "Thank you," I whispered instead.

The man sighed deeply, falling back onto his hands. "The Hunt," he muttered, turning his attention to the ocean, "makes monsters of us all."

The silence that drifted around us was a comforting thing. Together in grief, forever bonded through trauma and loss. I played with my bracelet, gazing out toward the fading sun. Normally, the sight would have sent a spear of fear down my spine. Night was approaching, and with the darkness came evil. Now I soaked in the colors, the tinges of fire red and burning orange, the hues of pink that sailed through the vibrantly blue sky. Still, old habits were hard to break. "I should go," I murmured.

The man sniffled, nodding sharply. "Life goes on," he bit out.

I smiled warmly, the void in my chest closing the slightest bit. "Life goes on," I agreed.

I pushed into the water. I was about to dunk my head underneath when the man's voice rose above the waves.

"What's your name?"

I stilled, my heart hammering. I looked over my shoulder at him. He was standing next to the cross, his hands in his pockets, a deep blush coating his ruddy cheeks. I grinned coyly. "What is *your* name, human? Tell me, and perhaps, if I feel like it, I'll tell you mine."

The man stammered out a laugh. "It's Rowan. Shaw."

"Rowan Shaw," I repeated gently, testing the name in my mouth. It didn't feel quite as soft and warm as Grayson's, but it *did* feel close. "My name is Evanora."

Rowan's face broke out into a smile, his eye twinkling. "It's nice to meet you, Evanora. Officially."

I could tell he wanted to ask if we would see each other again. But he closed his mouth, because in his heart, he knew we would.

So, with a smile and a small wave goodbye, I ducked into the looming waves and swam for home.

When I returned to the kingdom, the city was empty—no sounds of laughter floating through the square, no fluttering of hurried tails in the throne room. The pod had made good on their desire to leave. I hoped they were prepared for the unknown, for the trials and tribulations that were sure to greet them. I hoped they found what they were looking for.

But it was out of my hands, out of my control. And for the first time in my life, I was okay with not having any.

I took my time wandering through the city, feeling alone but not lonely. I stopped at the old houses, decaying and broken. I swept through the cluttered alleyways and soared underneath crumbling archways. Now unoccupied, the disrepair would only get worse. With no mermaids to fill the emptiness, the spaces seemed so much larger now, so much quieter—not cramped and full of noise, as I had once viewed them as a merling.

And I was okay with it.

Night steadily approached, and I found myself swimming along the path bordering the kingdom. My gaze drifted to the lanterns lining the white lava rocks. The lanterns that had protected our small world for an eternity. The lanterns that needed to be burning with my magic before even whispers of the day's end arrived.

They were unlit.

Shadows pressed in, sweeping through the undercurrent, tangling in the seaweed forests. The darkness stretched over the kingdom like a groping hand.

Fingers crackling with light, itching at my sides, I approached the lanterns.

And I swam right past them.

ACKNOWLEDGMENTS

First and foremost, the biggest of thanks to my dear friend Ashley. I remember the day I told you that I wanted to write a story about mermaids. We were eating donuts at Tim Hortons, and you nearly jumped out of your seat with excitement. Thank you for not only being my critique partner, but for being my biggest cheerleader. You've had my back since day one, and I love you with the white-hot intensity of a thousand burning suns.

A merry thank-you to Hayes, Kelsey, Brittany, and Paige for being stellar beta readers. You really helped me shape *The Hunt* into something magical.

Thank you to Yoanna Stefanova for providing developmental, line, and copy edits, as well as to Natalia Leigh for squeezing me into your schedule for proofreading! I'd still be stuck on the third draft if it weren't for you two!

Speaking of edits, thank you to literally EVERYONE who helped me with my book blurb: Sam, Natalia, Mandy, Hayes, Ashley, Paige, Bethany, Brittany, and Shannon. The blurb has seen many forms—some good, some very, very bad. The journey has been endless, just like my adoration for each and every one of you.

Thank you to Enchanted Ink Publishing for helping me format my novel! Doesn't it look so pretty?

Thank you to Selkkie Designs for creating the cover of my dreams! You took my scrambled ideas and shaped them into something less fever dreamy and more masterpiecey.

Big thanks to Rob Seib for the map artwork, because while my writing is considered average, my art skills are that of a preschooler.

Solid thanks to all the sorry souls who let me talk their ears off about writing. I was probably about to burst if it weren't for your kindness . . . and patience . . . and pity.

To my family, I offer a great and sincere thank-you. You've watched me create stories since I was a little girl and have always encouraged my wild imagination. You let me take out my computer during family visits to work when inspiration hit, and only got mad at me a couple times when I stayed up super late and forgot to turn down the thermostat. Thank you for your love, support, and patience.

And finally—Cale: love of my life, the peanut butter to my jelly. Thank you for being my daydreaming partner, my plot-twist analyzer, and my cuddles-on-demand machine when life felt like it was getting a little too hard. Thank you for letting me chase all the plot bunnies. Thank you for never asking me how much all of this cost.

Naomi lives in the Shuswap region of BC with her husband and her lazy—and occasionally sassy—polydactyl cat. Known for her lyrical prose and enveloping descriptions, Naomi has been telling stories since before she could properly hold a pen. Part-time OR nurse and full-time nerd, Naomi likes to spend her free time playing video games, eating candy, and coming up with book ideas that will make her mother blush.

Made in United States
Troutdale, OR
06/26/2025

32411347R00444